The Velvet Prison

Book One of The Chronicles of Samek

Alex Gold

Prologue

I murdered a man. Rannald, the leader of the Council, that august body which rules my world. I hurled a wave of energy into his chest, as if I were thrusting my hand inside, and grasped his heart with the power I wield. I squeezed: a short sharp deathly embrace. His heart stopped. He gasped for breath but to no avail. He slumped to the ground as the rest of the Council and all the others in the chamber rushed to his side.

I was thirteen years old. Young in time and experience, old in other ways. How was it that a child, an innocent and over-protected boy, could have come to taking a life at such a tender age? How had I reached such a state of desperation that my act seemed justified, was the correct thing to do?

This first book of the chronicle of my life will explain all, lead you through my story from my earliest memory to the day of the murder itself. And beyond the murder into the confusion of its aftermath, the apparent lull in hostilities between myself and the Council which allowed me to expand my already well-developed abilities in teleportation, drawing me finally to make the huge leap to travelling back in time, across the eight centuries to the year 2012, just at the cusp of the Chaos. The Chaos that would nearly, very nearly, destroy the world.

Chapter One

"What have you two boys been up to today," my benign uncle Kallan, who was not my uncle, asked in a bright voice, addressing me and my brother Adwin one evening in high summer as we sat as a family around the dinner table. I must, at the time, have been around eight years old, my brother five.

"We've been in the woods uncle," replied Adwin simply.

A hint of a frown passed across Kallan's well-tanned forehead, his bright blue eyes sparkling with mild concern, before he continued in his low mellifluous voice. "Doing what?"

Adwin and I glanced at each other, passing a telepathic message between us. "Playing," I replied laconically.

Our older twin sisters, Safya and Emaleen, five years older than me, picked up instantly that there had been a secret communication between me and my brother, but even at the age of eight, I was able to prevent them knowing the content of it. Out of the corner of my eye I saw Emaleen's pale eyebrows rise slightly.

"Playing what?" asked Kallan.

I flashed another silent message to Adwin, cautioning him not to share with the rest of my family everything we had done in the woods. As before, although I blocked Emaleen and Safya from hearing the words, I was not yet skilful enough to prevent them knowing *something* had passed between my brother and me. They glanced at each other, and then both leaned forward slightly, their knives and forks stopping in mid-air, as if sensing that something interesting was about to happen. Safya smiled vaguely at us, willing us to share what we had been doing in a kindly way. Emaleen's interest was far less benign and as she narrowed her slate-grey eyes I was irritated by her expression: like a cat smugly and lazily waiting for its prey to be cornered by a different feline. I was reminded that Emaleen had always been the more irritating sister.

Adwin was not as discreet as I was, more naive with his three years less of life to draw upon, wanting simply to share his feelings with others as a friendly and garrulous five-year-old child is wont to do. He did not pay much attention to my warning.

"We went to the magic place, with the waterfall and the pool of water, and we danced with the fairies and the tree spirits and the water spirits, and we looked for pixies and elves and..."

"What?" snapped my formidable mother Zelda, who was not my mother, suddenly involving herself in the conversation. "What is this drivel?" she continued, her gravelly voice ominously soft, silencing Adwin and piercing straight through the previously relaxed atmosphere of the dining room.

We all fell silent, and stopped moving. Adwin stared nervously at Zelda. Kallan and I sat tensely, not knowing what would come next or what to do. I sensed that Emaleen was continuing to enjoy herself, though she was wise enough not to make this too obvious. Safya flashed me a pained little smile, her big grey eyes filled with sympathy.

After an uncomfortable silence which seemed to last an age, but probably lasted less than a minute, Zelda leaned slightly closer towards Adwin, her bushy gray eyebrows drawn closely together over penetrating dark brown eyes, and asked again, this time in an even quieter yet more forbidding voice, "Well child. What did you say?" Her near-whisper demanded an answer.

Adwin did not reply, but looked helplessly at me, and then at Kallan and then at our sisters. From Kallan's expression Adwin knew that he could not help him. Safya's look of helpless impotence in the face of Zelda's tone of voice told my brother that she too could not come to his aid. And poor Adwin only needed the briefest glance at Emaleen to know that she *wouldn't* help him. He looked back at me, distress showing in his child's eyes, profuse apologies tumbling from his mind towards me. He looked back at Zelda, shocked to see how angry she seemed, and then looked hastily back at me, his young face desperate and completely at a loss as to what to do.

I took a deep breath, turned to Zelda, and explained in a voice tinged with defiance, "*You* made us learn about the magical things in the old world, the fairies, the pixies, the goblins, the water nymphs, the tree spirits."

Zelda turned to me, her anger now mingled with confusion. She shook her head slightly as if to indicate that what I had said not only made no sense, but certainly did not constitute any sort of explanation. As she did so, a single strand of gray hair escaped its tight confines, waving incongruously almost upright above her head. I knew I would have to clarify further.

"We like those things. We *love* some of them - the fairies, the elves, especially the nymphs and tree spirits. We imagine them living in our forest, coming out at night. Dancing and singing in the moonlight, splashing through the streams and pools and the waterfall. Going home again, back to the trees and the streams when the sun comes up. We invent stories about them when we go to the woods."

The silence that met this clarification was even more profound than before. But I saw that Zelda's anger had waned, and the expression on her prematurely wrinkled face showed astonishment, bewilderment even. She reached up and pushed the wayward lock of hair, forcing it back in line with the rest of its companions. I felt my brother's huge relief at having been saved from Zelda's wrath. Kallan had a slight smile on his face and was nodding kindly at Adwin and me, clearly approving of the content of our make-believe. Emaleen looked as astonished as Zelda, and even Safya showed surprise at my revelation,

After a long pause, Zelda shook her head slightly, once again liberating the undisciplined strand of hair, then looked straight at me, and said in a low growl so quiet that it was little more than a hoarse whisper, "But why, boy? Why?"

It was now my turn to be perplexed. I did not understand the question. I frowned, and cocked my head to one side. Zelda whispered again, "Why?"

"Why what?" interrupted Kallan, who also did not seem to understand the question.

Zelda turned sharply to face him, her bushy eyebrows lifted high in surprise. "Why would they make up such things? For what reason? Why would they utter such irrational notions?"

"They're children," replied Kallan calmly. Zelda shrugged in confusion, her face registering total incomprehension. "They're children," repeated Kallan, as if the repetition would explain everything. Zelda lifted her arms, palms upwards, in a gesture showing a complete failure to understand, and shrugged.

"Children play, Zelda," Kallan continued. "They invent things, they use things they've learned and then add to these to create make-believe worlds. Fantasies. Using their imaginations. All children do this."

"I never did," growled Zelda.

"And neither did we," added Emaleen in a slightly snide tone, crossing her arms smugly as she did so, her pale blond eyebrows lifted high. She spoke for herself and her twin sister, though Safya cast her a mildly disapproving look.

"Doesn't mean it's wrong," Safya mumbled in her gentle voice, so quietly we could barely make out the words. Emaleen snorted with irritation at her sister's intrusion with its implicit criticism of Emaleen's comment, of support for me and Adwin.

Kallan was not put off by the girls' distraction. "Well most children do. *Normal* children do," he added waspishly with the barest hint of a glance in Emaleen's direction, showing a side of himself Adwin and I had rarely witnessed. "It's good for them. They need it, so they can develop their imaginations, and..."

"They do not need make-believe to do that," interrupted Zelda. "I have made them all learn so much about the marvels all around them, the real wonders of the world, so why should they need to ransack foolish old stories rooted in superstition and ignorance to fire their imaginations?"

We all turned to Zelda, not quite understanding what she was saying, yet sensing she was on the brink of expressing herself more fully, more openly than any of us had experienced before. We all waited as she collected her thoughts.

"I am a scientist," she began in a loud and somewhat pompous tone. "I study the workings of the world, the real world, and what I see is full of marvels, awash with wonders, things that look like miracles. But they are not miracles. Everything has an explanation, a rational explanation. We do not always know what the explanation is, but there is one, and it is only a matter of time till we discover it. But even when we do understand how something works, so much of the world around us is so complicated, so intricate, so interwoven, that this alone is more miraculous, more *magical* than your fairies and pixies and nymphs. Why do you need them when you have the magic of how the trees grow, make leaves, blossom, produce seeds, and these tiny seeds, which look dead to us, just hard little lumps, then come to life and produce another tree, huge and imposing. The magic of mixing a couple of cells together and it turning into a new animal, or human. Watching the first new cell divide, divide again, over and over again and then the bundle of undifferentiated cells turning into all the diverse organs of the body, each one seemingly 'knowing' what it will turn into. Or the magic of weather patterns, of the water cycle - evaporation, rain, streams and rivers, ponds and lakes. It all looks like someone has come along and cast a spell to create all this unimaginable complexity, but no-one has made it. It has made itself, dragged itself slowly up by its own bootstraps over untold millennia to become the amazing, extraordinary place that we live in. Every new thing I learn is magic to me. I am enchanted by every discovery I make, entranced by every new revelation about the natural world. What need of silly old stories to fire the imagination!"

After this she sat back and breathed out heavily. We were all dumbfounded. None of us, not even Kallan, had ever heard Zelda make such a long speech, and certainly never waxing lyrical about anything in this way. We had all learned something extraordinary about her that evening. We would never have imagined that she saw the world in such a way, in such poetic terms. For all her usually robotic rationality, she still saw marvels and wonders all around her, every day of her life.

None of us had anything to say by way of reply to Zelda's lyrical speech. Uncle Kallan opened his mouth as if to speak, then snapped it shut as if thinking it better not to reply, perhaps simply marvelling at learning something new about Zelda despite knowing her better than anyone else, better than anyone else ever had.

Zelda looked around the table, registering our astonished expressions. Amazingly, the tiniest hint of a smile tugged at the corners of her normally tight lips, and an almost imperceptible narrowing of her eyes, the corner of each wrinkling slightly, with a sparkle in the dark brown eyes themselves. I simply could not decide which was more amazing: Zelda's extolling of the wonders of the natural world, or her amusement at our gaping mouths.

"Well, well, well," she rumbled. "If our boys have made so much of the ancient tales of magic and peasant folklore, I dread to think what they will concoct out of the nonsense of the old religions when they come to learn about those!" she said in a sardonic tone.

I jumped slightly in surprise. What were these old religions of which Zelda spoke?

We slowly resumed our meal in silence, Zelda still obviously entertained by our reaction to her unusual eloquence, Kallan not sure how to react, and we four children still almost in a state of shock. For one of the only times in our lives so far, the four of us sensed that we were all reacting the same way to events happening around us, all feeling the same astonishment to learn something new about this fearsome woman we called mother. Even Emaleen seemed to be sharing with us our great surprise. Our shared emotions spilled out of us, transferred telepathically between us, and none of us tried to block them, or even considered doing so. We were not communicating clearly in silent words, but with a simple outflowing of mutual feeling, of empathy, something more akin to a sensation than to a thought. Despite the confusion in our reactions to Zelda's revelations, the warmth that came from feeling at one with my sisters was rich and pleasurable. One look at Adwin's happy face showed me that he felt the same as I did. The four of us passed tiny glances between ourselves, and even hints of smiles, so greatly did the shared emotional experience affect us, causing us to need to communicate our feelings in gestures as well as directly into each other's minds.

As we finished our meal, Zelda stood up and began to move away from the table. As she reached the door she turned suddenly, fixed Adwin and me with a penetrating stare and said, "You two boys. Can I assume neither of you actually believes in any of this nonsense? That what you do in the woods is simply a game?"

I nodded vigorously, and assumed my brother would do the same. To my consternation Adwin was frowning, his dark hooded eyes tight with concentration, and he seemed unsure how to respond. I shot him an urgent silent message, so sharply that he actually jumped slightly in his chair. ~*Say yes!*~ I barked, straight into his head. He did not seem to understand why he should say yes, but he certainly took note of the urgency of my tone.

"Yes mother, of course," he began in a hesitant tone. "We just play. It's just a game."

Despite Adwin's non-committal tone, his answer seemed to satisfy Zelda who grunted slightly and shuffled out of the room. I breathed a sigh of relief, but sensed that neither of my sisters had been fooled by Adwin's reply. I glanced at the two girls, and gave them the slightest shake of my head. I felt a great need to talk to Adwin, and also my sisters.

I sent all of my siblings a silent message that we should talk privately between ourselves, and received their instant agreement.

"May we leave the table, uncle?" I asked Kallan politely.

"Of course, of course," he replied distractedly, waving his hand in a gesture of assent as he did so. He too was still full of surprise at the direction this most unusual supper had taken to note my unexpected courtesy, and perhaps he wanted to be alone to think over all that had happened. We four children leapt up from the table and raced out through the door. We moved rapidly through the house until we came to the plant-filled conservatory stretching the full length of the back of the building. The night was very warm, and all the outside doors were thrown open to let in the breeze. We dragged folding chairs from where they were stacked against one of the walls and ensconced ourselves among the thickest bushes in the hothouse. We knew we were alone, and could not be heard. We had learned from past experience that too much telepathic communication while in the presence of Kallan or Zelda was noticed by our absence from the normal conversation, and that this was disapproved of. And in any event, we still often chose to speak out loud, without using our telepathic abilities. My sisters in particular were jealous of their tight relationship with each other, and always found it intrusive when Adwin or I spoke directly into their minds.

For a little while no-one spoke. We sat in comfortable silence, enjoying the rare sensation of mutually shared emotion, of being at one with each other.

We were all a bit shy to start with, so unused were we to sitting together in amiable companionship, talking about events in our lives. Safya always acted in a gentle manner towards me, and especially towards my little brother who was a full eight years her junior, but even she seldom spent time with us, preferring to keep herself tightly bound with her sister. Emaleen was rarely kind to us, holding herself aloof from us, thinking us too young, too childish to waste her valuable time and energy on. After a few quiet moments Emaleen finally spoke, having first shot a tiny glance at her twin sister. "Do you really make up stories when you go to the woods, stories about magical beings from ancient folklore?" she asked, still not quite managing to keep the customary sharp tone out of her voice despite her genuine interest in our reply.

Adwin nodded vigorously. "Yes, yes," he said excitedly, speaking rapidly without pauses in his high-pitched piping voice. "We do. We really do. We know all the best places in the forest for the different creatures, where they all live, where they all spend the day and where they go at night. The elves live at the top of the trees, the fairies and pixies in little holes in the trees or under bushes and big leaves. And the best place of all is the glade where the wood nymphs come out of the trees to dance and sing with the water spirits at night. It's lovely there, so lovely and green with the pond and the waterfall and everything."

Emaleen looked at him, amazement showing clearly on her face. Safya too was obviously surprised, not only at what Adwin was saying, but by the excited tone he used. She turned to Adwin and asked in a gentle voice. "Do you really believe in all of this Addy?"

Adwin went very still at this question, not knowing how he should answer. He looked first at Safya and then at Emaleen. The expression of disbelief on Emaleen's face caused him to hesitate in answering, despite Safya's more kindly half-smile. He threw a silent question at me on the private channel that existed just between the two of us, but I answered in words. "It's alright Adwin", I replied out loud. "You can answer honestly." I did not want the twins to feel Adwin and I were keeping things from them, at this delicate moment of rare unity between the four of us.

Adwin paused for a moment, sighed, and replied in a slightly despondent tone, "No, not really I suppose. I know they don't exist. They can't exist. The old tales are just stories, nothing more than silly stories." He then looked up sharply, his childish features suddenly animated. "But when I'm in the woods it's so good, so strange, so different from anywhere else that I can almost believe it's all true. I can almost believe that all these magic creatures are real, but just out of our reach, just outside of what we can hear and see, but there anyway."

Adwin looked directly at Safya as he spoke. She smiled at him gently.

"He's right," I said, taking up the theme. "The forest really does seem magical, and it's easy to think of everything there being alive. Not just the trees and flowers and animals which we know are alive, but the rocks and stones, the streams and ponds, the waterfall...everything. The whole place seems to breathe. And what Adwin said about the magical beings being just out of reach, that's exactly what it feels like. As if, when we come into a clearing, or turn round quickly we almost catch a glimpse of one of them, but not quite, like they leave a trace behind, a shadow of themselves." I stopped talking, not knowing how else to describe it. Here we were surrounded by exotic plant life: could they not sense the life surging around us?

I looked at Emaleen to see her reaction to what my brother and I had said, to see whether she was reacting with expected derision. To my great surprise and even greater pleasure, I saw this was not the case, not at all. She sat quite still, leaning forward slightly with a strange look on her face, one I had never seen before. It was a mixture of contentment, and amazement, and what I could only decipher as eagerness. I glanced at Safya, noting how they looked exactly the same, their mouths slightly open, their gray eyes wide, their heads cocked to the side in identical fashion. For once even Emaleen seemed to lose her usual air of testiness and seemed genuinely intrigued. I took courage from their unprecedented reaction and made a bold suggestion.

"Why don't you come with us some time? To the forest," I asked.

They both snapped back in their chairs as one, mouths closing with a click of perfect white teeth. I knew they had never been into the depths of the forest, only skirted the edge of it. I had never known if this was through a fear of the woods learned from Kallan, or a simple lack of interest. Either way, I had never dared ask them before to accompany Adwin and me on our regular trips. I knew that this evening was so unusual that it might be one of the only opportunities I would have to do so. I longed to break through the barriers they had erected to keep us out, yearned to be closer to them, to know them as I felt I should. I had spent my whole life with only the five members of my family for company. I wanted so much to be closer to my sisters. I loved my brother, but sensed it was not good to spend nearly all my time with one single person, one tiny child for company. My sisters were older, and I could learn so much from them.

I waited anxiously for their reply. Adwin realised that the suggestion was audacious, and might be met with resistance, or mockery. But he too was caught up in the charged atmosphere that reigned that evening, and he sat quite still, hardly daring to breathe, his dark, hooded eyes frowning with tension, fearful of a negative reaction.

But it seems that the mood of bonhomie and empathetic telepathy had taken hold even of the often snappish and sarcastic Emaleen. She flashed a little smile, and answered simply, "Yes. We'll come. Some day."

Adwin breathed out loudly with relief. Safya breathed in sharply and looked at her sister. Emaleen merely nodded at her once, and was rewarded by an identical nod in return, two sets of pale blond tresses bobbing in perfect harmony. And that sealed it. They would come with Adwin and me to the forest, though no agreement had been made as to a day, and I did not want to push the point at this juncture, sensing it might cause my sisters to regret their promise. As was nearly always the case, Safya had simply followed Emaleen's lead.

After that, there seemed nothing more to say. By unspoken mutual consent, we all stood, put our chairs back against the wall, and moved through the luxuriant foliage of the conservatory to the door of the house, and then to our rooms to bed. Our trip to the woods would be fascinating, spending time with our sisters, and in our beloved forest. For the first time sharing our secret places with them, our private fantasies. I was thrilled to do so, but deeply apprehensive at the same time. What would they make of it all? What would they think of us after their trip to the woods? Would they fall in love with the forest as we had, or consider the whole excursion a waste of time? Worst of all, would they think our fantasies and make-believe puerile, belittling us in their own minds?

Chapter Two

I write these memoirs as an old man, an old man even by the long-lived norms of the time I write in the year 2916. That night, over a hundred years ago, in which I first shared my love of the forest with my family, I remember with such clarity, that it could have happened yesterday. But of course it was a long time ago, a very long time ago, in the year 2808.

I have been persuaded to commit the memories of my childhood, my youth, and all the rest of my long life to writing, lest they be lost. I was unconvinced for some time by the exhortations to do so, believing that enough is already known of me in this world, in this time, and in other times and places for that matter. But the pestering caused me to think a good deal about my early years, and I decided that there is much that is still unknown, that deserves to be told. In particular it seemed important to me to explain to those younger than me (a group which encompasses almost the entire population!) what our world was like then, and the ways in which it has changed so much since that time. Through the course of my memoirs I will try to elaborate as best I can how and why the world of the twenty-ninth century, a world which seemed so set and immutable, has changed so much in the hundred years or so since my story begins. There has been nothing short of a revolution in that time. A slow, ponderous revolution which is still underway, but a revolution nonetheless.

I therefore lay out all I can remember of my early years secreted away on the estate I lived on with my family, which we, as children always called 'the Compound' in our early years - such did it feel like a prison. I will elaborate my discoveries of who and what I am, my acquisition of the skills which enabled me to travel in time, and of my adventures across the centuries before the terrible Chaos which almost destroyed our world in the middle years of the twenty-first century, more than seven hundred and fifty years before I was born.

I beg indulgence if my memory is sometimes hazy, or I fill in gaps with descriptions of events as I think they happened, or sometimes even how they should have happened, but perhaps did not. I beg indulgence too if I misremember, and misdescribe, any of the many people I have encountered in my travels, good people, bad people, indifferent people. I plead for lenience that these chronicles should be taken for what they are: the reminiscences of an old man trying to commit to words a long, rich and eventful life. I must also crave forgiveness for my fondness for a certain style of language. As a very young man, even before I made my first jump through time, I discovered the joys of ancient literature, especially that of the eighteenth and nineteenth centuries. I so immersed myself in this literature that I became known for my quirky use of words and phrases, long-dead or moribund expressions which I hoped (and still hope) to revive, to revivify for future generations. I make no apology for my attempts to breathe life into old sayings and words: some of the ancient writers knew how to craft an expression, to turn a phrase, of such clarity and beauty that I see no reason not to try to emulate them.

My earliest memories are of a time when I was yet a tiny baby. I retain such memories, unlike other people, because of my unique provenance, unique at the time and still so. My mother, or the woman I always called mother, Zelda, created me from genetic material of nineteen ancestors, progenitors as we still call them. At the time I was created we believed that this had never been done before, though it transpired that we were wrong in our belief. What is true is that it has not been done since. Most other people in that time were created from between three and five progenitors, though my older identical twin sisters Emaleen and Safya, half a decade older than me, were created from nine progenitors. My little brother Adwin, three years younger than me, was created from twenty-one, though he seemed to be something of a failed experiment, carrying a range of genetic imbalances that caused him problems throughout his life. All of these experiments carried out by our mother were strictly forbidden, though this was never something that worried her.

My first memory, as I lay in my tiny crib, only days after being removed from the foetal tank in which I had gestated, was of an undifferentiated mass of impressions. I am immersed in a sea of blinding light of every named colour, and some yet to be named. Sounds envelop me in a cocoon of rustling, squeaking, scraping, scratching. Aromas pervade what I later learn are my nostrils, mouth, throat. Physical sensations press against what I will one day call my back, my legs, my head; and more sensations when I stretch those appendages I will designate legs and arms, and feel the ends of them contact hard and soft matter.

I cannot in fact separate colour from smell, from touch, and even from taste. My entire world is an endless explosion of sensory information, all-encompassing, indistinguishable, and overwhelming. The only glimmer of distinction is the vaguest awareness that I am something separate from the ocean of sensation all around me: that I am somehow in the middle of it, experiencing it, that it lies outside of me. I cannot fully perceive where I stop and it begins, but I sense that I am in some way discrete, unitary.

I gradually begin to perceive differences in the information streaming into me through my sensory organs. I notice that some of the time the light and colours seem dimmed, almost to the point of disappearing. The first time this happens it distresses me. Despite the almost overwhelming nature of the coloured luminosity, it is a warm sensation, a joyous sensation, and when it disappears my world suddenly seems cold and unpleasant. But then, almost miraculously, it reappears and the world once more overflows with shining, glowing hues.

I begin to notice that some of the aromas and tastes seem to create a sense of comfort and well-being in me, whereas others cause me to feel discomfort and even disgust. Something soft is pressed between my lips and I seem to know that I need to suck it. In fact, when it is first inserted into my mouth, it is as if there is nothing else in the world but that tiny thing. All other sensation fades into nothingness, and the entire focus of my being is concentrated in sucking, as hard as I can, on that insignificant, rubbery device. When it is removed from my mouth, for a brief moment I feel bereft, but am soon distracted by the blanket of sensations once more enveloping me. But I realise that the little article is regularly reinserted between my lips, and each time I am once again immersed in a tiny, focused world of sucking and swallowing, actions that bring a warm, almost sweet liquid into my mouth and down my throat, awarding me a profound sense of well-being.

I become aware that there is something much bigger attached to the tiny rubbery object, something that hovers behind it all the time I am drinking. Some of the sounds I hear also seem to be coming from this big something: soft, cooing sounds with a gentle undulating rhythm, sounds that pacify and comfort me, though I have no idea why. I notice that this large shape appears near me sometimes without offering me the little fluid-filled article. On these occasions, the gentle sounds still accompany the big thing, and I receive physical sensations at the same time - a feeling of being gently touched, stroked, caressed. As with everything associated with this large, moving object, the touching gives me a sense of extraordinary pleasure and contentedness, and I begin to long for the sensation again each time it finishes. I feel safe and at peace in the presence of this object which brings such sustenance and physical comfort.

Much less often I am aware of other shapes moving near me, their attention directed towards me. The larger of these appears rarely and never remains long. The sense I get of this one is peculiar and very unlike the others. This one seems to emanate no warmth at all, just a feeling of focus on me, of interest in me, but not personal in the same way as the other moving shapes. This one rarely makes much noise, just very quiet, low rumblings which seem to be directed backwards to itself, rather than towards me or anything else. At other times, two mid-sized moving shapes appear, always so close together that at first I cannot discern that there are two of them. Initially I perceive them as being one object, not tall, but wide. Gradually I perceive that they are in fact two, but apparently identical. They stroke me gently, murmur quietly, though whether to me or to each other I cannot tell, and I feel a sense of affection emanating from them towards me, stronger from one than from the other. This affection is pleasant, but it is not as strong as that coming from the big shape who provides me with sustenance.

I gradually perceive regularity in the changes which happen around me. The disappearance and reappearance of the light occurs with absolute regularity, though the light periods themselves are not always identical. Sometimes they are blinding and suffuse the colours of my world with a brightness that is hard to tolerate. With this there is always a sensation of increased warmth. On other occasions during the light periods, the brightness seems dimmed, less powerful, and in these periods there is a distinct reduction in warmth. The colours of the world around me also appear diminished and washed-out in these times: easier to bear but somehow disappointing, disheartening.

Slowly I begin to realise that colours are not the same as sounds, that taste is separate from smell, that touch is not the same as the thing doing the touching. I begin to discern that the things in my world have edges, boundaries separating them from each other and from the background they inhabit. The moving objects that loom over me look gradually more and more distinct the one from the other. They all have a roughly similar outline, but there are differences. The large one which provides sustenance has a thin halo of something bright all around the spherical part that makes up its highest part. I later come to know this gentle shape as my uncle Kallan. The two who are always together seem to have less surrounding their uppermost part, but it is light, and this light hue seems to flow around the spherical part and down beyond, across the wider part below. These always-together shapes are my twin sisters, Emaleen and Safya. The cold, irregular visitor, my mother Zelda, has a spherical top with little surrounding it.

I note that the moving shapes, the members of my family, always present the same side of themselves to me, and that their rounded top parts are configured with darker and lighter parts, and parts which seem to move, especially in conjunction with the noises that the objects make. I grasp the fact that the noises are coming from the moving lower part, a pinkish colouration that opens to reveal a darker space, fringed with white. I also grasp by observation of these noises, that they have significance. When there are two people together, there is regularity in the production of these utterances: one follows the other. And even when they are alone, I sense that the utterances are directed at me. With a blinding flash of comprehension, I appreciate that these people are communicating. The first moment this happens is when Kallan and my sisters are with me together. My flash of understanding causes a totally involuntary outburst of sound to gush from me, and the response in my family members is astonishing. For a moment they are absolutely silent, and then there is a flurry of loud, happy sounds from all of them at the same time, and at the same moment they turn from me to each other. When they turn back to me, the pink parts of their rotund upper parts are parted more widely than I have ever seen and they are emitting a loud, almost harsh sound, which nevertheless fills me with joy. I have produced my own first sounds, and witnessed what I will later learn is the laughter of others.

With this first flash of realisation, awareness of other distinctions in the world around me fall more and more rapidly into place. I now appreciate as a fact that the people moving around me are like me. I find it frustrating that I lack the ambulatory ability they seem to possess, but despite this shortcoming, I simply know that I am one of them. The noises they have been making begin to make some sense. What I originally perceived as a seamless flow of uninterrupted sound, I now begin to hear as a stream of separate units, laid out in a row, with significance in each series of utterances. Individual words begin to emerge, and each one I immediately grasp and remember. I rapidly learn that each person has his or her own special, individual designation which they call a name. The first one I met, the tall one who gave me the sweet liquid is Kallan. The others' names take me longer to discern, but I soon learn that the inseparable ones are called Emaleen and Safya, and the cold one Zelda. Even more amazingly, I seem to have my own moniker which they use in their utterances to me and between themselves: Samek. It is an extraordinary moment of profound emotion when I first realise this. I am more than an object. I have my very own individual word which sets me apart from those around me. I run this sound over and over in my head: Samek, Samek, Samek. I like the sound of it. I like even more what it signifies: that I am a person, an individual. And that I exist.

I rapidly learn words such as head, face, eyes, mouth, hand and so on. I see that I have arms and legs like the others who visit me. Though I am unable to move myself through space the way they do, I take great delight in the fact that I can move my limbs. I can wave them around, I can bend them, I can flex my fingers and even my toes to some extent. I learn that I can watch my toes wiggling by lifting my legs in the air. For some reason I cannot fathom, I am unable to lift my head at all, though not for want of trying. I can move it from side to side, but no more.

I can make noises, all sorts of noises, and these are nearly always met with laughter from the people I have come to think of as the group of things like me. I learn that I can evince a strong reaction simply by turning up the corners of my mouth and making a staccato gurgling sound at the same time. I realise that these people see this as me smiling and laughing at them, something that seems to give them huge pleasure. I do it often, as I adore the reaction it causes in them.

Kallan often picks me up, sometimes merely to cuddle and caress me, something I long for when I am alone. He occasionally passes me to the identical ones, but seems anxious as he does so, as if the little ones will somehow cause me harm. But I know no such fear. They, however, are anxious when they hold me, quickly returning me to Kallan or to my resting place. Zelda never holds me and never touches me. I know now that her interest in me, strong as it is, is somehow impersonal and distant. She is aloof and removed from the emotional connection between the other members of my group. The only exception to this is when she and Kallan are together with me, something that rarely occurs. Despite her gruffness and ill-temper, she nevertheless shows an obvious affection towards Kallan that she shows to no-one else.

My rapid acquiring of understanding of my surroundings, and of the words to describe my world seem natural and obvious to me. My reality is the only one I know, and I have nothing to compare it with. It is only as I grow older that I learn that the speed and ease with which I engaged with my environment was anything but natural and normal. It was breathtakingly rapid, and unprecedented in the history of humanity. I do not say this to brag, merely as a statement of fact. After all, I am something of an experimental fluke. My progenitors were deliberately chosen for their astounding range of abilities and talents, and their abnormally high intelligence. Little wonder then that the development of my consciousness should have been so expeditious. A pity that my physical development lagged so far behind, creating a peculiar disparity between my intellectual abilities and those of my rather normal baby's body.

I rapidly learned to talk, my vocabulary growing day by day at breakneck speed. It was not long before I could converse easily with the members of my family. Yet what frustration! I was still unable to move my own body, apart from rolling from side to side or waving arms or legs in the air. To experience the real world outside of my nursery, I had to rely on others to carry me, where they wanted and when they wanted. I was desperate to see and experience everything for myself, and Kallan, or sometimes my sisters took me out of my nursery, around the house, around the garden, but only for short periods. When I pestered Kallan to allow me more latitude, he merely laughed, then looked sternly at me and told me that for all my linguistic and intellectual precocity, I was still a tiny baby, and as such I needed mostly to rest and to sleep. This frustrated and even angered me, but there was little I could do about it but scream my displeasure, though deep down I suspected he was right. But these early months felt to me like some sort of imprisonment. I sometimes tried to persuade my sisters to disobey our uncle and take me out on their own, but they were unwilling to do this, partly through fear of Kallan's displeasure, but also because they sensed what Kallan said was right, and that a tiny baby like me needed rest, and not to be overwhelmed with too much novelty. I had no option but to soak up what I could on the occasions I was taken out, and otherwise to bide my time.

Chapter Three

As my intellectual and verbal abilities continued to improve, and I began to understand the world around me, I was able to make sense of my physical surroundings.

We lived in a large, rambling bungalow with many rooms. Apart from the room I slept in, Kallan and Zelda each had a sleeping room of their own; my sisters shared a room, and even shared a single large bed. Kallan, and occasionally Safya would carry me to a communal eating room with a big rectangular table in the middle, surrounded by chairs. Both table and chairs were made of dark wood which must at some time have been polished and gleaming, but which by this time showed signs of peeling varnish, discolouration and other minor damage. There were several rooms that were used for relaxation and leisure, though I did not understand any of this at first. These rooms were furnished with soft chairs and sofas, and other furniture and objects I did not begin to understand until later, when I was able to enjoy them myself. On the walls were childish pictures of trees and flowers in bright colours, and drawings of a person who I took to be Kallan. There were none that resembled Zelda, though I never discovered whether she forbade my sisters from drawing her, or putting up the pictures, or they simply had no desire to draw or paint her in the first place.

There were rooms where food was stored - a room for fresh food which was kept cool, a room for dried food with sacks and bags of all sorts of edibles, a room with refrigerators and freezers. Zelda insisted on us having enough to last a siege, such was her distrust of the outside world. There was also a small kitchen whose purpose I only learned much later. In my early years I never saw anyone actually prepare food: it seemed to simply appear as if by magic on the table, fully prepared.

At the back of the house was the conservatory running the entire length of the building, with bamboo frames between the panes of glass. Even the ceiling was made of glass. I later learnt that this was real glass, heavy old-fashioned glass, rather than the much more common perspiglass. This was always my favourite room as it was filled to overflowing with plants. There were pots everywhere, of all sizes, some housing small bushy plants covered with flowers of myriad colours, others larger green bushes. The biggest pots, almost as tall as Kallan and much wider, were home to trees, some of which reached all the way to the glass ceiling. Many of the trees had flowers, some tiny and unobtrusive, others huge and gaudy, begging to be looked at and smelt. The odours in the room were powerful and varied - the constant background smell of damp soil, the varied perfumes pouring from the many different types of flower, and the more subtle scents of leaves trying their best to compete with the blooms.

I was taken regularly by Kallan to a bright, cheerful room whose walls were tiled from floor to ceiling in shades of bright blue and vivid yellow, whose floor was darker yellow marble, cool underfoot, and whose ceiling was of the lightest sky blue, dotted with paintings of fluffy white clouds. Here I was bathed, under the watchful eye of my uncle, and occasionally my sisters.

After the glass room brimming with plants, this was my favourite. I loved the gleam that emanated from the shiny, brightly coloured tiles which, as the beams of sun flowing through the windows bounced off them, suffused the whole room with dancing shades of blue and yellow. Such joyous, living colours. Even on duller days, the room always seemed sunny, such was the effect of the colours on the walls. I was in the company of the person I loved more than anything in the world, and the occasion of my bath was always one of jollity, with much laughter and playfulness on the part of both of us. Safya regularly joined my uncle at my bathtime, and my antics in the bath seemed to cause them great joy and amusement, especially such simple things as blowing bubbles, splashing Safya and Kallan with water by striking the surface of the water with my hands, and even farting under water - something that even the often serious and sulky Emaleen found entertaining on the rare occasions when she assisted with my bath-time. Hearing my favourite people laughing this way encouraged me to play up to it, simply to be rewarded with such merriness again and again.

There were rooms where we children were educated as we grew older, and in which we also carried out our leisure activities. The two things blended, as we were all keen students, eager to devour whatever information and knowledge came our way, especially so as we were never allowed first hand experience of the outside world. We did not differentiate learning biology, physics, chemistry, history, geography, philosophy and many other subjects from activities such as painting, drawing, writing, playing musical instruments.

We were never allowed first hand experience of the outside world, so all our learning was vital to us, filling in for our otherwise woefully minimal experience of our world, our almost total lack of exposure to other people in our earlier years. Given my mother's scientific interest, we of course had access to all the latest technology to help us with our studies. The house had an integrated, multi-functional digital memory which not only ran everything in the house itself, but which also had in its memories the whole of human endeavour. Everything we could ever want to know was ours with no more than a question directed to the digital memory, and this included the sum of human knowledge from the times before the Chaos. Everything, that is, apart from how to properly interact with other people, with normal people, how to function appropriately in the world outside. And it was only later, much later, that I discovered how Zelda had limited our access to much of the basic information about our own world. Our mother's intention was always to keep us away from other people, buried in our ignorance of much that we would need to know in order to function normally in society.

As a tiny baby I was not physically able to access the huge amount of knowledge in the digital memory, but I pestered my sisters to feed back to me what they had learned each day. Safya, in general, was happy to help me, and even Emaleen occasionally, when she could be bothered. In this way, by the time I was finally able to walk and sit by myself, surrounded by all I needed to control the direction of my own learning, I had already imbibed a substantial amount of knowledge across a wide range of topics, albeit somewhat random knowledge due to the fact that most of it had been conveyed to me by five year old girls.

During my early years my main companions were Kallan and Safya, and to a lesser extent Emaleen. As I grew older, I was joined by Adwin, 'born' when I was three years old, and my constant companion from that time onwards.

Zelda always referred to Kallan as her brother, though they were no more true siblings than Zelda was my true mother. We children called Kallan uncle, for want of a better affectionate moniker. Kallan had been in Zelda's cohort at the Institute of Childhood, and was brought up with her. A few years after Zelda had removed the twins from their foetal tank, she invited Kallan to come and live with them, and to look after the twins, knowing that she neither knew how to look after them, nor had any desire to do so. Despite Kallan's initial reservations about raising children, he soon came to love his role, especially the fact that he could provide them with something unique, something that other children brought up in the Institutes did not enjoy: a presence in their lives like an old-world parent.

Kallan was tall, strong and robust - physically impressive. Despite living in an isolated house with only Zelda and us children for company, he always made a point of being well-presented, dressed simply but with style, his clothes of excellent quality. He tried to teach us the importance of appearance, and trained us to dress well, always to be clean and presentable. Year after year he also tried to get Zelda to be cleaner, tidier and better kempt, but to little avail. But he kept trying - leaving clean clothes for her and even sneaking into her room while she slept and removing her dirty clothes for washing. But as Zelda often fell asleep in her day clothes, this was usually difficult to achieve. Very occasionally (and generally on the extremely rare occasions there were guests visiting our home), Kallan put his foot down and insisted that Zelda shower, brush her teeth, comb her hair and put on clean clothes. Zelda was so astonished by his sudden change of temperament that she meekly acceded. But Kallan knew that he would rarely get away with such behaviour, and only insisted on occasion, often enough so Zelda did not become irretrievably submerged in her bad habits, but not so frequently that she might become defiant.

Kallan had thick, straight hair, almost completely white even when I first saw it. Though hair colour could easily be altered and never needed become white, he seemed to like its hue, considering it distinguished. He had intense blue eyes, marking an amazing contrast with the silvery sheen of his hair and his tanned skin. He smiled and laughed a great deal, deep crinkles appearing at the corners of his vivid azure eyes when he did.

Apart from our house, Zelda had a laboratory contiguous with the house, and occupying a large amount of land. The buildings were surrounded by a large garden, filled with all sorts of plants, and including a herb garden and even a vegetable patch lovingly tended by Kallan. Beyond what I could see from the windows and from my walks when carried by Kallan or Safya during my infancy, I could see that greenery stretched in all directions. I did not learn the full extent of this until some time later, when I was able to walk confidently under my own steam.

Zelda I saw infrequently during my earliest years: she had little interest in a developing child until it was old enough to express itself verbally and in an adult fashion. I was not unhappy that she was an irregular visitor to my room or to the other rooms we children spent most of our time in. Though we called her mother, she showed us no warmth or affection. I learned that she spent most of her time beavering away in her laboratory. I also discovered later that she was protective of her children, but I never knew if this was due to any sort of personal feeling for us, or merely because we were her lifetime's work, her greatest achievement, an investment. Kallan was the only person she seemed to genuinely like, but it was hard to discern in her manner much affection for him beyond a slight reduction in gruffness. Kallan was one of the only children in their cohort at the Institute who had liked Zelda, spending time with her, and even standing up for her against the other children, almost all of whom disliked her. For his support through those difficult childhood years Zelda was profoundly grateful and remained devoted to her cohort brother.

Zelda was unusually short for a person in our time. She had a slightly bowed upper back, probably from sitting such long hours at her studies, and scrawny legs. She moved with rapid, short steps, more like a fast shuffle than a walk. She was not good looking, with blotchy skin and eczema, despite the fact that such things could easily be cured. Zelda's hair was long, usually worn in a tightly bound plait. On one or two very rare occasions, we saw her hair unplaited, a mass of ringlets caused by it having been so tightly bound. On one such occasion, little Adwin said that she looked like a witch from the old stories. To our huge surprise, this amused her so much that from then on she sometimes referred to herself as the Bad Witch of the West, a reference we only came to understand much later.

My memory of Zelda is of a woman who seldom smiled or laughed. Life was a serious and not very pleasant business for her. In addition to her sombre manner, she also had a tendency to erupt into anger, at her children, the Council, the world at large, though never with Kallan as far as I was aware. It often struck me as odd that she should be so irascible, she who was in other ways so cool, clinical and detached. But her unpopularity as a child had instilled in her a deep-seated anger at people in general, and this was exacerbated by what she perceived as a lack of understanding of her work as an adult. As I came to know only too well as I grew up, Zelda's view of the world combined with the hostility of her peers, of many citizens, and of the Council, led to her being surprisingly short-tempered, frequently unable to control outbursts of extreme anger, even rage.

My sisters, I spent time with, more with Safya than Emaleen, though not nearly as much even with Safya as with my brother after he appeared. From my earliest times, I found both of my sisters enigmatic and hard to understand, even Safya despite her air of kindness, other times Emaleen, though for different reasons. They were Zelda's first successfully created 'children'. Both shared the same nine progenitors and as such were genuine twins sharing an identical mitochondrial commixture. The creation of the twins was the only time Zelda was successful in producing two fully viable embryos from the same batch, and so she decided to allow both of them to reach birth age.

They were tall with long fair, and unusual slate grey eyes. They both had the same habit of continually pushing their long locks behind their over-large ears, thereby accentuating this physical characteristic. As with most people of our time, they were healthy and robust, fit and with excellent immune systems. I soon perceived that they were 'thick as thieves', like one mind in two bodies, almost never apart, even sleeping in the same bed. Not only were they identical twins, but as the only two children in the house for the five years before my arrival, they learned to rely almost entirely on themselves for company and entertainment. This made them insular and self-involved, making it hard for other people to break into their tiny circle of intense sisterhood. This was even true for Adwin and me, who, though generally on fairly amicable terms with Safya, felt constantly excluded from real intimacy with either of our sisters. This was a particular problem for me, as I had three years of life with little company before my brother arrived.

My sisters were often silent, especially Safya, but this was because they usually communicated with each other by telepathy, and when they did speak to each other, they preferred to use a private language they invented which no-one else knew. I learned to understand and eventually speak their private language, but soon discovered that no-one else was welcome to use it. I also learned how to impose myself into their telepathic conversations, but this too was met with some hostility, so I quickly refrained from doing so. They spent a good deal of time alone, and even when in the company of others, their private, silently expressed language cut other people out of their circle of communication. Adwin and I always felt excluded, though we could if we wished have intruded into this circle. Kallan did not enjoy the same gifts that my brother and I were endowed with, so had no way of breaching the wall erected by my sisters. This always seemed to irritate him considerably, and to sadden him. He tried year after year to enter my sisters' private realm, but they never allowed him to do so. And his continual attempts to encourage them to spend more time connected to others were equally fruitless. With sympathy I watched his endless struggles, but knew he would always be rebuffed, kept strictly outside the tiny duality that my sisters had created for themselves. The most he managed was to encourage Safya, with some success, to help him with me and my brother.

Despite the twins' insularity, all four of us children shared a clear and powerful sense of connectedness. As we grew, we were to discover that we were unlike anyone else, unique, and that many people outside our home would come to view us with suspicion and hostility, even hatred.

Chapter Four

When I learnt to walk, I began to explore the gardens, and then the meadows and woodland surrounding our house. As a toddler, I was always accompanied. At first it was Kallan who took me out, though he showed almost no interest in straying beyond the gardens: even a stroll in the meadows was unusual for him. He seemed curiously uninterested in the area beyond this, indifferent to what he might encounter in the woods. With his fussiness about his clothing, perhaps he simply worried about tearing his garments if he ventured into the densely packed trees.

"Uncle! Uncle! - to the woods!" I would plead, time and time again. But he never acceded to my requests, just took my hand and helped me toddle around the garden. He pointed out the herbs and vegetables, the flowers and bushes, telling me their names. I never had the heart to tell him I already knew most of them, as he seemed proud of the fact that he knew all of them. He had a particular fondness for blue flowers, and his favourite was a large blue poppy.

"See these, Samek?" my uncle would ask, peering at me through vivid blue eyes. "They come from high mountains a long long way away. The seeds have to be almost frozen for a month before they germinate, and they are very unpredictable, but isn't it worth it? They are the most beautiful flowers in the world," he would sigh.

"Pick them?" I would ask, my chubby little hand reaching out to grasp the long delicate stems as I spoke. But he sighed again and say "No. They wilt if you pick them. They don't even last long left growing. But that is part of their charm. Such short-lived glory." I shrugged, not understanding what he was saying, and sulking slightly as Kallan thwarted my attempts to pick the blooms.

We would sit on the grass, or on one of the benches dotted around the garden and just admire the plants, watch the bees going about their busy lives, smile at the antics of small birds in the bushes. Kallan often spoke to me of his life with Zelda at the Institute, the life he had after the Institute but before coming to look after my sisters, and stories of them before I came along. I learned that before he came to look after us he had tried his hand at many activities, none of which really occupied his attention. He had tried painting, sculpture, dancing and acting, landscape and garden design, among other things. Each one proved mildly interesting for a while, but soon palled. He began to despair of ever finding anything that would hold his interest and give him a sense of purpose.

"Then Zelda asked me to come and look after her 'children,'" he told me one day. "I had no idea what she meant and was astonished to hear what she'd been up to. At that time there was only the girls. You hadn't been born yet," he added with a slightly wistful glance at me, perhaps wondering if 'born' were really the appropriate word. "Your sisters were very tiny at the time, just toddling around, not quite two years old I think. Zelda clearly had no idea how to raise children. In fact," he said with a wry smile. "It's amazing they survived those first few years at all, having been raised by then mostly by domestic automata!"

"I was wary," Kallan continued. "But Zelda managed to persuade me to visit, though I made it clear that I was making no promises. I came, met the twins, and knew they needed me. And that was that. I moved here then and have been here ever since. But even then I was very unsure. What did I know of raising children? More than Zelda I suppose," he added with a chuckle. "But that was not much of a recommendation. I insisted that I could leave whenever I wanted, and Zelda agreed. She could hardly refuse. Anyway, as you know, I didn't leave. And for what it's worth," he added, smiling at me. "I think it's worked out rather well, don't you?" I nodded vigorously and hugged my uncle, my short chubby arms not reaching even half way around him. I was profoundly thankful for his presence, shuddering at the idea of being without him.

"In fact," continued my uncle. "And I hope this doesn't sound too self-important. But I soon realised that being here, raising you children, that this was my purpose in life, providing the upbringing Zelda couldn't, or wouldn't provide." And again I sighed with the realisation of our lucky escape. Kallan was kind, thoughtful, considerate, almost never angry or short-tempered, amazingly patient - in all ways the opposite of our selfish, self-obsessed, irascible and angry mother. And in addition to this, because of his varied activities, all of which were things Zelda knew nothing about, he was able to provide us children with knowledge and interests far beyond the science and technology Zelda intended us to know. He allowed us all to be more rounded, to have more diversified knowledge, and provided us with a desperately needed element of normality in our otherwise highly abnormal lives.

When I was three, tiny little Adwin appeared, as if by magic. I was thrilled. Before that I had spent much time alone. Kallan was busy managing the home, and sometimes was away from the compound. Zelda was always too busy, and too uninterested, in spending much time with a tiny child. Emaleen never showed a great deal of interest in being with me, and though Safya did look after me and was always kind to me when we were together, she spent most of her time with her sister. I was immediately possessive and highly protective of my brother. He was mine. Even as a neonate, it was clear there was something wrong with him. In a time in which most illness had been eradicated, he regularly suffered from minor complaints, from lassitude and weariness. His skin was pale ivory, his eyes dark and encircled with brown rings, the contrast startling. I looked after him, protected him, cared for him. I included him in my activities whenever I was allowed. As he grew old enough to walk, I took him by the hand, showing him around our home, the gardens and meadows beyond the house. And eventually even to the woods encircling the estate. Though Kallan had always refused to take me to the forest, no-one had ever told us I could not wander at will there myself. The only thing Zelda ever showed us on the compound was the edge of it - the invisible 'fence' we were forbidden to cross, the border to our comfortable prison. But as small children, this limitation did not worry me: the estate was more than big enough to keep us happy and occupied. On very rare occasions our sisters joined us in the gardens, but more often than not Adwin and I were on our own.

We spent endless hours and days lost in our own world of imagination. Despite our access to unlimited information and knowledge through the digital memory available in the house, our world was narrow in other ways. Our circle of people was tiny: only our family and a very occasional scientist who came to visit our mother. We enlarged our world with our visits to the woods. This was genuine, wild woodland, not the manicured or tamed type that I later learned was the preference for most people near their homes. Zelda had acquired the estate partly for its isolation, but also because of its paradoxically protective wildness.

I learned that some people had a fondness for visiting the untamed, untouched parts of the world, though most people did not, and would avoid anything they perceived as uncontrolled and uncultivated. If anyone did ever happen upon the edge of the woods surrounding our home, they would not think to try and penetrate the dense greenery to see what was on the other side. If they did, they would soon come upon signs erected by Zelda warning them that they were about to encounter an invisible electro-magnetic fence that would prevent them crossing into 'private land'. Such a thing as private land did not exist in our world then, but Zelda never considered such restrictions to apply to her.

The woods were extensive, green, dense, made up of a huge variety of warm temperate trees, bushes and other plants. There were many evergreens, giving the forest the appearance of life throughout the year. But the deciduous trees were even more special: their variety through the seasons, from their bare brown bones in the winter, to the halo of pale green in the spring, to the fullness of darker green shading us in the hottest months, through to the yellows, reds and oranges of autumn. Some produced huge displays of flowers in the spring and early summer, but most of the colour came from the bushes and especially the carpets of small woodland plants that erupted into blues, yellows, pinks and whites from early spring right through the summer. Even now as I write so many years later displays of flowers still take me back to those innocent early trips to the forest. And the aromas of the blooms sitting in the vase beside me as I commit these words to paper fill me with a surge of nostalgia for those carefree days spent with my brother in our forest when I was still too young to know what the world was really like.

There were several small streams which meandered merrily through the woods, fullest in the spring, but flowing all year. And there were ponds dotted here and there where Adwin giggled with delight in finding frogspawn and tadpoles, small fish, and many types of insect from the tiny mosquito larvae wriggling just below the water's surface to the majestic dragonflies, jewels which hovered over the water or rested on stalks near the water's edge. He was not so enamoured of the adult mosquitoes which seemed intent on biting his soft young skin as soon as they emerged from the water's surface, the itchy welts causing days of discomfort. One of the very first benefits of the gifts I possessed was the ability to kill all such nasty creatures the moment I saw or heard them. My brother and I learned about these animals from seeing them in the wild, not just from the digital memory. We enjoyed the vision of water lilies emerging from the depths of the ponds, and then, against all logic, producing huge yellow or pink flowers in the midst of the dark, muddy waters. This seemed almost miraculous to us, though we were brought up firmly not to believe in miracles.

We played games of make-believe, imagining we were living in the wilds, finding all our own food, sleeping in nests we had made from piles of old leaves and bracken we had thrust into large holes in the bases of trees. We actually roasted nuts on fires we made, ate berries and drank water from the streams. We even tried to cook and eat some of the small fish we had managed on occasion to catch, but the bones made this almost impossible. Once, I tried to cook and eat a frog, but my little brother was so upset by seeing its charred little body when I teased it from the fire with a stick, that I decided instead to bury it, the way I had seen children do to favourite animals in some of the old stories.

Sometimes in our games of make-believe we were in our own times - children lost, or when we were in bleaker mood, abandoned, in the forest, unwanted by anyone. Then we planned how we would survive until we were able to find our way out and show ourselves to the world again, to be met either with joy (when we were lost) or guilt and outrage (when we had been abandoned). But one of our favourite games of this type was imagining we were back in the old world, the world before the Chaos.

Naturally, I only had the dimmest idea of the Chaos at this early age, and Adwin knew nothing beyond the vague details I imparted to him. I knew though, that the world before it and after it were different, utterly different, and that the conditions that created the Chaos could never happen again. I knew that no-one wanted things to return to what they were like before the Chaos. And yet, there seemed to me, in my childish innocence, to be a glamour associated with the old world. A tragic glamour, to be sure, but a glamour nonetheless. From my vantage point as a child of order and safety, the disorder, the untidiness, the disarray of the old world seemed appealing. Despite its dirt and poverty, its stupendous over-population, its pollution, its dangers, threats and perils, it seemed exciting, vibrant, alive, in a way I found hard to imagine in our own time. It is true my brother and I had little personal experience of our own world, but what small amount we knew had taught us that it was controlled, disciplined, restrained, everything in its place, everyone behaving with quiet civility, with little room for fancy or fantasy, originality, creativity or enterprise. Little wonder that we two small boys pined for a world we perceived as simply more fun, felt almost nostalgic for something we had never actually known, could not know, and which had never in fact existed the way we imagined it.

I learned to enjoy the company of animals in the forest. Adwin was much more wary, especially at first. Despite being a real forest, there were no dangerous animals here, as I had read existed in more genuinely wild forests and jungles. But we encountered several species of deer, foxes, badgers, hedgehogs, rabbits, numerous rodents, and a whole array of birds, as well as insects. We learned that if we kept very still we could observe them, and that some of them were less timid than others, even remaining near us after discovering our presence. One of the earliest abilities I discovered that I possessed was that of creating a calmness around me which seemed almost to hypnotise the animals close to me. I had no idea at the time how I did this, but by remaining immobile and thinking of stillness, I was able to exude a calming energy which affected the animals. With this, I was able gradually to approach the animals, and even stroke them, though some of them I felt no desire to touch or even approach, rats especially. Once he had overcome his reluctance, Adwin particularly loved to touch the deer, their soft, warm fur was like nothing he had ever experienced, and to touch another living thing was a thrill that rendered him speechless with joy. Despite my calming and almost mesmerising energy, they were still apprehensive, and quivered gently beneath his fingers. The slightest sudden movement, or noise from nearby disrupted my control, and the animal would tense, then suddenly bound away and disappear among the trees.

We learned to recognise individuals amongst the animals we most liked, and the bolder of them sought us out, seeming to enjoy our attentions. We helped this along by sneaking food out of the house which we gave to our favourites. We had little idea what different animals would eat, and learned through trial and error. At first we could not understand why the deer would not eat the cheese or meat we brought, or the badgers turned their noses up at the bread and rice we tried to feed them. We had to learn the lessons of nature the hard way when we discovered one of our 'friends' in the woods, a handsome red fox, eating one of our other friends, a cute and fluffy rabbit we had often petted. We had naively assumed they treated each other the way we treated all of them. I wanted to punish the fox for his betrayal, but even at my young age, I sensed that this would be wrong, that what he had done was normal, part of his nature.

Without our forest, Adwin and I would have had so much narrower a childhood. It not only kept us active, enjoying the sunlight and the fresh air, but opened up worlds to us that we might never otherwise have known. The world of nature, to begin with, but just as importantly, the world of imagination. Without these, our upbringing and education would have been restricted and narrow, and it is hard to see how we would have become the people we eventually did become.

As Adwin and I grew older, we went to the woods often. We continued to learn more about the natural world, the flowers and trees and animals, and about the strange world of living things that inhabited the ponds and streams. I was particularly fascinated by things that changed form, or grew at great speed. Tadpoles that grew legs, lost their tails and emerged from the water as tiny frogs and toads. Caterpillars that wrapped themselves in a hard chrysalis, seemingly unalive, then emerged resplendent some time later as flying creatures, fluttering wings iridescent in the dappled woodland light. Mushrooms and toadstools clustered around the base of trees, seemingly substantial, and yet growing from nothing to full size overnight. Tight green or brown buds on trees in the spring which, when we returned to the forest a few days later had blossomed into clouds of pink, white or yellow flowers entirely covering the tree, or which had unfurled into a mass of pale green leaves surrounding the tree with a downy coating of soft, light colour. I began to learn the science behind all of these transformations, but this did not hinder my enchantment of witnessing the changes. If anything, the science enhanced it, as it taught me how amazingly complicated our world was, yet with no apparent purpose, just as Zelda would later exclaim.

We continued to play our games of make-believe in which we were forced to survive alone in the woods, sometimes back in the times before the Chaos, and on other occasions in games of fantasy in our own era. We played more and more with the animals, honing our ability to control them as we did so.

A major transformation occurred in our game-playing after we had begun to learn about fairy tales, fables and myths from the old world. Our childish imaginations were fired by the forest creatures in stories of fairies and pixies, elves and goblins, giants and dwarves. We were enchanted to learn that in the distant past people had believed that there were spirits inhabiting the trees and rivers, waterfalls and woodland pools. Some of these had names: the trees had their dryads, the waters their naiads, or nymphs. I was under no illusion that such things were real - my upbringing was far too rationalist for that - yet I was thrilled by the idea of our forest being inhabited by a huge and varied population of such creatures, even if I was not able to perceive them. Adwin, in his earliest years, seemed more inclined to believe that these magical sylvan creatures were real.

We would wander around our forest kingdom, choosing the most likely spots for each type of mythical being to inhabit. The darkest and densest forest would obviously be home to the elves who were, so the stories told, shy creatures, denizens of the deepest greenwoods. I informed my brother that they built villages among the highest branches of the tallest trees, invisible from the ground, where they moved effortlessly from bough to bough and tree to tree. They only came down to the forest floor when it was absolutely still, mostly at night, and hunted the small animals using their amazing skill with bow and arrow.

The pixies, sprites and imps were tiny, living under bushes and even under the large spreading leaves of ground-dwelling plants, a particular favourite being the foxglove. We even saw pictures in one ancient book showing pixies wearing the spotted rose and white foxglove blooms as hats, protection against the rain. These creatures were not shy, but still did not like to be seen by human eyes. They would emerge when they felt it was safe, and delighted in playing tricks on unsuspecting wanderers in the woods - magically spiriting away their clothes if the human swam in a pond, or their food or bags if they rested on the ground and allowed themselves to fall asleep. It was said that if you found yourself a victim of such a prank, you could hear the silvery tinkling of tinny laughter (if you listened hard enough).

The fairies too were tiny, dressed in soft natural colours, and with translucent wings which reflected light in iridescent greens, purples and blues. They lived in tiny dwellings made of leaves drawn together and sealed with tree sap, providing a safe, yet unobtrusive home in the woods.

Perhaps through fear of encountering one, Adwin decided that giants would be too big to inhabit our woods. Dwarves of course, though small, needed more space to live and work. But goblins were another matter. They were small, wicked creatures, hiding in wait for innocent travellers, and then leaping out to beat them, rob them, and even kill them. We were both alarmed by goblins, but when we learned that they normally lived under bridges we felt safer: there were no bridges in our forest.

The place we felt the most likely to house spirits was our most treasured spot in the entire forest. In one of the darker parts of the woods there was a clearing we discovered on one of our perambulations around our demesne. One of the streams which ran through the forest approached the clearing some seven metres or so above the forest floor. It cascaded over the top of a semi-circular rocky outcrop, its small, fast flowing waterfall ending in a small pool. The rocks of the outcrop were alive with ferns and mosses, and even some intrepid flowering plants which clung tenaciously to the damp, glistening cliff. Small birds flitted to and fro in and around the sparkling, tumbling water, and small flowers and other water-loving plants encircled the crystal of the pool whose water was tinged with the lightest trace of green. At one end of the pool the stream once again took up its journey on through the forest. The water in the pool was so clear that it was almost luminous, reflecting the stippled light that managed to penetrate the canopy of greenery above, emitting an emerald-tinged glow. The glade was thus suffused with an almost tangible greenness, a symbol of two of the gifts of nature - the opulence of foliage and the vitality of water.

This, our private and secret glade, Adwin declared to be the place where the spirits of the trees and the nymphs of the water would live. Why would they chose any other, when this one was perfect? On the mossy trunk of a large fallen tree near the edge of the pool we would sit, gazing in wonder all around, and talk about the water nymphs and wood spirits, how they would emerge on a summer evening, especially under a full moon of course, and dance and sing, holding hands, cavorting in circles large and small in and out of the pool, among the trees surrounding the glade, through the waterfall itself, causing eruptions of pearly-white foam to sparkle under the light of the moon, their voices high and clear, their laughter bright and bell-like. As the night waned and the first glimmer of the rising sun appeared, they would quietly fade away, back into the trees, the pool, the waterfall and stream, to peacefully while away the time until they next emerged to cavort in the safety of their woodland home.

After we had recounted the details of the nymphs' and wood spirits' nocturnal merriment, Adwin and I would sit in absolute silence, as still as the rocks under the waterfall. We would strain to hear the tinkling voices of the nymphs and spirits, the delicate fluttering of the fairies' wings, or even the mocking laughter of the imps and pixies. But all to no avail. No such things existed. I knew this to be the case, and yet, and yet...even I longed for them to be real, yearned to see them, to hear them, to be drawn into their magical realm, to dance with them, play with them, sing with them. Even as a small child, I had a dim understanding that the old world, before the Chaos, for all its disorder, its misery and filth, its ugliness, had enjoyed a rich and vivid imaginative realm beyond the comprehension of most of the people in my own time. One of the saddest, and most enduring, effects of the Chaos was to wipe out thousands and thousands of years of inventive creativity, so many of the stories and fables, tales to delight the soul.

After a long span of utter stillness and immobility, I would sigh deeply, slowly stand up, and drag myself from the bewitching dell, my brother reluctantly in tow, to make our way haltingly home, unwilling to break the spell we had created with our imaginations, sad to leave our fantasy world behind. Our consolation was that we could return soon, and once again weave our own form of magic.

Chapter Five

Some time after the strange dinner at which Adwin and I had confessed to our games of fantasy in the forest, I managed to finally convince our sisters to make good their promise to come to the woods with us. I woke early on the day we had decided upon for our trip, and lay for a while in bed, thinking about the strange dinner and the unheard-of friendly familiarity shared with our sisters after the meal, and their even more unexpected agreement to come with us to the forest.

As I lay there, enjoying the birdsong from the bushes outside my bedroom window, planning the trip to the woods and what I would show our sisters first, a shadow crossed my mind. Perhaps the twins would have second thoughts and would now have changed their minds. Perhaps they would not come with us after all. Perchance their amiableness and consent had been evoked merely as a response to the strange atmosphere which had reigned at that supper. And I knew that even if Safya wanted to join us, if Emaleen refused, her sister would stay at home too.

I cast a mindthought to Adwin to see if he was awake, and received a chirpy ~*Good morning*~ in reply. An unusually chirpy response from him, especially at the start of the day. I could sense he was as enthusiastic as I was to spend a day with our sisters, eager to share our special places with them. I got no feeling that he had any doubts about their agreement to come. Adwin was a more trusting soul, more naive perhaps, and took the girls at their word.

I got out of bed, dressed quickly in comfortable clothes, suitable for a day in the woods, and made my way to the dining room. I ate a simple breakfast of toast and butter washed down with milk. No-one else was in the room and I assumed they had all breakfasted before me. As I was finishing, Adwin came into the room, slightly flushed as if he had been running, beaming an unusually wide smile as he approached me. He was carrying two rucksacks, both of which were bulging, and, judging from his stumbling walk, too heavy for him.

"I've packed food and drinks for us all for the whole day. I don't know how long we'll be out, but it's better to be safe than sorry." He then laughed, and continued, "I can't imagine the girls eating nuts and berries, or a rabbit cooked on an open fire, or drinking water from the stream!"

I laughed too. My sisters were very particular about what they would and would not eat or drink, and fussy about dirt and cleanliness. I hoped Adwin's choices would be acceptable to them. At this thought, I wondered what they would really make of the forest. Would they share our delight in the sheer vibrancy and aliveness of it all, or would they think it all dirty and grimy, muddy and wet? Would they find it alarming, frightening even?

Adwin picked up on my unspoken concerns. "What are you worried about?" he asked.

"It doesn't matter," I replied, deciding to keep my concerns to myself. "Shall we go and see if they're ready?"

My brother nodded eagerly, his dark curls bobbing as he did so. He then turned and began to move towards the door, struggling gallantly with the two bags. I caught up with him and took one of them from him. He flashed me a smile of thanks.

When we reached our sisters' room, we knocked gently. We waited until we heard Emaleen shout that we could come in. Despite the invitation, we were hesitant to open the door and enter, as we had never felt ourselves welcome to enter this private space. But on the basis of Emaleen's call to us, we gingerly entered the room.

The girls were sitting on their large bed, both dressed in flimsy, floaty loose-fitting tunics, open-toed sandals on their feet, and floppy straw sun bonnets over long blond hair. I quickly suppressed the desire to laugh at the sheer inappropriateness of their clothing. They noticed my reaction, and seemed put out. A tension arose between us that I was keen to lay quickly to rest.

"I think you should wear sturdier clothes and shoes. There are lots of scratchy plants in the forest. You should put on trousers, or at least shorts, and proper shoes. And take a jumper."

"A jumper?" asked Emaleen in a surprised voice, a hint of irritation in her tone. "It's high summer!"

"Yes," I continued patiently. "But it can get cool in the depths of the woods where there isn't much sunlight."

I wondered if I had said the right things, referring to the scratchy plants and lack of sunlight, but if they came to the woods as they were, so inadequately prepared, their experience of it would inevitably be tarnished, perhaps to such an extent that they would not want to make the trip again. It was important to me that they should have the best exposure to the forest possible, and this meant being properly dressed. Emaleen had a tendency towards impatience, especially with me, and I did not want to furnish her with more reasons to find me annoying.

There was a short pause and I knew they were communicating silently. I waited, and did not attempt to intrude or listen in, knowing how hostile they were to this. They then both stood up and Emaleen said, "That makes sense and I suppose you know what it's like there. But maybe it would better if we postpone our trip, or even cancel it if it's so unpleasant in the woods?" I was disappointed at my sister's words, feeling that she was merely looking for an excuse to renege on her promise. I insisted that it was not at all unpleasant, just that bushes and trees could scratch and tear nice clothes, and sturdy footwear was essential. My sisters stared at me for a few moments after I had spoken, silent communication passing between them. Adwin grew impatient.

"You promised you'd come," he said slightly tetchily, crossing his short arms and pouting slightly. "You promised." Another silence ensued. Safya turned to her twin, a look of entreaty on her face. She then turned back to us, smiling. Emaleen sighed lightly as Safya spoke.

"Of course we'll come," she said. "We said we would. And we'll change our clothes if you say we need to. We've never been there. We'll get changed and meet you in front of the house in a few minutes."

I nodded, and Adwin chimed in in a much jollier voice, "We've got food and drink for all of us for the whole day." Emaleen looked at him, her grey eyes wide with surprise. Clearly she had not given any thought to food or drink. Perhaps she was also surprised to hear Adwin talk about "the whole day". I was annoyed with him for saying this, but it was too late to take the comment back.

Safya, noting her sister's expression spoke quietly to her. "We promised, Emmy, we promised." Emaleen's look of surprise faded and she shrugged.

"Well get out then," she snapped as she shooed us out the door. "And let us get changed." We sauntered to the front door, and waited outside in the morning sun.

As we were waiting Kallan came out of the house. "What are you two up to?" he asked, mock suspicion in his voice. "We're going to the woods with Emaleen and Safya," Adwin offered before I could warn him not to. As I had anticipated, Kallan did not look happy with this news. He frowned and shook his head, saying, "Why are you taking them there? It's bad enough you two disappear off there so often, but they've never been."

I shrugged, and said simply, "We asked them to and they said yes." Kallan looked at me to see if I was telling the truth, and decided to believe me.

"Perhaps so," he went on. "But I still don't see why they agreed." He was answered by Safya's voice behind him as she and Emaleen emerged from the house, "Why not uncle? We've never been and they seem to love it there. Maybe we've been missing something all these years," and she laughed. Even Emaleen smiled.

Before Kallan could raise any more objections, Emaleen, taking the lead, swept past us all and indicated with a jerk of her head that we should follow her. It was always hard to persuade Emaleen to do anything, especially with me and Adwin, but once she made up her mind she acted decisively, impatient if anyone thwarted her or even slowed her down. Adwin and I needed no more encouragement, and hurriedly followed in her footsteps, Safya beside us, flashing us a little smile as she trotted along in her sister's wake as usual. I glanced briefly around once at Kallan, and saw that he was shaking his head, an expression of irritation mixed with concern on his face. I hated to annoy or upset my uncle, but was so happy to be racing off to the woods with my sisters for the first time, that not even Kallan's disapproval could dampen my spirits.

The day was perfect, already warm at this early hour, but with a gentle breeze and fat white clouds in the sky. We were all in a high state of excitement, and I quickly put away the doubts that I had about my sisters fulfilling their promise. Even Emaleen, often tetchy and guarded with her emotions, now seemed excited. She walked determinedly through the gardens and the meadows, in a straight line to the dense trees of the woods. Safya caught up with her, but we little ones had to pump our short legs at a rapid pace, and even so we did not catch the girls up. But we did not want to be left too far behind. None of us spoke, but were all intensely aware of each other's high moods, unusual in our sisters, as we walked fast with a spring in our step.

As the twins approached the first row of trees, they slowed a little, allowing Adwin and me to catch up. I sensed a frisson of hesitation in them, the tiniest indication of apprehension as their imminent entry into the forest loomed ever closer. Again my doubts bubbled to the surface of my mind: would they go through with it? Would they take the plunge and immerse themselves among the trees? My sisters did not seem to be cowards, especially Emaleen, but I wondered if their restricted movements thus far would render them fearful of stepping beyond the safe boundaries of the meadows. My fears instantly dissipated when, as we caught up with our sisters, they turned to us, smiled broadly, and in perfect unison said, "Shall we?"

We all laughed, even Emaleen, and Safya chortled loudly in a free and abandoned way I had rarely heard. We all ran forward, plunging through the first closely packed line of trees. For the twins, this was the boundary between the familiar, the regular, the world of light; and the unknown, the strange, the shady world of the forest.

The next few hours were some of the most marvellous of my short life, and I knew without asking that Adwin felt the same. We showed our sisters everything. Every place that was special to us we took them to, showed them, explained to them. The merry gurgling streams, the still waters of the placid ponds, the biggest trees, the richest and most colourful flowers, the glade with the cascading silver waterfall and the clear emerald pool. We introduced them to some of our animal friends, suggesting they might like to touch them. Emaleen refused, but after some hesitation, Safya seemed enraptured by the experience of stroking live deer, of picking up and petting real rabbits, of letting badgers and hedgehogs sniff her fingers, though I had to ensure that the badgers were calmed before doing so lest they try to bite my sister's fingers and ruin the happiness of our day out. Adwin proudly told them where the fairies, pixies and elves would live, how the dryads and water nymphs inhabited the streams and waterfall and pools, and how all of these would come out when no-one was around, to play, to sing, to dance in the moonlight. Safya seemed entranced, more than willing to join us in our make-believe, happy to be drawn into the imagining of the magic and mystery that pervaded the forest. Even Emaleen, though less enthusiastic, was at ease, relaxed, seeming to enjoy herself. Adwin and I were elated, that our sisters were sharing with us the wonders of our private world, and that even Emaleen showed not the slightest trace of derision or mockery. If I had not known better, I would have said that the forest was working its magic on them. I had never seen them behave like this, so open, so cheerful, so chatty and communicative. Even Safya spoke a good deal, enthusing about what she saw. She was always the kinder, the more considerate of our sisters, but her usual demeanour was quiet, laconic in the extreme. This was like a bright new beginning between the four of us, and I was ecstatic.

Adwin announced that we should stop in our favourite glade to eat: the most perfect and magical place in the forest. We sat directly on the dense, soft moss that grew near the edge of the pool, emptied the contents of the rucksacks, and ate hungrily with our fingers, washing it down with the juice Adwin had brought, drinking it straight from the bottle. I had never seen the twins eat with such abandon. And with their hands! Without even washing them first! And sharing a drink with us from the same bottle! We laughed and chatted and joked all the while, revelling in the tangible atmosphere of water and plants and soil surrounding us in the glade. When we finished, we all lay back, hands behind our heads, and gazed contentedly upwards, at the rough bark on the trunks of the tall trees, the canopy of all manner of greens of the leaves high above, and at the little patches of blue sky we could glimpse between the leaves, white clouds slowly passing across.

I think we must have dozed, or perhaps merely allowed our thoughts to drift without direction in the warm air of the afternoon. The sound of the water cascading across the rocks of the outcrop and splashing gaily into the pool, the gentle buzzing of bees in search of flowers as yet unvisited, the soft rustling of the leaves caught in the breeze - all of this was hypnotic, lulling us into a semi-somnolent state of tranquility. Time stopped, or at least seemed held in suspense, but not as if waiting for something to happen. It was as though nothing existed outside of that magical glade, on that one marvellous afternoon in summer. We were trapped, willingly, in a suspended moment in time: a perfect, exquisite point in time, never before experienced and never to be experienced again. The glade was the gently beating heart of the living forest, and we were blessed to have been permitted to enter this enchanted place, allowed to share its magic, even for this one brief period. These memories flood my aged mind as I write as an old old man, and I am so overwhelmed by painful nostalgia that I almost weep.

All good things must come to an end. Despite the sensation of timelessness in the glade, this was an illusion. We had no conception of the passing of the hours, yet the gradual drop in temperature, and the barely imperceptible waning in the brightness of the light began to intrude upon our awareness. The afternoon was moving inexorably onwards, and we noticed a chill invade us. None of us wanted to move, to break the spell that was gripping us with such tenderness, yet eventually we had no option.

Emaleen was the first to sit up, shiver slightly and rub her hands on her upper arms. She took the jumper that she had been using as a pillow and pulled it on. We all followed suit. We packed the picnic away and stood up, stamping our feet slightly and waving our arms to bring a little heat into them, and to get our circulation moving properly again after a long period of stillness.

"It'll be warm still outside the forest," I promised the twins. "It gets cold much earlier here under all the trees. And the spray from the waterfall makes it even cooler."

Safya picked up the rucksacks, handing one to her sister.

"It's time we carried the bags," she said softly. Emaleen raised her eyebrows slightly, but did not object as she hoisted the bag onto her shoulders.

We moved grudgingly away from the centre of the glade, towards the surrounding trees. As we reached the edge of the clearing, as if with a single mind, we all turned, gazed wistfully around the perfect beauty of the glade, sighed, turned away and moved in among the trees.

We walked in silence, each trying to hold the atmosphere of the magical glade in our minds as long as possible. We joined our thoughts and images together, strengthening the effect of individual memory, allowing us to remain immersed in an almost tangible recreation of the otherworldly glade. But as we moved closer to the edge of the trees where the light grew ever stronger, the warmth began to return, and it was harder to maintain the image of the clearing. With each step towards the open ground beyond the trees, the feeling of still being in the glade faded, step by step, moment by moment. By the time we emerged, blinking slightly into the bright late afternoon light, we had lost the shared image of the green shady forest heart, and were once more plunged into the luminous world of reality.

We had emerged from the forest a long way from the house, almost on the opposite side from where we had entered. The area we found ourselves in was open, dotted here and there with a lone tree, and occasional clumps of bushes and flowering plants. It was late afternoon and the sun was no longer high overhead, yet it was still strong, casting long shadows across the grass. Despite the sense of loss we were all suffering, it was pleasant to return to the warmth of the sun.

I looked around, realising that we were very close to the fence. We were all able to sense its presence, the energy it emitted keeping other people out. And keeping us in.

"Shall we go closer?" I asked, knowing that they would all know what I referred to. After the briefest glance at her sister, Emaleen nodded. We moved slowly across the grass towards the fence, invisible, yet clearly marked to us by the waves of perceptible energy flowing horizontally and vertically. As we approached it, its presence grew more and more obvious, more and more physical. When we were mere metres away from it we stopped as one, finding it too uncomfortable to move any closer. We felt it as a heat, a prickly, unpleasant heat on our skin, our hair, entering our eyes and mouths. We also sensed it in our bodies, as a juddering which caused discomfort and, we suspected, would cause pain if we got any closer.

We stood quite still, as close to the fence as we could, staring at it. The experience was peculiar because there was nothing to see, nothing visible to indicate the presence of such force. As far as the eye perceived, the land on the other side of it was identical to the land this side - the grass, trees and bushes continued seamlessly across the divide. Yet the sensations that the invisible barrier imposed on us left us in no doubt that it was there, and that it was real. For all the comfort of our home, the loveliness of the gardens and meadows, the extensive splendour of the forest, we were in a prison. A large, delightful prison, but a prison nonetheless. A wave of frustration and anger passed between us, a feeling of helplessness and resentment towards Zelda, that she believed it to be her right to control our lives in this way.

Before we could say anything, we saw a small herd of roe deer on the other side of the fence. They were moving determinedly directly towards the fence. We were not surprised to see the deer, but were certainly perplexed to see that they were moving straight towards the fence.

~*Can they not sense it?*~ Safya mindqueried silently to the rest of us. I just shrugged, as I had no idea. I knew that animals usually had more acute senses than humans, ordinary humans at least, but was in the dark as to whether they could perceive the energy of the fence.

I dithered about whether we should shout a warning to the deer, but before I could do so, the leader of the herd reached the fence, and to our utter astonishment, walked straight through it, emerging completely unharmed on our side. The other deer followed, seeming equally untroubled by the barrier, unaware of its existence. I looked at my sisters and Adwin, and we shared feelings of confusion with each other. Safya was so amazed, that this prompted her to speak out loud. "What just happened? Why didn't they get hurt? Can't they feel the energy?"

No-one answered, as no-one had an answer. The only thing that was clear was that they were not affected by the force of the fence and could pass through it unscathed. Presumably they did so regularly, in pursuit of fresh food. I wondered if all animals could pass through the fence in the same way, moving at will from one side to the other. I saw no reason why this should not be the case. If a large deer could do so, then why not all the other animals, nearly all of which were smaller.

"Do you think we can pass through like they did?" asked Adwin. Emaleen turned to him, interest showing on her face. We all took a step towards the fence, but the discomfort became so intense that we quickly stepped back again. We all knew that we could not pass across the energy field without serious harm. For some reason, we were prevented from doing what the deer could do. Or perhaps it would be better to say that the deer were able to do something we could not.

After a few moments, Emaleen offered a suggestion.

"Perhaps it only affects us."

"Do you mean just us four?" Adwin asked.

"No," she replied, turning a withering look on him. "What a stupid suggestion. How would it only affect just us four?" Adwin was crushed. "I mean us humans," continued Emaleen, indifferent to Adwin's reaction. "It has to keep other people out too, obviously." We all thought on this for a moment and then I pointed out,

"But it stops air vehicles too, and ground vehicles, or so Zelda's always claimed, and I assume she's right. That's the whole point of the fence - to keep everyone out, and most people who tried to come in would be in some sort of vehicle." We thought again for a moment.

"Yes," agreed Emaleen. "But there are always people in them, and maybe that's why it can stop them. Or maybe it stops anything metal, or mechanical."

We stood for while, staring longingly across the invisible barrier that marked the edge of our jail. I tentatively put out feelers towards the fence, to test exactly what the energy was, and how it worked. The others sensed what I was doing, and waited silently for me to finish. None of them had the ability to do anything like this, so none of them could help. I was on my own. I closed my eyes as I found this made such probing easier and clearer, at least this helped when I was so young and lacking experience. After a short while, I withdrew the mental probes, and said,

"It's quite simple really. It seems to interfere with human brain waves by emitting electromagnetic waves of the same strength and frequency. This makes it painful and distressing for a human to get close to it. Other animals' brain waves aren't the same, and it's so accurate it doesn't affect them at all. I'm not sure why it causes problems for machinery - maybe the electromagnetic waves disrupt their systems. I think the force field must be coming from something buried in the ground, all along the perimeter."

As I seemed not to be about to offer any practical solutions, Emaleen asked impatiently,

"All very interesting I'm sure. But can you stop it, or disarm it so we can pass across?"

I thought for a moment, and then replied.

"I think I could, though I might need to practise a bit first, but I don't know how to do it quietly."

"What do you mean, quietly?" asked my sister, even more impatiently, hands on her hips in a familiar gesture of irritation.

"I mean without Zelda knowing," I replied. This piece of information silenced Emaleen, and her impatience evaporated. She knew what I meant: that Zelda would have monitors in her laboratory telling her instantly if there had been any malfunction or breach in the fence. And she would know where it had happened, perhaps even be able to detect that I had breached it. Safya also knew immediately what I meant, but I had to explain it to little Adwin. He nodded wisely after the explanation, and asked,

"Can't you just, I don't know, maybe carry yourself and us across without messing up the energy?"

I smiled indulgently at him, and shook my head.

"No. I don't know how to do that." A thought crossed my mind. I turned to my sisters and asked them if they were able to do something like that, to move themselves through space. They looked surprised, and Emaleen said,

"No." She then paused before continuing, a small frown of concentration on her face. "But I don't see why we couldn't learn. Mother has probably never raised the possibility because she doesn't want us to be able to leave the compound, and that would make it too easy."

We all paused for a moment, realising that this might one day be the best solution for coming and going from the estate without Zelda being able to do anything about it, but until we learned how to do so safely, this must remain a fancy. It certainly would not help us today, or any time in the near future. I had already learned that people regularly moved around our world in this way, teleported, but did not know how they achieved such an act. The means must exist, but surely it was not achieved by an individual human using only the power of their own brains?

We sensed each other's frustration at our inability to cross the fence, and we were irked by the knowledge that acquiring the skill to teleport would take us a long time and a great deal of effort to learn, if it were ever possible. But suddenly Adwin offered an unexpectedly simple possible route out of our current dilemma.

"Couldn't you just turn off the monitors?" he asked.

I saw Emaleen's look of contempt at Adwin's suggestion, and this time I agreed with her. I was about to dismiss his suggestion as simplistic and childish, but suddenly realised that he may be right. Perhaps I could disarm the monitors without Zelda knowing, and then learn how to breach the fence with impunity, also without Zelda's knowledge. We could cross over, see what was on the other side, and then after returning I could re-start the monitors again without Zelda being any the wiser.

I laughed out loud, and clapped my brother on the back.

"Brilliant Addy," I said loudly, using his pet name. "I think that might work!"

We all laughed, even Emaleen, and began to head back to the house. If I was going to break into Zelda's laboratory over the next few days, it would be better not to arouse suspicions by being out too late. We returned home well in time for our evening meal, in high spirits from having spent such a special day together, and with a shared secret: that we may soon be able to escape our prison, albeit briefly, and that we would learn all we could about teleportation to see if we could eventually move ourselves at will out of the compound. These thoughts made us all very jolly indeed. So much so that Kallan spent the entire meal casting us suspicious looks, though none of us would divulge the cause of our good-humour.

Chapter Six

I was impatient to find out if I could disarm Zelda's monitors which told her of a breach or malfunction in the fence. I was not entirely sure if such monitors existed, but could not imagine that our mother would have set the system up in such a way that any problem with the fence would not immediately be brought to her attention. Her obsession with privacy, and with keeping us confined to the compound would certainly have caused her to arrange the security of where we lived as tightly and effectively as possible. I had never seen anything that might function as a monitor of any sort in the house itself, so surmised that these must be located somewhere in the collection of rooms that made up Zelda's laboratory.

Only a few times in my life had I ever been in the laboratory, and when I asked my sisters, it turned out that this was the same for them, despite the five extra years of of life they had known living on the estate. Adwin, at only five years old, could not ever remember having been there. It was strange that we all knew the laboratory to be strictly out of bounds, despite Zelda never having made this explicit. The only times my sisters (or I) had been into the laboratory was with our mother, and by specific invitation, and then only to be shown some small part of her work.

I knew it would be difficult to find a time to enter the laboratory and to have long enough to locate and then, with luck, disarm the fence monitors. Not only did I not know my way around, but Zelda spent much of her time in the laboratory, and was unpredictable as to when this might be. She worked there at any time of the day or night, without a clear pattern. Obviously she did leave to eat (though often she ate on the job), and to sleep, but without predictable hours. All I could do was to set a subtle trace on her movements, and knew that I would probably have to act quickly when the right time came, when she seemed to be leaving her work for a period long enough for me to do what I needed to do.

During the days immediately after our trip to the forest, no such opportunity arose. Zelda was as devoted to her work as ever. The only time she left the laboratory for any length of time was deep in the night, and I had already decided not to allow my trace of her movements to wake me from my own sleep, as I would need to be fully alert to achieve my goal. To have any hope of success I needed to succeed the first time, so as to prevent any possibility of Zelda discovering my activities before I accomplished my task.

It was not until early one morning almost a week later that the opportunity finally arose. I was in the study room with my sisters when the trace I had placed on Zelda's movements alerted me to the fact that she had left the laboratory, after an uninterrupted period of nearly twenty hours of lab work. The information I received gave me to believe that she was exhausted, and when she stumbled into her bedroom slamming the door behind her I knew that she would sleep deeply for the best part of a day. Emaleen instantly sensed my shift in mood and my tension.

"Now?" she asked. Safya looked up sharply at the tone of her voice, quiet yet excited. I nodded.

"Yes," I replied with a lump in my throat. I was truly fearful of what would happen if I were caught. Zelda did not take kindly to disobedience from any of her children, which we had all discovered at one time or another to our cost, and she was more than willing to impose punishments for even the slightest infraction, the most minimal sign of defiance. At that time, at the age of eight, I had not yet learned to physically resist Zelda's wrath, a skill that was still some years away. We children had all suffered our mother's ire, her favourite punishment being to lock us in a small, dark, dank room underneath the house with no food or water to "contemplate your misbehaviour". The room had no light, or none I had managed to discover in my several sojourns there. Each time, after finally overcoming the petrifying distress of being totally alone in the pitch black sufficiently to rouse myself, I had moved slowly around the room, sliding my hands along the damp walls in search of a source of light, but always to no avail. In truth, I do not think Zelda ever left us in the room for long, but to a child it felt like an age. An age of fear, of anguish, of true terror. I never forgave Zelda for this, and could not understand why she did not simply slap us, or even beat us. Later in my life when I reminded her about this cruel psychological chastisement, and asked her why she had not just hit us, she had looked shocked at the suggestion, replying that "it would have been wrong to use corporal punishment on children. Immoral!"

Returning to the present, I continued to speak to my sisters.

"Stay here and carry on as normal," I managed to force out, my voice trembling with anxiety. "I'll be back as soon as I can." Emaleen nodded, Safya smiling at me with encouragement.

I left the room and moved briskly through the house towards the laboratory area at the back. I had to force myself not to run or appear in too much of a hurry. I walked determinedly, but not so fast as to arouse suspicion if I bumped into Kallan. He knew me better than anyone, and was highly perceptive, and I was not sure I could deceive him, especially in my heightened state of excitement and agitation.

At the far end of the house I came to the door connecting it to the laboratory complex. As usual, this door was firmly closed, though not locked. The demarcation between the house and the laboratory was so clear that Zelda had no need to lock the door: we would not have considered going through it under normal circumstances. As my hand approached the control panel beside the door, I hesitated, my hand stopping in mid-air. Though the door was not locked, I wondered if it was monitored, if Zelda kept an eye on anyone passing through it without permission. I quickly scanned the door frame and the control panel, and as far as I could tell, there was no evident monitoring in place. In any case, I had to take the risk. I passed my palm in front of the control panel and the door slid silently open.

It was dark on the other side of the door, but the lights were motion-activated, as they were throughout the house. I took a quick, sharp breath, and stepped briskly across the threshold before I lost my nerve. The lights blinked on the moment my foot entered the room. I remembered from my rare visits to the laboratory complex that the first few rooms were used for record keeping, and were filled with cabinets and cupboards all overflowing with papers and files. Astonishing as it may sound as I write these memoirs in the thirtieth century, Zelda kept physical records of all her research as well as the usual electronic data storage. She regularly told us that digital storage could be corrupted, either by accident or by design, and she was obsessed with the idea that one of her enemies would somehow access her data storage and destroy it. So she printed everything, some on microfile but some on actual paper (believing this to be the most durable medium), and kept all of this stashed away in these first few rooms of her laboratory. The paper she used was very different from that which the ancients had made use of. This was in truth a paper substitute, almost indestructible, which nevertheless looked and felt like normal, old world paper. It was coated with an imperishable layer of material, only a few molecules thick which was added on top of the ink as part of the printing process, allowing hard-copy storage of material for those who wished it. Despite this, most information was not stored on paper, but only in electronic form. Zelda was one of a rare breed of scientist who obsessively kept all her data and information in both physical and digital form.

Hastily I passed through the data storage rooms, making my way towards the laboratory proper further back, knowing that any monitoring equipment would be here, among all the other instruments and most likely in the control room in which Zelda spent most of her time, as far as I was aware. If she had installed monitoring devices she would want to receive their warnings as soon as possible.

I moved through rooms filled with scientific equipment of many different types. Some of them I recognised, but quite a few I did not know and could not begin to fathom the uses of. Perhaps if I had longer to contemplate them and consider them more fully I would be able to understand them, but I did not tarry as I had a mission to fulfil. After a number of such rooms I came to a larger room, in the middle of which was a big empty table above which I assumed Zelda would extract information from the digital memory the same way we did. In front of the table was a well-worn chair on castors, and I knew instantly that this was the centre of Zelda's web, where she spent most of her time thinking, working and analysing data. Along the back wall was a row of silvery metallic containers, each a little under two metres tall and a metre wide, cylindrical, with a clear glass panel on the front. Slim pipes of many different colours were connected to each cylindrical tank, the other end of each disappearing into the wall behind.

Although I had no time to waste, I was intrigued by these objects and moved towards them to have a closer look. By straining my head backwards, I could just see into the cylinders, but I was too small at that age to get a clear view inside. So I dragged a chair over and placed it right in front of the middle cylinder. I chose a chair without castors so I could stand on it safely, and grimaced as the sound of the chair being dragged across the floor reverberated around the room. I stopped to look around and listen. I seemed to still be alone, the noise not having attracted any attention. By standing on the chair I was able to see through the glass panel into the tank itself. It was filled with a faintly blueish but otherwise clear liquid, which, as far as I could tell, was viscous, as close to the texture of syrup as to water. Affixed to the inside wall of the cylinder was a much darker blue circle of thick jelly about eight centimetres in diameter, a centimetre or so deep, and through this passed the coloured pipes from outside the cylinder. I went up onto tiptoes and pressed my face up against the glass panel as I peered into the tank. I could not work out what these cylindrical tanks were at first, but with a flash of realization I knew they were foetal tanks, almost certainly the very tanks that had housed my sisters, Adwin and me during the time as we grew from single-celled zygotes into fully formed babies. I surmised that the coloured pipes delivered all the necessary nutrition to the foetus, and that the balance of different nutrients could be altered as required by changing settings on the control panel on the front of each cylinder. The jelly circle must somehow join up with the placenta produced by the foetus, acting as an artificial uterine wall, a conduit for the sustenance passing into the body of the embryonic child.

As I stood on the chair staring into the foetal tank I was overwhelmed with emotion, dumbfounded as I contemplated my own origins, the first months of my existence floating silently, suspended in a blueish jelly, life-sustaining nutrition being fed through pipes flowing through the placenta attached to the wall of an artificial womb, thence to me via my umbilical cord.

I was so dumbfounded by what I was looking at that I almost forgot why I had come to the laboratory in the first place. After a long pause, I shook my head vigorously from side to side in an attempt to snap myself out of my torpor, and my body shuddered into action.

As I looked around the rest of the room, I noticed that on the wall running adjacent to the tanks were a number of rectangular panels of the same dark glass as the ones on the fronts of the tanks, but most of these glowed faintly, indicating their present usage. I jumped down off the chair and pulled it behind me as I walked along the wall, cringing again as it scraped along the floor, not strong enough at my young age to lift it. As I did so, each panel came to life as I passed it, lighting up more brightly. I moved swiftly past each one, only vaguely noticing what the function of each panel was, until I reached one with the words "Perimeter Fence" helpfully throbbing in red, back-lit lettering. I clambered up onto the chair which I had placed in front of the panel, and waved my hand across the screen. The whole panel came fully to life, showing brightly lit letters and numbers, buttons and symbols, and in the middle what looked like a diagram of the actual perimeter fence in its entirety, encircling the whole estate. A thought passed across my mind that installing the fence must have been a huge task for my mother at the time she did it, and I wondered how she had actually achieved it. I assumed she would have set automata to the task of actually laying the equipment under the ground, but it was nevertheless a major undertaking. Perhaps the compound already had a protective fence in place, and that had been one of its main attractions to Zelda? This seemed extremely unlikely though as privacy was not highly prized in the world outside, something I only learned much later.

I did not dwell long on these issues, but instead scrutinized the surface of the control panel, trying to ascertain how it worked. It was not complicated, and after only a short time I was able to see how it functioned, and more importantly, to see how to switch off the warnings given for breaches of the fence. There was a dual visual and auditory alarm raised both for malfunction and breach of the fence, and I quickly pressed a few of the symbols on the screen, disabling both types of warning. I smiled to myself at how easy it had been to fulfil my mission, but then remembered that I would have to get safely out of the laboratory and back to the study room, and that after we had been out beyond the fence and back, I would be obliged to return to this room as soon as possible and reset the alarms to their normal functioning so as not to raise Zelda's suspicions. This would not be easy as I would again have to wait for the right time, when Zelda left the laboratory area for a sufficiently long period.

There was no time to waste, so I leapt off the chair, dragged it back to where I had found it, and hurried from the room, glancing back as I did so at the foetal tanks, casting one final contemplative look at the place I must have spent the earliest part of my life.

Chapter Seven

On my way back to the study room to tell my sisters that I had succeeded in disabling the monitors, and to hurry them out of the house towards the fence, I stopped at Adwin's room. He had not been at breakfast and had not yet appeared in the study room, and I wondered where he was.

I let myself into his room, and saw that the photochromic perspiglass in the windows was still dark and smoky, despite it now being full day. I saw a shape in his bed, and tiptoed over to see why he was still abed. As I reached the edge of his bed, he sat up. He had not actually been asleep, and knew the moment I had entered his room.

~Hello Samek,~ he mindspoke in an artificially perky voice. I knew instantly that he was not well, even before I noticed his unusually pale skin and dark rings below his eyes.

~Hello Addy,~ I replied silently. *~What's the matter?~*

He shrugged slightly, a small tight smile playing at one side of his mouth.

~I'm not sure. Just the usual. I'm really tired and slept badly.~

He sensed my anxiety, and continued.

~Don't worry. I'll be fine once I've had a good rest.~

I hesitated for a moment, and he asked, in a normal voice, "What's the matter with you? You seem in an odd mood."

I smiled at him reassuringly, and replied, "No, I'm fine. Still shaking a bit from going into the laboratory. Imagine if I'd been caught! But I wanted to come and get you to go out to the fence with Emaleen and Safya."

"Now?" he asked, sitting fully upright in his bed. I nodded. "Why now?" he continued. Before I could reply his dark eyebrows shot up and he asked in an excited whisper, "Did you turn off the monitor?"

I nodded again, and saw his almost black eyes sparkle with animation, despite his poor state of health. He threw the sheet back and swung his short legs over the side of the bed. As he began to stand up from the bed, he clapped his hands twice activating the perspiglass in the windows which now rapidly lost their smokiness and became clear. The sun flowed in, flooding the bedroom with cheerful yellow light. Adwin looked even more pallid and drawn in contrast to the lively colours that filled the room, sunlight bouncing off the walls and ceiling.

"You aren't well enough to come," I said quietly, gently putting my hands on his shoulders in an attempt to guide him back onto the bed. He shook off my hands and said in a tetchy voice,

"Yes I am! I just need to wash my face and have something to eat and I'll be fine."

I was not sure what to say. I was frustrated and even felt annoyed with Adwin that he was unwell just at the moment when I had managed to penetrate Zelda's laboratory and disarm the perimeter monitors. It would not be easy to do this often, and I did not want to risk them being out of order for too long in case Zelda discovered the fact, hardly daring to contemplate her anger if she found out. I badly wanted to try and cross the fence as soon as possible, but knew that Adwin would be crestfallen if we went without him. I simply did not have the heart to even suggest it to him, despite my unfair irritation with him. As I had done every time he was unwell, I gently mindprobed his body, examining him to see if I could ascertain exactly what was wrong. But as always, I could not obtain a clear picture of the problem. Perhaps I was simply too inexperienced at such things, lacking the necessary skill. Or perhaps it would always be beyond my abilities. No matter my unprecedented skills and abilities, I would always have limitations. Something had clearly gone profoundly wrong during his time in the foetal tank, and I was unable to discover precisely what. Or, I thought, perhaps Zelda was not such an accomplished geneticist as she believed. This possibility caused me a little flush of pleasure, that my vain and self-important mother was perhaps not all that she claimed to be.

I could, however, provide him with temporary relief from the symptoms, furnish him with additional energy for long enough to allow him to accompany us on our trip. I told him I would do this, but that when we got back to the house he would have to go straight to bed. I knew that artificially boosting a sick person's vitality would have repercussions, as all it did was mask the symptoms, and not work as any sort of remedy.

"Are you sure you want to do this?" I asked. "You know you'll be worse afterwards."

"Yes!, he snapped. "Just do it!"

I took his hands - something which at that young age helped me carry out the activity more efficiently, and suffused him with my own excess energy, allowing it to flow into him. At the same time I caused analgesic waves to pass into his mind, dulling his perception of the aches of whatever ailed him. As I did this, he visibly took on a healthier colour, a slight flush appearing in his ivory cheeks, his dark eyes glistening more brightly. He sighed deeply, and then smiled widely. After a few moments I let go of his hands. He splashed his face with cold water in the basin in his room, and dressed as quickly as he could manage. As he did so I mindspoke to our sisters, telling them what I had done in the laboratory, and urging them to be ready shortly to make the short trip to the fence. I warned them to do so unobtrusively so as not to arouse suspicions, but they assured me there would be no impediment as Kallan was nowhere to be seen.

As before, we met just outside the front door to the house. And as then, Adwin and I carried bags which we had filled in the kitchen with food and drinks. Safya took the bags from us, passing one to her sister. Before Emaleen could object, Safya spoke in low voice. "We're bigger than them." Emaleen pursed her lips but took the proffered bag without comment.

We had no idea how long we would be out. I was fairly sure I could get us across the fence, but it was just possible that I was mistaken. And even if I did, we could not predict what we would find on the other side, or how long we would want to remain there.

We did not speak, but knew that we were all in a heightened state of excitement: today we would transgress the boundaries of our prison home for the first time in our lives! It was hard to believe, and we struggled to control our emotions as we contemplated the reality of it. Even Safya's usual barrier against showing what she felt was not in place, and she radiated emotion. We walked very briskly away from the house before anyone might see us, across the well-tended lawns, straight towards the fence.

At its nearest, the fence passed fairly close to the house, but we knew that this would not be the most sensible place to cross: we could just be seen from the house itself. We did not fear Kallan, though did not want him to intrude into our plans. And Zelda - we most definitely did not want her to have the slightest idea of what we were up to, knowing how strictly she had forbidden us from even approaching the fence. As we neared the perimeter, we approached it obliquely as it snaked away from the buildings, covering our intent with what would look like a haphazard trajectory. When the fence passed behind several small copses of trees and tall bushes, concealing us from any eyes looking from the house, we walked directly towards it. When we stood in front of it, we stopped and glanced around. We were unable to see the house at all, and knew that we were completely hidden from view. We were too impatient to walk any further, so decided that this spot would suffice. We stopped.

"Are you going to switch the fence off?" Emaleen asked me, without preamble, tension making her even more impatient than usual.

"No," I replied. "I'm not sure if I could do that, or if I could, I couldn't be sure I'd be able to return it to exactly how it was before."

"So how are we going to cross?" asked Safya, her tense voice betraying her nervous anticipation.

"I'll have to make some tiny changes to our brain waves," I replied, to which all three of them started in surprise. "I told you that the fence works by emitting electromagnetic radiation at exactly the same strength and frequency as human brain waves," I explained. They all nodded their heads. "Well," I continued. "If I alter the waves coming from our brains just a little bit, it should be enough to allow us to pass across the fence without us feeling any painful disruption of our brain waves, the same way the animals can do it."

Adwin let out a short, sharp laugh, and said, "So you're going turn us into sheep who will follow you blindly?" We all laughed at this, even Emaleen, and I went on,

"Sort of, I suppose, or at least give us brains that aren't quite human!" We chuckled again at this idea. "It's probably best if I slightly alter the alpha waves. Gamma and beta we need so we can think." Adwin looked confused, too young to have studied such things, but my sisters nodded in agreement, knowing what I was telling them. A slight, and temporary, alteration in alpha waves was likely to be the least problematic for us, though I did not think a change in any of the other types of wave for the very brief period needed to cross the fence would cause any harm, or even any perceptible effect.

"Are we ready?" I asked. They nodded their agreement. As earlier with Adwin, I decided I could more easily effect the modification in brain wave if we were physically connected. We all linked hands and I closed my eyes.

~I'll need to go into your heads,~ I warned, tacitly asking permission to do so. I received permission from them all by return, accompanied by a little smile from Safya. I entered their minds, travelled along the dizzying maze of axons and synapses until I located the spot in each of their brains which

were emitting alpha wave energy, and subtly altered the rate of emission, changing both the intensity and frequency of the charge being given off. I did the same in my own brain.

After a short time I opened my eyes and mindspoke,

~That's it.~

We unclasped our hands and looked at each other. For a moment we all stood completely still, no-one wanting to make the first move. I decided that I would have to shepherd my siblings, so I began to move gingerly towards the fence. It felt peculiar, almost wrong, to be walking straight towards the perimeter of our world, especially as we knew that the last time we had tried this we were driven back by the severe discomfort caused by the energy being emitted. But this time we felt nothing, no distress, no discomfort, no pain. It was as if the fence did not exist, or was not switched on. We could sense there was something being emitted into the air, but we did not feel it physically. We just had a dim awareness of it. We moved closer and closer to the fence, and as I reached it, I squared my shoulders and walked straight through it. The others followed immediately behind me.

The crossing itself was a huge anticlimax: I felt nothing. One moment I was inside the compound, the next I was outside of it. I even knew the moment when half of me was on one side, and half on the other as I straddled the barrier's energy field. I stopped a few paces from the fence and turned round. Adwin and my sisters stopped beside me and also turned round. We all stared back the way we had come, across the invisible boundary which had kept us imprisoned all our lives, across which we had been forbidden to tread. But the landscape was identical on both sides, and as the fence was invisible, we perceived no difference at all from one side to the other.

I relieved myself of the effort of modifying my siblings' brain waves. We turned full circle, looking all around us, eager to find something new and unfamiliar to see on the outlawed side of the boundary, but to no avail. We saw exactly the same combination of grassy meadows, dotted here and there with bushes and clumps of flowering plants, occasional lone trees, and sporadic little copses. We looked up to see an identical blue sky, woolly clouds scudding across it. Just like the deer we had seen traversing the perimeter the time before, everything else seemed oblivious to the presence of the fence. I struggled with disappointment, disheartened not to find myself immersed instantly into a new world of fresh and strange images and objects, a rare land of brightness and wonder. It was pretty, to be sure, but so was the compound itself. I was rendered mute and immobile by the sheer sameness of it all. My siblings clearly felt the same.

Eventually I decided we needed to do something. I snapped myself out of my disappointment-induced torpor and turned to the others.

"Now we're here," I began in a voice as cheerful and normal as I could make it. "We might as well have a look around." Adwin brightened up at this suggestion, and forced a slight smile onto his face, though I was once again made painfully aware of his lack of robustness, light sweat glistening on his pallid skin. Emaleen and Safya did not respond. I glanced at Adwin and with a slight movement of my eyes, indicated towards the girls, annoyance at the twins showing on my face. Adwin took the hint and immediately began in a bright voice to encourage us all.

"Come on you lot, come on. We're outside for the first time. A week ago we'd never have thought it was possible and now here we are. Let's have a look around, away from the fence, see what we find." Our sisters responded slightly in body, turning to face Adwin. Safya remained emotionally impassive, though forced a smile at Adwin in the face of his enthusiasm. Emaleen scowled at everything around her, disappointment having thrown her into a temper. She stood with hands on hips, but when Adwin grabbed a hand of each of our sisters, and began dragging them away from the estate they had little option but to go with him. I followed closely behind. As we moved further from the boundary of the estate Safya began to walk a little more lightly, and I sensed a slight shift in her mood. She still showed no real interest, but this was at least an improvement. One glance at Emaleen made it clear that her ill-humour had not abated in the least, and she dragged her feet as little Adwin struggled to pull her onwards. From past experience, I feared that Safya would eventually follow where Emaleen's mood had already travelled.

We wandered away from the compound, across the grassy fields, through copses and thickets, across small bubbling streams, and around marshy ponds filled with the sounds of buzzing insects and croaking frogs, bullrushes and yellow iris growing all around. We skirted the edge of a larger wood but did not enter it, not wanting to risk getting lost in its darkness. Despite how familiar and ordinary it all felt, Adwin and I grew more and more carefree, a lightheartedness invading us as we came to accept the truth that we had breached the walls of our prison. This simple, yet profound, fact alone liberated us, and we chatted merrily, commenting on everything we saw, pointing at birds as they swooped by, laughing at the antics of rabbits capering across the fields. We stopped at the side of a pond, dropped onto our bellies and peered into its green waters, delight in our voices as we saw tiny silver-sided fish darting brightly through the dappled watery light.

Emaleen did not share our enthusiasm. She did not complain as we took her and Safya further and further from the estate, but she offered no comments on our surroundings, no collaboration in our playfulness. I would even have preferred verbal evidence of Emaleen's sulky demeanour, but it was as if she could not even muster the interest to engage with her surroundings in this way. Safya tried to show some enthusiasm, but affected by her sister's mood, she gradually withdrew into a silent place, barely even looking around her. Whatever she felt herself, she seemed to have decided to emulate much of her sister's attitude. I tried hard to ignore their demeanour, tried not to let it dampen my excitement in exploring the new world. But it was difficult to shut out the dark-clouded atmosphere that enveloped Emaleen, the apparent indifference of Safya. I knew that they had suffered disappointment on crossing the fence, but did not fully understand why they seemed so profoundly disheartened. I had also hoped for more, yet I was enjoying the simple fact of liberation from the comfortable jail I had spent my life in thus far, and happy to be doing so in my little brother's company. And I knew that if we had escaped once, we could do so again. I knew that somewhere far beyond the horizon lay another world, one filled with people, with towns and cities, a truly new and exciting world just waiting for us to discover it.

We stopped beside a particularly fast-flowing brook, its frothy white-capped waters rippling across its pebbled bed, the gurgling and splashing of the water mingling with the clattering of tiny stones as they were flung together over and over again by the racing stream. We ate there, watching the kingfishers hovering over the brook, then plunging into the water, wings folded against their sides, arrows of blurred orange and blue, to emerge moments later with tiny glittering fish wriggling pathetically and pointlessly in the tightly-clamped beaks. Still Emaleen and Safya showed no delight in such beauty, Emaleen persisting with her scowl, Safya watching with only faint discernible emotion as the little birds gracefully repeated their frolics over and over again. I forced myself not to react overtly to my sisters' behaviour, not to chide them for it, or interrogate them as to the real reasons why. But as the day went on, I felt them slipping further and further away from Adwin and me, sensed them sliding back into their usual withdrawn behaviour towards us and towards the world at large. Even Emaleen's sulks gradually faded, but only to be replaced by a look similar to that of her sister, an expression of apathy, of remoteness from their surroundings.

I despaired at how they were responding, but gradually came to accept that it was not merely the disappointment at the world outside the estate, but something much deeper. There was something so profoundly inward-looking about Emaleen and Safya, especially Safya, so uninvolved were they in the world outside themselves, that they were simply reverting to their usual selves. The dashed expectations of the world outside the estate simply acted as a catalyst, returning them to their self-involved and internalized world more quickly than it might have done. I understood that their outward-focused behaviour in the forest a week before, and in the week since, *that* was the oddity, *that* was the anomaly, and now they were returning to where they felt safe, to what they knew. I sighed deeply, my sadness as this realisation so strong that Adwin gasped as he saw the expression that I tried not to show on my face. I turned to him and smiled wanly, trying to reassure him that I was alright. He gave me a crooked smile, the frown between his black eyebrows showing me he was worried about me and not convinced by my forced smile. I shrugged slightly and mindspoke just to him.

~It's ok Addy. I'm fine.~

But *he* was not fine. His eyes showed his exhaustion and pain, his face even paler than it had been that morning, an unhealthy sheen of cold sweat on his white skin, the contrast between this and his deep, dark eyes stark. I was alarmed. I was able to help him briefly by reducing his pain a little and giving him a burst of energy, but knew that the more I did this, the more he would have to pay it back later.

"It's time we went home," I said suddenly. "I'm tired. And we don't want Zelda or Kallan to wonder where we are. Especially Zelda." Adwin looked at me gratefully, and stood up. Our sisters followed suit, more slowly, showing indifference even in returning home, despite their clear lack of pleasure at being outside the compound.

We wasted no time getting back to the fence, and as we approached it I told everyone to join hands to allow me to make the minor alteration to our brain waves as before. We crossed the fence without incident, hands still firmly grasped together, then made our way to the house by the most direct route. We were silent, neither speaking out loud nor mindspeaking. I felt Adwin and I had lost our sisters again, and I doubted if we would ever enjoy the same intimacy and affection we had had with them in the past week. Adwin himself seemed unaware of their emotional disappearance, so focused was he on dragging himself the last distance to the house, and to his bed.

As we came through the front door Kallan was waiting for us in the entrance hall. He must have seen us from the window. He stood with folded arms, a look of concern mixed with irritation on his tanned face, his bright eyes glittering with worry. He glanced at the girls and stepped backwards slightly in surprise as he recognized their usual impassive features, wondering fleetingly what had happened to wipe the recent change in mood from them so suddenly. He then frowned at me, disapproval radiating from him, but when he saw Adwin, all annoyance and reproof vanished from his features. His face registered nothing but distress, deep concern at the colour of Adwin's skin, the obvious pain in his eyes and his laboured breath.

"Adwin!" Kallan cried, rushing towards him, just in time to catch my little brother as he fell forward, fainting into Kallan's arms. My uncle looked at me with an enigmatic expression I could not fathom, picked my brother up and raced off with him towards his bedroom. As he did so he shouted back at me.

"Get his medicine and bring it as fast as you can. You know where it is." I jumped into action, rushed into the kitchen, grabbed the bottle of liquid medicament that seemed to help Adwin when he suffered this way and dashed back with it to his room. By the time I got there Kallan had already undressed him and put him to bed. Our uncle was sitting on the bed, gently wiping my brother's face with a damp cloth, cleaning the day's dirt from his cheeks and forehead as well as cooling his skin. I poured a measure of the medicine into the bottle cap and offered it to my brother. He drank it, shuddering slightly at its bitter flavour, still managing to thank me with a weak smile. Kallan clapped twice and the windows immediately clouded over, becoming dark gray and opaque as the glass responded to his signal.

Adwin lay his head back on the pillow. Kallan stood up, bent over him and kissed him, lips feather-light on his sweat-beaded forehead. Adwin sighed, yawned, and closed his eyes. The medicine calmed him, and caused him to sleep, and always seemed to help him rally after a spell of sickness. Kallan indicated to me with a small tight movement of his head that we should leave. I followed him as he left the room, the door sliding silently closed behind us.

A few paces down the corridor he turned and stopped, folded his arms across his chest and fixed me with a menacing glare. I halted in my tracks and stared down at the floor, not daring to look him in the eye.

"Samek!" he hissed in an ominously quiet voice. "Look at me!" His tone gave no option but to obey, and I fearfully lifted my gaze slowly from my feet towards his face. He was livid, his piercing blue eyes blazing with anger and indignation. When he spoke again his normally soft voice crackled with quiet anger, dropping both in depth and in volume.

"What did you think you were doing, taking him out like that? I saw him this morning, and told him to stay in bed. I came back a bit later and he was gone. You were nowhere to be found, and the same with Emaleen and Safya. You know how delicate he is, how he needs to rest and sleep when he's having one of his episodes." He peered at me even more intently, his eyes boring into me, as he spoke in a louder voice. "What on earth were you thinking? For shame, Samek, for shame!"

And I truly felt shame, real, tangible, physical shame. Kallan was the kindest, gentlest and most patient person imaginable, yet here he was shaking with quiet rage at me. I was scarlet with mortification, my face burning hot, actually feeling dizzy from the painful, raw emotion flooding my body and mind, made all the worse because I knew Kallan was right. But what could I have done? I could not have gone out that day without little Addy - he would have been inconsolable. I could not delay the outing - if I had done, my brother would have blamed himself and been riddled with guilt. But none of this could I tell Kallan, as to do so would have necessitated me confessing why we had to go out that very day, go out without delay, and this was something I could not tell him. He would have fiercely disapproved of me having gone into the laboratory and disarmed the monitor, and would have found our plan to cross the fence equally reprehensible. I knew that I could not defend myself from Kallan's ire and censure. There was nothing I could do but apologize, so I quietly mouthed the words "I'm sorry."

"What was that?" he asked harshly. "Did you say something?" I steeled myself and said in a hoarse whisper,

"I'm sorry."

"Humph", was Kallan's terse reply. He was clearly not mollified and I knew there was nothing I could do. We stood in awful silence for a short period, which felt endless to me. I looked into his distraught eyes as he said in a thick voice, "Get out of my sight. I am *so* disappointed in you."

I burst into tears, appalled at my uncle's words. His anger was awful to endure, but not nearly as distressing as his disappointment. I turned on my heel and ran away from him as fast as my short legs would carry me back to my own room, to lock myself away from Kallan's rage, Adwin's illness and my sisters' renewed withdrawal from the world.

Chapter Eight

I was distraught as I threw myself onto my bed, tears still flowing liberally from my now red and inflamed eyes. I very rarely wept, and found the experience disagreeable, emotions clouding my thoughts as the salty tears obscured my vision. I felt I had been treated most unfairly by Kallan, but despite feeling his anger had not been justified, I nevertheless squirmed with shame at suffering his disappointment. It is true that Adwin should really have spent the day quietly in bed, recovering his strength and health, yet he was the one who had insisted on joining us on our trip outside the compound. Nothing short of physical restraint could have stopped him, and certainly not my efforts at persuasion. And surely I was not culpable for Adwin's worsened state of health?

My weeping eventually wore me out, and as it abated, I drifted into a light and unsatisfying slumber, outrage at my unjust treatment still rankling me, combined with the distress of disappointing my uncle. I woke with a start when I received an indication that Zelda had left her laboratory. I had set up the proximity alert before we got back to the house, eager to once again enable the fence monitors to function as they should as soon as I could, before Zelda could discover my original misdeed.

My thinking was still clouded from my slumber, made worse by the emotional turmoil I still felt after Kallan's castigation of me. I did not think I was a person to harbour a grudge, but my outrage at Kallan's treatment of me was slow to abate. If I had been fully alert, and not so immersed in my self-pity, I would have investigated further to see if Zelda's departure from the laboratory seemed likely to be of sufficient duration to allow me to undo my earlier deed. I stood groggily up from my bed, bottom lip still thrust out in a pout, and made my way briskly to the door into Zelda's private work rooms. I crossed the threshold into her private area, and moved quickly through the outer rooms, straight towards the room housing the foetal tanks and wall panels. I did not stop once to check if I were alone, or whether Zelda remained outside the laboratory. Once in the room with the fence monitor, I pulled a chair over to the panel which controlled the fence, careless this time of the noise it made, climbed up onto it, and hastily re-activated the monitor.

As I finished and breathed a small sigh of relief, I was startled when a loud gravelly voice behind me spoke.

"What in heaven's name are you doing?" Zelda had entered the room without making a sound, only to find me balanced on a chair, fiddling with one of her control panels. As I was not yet fully awake, and still smarting from Kallan's words, I had been careless, too preoccupied to notice the proximity alert I had set up to warn me of Zelda's approach.

I was so taken aback by my mother's presence, that I turned too fast, lost my balance, and fell from the chair, landing clumsily on the floor. I felt a sharp pain in my elbow as it hit the floor, but before I could cry out or begin to right myself, Zelda moved with surprising speed across the room, grabbed my collar and lifted me bodily off the ground. For a moment I hung suspended in front of her, our eyes level. Her look of shock was so intense, her eyes wide, her mouth gaping open, her bushy eyebrows almost in her hairline, that I felt an incongruous desire to laugh. When I pictured the two of us, both equally stunned, me swinging before her, my feet some way off the floor, this desire overwhelmed me and I laughed out loud. I was so appalled to have been caught red-handed that I could not stop laughing, hysterical guffaws gushing uncontrollably from my mouth.

This rendered Zelda even more bewildered, and she seemed frozen with indecision. She simply stared at me as if I were mad, my wild laughter causing me to swing slightly in the air, my shirt up around my ears as gravity pulled me in the opposite direction from her iron grip. All I could think through my almost hysterical laughter was how strong Zelda was, so much more than I would have anticipated. Eventually, as my gales of laughter began to wane, Zelda finally noticed that I was suspended, supported only by the muscles in her right arm. She lowered me to the floor, staring intently at me all the time. I pulled at my shirt until it once more sat normally on my torso, busying myself with this so as to avoid having to look at my mother's face.

"Well child?" she said finally, as it became clear that I was not about to offer an explanation. "What are you doing here? What were doing with that control panel?"

I shot her a quick glance from under my eyebrows, and was astonished to see that she no longer seemed angry. She just looked surprised and confused, not having a clue what I could possibly have been doing.

She waited, staring straight into my eyes, clearly expecting an explanation. I glanced at the door, but knew that there was no escape. Even if I could dodge past her and race back to the house, what would be the point? It was not as if I had anywhere to hide. I also knew that there was no point in lying: the truth would come out before long, and my situation would then be even worse. I took a deep breath.

"I was turning the fence monitor back on," I said. She looked even more confused, her eyebrows arching even higher up her forehead. My comment made no sense to her. She waited again.

"I came in early this morning and switched it off," I added, as if this made things clearer. This time she lifted her hands in a gesture of utter bewilderment, shaking her head as she did so. Another long silence ensued. I knew I would have to confess to having crossed the fence, gone outside the compound, taking my siblings with me. I feared her reaction, but was backed into a corner from which I could only extricate myself with a full revelation.

"We crossed the boundary, went outside, outside the com..the estate. We spent the day there exploring, and then came home again."

Zelda's jaw went slack, and she peered at me even more intently than before. "How did you cross the fence? You should not be able to cross it. It must have hurt you." I shook my head, but said nothing. "How did you do it?" she asked, genuine curiosity in her voice.

"I changed our brain waves slightly so they didn't match the energy coming from the fence any more. Just for a few moments. Long enough to get across."

Zelda moved slightly away from me, and sat down heavily in one of the chairs behind her. She stared at me with the strangest expression I had ever seen on her face. Her dark eyes narrowed and she put a hand to her head to smooth a few unruly locks back into their usual strict place. She then leaned forward in the chair, and spoke in an unexpectedly quiet voice, her tone low and gravelly.

"Well, well, well boy," she began. "I knew you had the potential to be the most extraordinary person our world has ever known, but I did not anticipate you showing such abilities so young. How old are you now? Eight?" I nodded. "But how did you know how the fence worked?" she continued. "How did you know what to do?"

I shrugged slightly. "I was able to probe the fence a bit with my mind, and it was clear to me how it worked. I wasn't sure I could switch it off, but did think I could change our brain waves so they didn't match those coming off the fence."

Zelda nodded and looked thoughtful. "But why did you deactivate the monitor if you did not alter the energy from the fence?" she asked.

"I knew you'd have monitors telling you if there was a breach, and didn't know if these would go off when we went through, even though our brain waves were different from the fence's," I replied.

"But you did not need to deactivate the monitors if you altered your brain waves," my mother answered. I frowned slightly, not understanding her point. She continued. "Animals pass across all the time without setting off any monitors because their brain waves are different, a point you seem to know. I set it up this way so as not to be disturbed each time a deer or a fox crossed over. So you did not need to trespass into my private rooms to deactivate the monitors." She smiled at me slightly, a mean little smile telling me that for all my cleverness in working out how the fence functioned, I had not reached this obvious conclusion, had not in fact needed to risk her anger by being caught in her laboratory.

I was annoyed with myself, that I had put myself in such a foolish position, an unnecessary position, had allowed my mother to catch me and discover what I was about. I looked at my mother, noting that the little smile had faded from her face. She was frowning as if something was nagging at her mind. Once again she checked the state of her tightly drawn back hair. After an uncomfortable silence during which I wondered what my mother would do next, she looked up sharply.

"But why did you want to leave the estate?" she asked, bafflement again clear in her voice, this time tinged with the beginnings of anger. I swallowed hard, images of small, damp, lightless rooms leaping into my mind.

"Because we never have," I managed to squeak out in my high child's voice. "Because we've never seen the world beyond. Because we are locked up here, not allowed to leave..." I stopped in mid-sentence, fearful that I might have gone too far by suggesting we were imprisoned, wondering if mention of being locked up might have put such an idea into my mother's head. But her reaction was unexpected.

"Who is *we*?" she asked.

"Me, Addy, and our sisters," I confessed.

"And do you all feel that you are 'locked up', or is it just you that feels like that?" she asked in a tight voice.

I gulped, but immediately replied, "All of us."

She dropped her head, nodding, as she assimilated this information.

"Why did none of you ever mention this?" she asked at length. "Especially Emaleen and Safya. They are hardly children any more. They are on the verge of becoming women. Why did they suffer this in silence?" Again, she appeared utterly nonplussed, confusion having replaced any trace of incipient anger. I did not know what to say, so kept my silence. I was not about to admit to her that she frightened us, that we thought of her as our mad jailer, unpredictable and irascible, prone to outbursts of anger, even at her best not showing us much beyond ill-temper, impatience and coldness, punishing us for every tiny infraction or disobedience.

I squirmed where I stood, desperate to get away from her, out of this awful room, yet knowing that I would have to remain to see the event run its course.

"You are not prisoners," she said suddenly in an unusually emotional voice. "The fence is there to protect you, to keep other people out."

"But it keeps us in!" I wailed in a whiny voice, unable to control my outburst as I actually stamped my foot. Zelda looked startled. I gasped at my own foolishness. Surely I had gone too far this time. But again, my mother's response took me by surprise.

"Yes," she replied, in a voice heavy with feeling. "But for your own good, to protect you. People outside will not understand you, any of you. They will not understand what I have done here. They will say terrible things about me, and about you. Especially about *you* Samek." I looked so distressed by this curious revelation that she knew she had to explain further. She moved towards me, her chair bumping forward as she did so. To my utter astonishment, she took both my hands in hers, for the first time in my life. She looked me in the eyes and I was dumbfounded to see what I could only describe as compassion in her expression. I had never seen Zelda show any such emotion, not even to Kallan. Indeed, I had imagined her incapable of such feeling. I was transfixed, rooted to the spot by Zelda's intense stare, and could not have moved even had she not been grasping my hands.

"You know who you are," she began. "You've had all of that explained to you. That I made your sisters from nine progenitors, you from nineteen. And your brother from twenty-one," she added with the tiniest hint of a frown the reason for which I did not understand at that time. "What you do not know," she continued, "Is that what I did in creating you, all of you, is forbidden, strictly forbidden."

"But I thought you said everyone in the world has lots of progenitors," I interrupted, confused.

"Everyone in the world has more than the biological norm of two," she continued. "But most people are made from three or four, a few from five. But it is absolutely prohibited to make a person from more than five. This is such a strict prohibition that it is almost a taboo, even to talk about it. That is why I fell out with most of the other scientists I have ever worked with - I wanted to make people from more than five, and even tried sometimes. But when I discussed this with my colleagues, they were horrified. And when I was caught a few times experimenting, I was thrown off the research straight away. And that is why I work alone. I came here, to this house, and began my own experiments. And nobody outside really knows what I have been doing here, nor would they be able to imagine that I have succeeded. I knew that I could succeed in creating humans from more than five 'parents', far more than five actually. After years of failed attempts, I finally made your sisters. It took five more years to successfully add more progenitors to the mix, and this led to you, my greatest success. Three more years, hundreds, perhaps thousands of failures, and finally I made your brother." Again, at the mention of my brother, a fleeting shadow crossed Zelda's eyes, but I barely noticed this, so astonished was I to be described as her 'greatest success'. I did not think I had done much to warrant such a compliment. I just was who I was. And what did this mean for Adwin? Surely Zelda's last work should be the most proficient?

I glanced back at Zelda as she stopped and drew breath, unused to making such long speeches. I just stared at her. I knew some of what she told me, but did not have an inkling that what she had done in making my sisters, Adwin and me was forbidden. I shuddered with apprehension at what this might mean. That there were people who had authority over Zelda. And what would people outside consider me and my siblings to be, us having been created by means of a taboo process? Would they consider us criminals, or even freaks?

As if following my thoughts, Zelda continued her explanation.

"Young man," she said quietly. "You need to know that other people out in the world will not understand that you and your siblings are extraordinary, unique - marvels of nature combined with technology. They will only see you as products of something banned, something awful, something abhorrent. They will see you as abominations, grotesque distortions of nature. Ridiculous I know, as they are all products of the same basic process, but people are not rational." She paused, looking keenly at me. I was visibly upset by her revelations, but she sensed I was not completely convinced. "They will see you as monsters, Samek, monsters."

I gasped, repelled by the word she had just used. I began to protest, pulling away from her, struggling to extricate myself from the grip of her strong hands and her fierce stare.

"We're not monsters," I wailed. "I'm not a monster."

"To them you are," she went on, a nasty tone creeping into her voice.

I knew I should not have reacted to her words in the way I did, should have feigned indifference to her attempt to scare me with the spectre of the hostile world outside. I was aware that she was trying to frighten me, to create an image of the world beyond the estate which would so alarm me that I would not try to leave again. I was angry with myself for being so easily scared, yet had so little knowledge of anything outside my home that she succeeded, at least in part. I knew I was no monster or freak, yet I could not contest what Zelda had said. Until I had more experience, I had to accept her words. She saw that she had won, at least for now. A spiteful smile spread across her blotchy face. Content with what she had achieved, she let go of my hands.

"You can leave now, but do not let me catch you in here again," she said. "Next time I will not be so lenient. And I think you know what that means!"

I needed no more encouragement than this, and darted towards the door. As I rushed through it, she shouted at me. "But do not forget. You are not a prisoner. You can leave whenever you want!" And she laughed sneeringly as I raced back to the main body of the house, away from her, from her laboratory, and away from the revelations I wished I had never heard. And as I fled, I realised that it was not leaving the compound which had changed the way I viewed the world: it was returning home that had turned my world upside-down. My velvet prison was my sanctuary.

Chapter Nine

As the days passed following the trip outside, Adwin slowly recovered. I spent a great deal of time with him as he did so, taking him his food, helping him eat, reading him stories and singing songs to him. Sometimes I just sat on his bed in silence as he dozed, gently stroking his hair or dabbing his face with a cool, damp cloth. As he improved, we played cards together, and some board games which Zelda insisted were exactly the ones played before the Chaos. She had taught us a game she called chess, or sometimes shah, but Adwin was not up to the levels of concentration required to play this properly, and even when he was well he did not take it very seriously. He was, after all, only five years old, and a game of strategy such as this was simply too slow and dull for him. We played a much simpler game at Adwin's behest, using the same black and white chequered board, which Zelda said was called draughts or checkers. We also spent a great deal of time reminiscing about our single trip beyond the fence, and chatting animatedly about our forest which we would soon visit again. Adwin kept insisting that I visit it alone, knowing how much I missed it, but I never did. It somehow felt wrong to be there without him, especially when the reason was his illness. I just reassured him that it would all be the same when we returned, and that it would not be long until that time.

Kallan's anger towards me gradually subsided, although I could not forget his profound disappointment at my action, and each time I remembered it I cringed inside. Adwin kept insisting to Kallan that he was responsible for his own actions, but as I was the older brother, I did not think such insistence carried much weight with our uncle. Eventually Kallan let the matter drop, ostensibly accepting Adwin's word. I knew that Kallan hated being angry with any of us. It upset him, and created a difficult atmosphere in the house. He seemed almost grateful to have a reason to abandon his ill humour towards me, and things returned to normal.

Zelda kept very much to herself and to her workrooms. We barely saw her, even at mealtimes, and on the few occasions we did, she was introspective and taciturn, barely exchanging more than a word or two with any of us, even with Kallan. I was glad of this, and tried to avoid any contact with her at all, my feelings still raw, hurting from her revealing to me how other people would see me and my siblings. When she passed me in a corridor or when leaving a room, she turned an obnoxious smile on me, a combination of triumph and sheer unpleasantness. I glared back at her, as much as I dared, and rushed away before she could react. Every time I saw her, I wondered why I had not been punished for breaching the forbidden sanctuary of her laboratory, and waited with nervous anticipation for such to occur.

Emaleen remained aloof and distant, though not as much as she had been before the strange dinner we had had with Zelda which led to our crossing the fence. She never quite removed herself from me and Adwin the way she had previously done, though equally never showed anything like the closeness and affection that had lasted so briefly, only to be extinguished by the trip across the perimeter. With Safya, things were different. A few days after we had crossed the boundary, I heard a quiet knock at my bedroom door one evening as I prepared to go to bed. This surprised me, and my surprise grew when Safya leaned her head tentatively around the door.

"Can I come in Samek?" she asked in a quiet, timid voice. I was almost too taken aback to respond. She had never come to see me alone, without her sister. She took this as a negative response and began to mumble apologies for disturbing me. I quickly rallied.

"Yes, yes, of course Saffy. Come in," I replied, forcing a smile onto my face. She hesitantly crept around the open door, responding to my smile with a tentative little grin. She stood in front of the door, seeming uncertain what to do next. I took the initiative, despite being five years her junior, and sat on the bed, indicating with a pat that she should come and sit beside me. She moved slowly across the room, gently lowering herself to sit next to me. A long silence ensued. Finally, she sighed, and, without turning her head to look at me, spoke quietly.

"I'm sorry Samek, really sorry about the way I behaved the other day when we crossed the fence." I remained silent, not knowing quite how to respond. She sighed again and continued. "You went to a lot of effort to get us across, disarming the monitors, changing our brain waves, and then me and Emmy, well, we just reacted badly. Or rather, Emmy reacted badly and I just went along with her, copied her. As I always do," she added, a wistful tone creeping into her voice.

I did not know what to say. I had wondered if she really felt the same profound disappointment as her sister on discovering that the land beyond the fence was no different from our compound, whether she too had expected much more. And I was amazed that she felt guilty enough to come and make amends. We sat in silence until I turned my head to look at my sister.

"What did you really think Saffy, when we crossed the fence? Did you feel the same as Emaleen?"

After a pause, my sister turned her face towards me. She tucked her long blond hair behind her large ears and shyly, a tiny smile pulling at one corner of her lips, looked at me straight in the eyes.

"No," she replied simply. "I was thrilled to be outside, beyond the fence for the first time in my life. I know it all looked the same as inside, but...but it really wasn't the same. I...it...somehow..." she said, seeming to struggle to find the words to describe what she had felt. "The difference was huge. Inside. Outside. For the first time not locked in, with the whole world around me, just there, ready to be explored. I felt...free."

"So why did you act the way you did then?" I asked, trying to disguise the peevish tone in my voice as I remembered the way she had behaved, her apparent indifference almost matching that of her sister. She shrugged her shoulders, dropping her gaze as she seemed unable to continue to look at me directly.

"I...I...you know I always just go along with Emaleen."

"Yes. But why?"

"I just do. I always have done. I can't help myself. I just follow her lead."

"But I don't understand why Saffy. You're not Emmy. You're separate. You're a different person." She just shrugged again, turning her face away from me, looking down at the floor in front of her feet.

"I know full well how bossy she is," I continued, unable to mask the petulant tone in my voice. Safya's head snapped round, a fleeting look of irritation on her face at my criticism of Emaleen.

"Yes," she replied, her expression softening. "She is bossy, with you and with Adwin. But not with me."

"Then why do you do what she does? Why do you just copy her?"

"I just do. I always have done. It seems...it's just the way we are, the way we work together. She leads and I follow. It just seems the right way, the way things should be."

I did not know how to counter these statements. I could reiterate that she was an individual, separate from her sister, and that she should make her own decisions, but I suspected that my words would fall on deaf ears. For thirteen years my sisters had been bonded in a way I could never understand. Surely the patterns of behaviour they had developed were fixed, or at least beyond my ability to intrude into, to affect in any way?

"Anyway, Samek. I'd better go. Emaleen will wonder where I've been and I don't want her to know I came here to apologise to you. She wouldn't approve. But I am really sorry and wanted you to know that I'm grateful for the trip outside, really grateful." I nodded as she stood up and left my room. I was truly surprised that Emaleen had no inkling that Safya had come to see me to make amends. Perhaps there was hope after all that Safya could break free of Emaleen's control, could assert some independence when she felt it necessary.

I was pleased that Safya had come to talk to me, and felt warmer towards her than I had ever done. But I frowned as I remembered Emaleen's reaction to crossing the fence, as I considered how dominant she was in the relationship with her sister, how Safya had meekly followed her sister's lead that day. But in the end I simply had to be thankful that she and I now shared a little more familiarity and friendliness than we had known in the preceding years.

I chose not to share Safya's visit to my room with my brother, lest he blurt it out to Emaleen, something Safya seemed keen to prevent. And until Adwin's health began to improve, I did not share with him what had happened in the laboratory with Zelda. When I felt that he could cope with it, I told him everything. He was as perturbed as I was to think that other people would see us as monsters, would fear and despise us.

"But we haven't done anything wrong!" he cried. "We are just us. We didn't choose to be what we are!"

I couldn't disagree with him, and had no answer to his complaint. His interest in passing over the boundary again evaporated, such was his fear of the reaction of other people when we came across them in the world outside. I wondered if I should have told my brother what Zelda had said, but in the end knew that I had had no option: he would have found out sooner or later, and better that I tell him than Zelda do so and distress him even more.

When I spoke to my sisters about Zelda's awful revelations, they were disturbed, but not nearly as much as Adwin. At nearly fourteen, they were much older, and had endured so many more years of exposure to our mother. From Kallan too they had heard more stories of the world outside, some cautionary, but many which caused them to doubt much of what Zelda said.

Curiously, Emaleen seemed undecided as to how best to proceed with what I had learned, and for once, her sister took the lead. I waited impatiently as they engaged in a brief, but apparently animated telepathic discussion, at the end of which they turned to me.

"Kallan must know more," said Safya in her usual quiet voice. "Let's go and talk to him."

This was sensible, so we went to talk to our uncle, to ask him how other people would really see us. When Adwin heard what we planned to do, he insisted on coming with us, determined not to be left out of such an important conversation. He dragged himself out of his bed and followed us out of the house, wrapped in a loose bedroom gown, soft slippers on his feet.

We found our uncle sitting quietly in the garden, sipping a cool drink, watching the swallows swooping through the sky and catching insects on the wing. He smiled warmly when he saw us, even at Adwin. The day was mild and calm, and he knew that our brother needed to get out into the sunshine, away from his sick room. He raised his silver eyebrows, however, at Adwin's inappropriate indoor clothing, but held his tongue.

We sat down, Adwin and I on either side of Kallan on the bench, the girls sitting on another bench the other side of the narrow path. We did not know how to start, how to broach this subject of such importance to us. We assumed that Zelda had not told Kallan of my discussion with her, and preferred our uncle to remain in ignorance of what I had done. He looked at us, curiosity on his face, aware from our uneasiness that we wanted to talk about something that mattered, but unsure how to begin. He started for us.

"Well, children? You're all rather tense. What is it?" We glanced at each other, still unable to begin. "What is it you want to ask? You know you can ask me anything." Another uncomfortable pause ensued. "Is it about your trip outside, across the fence?" he prompted.

I felt a flutter of embarrassment run through my siblings and me, knowing how we must have vexed our uncle with our trip outside. Yet we also thought he would be appalled to learn that we considered ourselves prisoners. He was well aware we had never left the compound before, but it probably never crossed his mind that we had desired to do so. And even if he had, he would surely have felt hurt to know we felt imprisoned.

Emaleen lost patience with our dithering, and launched straight in.

"What do people outside think of us?", she asked bluntly. The directness of the question caught Kallan unprepared, actually caught us all by surprise.

"What do you mean? Which people?" Kallan asked in a confused voice.

"Anyone. Everyone," replied my sister tersely, a scowl marring her fine, even features.

We all looked keenly at Kallan, waiting anxiously for a reply, but instead were astonished to see him blush furiously, squirm in his seat, and wring his hands together in distress. He was mute, seemingly unable to respond to Emaleen's question. He looked all around, his head darting from side to side, everywhere but at us, as if seeking an escape route or someone to rescue him. Our anxiety grew as we witnessed this strange reaction from our uncle, this highly unusual silence in someone normally so communicative and affable.

After a long agonizing pause, Kallan coughed lightly, clearing his throat. He took a deep breath, and stated simply in his soft voice. "No-one knows about you."

We sat back sharply almost in unison, so unexpected was this answer. How could four children, the oldest close to fourteen years old, have lived so long without anyone outside knowing of our existence?

"What do you mean?" asked Adwin in tones of utter confusion.

"Nobody knows you exist," said Kallan. "Or at least nobody beyond a few scientist colleagues of Zelda's, and even they don't know anything like the full story." We sat in speechless astonishment, not knowing how to react to this most unexpected of news.

"I...I don't understand," I finally stammered. "Why doesn't anyone know we exist?"

"Zelda felt it best not to let anyone know. She thinks it's safest that way," continued Kallan, with the faintest emphasis on the word 'she'.

"Safest!" snapped Emaleen harshly. "Safest for who? For us? Or for her?" She was angry, her voice dripping with bitterness.

"For all of you, Emmy," Kallan continued in a quiet voice. "For Zelda *and* for you." Emaleen scowled at this answer, Safya followed suit, a matching though less convincing scowl darkening her features. Adwin and I merely frowned with incomprehension. A dim thought hovered at the edge of my mind, an unwanted and unpleasant thought that forced its way into my consciousness: if it is not safe for people to know we exist, what will the risk to us be when they eventually find out? Was calling ourselves prisoners a strong enough description of our situation?

I voiced this thought aloud, and Kallan turned to me, compassion radiating from him.

"I don't know my dear. I really don't know. But Zelda thinks the longer you are kept secret, the safer you'll be. Now that you're growing older it wouldn't be possible for anything to be done about you all, about the fact that you exist..."

"Done about us? Done about us?" Emaleen shouted, interrupting our uncle, leaping up off the bench as she did so. "What in the name of buggery does that mean??" Kallan jumped at my sister's profanity, amazed she even knew the word, never having heard her use such language. None of us had ever heard her speak this way. She was furious, standing with hands on hips, stamping her foot on the gravel of the path, long blond hair blowing in the breeze.

Kallan tried to reach out to her, to take her hands, to calm her, but Emaleen snatched her hands away, face red with rage, slate-grey eyes ablaze. Safya sat utterly still, but with the same flush of fury mirrored on her face. Looking at them, I realized that they had jumped to a conclusion I had not, something I could not imagine. Kallan knew there was no point beating around the bush.

"Zelda thinks that if the Council had found out about you when you were in the tanks, or even as babies, they would have issued an order for you to be destroyed."

This statement was met with the most profound silence I had ever experienced. I was so flabbergasted, so overwhelmed with the reality of what Kallan had just said, that the world seemed to stop, the breeze died instantly, and even the birds stopped singing.

"Destroyed?" whispered Adwin in tones of horror. "You mean - killed?" he continued, his voice barely audible. Kallan nodded, sighing deeply, his face awash with unhappiness and tenderness. He was so upset by what he had told us, so distressed by our reaction, that he was unable to speak. His eyes filled with tears and suddenly he put his head in his hands so he did not have to look into our distressed eyes. We did not weep, shock preventing us from such a facile release.

"Are we safe now?" I asked suddenly. I was not sure Kallan had heard me. I tugged at his sleeve and asked again, louder this time. "But are we safe now?" He looked at me through red, teary eyes, shrugging as he did so. He managed to blurt out, "I don't know. I think so, now you're older. Zelda thinks so."

I was not greatly reassured by this, but what could I do? I looked at my sisters, their faces registering a mixture of outrage and disbelief. We all knew what this might mean: Zelda was right when she said outsiders would consider us monsters. If they did not, why order our destruction? Surely no-one would order the extermination of a child if it was not considered a threat?

Emaleen suddenly looked up sharply, and I knew a thought had entered her head. She turned to Kallan and demanded, "You said the Council would order our destruction, yes?" Kallan took his hands away from his face and looked at Emaleen through blue eyes rimmed pink, not knowing what she wanted to know.

"Yes," he replied hesitantly. "Why?"

"The Council isn't everyone," stated Emaleen. "Mother is always telling us the Council doesn't represent anyone, or at least doesn't represent everyone, and that lots of people don't like them, hate them even. She's always told us not to trust the Council, that they act to suit themselves."

Kallan's wavering voice returned to normal as he replied, "I suppose that's true, though Zelda may have a jaundiced view of the Council, given their hostility to her."

I knew all about this, how the Council members were, according to Zelda, responsible for all of her woes when she was a scientist in the world outside. They were always behind her removal from projects and experiments, always persecuting her for her beliefs and actions. They were the ones who drove her to remove herself from the world, to work in isolation out of the gaze and cooperation of society. We had all heard such rantings from Zelda all our lives, and had no reason to disbelieve her. After all, we had never met a single member of the Council, or indeed anyone else from the outside world. Zelda was so consistent in her condemnation of the Council, so relentless in her vituperation that we could not help but to have been deeply influenced by it.

As it dawned on me what Emaleen was trying to imply, I began to feel better, less distressed. If it was only the Council that hated us to the extent of wanting to see us eradicated, this did not necessarily mean that other people felt the same way. It did not mean that everyone would see us as monsters. And if the Council acted out of rational self-interest rather than on the basis of emotional response, perhaps the world at large would not respond to us, emotionally, as monsters. I grasped at this idea. It made our predicament less problematic. Perhaps when people learned about us they would not react in the extreme and hostile way Zelda had suggested. Perhaps this was merely *her* self-interest, wanting to keep us to herself, wanting to keep her own illegal behaviour out of the public domain.

The mood lightened dramatically. As Kallan perceived this, he too felt less upset, though was wary that we were perhaps too quickly assuming that the Council was the only problem, that other people would not react towards us in a hostile manner. But he was at least glad that our distress had waned. The reality of our situation he could do nothing about, so what use in us being thrown into a long-lived state of torment about it? Nobody could predict or control how people outside would react to us when they finally found out, so what would be achieved by torturing ourselves over this?

Safya smiled gently at Kallan. "Thank you uncle. For telling us the truth," she said quietly, keen to reassure him that he had been right to do so.

"Better to know what people might think, in case we ever meet them," she added. Kallan looked at her sharply as she said this, but I agreed with her. It was preferable to be enlightened than to live in ignorance, especially as we now knew how to leave the compound and may come across other people at any time. We left Kallan alone in the garden, still visibly agitated, but calmer than moments before. We headed quickly to the girls' bedroom to discuss the momentous truth we had just uncovered. We chose to remove ourselves from our uncle's presence before engaging in further discussion, knowing how it irked Kallan if we mindspoke to each other in his presence.

When we were safely inside their room, the door firmly locked behind us, I began. "We can leave again, cross the fence, and there's nothing he can do to stop us."

"But what's the point?" queried Emaleen bluntly. "We know there's nothing outside of any interest, not for kilometres and kilometres. Zelda's always bragged at how remote and unknown the estate is."

I knew my sister was right. For all that Adwin and I had enjoyed our day outside our prison home, as had Safya as I later learned, it offered nothing new, nothing we could not find inside the perimeter, apart from the simple fact of being outside. We knew that in the outside world people travelled around in a range of vehicles, some on the ground propelled on wheels or on cushions of air, and for longer journeys high in the sky. We had seen these in our studies, racing across the surface of the world or up in the clouds, conveyances large and small, from tiny single person pods to large communal transports. Yet we had never seen one from the estate. And we were sure that neither Zelda nor Kallan owned any such vehicle, or surely we would have seen it in our explorations of the house and its environs.

We sat in silence, frustrated by the fact that we now knew how to leave the compound, but not knowing how to travel any distance from it. It was as if the boundary of the estate had simply moved a little way beyond its actual border. After a while my sisters and I were startled when Adwin suddenly piped up in a high-pitched excited voice, "But how does Kallan get out?"

I stared at him, impressed that he had thought of this, young as he was. Kallan left the estate fairly regularly, telling us that he was going to visit friends. Zelda clearly did not approve, and stomped about making her opposition clear. Yet Kallan still went. He dressed up for the occasion, wearing his best clothes, his white hair beautifully coiffured, gold or silver jewellery sparkling as the light caught the polished precious stones embedded in the metal. He made a point of saying goodbye to us all, laughing at our displeasure as he left us, abandoning us to our own company, or that of Zelda. He was usually gone for at least a day, and sometimes for longer. Yet we never actually saw him leave, or return. We never heard the hum of a vehicle taking off or landing. It was obvious that he must have some other way of getting to and from the estate.

We frowned with concentration, trying our best to understand how Kallan could exit and enter our home. Suddenly Safya leapt off the bed, clapping her hands animatedly, a huge smile spread across her face.

"Teleportal! There must be a teleportal on the estate!"

"Of course," agreed Emaleen. "That's the only way he could come and go without going across the fence."

I was confused. The word teleportal was not familiar to me. I knew what teleportation was as I had come across the concept in my studies, but what was a teleportal? Adwin and I looked to the girls for elucidation. Emaleen glanced at her sister, nodding to her to explain. Safya smiled slightly. Her excitement seemed to overcome her usual taciturnity.

"When were younger, maybe a bit younger than you Addy, we came across teleportals as part of our studies on teleportation. When we asked Zelda what a teleportal was she was livid, though we had no idea why, not that that was anything unusual! Anyway, she shouted at us to forget all about teleportals and rushed off. Her anger made us even more eager to learn about them, but when we tried to find out more, we couldn't. It was as if all references to them had been removed from the digital memory, and no matter what we tried, we never came across them again. Eventually we gave up looking."

She stopped, as if tired from her unusual talkativeness. Realizing this, and seeing confusion still on the faces of Adwin and me, Emaleen picked up the explanation. She stopped for a moment to collect her thoughts, trying to remember what she had learned about this topic all those years before.

"We all know what teleportation is - just disappearing from one place and appearing in another a moment later. I've no idea how it works, but it seems to be common, used by lots of people. A teleportal, often just called a portal, is a machine that does this. As far as I remember it's usually quite small, though maybe some of them are bigger. All I can remember about the ones we saw images of is that they were big transparent cylinders or cubes, about as big as one of our shower cubicles. They stood on the floor, usually near the side of a room, though I think they could be anywhere. They weren't very tall, but higher than an adult, and sealed at the top. The small ones only fitted a single person, the bigger ones maybe a small group, five or six people." She stopped and looked at Safya, who took up the explanation.

"You stepped up into the container. I think there must have been some sort of machinery in the base of it, and maybe more in the ceiling of it. It closed over, sealing you in, and I assume you activated it by telling it where to take you. And then it just sort of sent you where you wanted to end up."

"But how did it know to send you to the right place? How come it didn't just send you off anywhere?" asked Adwin, genuinely concerned.

"I'm not sure," replied Emaleen. "I can't remember too well, but I think it sent you to another teleportal, the one you told it to send you to, so there was no danger of getting lost. It's a bit like the way pieces in chess or draughts can jump around the board from one square to another," she explained, using imagery Adwin would understand.

Adwin and I were amazed to hear about teleportals, yet it seemed to make so much sense. It certainly explained Kallan's seemingly easy trips to and from the house, and the lack of any visible means of transportation. I suddenly felt excitement, so much that I was barely able to get my words out.

"We have to find it, get it to work," I said breathlessly. "Then we can bypass the fence, and go wherever we want, as far as we want."

We stilled instantly at this realisation, freedom beckoning, so near that it was almost tangible.

"We know it's not anywhere in the house, or outside in the gardens or woods," said Emaleen pensively. "So it must be somewhere in Zelda's laboratory." She turned to me and asked, "Did you see anything like a teleportal when you went in there?"

I reflected for a moment, running through my mind all I had seen in my hasty traversing of the various rooms on my way to the foetal tank room.

"No," I said confidently. "There was nothing like that. But there are quite a few other rooms I didn't go into, or didn't get to. We need to explore those."

"You should have had a look in them while you were there," said Emaleen irritatedly. "Why didn't you?" I bristled at her annoyance.

"I had to get in and out as quickly as I could before Zelda came back. And I still got caught anyway!" I added angrily.

"Stop carping Emmy," said Safya unexpectedly. Emaleen turned an astonished look on her sister. "Samek did everything he could, so leave him alone."

Emaleen remained silent, this day of startling events never seeming to end.

After a pause, we nodded in unison, even Emaleen, each filled with apprehension at the task ahead, knowing that Zelda would be outraged if she caught us scouring through every private room of her laboratory complex, especially as we would be looking for something she would not want us to get our hands on. I was, however, filled with a steely determination to find the teleportal. I had come to realise that the prison we were in was far wider than we had ever imagined.

Chapter Ten

As usual, Zelda was rarely out of her laboratory complex over the next few days, and I still worked hard to avoid her, to keep out of her sight and mind, lest she decide to inflict a punishment on me for my earlier transgression. I maintained a proximity alarm on my mother, but it seemed the only occasions she left for any length of time were late in the night, when we children were sound asleep. As before, I judged this a poor time to risk breaching the boundary to Zelda's private rooms, in search of the teleportal we so desperately wanted to locate. My subconscious alarm would fire, waking me, but I would then have to rouse the others in the dead of the night. We would be sleepy and unfocused, lacking attention, thereby risking discovery or simply being unable to concentrate well enough to actually locate what we had set out to find.

During the days, we spoke occasionally in whispers, or mindspoke if we thought we could be overheard. It was clear that we were on edge, tense with the anticipation that we might soon have within our grasp the means to leave and re-enter the compound as we willed, without Zelda having the slightest idea that we had done so. But as the days passed without being able to explore the laboratory, we grew ever more strained and impatient, our goal so near and yet seemingly so far. Despite our best efforts to hide the anxiety we felt, we were unused to such behaviour, rarely having had a need to dissimulate in this way. Adwin and I were visibly tense, Emaleen even more surly than usual. And Safya's taciturnity was stamped with an almost permanent frown. As such, Kallan was able to sense that something was amiss, that all four of us were not behaving in our usual way.

"What on earth is going on?" he asked one evening at supper, as we all sat in stony, tense silence. We jumped at his sharp tone, but instead of answering, we stared down at our plates, unwilling to look at him directly.

"I asked you, what is going on?" he repeated, in an even more spiky voice, clearly irritated. As this was met by an even more determined silence, I decided I would have to say something.

"Nothing, uncle. We're all just a bit tired."

Kallan looked at me in astonishment, disbelief obvious on his face at this patently foolish reply.

"And why would that be?" he asked scathingly. "All you've been doing the whole day is mope around the house. I hardly think that would render the lot of you mute with exhaustion!"

We had no reply to this, and simply stared even more intently at our plates, guilty expressions on our faces. Even Emaleen looked embarrassed, an expression rarely seen on her face. From the corner of my eye I saw Kallan raise one silver eyebrow, scrutinising each of our faces one after the other. When it became clear that my words were the only reply he was going to get, he huffed loudly, mumbling, "Well let's just hope it's nothing foolish or dangerous again," and left it at that. The rest of the supper passed in uncomfortable silence, and I was relieved to finish and rush off to my own room.

Later that evening the four of us met in the conservatory at the back of the house, our whispers turning immediately to the only subject we could focus on: when would we be able to go and look for the teleportal. As we were griping as usual about Zelda and the fact that she never seemed to leave her rooms, my alarm system told me that she had left the laboratory. I held up my hand, and the other three fell silent. I tracked her movements as she moved through the house. Unusually, she went to Kallan's room, finding him there reading quietly. I knew my uncle would consider it wrong for me to follow Zelda into his room, but I sensed something odd was happening. I decided to breach their privacy and listen in to their conversation, something I would normally never do, as I feared I might later blurt out something I could only possibly have learned by eavesdropping on a private conversation. I silently told my siblings what I was about to do. My sisters nodded eagerly, the first time in days their features were not blemished by a dark frown. Adwin looked uncomfortable, but gave the tiniest nod of assent.

What I heard was completely unexpected. Zelda informed Kallan that she was "going out for a while", and that she did not know when she would be back. When Kallan asked what she planned to do, he was clearly taken aback when Zelda informed him that she wanted to visit an old scientist colleague, one of the handful who had shown a guilty interest in what she was trying to do. I knew from Kallan's reaction that this was a very infrequent occurrence, though I also heard them briefly discuss the scientist in question, and it was apparent that Kallan had met her before, in fact that he seemed to know her well. He smiled at Zelda and told him to take care outside the estate, to remember that "you have a lot of enemies out there, so best not to be seen." Zelda nodded, well aware of this fact, then left my uncle's room.

As I listened in to the conversation, I shared it with my siblings, so we all heard Zelda's unusual announcement. I then tracked her as she returned to her laboratory, stopping briefly at her own bedroom to change her clothes. As she entered the laboratory, Emaleen threw a mindspeak at us so sharply that it felt like a shout.

~She's going to use the teleportal!!~ she silently shrieked. We all leaped off our seats with excitement, knowing that she was right. *~Don't lose your focus Samek. Follow her!~* she commanded.

I grasped instantly what she meant: Zelda would lead us straight to the portal. I shook my head to clear the cloudiness caused by eagerness, and locked on to Zelda again. She moved briskly through room after room, stopped for a moment in the foetal tank room to pick something up from the table, then continued on through several more rooms until she entered what I knew must be the last room in the laboratory complex. I saw, through Zelda's eyes, that it was a fairly large room, empty apart from a large rectangular box with clear walls, sat on a small platform, and sealed across the top with a metallic layer about ten centimetres deep. I showed the image to the others, and both Emaleen and Safya mindspoke at exactly the same time, and in exactly the same jittery tone.

~That's it!~

Zelda stepped onto the platform, the open door of the cubicle sliding softly closed behind her. She spoke briefly, too quickly for me to hear clearly, and in an instant, just disappeared.

I broke the connection to the image, standing absolutely still in shock. I saw the others did likewise. Though we knew that teleportals existed, and what they did, this did not prepare us for the reality of watching someone simply disappear; there one moment, gone the next.

After a few moments of utter stillness, we all looked round at each other, and laughed to see the boggled expressions on each other's faces. Emaleen took control of the situation and barked a curt command.

"Now. We have to go now. She's not here."

We needed no further encouragement, and rushed out through the dense foliage of the conservatory towards the laboratory. I quickly checked if Kallan was still in his room, and to my relief found this to be the case. We did not tarry, and soon found ourselves at the laboratory door. After a fractional hesitation, Emaleen waved her hand across the panel next to the door, and it glided smoothly open. She looked at me, as I was the only one who knew his way around the labyrinth of rooms. I stepped through the door, followed by the others, and made my way directly to the room with the foetal tanks. I perceived curiosity from my siblings as they looked for the first time upon these containers, the ones I informed them they had gestated in. Their curiosity was tinged with wistfulness, a desire to stop and inspect these objects, understand the artificial wombs that had nurtured them. But they knew we did not enjoy the luxury of time, and any exploration of the tanks would have to be done another day.

I led them through the remaining rooms to the final chamber, where we knew we would find the teleportal. As we entered this chamber, we stared at the transparent booth in front of us, neatly pushed up against the back wall. It looked unimpressive, not much bigger than a large shower cubicle, as Emaleen had described it, with room for perhaps four adults. It had a metallic base and top, the walls completely see-through, presumably made of perspiglass, strong yet flexible. Despite the booth's lack of visual interest, we quivered with excitement, breath shallow and rasping. Liberty stood before us, waiting for us, literally within our grasp.

We moved further into the chamber, coming to a halt right in front of the portal. We stared at it, into it, around it, trying to summon the courage to open its door, to step inside. Before we could rouse ourselves to do so, I heard the faintest hiss, a barely audible sibilant sissing sound, coming from the machine. All four of us echoed this with a collective inward gasp of breath, followed by a moment of strained tension as we waited to see what the sound signified. We stopped breathing.

To my horror, Zelda reappeared in the portal as abruptly as she had disappeared. She was facing us, and her expression was thunderous, her cheeks mottled red, almost purple, the scaly patches of eczema even more livid than usual, her eyes narrowed with rage. We were transfixed, unable to move a muscle as if we had been turned to stone. There was nowhere to hide, no point in running even if we had been able to move.

The door to the cubicle slid open. Zelda stomped out and stood right in front of us, her face barely a finger's breadth from ours, her enraged glare boring into us as she moved her eyes across the row of fearful gazes in front of her. I especially was numbed with fear, having so recently been caught snooping around in my mother's private domain. She was so furious that she seemed unable to produce a sound. Her rage coursed out of her, flowing around us, enveloping us in a torrent of palpable fury. After what seemed an age, she finally found her voice.

"How dare you. How dare you all. You, you, you and especially you," she said in a menacingly quiet voice, almost a whisper, jabbing a finger at each of us in turn as she spoke the final sentence, the last jab at me. "You have no right to be here," she went on. "No right to be anywhere in my private quarters." She turned her ferocious gaze directly on me. "And you," she said, again accompanying her spat words with an aggressive thrust of a finger. "*You* are the worst of the lot. I only told you a few days ago never to come in here again. What do you have to say for yourself?"

I quailed under her gaze, swallowed hard several times to try and lubricate my dessicated throat, aware that her anger would only increase if I did not make some sort of reply. Visions of terror in a black, sealed room wavered before my eyes. But before I could bring enough moisture to my mouth to allow me to speak, Emaleen interrupted in an angry, yet still fearful voice.

"Why shouldn't we come in here? Why are you so special that you have this to yourself? We live here too, we're part of this 'family' as much as you are!"

Safya, Adwin and I stared at our sister, appalled at her tone, horrified at the reaction this would evoke from Zelda, yet at the same time filled with admiration. We felt our sister's trepidation, but despite this she had mustered the courage to shout at Zelda, risking bringing further ire down on her own head.

Zelda turned to glare at her, stunned that this child had dared to speak to her in such a way. For a long while she fixed Emaleen with her gaze, unblinking, trying to stare her down. But my sister refused to succumb, glaring back at our mother, rage blazing in her own slaty eyes. The fraught emotions pouring out of them both were almost painful for me to experience.

To our utter astonishment, Zelda suddenly laughed. A harsh, barking, unpleasant laugh, to be sure, but a laugh nonetheless. It was the last sound we expected to hear coming from her mouth. Emaleen was so taken aback by this unexpected reaction from Zelda, that her own fury wavered, anger diminishing suddenly by a large measure as she took a step backwards. The atmosphere in the room shifted abruptly. We all breathed out, relief flowing through us. But Zelda was not appeased, merely less furious than moments before. She spoke suddenly, at a more normal volume, her growling voice still dripping with anger.

"I do not think I need to ask you what you are doing here. The fact I caught you all staring longingly at the portal here tells me everything I need to know. What did you think - that you would port in and out as and when you want, expecting me to be none the wiser? Do you think I am that stupid, not to know what goes on in my own home?"

"Why did you come back?" snapped Emaleen, still smarting at Zelda's treatment of us. "Why weren't you gone longer?" she added, just managing to remember not to suggest we knew the reason for her trip. If our mother found out I had eavesdropped on her conversation with Kallan she would be incandescent with rage. But she still picked up something from what Emaleen had said.

"How do you know how long I was gone young lady?" she asked sharply. "How do you know when I left?" She peered at Emaleen, eyes narrowed ominously. My sister was startled and flushed slightly.

"We saw you just a little while ago," I interrupted hastily, "Leaving Kallan's room, heading here."

Zelda turned to me, a nasty look on her face. "Well, well, well. Did you now? But how did you know I would be going anywhere?" she growled.

I swallowed hard, and knew that when I replied I was going to do something I never thought I would dare to do to Zelda: I would use my gifts to cause her to believe whatever I told her. I balked at this, but felt I had no option. If she pursued her line of questioning, she would soon unearth my dirty secret: that I had tracked her, and eavesdropped when she spoke to Kallan. I could not risk her discovering any of that. So when I replied, I had made sure that she was already predisposed to believing what I told her, and I had warned the others silently ~*Don't contradict what I say.*~ I wanted to run no risk that they would inadvertently apprise Zelda of my ability to eavesdrop at a distance by a careless comment.

"We didn't know for sure, but we were impatient to find the teleportal. We knew there had to be one in your laboratory - otherwise how could Kallan go and visit friends the way he does? And we knew it had to be in your rooms. We couldn't wait any longer, and just hoped that if you had gone off somewhere you wouldn't be back for a while." I had stuck more or less to the truth, always the best option in such a situation, but deliberately made her accept what I said as sufficient explanation of our behaviour. She nodded her understanding, and seemed to be satisfied, seemingly unaware how I manipulated her reaction to my words.

My relief was huge, but as I breathed more freely, Adwin asked me, ~*If you could make her stop asking more questions, why couldn't you get rid of her anger earlier?*~

It was a good question, and the the first thing that crossed my mind was that if Zelda felt her anger wane for no good reason, she would know very well that one of us had caused it to do so, and this could only be me. But then I realised in addition to this, that when faced with such monumental rage, I was unable to react rationally. I was overwhelmed with the outpouring of emotion, and this disrupted my ability to tap into my gifts. I would have to think about this quietly later on. What use my abilities if they could so easily be disturbed? I also wondered if any of my siblings could have reduced Zelda's anger with their own abilities, but perhaps they did not realise this, or were unwilling to try.

My cogitations were interrupted by Zelda saying, "You surely did not think I would leave the estate without setting up warnings did you? And after master Samek's unsanctioned 'visit' to my laboratory so recently, surely you did not imagine I would not take measures to protect my private space?" She chortled at the surprised looks on our faces. Clearly we had not considered such a thing.

"That is how I knew someone had broken into my rooms, so I came rushing straight back. I did not expect to find the four of you staring like idiots at the portal at the very moment I arrived back." She laughed again, loudly and raucously. "You should have seen your faces when I popped up in front of you. Talk about guilty!" She laughed on and on, the image of our horrified, culpable faces causing her such merriment that she could not stop laughing. Eventually her guffawing caused her to have a coughing fit, which we were relieved to note stopped the derisive laughter.

When she had caught her breath, she said, "But why did you think there was only one portal in the house anyway? There are several others."

We looked round at each other, puzzlement on our faces. Zelda seemed to be enjoying our confusion.

"There's a big one at the back of the house," she continued. "In the store rooms off the kitchen. It is a really old model, but still good enough to bring in inanimate material, and things like that. And there is another one, a small one you have seen hundreds of times, in the kitchen itself."

We looked even more confused, so Zelda continued in a tone of unpleasant glee, "How else do you think we get our food? And the big one we use for furniture, tools, other things like that."

With a flash of comprehension I saw the small teleportal in the kitchen in our minds. It sat on a table along one wall, an opaque perspiglass cube-shaped box, each side about the length of an adult's arm. It was so familiar to me that I had never questioned what it was. I felt dismayed at my lack of inquisitiveness about the box, but knew that my siblings had not shown any more curiosity than I had. Perhaps this was simply evidence of our young age, that despite our precocious maturity in many ways, in some respects we were still very much children.

"It is also a fairly old model, but adequate to get our food delivered," Zelda continued in almost conversational tone. It seemed that our shock at discovering that there were portals in the house we did not know about, despite seeing one of them on an almost daily basis, and our lack of curiosity about how we actually received food and other products caused Zelda's anger to abate. Now she seemed to be simply enjoying herself.

"But *how* do we get our food, and everything else? Where does it come from?" snapped Emaleen, tossing her long blond locks with irritation.

Zelda turned a mocking look on my sister. "We just order it and it turns up," she said simply.

"How?" Adwin piped up, no wiser after Zelda's terse reply.

"That is just the way it works. You order things and they appear. We tell the portal what we want. The order goes to one of the central distribution hubs if it's in stock there. If not, it gets sent to the appropriate factory, or workshop, or farm, telling them what we want and where we are, and they immediately arrange for it to be teleported straight into our home. If it is a regular product, it is quick. If it is not so usual, we can search the digital memory by category, or name or however we want, and choose. And if it is really unusual, or never been made before, we can put in an order for this to be done, and when it is ready, hey presto! It arrives in our home portal. The other option is to have instructions sent to a 3D printer which then prints the thing you want, though this is usually slower than teleporting it."

I was utterly dumbfounded by these revelations, presented to me and my siblings in such a matter-of-fact way by Zelda, as if they were something mundane, humdrum. Yet to me this seemed like magic. We were surrounded by everything we needed, and I remembered that when one of us asked Kallan for things we did not have, they just appeared shortly after. Yet I had never thought to question how. It had never crossed my mind, for when there is never any scarcity why should one dwell on the reasons for this?

It was disconcerting that something so extraordinary should have seemed so commonplace to me, so unworthy of enquiry. I wondered if perhaps this was always the case, that the things surrounding us on a daily basis we simply took for granted, did not question, did not investigate. It was as if they were simply part of our environment, and as such they did not stand out, did not protrude from the background of that which constituted our everyday horizons. If this were true for something as phenomenal as being able to order whatever we wanted, and for it to appear in our own home as if by magic, then surely I must be constantly failing to apprehend all sorts of other everyday marvels, all sorts of other wonders meriting investigation, or at least notice. I seemed to have no trouble feeling a sense of wonder at the world of nature, so why did this not also occur with the world of everyday objects which surrounded me in my home? I sighed, and knew that I would have to think about this.

There was a hiatus, a tense pause. Zelda seemed unwilling to share any more information, and none of us seemed to know how to extricate ourselves from the difficult situation we were in. So far, there had been no talk of punishment, and we were keen to keep it that way. We all stood quietly, glancing at each other, Zelda faintly triumphant, we children abashed. Zelda put us out of our discomfort by announcing abruptly, "Well off you go, out of my rooms." We did not move at first, until she yelled, "Now! Get out! Fuck off and do not come back!"

We needed no further encouragement. We turned and fled, Safya, Adwin and I simply relieved to be removing ourselves from Zelda's presence, but Emaleen still scowling as she moved towards the door. As I turned, I was slightly surprised to see a pensive expression on Zelda's face. And as I moved to the door, I could feel her intense gaze boring into our backs. I did not have the courage to go into her mind to find what she was thinking, glad to have got away so lightly from this, my second violation of the absolute privacy of Zelda's laboratory, not to mention violating the privacy of my uncle Kallan by listening in to private conversations. Zelda was unpredictable and might yet decide at a future point to inflict punishment upon us for our dreadful transgression.

Chapter Eleven

I spent a restless night, struggling to fall asleep after the encounter with Zelda beside the portal. My mind was spinning with thoughts of what I had learned, about the ordering and delivery of all that we desired, about the blindness I suffered towards all that surrounded me daily, and about the portal itself. I still found the idea bizarre and truly disconcerting that an object could simply disappear from one place and almost instantly materialise somewhere else. And the notion that this could also happen to a living creature, especially to a human being, was almost too much to comprehend. How did it work? How did a person cease to exist in one location, yet reappear in another? I could not imagine the actual process, the technicalities of the physics required to perform such a wonder. I had only the most basic knowledge of physics at that age, and nothing I had learned offered me any solution to the problems I was grappling with. When I searched the digital memory, there was only a brief mention of teleportation with no detail of the science. What else had Zelda removed from the digital memory? I dared not ask her or Kallan.

Even after I had finally managed to doze off, I suffered a restless night, my sleep fitful and disturbed as I tossed and turned in bed, my mind seething with ideas and images. Normally I could control my thoughts, but this night was strange, and I failed to do so. The best I could manage was to calm my unsettled mind by a smidgen.

I awoke early, and finding myself fidgety and restive, decided to get up. I dressed, left my bedroom, and went to the kitchen to see if there was any food prepared for breakfast. As I entered the room, my gaze was drawn straight to the teleportal on the table against the wall. I went over to it, stopped, then looked at it from all angles. It was made from an opaque, greyish-blue perspiglass, a dull, glassy sheen reflecting back from its unremarkable surface. I ran my hands over it. It felt exactly as I had expected, exactly like every other piece of perspiglass I had ever felt: cool to the touch, hard, lacking any notable features. On the very left-hand end of the side of the cube I saw a small matt blue circle, a few centimetres across. I carefully moved my right hand towards it, extending my index finger as I did so. As the tip of my finger approached the circle, and just before it made contact, I heard a tiny hiss and felt an infinitesimal spark of energy leap across from the circle to my fingertip. The front of the portal slid smoothly sideways, stopping only when the entire inside space was fully revealed.

I peered inquisitively into the box, but to my disappointment, saw nothing. Just an empty cube. But as I moved my head away from the front of the portal, I noticed that the front of the box began to glow faintly. As I watched, the surface of the frontal facade glowed ever more brightly as the dormant control panel of the portal came to life. After a few moments, the increase in luminosity halted. I moved to stand in front of the panel. It was lit in various colours, covered in symbols and numbers. I did not understand the symbols at my young age of only eight, never having seen them before, but wondered whether the user could touch the symbols and numbers in specified sequence to indicate precisely what food he wanted sent, and in what quantity. Then I remembered that Zelda had said that you could simply tell the portal what you wanted, and it would be delivered. I glanced around the kitchen and saw that, as usual, breakfast was ready and waiting. Kallan had always seen to this, though I had thought he always prepared the food himself having watched him do this many times. On the occasions I had seen him open this simple cube and remove food from it, I had assumed it had manufactured the food itself, or perhaps cooked it. I had never considered that it was a portal for food made somewhere else and then teleported in its entirety straight into our home. I smiled vaguely as I remembered how surprised I used to be that the same box could make such diverse offerings as chicken pie, or ice-cream, but like everything that is seen daily, I soon forgot my initial wonder and merely accepted the everyday reality.

I turned back to the glassy cube. A shiver of thrill ran through me as I made up my mind to try and order something, just to see if I could make it work. I stood right in front of the portal and, after a moment's reflection, said in my high boy's voice, "Two pieces of buttered toast with two scrambled eggs." I was not sure which part of the portal to speak to, but thought that it would probably suffice to stand directly in front of it, and speak in a strong voice.

I waited a moment, and nothing happened. I was frustrated by this, not knowing what I had done wrong. But as I watched the portal, it occurred to me that it would not know that the eggs on toast were all I wanted to order. Perhaps it was waiting to see if I had finished for the moment, or wanted something else. I did not know exactly what to do, but remembered Kallan as he often stood in front of the cube, mumbling quietly as if speaking to it. This slightly odd behaviour now made sense to me. I decided to say what I had heard him say on a number of occasions before taking food from the box.

"Ok. That's all," I said firmly. Almost the moment I finished saying this, the front of the cube slid across the portal until it dropped back into place, clicking shut. Nothing seemed to happen after this, but I sensed a minuscule tingle of electromagnetic energy coming from the device. A moment later, with a single high-pitched chime, the front slid open again. I laughed in astonishment to see two pieces of toast covered in scrambled eggs lying steaming slightly on the bottom of the box. I realised I should also have asked the machine to put them on a plate, but it was not difficult to reach in and grasp the crisp toast in my hands and carry it across the kitchen to a plate.

I took my miraculous food into the dining room, which I found empty at that fairly early hour. But as I was eating, my sisters came in, carrying some of the breakfast Kallan had left in the kitchen with them which I had ignored in my eagerness to try out the portal. They looked surprised to see me tucking in to scrambled eggs on toast, and Emaleen demanded to know where I had got them. I chuckled, led my sisters back into the kitchen, and repeated the process I had carried out with the portal. We all stood laughing as the box opened revealing four pieces of egg-covered toast, and this time on a plate! We were making so much noise as we delighted in our new toy, that Adwin heard us as he toddled along to the dining room. He joined us, and was equally entranced by this marvel we had overlooked for so long.

Adwin demanded chocolate-covered marzipan, accompanied by hot banana milk, and shrieked with childish pleasure as the box delivered these treats. We saw that even without specific instructions as to quantity, the box made a choice and delivered a fairly conservative amount of each item ordered. I assumed one could increase or decrease the quantity, but the cube defaulted to a sensible choice if not given precise instructions. Strange though, I mused, that it had not made the same assumption in relation to a plate. Perhaps our machine was old and weary, not the best model available? Or perhaps the lack of a plate was a hygiene measure? The food itself would surely have been produced by automata in a sterile factory, but could the same be said of the plates?

We then got rather carried away, ordering a whole range of foodstuffs: more chocolate, biscuits, exotic fruits, rice pudding, several varieties of cake, and even some savouries. We commanded the machine to send us chicken and mushroom pies, roast beef, hard boiled eggs. With each new food, we whooped with laughter, clapping our hands, removing it from the portal as quickly as we could so we could demand more. We piled plate after plate, bowl after bowl on every surface of the kitchen, and when we ran out of space, on the floor. We were delirious with the sheer joy of being to speak our wish, and having it fulfilled. We knew there had to be good scientific explanations for what we were witnessing, but to us it seemed like magic, like the wizardry of old that we had read about - witches and warlocks who had learned the arcane secrets of the physical world and who could perform miracles with the merest movement of their magic wands, or by incanting magic spells.

Our revelry was abruptly dashed by the outraged voice of Kallan behind us, stentorian in its thunderous tone.

"What in the name of hell are you doing!!?" he roared. We leapt into the air in unison, shocked out of our merriment by a tone and volume we had never heard him use before.

We turned quickly, blanching as we looked up at our uncle. He loomed over us, taller by far than Adwin or me, and by some margin over the girls. He was a big man, tall, broad and robust, and his righteous anger seemed to augment his natural sturdy form as he dominated us by his sheer presence. Yet as I glanced at him nervously, I saw he was not really angry - he was flummoxed, at a loss to understand what was happening in *his* kitchen, and why every surface, even the floor, was covered in plates overflowing with food. He gazed around at the bowls and saucers, large plates and pans, some sizzling hot and steaming, others piled high with cold foodstuffs, his tanned brow furrowed in confusion.

He turned back to us, and we cringed under the withering gaze of his vivid blue eyes.

"Well?" he demanded in a tight, clipped voice. "Would one of you be kind enough to explain yourselves?" he added in a tone dripping with artificial politeness. No-one spoke. I glanced rapidly at the door to see if escape was possible, but Kallan saw the direction of my eyes. He crossed his arms over his chest and seemed to grow even larger. I saw that flight was not an option, so I decided to simply speak the truth.

"We found out from Zelda yesterday that this box is a teleportal, for food. I tried it this morning and it worked, then the others tried it too, and it kept on working." I stopped, and peeked up at Kallan. He glared down at me, clearly not intending to help me, and not yet satisfied with my reply. I swallowed and continued. "We got carried away," I whispered, and dropped my eyes to the floor.

"You don't say!" replied my uncle, his tone dripping with scorn. "And what did you plan to do with all this food?" he asked. Again, no-one answered. "Well?" he asked ominously. "I'm waiting." And he actually began to tap his foot on the floor with impatience.

I glanced at my siblings, my expression a desperate request for help. But none of them would look at me, and their total lack of response told me that I looked in vain for help from them. I mindspoke a loud, cross message at them, making them flinch, as I had intended. I took a deep breath, and looking up at Kallan, replied.

"We didn't plan to do anything with it. We just ordered it, kept ordering it. We didn't think."

"Humph," he replied, though I noted that his foot had stopped tapping.

"You didn't think?" he queried sharply. "That much is obvious. What am I supposed to do with all of this? It'll all go to waste."

"Not all of it!" I wailed, wounded by his patent exaggeration. "Some of it will last and..." but I stopped in mid-sentence as Kallan's foot began to tap again.

I waited, gazing intently at the floor, eyes darting to and fro, trying to find even a small expanse of tiling uncluttered with overburdened crockery. I could see no way out of this uncomfortable situation. We had behaved childishly, and there seemed no escape.

But amazingly, salvation shuffled into the kitchen, and even more astonishingly, in the form of Zelda. She glanced abstractedly around the kitchen, shrugging slightly as she took in the picture of domestic chaos all around, seemingly impassive in the face of such disorder, as if it were a common, everyday occurrence.

"I want to talk to you," she said without preamble, smoothing down her already smooth hair as she did so. I looked up as Kallan rounded on her.

"What did you want to talk to me about?" he asked brusquely, not at all happy to be interrupted in upbraiding his wayward children.

"Not you Kallan," Zelda replied. "Them," she added, jabbing her finger at us as she spoke.

I did not know whether to find relief in this, or further trepidation. Was this the moment which Zelda had chosen to reveal her chastisement of us for breaching the walls of her laboratory? I glanced at Zelda, sensing that she was in a good mood, good for Zelda, that is, and that she was in brisk, businesslike mode. I was taken aback at her unusual mood, but as it seemed to provide us with the escape we were seeking, I did not question this providential development.

"What did you want to talk to us about?" Emaleen asked hastily, fearful lest our escape route be blocked by inaction.

"I have an offer to make you," she replied. "About the teleportal."

We looked at each other sharply, our curiosity piqued, unable to guess what she would say next. Even Kallan looked intrigued, unfolding his arms and stilling his tapping foot.

"I have been thinking about yesterday evening, about finding you all gazing longingly at the teleportal in my laboratory," she said. Kallan gasped, turning to us with a deep frown between his neat silver brows, concern mixed with exasperation showing on his face. Before he could begin to berate us for our intrusion into Zelda's private domain, Zelda waved her hand at our uncle, shaking her head as she did so.

"It is of no consequence now," she said. Kallan looked surprised at her unusual equanimity, but said nothing.

Zelda looked at each of us in turn, then continued, seemingly oblivious to the fact that we were conducting the conversation in the kitchen, surrounded by copious quantities of unwanted and unusable food, disarray in all corners of the room.

"As I said, I have an offer to make you." We stared at her, and she continued.

"I will teach you how to use the teleportal in my lab, but on conditions." Our eyes widened further in astonishment, and we waited in anticipation, silent and eager to hear what else she had to say.

"I shall teach all four of you, but for the moment only the two older children, the girls, will be allowed to use it to leave the estate. As and when I judge you boys to be ready, then I shall let you leave too. You're too young at present."

I was filled with indignation at this, and began to speak, to argue with Zelda, but she cut me off abruptly, lifting her hand with her palm towards me, then continuing in a loud voice.

"The girls will not travel to another portal. They will only go to places devoid of people, for their own safety."

We stood absolutely still, taking in what Zelda had just said. Kallan was the first to speak.

"But is that wise Zelda? Is it safe for the girls to leave the estate, and especially to places there are no people?"

"It's a damn sight safer than going where there *are* people!" Zelda chuckled in reply. Kallan shook his head slightly, unconvinced, and began to speak again.

"Shush, Kallan," she said, our uncle so surprised by this command that he did not speak. Zelda then sighed slightly.

"I spent most of the night thinking about things, after finding the four children staring longingly at the portal yesterday. I realised I cannot, in the end, stop them leaving, much as I would prefer them not to. They are not prisoners, whatever they might think," she said, with a wry glance at me. "And the girls are nearly adults," she added with something resembling a smile at my sisters. "Better that I teach them properly, and impose restrictions in return for this, rather than they break into my laboratory again, try to teach themselves, and end up causing all sorts of mayhem, and travelling to who knows where. They seem to be showing disobedience at an alarming rate." I cringed at her final comment, but Emaleen seemed able to ignore it.

"But how do you travel if there's not another portal at the other end?" Emaleen asked reasonably, though her tone showed impatience. "Isn't that dangerous?"

"Not if you know how to use your base portal properly," replied Zelda. "Most people do move from one teleportal to another, but it is not strictly required. You can access all the necessary energy, and use the technology of the one you leave from to take you wherever you want. You need to give it a precise location, with exact three-dimensional coordinates, and it is fine. And to come back, you just tell your home portal you are ready using a small electronic location device most people have implanted into their heads as children, and it takes you home." Seeing a wall of confused expressions, Zelda continued.

"Obviously I never had any of you fitted with these devices, as I do not approve of them, so you will have to carry something instead, though I imagine you will eventually be able to instruct your home portal without this using your gifts."

"But," Adwin piped up, suddenly finding his voice, then asking indignantly, nodding his head in my direction as he did so, "Why can't we go out as well? Why do we have to wait?"

"Because *you* are too young, and because that is one of my conditions," snapped Zelda, silencing him. I wanted to argue with her, as Adwin had started to do, but one look at the resolute expression on my mother's stern face made me realise that this would be pointless. Adwin flashed me a silent mindmessage asking me to force Zelda to change her mind, but I replied, also silently, that I didn't dare, that she would probably know what I was trying to do.

"But how does it work?" asked Safya, surprising us all with her sudden interjection.

Zelda looked pensive, pushing back a few locks of hair that had managed to escape the usually strict confines of her scraped-back style in all the excitement. After a pause, she said, "I very much doubt you would understand. Perhaps when you are older and have mastered quantum physics," she added, smiling wryly to herself. She knew well that neither Emaleen nor Safya had ever shown the slightest interest in physics, quantum or otherwise. Adwin and I were too young to have begun such advanced studies.

"Please mother," cajoled Emaleen, impatience colouring her voice, despite her obvious attempt to mask it. "Just give us some idea."

Zelda chewed her bottom lip, and picked at one of the eczema crusts on her chin.

"Alright," she replied at length. "But it will be very basic." We nodded our assent, and she explained.

"The base portal, the one you start in, reads your molecular makeup, at an atomic level, atom by atom, sub-atom by sub-atom. It makes a full, perfect copy of you which it then transmits somewhere else, either to another portal, or to the coordinates you have instructed it to. At the other end, this copy is reassembled, again atom by atom, into a complete and faultless copy of you. I am not going to confuse you by trying to explain how it actually transmits the data in the copy, so that will have to suffice for today. But it is all to do with quantum entanglement."

She stopped and looked at us. Kallan too turned from listening to Zelda to see our reaction. Our responses ranged from befuddled on the part of Adwin, to shocked on the faces of Emaleen and Safya, to appalled on my part.

"But what happens to the original, the real person, the one who got into the base portal in the first place?" I asked breathlessly, almost dreading the answer.

Zelda, as usual lacking all sensitivity and tact, said artlessly, "It disappears. It is wiped out."

"What do you mean?" asked Adwin in a confused tone, roused from his befuddlement by the glimmerings of understanding of what Zelda was saying. "What does 'wiped out' mean?"

"Just what it sounds like child. It is destroyed," replied Zelda, almost surprised at the question, as if it were obtuse. On seeing four identical expressions of panic on our faces, she stated impatiently, "Well you cannot have two versions of the same person at the same time, and in two different places." She said this in such a matter of fact way, clearly seeing this as obvious, surprised that we had not understood it immediately.

"But how do you know who you are after you've gone through the portal?" wailed Adwin, deeply upset by what he had just heard. Zelda looked confused by the question.

"But you are still *you* after the journey," she replied. "You are the same person. As I said, you are copied perfectly right down to the sub-atomic level. Obviously you are the same person." She did not seem to know how else to explain something that to her was so obvious.

"But what about our feelings, our memories, surely they're not molecular?" asked Safya in a quiet voice.

"Yes, they are," replied Zelda. "What are humans after all but chemicals and electrical impulses. Our memories, our feelings, our thoughts, *everything*, is nothing more than sparks of electricity and chemistry. So when a perfect copy of you is made, all this is copied too, and reassembled in exactly the same form it was to start with."

"But what about the soul?" whimpered Adwin, ever more distressed by what he was hearing. Zelda guffawed at this, especially from the mouth of such a small child.

"The soul?" she sneered. "You speak some rubbish Adwin, and that's a fact. You know perfectly well there is no such thing, it is just ancient superstitious mumbo jumbo, a ridiculous 'explanation' given by people without the science to understand how a human really works, how our brains and bodies genuinely function. No more of such foolishness now!" And Adwin was silenced, his head dropping forward, his fringe almost covering his dark eyes which gazed down at the floor. His bottom lip quivered and I knew he was on the edge of tears. I moved to stand right beside him, linking my hand in his. It seemed so unfair to dismiss the worries of a small child this way.

"What do you think Kallan?" queried Safya in a quiet, pensive voice. "You use the portal often. Don't you worry about being, being..." she struggled to find the right word. "…Erased, and then recreated? Doesn't it concern you that you might not be the same person at the other end?"

Kallan, who had not contributed to the conversation, seemed surprised to be asked for his opinion. He did not answer immediately, stopping briefly to think. "No," he replied simply, "I don't worry about it. To be honest, I've never given it any thought. I've been using the portals so long, since I was a small child, that I can't really remember a time before that."

"But each time you're destroyed by the machine," Emaleen interrupted in a prickly voice, unsatisfied by Kallan's reply.

"It doesn't feel like that. It just doesn't feel like that at all," replied Kallan. "Every time I've done it, I've come out the other end feeling exactly the same as when I went in. I'm the same person. It's just the location that's changed, not me."

"But how do you know that?" persisted Emaleen, hands on her hips, her tone ever more jagged.

"I just do. I just *know*," Kallan insisted resolutely.

I had no reply to Kallan's absolute insistence. I had no personal experience of teleportation, so nothing to measure against my own perceptions. The silence from my siblings suggested they felt the same. After a moment's silence, Safya spoke hesitantly.

"Does everyone feel like you, uncle?" she asked.

"To be honest, no," he replied, after the briefest hesitation. "Some people are wary of using the portals. Actually, some people are so worried by the idea that they refuse point blank to do so. Ever. They are convinced that it somehow messes you up, re-creates you differently the other end, despite all evidence to the contrary. In fact, some of these people take such an extreme view of teleportation that they won't even have their food delivered this way. They believe that the process alters the chemical structure of the food, and that this could have long term consequences for your health. They'll only take delivery of other things via a portal - furniture, tools, books, machinery and so on. But they're extreme. Some other people try to avoid teleporting as much as they can, so if their journey is short, they use more conventional means of transport, and only use a portal if the distance is long."

"But most people, nearly everyone in fact, is perfectly happy to use the portals as often as they want. And to eat food that has come through one," added Zelda, keen to make this point clear to us. "And your bodies are almost entirely made up of food that has moved around the world, molecules disassembled and reassembled thousands, millions of times."

Emaleen and Safya looked thoughtful, allowing the new ideas to run through their minds, though Emaleen still seemed irritated. Adwin remained visibly unconvinced, shuffling on the spot, eyes still staring at the floor, his whole body radiating despondency. I squeezed his hand for reassurance, not to persuade him, but to let him know I shared his concerns.

"What happens if the process is interrupted?" queried Emaleen suddenly. "Surely that's a disaster?"

"No," replied Zelda. "If there is any interruption, and this is *extremely* rare, the home portal will always bring you back immediately. I have never heard of anyone suffering any untoward consequences of an interruption. And," she continued after a brief pause, "We have been doing this now for hundreds of years, so we would know if there were any real problems. We have had generations of people teleporting all the time, without any evidence that any damage is done either in the short or the long term. If that were the case, we would know by now."

Zelda's words made sense. The millions of people who used teleportals regularly, and who had done so for generations, were a living, on-going scientific experiment. In a long-lived population, any damage to their genetic make-up, or to their cells, right down to a sub-atomic level, would surely have come to light long before if teleporting caused a build-up of harm. I squeezed Adwin's hand again, this time sending him a mindmessage. He turned a bleak face to me, shaking his head slightly, and replied.

~I'm not worried about cells, atoms, things like that. I'm worried about the things we can't see. Thoughts, feelings, memories and...and the soul, whatever Zelda says. All the things that make us who we are, that make us human.~

I was a little surprised to hear Adwin's comment, remarkably mature for such a young child, even one with his special abilities, but I had no reply. Although Zelda could not hear our silent conversation, she could see Adwin was still troubled. This seemed to irritate her, and she turned to him and said sharply,

"No-one is forcing you to use the portal, boy. If you do not want to learn how to use it, then don't. You would be doing what I want given that I do not want any of you to leave the estate." Adwin glared at her, unsure how to react. He was deeply concerned about the effect that teleporting might have on him, yet also did not want to be excluded from learning how to use the portal. Being left out, unable to do something the rest of us could do might be worse than the possible negative effects of travelling through space.

"You, Samek, can probably learn how to move yourself without using a portal at all, not even a base portal," said Zelda suddenly. I blinked with surprise at this odd comment.

"What do you mean?" I asked. Was this some kind of sarcastic comment, a joke on Zelda's part?

"With your gifts, you should be able to learn how to move small objects, and if you can do that, you can learn, with experience and commitment, to move living creatures and eventually people. Yourself, and anyone else."

I was staggered by Zelda's matter of fact statement.

"But how can I do that," I asked, "If I don't really understand how it works?"

"The gifts I bestowed upon you are so extensive," replied Zelda, arrogant pride in her voice, "That you do not need to understand the details, the physics, to be able to put the process into place. Your brain should be able to do what the portal's quantum processor is doing, but more efficiently, with such facility, that you will be unaware of how it is doing it. In fact, it should be so rapid, so smooth and effortless for your brain, that I am not sure you could ever follow its activity. I do not think you could bring the process to your consciousness, even if you wanted to."

I found Zelda's comments hard to comprehend, and her smug reminder that she had created me irked me, but I shuddered with excited anticipation at the idea that with practice there was no reason why I could not master the skill of moving objects through space.

I grasped instantly what this meant. That once I had acquired this skill, nothing could stop me leaving the compound as and when I wanted. Zelda's prohibition on me using the portal would be meaningless. And I might be able to take Adwin and my sisters with me. I glanced at Zelda. Her wry expression told me that she had reached the same conclusion. I was immediately fired with the desire to learn how to do so, as quickly as possible.

"Well that is that then," Zelda said, interrupting my thoughts. And at that she turned and shuffled out of the kitchen, leaving the rest of us behind. We children began to move towards the door, only to be blocked by Kallan's bulk.

"Oh no you don't," he said sternly. "I'm not clearing up this food on my own. You can all help."

We groaned in unison, but knew that when Kallan was in determined mood, he brooked no refusal. Under his supervision we began to move all the imperishable food into the store rooms behind the kitchen. It was laborious and we moaned throughout the procedure.

"You'll be doing a lot more housework for me in the future," Kallan laughed as we carried load after load from the kitchen. We decided to have all the perishable food taken out into the forest - something would eat it, even if some of it only fed the worms, the fungus, the bacteria. Kallan instructed our domestic automata in this task.

I asked Kallan what to do with all the plates and bowls - surely we had more of these than we needed already? He asked me to stack them all in the large teleportal in the store room, and from there he instructed it to send them back to the warehouse. Again, the speed and ease of such action amazed me.

After this Kallan left the kitchen, satisfied that it had been returned to its usual clean and tidy state. Emaleen had become bored once all the food had been sent away, and had gone back to her room, Safya trotting along behind her. Adwin too left once the crockery was safely stocked in the portal. I was the last to leave the kitchen.

As I did so a pang of hunger reminded me that I had only taken a few bites from my eggs on toast before being distracted by the excitement of ordering cascades of food. Though it would be cold by now, I decided to return to the dining room to retrieve it. Just before I got there, I heard voices speaking quietly in the dining room. Zelda and Kallan. And by their hushed tones I knew that they did not want to be overheard. I crept closer to the door, open as doors in the house usually were during the day, especially in warm weather. If I peered through the crack on the wall side of the open door, I could just see my mother and uncle. I realised that eavesdropping was starting to become a guilty pleasure. I stood absolutely still, barely breathing, in case I made any noise. The last thing I wanted was to be apprehended listening in to private conversations.

"When will you be back?" I heard Kallan ask, in barely more than a whisper.

"I'm not sure," replied Zelda, equally sotto voce. "Perhaps today, but more likely I shall stay a few days so I can see what they are working on."

"Are you sure that's a good idea?" queried Kallan, "Staying too long outside? What if the Council finds out? You know how much they hate you, are out to get you. If they knew you were out there, unprotected, I dread to think what they might do." Zelda tutted lightly by way of reassurance.

"No-one will find out, and especially not those bastards on the Council." I sensed Kallan was unconvinced. "I told you, I shall stay with Marna, and you know her, she is entirely trustworthy. We have known her so many years, since we were children, that she has had endless opportunities to betray me if she had wanted to." Perhaps this Marna had been part of the cohort raised with Zelda and Kallan at the Institute. "And she understands my work. She works in a similar field." Clearly Marna was a scientist, an expert in genetic engineering like Zelda. "You know it was the others on the project who got me thrown out, not her. She actually argued on my behalf."

"Yes I know, Zelda," Kallan replied. "But you said that she works with another scientist and you don't know the other one," he persisted.

"True," conceded Zelda. "But Marna insists she is reliable, and I trust Marna's judgement."

"Reliable isn't the same as trustworthy," Kallan protested. "Is it really safe to meet her and to discuss your work with others you don't know?"

Zelda said nothing, but I felt my shoulders shrug in harmony with hers. She offered no further comment, and Kallan persisted.

"Why, Zelda? Why are you doing this now? You've worked alone so long, I don't understand why this need to share all of a sudden."

"Precisely because I have worked alone so long," Zelda sighed. "Frankly, I am tired of it. I am tired of having nobody to discuss my work with, or at least not in person. Despite my regular contact with Marna, conversations at a distance are not the same as discussions in person, with the results of your work actually in front of you. I need to collaborate. I have run out of steam, have no more energy to pursue all of this on my own."

Her tone was so dejected that I was amazed. I had never heard this side of Zelda before, the vulnerable, lonely person. I had always seen her as utterly self-sufficient, needing no-one, yet here she was confessing a desire to share her thoughts and ideas, even at some possible risk to herself. I did not understand what possible danger Zelda could face from the Council, yet her and Kallan's anxiety clearly showed that such peril was real. Zelda often seemed to show signs of paranoia at the outside world's attitude towards her, but Kallan did not, so I took his unease seriously.

I saw Kallan move across to Zelda, and put his arm around her shoulder. I was flabbergasted by this, and even more by Zelda's reaction. I sensed her overflowing with emotion, with gratitude for Kallan's affection and support, and with a strange yearning for something I could not quite ascertain. The totally unexpected stream of sentiment from Zelda, combined with the equally strong reaction of sympathy and compassion from Kallan threatened to overwhelm me. I was toying with the idea of creeping away before I was caught, escaping from this deeply troubling and uncomfortable situation, when Zelda spoke again.

"And I plan to invite both of them back here," she said.

Kallan gasped. "Really?" he asked in a breathless voice. "You've almost never had visitors here, and not for years."

"True," Zelda agreed. "But I long to show some fellow scientists my work, my actual equipment, and explain to them how it all works, discuss it with them as colleagues. And I have also been thinking about our children," she went on.

Kallan started a little at his final comment. "What about our children?" he asked, a trace of anxious suspicion in his voice.

"Finding them there, beside the portal," Zelda began, not quite sure how to put her thoughts clearly into words. "I want to protect them from the outside world, from people who will fear them, hate them even. Yet in the end I cannot keep them here forever. I should have thought about that when I made them, but I was so focused on the science I gave no thought to the future, to *their* future, that for all their unusual provenance, they are just people after all, just children. And they will one day have to meet other people, go out into the world. They have hardly ever met anyone else, have almost no experience of anyone outside the family. And little Adwin has never met a soul outside of this house. If this carries on much longer they will be so socially inept that they will never be able to function in the outside world." And after a brief pause, she added, "After so long, it may already be too late for the twins."

She stopped, wearied by such a long speech and from the unexpectedly powerful emotions she was feeling.

"I can't tell you how overjoyed I am to hear you say that my dear," said Kallan, profound relief in his voice. "I worry about them all the time, what will become of them. They need other people. Emaleen and Safya have already been kept apart from other people for so long that I worry for them too, especially Safya who's even more strange than her sister, but Adwin and Samek seem reasonably normal, fairly well-adjusted given the circumstances, at least for now. But it's vital for them to learn how to deal with strangers. I'm wary of outsiders coming here, but the benefits to the children must outweigh any possible risk."

I stood transfixed. To hear Kallan and Zelda discuss us was curious enough, but to know that both Kallan and Zelda saw my sisters as strange, Adwin and me as reasonably normal, this discovery was amazing. And the most astounding thing of all, which left me almost unable to breathe with excitement, was that we were to have visitors. I could barely remember the rare times Zelda had invited strangers to our home, when I was very tiny. And on these few occasions, Zelda had kept them entirely to herself in her laboratory. In truth, I did not remember ever having met them, so cloistered had they been in my mother's rooms. I knew that since Adwin had appeared, we had had no guests at all, and assumed that my sisters had probably never actually met the rare visitors any more than I had.

I had no clear memory of ever encountering a person I did not know almost as well as I knew myself. What would it be like, what would it feel like to be faced with complete strangers? How would I cope with having to talk to them, ask them questions, answer questions about myself? Would they think of me as a freak, some sort of anomaly of nature, or would they just treat me as the eight year old child that I was?

I moved quickly, racing away from the dining room, all thought of toast and eggs forgotten. I had to tell the others. But as I ran through the corridors I wondered if I should tell them. What would the effect be on them? Adwin, I knew, would feel like me, apprehensive, nervous, yet filled with excited anticipation. Emaleen and Safya's response might be much more negative. I knew Kallan was right in describing them as strange. In fact, this was an understatement. I realised that their reaction to the news was completely unpredictable. I had no way to know what effect it would have on them. But if they reacted badly Zelda might cancel the visit, or Kallan forbid it. This, I could not risk. I was desperate to meet other people, real, normal human beings. So I decided to keep the news to myself. I could tell Adwin, but I knew he would not be able to dissimulate his thrill at the news, and Emaleen and Safya would surely perceive this. I persuaded myself that he might even prefer the shock of discovery at the last minute, rather than anticipate it in advance. I felt a twinge of guilt keeping such huge news from my brother, but all in all, decided this was for the best.

I stopped running, forced myself to be calm to prevent my sisters sensing my huge excitement, and walked slowly towards the study room, to try and carry on with my normal daily activities, keeping the turmoil inside me suppressed as best as I could.

Chapter Twelve

As I waited impatiently for Zelda to return from her trip outside, hoping desperately that her colleagues would be with her when she returned, I hid my agitation from my siblings.

Adwin was often with me during the days I awaited our visitors. I found it desperately hard not to share with him the momentous news, but I could not risk him blurting this out to Emaleen or Safya in his excitement, or them simply perceiving his heightened state of excitement and winkling the truth from him. I was even more worried he would say something to Kallan, thereby apprising my uncle of the fact that I had eavesdropped on a private conversation with Zelda. I justified my deception of Adwin by reminding myself how vital it was to both of us that the visit not be jeopardised. At least that is what I told myself. But it was certainly true that my brother needed to meet strangers as much as I did.

After breakfast one day I went back to my room to change my clothes for the outdoors, planning to go into the garden, but as I was about to leave my room, I sensed a frisson of agitation flowing through the house, a sensory commotion coming from Adwin, Emaleen and Safya simultaneously. I rushed out of my room, following the trail of agitated emotions, and this led me to the main living room of the house, the room we often spent our evenings in together.

I barged into the room, stopping cold in my tracks at the door. Kallan arrived just behind me, pushing past me to enter the room. The rest of the family was already there. Emaleen and Safya just in front of me by the door, Zelda in the middle of the room with Adwin in front of her. But what stunned me was the vision of two strangers, two total strangers, simply standing near Zelda. One of them, a woman of about Zelda's age stood beside my mother, the other a woman a little younger than Zelda, a little further away from her on her other side. Little Adwin, only five years old, was stupefied, shocked into absolute silence by what he saw, apprehensive enough that Kallan had felt he needed some physical reassurance, moving up beside him and gently taking his hand. My sisters stood as still as statues, numbed by the appearance of strangers in our home, in our living room, ready to meet us.

A wordless, strained silence ensued, broken abruptly when Safya screamed and rushed from the room. The newcomers jumped at Safya's screech, not knowing how to respond. Zelda scowled in anger at Safya's behaviour, embarrassed in front of her guests. Kallan gave no reaction at all, merely standing calmly, his hand still clasping Adwin's, and smiling faintly at the interlopers.

After another tense silence, Kallan released Adwin's hand, pushing him gently back towards me, then moved forward, hand outstretched, to welcome the guests.

"Welcome to our home," he said quietly. "Marna! It's truly lovely to see you again after all this time," and he placed a kiss on each of her cheeks.

"Kallan," the woman called Marna replied warmly, throwing her substantial arms open wide as she spoke. "It's simply fabulous to be here, to see your home, and especially to see you again." Kallan smiled broadly at this comment, then turned to the other visitor.

"I'm Kallan," he said, smiling directly at the other stranger. Marna took this as her cue, and introduced them.

"This is Yenifa," she said, indicating the other woman.

"I'm so pleased to meet you," said Kallan, "And to welcome you here. Please, make yourselves at home, and anything you want, just ask." Yenifa said nothing, merely nodding slightly to Kallan. My uncle then turned to Adwin and me, beckoning us forward. I walked cautiously towards the strangers, pushing Adwin in the back as I neared him. He moved forwards too, with reluctance.

"I'd like to introduce our boys," Kallan continued. "The older one is Samek, and the baby of the family is Adwin." Yenifa looked surprised by the use of the word 'family', and her reaction puzzled me. Before I could question it, Emaleen spoke out, addressing Yenifa directly from where she stood near the door, hands on hips.

"Why do you look so surprised?" she asked in a loud voice filled with challenge.

"Emaleen!" snapped Kallan. "Don't be so rude to our guest." He turned to Yenifa with a faint smile of apology, and seemed about to speak again, when Marna preempted him.

"It's not rude, Kallan," she said with a wide grin. "Actually it's a reasonable question. And I'll answer it on Yenifa's behalf," she said turning her smile on Emaleen. "Family isn't a word you hear often, and certainly not in a situation like this." Emaleen frowned slightly, but before she could speak, Marna continued her explanation.

"Children in the same cohort, brought up together in the Institute, are sometimes referred to as brothers and sisters, and the whole cohort occasionally called a family, but the term is never applied to a group of people like this one, a cross-generational group living together. You live in an extraordinary household, quite unlike any other, made up of an adult man and woman, and a selection of children. I doubt such a thing's existed since before the Chaos. I've heard Zelda refer to her family before, although to be honest," she continued with a chortle, "I've know Zelda long enough that I shouldn't be surprised by any aspect of her life!" Even Zelda smiled slightly at Marna's final comment, looking almost smug, as if Marna had paid her a compliment.

They each held out a hand and Adwin and I gingerly shook each of them in turn. Yenifa's hand was thin, cool and clammy, reminding me of a dead fish. Marna's was warm and smooth, her fingers chubby. I knew from imagery in the digital memory that this was a common gesture among strangers upon first meeting and followed Kallan's example, but I was self-conscious and shy, uncomfortable performing this strange ritual for the first time, the very first occasion I remembered of meeting strangers. Adwin seemed even more awkward than me, grasping each proffered hand in his own little hand briefly, before rapidly letting go, stepping back a pace, and looking shyly down at the floor.

I liked Marna on sight. I guessed from the conversation I had overheard between Zelda and Kallan that she was one of their cohort, a 'sister', raised with them. She exuded affability and kindness, which surprised me. I had assumed that this person, the only person who had supported Zelda's work, had argued on her behalf, would be like Zelda: driven, unemotional, cold and aloof. Yet she was not at all like this. I did not need to probe her mind to know how easy-going and pleasant she was: this flowed out of her, wrapping all of us in its warmth.

She was taller than Zelda, about the same height as Kallan. She was rotund, which amazed me as I had never seen anyone this shape. Her clothes fitted badly, her adipose tissue threatening to burst through every seam, from behind every button and zip. She had thick brown wavy hair which seemed to have a life of its own as it emerged in all directions from her scalp, unkempt and untidy. I wondered why she was overweight. Surely this was not necessary? Surely this could be fixed? I only learned much later that she cultivated her image carefully, aware that someone of her shape, and with her disordered sense of dress, would not be seen as a threat, would in fact be considered risible. As her views on many subjects were little short of iconoclastic, she felt her deliberate lack of personal care and matronly form protected her from scrutiny. She had deep set, kindly dark blue eyes, curiously well-shaped eyebrows overshadowing them. As I appraised her frankly, she smiled broadly at me and winked. I blushed, and looked away.

Yenifa I found inscrutable. She did not come across as unpleasant, it was just that I could not sense any clearly discernable emotion coming from her at all. I wondered if she was able to block it, but did not dare to probe her to find out in case this were true. She would certainly be able to sense my juvenile attempts at reading her if she had such a gift. She was very tall, taller even than Kallan, but much thinner. She had a curious way of holding her arms tight against her sides, fingers curled in towards her palms. In fact, Adwin, recovering from his initial shock, sent me an amused message.

~She looks like a stick insect!~ I struggled not to laugh, and warned him to be careful, that she might be able to hear him. But he was right. Her height and thin body, and especially the way she kept her arms in place looked for all the world like a human-sized stick insect.

She had reddish-blond hair, pulled tight into a severe bun at the back of her head. Her eyes were light brown, flecked with hazel, her eyelashes and eyebrows a slightly darker hue than her hair. She was plain, her appearance brisk and matter-of-fact, appropriate I supposed in a scientist. She wore simple clothes - loose trousers, soft shoes, and a long-sleeved shirt left untucked over her trousers. I felt her scrutinise me back as I looked at her, and quickly averted my eyes, moving them back to Marna.

"I apologise for Safya's rudeness," Kallan said suddenly, interrupting my appraisal of the newcomers. "I shall talk to her later and tell her to make her own apologies. Emaleen can apologise here and now." But by way of response, Emaleen snorted and stomped out of the room.

"Emaleen!" barked Kallan at my sister's disappearing back.

"Now, now. There's no need," assured Marna, smiling calmly, apparently unperturbed by Safya's extreme reaction and Emaleen's rudeness. She was the perfect guest, acting as if Safya's screaming and fleeing the room were a perfectly normal reaction to visitors.

"Humph," was Zelda's response to Marna's courtesy.

"Are you hungry, thirsty?" asked Kallan, turning back to the guests, and smoothing over the slightly awkward moment. "Would either of you like a drink or something to eat?"

"No thank you my dear," replied Marna amiably. She turned to Yenifa, who indicated with a shake of her head that she too needed no refreshment.

"Well, I'll show you to your rooms, and then I imagine Zelda will want to whisk you straight off to her workrooms, to show you what she's been busy with," Kallan continued with a smile. "I'm sure the three of you will have plenty to talk about."

At that, Kallan turned aside and gestured that the guests should proceed out of the room before him. They did as indicated, followed by Kallan. Zelda left after Kallan, telling her visitors that she would come and find them in a short while to take them to her workrooms.

Adwin and I stayed in the living room, staring at each other. I still did not tell him that I had known about the imminent visit. I knew he would be angry with me for keeping such a momentous piece of information from him and he would not accept my reasons for it. We shook our heads, eyes shining with excitement, mouths stretched wide in foolish grins. For all that I was expecting the visit, the reality of it hit me like a slap to the face, knocking all my composure out of me. Adwin clearly felt exactly the same, despite his initial nervousness. We could not wait to see the visitors again, to talk to them, ply them with questions about the outside world, tell them about our lives, our interests, our hopes and dreams.

I took Adwin's hand and pulled him from the living room. He shared his elation with me: ~ *This is the most exciting day of my life!*~

We knew that there was an outside world and knew a great deal about it, but having people from that world suddenly appear in our familiar environment was even more exciting than the distant prospect of us eventually travelling to that world.

Chapter Thirteen

Marna and Yenifa stayed with us only for a few days, but to Adwin and me, these were some of the most exhilarating days of our lives. It is hard to describe how profound the effect on us was of meeting new people for the first time ever, real people who spent their lives in the world outside, people who had seemingly endless stories and anecdotes, descriptions of what went on in the mysterious realm beyond the boundaries of our comfortable prison.

Although most of the time the guests were at our house Zelda kept them to herself, Kallan insisted that we all eat our meals together. He raised this with Zelda the very first evening, as Marna and Yenifa readied themselves for supper. Adwin and I were already sitting impatiently at the dinner table, anxious to meet the guests again, brimming with queries and questions we wished to put to them. Kallan and Zelda arrived together, clearly finishing a conversation they had begun on the way to the dining room.

"I absolutely insist you bring our guests to eat with us, at least lunch and dinner, if not also breakfast," Kallan said as they entered the dining room.

"Hmmm," was Zelda's only reply, and the look on her face implied that she was not persuaded by Kallan's insistence.

"You yourself said that one of the main reasons for bringing them here was to expose the children to new people. How is that going to happen if you keep them secreted away in the laboratory the entire time they are here? How are these boys," he said, indicating Adwin and me with a sweep of his arm, "Going to learn how to deal with strangers if they don't get to spend time with them?"

Zelda did not reply, but looked slightly sheepish, knowing that Kallan was right. After a pause during which Kallan fixed our mother with a forthright stare, she finally conceded.

"Very well," she granted. "I shall make sure I bring them to lunch and dinner every day. But not breakfast. I draw the line at that!"

Kallan nodded, and turned towards the table. As he did so he caught my eye and smiled slightly, a hint of triumph on his face. He had achieved what he wanted - something of a victory where Zelda was concerned.

Shortly after this, our guests arrived. Marna smiled broadly at Adwin and me as she entered the room. Yenifa merely nodded vaguely in our direction, her stern features immobile. Kallan invited them to sit, and then told Adwin and me to go and fetch the food from the kitchen. We raced off to do his bidding, carrying back a number of bowls and platters filled with all manner of tasty dishes.

"Kallan!" exclaimed Marna. "You certainly know how to keep a woman happy!" She gazed greedily at the steaming platters. Kallan, oddly, blushed lightly at her comment. On seeing this, Adwin turned to me, a questioning look on his face. I shrugged, indicating I had no idea what had caused Kallan's blush.

The crockery and cutlery were already on the table, and Kallan invited the guests to serve themselves. Marna helped herself to generous portions of everything on offer, creating a huge heap of food on her plate. I was highly amused by this, and even more so when she turned to me and said,

"I absolutely have to keep my strength up - I'm a growing girl! Growing sideways it's true, but growing nevertheless!" Adwin and I joined in her laughter. I liked her more all the time.

Yenifa took small, precise quantities, but only of certain foods. As far as I could tell, she deliberately avoided all the nicest food - the roast chicken thighs, the fried aubergines, the creamed mashed potatoes, and only helped herself to vegetables, grilled white fish and a tiny portion of boiled rice.

Kallan then served me and Adwin before himself and Zelda. Neither of my sisters had come to the table. Safya presumably because she simply could not cope with the reality of guests in our home, Emaleen in solidarity with her sister. As Kallan served the food, Zelda leaped up, and walked briskly in the direction of the kitchen. When she returned she was actually smiling, brandishing a bottle of white wine.

"I have been saving this for a special occasion," she announced. She opened the bottle and poured wine for the adults. Yenifa stopped her with a tiny gesture when there was only a finger-full in her glass. Marna lifted her full glass, and said, "A toast to our hostess Zelda and our delightful host Kallan, and of course to the lovely young men making up the rest of the party." Adwin and I smiled broadly to be included in the toast, and lifted our glasses of fruit juice so we could be fully involved.

"Delicious! Absolutely wonderfully delicious!" exclaimed Marna after taking her first sip, smacking her lips loudly as she did so. She rapidly took another much larger gulp, almost emptying her glass this time. Zelda refilled it. Yenifa took the tiniest sip imaginable, and smiled politely.

"Yes," she said in a flat tone. "Very nice."

Adwin could no longer withhold his impatience, and began to fire questions at the guests. Marna, in between large mouthfuls of food, answered all of them genially. Yenifa too gave occasional answers, but always in clipped tones, briskly and without elaboration. In between she picked at her food, spearing small morsels with her fork and passing these to her mouth. Despite the tiny size of each mouthful, she seemed able to chew it for a long period, making each piece last a remarkable length of time. After each swallow, she stopped and put her knife and fork down, leaving them on her plate for a few moments before picking them up once again, carefully, as if they would burn her. Marna's cutlery never stopped moving - flashing to and fro as she cut her food, piled as much on each forkful as she could, actually leaning in towards the table so as not to risk anything toppling off the over-full fork as it moved from plate to mouth, shovelling it into her maw as fast as possible, and then repeating the whole process as she chewed the huge mouthful of food. As she munched each stack, she made strange noises, almost humming with pleasure.

Adwin, surprisingly chirpy, could not contain his child's excitement, asking a long series of questions. He was, after all, only five years old. He asked things like, "So where do you live? What do you do? How do you have fun? Do you have lots of friends," and even such intrusive queries as, "Marna, why are you so fat?", or "Yenifa, why do you never smile?" And even, "Yenifa, are you a man or a woman?" Eventually Kallan interrupted the stream of queries.

"That's enough Adwin. Let our guests eat in peace," he said in a quiet yet firm voice. Marna just smiled and said through a mouthful of mashed potato,

"It's fine Kallan. It's absolutely marvellous the boy has so much curiosity. You've done such a super job raising him. Both of them actually."

As before, Kallan reddened slightly at the compliment. This managed to silence Adwin for a while, and we all ate quietly. Marna quickly finished her second glass of wine, and then a third. Zelda was obliged to fish out a second bottle from her stash in the kitchen. But to our great surprise, she almost matched Marna with her quaffing. We had never seen Zelda drink more than the occasional small glass of beer or wine, and were astonished at the effect her drinking had on her. She became more animated, louder, actually laughing at Marna's anecdotes. Kallan smiled benignly at Zelda, demonstrating by his lack of surprise that he had seen her like this before, but perhaps not for a long time. I could not remember ever having seen my mother inebriated.

As the meal ended, Zelda announced that she and her guests would now return to the laboratory, to continue whatever it was they had been doing before supper. I was amazed that they could even consider returning to work, given the amount of wine she and Marna had put away. But what would I know? I was a small child with only eight years of life, and no experience. Perhaps adults regularly guzzled large quantities of alcohol and saw no reason not to then return to their everyday activities. I found the idea amusing that Zelda and Marna, with exaggerated bonhomie brought on by their drinking, would impose themselves on Yenifa's dour demeanour. The contrast could hardly be greater, and I wished I could watch as these two bellowed and guffawed, Yenifa cringing at such clumsy and boorish behaviour.

Zelda and Marna stood up and moved to the door, followed briskly by Yenifa with her small, neat steps. I sensed that for all her disquiet at Zelda and Marna's conduct, she saw this as preferable to being left with Kallan, a man she did not know and had little to say to, and even more so with us, two small and over-excited boys.

Adwin and I sat pouting, filled with a huge sense of disappointment, that we had not had longer to pursue our inquisition of the guests. Kallan smiled at us fondly, knowing what we would be feeling.

"You can pester them again tomorrow, at lunch and dinner, and maybe even breakfast, despite what Zelda said," he told us in an amused voice.

We did not like to be told we had been pestering, and both pouted with even greater vigour.

"You can put those bottom lips away immediately," said Kallan tartly. "You know I can't abide sulks."

We continued to glower at him, but our sullenness was so ineffectual that he just laughed. This of course made us scowl even more, but Kallan merely stood up and left the room, laughing as he went. As he approached the door he turned and said, between chuckles, "You two can clear up."

My brother's face showed outrage, and I assumed my own mirrored his.

"That'll teach you to pout at me!" Kalan said, chortling loudly as he left the room.

We sat in silence, burning with indignation at Kallan's laughter. How humiliating, to work up one's best scowl, only to be the butt of someone else's humour. To be so impotent as to cause laughter by one's sulks, rather than offence. How I longed at that moment to be grown up. Adults took each other's sullen moods seriously. Children could simply be laughed at.

Eventually, realising there was little point in maintaining my grouchiness, I sighed, and began to clear away the crockery and cutlery from dinner, nodding to my brother to garner his help.

Over the next few days, all our sulks forgotten, we were able to pester the visitors at every meal. As Kallan had said, they also joined us for breakfast each day, presumably considering it polite to do so. So for about three hours a day my brother and I enjoyed the unprecedented luxury of finding out about the unknown and baffling world outside our velvet cage. Sometimes we fired question after quick question at our captive informants, other times they offered more lengthy descriptions themselves. Or to be precise, Marna offered these, Yenifa restricting herself to giving curt answers to direct questions, or brief interjections to Marna's contributions. Kallan and Zelda joined in, and we learned more about our mother and uncle, about *their* lives before coming to live in the house, than we ever thought possible. We realised that in future we could ask *them* about the great big world outside, and would not need to rely on the rare visits from Marna and Yenifa. Yet for all this revelation of Kallan and Zelda's knowledge of the outside world, it was the visitors who captivated our imaginations. Not only was Marna so forthright, so garrulous, that stories and yarns, reminiscences and tales poured out of her, but she and Yenifa were strangers. Total strangers. The first we had ever met. Or at least, the first I could ever remember having met. No matter what happened to me later in life, no matter who else I would meet or where else I would travel, I would never forget those first joyous, momentous days in which the fact of other people was unveiled to me for the first time.

During the entire visit, Safya refused to leave her room, so appalled was she at the idea of visitors. Emaleen was clearly conflicted. On the one hand she had a strong desire to support her twin sister, not to abandon her alone in their room, yet she also had great curiosity for the visitors, for who they were and what they represented, for the stories and tales they could tell. Inquisitiveness trumped her desire to show solidarity with her sister, and by the second morning of the visit Emaleen joined us at every meal, avidly soaking up all she heard about the outside world. But as if making a small gesture of support for her sister, she did not ask any questions herself of our guests, contenting herself with merely listening to the replies to the questions we boys plied our guests with, a well-rehearsed glowering expression on her face throughout. What an effort she must have made to maintain her stony silence!

When the time came for Marna and Yenifa to leave, Adwin and I were disconsolate, woebegone with the misery of being once again plunged back into our old environment, the novelty of new people snatched from us. But as Yenifa formally shook our hands, her palms moist and sticky, and Marna enveloped each of us in a tight hug, our moods lifted dramatically as she whispered to each of us as she did so, "I'll be back soon. I promise."

We hugged her back with as much fervour as we could muster, copying the warmth and sincerity of her embrace as best as we were able. Kallan too received a huge hug from Marna, and as he moved out of her arms, he was smiling broadly.

Zelda shepherded her guests back towards the laboratory, and the last we saw of them was as the door to her private rooms slid shut. But our mood of dejection soon evaporated as we contemplated what Marna had shared with us privately: that she would soon return. As I turned to Kallan, I saw a strange, enigmatic smile play on his lips, at odds with the slight sadness in his eyes. We moved away from the door, to take up our normal lives once again, after the unprecedented novelty of strangers in our midst.

Chapter Fourteen

True to her word, Zelda instructed us in the use of the portal in her laboratory. It was not difficult. In fact, we were amazed how easy it was. Although Zelda had forbidden Emaleen and Safya from travelling to any other portal, which were always located where people were to be found, she nevertheless showed us all how to do this. This was the easiest process of all. Each portal had a unique numerical code, and this could either be entered on the panel inside the portal, or more usually simply spoken clearly from outside or inside the portal. Travelling to a location without a portal was marginally trickier, but not by much. All that was required was to code into the panel, or speak, a precise end point, given in three-dimensional geographical coordinates: longitude, latitude and height above sea level. The entire planet had been mapped in this way over the centuries by drones, always flying at the same height above the level of the sea to give pinpoint accurate locations. The final step for both processes was to indicate that the person wanting to travel was ready. The quantum processor in the portal did the rest.

Early on, Emaleen raised a genuine concern when the destination was not another portal, and was a spot the traveller had not been to before: how to ensure that the location was not in the middle of a boulder, or a tree, or some other dense object? To materialise in a place already occupied by something else would surely be disastrous. The same exact spot could not be simultaneously occupied by two competing atoms. Zelda reassured us that this could not happen, that the computer would know if this were the case, and would only be able to reassemble the traveller in a space with a solid base and only occupied by atoms such as air that could be easily displaced, if necessary slightly away from the given coordinates.

"I have another question," continued Emaleen. "How do we get back home, to our home portal, if we're nowhere near another portal?"

"That is not a problem," Zelda replied. "As I explained before, whenever someone teleports, whichever portal they last passed through automatically tracks that person, wherever they go. Normal people have a small electronic chip embedded in their skull as a small child and this allows the portals to track them. I object to putting chips in people, so none of you children have them. Therefore you girls will need to carry a small electro-magnetic device to achieve the same result. With your abilities though, you should be able to send a signal yourselves to the home portal. When you first travel, try sending a signal directly, and if that does not work, then use the tracking device."

"Is it really that simple mother?" asked Safya quietly, unexpectedly joining in the conversation.

"Yes, it really is," Zelda replied. "This technique has been around for so long, that it is fool-proof. Any hitches were ironed out long ago."

"Do lots of people go to places without portals?" Adwin asked, fascinated despite the prohibition on him actually using the portal. I scowled at him, as we had agreed that we would not talk during the demonstration by way of protest at our exclusion from teleporting at this stage.

"No, not really," replied Zelda. "Most people prefer to go from portal to portal. Not because they do not trust the tracking devices in their heads, but because they see no reason to travel anywhere unpopulated!" And she laughed at this idea.

"Have you travelled without a second portal?" Adwin persisted.

"Yes of course, many many times," Zelda replied. She laughed again. "Far more times than to another portal. Do you really think I would want to be visiting places full of people?"

Adwin knew that this would, of course, not be the case, and smiled slightly.

"Do you want to try?" Zelda asked suddenly, addressing Emaleen and Safya.

They looked startled at the question, not thinking they would be using the portal so soon. They glanced at each other, passed a silent communication between themselves, turned back to Zelda and nodded in unison, identical long blond hair shimmering.

"We shall send you somewhere nearby to start with, perhaps just to the other side of this room," Zelda said as she passed her hand across the front of the portal, thereby causing it to open. "Get in then," she said briskly to the girls.

They looked at each other again, then entered the portal, with the slightest hesitation as they each passed over its threshold. They turned round to face outwards, slate-blue eyes gleaming with anticipation, tucking their long hair behind their big ears in preparation for the event.

"Just a moment," said Zelda as she went over to a cabinet against the wall. She opened one drawer after the other, rifling through the contents of each one, mumbling crossly as she did so. Eventually she seemed to find what she was looking for. She came back to the portal and passed a tiny dark rounded cylinder to each of the girls, each smaller than her thumb.

"These are the trackers. I shall have to find you something to hang them on round your necks, but for now just hold them." They took the tracking devices, closing their fists securely around them.

"Ready?" asked Zelda. They nodded. Zelda passed her hand across the front of the portal, and the transparent front slid across, shutting with a gentle click. Zelda then said "five metres north", and "ready" in a clear voice. I sensed a small surge of energy, and heard the faintest hum. For a moment Emaleen and Safya stood quite still inside the portal, then suddenly, with no warning, they disappeared. As this happened there was an almost imperceptible increase in the luminosity inside the portal, a tiny augmentation in the glow of the light, combined with the faintest impression of a sparkling metallic radiance. But only for the briefest of moments. Adwin and I stared open-mouthed at the portal. Despite knowing what would happen, actually witnessing our sisters simply pop out of existence before our eyes was astounding, and deeply disconcerting.

As we stared, eyes bulging out of our heads, a loud, amused voice shouted at us from behind.

"Oy! Over here! What are you lot staring at like idiots?" It was Emaleen. Adwin and I spun round, and there were Emaleen and Safya, standing calmly on the other side of the room, smiling, as if nothing had happened, both grinning widely. When I had recovered slightly from my shock, I asked, in a shaky voice, "What did it feel like?", forgetting in my surprise to maintain my silent protest. Emaleen paused for a moment, to consider her answer, and her sister spoke first.

"Nothing much really," she replied softly. "It felt like someone was pushing me very gently, and then pulling me the other end, but again, only really gently. Otherwise nothing." She looked to Emaleen who nodded in agreement at this description, a wide grin still fixed on her face. After a brief pause, Zelda told them to try and activate the portal again themselves, to take them back, without using the trackers clasped in their hands. They turned to the portal and frowned slightly in concentration. Again I sensed a minuscule surge of energy and noticed a hint of a glow inside the portal from the corner of my eye. But nothing happened. The energy subsided, Emaleen and Safya still standing in the same spot.

They looked confused, and disappointed.

"Try again," Zelda encouraged. "It might take a few attempts."

They did as bidden, and this time it worked. As before, they simply vanished before our eyes, and in the time it took us to spin round to face the portal, had reappeared inside it, the same delighted smiles on their faces.

"Excellent," said Zelda in an unusually jolly voice. "Excellent," she repeated. "I thought you could do it yourselves. But you must take the trackers with you at first, especially as you travel further afield." The girls nodded at the wisdom of this advice.

"Can we go again?" asked Safya animatedly, her excitement overcoming her usual reticence.

"Why not?" said Zelda with a brisk chortle. "You know how to do it now."

"But how do we know the coordinates of where we want to go?" asked Emaleen reasonably.

"Talk to the panel there behind you. Give it a rough idea of where you want to go and it will show you a bird's eye image of that area, from high above. You can then just tell it how to zoom in, go left, go right, whatever, and when you have seen the spot you want, tell it to pause and it will give you the coordinates. Obviously it will remember this, and remember who you are, so if you want to go there again it should be easier the next time. It will have a record of all the places you have visited, or even just looked at on the panel, so you can choose from these in the future if you do not want to go anywhere new."

The girls communicated silently with each other, then Emaleen turned to the panel. There was a small ridge of hills we could discern in the distance if we climbed onto the roof of the house, which we called the hazy hills for obvious reasons. Emaleen told the portal that she wanted to visit those hills. From where I stood outside the portal I could not see what the panel showed, but after giving some instructions to it, Safya suddenly told it to stop. A voice from the panel gave out coordinates, and Emaleen told the portal to take them there. As they vanished, Zelda shouted at them to take care not to lose the trackers in case they needed them.

After this, I felt a sense of anti-climax. I glanced at my brother, noting the frown on his face. I turned back to the portal and looked at the empty perspiglass box, not knowing when my sisters would return.

Zelda turned to us and said in a matter-of-fact voice, "Well that is that then. No point hanging around in here." I could not argue with what she said, but was loathe to leave. From his reluctance to move, I gathered that Adwin felt the same. We had to drag ourselves away from the portal and out of the room. As we moved slowly and reluctantly through the rooms of the laboratory behind Zelda, I noticed a door on my right I had not heeded before.

"What's in there?" I asked Zelda, as much to delay leaving the laboratory complex as through actual curiosity.

Zelda ignored my question, putting more pace into her step suddenly. This piqued my interest, so I repeated the question, this time more insistently, actually stopping as I did so. Zelda turned on me and spoke sharply, in an unpleasant voice.

"Nothing. Nothing of interest to you!"

I was taken aback by the vehemence of her tone, and knew instantly that there must be something behind that door that she did not want me or Adwin to see. I tried to probe Zelda's mind to see if it carried any images of what lay behind the door, but there were no clear pictures. I sensed she knew I would try to probe her, and was deliberately clearing her mind of useful images.

"And you can stop that!" she snapped, obviously aware of my attempt to see her thoughts, shocking me by her immediate perception of what I was doing. Was she gifted in some way to be able to sense my mental intrusion? Was it normal that people could perceive an uninvited probe of this type? Surely not as I had gone into Zelda's mind before with no indication she knew. So had she learned to do this since the first and only time I had done so? What a worrying thought. Zelda turned away from me, moving off at a very brisk pace.

"Come on," she ordered. "Time to leave." Her crisp tone brooked no opposition, so we scurried to catch up with her, following her to the door into the house. As we reached it, she stood aside, indicating with an impatient gesture that we should pass through. As we did, she caused the door to close behind us as she returned to her rooms.

Adwin and I moved dejectedly through the house, deeply disappointed that we were not with our sisters, travelling outside the house. But we did not dare cross Zelda in this. And I was at this point unable to teleport myself or Adwin, or any other living thing.

My innate abilities were unprecedented. And this is not merely a figure of speech. Though Adwin had been fashioned from the genetic material of more progenitors than me, something must have gone wrong in his creation as he did not seem to enjoy my unprecedented gifts. Outside of a tiny number of scientists, mostly other renegades like Zelda, no-one, not even highly experienced genetic engineers, were able to imagine producing a viable embryo from such a number of progenitors. Much beyond five was considered impossible and liable to lead to the creation of genetic mutants with no chance of a viable life. Thus, in the centralized Embryo Production Units, the absolute limit of progenitors permitted was five. Most people were, and still are, created from three or four, but in special cases, five is permitted.

The strict upper limit of five was the main reason Zelda no longer worked with other scientists in officially sanctioned genetic research or embryo production. Every team she collaborated with, every unit and organisation she worked for, simply restricted her too much, at least as far as she was concerned. She was either told to leave for carrying out work which was forbidden, or for arguing so vociferously with other scientists in her unsuccessful attempts to get them to expand the remit of their own work.

Even by the time she created my sisters, Zelda had already worked alone for some years, with only a handful of other dissident scientists knowing anything about her work, and occasionally visiting her, before she had created any of her children. But even when they did, she remained secretive and protective of what she had learned, suspicious they might report her outlawed experiments to the Council, or steal her ideas for themselves.

Zelda knew that, despite my unique and exceptional combination of innate abilities, these would still need to be trained, to be brought out and moulded so that I could make the fullest use of them possible. As she worked alone in creating me and my siblings, so she was also alone in designing an appropriate education for us.

By the time I came along, she had refined this education with Emaleen and Safya. My sisters' innate gifts were not as obvious as Zelda had hoped for. It was clear from an early age that they were able to communicate directly between themselves without speaking, but this ability was never taught to them. Zelda knew that several of their progenitors had enjoyed reasonably well-developed psychic abilities, in being able to sense what other people were thinking and feeling, and in being able to communicate to some extent by telepathy. Zelda had hoped that the combination of different progenitor genes would enhance these abilities, but her success in this was moderate. In fact, despite Zelda's early attempts to draw out and develop the skills the twins possessed, she achieved remarkably little success. They were able to communicate with each other by telepathy, and with Adwin and me, but only to a very limited degree with Zelda or Kallan. It seemed their ability in this required the other party to share a similar level of capacity, and this disappointed Zelda. She eventually abandoned the attempt to try and expand their ability further.

Because of her disappointment in Emaleen and Safya's abilities, and in her failures to enhance these abilities much through training, Zelda paid less attention to their upbringing and education than she should have. She merely insisted that they have a good general education, with specific focus on the sciences, but beyond this she left it to Kallan.

Our scientists at the time had wide-ranging, and thorough knowledge of the workings of the brain, of the areas responsible for specific thoughts and ideas, and on the synaptic pathways created and maintained for particular thoughts and functions. Many activities, and even ideas, were known to activate more than one part of the brain. The neural pathways for even a simple action or notion are complex, very complex. Knowing our way round the functioning of the brain had been the first stage of my training. I was born with a brain which already enjoyed elevated levels of electromagnetic activity, and the next stage of training involved harnessing and controlling the energy created by this activity.

I practised throwing this energy at inanimate objects first - rocks and stones, chairs and tables, anything and everything within my purview. From there I moved up to static, living things such as trees. Obviously I was not trying to influence the rocks and trees, but I was able to discern if the beams had hit their targets, and to ascertain roughly what strength they had. When I began and lacked experience in controlling the intensity of the beams, I caused small scorch marks to be left on the surface of the object targeted. Later, as I became more adept, no marks were left on the surface, but on breaking the object open I saw tiny burns inside, an unplanned and unwanted outcome. Energy at too high a frequency caused a substantial burn, and this could be wide if the energy waves were themselves too wide, and deep if they were too short. Clearly, if I were ever to use such a power on people, I knew I would have to gain complete control of the level of frequency of the waves, and leave no mark whatsoever on either the outside of the person's head, or inside their brain.

It never occurred to me that there might be ethical problems with using my powers on people. I never considered that it might be immoral to learn to control people by altering the functioning of their brains in order to stimulate completely artificial images, feelings, ideas and thoughts. I was very tiny when I began my training, perhaps as young as two years old. I was a toddler, so could not be expected to consider the moral implications of the skills I was acquiring. Zelda must carry the blame for teaching me, for bringing me to a knowledge that would allow me to have dominion over the thought processes of other people, ultimately to subordinate their free will to my own. And Zelda never showed the slightest interest in exploring the morality or possible misuse of such abilities: to her, all use was valid and its ends were justified by the means. In the wrong hands, such ability could be catastrophic, but neither I, nor Zelda, had any intention of sharing what I had been born with, and had later honed into a most effective weapon. And as I grew older, I learned just how irresistible it was to make use of my gifts to achieve my ambitions and goals, sometimes to an extent that was unethical, immoral even.

~I'm going to try moving living things,~ I mindspoke to Adwin as we walked away from Zelda's quarters. He smiled at me, immediately understanding why the thought occurred to me at this precise moment, just after seeing our sisters successfully use the portal. He nodded enthusiastically, and he trotted along behind me towards the garden, talking loudly though not necessarily to me. "How exciting! Moving living things! I can't wait!"

Once in the garden, I looked around for something to begin with. I settled on a small bushy plant growing under a tree. It was only about a foot high, with large, dark green spiky leaves, and a stem ending in a yellow bell-shaped flower. It seemed a good starting point, as it was growing alone and was small. I stopped near it and pointed at it. Adwin nodded and waited. I concentrated. The plant vanished, as it should, but when we walked round to the other side of the tree, to where it should have reappeared, we were disappointed by what we found. Instead of a healthy green plant standing to attention out of the soil and topped with a vivid yellow bloom, there was a pile of verdant mush, decorated with a blob of yellowish-brown matter. I looked at Adwin, and we quickly scooped up the wreckage of the plant, hiding it in bushes nearby, so Kallan would not know what I had done.

I selected another plant, this time a little further from the house, and thereby a little further from possible discovery. I paused briefly and tried again. But with similar result. Again, we hid the evidence and once more essayed a teleport, this time with a small, scruffy bush. But with no more success. I tried over and over again, but never achieved the desired result. I attempted different ways of moving the herbaceous objects, but each time with the same failure. Though the results were different, the outcome was always the same: the destruction of the plant. Sometimes it merely reappeared as a gooey mush, as the first time, other times it came back into being with its parts in the wrong places. A few times it simply failed to materialise at all, and I wondered where it had ended up. Were there now plants and parts of plants floating around somewhere, or were its molecules so divorced one from the other, that they could never come together again in any recognisable form?

After many hours, and multiple abortive attempts, I accepted defeat, and gave up. As Adwin and I sat dejectedly on the lawn a little way from the house, I noticed a large beetle blundering through the grass, its iridescent blue and green back reflecting the light of the sun as it moved clumsily through the stems, apparently at random. I watched it for a moment, then looked up sharply at Adwin. I raised my eyebrows in question, and he nodded. My heart beat faster as I contemplated what I was about to do: to try and transport a living creature, an animate being, for the very first time. I concentrated on the animal's glossy back, and then put the teleporting process into motion.

Adwin and I both jumped backwards as the unfortunate creature exploded with a loud pop, tiny particles of lustrous carapace flying through the air, catching the light, but mingled with blood and tattered pieces of internal organs. I moved away in disgust, Adwin following closely behind. As we crossed the path beside the lawn, a purple and cream butterfly flapped by in front of us. Almost without thinking I set the porting in motion. The poor thing went the way of the beetle: it burst. But this time, along with the inevitable splash of skin and organs was a puff of lilac smoke, all that remained of the delicately coloured cells of the butterfly's wings.

I was disheartened, but not ready to abandon my efforts. I tried moving a couple of ants as they busily crossed the path in front of me. They simply disappeared, and I could find no trace of them. I attempted to teleport a large fat worm which had come to the surface in search of humus, incautiously popping its head out of the ground as it did so. The doomed beast ended up nothing more than a tiny pile of brown and pink sludge nestled among the grass stems. I was by now beginning to despair. I saw a flock of small birds pecking as they hopped around the lawn. I turned to Adwin, who looked crestfallen at the prospect of their fate if I tried to teleport them. I frowned to see his expression, and decided that enough was enough, at least for the time being. In fact, I resolved not to attempt to move any living thing, animal or plant. It not only seemed cruel to destroy large numbers of hapless creatures and unfortunate plants, but even more so was it dispiriting, creating in me a sense of disillusionment at the whole process. If only I had been able to locate a swarm of mosquitoes, or a nest of wasps, or unearthed a cockroach den that day, then I would have had so much fun practising on these repugnant and worthless creatures as I caused one after another of them to explode, disappear, be destroyed. But I was out of luck.

So with my definite conclusion now reached, Adwin and I left the garden, easily leaving our disappointment and disgust behind as we turned our minds to the supper we were about to enjoy, to be expected in two young boys. We were, after all, only five and eight years old.

Chapter Fifteen

Time passed, and life went on much as normal. I still struggled to master teleporting of living creatures. After my failed experiments, during which small creature after small creature either died in the process or had to be killed as it was so badly injured that survival seemed impossible, I became disenchanted with the process. The only silver lining to the cloud of failure was being able to destroy large numbers of the vile insects whose purpose I could never fathom: wasps, mosquitoes, cockroaches in ascending order of repugnance. Despite the pleasure in removing some of these horrid little beasts, I decided to stop trying. No matter how many I killed, there were always more.

I occasionally wondered about the door in the laboratory that Zelda was so adamant I should not enter. What could be in there that she so fervently did not want me to see? As neither Adwin or I were permitted to use the portal, we had no reason to be in Zelda's private domain. There was only a single occasion when Safya asked us to go with them to the portal. This was the first time our sisters travelled without their tracking devices, and Safya wanted us to wait by the device to instruct it to bring her and Emaleen home in case some unforeseen problem occurred.

"Stop fretting Safya," chided Emaleen, visibly irritated at her sister's request that we accompany them to the portal. "We're more than competent to get ourselves back, without resorting to asking little boys to help us."

"I'm sure we are," replied Safya calmly, ignoring her sister's tone. "But what harm will it do to have them there, just in case? We can get them to stand there just the first time, when we practise." Emaleen shrugged and replied tartly, "If you insist Saffy, but it's all very silly since mother told us there's an emergency control which brings back the last traveller in case of problems."

In fact our sisters returned almost immediately without our help after their practice leap, and set off straight away again into the great outside world. Adwin and I were left alone to find our way back to the house. Zelda did not seem to be in the laboratory, so we took our chance and rushed to the forbidden door. We found it locked, so securely, that nothing we did would cause it to open. Even with my abilities, I could not open it. Adwin seemed keen to keep trying to open the door, but I did not dare tarry long, in case of discovery by Zelda. Her extreme reaction to me the time I had questioned her about what lay beyond the door was still vivid in my memory, and I had no intention of risking such ire again. But my curiosity about the room beyond the door was further inflamed by the security Zelda had clearly put in place to prevent intrusion. I knew I would have to find a way through at some point.

Emaleen and Safya continued to teleport often, and no longer felt the need to take their trackers with them. No matter how far they went, they were easily able to instruct the home portal to bring them back. They became ever more self-involved. The brief period we children had enjoyed of heightened intimacy and affection became no more than a distant memory. Even Safya, never sharp or unkind with her little brothers, became more distant, her absences from the estate mirrored in her emotional absence. I remember now, as I write these memoirs so many years later, how little I knew my sisters at that time, how little they allowed me, or anyone else, to enter their private mental world.

Safya seemed willing to share with her little brothers where she and Emaleen went, but Emaleen was adamant that they should not divulge this information.

"It's nothing to do with them Safya," she would say when Adwin or I pestered one or both of them for information. "It's our adventure, not theirs." Safya looked as if she were considering disobeying her sister, but in the end she complied, shrugging slightly at me and my brother, an expression on her face which seemed to say, "I'm sorry. But what can I do?"

Despite this, I managed to piece together a few scraps of information, and came to the conclusion that they had discovered the joys of outdoor life, especially hill walking and then mountain climbing. I knew this from tiny hints Safya dropped on occasion, but mostly from the clothes the twins wore and the equipment they carried on the few occasions I managed to see them on their way to the portal. They had learned a great deal since our trip with them to the forest, learned to respect the natural world and enter it properly dressed and provisioned.

On Emaleen's insistence, they even kept their departures and arrivals private, ensuring nobody was around as they made their way from their room to the laboratory. They were usually only away a day, but sometimes stayed out overnight. Kallan was deeply concerned that they left the house so often, and even more so when I confided in him my thoughts about their destinations. But when he raised these with Zelda she dismissed them, saying that they were well able to look after themselves, and that in any case, she had agreed to allow them to use the portal provided they did not travel anywhere near other people, so as long as their trips were only to remote areas in the wilds, she was not going to intervene. It was precisely these destinations which caused our uncle such concern.

In the meantime we had regular visits from Marna, often, but not always, accompanied by Yenifa. I relished these visits, always fired with eagerness to spend as much time with the guests as I was allowed. Adwin seemed even more enthused, plying the visitors with endless, potentially annoying questions about the outside world. Marna was infinitely patient with him, always answering every question genially and fully, and often with great humour, beaming smiles filling her rotund face. Yenifa too seemed willing to respond occasionally, but her replies were much more curt, and never amusing. She was not exactly unpleasant, but was a singularly humourless woman, dour and severe in her behaviour, and her appearance. She always dressed in much the same way: plain, sensible clothing, always a long shirt over loose trousers in earthy colours such as brown, dark green, dirty yellow. She kept her reddish-blond hair pulled tight into a neat bun on the back of her head, no make up or ornamentation of any sort. She seemed never to smile, her features fixed in what looked like a permanent frown, though whether this was due to a generalised disapproval of the world, or merely persistent concentration, I could never decide.

During one of their early visits, Adwin, pestering the guests as usual with a barrage of questions, suddenly asked,

"Do you want to come to the forest with us?"

"The forest, my dear?" replied Marna. "What is that, or perhaps where is that? It sounds wonderfully exotic!"

"Just on the edge of the compound," Adwin blurted out, quickly correcting himself. "I mean the estate. Not far. We can walk there and me and Samek can show you our special places where the woodland creatures live and all our friends in the forest."

"Sounds delightful Addy," replied Marna. "You can show us round. What do you think Yenifa, shall we go to the forest with the boys?" she asked, turning to the dour woman beside him.

Yenifa looked bemused by the question.

"Why?" she asked in her flat voice. "What would we do?"

"We'd wander round, chat, show you everything, introduce you to the animals. Things like that," replied Adwin, slightly defensive at Yenifa's tone. She frowned.

"But why would anyone want to spend time wandering aimlessly around a forest? What would be the point? What would be the purpose? What would be our goal?"

"You sound exactly like Zelda!" said Marna with a chuckle. I agreed. Zelda too would find the idea of spending time with other people alien, just for the pleasure of doing so. Given the similarities between Zelda and Yenifa it was odd that they grated against each other, and the atmosphere between them seemed permanently stiff and strained. It was possible that they found each other interesting at a professional level only, but did not enjoy being together generally. Perhaps they were simply too alike, and the similarities jarred with each other. Perhaps it was uncomfortable to spend time with someone who brought home one's own foibles and inadequacies so clearly.

Zelda got on well with Marna, though it was hard to see how Marna would rub up the wrong way against anyone. Even Yenifa seemed relatively relaxed when together with Marna, though they always talked only about their work. Marna and Kallan seemed to adore each other, laughing and joking, teasing each other gently, smiling at each other's jokes, endlessly tactile as they lightly touched each others shoulders, arms, backs. I was fascinated watching the different relationships between Zelda, Kallan, Marna and Yenifa play out before us. With my woefully limited social experience, it was difficult for me to keep track of the network of cross-currents in the affiliations between just these four people. It seemed terribly complicated, and never remained constant. The nature and intensity of communication and rapport between the four adults shifted relentlessly, waxing and waning, rippling between them, and appeared to be as unpredictable as the gushing of the forest waterfall as it cascaded over the rocks, splashing in endlessly different patterns into the pool below.

Little by little, however, as I observed the adults keenly, I began to see through the mist of confusion and recognise that there were in fact patterns in their behaviour, and that it was not nearly as random as it appeared on the surface. The abrasive nature of the rapport between Zelda and Yenifa always created a tense atmosphere, yet they both worked hard to avoid actual disagreements or heated exchanges. It became gradually easier to predict that whenever they were together, they would discuss some element of their work, practical or theoretical, their voices starting softly, becoming slightly louder, then louder again, but just before it seemed an altercation would break out, there would be a lull in their conversation, seemingly by tacit consent, after which they would be over-polite for a short while, before the whole dance began again. Between Zelda and Marna, there was a calm, easy manner. They mostly discussed some scientific issue or other, but lapsed regularly and naturally into reminiscences about their shared upbringing in the Institute, or when they had worked together on some scientific project or other. There were also frequent silences, calm, unworried silences, showing how comfortable they were with each other.

Marna and Kallan were the most intriguing of all. At first I found their teasing and banter troublesome, suggesting as it did an underlying tension or even hostility. But as I watched them, I came to see that the reverse was true. That they were extremely fond of each other. I was not sure if the gentle mockery was a way of masking the mutual affection, or whether it was simply that two people who are secure in the knowledge of how much the other likes them are able to goad each other knowing there is no risk to the basis of the relationship. I also noted how they touched each other a good deal, gently, lightly, on various parts of their bodies. The contact was always fleeting, sometimes so light that I barely saw it.

We children were sometimes tactile with each other as all children are. Adwin and I especially often play-fought, or walked hand in hand, or with an arm over the other's shoulder. My sisters regularly walked with arms linked. Kallan hugged all of us frequently, and even occasionally put his hand on Zelda's shoulder or across the back of her hand. Yet I sensed that when Kallan and Marna touched with the gentlest and briefest of caresses, this meant something quite different, though it seemed as if neither of them was fully aware, in a conscious way, of the caress ever having occurred. I could not make sense of what I observed. Adwin and I discussed it at great length, but failed to reach any conclusion. In the end we decided we would have to wait till we were either older or more socially experienced before we could begin to comprehend such subtleties of behaviour.

Emaleen and Safya continued to treat the visitors exactly the way they had the first time they had met them. Emaleen joined us at mealtimes and, despite her gruff exterior, I sensed she enjoyed hearing of the world outside. Occasionally, she even forgot to maintain her silence. Beyond this, she had few dealings with our guests. Safya mostly remained in her room, and on the extremely rare occasion that she bumped into Marna or Yenifa in the house, she would shriek and race away as fast as she could. Generally she was acute enough to always know when a visit was happening, and on these occasions she locked herself in her room, refusing to emerge until the visitors had left. Kallan and Zelda both remonstrated with her over this, telling her time and time again how rude she was, that it was essential she learn how to deal with strangers, that her behaviour was harming no-one but herself, but nothing ever made her behave differently. In the end even Kallan gave up trying.

About a year and half after Marna and Yenifa's first visit to the house, there was an unexpected development. Marna and Yenifa made one of their regular visits, but this time accompanied by another person. I was not yet ten years old, yet this would be only the third stranger I had ever met, or could remember meeting.

I sensed the arrival of the guests as I always did having put a tracker on the portal, and at the same moment knew that there were three of them from the three little surges of energy. Adwin and I were playing in the garden, kicking a ball around the lawn, much to the annoyance of Kallan, as this inevitably led to plants being damaged. Adwin looked at me keenly through intense inky eyes, curly dark fringe flopping over his brow, as I stopped in mid-kick, head tilted to one side as I perceived a new arrival.

"What is it?" asked Adwin inquisitively, peering at me.

"Quick!" I shouted. "There's someone else. A new visitor with Marna and Yenifa!"

Adwin leaped with surprise, not doubting what I said. Abandoning our game, we raced as fast as we could into the house and to the living room. We were so quick that we arrived in an empty room. We looked around disappointedly, then rushed straight off to the door to the laboratory through which we knew the visitors would emerge with Zelda. Just as we arrived by the door, it slid open, and Zelda came through, Marna and Yenifa following her. We greeted Yenifa politely as usual, and Marna with genuine affection. She gave us both a friendly hug.

"My my, gentlemen. How big you've both got!" she said with a smile.

We laughed at this, knowing she was merely being genial - we had only seen her about a month before, so could hardly have grown markedly in this time. Behind Yenifa we perceived a shadowy figure, hanging back slightly, perhaps shy to cross into the house.

"Come on Devid," Marna encouraged jovially. "Don't just stand there like a wet blanket. Come into the house!"

The man called Devid slinked through the door, sniffing loudly as he moved. I recoiled slightly as I peered at him. I sensed something unpleasant about him, something shifty and untrustworthy. I remembered the conversation between Kallan and Zelda I had eavesdropped on all that time ago, and Kallan's concern that someone untrustworthy might one day enter our home. That was exactly the word he had used: untrustworthy.

I could not determine exactly what it was about this man that caused me such aversion. He was neither tall nor short, of slim build, light brown hair cut fairly short and pushed back from his forehead, hazel-green eyes, and moderately good looking in an unremarkable way. His clothes looked to be of good quality: trousers and a short-sleeved shirt, both in a dull olive green, brown suede shoes on his curiously tiny feet. The only slightly unusual thing about him was that he sported a short, neat little beard and moustache, an affectation in a time when facial hair was not in fashion.

I wondered if I should raise my concerns later with Kallan, and perhaps even with Zelda, but was not sure they would take them seriously. I had nothing to back up my strong impression of his faithlessness, and so little experience of other people to give my sensations depth. I would simply have to wait and see what transpired, surreptitiously watching him for evidence of wrongdoing, for confirmation of his malice.

Zelda ushered the guests further into the house, towards the living room, Adwin dancing around behind them, dogging their every step. When we all arrived at the living room, Kallan was already there, a tray with steaming coffee and cups resting on the sideboard at the side of the room.

"Oh!" he said, clearly surprised to see a new visitor. "We have another guest. How nice," though I thought I saw a flicker of disquiet pass across his face as he looked at Devid for the first time. But the shadow quickly passed as Kallan regained his composure and his usual host's charm. He shook Devid's hand, and then turned to Adwin.

"Addy dear, go and fetch another cup. I was only expecting Marna and Yenifa." Adwin did not want to leave the room, to leave the new guest. He hesitated, still jigging with excitement, until Kallan frowned at him and nodded sharply towards the door with his head. My brother rushed off as fast as his little legs could carry him, so as to be back as soon as he could and not to miss any of the excitement. I stayed where I was, quite still, staring at Devid. He turned to face me directly, and just stared, with no expression on his face. Yet I had to work hard to repress a shudder as I contemplated the look in his eyes: ostensibly bland and neutral, yet with something behind the vapid mask that was frankly noxious. No-one else could see his expression from where they stood, and I sidled in behind Kallan to evade the baleful gaze Devid had turned on me.

After a short pause during which Kallan greeted Yenifa formally and Marna affectionately, and then invited everyone to sit down, Adwin came hurtling back into the room, coffee cup in hand. As Kallan took the cup from him, he mindspoke to me.

~What did I miss? There's a funny mood in the room.~

~Not now, Addy, I'll tell you later,~ I replied. *~But don't trust the new one. There's something horrible about him.~*

Adwin glanced surreptitiously at Devid, but jolted as Devid instantly turned his gaze on Adwin, wrinkling his nose as if about to sniff again. Adwin did not need my abilities to sense something menacing about Devid.

~I see what you mean. Let's get out of here.~

I indicated my consent, and asked Kallan if we could go and finish our game. He turned smilingly to me and said yes, but to be back in time for supper.

As Adwin and I scrambled from the room, I made the mistake of glancing over my shoulder, to see Devid's gaze following me. I could no longer restrain a shudder at the sinister look in his eyes, a tiny, malevolent smile lifting the corners of his full red lips. As I hurried from the room, I could not help but wonder: why did Devid seem to dislike us so much?

Chapter Sixteen

Adwin finally managed to persuade our guests to come with him to the forest on this occasion of Devid's first visit to our home. "Please," he would wheedle, time and time again, over the dinner table, and even dancing around behind the guests as they left the room. "Please come with us. I want to show you my special place and my animals. Please please please." Eventually his pestering bore fruit.

Marna had always seemed keen, at least on the surface, Yenifa decidedly not, yet even Marna had yet to set foot any further from the house than the garden. It was not only Yenifa's reluctance to join us, but also the simple lack of time: most of each visit was occupied with Zelda in her laboratory. Our time with the guests was predominantly limited to mealtimes. But on this visit, Devid proved an unlikely ally, eager to survey not only the whole house, but also to venture further afield into the gardens and meadows, and even the forest beyond. In fact, he seemed particularly inquisitive about the forest, after Adwin had waxed lyrical about it the first evening at supper, this time supported by my own enthusiastic comments. I disliked Devid, but could not imagine what harm it would do if he were to accompany us all to the forest. And it would be a great joy to show Marna our special and magical place.

The next day was mild, slightly breezy and with a hint of rain in the air, but pleasant enough to warrant an outing. As was usually the case, the guests joined us for breakfast. Adwin and I were already there, and Zelda came shuffling in as we ate, looking for her visitors. She assumed that they would retire immediately after the meal to her private area, to continue their discussions and investigations of her scientific work. But by the time Zelda arrived, Adwin's enthusiasm, aided by his relentless encouragement of the visitors to join us in a trip to the forest that morning, meant that the decision had already been made.

Zelda began to argue against such a trip.

"It is such a waste of time," she began. "A total waste of time."

"I find I have to agree," added Yenifa. "I can't see the purpose of it."

"Oh you two!" remonstrated Marna as she threw her arms into the air, glaring at Zelda and then Yenifa, a look of mock sternness on her face. "Just look at the shining faces of your boys. They are so keen to get us to their precious woods. I haven't the heart to disappoint them, especially as we've agreed we'd go," she said in a jovial tone. "And it sounds absolutely marvellous to get outdoors into nature," she added. "Both of you could do with showing those ghostly-white faces to the sun from time to time!" And at that she winked at me. I struggled to restrain a chortle.

Zelda looked as if she were about to disagree again, but Devid interrupted before she could do so, prefacing his comment with a little sniff.

"I would very much like to see the forest too," he cajoled, using his status as a guest, and a new guest at that, to put pressure on Zelda. Zelda knew she was beaten.

"Very well," she said grumpily. "But only a quick trip there and back. No dawdling and messing around once you are there."

Marna pretended to look contrite. "Yes boss!" she said, and this time winked at Adwin, who responded with a high-pitched giggle.

"I did not mean you Marna, or Devid," interjected Zelda, embarrassed that her guests may have interpreted her bossiness as applying to them.

Even Yenifa smiled slightly, very slightly, at Zelda's discomfiture.

Marna laughed out loud. "Don't look so flustered Zelda. I'm teasing you."

Zelda was singularly unamused at this. She *never* took well to being mocked, teased or taunted in any way whatsoever. She was used to being taken seriously, even by those outside who hated and feared her. And any type of ridicule took her back to the days at the Institute, when most of the children had taken huge pleasure in endlessly needling her, making jibes about her unattractiveness, her short stature, her unappealing personality.

Marna noticed Zelda's expression of umbrage and turned to her, looking her straight in the eye, saying gently,

"Zelda, my dear friend. You know I would never really mock you. I was always your friend, even back there when we were children together. So let's stop all this outrageous sulking and get on with the marvellous business of the day."

"Hmph," Zelda replied, but her features had cleared somewhat of their irascibility.

Adwin leapt up from the meal, nodding at me vigorously as he did so. "Meet me at the front door as quickly as you can," he directed. "But there's been lots of rain so you must wear boots or sturdy shoes. There'll be water and mud everywhere." From the look on her face, this last comment clearly did not endear the visit to Yenifa. Marna saluted my brother, acknowledging the fact that he was ordering our guests around, despite being only six years old. Adwin giggled and raced off, and I threw a little smile at Marna as I followed quickly behind him. As I left the room I heard Kallan say that as the guests had not brought boots or even sturdy shoes, not expecting to be dragged through mud, he would go and try to find some that would fit them.

We all met a little while later as agreed, and took the three scientists on a trip to our forest. Zelda did not accompany us, nor Kallan. My little brother looked as elated as I felt to be heading up the group, to have the responsibility of leading these adult outsiders into places they had never been, places that we knew and that they did not. Neither of us had never been in such a position. Even in our own family, my brother, at six years old, was the youngest, always at the bottom of the pecking order, my own status at the grand age of nine not much higher, yet here we were, taking precedence over three highly educated, knowledgeable grown-ups, demonstrating and explaining things to them in which we were the experts. Adwin, face beaming with pride, led the walk to the forest, egging the others on throughout with commands. "Come on. Hurry up. Don't dawdle. We don't want to miss anything," to the amusement of Marna, the bafflement of Yenifa, and the irritation of Devid.

The morning was a blur of happiness for me. Marna, as always, was a joy to spend time with. Genial, jolly, and kind as ever, I also saw a different side to her. As a scientist, she was fascinated by everything, and it was clear she had not spent much time, if any, meandering through woodland. She wanted to know the name of every plant we saw, how it grew, did it flower, did its leaves die in the winter, how big do you think it will get, what do its seeds look like, and on and on. I knew much of the information she sought, Adwin much less so at his younger age, yet she treated us both with the respect of colleagues who were more knowledgeable than her in our field. She nodded at our answers, acting as though each one must be correct. I had never felt such status, to be the imparter of information, and the sensation was invigorating. Unexpectedly, Yenifa too, seemed different. As with Marna, the scientist in her came to the fore, and she engaged keenly with everything around her. She too had clearly spent little time outdoors, presumably because she was just too busy in the laboratory.

We encountered animals too, and as with the plants, Marna and Yenifa alternated in asking a long series of questions about each of them. They knew most of their names, but nothing about their habits. How did we tell the males from the females, what were their mating habits, what did they eat, and so on. I was especially flattered by the questions about mating habits. As children, some adults may have felt such discussion to be inappropriate, but neither Marna nor Yenifa seemed to consider this, and with this topic they treated us with respect, astonishing given our youth. I even showed them how I was able to almost hypnotise the animals into remaining still, enabling us to approach them and stroke them. Marna was thrilled by the experience, a huge grin filling her wide face as she caressed a tractable doe with her chubby fingers. Yenifa approached, touched the animal once before rapidly withdrawing her hand and forcing a tight smile onto her face. Devid did not join in, hanging back behind us where I sensed his intense focus on me.

In the waterfall glade, we stopped to rest. *~Best not to tell them anything about wood nymphs and water sprites, fairies and goblins,~* I mindspoke to my brother. He nodded his agreement, clearly enjoying the sensation of being treated with respect, and wanting to say nothing to undermine this. As with Zelda, I suspected that these scientists would consider any comments about magical beings of folklore to be risible, childish. I wondered if Marna, on her own, might be amenable to our stories, but Yenifa most certainly would not be. Best to err on the side of caution.

Yet, they were clearly enchanted by the simple natural beauty of the forest clearing with its dappled light, the gentle splashing of the waterfall as it hit the pool, the emerald waters of the pool itself, the dense green moss of the forest floor. I thought it was clear from their reaction to this exquisite place that they had never experienced anything like it. They were happy to sit for a while in silence, drinking in the bewitching atmosphere of this, our most cherished spot.

I was keenly aware of Devid throughout the entire visit. Unlike his colleagues, he barely spoke throughout the walk. He simply followed along, watching everything intently through narrowed hazel eyes, as if trying to commit the experience to memory, sniffing and snorting lightly as he walked. I desperately wanted to probe his mind, to know what he was thinking and feeling, but I did not dare, not knowing if he would be able to sense my intrusion the way Zelda seemed to have learned. But I did not need to use my gifts to feel that he was devious, that whatever the reason for his eagerness to visit the forest, the motive would not be a good one. I tried to shut him out of my feelings, not to allow him to impair my intense enjoyment of this special day. I was not entirely successful in this, and his presence sat like a noisome weight on my mind, always there, ever menacing. Adwin appeared far more successful at simply cutting Devid out of the picture. My little brother was clearly enraptured by the entire experience of the morning in the forest with our guests. Nothing could dampen his spirit or corrode his pleasure, and I was happy for him.

As the day wore on, I knew we would have to return to the house. Zelda would be livid if we kept the guests, *her* guests, away from her for too long. When I suggested that we return, I was met with a howl of resistance from Adwin. "Noooo!" he wailed. "Not yet. Please not yet. Just a bit longer. A few more minutes. Please please please!" I shook my head, silently mouthing the single word 'Zelda' at him. He crossed his arms and pouted, but gave up resisting as the thought of an angry Zelda entered his mind.

With a heavy heart I led the three adults out of the forest, back to the house. All five of us were silent on the return journey. I tried to maintain the unique experience of primacy as long as we could, before I was once more relegated to the bottom of the social pile, or nearly the bottom. Only Adwin ranked below me, and he was marching ahead on his little legs, his monumental sulk perceptible even as I walked behind him, visible in the set of his shoulders, the angle of his head. Marna seemed enraptured with all she had seen, and I assumed her mind was filled with the novelty of it all. Even Yenifa looked almost content with the day's outing. Devid I could not fathom, though I noticed him still looking around, eyes darting to and fro, never settling long on anything.

At one point we passed not far from the perimeter fence. Although there was nothing to show the fence existed, it being entirely electromagnetic, Devid seemed to peer even more intently in its direction. I shuddered slightly. Perhaps he did enjoy special gifts, or at least some heightened mental ability. Or perhaps I was reading too much into his behaviour, over-interpreting everything he did due to my lack of trust in him. I tried to ignore him, but as we approached the house, I could not help feel that he was not merely visiting us in order to get to know Zelda, but that he was surveying us, studying and analysing everything he saw, inside the house and out, filing it all away in his memory for some future, as yet unascertained, purpose.

Zelda came to meet us almost as soon as we came through the door. Her face showed impatience that we had been out so long. She started to usher the guests in the direction of her private area, but Kallan descended upon us, instructing us all, guests included, to go and change our footwear, wash our hands, and come straight to the dining room for lunch. We must, according to him, all be starving after our long morning enjoying the delights of the forest. Zelda was seriously put out and began to remonstrate with Kallan, but one imperious glance from him, a single silver eyebrow raised, and Zelda was silenced. For the second time in one day, she knew herself beaten. We all obediently moved off to our rooms to prepare ourselves for lunch. As we did so, Marna turned to Adwin and me, and said, in tones of genuine warmth, though somewhat overblown language,

"Thank you so much, both of you. That was truly one of the most marvellous mornings of my life. You were both absolutely perfect guides." To our astonishment, Yenifa also managed a tight smile at us as she nodded her agreement. I had never seen her look so pleased. Devid just stared at us, his gaze boring into us. I blushed at Marna's comment and rushed off, Adwin in tow, his sulks marginally appeased by Marna's thanks.

Zelda had the pleasure of her guests for the rest of the day after we had eaten. We all met again at dinner that evening, which was later than usual due to the unusually late lunch. Safya, as always when we had guests, refused to join us, and this evening, Emaleen had opted to eat with her sister in their own room.

The atmosphere at dinner was odd. Not exactly strained, but it was obvious that something unexpected had occurred among the scientists that afternoon. Kallan looked at Adwin and me, indicating by his expression that he too noticed the mood. We began the meal in silence. In truth, Zelda was little different from usual in that she so often showed irritability and lack of sociability, but the other three seemed to be in a state of mild shock. I found this most confusing, and shared my feelings silently with Adwin. He shrugged slightly to show that he too was nonplussed and had no explanation to offer for the peculiar atmosphere.

Eventually Kallan became impatient at the stony silence.

"Have you all had an interesting afternoon?" he probed, not quite wanting to ask a direct question.

Zelda looked up, and answered curtly, "Yes."

When the others showed no inclination to add anything to Zelda's single word, Kallan persisted.

"So, what was interesting about it?" he asked, more pointedly. He still got no reply. He stared directly at Marna, neat silver brows lifted lightly in query, knowing that he had the best chance of a response from her.

"Well Marna, my dear," he queried in a silky voice, "what *have* you four been up to?"

Marna squirmed slightly in her seat. It seemed she was always susceptible to Kallan, and never wanted to offend him. Yet clearly there was something that none of them, most especially Zelda, wanted to impart to Kallan or either of us children at the table.

"Marna?" Kallan insisted, still in a soft and persuasive tone, looking directly at her and smiling benignly. Zelda was glaring at Marna, but Marna was doing her best to ignore my mother. I waited with baited breath, hankering to know what the four scientists had been up to. Adwin too had stopped eating, watching the interplay between the adults with obvious fascination.

After a tense pause, during which Kallan sat quite still, his smile fixed on his face, his gaze at Marna unwavering, Marna crumpled, as Kallan knew she would.

"Zelda showed us her experiments, the foetuses that didn't succeed," she admitted finally.

Zelda growled her disapproval. Yenifa looked embarrassed. Devid sat stiffly, watching every tiny part of the interactions happening around the table, his nose twitching with anticipation, though for what, I was not yet sure. Kallan sat back sharply in his chair.

"What do you mean?" he asked, frowning. "What foetuses that didn't succeed?" He genuinely had no idea what Marna was talking about.

Zelda growled again. Marna looked at her forlornly, wriggling with discomfort, blushing with embarrassment. Zelda shook her head violently, indicating that Marna should offer no further information. But Kallan was not so easily put off.

"I asked you, Marna, and you Zelda," he persisted, his tone now hard and metallic, "What foetuses?"

Marna shrugged at Zelda, her fleshy face showing acute apology. She turned back to Kallan and said simply,

"The ones she worked on which she couldn't quite bring to full term because they weren't viable."

Zelda let out a loud, angry breath and sat back in her seat with a thump. Kallan looked confused and turned to Zelda.

"You never told me you had actual foetuses which didn't work out," he said accusingly.

"Don't be naive, Kallan," Zelda said defensively. "You knew my experiments involved many, many failures before I had any successes."

"Yes," said Kallan in the same hard tone. "But I assumed you knew they were failures early on, when they were no more than a bundle of cells. Or at the very least that if they were more developed than this, you'd have destroyed them." He turned abruptly to Marna, knowing he was more likely to get an honest reply from her than from Zelda.

"How big are they?" he asked her.

"Small," replied Marna in an unsure voice.

Kallan sighed loudly in exasperation.

"Obviously they're small," he snapped in an impatient tone. "*All* foetuses are small. But how small? Or better, how big? How old?" He stared at Marna angrily.

Marna floundered for a reply, but eventually said, in a quiet, abashed voice,

"Some of them are almost full term."

Kallan gasped. Zelda growled again. Marna looked down at her empty plate, clearly wishing the ground would swallow her. I stole a quick glance at Devid, and was appalled to see that he seemed to be enjoying himself, a small, nasty smile lifting the corners of his red lips which almost glowed through the brown moustache and beard, his eyes twinkling with what looked almost like amusement. He noticed me look at him, and turned his unpleasant gaze on me. His eyes bored into me. As he looked at me, I saw with absolute clarity that his expression when he stared at *me* was no longer one of amusement. Instead it was a glare of something truly unpleasant, contempt or perhaps even disgust. I jerked back in my seat and tore my eyes away from his. Why would he view me with such antipathy, almost with anger? And why now? Since he had arrived he had looked at me with distaste, but this was something totally different, and new, and only since spending the afternoon examining the unviable foetuses in Zelda's laboratory.

I wondered where the foetuses could be, as I had seen most of the rooms in the laboratory complex. I realised with a start that they must be behind the locked door I had seen, the time Zelda had reacted so angrily when I queried what was behind it. But what did these foetuses look like? What was it about them that seemed to have so affected Devid that he now looked on me with such aversion.

My thoughts were interrupted by Kallan, pursuing the issue.

"Please tell me they are no longer alive, Zelda," he said in a voice filled with despair.

"Of course they are not alive," she replied loftily, as if the question were irretrievably stupid. "What a ridiculous suggestion!"

"So where are they? How are they stored?" snapped Kallan, ever more exasperated.

"If you must know," replied Zelda testily, "They are in glass jars filled with preserving fluid."

Kallan looked disgusted, but still persisted, wanting to know the whole truth.

"But why have you kept them? Why didn't you destroy them?"

"Destroy them??" shrieked Zelda. "This is my life's work. They are a record." She stared at Kallan and offered no more, as if this were an adequate explanation.

A heavy pause ensued. Adwin suddenly gasped, as if a realisation had just hit him.

"Did you kill them or did they just die on their own?" he asked Zelda accusingly, his high and piping child's voice intruding into the adult conversation.

Zelda was totally unprepared for the question, especially from the youngest member of her family, and merely stared at Adwin dumbfounded. Zelda's silence and mixed expression of shock and guilt told us what we needed to know. She had killed them. She had let them reach almost full term, and then she had killed them and preserved their bodies for future research.

Adwin burst into tears and ran from the room. I was torn by an urgent desire to follow him and comfort him, yet also by my intense need not to miss any of the shocking revelations that were flowing thick and fast around the table. I saw the look of disgust on Devid's face as his eyes followed my brother fleeing the room. I was utterly confused as to why his hostility to me seemed also to attach to Adwin. What had we done to deserve it? I knew it had to be connected to what Devid had witnessed that afternoon in the laboratory. And would Devid also show such antipathy towards my sisters when he got to know them?

Another intensely uncomfortable silence ensued. Yenifa had remained silent through the entire discussion, and still made no contribution. She seemed unwilling to offer any comment, and sat quite still, a look of deep embarrassment on her severe features. I could not ascertain what she thought or felt about Zelda's experiments, but did not think they would cause her discomfort in themselves. Her subdued manner was likely to be due to social distress, not being used to such angry and frank exchanges. I assumed that she would have been fascinated by Zelda's experiments, and would not have given a second thought to the morality of what Zelda had done. Yenifa was a hard-minded scientist, for whom scientific progress would surely trump any ethical dilemmas, if she even considered such dilemmas to exist.

Kallan was appalled, and visibly distressed. Looking back at this as an old man, I could only assume that it had never crossed his mind that Zelda's experiments would lead to such a distasteful outcome, though perhaps he should have thought through the ramifications of Zelda's research. If he had done, perhaps he would have contemplated such an eventuality. His oversight seemed to make him angry with himself, adding to his distress.

"What did they look like?" I suddenly threw out, mostly at Marna, but at anyone who would answer me. The moment the words left my mouth I regretted them. I was not at all sure I wanted to know, but my curiosity had got the better of me.

I was surprised when Devid answered me, informing me with relish in his nasal voice.

"They're monsters. All horribly deformed. Some with huge bodies and no limbs, some with arms and legs the wrong way round, others with lots of eyes dotted all over their heads, or huge gaping holes in their faces so you can see inside, or with their internal organs on the outside or..."

"That's enough!!" shouted Kallan, making everyone jump. "You will not say another word on the matter!" He glared at Devid with such a forbidding expression on his tanned face, that Devid was silenced.

I stared open-mouthed at Devid's descriptions. I knew he had taken pleasure in telling me the awful details, had enjoyed watching my expression grow more horrified at each revelation, yet I did not disbelieve him. And Marna's shamed reaction to what Devid said told me without doubt that Devid's depictions were true. I wished I had never heard them, wished I had never asked the question and given Devid the opportunity to fill my mind with such hideous images. Tears began to well in my eyes as another unwelcome thought intruded into my mind. I turned to Zelda and asked in a quavering voice,

"Why don't my sisters and Adwin look like monsters?" And I continued in a tiny voice, little more than a wobbly whisper. "Why don't I look like a monster?"

Zelda turned her gaze on me, fury clear on her red blotchy face, fury that Marna had succumbed to Kallan's questions and had blurted out to Kallan and us what she had seen, rage that Kallan had persisted in his questioning, and incensed at Devid's lurid descriptions of the dead foetuses. She took her rage out on me, replying in a quiet but savage tone,

"You," she said, jabbing her finger at me as she spoke. "You are as near to being a monster as I could make you while ensuring you at least look human."

For a moment, I did not understand what she was saying. I knew I did not look like a monster. But then it hit me: she was saying that I *was* a monster, I just did not look like one. I burst into tears and fled the room. As I flew through the door, my last impression was the look of revulsion I saw on Devid's face from the corner of my eye. I suddenly understood the basis of his disgust: he saw me and Adwin as monsters. Our provenance was such that we were no different from the dead foetuses floating pathetically in their fluid-filled tanks. I could not help but wonder whether such antipathy and aversion would have repercussions for Zelda or any of us, and that Zelda's decision to allow him to see the tiny corpses had been a huge mistake.

Chapter Seventeen

I rushed to Adwin's room as I fled the dining room. I found him sobbing on his bed. I threw myself down next to him. Adwin was distraught, inconsolable, despite not having heard the most upsetting part of the discussion. He had left the room before Devid had described the foetuses with such delighted malice. As his crying slowly ebbed, I knew I could not tell my little brother what I had heard. I felt an intense need to protect him from the horrors described to me. He was not as robust as me, either physically or mentally. He suffered more from illnesses than I did, and his heart also sickened more easily than mine when he confronted some of the awful realities of life. He was prone to anxiety and to sickness, the latter of which I was beginning to think might stem from his delicate mental state. I knew I would never tell him what Zelda had said to me just before I fled, that I was as close to being a monster as she could make me while ensuring I *looked* human. If this is how she described me, then surely it would also apply to Adwin, created from even more progenitors than I was.

Adwin's tears took a long time to abate, but eventually his weeping shuddered to a gradual stop, and his breathing calmed. All that time I just lay beside him, stroking his hair, humming gently to comfort him.

Eventually we lay quite still, each wrapped in our own thoughts. I sensed that outside the room things were happening. I threw out a probe, and saw the three guests had returned to their own rooms, and were packing their small bags. They were leaving. Even without looking for Zelda specifically I could clearly sense her. Her fury at Marna and Devid, and even Kallan, was so intense that it pervaded the house, like the stench of rotting eggs. Marna was mortified, desperately unhappy to have angered her old friend this way. Devid seemed smug, and simultaneously self-righteous. I sensed that he was well pleased with the outcome of his visit, even though disgusted and angered at what he had discovered. Yenifa's reaction, as always, was so enigmatic as to be unfathomable. I wondered if she enjoyed some gifts, to allow her to block so effectively any outflowing of emotion. Or perhaps she simply did not have any emotion to block in the first place.

I knew that Zelda was in her laboratory, storming around, unable to sit or calm herself. She had not even had to order the guests to leave: they knew the visit was at an end. After they had packed their bags, they made their way to the portal room, tentatively moving through the rooms of Zelda's private area, hoping they would not encounter her as they went. She heard them, and made sure she did not see them as they left the estate through the portal. She wanted to run to them, to shout at them, berate Marna for her betrayal of trust, scold Devid for his salacious depictions of the foetuses, but such was her anger that I assumed she did not trust herself not to actually strike them. So she let them leave the house alone, without being seen off. Kallan too had diplomatically withdrawn to his own room, not feeling there was anything useful to be gained from a final farewell, and keen to avoid Zelda's wrath.

A little time after they had gone, I heard a light tap at Adwin's door.

~*Can we come in?*~ mindspoke Safya tentatively. I glanced at Adwin's tear-stained face and he nodded his consent. I passed this to the girls who let themselves into the room. Their expressions showed they were worried, and I knew that their gifts were sufficient to allow them to sense the intense, heightened passions both during the conversation in the dining room, and afterwards, pervading the house.

"What happened?" asked Emaleen without preamble but reverting to normal speech, as they both sat on the end of the bed. I sighed, not quite knowing where to begin, or how much to tell them. In the end I recounted most of what had transpired around the dinner table, leaving out Devid's ghastly images and Zelda's final barbed comment. I felt a need to give some explanation to my sisters, and also to Adwin, as to why Zelda's ire was aimed at Devid as well as Marna, but I simply said that Devid had backed up Marna's tale. After telling my sisters all I judged wise about the dead foetuses, they sat in immobile silence, conflicting emotions clear on their faces. On the one hand, they were intrigued to hear details of the failed experiments, the very experiments that had led to them, to me, to Adwin. But on the other hand, they were appalled by the revelation that Zelda had not only allowed the failed foetuses to reach full term, but had then killed them, keeping their corpses preserved for future research. How close had each of us come to being terminated in like manner?

Safya's face showed more than just concern mixed with curiosity. She looked pensive, and just before she spoke, I knew what her questions would be, and was filled with dismay.

"How were they not viable? What was wrong with them?" she asked in a tone of genuine puzzlement.

Before I could muster the correct answer, Zelda suddenly burst through the door. I had been so distracted by Safya's questions, preoccupied with how best to reply to them, that I had not perceived our mother's approach.

"There you are!" she shouted. "Good. All four of you. That is even better." She stopped and stared at us. We gaped at her. She was flushed, her skin blotched with anger, her hair escaping in many wild strands from its usual bondage, as if she had been running her hands through it over and over again with little success. Her dark eyes blazed with a crazed look we had never seen before. A strange, icy fury had taken hold of her. Oh, we had seen her angry before, at us, at her work, at the Council, at the whole world, but never like this. There was a feral look in her eyes, the expression of a wild predatory animal on the verge of a kill, or of a madwoman about to launch into some demented act. We all cringed as we sat on the bed.

"Come with me!" she commanded in a cold voice almost devoid of emotion, despite the freezing rage that flowed from her. Nobody moved. "Come with me!" she said again, enunciating each word slowly and viciously. Again, nobody stirred. She launched herself at the bed, and before I could evade her, she grabbed me by the hair.

"You!" she snarled at me. "You who wants to know so much, asks so many fucking questions. I have something to show you." And she literally dragged me off the bed, my curls gripped in her iron grasp. As she dragged me towards the door, she turned abruptly to the others sitting mute on the bed and shouted,

"And you lot too. Follow me. If you don't there will be hell to pay." I winced in pain as she pulled me along behind her, the others slowly standing up and gingerly following.

She marched me through the corridors of the house to her laboratory. Just before we got there, Kallan appeared, having heard the commotion.

"What is going on?" he demanded imperiously of Zelda, neat silver eyebrows raised high. She turned her feral gaze on him. Kallan looked shocked, but did not flinch. Zelda replied,

"I am going to show this little busybody what he wants to see, and the rest of them too." Kallan stood stock still, undecided how best to respond. But as Zelda continued on her way, Kallan trotted along behind.

My mother dragged me through the rooms of her private area, my siblings and then Kallan following at what they felt was a safe distance. We arrived at the locked door I had asked about all that time ago, when Zelda had responded so angrily to my queries about it. I knew without any doubt that this was where she kept the foetuses. She spoke a code into the control panel beside the door, and it slid open. She let go of my hair and pushed me into the room. As she did so, she gestured impatiently at the others that they should follow me. She brought up the rear, her expression of anger by now having been replaced by one of cold, icy steel which chilled me even more than the ruddy rage it had replaced.

As I entered the room, the lights flickered on automatically. I stood dumbfounded by what I saw. The room was very long and fairly narrow. The whole way down each wall was filled with a row of transparent perspiglass tanks, each set on a solid base so that the top of the tank itself was at about the height of an adult. I estimated that there must be approximately forty or perhaps fifty such tanks on each side of the room, stretching away in the distance. Each was lit from inside, seemingly from the top of the tank itself, and was filled with a faintly yellow clear liquid. I strained to see what was in the tanks above my head, and Zelda decided I needed to observe clearly what each contained. She lifted me up physically so my eyes were level with the middle of each perspiglass container. I cried out in horror at what I saw in the first one, struggling to extricate myself from Zelda's grasp, but she held me so fast that I could not move. As on previous occasions, I was struck by how strong she was. I looked away, but with her right hand she forced my face forwards and ordered me to look.

I gazed at the object floating in the yellowish fluid, feeling repugnance combined with gross fascination. It was clearly a human foetus, its size showing it must have been almost full term. Its overall body shape was normal, and it was curled lightly into a foetal position. But at the back of its head an eye, wide open, gazed vacantly out from among the downy hairs on its scalp. A single, over-large blue eye, encircled by pale eyelashes, fixed forever open, seeming to look out, yet with no expression on its dead surface. Zelda laughed harshly at my obvious shock, and moved to the next tank. Here I saw another foetus, slightly smaller, this time with no legs and arms, just little stumps where the limbs should have been, the bones of the stumps actually protruding through the skin. And to the next one, a tank with a single foetus, but with two heads, partially conjoined, the facial features melded together, looking like a reflection in a distorting mirror.

On and on Zelda carried me down the row of horrors. A tiny baby with a full simian tail, its whole body covered in thick black hair. I shuddered as I realised that this experiment must have involved monkey genes in addition to human, and the thought came to my mind that perhaps *my* progenitors were not all human! Was I inhuman? I trembled at the thought, and tried to put it from my mind.

Another submerged baby had an unnaturally curved back, a crest of bones protruding down the whole line of the unfortunate's spinal column like an ancient reptile. On and on down the corridor of horrors Zelda carried me, vision after grotesque vision presenting itself before my aghast eyes.

My body stilled as I was manhandled along the line of outlandish sights. My senses were so overburdened that I was no longer able to struggle. I fell limp in my mother's arms, and she judged it safe to let me go. I dropped heavily to the floor, my head in my hands, and wept. I sobbed and sobbed, as my siblings stared in silent terror at the rows of foetuses. Kallan fixed Zelda with a gaze of disgust and profound reproach for what she had done with the foetuses, and even more for what she was doing to us. Zelda stood behind me, unmoved by my misery, by my siblings' horror, oblivious to Kallan's opprobrium. What sort of monster was she to subject a nine-year old boy to this?

I could not stop weeping. Zelda began to shuffle impatiently behind me, seemingly almost bored now with my reaction. Abruptly she decided to leave, and walked briskly back down the avenue between the two rows of monstrous deformities. She swept past Adwin, Emaleen and Safya, ignoring them, and even discounting Kallan's obvious outrage at her behaviour. As she neared the door, she could not seem to resist a final, wounding shot.

"Let yourselves out," she began, dark humour obvious in her tone, "When you've finished saying goodbye to your brothers and sisters!" And at this she laughed nastily and left the room. Emaleen and Safya rushed out straight after her, desperate to remove themselves from the horrific visions before them. Kallan followed rapidly in their wake, perhaps to berate Zelda for what she had done, seeming almost to forget the two little boys left alone in the dreadful room in his haste to pursue Zelda.

Adwin moved slowly towards me, dropped down onto his knees beside me, put his arm across my shoulder and rested his head against mine. He said nothing, merely offered his unconditional comfort, and love. I pressed my head against his as we kneeled together, silent, enveloped in a shared horror at the sights all around us, yet also cocooned in our affection for each other.

Little by little my sobs abated, and as they did so I became aware of my aching knees from my heavy fall to the floor. I dragged myself to my feet, pulling Adwin with me. We looked forlornly at each other, determinedly avoiding the sad, heartrending creatures all around us, floating forever in their translucent prisons, victims of an amoral scientist who saw nothing wrong in what she had done. What kind of ghoulish logic made her keep these sad, dead monsters?

We two living victims made our way slowly from the room, back to the safety of the house, determined never again to visit that terrible room. I knew, however, that I would never be able to expunge its ghastly contents from my mind.

Chapter Eighteen

After the nightmare of the forced visit to Zelda's chamber of horrors, life slowly returned to normal for me and my siblings. Or as normal as it could be after what we had witnessed. Adwin and I returned to our studies, to our trips to the forest, to our games in the gardens. Emaleen and Safya left the estate even more often than before, perhaps feeling that by doing so they could leave behind the harrowing images of the dead foetuses and escape their dysfunctional mother. I wondered whether their trips abroad were successful in this, gave them any relief, and decided that it was unlikely. As far as I was concerned, *nothing* could ever erase from my consciousness the monstrous, tragic and heartbreaking sights I had seen.

Zelda kept even more to herself than usual, rarely joining us for meals, nor to socialise in the evenings. We were profoundly glad of this, as we did not know how to deal with her, and now felt a genuine fear when in her presence. We had feared her moods in the past, dreaded her punishments. She had never been an easy woman to get on with, and was almost permanently irascible and ill-tempered, and now we felt a sense of foreboding when with her, a feeling that she could explode at any moment, once again subjecting us to an experience as ghastly as the room full of tiny lifeless cadavers. More and more Zelda seemed like our jailer.

Kallan too was in a most difficult mood, clearly still livid with Zelda, with underlying sympathy for us, yet unable to overcome anger at Zelda to show us the usual kindness and affection which were his norm. Mealtimes and other occasions where we spent time with Kallan were tense and uncomfortable, and we tried to limit their duration as much as we could.

Adwin and I were thus thrown very much onto our own resources. But this did not worry us unduly. We relished each other's company, and during this fraught period, we were able to please ourselves with how we spent our time. Nobody seemed to involve themselves with our education, our games, our leisure time, and we made the most of this.

Despite our contentment in running our own lives during this period, we did not enjoy the strained atmosphere in the house, envious of our sisters and their ability to flee when it suited them. The other major disadvantage for us was the lack of Marna. We loved her, for her joviality, her obvious affection for us, her transforming of the mood of the house into one of jollity and lightheartedness. Her almost miraculous ability even to draw out a different Zelda from the one we were usually subjected to, to make Zelda simply *nicer*. How we could use Marna's magic now! Kallan too was always smiling and happy when Marna was around, almost boyish in his upbeat and cheerful demeanour.

Adwin made the mistake one day of asking Kallan when Marna would visit again. He was wise enough not to even attempt such a question of Zelda, even were he to be long enough in Zelda's presence to do so. He told me he felt it would be safe to ask Kallan, given our uncle's tender sentiment towards Marna. Adwin encountered Kallan as our uncle was leaving to visit friends in the outside world. I was further down the corridor, but saw the interaction clearly. As Adwin asked Kallan. "When will Marna visit again?", Kallan turned an empty stare on my brother, bright blue eyes cold and eerie, and barked, "Never!" in a deeply unhappy voice. And that was that. No further explanation was offered, and he turned and left Adwin standing stupefied in the corridor. My brother was crestfallen at the prospect of not seeing Marna again, of our prison once again consisting of the two of us, Kallan and Zelda and our sisters. And it was especially empty as we rarely saw Zelda or our sisters, and Kallan now seemed aloof and distant. I bemoaned my inability to contact Marna directly, to seek her succour in this time of need.

Gradually however, Kallan's natural warmth reasserted itself, and we noticed that each time he returned from a visit away from the estate his mood had improved. We were deeply relieved at this, and when I surreptitiously probed his mind after one of his visits I was taken aback to sense Marna in his thoughts. I saw clearly that he had been visiting Marna, and I was not at all surprised that the visit had ameliorated his mood to the extent it had. He loved Marna as much, if not more, than Adwin and I did. He clearly felt strong emotions for her, emotions I did not fully understand at that age, adult desires that mystified me. I did not worry unduly that my comprehension was so opaque: all I cared about was that the Kallan I knew and loved had been returned to me. And I had Marna to thank.

My brother, in the meantime, continued to put pressure on me to return to my experiments with teleporting living things.

"Come on Sammy," he would whine in his high-pitched voice, sometimes so impatient with my reticence that he would actually give me a little punch on the arm, a deep frown of displeasure showing between his dark brows. I had to suppress a desire to laugh at his annoyance, knowing this would offend him.

For a time I was wary of returning to my experiments, as my previous attempts had been met with such spectacular lack of success, but Adwin assured me that this would no longer be the case, cajoled me, pressured me over and over again. "Pease Sammy, please. I know you can do it. I have faith in you."

Eventually I capitulated, giving in to his relentless pestering, as much to stop the harassment as for any other reason. I was amused by my little brother's child-like confidence in me, but singularly unamused by my continued abject failure in mastering this skill. No matter what I tried, disaster was always the result. Eventually, disgusted with my lack of success, I abandoned the experiments. I would leave it to my mother to kill harmless creatures.

Chapter Nineteen

I had long assumed that Zelda, and especially Kallan, had regular contact with the outside world. Neither of them possessed the ability to mindspeak, to communicate directly with the brains of other people, so they must surely use one of the various technical means available. I had never had cause to use such apparatus, not knowing anyone on the outside, but knew that we had a range of them in the house. The simplest was a vidiscreen, a rectangle inserted into the wall which the speaker sat or stood in front of and spoke to the person at the other end, the talkers able to see each other as they spoke. I had seen such a device in Kallan's room and he had told me that these were a very old idea. But despite their antiquity, in the days of my childhood, many people still found them adequate, especially for simple communication.

The more modern version at that time, a 3DV (short for three dimensional viewer) created a holographic image of the person talking, and this was then transmitted to wherever the other person was located. In this way, a three dimensional image of the speaker appeared to actually be in the same room as the person spoken to. Similar looking to the older appliances, these were often no more than a panel incorporated into a wall that the speaker stood in front of, or into a ceiling which the speaker stood beneath. This apparatus not only created the holographic image, but also transmitted whatever the person spoke. The machine made a perfect image with an almost life-like density. I enquired if we had such a device in our house, but was answered in the negative. Zelda, as I was informed, felt no need of equipment which could either convey or receive life-like images of outsiders from or to our home.

Apparently, tiny portable devices known as mobies (a contraction of mobile viewers) were also available which attached to headsets. These transmitted voice and picture to similar devices, or also to the fixed appliances in people's homes. Some of these were even capable of creating and sending holographic images, though not of the same quality as the 3DVs people had in their homes. But these headset-borne mobies had the huge advantage of mobility and usability wherever a person happened to find themselves, and were, apparently, hugely popular.

Zelda had once explained to me that there had been a plan, a long time before, to develop tiny devices which would achieve the same effect as mobies, but which would be implanted directly into the cerebral cortex of an individual who wished it. There had even been experiments carried out of embedding them into babies' heads, though this had been highly contentious at the time. In the end, the experiment was short-lived and all such research was abandoned soon afterwards. As the experimented babies grew into childhood and learned to speak, it was clear that their social development was profoundly impaired. They seemed to prefer to connect to the world via their implanted communication devices, and not to show a normal inclination to connect directly with the people around them. They were socially isolated, showing no desire to talk, to play, to engage at all with others in their vicinity, only wanting to be in direct contact with the small number of others in the experiment.

I remember wondering, when Zelda first told me about this doomed experiment with the full implants, whether excessive use of telepathy could lead to the same result. Perhaps in Safya's case this was indeed what happened, and to a lesser extent even with Emaleen. But a telepathic baby is still present in the world in the way the cortex implant babies were not. The vision of a telepathic baby is not interrupted or distracted by the use of telepathy, nor any of their other senses. It seemed that the cortex implant babies suffered something close to full sensory deprivation, at least in relation to the immediate world around them. This was not the case with my sisters, and Adwin and I simply did not use telepathy enough for such ever to be a problem. And as far as I was aware, telepathy was unusual, and very few of those who could use it did so to the well-developed level that my siblings and I were able to use it to communicate.

Mindspeaking only appeared as the technology for creating multiple-parent foetuses improved, and only in a very small percentage of the population. Zelda always claimed that the Council deemed it undesirable and antisocial, to produce people who could communicate secretly, without anyone else knowing what they were saying, and that the ability to mindspeak was only ever a by-product of multi-parent babies, never a deliberate policy. When I learned this, I could not help but wonder what the world would make of four children whose ability in this field was so highly developed. Would this be yet another reason for the world at large to fear and hate us?

For those unable to mindspeak, the mobies were more than adequate, and did not carry the profound social disturbances shown by the babies with the implants. In addition, I learned that some of the experiments using implants were unsuccessful on a more physical basis: the babies' bodies did not develop normally because these tiny children were so mesmerised by their introspective and obsessive communication that they refused to move, to try to crawl or walk, to carry out a normal range of activities essential for the human body to develop as it should. Thus the experiment was rapidly abandoned and nobody had seriously suggested trying it again ever since. I wondered what had happened to the unfortunate subjects of the failed experiment, but neither Zelda nor Kallan seemed able, or willing, to tell me. All that was left of the experiments was the tiny tracking device still implanted into babies' skulls to help them in their use of portals as they grew up.

Apart from Kallan's vidiscreen on the wall, I assumed there must be another one either in Zelda's bedroom, or in her laboratory. She had mentioned on a number of occasions her conversations with Marna (and more rarely with other scientists), and from this I concluded she must have meant via vidiscreen. I presumed she also received messages from her colleagues outside by the same method, though I had never witnessed any such message being received myself.

One afternoon, a little before my tenth 'birthday', Adwin and I were in the garden with Kallan, helping him to prune bushes and weed the flower beds. Although all such work could easily have been undertaken by specialist horticultural automata, Kallan derived great pleasure from tending the garden himself, and was keen to impart the same enjoyment to us. He still had all large-scale or risky work carried out by automata, such as pruning fully-grown trees, excavating substantial quantities of soil or moving rocks, but most of the planting and subsequent care of flowering plants, bushes and vegetables Kallan did himself, with our help when he could persuade us. I was never sure if we were not more hindrance than help, as he not only had to instruct us in relation to every single thing we did, he also had to oversee us in our tasks for fear that we might damage some of his precious plant life. Yet he persisted in requesting our company in the garden, teaching us all he knew, and seemed to enjoy our presence there when he was at work, quietly telling us the names of the plants and explaining the horticultural techniques.

We all three looked up sharply from our tasks when Zelda came racing out of the house, shouting incoherently as she did so. She almost never came into the garden, so this alone piqued our curiosity, and her odd behaviour merely added to our interest. She came straight towards us, gesticulating wildly as she stormed across the lawn, bellowing all the while, the scaly patches of dry, red skin on her cheeks and forehead even more livid than the rest of her face, so flushed with anger was she.

She stopped in front of Kallan, but there was no diminishment in the volume or incoherence of her gibberings. Kallan waited a moment to see if she would calm down, but when it seemed not, he interrupted her sharply.

"I can't understand a word you're saying Zelda," he stated. "Stop shouting, take a deep breath and tell me what's happened."

For a moment it seemed that Zelda had not even heard him, so caught up was she in her rage. But after a few more moments of fulmination, she blinked a few times and fell suddenly silent. Kallan waited quietly, his neat silver eyebrows raised slightly in query.

"I...I," Zelda began. "I cannot believe it. How dare they? How dare they? Who do they think they are? The bare-faced fucking cheek! The outrage of it all!"

"Who, Zelda? Who are you talking about? And what have they done?" prodded Kallan, in an attempt to get more sense out of her.

She fell silent again, stormy fury contorting the features of her face, bushy eyebrows dancing. Adwin and I stood absolutely still, partly in the hope that she would not notice us while in such a mood, and partly out of an intense curiosity to know what had caused her such ire.

When she felt able to speak, she said in a quiet yet fierce tone,

"The Council. The fucking Council."

I knew from Zelda's use of such an expletive that she was truly incandescent with rage. I was aware from her tirades against the Council over the years just how much she despised that body, and most of its members, but I had no idea what they had done this time to evoke such a response. Neither did Kallan, but like me, he was keen to find out.

"Well," he persisted. "What have they done now?"

"I can barely believe it," Zelda began to explain, calming a little as she did so but anger still clear on her face. "But they have actually had the audacity to send me a message here, to my own private home, demanding my presence to explain my activities here at the house. Demanding! Who the fuck do they think they are? They have no authority to go round demanding anything of anyone, and especially not of me. And as if that were not bad enough, they have also demanded that when I come I am to bring all of the children."

"The children?" asked Kallan sharply, concern in his tone. "What have the children got to do with anything?"

"They want me to explain why it is I have been conducting illegal experiments in creating children from more than five progenitors, and they want to see 'the results of my experiments' as they refer to the children, so they can decide what the best course of action is."

"What do they mean 'the best course of action'?" queried Kallan in a worried tone. "And how do they know about your experiments and about the children?" he added, confusion mixed with concern on his face, tanned brow furrowed deeply.

Zelda flushed bright red again, the full force of her fury returning with a vengeance. She was so choked with rage that for a few moments she could not speak, and her renewed ire only served to augment Kallan's misgivings. When she was finally able to communicate coherently, she said in a low, ominous voice,

"That villain. That viper we allowed into our own home must have told the Council what I have been doing."

"Marna?" shouted Kallan in a distressed voice, unable to believe what he had just heard.

"What? Who?" replied Zelda, visibly puzzled by Kallan's outburst. "Of course not Marna. *She* would never do a thing like that, and anyway she's known about it since the start, so why would she only tell them now? No, I mean that poisonous intruder they brought with them last time they came. Devid."

I gasped, all of my worst fears about Devid being made real by Zelda's revelation.

"Samek knew he was untrustworthy!" my little brother blurted out.

Zelda and Kallan turned to me sharply, ignoring Adwin though he had been the one to speak.

"Then why did you not say something?" asked Zelda menacingly.

"I, I don't know," I stammered, casting an angry glance at my brother. "I had nothing to go on, just a feeling. He used to look at me with a horrible, evil expression on his face, and it got worse after he'd seen all the dead foetuses..." I stopped in mid-sentence, appalled at what I had just done: I had brought up the subject that had caused such a rift between me and Zelda before. But this time Zelda seemed unperturbed by my utterance.

"Well now we know why," she continued. "I assume he found the whole idea repugnant, making babies from so many progenitors, keeping some of the failed experiments, bringing up the successes here at my own home, treating them, treating *you* as normal, as real children. This seems to have upset him to a ridiculous degree, so he went to the Council to report me." As she spoke, she flushed again, anger rising, her facial features distorting as she contemplated Devid's betrayal, red blotches glowing more brightly.

"Do you think it's possible he came here knowing something about it?" asked Kallan. "Wanting all along to find out for himself so he could report it?"

Zelda looked surprised at Kallan's query as if such a possibility had not occurred to her, and as she seemed about to deny this, Adwin interrupted.

"I'm sure he knew something," he stated. The astonished expressions on the faces of both Zelda and Kallan told my brother he needed to furnish further explanation. He looked nervous at their intense attention. He swallowed loudly and continued. "Samek told me that right from the moment he met him he gave him dirty looks that frightened him. And he gave me those horrible looks too. And the looks just got worse after...after..." my brother stammered. I decided to save him.

"They got worse the longer he was here," I said, finishing my brother's sentence, but avoiding further reference to the ghastly hall of horrors. "But the horrible looks were there from the start," I continued, as my brother nodded in agreement. "And if he hadn't known anything before he got here, why would he have looked at me like that?"

Neither Kallan nor Zelda questioned Devid's hostility towards me from the outset. My comments made sense. "Yes," said Kallan. "I remember that at that first meeting there was a curious tension. Devid had an odd attitude."

"But how did he know?" My uncle continued, to no-one in particular. "Someone must have said something."

"That is not that surprising," replied Zelda. "A few people apart from Marna and Yenifa knew what my interests were and have known for a long time. I imagine even the Council had some idea. I was thrown off group projects for those very ideas, so they were not unknown. But still, it is odd that he seemed to arrive with such a biased view in the first place. I hate to say it, but I think either Marna of Yenifa must have said something."

A long silence followed, eventually broken by Adwin.

"Marna wouldn't have said anything. She's our friend. She'd never do anything to hurt us," he whined in a distressed tone.

"I agree with you child," replied Zelda unexpectedly. "Kallan and I have known her all our lives, and she is the most reliable, the most honourable person you could hope to meet. In addition to which, as I said before, she has known about my work, about you children, for so many years that it would make no sense for her to suddenly say more than she knows is safe to someone she does not know. It must have been Yenifa," she added with finality.

None of us could disagree with Zelda's comments, but the situation made little sense. Why would Yenifa, usually so taciturn and unforthcoming in every way, why would she have told Devid about Zelda's work, and about us children? She might have hinted at something, enough to pique Devid's interest, but what possible reason could she have had to impart more information than this? Yet Devid's behaviour indicated with great clarity that he was well abreast of the activities in our home, and its inhabitants *before* he came to visit.

I struggled to think of answers to these queries, but without success. Finally Kallan intruded by saying,

"I'll ask Marna. She'll probably know. She knows Yenifa well, has known her for years. If anyone can tell us, it'll be Marna."

Zelda nodded at him, indicating that this was our best option, our most likely method of ferreting out why Yenifa would have told Devid so much even before he was given permission to visit.

Kallan strode straight off towards the house, intent on communicating immediately with Marna. Zelda followed him, leaving me and Adwin alone in the garden. We looked around, decided to abandon our ineffectual plant-tending activities, and made our own way back to the house. I for one wanted to be as close to Kallan as I could, so I would know as soon as possible if he had discovered the real reason for Yenifa's unexpected behaviour.

Chapter Twenty

Kallan was absent for several days, during which time Adwin and I could barely sit still or focus on anything. We were so impatient to hear what had really happened, why Yenifa had told Devid about Zelda's work, and why she and Marna had asked to bring Devid to our home in the first place.

Zelda we saw very little. As usual, she disappeared off to her work place, emerging rarely, and then only to eat or sleep. But on the few occasions we encountered her in passing, she was oddly pleasant, actually smiling and greeting us. She seemed to feel that we were all involved in something together, sharing an anxious desire to uncover the truth. And in fact, we had been forced together by the Council's demand. I managed to blurt out a query to Zelda as she walked past us one day as to what she intended to do about the Council's edict, and she just laughed, saying,

"I plan to ignore it. All my life I have ignored every other communication I've ever received from that contemptible lot."

Our sisters were not at home, though I decided to break one of my own rules and mindspeak directly to them, to tell them what had happened. When I first attempted to do so, as usual, they blocked me, but I was able to indicate by the insistent and fretful tone of my attempted intrusion that what I had to say was important, though I had to resort to causing them some real discomfort to breach their barrier. Shortly after throwing such a message out to them, Emaleen contacted me directly.

~What do you want?~ she snapped, irritation apparent in her tone even mindspeaking at a great distance. *~It had better be good or there'll be trouble.~*

I ignored her snappish mood and briefly explained all that had occurred, giving details as fully as I could. Since there was no new information, and I had no idea when such would be available, Emaleen said that they would remain where they were for another day or two, returning as originally planned. Emaleen, all annoyance now evaporated in her desire to find out the truth, made me promise that I would contact her the moment Kallan returned.

Adwin and I were restless, but I decided there was one thing that might distract me from my impatience: learning as much as I could about the Council. I had heard the basics about this important, official body, but as I had had no dealings with it, and its jurisdiction did not seem to reach into my home, I had never paid it much regard. In addition, as a child, I had little forbearance for the details of such a distant body. I felt that now was the time to remedy my past indifference. Adwin, not yet seven years old, still showed little inclination to follow me in my studies. But what I learned amazed me.

The Council, based in our biggest city of Beyra, was the administrative body of our world, the closest we had to a governing organization. The members did not all live in Beyra, but regularly travelled there to conduct Council business. In that time of absolute equality between all citizens, there were no actual rulers as such. But I knew from Zelda's fulminations against the Council that they believed themselves to be 'more equal than everyone else' (as she always put it, apparently lifting this idea from some famous book from the old world). In other words, that the much vaunted equality was nebulous, more of an idea than a reality. But even those who believed in the truth of it knew that a world with a population of around 100 million people needed some form of administrative governance. Hence the existence of the Council, whose origins dated right back to the early days after the Chaos, as the tiny remnant surviving populations began to emerge from their hiding places, and started to make contact with each other.

Even then, those frightened, desperate people were aware of the need for a small, centralised group of people to guide humanity as it began its long and painful climb to a point where its survival seemed no longer to hang in the balance. The few thousand survivors from the teeming billions who had died in the Chaos had an urgent need of leadership, and a small group of them was chosen to take responsibility for the others, to direct and inspire, taking the burden of survival onto their shoulders. On the few occasions Zelda had delved into the history of the Council with me and my siblings, she had talked of these first leaders in glowing terms, spelling out what a huge responsibility they accepted: nothing less than the continuance of our species. But she had nothing but contempt for what the Council later became. In her opinion, this body now saw itself as a ruling body, an elite group, whose orders and edicts had to be followed, and not what it should be, what it had been at the beginning - a team of leaders chosen for their skills, abilities and personalities to lead humanity out of the darkness of the Chaos towards the light of the future.

I knew that the Council was made up of twelve people, but I had little idea of who they were. Apparently, they were chosen every five years by a process lasting many months, a process that seemed complicated and opaque, involving discussions between a huge range of different interest groups (social, scientific, artistic, professional, geographical, and so on) as well as interminable discussions (according to some of the information I found) in the narrowcast and other media. Slowly, through a process of elimination, the large number of people recommended at the start of the process was whittled down and eventually only twelve were left. These twelve people made up the Council for the next five years. It seemed that on occasion, the same people were re-chosen, so a few Council members at any time have been members for more than five years, and in the Council of that time, for substantially more.

Thoroughly confused by the whole selection process, I became even more so on discovering that the Council can be dissolved, again by an impenetrable process of disapproval from a wide range of interest groups. On rare occasions individual Council members have been removed, either by the rest of the Council, or by yet another muddy and unclear process of scant interest to a child. If any member was removed, or the Council was dissolved, the vacancy would be filled as quickly as possible, as twelve seemed to be considered the minimum number required to administer our world.

Although the Council had responsibility for overseeing every activity, in practice different members took on different duties, authority having been delegated to them to do so by the full Council. While this was essential for decisions to be made, it gave individual Council members huge influence and sometimes real power to make decisions, often with little or no scrutiny, leaving the rest of the Council and the world at large unaware of what had been decided, or on what basis such decisions had been made. As I read about this aspect of the Council's functioning, I remembered this was one of Zelda's principle bugbears: that not only did the Council as a whole see itself as unaccountable, but each individual member did not consider him- or herself answerable to anyone, not even, on a day to day basis, to the Council itself.

There was a Speaker of the Council, nominally the head of the organisation. As with the Council itself, this was in theory a purely administrative role, but in practice carried substantial weight and control. I knew the name of the present Speaker - Rannald - as this was the name which came up most persistently in Zelda's rants against the Council. Rannald was the object of a good deal of Zelda's bile, Zelda considering him to be behind much of the Council's endless hostility towards her. She always described him as pompous, arrogant, full of himself. Rannald was one of the two members who had been on the Council for a long time, this being his fourth successive five year period, and his second as Speaker.

One of the roles the Council fulfilled was to issue what were called Rulings which people were supposed to follow, though I had no idea how these were enforced, or even whether they could be. In truth they were more like guidelines for appropriate behaviour than anything more binding. We had no actual laws in our world, and there would be no point in having laws in any case, as we possessed no infrastructure to enforce them even if such existed: no police or army, no courts, no judges, no prisons, no official sanctions at all for misbehaviour of any type. I had been taught about nation states of the old world, how they possessed complicated structures for the passing of laws, and the enforcement of these. Even the most free and liberal of the old world states had intricate infrastructures for the governing of their people. In our world, we had no such formal frameworks.

As I puzzled over the knotty problem of how it was in our world that people's behaviour was controlled, I remembered discussions I had had with Kallan on this topic. He explained to us that behaviour was regulated by intense, persistent social pressure. This seemed to work much more effectively than might be imagined due to the fact that people were all created using strict scientific criteria, and so only people likely to behave were produced, and especially those who were most likely to be law-abiding and highly susceptible to social pressure. Science had been used to dramatically speed up the process of evolution, to produce the most law-abiding and well-behaved people with the greatest sense of social conscience. A keen sense of shame seemed also to be a major factor in effective social control. Yet the processes used were clearly not without error. We remembered Kallan laughing as he told us that occasionally somebody like Zelda was thrown up, and this made the Council's job almost impossible when it came to controlling people like her, people who simply would not follow the Rulings and would do what suited them. The Council at that time (and the world at large) had no experience in dealing with people like Zelda, no precedents to work from. As such, they had always struggled to know what to do about oddballs like our rebellious mother.

I read the names of all the Council members, but only a few of them stood out - those that had figured prominently in Zelda's diatribes. Apart from Rannald, the other name for whom Zelda reserved her most strident invective was Helna, who had been on the Council almost as long as Rannald, and usually described by Zelda in terms such as "that odious little dwarf", or "that obnoxious little midget". Most of the other names were not familiar to me, with the exception of Lenora whom we had heard Zelda mention in relatively positive terms. It seems that this "tall and impressive woman" (her height perhaps being the reason my mother described her as impressive) was not hostile to Zelda in the same way as some of the others. Of the remaining names, I did not know what they thought of Zelda or her research.

Thoroughly confused by the arcane workings of the Council and of its appointment, at least I now had a clearer idea of a few of the main players. And having researched and learned all I could about this body, I had little else to do but wait for Kallan's return.

I did not have to wait long, though at my young age, not quite ten years old, those few days felt interminable. I played outdoors with Adwin, wandered in the forest, read my favourite stories, yet nothing really captured my attention. Most of the time I speculated wildly with my brother on the possible reasons for Yenifa's behaviour, all of which speculation was probably specious, given our woeful lack of acquaintance with people and with the outside world.

As we sat in the garden one day spinning our ridiculous tales of Yenifa's betrayal, I sensed a tiny burst of energy, indicating that the portal had been activated. This could only mean one thing: Kallan had returned. Adwin saw me look up sharply, guessing what this had to mean. We leapt off the grass and raced back to the house. I threw a hasty message to Emaleen as I had promised to do, informing her of Kallan's return.

By the time we arrived at the door leading to the laboratory through which I knew Kallan would soon pass, Emaleen and Safya were already there. They were dressed in outdoor clothing, large rucksacks on their backs, sturdy boots covered in mud on their feet. Despite my agitation, the thought crossed my mind that Kallan would be cross to see the muddy footprints my sisters were leaving on the polished wooden floor.

We nodded to each other, not needing to speak. Emaleen and Safya took off their bags, dropping them heavily to the ground. As they did so they seemed to notice their boots, and removed them. Safya, with a guilty expression, swiftly kicked them out of sight under a nearby table as quickly as she could. We stood, all fidgeting with impatience, for what seemed an age. I began to fear that Kallan would not come into the house, but would instead remain with Zelda in the laboratory, explaining only to her what he had learned on his trip outside.

But I had no need to fear, and after what was in reality a short wait, I sensed Kallan and Zelda approaching the door from the other side. I waved my hand over the panel causing the door to slide open. Kallan and Zelda looked mildly surprised that the door seemed to open of its own accord, but immediately spotted the four of us on the other side of the door, Adwin and I jigging up and down restlessly.

"Follow me," Kallan commanded as he swept past us, Zelda stumbling along in pursuit. I breathed a huge sigh of relief as I had feared our uncle may not include us in the initial revelations of what he had learned. It was clear he felt that we needed to hear what he had to say as much as Zelda. It was also clear that he had not yet told Zelda anything. Despite my anxiety, I almost laughed to see my mother trotting along behind Kallan, struggling to match his long strides, a look of patent impatient eagerness on her face.

As the smallest member of the family, little Adwin had to run to keep up as we were dragged along in Kallan's wake. Only when we reached the living room did Kallan slow down. He plopped himself down in one of the armchairs, indicating that we should all sit down, and when we had done so, he began.

"You won't believe it," he said. "The things I've found out! Two things actually. I'll start with the first as it's almost funny. The second is not funny, not funny at all."

We all sat forward, quivering with suspense.

"I'll start by telling you all that Marna is ashamed of having asked to bring Devid along. She can't believe that she didn't see what Devid was like, and is so appalled that she allowed such a creature to come into our home. She's mortified and thinks she will no longer be welcome here. I assured her that she would *always* be welcome here," and at this comment he looked fixedly at Zelda. Zelda looked away, embarrassed that she had forbidden Marna from visiting for so long, yet still chafing at what had happened on her last visit.

"Please uncle, please please please just tell us what you found out!" begged Adwin in a whining voice, squirming in his seat. He was not interested in whether Marna felt guilty about Devid or not. Like the rest of us, he was desperate to learn what had really happened. Kallan turned and spoke directly to him.

"Calm down Addy, I'm getting to it. I just wanted you all to know how badly Marna is feeling. Anyway, she told me that it was Yenifa who wanted Devid to be allowed to visit, and when Marna, who'd never met Devid, told her that she wasn't sure if she should ask, apparently Yenifa implored her to make the request of Zelda. Marna didn't understand Yenifa's insistence, but Yenifa didn't let up. Marna finally got fed up with her endless pestering, and asked Zelda if Devid could visit. Marna herself only met Devid for the first time shortly before his first visit, and only then because she had insisted on it. And you all know what happened when Devid came here." We all nodded slightly to show we understood what he meant. Kallan continued.

"But when I pushed Marna on why Yenifa was so insistent, she didn't want to tell me at first. Actually, she claimed she didn't know, but I knew she wasn't being truthful so I made her tell me, told her that she owed it to us to be honest, given the problems that Devid's visit has caused us. Eventually she confessed. She herself had to force the information from Yenifa, and had to threaten to report *her* to the Council for her visits here if she didn't tell Marna everything. A rather risky threat, since Marna would be implicated too."

Astonishingly, Kallan stopped at this point and chuckled, clearly finding what he was about to tell us amusing. I clenched my fists with impatience as I waited for him to continue. Emaleen could not hold her tongue.

"Uncle! Just get on with it!" she snapped. Kallan ignored her intrusion.

"Apparently," he went on, still smiling broadly, "Devid has been wooing Yenifa for some time, and, according to Marna, simply to get to visit here."

Zelda sat back in surprise. A little shy of ten years old, I did not understand what Kallan's comments meant, and glancing at Adwin, I knew he was no wiser than me. My sisters did not appear so perplexed, as if Kallan's comments made more sense to them. I wondered if they really understood, or simply wished to appear as if they did, wanting to seem more worldly with all of their fifteen years than their younger siblings.

Kallan sensed the confusion in me and my brother and explained. "Devid is not a bad looking young man. Quite attractive really. Or he would be if he didn't look so shifty. And Yenifa is, let's just say she's plain and leave it at that." At this, he and Zelda chuckled in unison.

"Apparently Yenifa met Devid a little while ago," continued Kallan. "When they were both working on some project related to eradicating the final few congenital diseases that still linger on despite our techniques of foetal production. She's normally such a stiff, cold person, seemingly uninterested in relationships or sex, but she confessed to Marna later that she felt an instant attraction to Devid. And even more astonishingly, he showed signs of reciprocating her feelings, and made sure he spent as much time with her as he could, flirting with her, flattering her, and so on. As an unattractive middle-aged woman with little experience of men - if any! - she was bowled over by his attentions."

"You surely don't mean they...?" asked Zelda elliptically, a tone of faint disgust in her voice.

"No, no, no!" squawked Kallan, guffawing at the very idea. "That's the whole point. He didn't have *any* interest in her, and was just using her. He must have found out that she knew Marna, and that Marna was a good friend of yours Zelda, and he manipulated her to get closer to you. One evening he even managed to get that dessicated, uptight old trout drunk, and she was so unused to the effects of alcohol and so overwhelmed by the attentions of a good-looking man, that she seems to have told him all about her visits here, and all about your work Zelda."

Zelda looked outraged, colour flooding into her face. She was about to erupt, but Kallan held his hand up to stop her.

"Let me finish, Zelda," he said in a commanding voice. She immediately subsided and Kallan continued. "Devid presumably couldn't believe his luck. He'd got the information he'd wanted, and to reiterate what I said earlier, no, nothing happened between them. He hadn't even had to dip a finger into that dried up old prune to get what he wanted!" And for some reason I could not fathom, he went off into gales of hearty laughter at his final comment, a comment I did not even understand.

"And after that," he continued when his chortles had subsided enough for him to speak, "He pressured her to get permission to visit, and she, the poor misguided fool, pestered Marna until she gave in."

At this he stopped to catch his breath. After a few moments, Zelda looked at him sharply, and said,

"That is funny, or it would be if it had not led to her bringing that creature here. But you said you found out two things, and the second one was not funny. So what is it?"

A dark, angry look crossed Kallan's normally benign face. He seemed unable to express his thoughts immediately, taking his time to chose his words. I sensed he was also anxious about Zelda's possible reaction to what he had to tell us, and this only caused my impatience to grow. I emitted a silent suggestion that he begin at once, ensuring it was subtle enough that he was not consciously aware of it. Safya discerned instantly what I was doing, and quietly sent me a message of support, accompanied with a tiny smile in my direction. And my gentle mental pressure seemed to work.

"I hate to even begin to have to tell you all what I'm about to tell you," he began, somewhat verbosely. "But Devid didn't just come here for himself, just to find out more about your work Zelda or out of personal interest or distaste." He paused briefly, giving his next comment a dramatic flourish that he seemed unaware of.

"Devid is Rannald's nephew," he stated.

Zelda gasped and sat back in her chair, mouth opening and closing like a fish on a river bank, stunned by the revelation and incapable of a coherent response. I was bewildered, and sensed that my siblings were too. I had heard the word nephew before, but only in the context of my studies of the old world, or occasionally used by Kallan. Before I could formulate a sensible question, Emaleen leapt in.

"What do you mean Kallan, his nephew? What sort of nephew? You mean like you sometimes call Addy and Sammy your nephews?" she asked in a tone of impatient incomprehension.

Kallan turned to her, and then to all of us, noting our flummoxed expressions. Zelda was still sitting rigidly in her chair, mouth still flapping open, as yet unable to respond. Kallan decided to fill the gap while Zelda collected herself, to explain to us what a nephew was to most people.

"No Emmy, not the way I use the word," my uncle began, before continuing. "You know that children, other children that is, are raised in the Institutes?" he began. We all nodded in unison, fully aware of this fact. "Well," he continued, "that's only up to the age of fourteen. After passing their fourteenth birthday, every child is sent to live for the next four years in an adult home, to complete their education and to learn how to become normal grown-ups, how to cope with life in the outside world on their own."

I was amazed. I had never heard of such a thing, and had probably just assumed that a child left the Institute on reaching full adulthood to take up their place in the world. But it made sense - otherwise how could such sheltered young people make the transition from the protection of the Institute to the responsibilities and freedoms of the outside world without guidance?

"But who do they go to live with?" Adwin piped up. I nodded as this was a good question.

"Oh that's decided years and years before," replied Kallan. "Every child is allocated an adult mentor from a very early age, usually around the age of about five. That adult has regular contact with the child, which they call their nephew or niece, visiting them often at the Institute, getting to know them, being involved in their education and development and so on. So by the time the child takes the huge step of leaving the Institute, he or she already has a long-standing relationship with their uncle or aunt, as the adult is called."

"What if they don't get on, or don't like each other uncle?" asked Safya quietly.

Kallan turned to her and replied, "They'd know long before they live together whether there was a problem, Saffy, and if they don't get on while the child is still in the Institute, another adult is chosen instead. Some children go through a few before they find one they feel comfortable with, and vice versa. Nobody's going to force two people to continue such an important relationship against their will."

"Have you ever been an uncle?" asked Adwin. "I mean an uncle like that, not an uncle like our uncle," he clarified, though not very clearly.

Kallan smiled at him fondly. "No," he replied. "Not everyone is chosen as there are far more adults than children, and the allocation is random. Some adults get to do it more than once in their lives. But everyone values it highly. It's an essential part of the upbringing of the next generation, to properly socialize the youngsters."

"So *we* won't be properly socialized then?" queried Emaleen suspiciously.

"You have me and Zelda, and each other," Kallan replied gently. "And have actually lived a life quite unlike other children. You've had a home since you were born, a home with brothers and sisters, Zelda and me. You've been socialized since your very first days, so don't worry about that."

"Has Zelda ever been an aunt?" persisted Adwin, wanting to know everything.

"No," replied Kallan with a slight smile in Zelda's direction. "I suspect the Council ensured that that never happened. They wouldn't think her a suitable person to be responsible for the upbringing of children."

Given our domestic situation, I was disconcerted by Kallan's last comment, but before I could formulate an appropriate question, Zelda regained her composure.

"So Devid is Rannald's nephew?" she asked Kallan, though only for emphasis, as she had clearly heard him the first time.

"Yes, Zelda, as I said," confirmed Kallan. "Apparently he and Rannald were so happy with the arrangement, that Devid lived with him until only last year." Kallan turned to us to offer further explanation of this last statement.

"A child has to stay with his or her uncle or aunt for at least four years, but there's no obligation to move out after the four years. Some people want to become fully independent at the age of eighteen, and that's fine, but many people stay with their aunt or uncle for longer than this, sometimes much longer. I've even heard of people living together for the rest of their lives."

"Yes thank you, that is all very interesting for them," interrupted Zelda testily. "But the important point is that Devid is even worse, even more dangerous to us than I thought. If he is close to that villain Rannald, do you think Rannald is behind Devid coming here?"

"If you had let me finish what I was telling you," replied Kallan turning to Zelda, his own tone showing mild irritation, "I would have told you that. According to Marna, who had to force it out of Yenifa, it was Rannald who arranged for Devid to meet Yenifa in the first place, and Rannald who had instructed his nephew very clearly as to how to inveigle his way into Yenifa's affections, with the aim all along of worming his way to an invitation here."

At that, Kallan stopped, feeling he had explained well enough. I was deeply disconcerted by what I had heard, though not fully understanding all the ramifications. I knew that what had happened was bad, very bad, and the fact that Rannald was behind it all rendered it something else: dangerous and threatening to our family and our home.

I looked at Zelda, and her expression was difficult to read. She seemed unable to decide if she was enraged, or outraged, or alarmed by what Kallan had imparted, or perhaps all three at the same time. Expressions flowed across her face in waves as she rubbed the sides of her head with her fingers, pushing unruly strands of hair back into their otherwise tight arrangement, a clear sign in her of distress. Kallan waited quietly to see how she would respond. My siblings and I also waited, but without Kallan's patience. We had no idea what Zelda would say, or whether she would erupt in rage.

After what seemed an age, she sighed deeply. "What is done is done," she stated in a resigned tone, the anger and outrage seeming to have evaporated. "And I should not really be surprised. Rannald and his vile cronies on the Council have been out to get me for years, but have never had enough ammunition. Now they will have plenty."

She stopped talking, and after a short pause Kallan asked in a quiet voice, "So what will you do? What will *we* do?"

Zelda looked at him, a surprisingly gentle expression on her face.

"We will do nothing for the moment. And when they start to pester, well, I think I shall eventually reply, but only after keeping them waiting as long as I can." She stopped and chuckled, surprising us all. "When I get round to it, I shall send them a message telling them I have no intention of responding to a command from them and that they have no right to command any citizen, but if they ask politely, then perhaps, only perhaps, we might consider coming to meet them."

Kallan laughed gently too, imagining the Council's outrage at Zelda's reply. Before he could say anything by way of reply, Zelda turned to me.

"How is your teleporting going?" she asked suddenly. I was taken aback by the abrupt change of topic. After a pause, I replied quietly. "Slowly."

"But can you teleport yourself yet, or other people?" my mother queried irritably.

"No," I said quietly after the briefest of hesitation. "Though I think I probably could. I just haven't tried yet, haven't had the courage to try." I chose not to share with my mother that I kept failing at moving other living things, plants and animals, and had given up trying in disgust at my lack of success. I had, once or twice, tried to move myself and the process seemed completely different from moving another object. But each time, at the last moment, just as began to feel a slight pull on my body, I lost the courage to continue, abandoning the attempt. I did not understand why it felt so unlike trying to move other living things, but knew that it was of a different nature. Perhaps simply being the object in which the brain, the agent of motion of that very object was located, fundamentally altered the process?

"Hmm," replied Zelda to my comments, looking pensive. "Well get on with it. When, or should I say if, we go to visit the Council, we need to make a splash, a dramatic entrance. I want you to take all of us there, teleport all of us there at the same time, so we just appear out of nowhere in front of them. There are a few other things I shall need you to do at the meeting, and you lot will need to help Samek," he added, looking directly at Adwin and my sisters.

"*We* won't be going!" shrieked Safya in an unusually loud voice, horrified at the prospect.

"Yes you will!" barked Zelda. "Yes you bloody well will! The Council need to see we are united. And not only that, but Samek will not be able to do what I want him to do on his own. It will take all four of you, with your combined abilities, to teach them a lesson they will never forget, and get them off our backs."

Her tone made it clear that Safya had no choice but to do what Zelda bade, and my sister was wise enough not to try and argue the point, though her look of distress did not abate.

"Well that is that then," Zelda said suddenly. "We have a plan. Samek, get on with learning how to teleport yourself and the rest of us. I shall ignore the Council for now, and only reply when I am sure you can port us easily. And in the meantime I shall be working with all four of you children on my plan for showing the Council they cannot push us around. So no disappearing off into the wilds for a while ladies," she added, looking meaningfully at Emaleen and Safya, being rewarded by a slight scowl from Emaleen.

At that she turned and left the room. I was filled with pride that she saw me as pivotal in her plan for the Council, but at the same time awash with worry that I would disappoint her, either by not learning to teleport people as quickly as she would like, or by failing in the actual plan when in front of the Council. Realising there was not a moment to waste, I bounded out of the room, followed closely by Adwin, to begin thinking about how best to practise teleporting myself and other people. How did one learn such a thing except by doing it? Yet what a huge leap into the unknown, what a terrible risk for what might happen in the event of failure.

Chapter Twenty-One

I dithered and procrastinated, and could not bring myself to simply try to transport myself. It was such a huge step to take that each time I brought myself close to making the attempt, I could not bring myself to do it. There were no small steps that could be taken by way of build-up to the actual event, nothing that could be practised: it was all or nothing. And so far, I had opted for nothing every time, at least beyond the first few moments of setting the process in motion. I had tried and tried to teleport living things, plants and animals, so far with no success. I had, some time before, abandoned my experiments, so disgusted was I with my endless failures. And the few occasions on which I had begun the process of porting myself I panicked and stopped the process. As I had already discerned, it felt utterly different when it was *my* brain beginning the process of moving *my* body, rather than moving a different object. I had no idea why this was the case, but just knew that it was so. The unity of mind within a body somehow profoundly affected the nature of teleporting though for some reason I could not fathom.

Adwin was always with me as I tried to work up the courage to take the leap, quietly encouraging me with his presence, but for once, not attempting to push me or badger me in any way, even on the rare occasion when I began to port myself but curtailed the action as soon as I felt myself being pulled out of the place I was in. My brother was acutely aware of my concerns, and fully understood the reasons for them. He shared my disquiet. After all, if I failed, he could lose his brother and closest companion. I sensed ambivalence in him, mirrored by my own. Yet we both knew that one day I would simply have to hurl myself into the unknown. In theory, I had no doubt that I could port myself by imagining myself in the place I wished to end up. There was no rational reason why I should fail. And yet, and yet...the implications in the event of failure were almost too awful to contemplate.

One day, a few days after Zelda's command to me to get on and learn to teleport people, Adwin and I were surprised when she appeared at the door of our study. She stopped, looked at me, and asked bluntly,

"Can you do it yet?"

I hesitated, then answered quietly, "No. Or, maybe. I don't know."

"It is a simple yes or a no answer, boy," she snapped. "What you mean is you have not yet tried."

I nodded slightly, indicating that she was right.

"Why?" she asked in an oddly distressed voice. "I need you to be able to do this, and soon."

"I...I...I'm frightened," I stammered.

She was taken aback by my reply, and replied, "Frightened? Of what?"

I thought her question obtuse, but did not dare say so. Instead I answered simply, "Of failure."

"Oh!" was her reply. "But what is there to fear? After all, if you fail, you will not know anything about it!" she said with a slightly unpleasant chuckle.

"That might not be true," stated Adwin in his high boy's voice, coming to my defence. Zelda turned to stare at him, as if noticing him for the first time. Adwin bravely glared back at her, not dropping his gaze, and replied,

"He might half succeed, and reappear deformed, or inside out, or something else horrible like that, but still be conscious and alive, still knowing what's happened."

Zelda and I both stared at Adwin, our mouths open. It seems that neither of us had imagined such a possibility, and I for one did not much appreciate Adwin's flight of imagination.

"Well that will help your brother work up the courage to port himself!" Zelda snapped at Adwin in a sarcastic tone. "If you cannot offer anything more useful than that, you had best leave us alone."

"No!" I said loudly. "He stays. I need him here, for moral support."

Zelda laughed at my comment, clearly finding such an idea risible, but then shrugged.

"Have it your own way, but you young man," she said jabbing her finger at me. "You are porting yourself now. No more delays. No more putting it off."

I began to argue, but she turned such a look of venom on me that I decided that the risks of teleporting might be a lesser evil than incurring her wrath. In truth, I knew she was right, and that there was no reason to put it off any longer. I took a few deep breaths, calming myself for the moment when I would transport myself for the first, and I hoped not the last, time. I nodded once at Adwin, who smiled nervously at me, a look of such open faith in me on his face that I faltered in my resolve. Zelda sensed my hesitation and seemed on the verge of bearing down on Adwin, with what intent I could not fathom. Before she had the chance to move, I set the porting process in motion, holding my breath with sheer terror as I did so.

The actual event was a huge anti-climax. All I felt was a slight energy surge, and then as if someone was pulling me gently from the side. The next thing I knew I was looking at Zelda and Adwin again, but from the other side of the room. I blinked several times, barely comprehending my success. The process had been so swift and smooth that for a few moments I was not even sure I had been successful. I only knew for sure when Adwin leapt up and down, whooping with delight and clapping his little hands, his dark curls bouncing. Even Zelda was swaying from one foot to the other, knocking her hands against the sides of her head, a broad smile spread across her face. They both rushed up to me, Adwin enveloping me in a huge hug, and Zelda patting me on the shoulder, almost shyly.

Adwin was so overcome with relief that he was incapable of speech, just grasping me in a bear hug far stronger than I would have thought him capable of at his tender age of six. Zelda was muttering words like "Marvellous, fantastic, superb", and neither she nor I knew to whom she was talking. After a few moments, Zelda suddenly said,

"Do it again boy, before you lose your pluck." I realised that she was right. It was vital to transport myself a few times immediately, to consolidate my confidence that I could do so on demand. I extricated myself from Adwin's embrace, stepped back a pace, and jumped again. This time I appeared behind them, and laughed to see their backs as they remained staring at the spot I had just disappeared from.

As they spun round to face me, I flashed them a smile, and ported again. This time I took myself outside, and waved at them from the garden on the other side of the window. I jumped again and again, around the garden, in and out of the house, until eventually I returned to the study where I had begun the great adventure.

"Now take one of us," demanded Zelda. I looked at her with astonishment. Had I not achieved enough for one day? As if hearing my silent question, she continued,

"You cannot stop now. You have to prove to yourself you can move other people, more than one person at the same time."

Adwin rushed up to me. "Take me! Take me!" he pleaded. "It must be so much fun to jump around like that!" I smiled at him.

And his confidence in me filled my heart, so I grabbed his hand and ported us both, first to the other side of the room, and then, as before, outside, back inside, around the garden. The only time I failed was when I let go of Adwin's hand and ported myself without physical contact between us. As I had guessed, he remained exactly where he was, and only I moved through space. I did not dare try to bring him to where I had landed, given my many earlier failures with other living objects. I was puzzled, though soon realised that, for whatever reason, I was only able to take a person with me if I was actually touching them. This obviously meant that I would be unable to bring someone from another place to where I was - the only option being for me to travel to them, grab them, and drag them back myself.

I quickly resumed my rapid leaps, once I had grasped my brother's hand again. Zelda could not keep up with the speed and agility of my teleporting, but I heard her shouting at me from the open window of the study,

"Come back. Take me too. I need to see you can move three people." So I transported Adwin and myself back to the study, and before Zelda could react, I grasped her hand in my free hand, and ported all three of us. Again, I moved us all over the house and the garden, and even further afield, as far as the forest. Each time, no sooner had we popped up in one location, almost before we would catch our breath, I took us off somewhere else.

Eventually, I stopped, feeling suddenly tired, and noticing the expressions of disorientation mingled with exhilaration on my companions' faces. I had been somewhat overzealous, elated by the joy of success, buoyed by Adwin's excitement and Zelda's triumph, and knew now that such an activity was energy-dense, taking a toll on my resources. I hoped that with practice I could learn to teleport more efficiently, using less energy. But for the moment, I knew I needed to stop, lest I lose concentration and disaster ensue.

"Well done, my boy, well done", said Zelda, in a tone of warmth and pride such as I had never heard from her before. It felt so peculiar to receive such approbation from her that I was immediately bashful, blushing and looking shyly down at my feet. The next instant I was overwhelmed with confusion when she actually turned to me and embraced me, pulling me close to her in a tight hug for the first time in my entire life. My jailer had become my mother. Her emotions were powerful, flowing out of her and wrapping me in an embrace almost as strong as that of her arms. I was overcome, having no precedent for dealing with such feelings coming from Zelda. Though I could not see Adwin as Zelda pulled my face into her shoulder, I sensed that he was as dumbfounded as I was at Zelda's behaviour. Zelda too seemed barely able to cope with such strong emotions, and suddenly released me, turned away and shuffled off towards the door, but still muttering as she went,

"Excellent, superb, marvellous."

I was left standing like an idiot in the middle of the room, unable to move. Gradually my senses returned to a state something more like normal. I felt a wide grin on my face, and, turning to look at my brother, saw the same expression on his face. We could not wipe the beaming grins from our faces, stretched so wide that our cheeks ached.

We were still standing grinning inanely at each other some time later when Kallan put his head round the door. He looked at us curiously, wondering what we were doing, standing immobile in the middle of the room, staring at each other with huge grins plastered across our faces. I sensed that he considered asking, but then thought better of it, so simply shrugged, told us to get ready for supper, and left the room.

Even after Kallan's interruption, I found it difficult to move, which was ironic since I had done nothing but leap around the estate that afternoon. But I understood the enormity of what I had done. From this moment onwards, I could take myself, and Adwin if he wanted to come, and we could travel anywhere. We could visit the places our sisters loved to visit, and unlike them, we were not limited by having to be anchored to a home portal. We could literally teleport anywhere, and from there to anywhere else, and always return home in the blink of an eye. The prospect of being able to visit other people's homes, travelling to towns and cities was daunting and thrilling in equal measure.

We finally roused ourselves from our torpor, and as we walked slowly to the dining room, our minds were so filled with these possibilities, that our thoughts were barely coherent. We shared the jumbled ideas and images surging through our minds, partook of the shared joy of anticipation, however rambling and disjointed this was. This was a day I would never forget.

Chapter Twenty-Two

A few days after my momentous success at porting myself and Zelda, I wondered what was happening with our summons by the Council. I asked Kallan, and he said that he had no new information, that we would have to wait for Zelda to update us.

While I waited, I took the opportunity to practise my new skills, taking Adwin on a number of trips around the compound, and especially into the forest. At first I lacked the courage to transport us outside the boundaries of the estate, but one day, as we were preparing to return from the forest, I smiled conspiratorially at Adwin, and before he could react, I grabbed his little hand and ported us beyond the fence.

"I love it!" he shrieked with pleasure as I transported us through space. "It's great, this flitting around!" And I realised that he had given my new ability to teleport people without a portal the perfect name: flitting. It was so unlike using a portal, that it needed its own special word.

I had learned how to ensure a flit would not cause us to emerge inside a tree, or a boulder, using the same basic technique as did the portals. If I attempted to do this in error, the result would be to appear in a space as close to the original plan as possible. It would be disastrous to emerge inside another solid body, two sets of molecules endeavouring to occupy the same crowded atomic place. What seems to our human senses to be empty space is of course no such thing, yet to appear in what looks like a safe place is secure enough, the molecules of the air being sufficiently widely-spaced to allow our relatively solid mass to be reconstructed without incident.

My brother and I stood just outside the invisible boundary to our enclosed world, staring back at it. This was not of course the first time we had travelled outside our confines, but it had been so easy this time, and I felt no sense of guilt, of having done anything wrong. Zelda had pressured me into learning how to port myself and others, so she could hardly criticise me if I used my power to escape the velvet prison we inhabited.

There seemed little point in moving around the area just outside the estate: we knew from our last escape that it offered nothing that we could not find within its boundaries. Yet I lacked the courage to take us further afield, having absolutely no experience whatsoever of the wider world outside. I knew in theory where other people lived, the location of towns and cities, and even of our nearest neighbours' homes, a substantial distance from our estate. My imagination had been fired by the stories told to us of the outside world by Marna and Kallan, and occasionally by Yenifa and Zelda, yet I was fully aware that none of this prepared me in any way for the realities of the world at large. I was, after all, not yet ten years old, and though far older than this in terms of intellect, and even maturity in some ways, in other ways I was little more than a baby. In my entire short life I had met eight people, five of them members of my own family, the other three scientists. I was wise enough to know that these eight people did not provide a cross-section of society from which I could extrapolate anything useful about humanity in general.

Adwin proudly informed Emaleen and Safya one day that, "he can now teleport people. As long as he's touching them that is."

"That's nice Addy," replied Safya, smiling gently at his enthusiasm.

"We've been able to teleport for ages," added Emaleen with an ostentatious sigh, as if the fact were uninteresting.

"We even went outside once," Adwin retorted. "Right across the fence. Right to the other side."

"Well hoorah for you. All the way to the other side of the fence!" sneered Emaleen scornfully, actually laughing in a derisory tone at what she saw as our obvious lack of valour.

"That's mean, Emmy," Safya berated her sister. But I was not sure that Safya was any more impressed by our exploits than Emaleen. She was simply a kinder person.

Adwin was incensed on my behalf at Emaleen's mockery. "You're just envious of Samek that he can do it on his own but you always need to use a machine," he snapped. I was unmoved by Emaleen's attitude: after all, whatever she thought of her and her sister's abilities, mine were so much the greater. As Adwin had pointed out, I could teleport using my own gifts whereas they needed to use a portal, and would always be limited in this way. And I was much younger than them, much less experienced or practised, so I knew that I was only at the start of a huge expansion of my powers, whereas they had probably reached the limits of theirs.

I had planned to offer to teleport my sisters around the compound, and perhaps even outside of it, but faced with Emaleen's derision, I decided not to make such an offer, not even to Safya. Let them teleport themselves wherever they wished, anchored to the home portal as they always would be, only able to leave and return via the machine and not under their own volition. I would one day travel as far and wide as I willed, without limit or restriction, and Adwin could come with me. I was smug in my powers, and as such Emaleen's scorn simply washed over me.

All four of us did have common ground however in our inquisitiveness about Zelda's intentions towards the Council. She had made it clear that she had formulated a plan of action, and that all four of her children would be key elements of the plan, but as yet we had no details. Zelda was not a woman to be pushed, so we simply had to wait until she was ready to share her ideas with us.

In truth, we did not have to wait long, but even when Zelda called for us to elucidate, she kept the details of the plan secret.

"I have called you all here today, and Kallan," she began in a pompous and oddly formal manner, nodding at our uncle. "To tell you something of my plan for the Council. And by the way, they have been badgering me again, several times, with demands that I reply to their summons to attend a Council meeting."

"Have you replied yet?" asked Kallan, posing the question on all of our minds.

"Yes," chuckled Zelda. "And just like I told you before, I just sent them a message, a *written* message, saying that they have no authority to summon anyone, and that I do not respond to such summonses, but that if they ask politely, I might, just *might* consider their request and come along to meet them."

She laughed outright at this, finding her own reply to the Council highly amusing. Kallan laughed gently too, though none of us children understood what was so funny. Was it the fact that she had sent a written message? I knew that such a thing was almost unheard of, and as such, perhaps it implied a subtle insult? Or was it the outrage Zelda knew the Council would feel about the wording of her message, that they had no authority, but that she might *consider* their request, but only if they asked politely? Her message implied a total lack of respect for the Council, for its powers, for its ability to control citizens, and presumably this tickled Zelda, and Kallan too.

"I still don't understand why the Council hate you so much, and why you hate them so much," said Emaleen out of the blue.

Zelda turned to her and replied, "I have already explained to you how they hate my work, always have done, and have been determined for years to hound me out of research, of working with colleagues."

"I know that mother," Emaleen replied tetchily, tossing her head and shaking her long blond hair as she did so. "But is that the only reason?"

Zelda did not reply, but the tiny glance she flicked at Kallan suggested that there was more to it than she was admitting. After a pause, Kallan said quietly,

"I don't see why they shouldn't know. After all, they'll be meeting the Council before too long as I understand it." Zelda stared at Kallan for a few moments, then nodded very slightly, reaching up to push a wayward strand of hair back into its usual confines.

"You tell them," she indicated to Kallan. "I cannot trust myself to explain it without getting angry, and it is better they hear it calmly."

Kallan nodded back and explained to us why the antipathy between Zelda and the Council was so intense. To our astonishment, we discovered that Rannald, that smug and puffed-up leader of the Council, had been in the same cohort at the Children's Institute as Zelda, Kallan and Marna. They were all the same age, and had been brought up together to the age of fourteen, living in the same communal home, studying together, playing together.

According to Kallan, Rannald had disliked Zelda as long as any of them could remember, and over the years they spent in such close proximity, the dislike blossomed into hatred. Kallan was not entirely sure what the origin of the antipathy was. Rannald had been a handsome boy, a fact which always rankled with the frankly unappealing Zelda. But perhaps it was simply a clash of personalities as Rannald and Zelda were two of the strongest characters in their cohort, though neither of them popular. Perhaps it was competitiveness, given that they had been the two most intellectually competent children, and as far as Kallan remembered, they always struggled to outshine each other in every intellectual endeavour. Perhaps, Kallan told us with a mischievous smile lighting up his blue eyes, it was the fact that Rannald was even more unpopular than Zelda. Zelda actually laughed at this, giving Kallan a wry look as she did so. Zelda had had Kallan and Marna, always her close friends, ever ready to come to her defence, whereas Rannald had not had a single good friend at the Institute. He had had a coterie (to use Kallan's word) of almost equally unpleasant followers, but none that could be described as a true companion. And from his position of hatred towards Zelda, Rannald had never budged. To be fair, Zelda gave back almost as good as she got, and the antipathy between the two of them had, if anything, become even more intense over the years. Kallan smiled as he recounted Zelda's incandescent rage first when Rannald was appointed to the Council, and even more so when he was made Speaker.

I was glad that I was too young with all of my nearly ten years to have witnessed Zelda's anger on these occasions: her fury was something we had all suffered from time to time. I wondered if my sisters remembered those particular bouts of ire as they were a full five years older than me. But Kallan's tale helped us all to understand Zelda's regular tirades against the Council: not only had they always thwarted her in her work, but one of their members, now their leader, was a long-standing foe of hers. It was a combination hardly likely to create good relations between Zelda and the Council. And for Zelda to have discovered recently that Rannald's nephew, Devid, had actually wormed his way into our home had been almost too much for our mother to bear.

But Zelda was a canny woman, and despite her anger at the recent summons from the Council, she had clearly decided to turn it to her advantage. We would all attend a Council meeting, and Zelda would use the occasion to teach the Council a lesson. She would not, at this stage, give us full details of her actual plan, but she did inform us that the four of us would have to work together to learn to combine our abilities. Adwin and my sisters would have to learn to use their abilities in combination with mine, letting them flow together to create a much stronger effect than any of us could manage alone. Zelda was convinced that the sum effect of blending our powers and abilities would be far greater than merely twice, or three times our individual abilities. She began to explain why to us, but we clearly found the reasons so arcane, that she abandoned the attempt.

"Just take my word for it. And," she continued, "When you have worked on that for a while, come and see me again and I shall explain my actual plan." We waited to see if she would add more, but she seemed unwilling to divulge any further details at that stage. I was frustrated by the lack of clear information, but intrigued at what she was contriving in order to teach the Council a lesson.

"I still don't understand," I said to Kallan suddenly, changing the subject. "Why all of the children in a cohort don't get on better. Aren't you all clones?"

Kallan was visibly shocked at my question, so much so that it took him a few moments to reply.

"Clones?" he asked incredulously, vivid blue eyes wide. "Why on earth would you think we are clones?"

"I...I don't really know. I just assumed that you were all produced from the same stock, and that's what a cohort is. That you're all the same," I replied, lamely.

"What a strange notion," said Kallan. "Of course we're not clones. Don't you think we look different? And if we were clones, wouldn't we all be the same sex?"

I was abashed at his reply, realising how foolish my assumption was. I had obviously never really given it any thought.

I had never seen Rannald, though I had seen images of his arrogant face, and he looked nothing like Marna, Zelda or Kallan, just as they did not look much like each other. And of course, two of them were male, two female! By definition, clones all had to be the same sex.

"Humans are never cloned," interrupted Zelda, in a mildly affronted tone. "What an idea!"

"Why not?" demanded little Adwin with a deep frown just visible beneath his floppy dark fringe, as ever jumping to my defence.

"It would be wrong, unethical, *undignified*," replied Zelda. "A human being is unique, one of a kind. It would be unthinkable to create a...a *litter* of humans, for want of a better word."

"But where does that leave me and Emaleen?" asked Safya with real concern in her voice. "We're not unique. We were made from exactly the same group of progenitors." She stared at Kallan and then at Zelda, but neither of them seemed willing or able to answer her perfectly reasonable question. Safya opened her mouth to persist with her query, but Adwin spoke first, causing Emaleen to scowl at him for interrupting her sister.

"But animals are cloned," he said, not easily put off his earlier query. "I know that farm animals are always cloned."

"Of course," replied Zelda, as if the issue were glaringly obvious. "Animals would not care whether they were clones or not. How would they know? So what difference does it make? They do not give a fig for dignity or uniqueness. And it is far more efficient for food production to make hundreds, even thousands of identical creatures from the same egg. And any genetic adjustments made to the fertilised egg straight after fertilisation are then passed automatically to every single animal in the batch. But we could never do such a thing with people."

Emaleen and Safya both stared at Zelda in frank disbelief at her disingenuous comments. But before either of them could remonstrate with her, Kallan intruded back into the conversation, causing the scowl on Emaleen's face to deepen, now mirrored by an almost identical moue on her sister's face.

"That's all very well and noble, Zelda my dear, but you know as well as I do that such sentiments didn't always hold sway."

Zelda looked at him, and after a short pause said sharply,

"Well tell them then!"

Kallan explained to us that long ago, even before the Chaos, the technology for producing clones had been developed. The early part of the twenty-first century saw huge advances in such procedures, and by the fourth decade of that century farms in the richer countries were using the technology regularly, working with laboratories to produce cloned animals in huge quantities. It was much harder for poorer countries to avail themselves of the new techniques because they were still very expensive. This information, Kallan told us, was merely by way of background, and as we knew, cloning of farm animals was always used nowadays.

After the Chaos, as the tiny groups of survivors left their hiding places, they emerged into a world in which many, many species of plant and animal had been wiped out, dragged down by the human-engendered disasters of the Chaos. Early on, before the Chaos proper had begun its destructive course, some prescient humans foresaw the future, and began to save plants and animals, or at least enough of them for them to be resurrected after their annihilation. Some durable physical parts were saved, notably plant seeds, but predominantly those farsighted people saved DNA. They raced to take samples of the genetic material from as many animals and plants as they could before they disappeared, and stored these as best they could. They accelerated the process dramatically as it became clear that disaster could not be averted, that the Chaos had entered a stage from which there would be no return. And thanks to these prescient people, the survivors of the Chaos, once they had managed to ensure their own futures by providing themselves with the basic necessities of life, were able to turn their attention to resurrecting as many of the extinct animals and plants as they could.

Despite the best efforts of the collectors of DNA, in the end they were only able to harvest and store a small percentage of the world's living things. A surprising number of hardy creatures survived the Chaos - the ones everyone expected like cockroaches (as I had already guessed) and scorpions, but also many others among the insects, the molluscs, a few fish, even some tiny mammals, other tiny creatures such as the tardigrade, and many, many microorganisms such as amoeba, bacteria and so on. Enough plants also survived to provide a basis for the post-Chaos food chain. The most shocking thing for the survivors was the fact that not a single large animal survived. The largest living creatures the human survivors encountered were the scorpions and rats. All other larger mammals, reptiles, birds, fish and amphibians had perished, wiped out by the activities of humans.

This was a devastating discovery, and only partially ameliorated by the stored genetic material. As soon as they were able, and this was not for several generations after the emergence into the new world by the remaining people, they began to utilise the cloning technology that itself had been preserved, and began to re-populate the world with creatures and plants that had been eradicated. But even by the time I was a child, nearly eight-hundred years later, our world was not remotely as diverse as the one our ancestors destroyed. We thought then, as we still do, that we have a wide range of animals and plants, domestic and wild, and feel smug that we were able, god-like, to bring many of these back to life. But most of the old life forms are lost to us for ever. There was nothing left from which we could resurrect them. Evolution is once again working its magic to create diversity, but it is a slow process, and our world has, as yet, seen little evidence of it in action.

Once the remaining people were able to think of cloning dead animals and plants, questions were raised as to whether we should use the same technology to increase our own population again. The entire human population surviving the Chaos numbered no more than a few thousand, the most optimistic estimates putting it at around three thousand. Would it not be a good idea, an imperative even, to increase our population more rapidly, the better to ensure our species' continued survival? According to Kallan, this led to bitter and acrimonious arguments. Some people were indignant that the issue had even been raised, pointing out, quite reasonably, that the enormous, and ever-expanding human population before the Chaos had been the very catalyst for the Chaos itself. Others, while not denying this basic fact, made the valid point that a tiny population, so small as to be at risk of extinction, could not be compared with the billions upon billions of people crammed onto the planet at the time of the Chaos.

This dispute, seemingly, could not be solved, until one young woman, a shy and diffident person so Kallan told us, took the courage to wade into the debate. She reminded everyone else that one of the main problems leading to the Chaos was not merely the endless growth of the human population by natural means, from seven billion in the early part of the twenty-first century to nearly fourteen billion only forty years after this, but that the ruinous explosion of the population only occurred after the middle of that century when human cloning began. Kallan paused at this point of his tale, for effect, and as he had expected, all four of us children stared, mouths gaping, eyes wide with wonder. The tale told by Kallan was so gripping that even Emaleen had forgotten her earlier anger.

After Kallan had enjoyed the effect of his revelation he went on to explain to us that, unknown to most people, human cloning had actually begun long before it became obvious. The richer countries, with their relatively low birth rates and technological abilities to feed their populations, were able to keep food production more or less in line with numbers of people. They were also either fortunate enough to be located in parts of the world with sufficient rainfall, or wealthy enough to be able to supply their inhabitants with desalinated sea water. But many, if not most, of the poorer countries did not have such luxuries.

As the water ran out in many countries due to the pressures of agriculture and manufacturing for an ever-growing population, and the polluting of the remaining water sources, the poorer countries became more and more desperate. They appealed to the richer countries for help, and at first, some help was forthcoming, but as the numbers of people continued to grow exponentially in the poor countries, yet remained stable in the rich ones, the poor began to move en masse across seas and borders, desperate to reach the richer countries. For a while, the humanitarian attitudes of the richer countries held sway, and large numbers of refugees were allowed to settle, but the unchecked population growth in the poorer countries soon made this untenable. The rich countries, fearing being overwhelmed by numbers of people far larger than their own populations, eventually slammed their borders shut, policing them with all means at their disposal.

At first the poorer countries had little response to this, and merely carried on as they were, their water supplies diminishing all the time, their populations growing incessantly, their food supply not keeping pace with their numbers. Then at some point, though Kallan said it was never clear exactly when it happened, or who began the process, some of the poorer countries began to artificially increase their populations.

"But why??" cried Adwin, unable to understand what the possible reason could be.

"Patience, my dear. I'll get onto that in a moment," replied Kallan calmly, and continued.

The idea, as far as Kallan could recall, was to become big enough to be able to invade any other country and overwhelm it by sheer weight of numbers. From what happened afterwards, it seemed that the countries called China and India were the two prime movers of this policy. Both of them already had enormous populations, and were, in fact, by far the two largest countries in the world by number of people. India had severe problems with water shortages, for, despite being copiously provided with rain during and after the annual monsoon, and with water carried through the country by huge rivers, the vast population had simply used far more water than was available, and despite the monsoons and the rivers, the usage each year of this most precious resource hugely outstripped supply. China, not being blessed with the monsoon, still had huge rivers and a plentiful rainfall, and in most of its regions did not suffer the same evaporating heat as did India. These two enormous countries stared at each other's resources, such as they were, across the massive barrier of the Himalayas, the highest mountains in the world.

Eventually, so Kallan surmised, China felt that its population, artificially enhanced at breakneck speed by cloning hundreds and thousands of people from single eggs decided that the time was right to attack India, before India could attack it. Kallan added some detail that he clearly found deeply distasteful - that the Chinese authorities (and possibly also the Indian) forced all women of childbearing age to act as surrogates to multiple cloned embryos at a time, and used the newest technologies to allow the prematurely born foetuses to survive, having been removed from the woman's womb after less than half the normal term. In this way, a woman could produce what amounted to a litter of babies in only around five months, and could then have another batch of embryos implanted immediately into her womb.

The Chinese led the Indians in such technologies, and never having been a democracy so not having to consider such inconveniences as elections, it was easier for them to out-breed the Indians by this method. Were China to succeed in its plan, this of course would entail wiping out the entire existing population of India. The war was not over territory, but water, so what would be the point of owning India if the original people were left there, still using as much water as previously?

When China attacked India, the Indians knew what the outcome would be if they lost, because they had exactly the same plan for China. This being the case, the war was the most brutal in the history of the World, as losing was not an option for either side. Other countries in Asia also got involved, either by default or by deliberate action, joining the side they thought would win, mostly on the side of China. The rest, as Kallan reminded us, was history well known to us: how this pan-Asian war of utter destruction and slaughter, eventually involving nearly half the World's population, we look on now as the step which took humanity over the brink and on a course from which there was no return.

"Yes, yes," Emaleen interrupted testily. "But what has all that ancient history got to do with people *after* the Chaos cloning humans or not?"

"Oh, I'm sorry - I forgot to get to that," tutted Kallan with a smile, realising that he had missed out the whole point of the story.

"Once the shy young woman had successfully reminded everyone what had happened after human cloning had been used in the past, the survivors made a very definite decision, the very first Ruling I suppose, never to allow human cloning again. And that decision, that Ruling, was clearly the right one, because, as Zelda so rightly said, human cloning is wrong, unethical and undignified. We are, after all, each of us unique, and the special nature of being human must be preserved."

I was not entirely convinced. I thought of some of the forest animals, the deer, the foxes, the badgers, all of which I could easily tell apart the one from the other. Although these wild animals were not produced by cloning, did not the domestic animals, the cows, the sheep, the pigs, deserve the dignity of uniqueness? I dared not share these thoughts, as it was clear that both Zelda and Kallan felt that there was simply no problem with cloning farm animals, based on the premise that since they had no consciousness of having been cloned or not, what possible difference could it make?

My sisters seemed even less convinced than I was, for obvious reasons.

"But we are twins," insisted Safya in worried tones, returning to her earlier query. "Does that mean we're not unique?"

Kallan looked at her helplessly, then turned to Zelda for rescue. Zelda sighed loudly and answered Safya's question.

"You are twins, that is true. But as you were made from so many progenitors, it is not the same as two ordinary, old world twins, and it is not the same as the clones made on farms. They are all made from a single reconstructed egg. You are both made from splicing and reorganising DNA from nine separate people." She stopped, apparently feeling that this explanation was sufficient, but Safya simply stared back at her, unconvinced. Zelda sighed again and continued.

"That is more than enough science for one day. And history for that matter," she said, truncating any further discussion. "Now you know all the reasons why I hate the Council so much and why the hatred is reciprocated. All the more reason why you four very special young people need to get off and start practising what I have asked of you, so we can slap those smug bastards square in the face. Figuratively, obviously, though how I would love to give that Rannald and a few of the others on the Council a swift backhander across their arrogant cheeks. What pleasure it would give me to see the marks of my fingers across their pompous jowls!"

Kallan looked amused at Zelda's comments, shaking his head slightly as he smiled.

"Well?" said Zelda sharply to the four of us. "What are you waiting for? Get out of here and get practising. I want you perfect as soon as you can, so no dilly-dallying or shilly-shallying."

At that, she turned and shuffled out of the room. Kallan looked at us more kindly, adding,

"Come on then, off you go and do as you've been asked. I don't have the same hatred of the Council as Zelda, but how I will enjoy seeing them brought down a peg or two."

At that, he also left the room. We four remained still for a few moments, and then followed him out, intending to begin our joint activities immediately, thrilled at the idea of being the central element of Zelda's great plan.

Chapter Twenty-Three

In truth, we found it somewhat difficult to learn how to work together as we had no clear idea the uses to which our joint activities would be put. We also struggled to think of ways to practise our combined powers: we feared that enhancing the level of our abilities in this way might be damaging or harmful to our immediate surroundings. Moreover, we had grown increasingly apart, especially from Emaleen. Nevertheless, we persisted in our attempts, and certainly honed our ability to fuse our skills, feeling a surge of energy and competency as we did so. Although we were new to the experience, it felt as if by working together we should be able to achieve far more than we could working alone. And that the sum of what we would achieve would be greater than the individual parts.

Zelda asked us one day if we believed that we could make people obey our will.

"I'm sure we could," replied my brother, sounding more confident than I suspected he was, and certainly more sure than I myself felt. But Zelda appeared content with his reply. Fortunately, Zelda did not pursue her question. We struggled to know exactly how to practise, how to develop, our combined energies, and I was glad Zelda did not ask us any specific questions about our abilities.

As we continued to practise, we wondered what the great plan would be for the Council, to give it the sharp lesson that Zelda was threatening. But until she was completely happy with our progress, she would not be drawn on a single detail of the plan, and we simply had to wait.

As we worked on improving our mutual skills, I pondered on what Kallan had told us about human cloning, especially before the Chaos. I knew a little about the technological abilities of the pre-Chaos science in this field, but was nevertheless astonished that it was so well-developed before the Chaos. I simply could not understand how our ancestors, so precocious in their understanding and manipulation of the science of cloning (and indeed the creation of multi-progenitor babies), could be so backward in other respects. How did such people, so clever and skilful in so many ways, allow their world to be dragged to destruction, to the utter and all-encompassing disaster that was the Chaos? I could not reconcile the conflicting knowledge I had of the simultaneous brilliance and rank stupidity of those pre-Chaos scientists. But perhaps my judgement was unjust. Perhaps the sheer complexity of the old world with its teeming billions, its hundreds of separate countries and peoples, its thousands of languages and cultures, its manifold competing religions and political ideologies, made it impossible to impose order, to salvage what was good, ultimately to rescue the world from its headlong plunge into the chaotic abyss. Did those scientists with their dazzling brilliance simply bury themselves in their work, bury their heads in the sand as order disintegrated all around them?

I knew that the techniques of cloning, and of producing foetuses from many parents, were in fact the same as they had been before the Chaos. There were, of course, differences between then and now, but they were differences of detail and not of essence. We can now produce even more clones from the same original blastocyst, and with far fewer errors than the pre-Chaos practitioners. And when creating multi-progenitor foetuses, they only had a rough understanding of which genes, or epigenetic factors, were responsible for specific aspects of development of an organism, or for identifiable causes or progress of disease. We have a much more profound, precise, and subtle understanding of all these things, and as such, we had almost eradicated genetic disease even by the time I came into the world. Almost, but not quite. We too still lacked a full understanding of these matters, but progressed inexorably towards full comprehension. We could not only produce people without actual genetic disorders, but also lacking the propensity to develop most maladies. Occasionally someone was brought to life who did still manifest genetic disease, or who developed it later in life. Even then, we were generally able to solve such problems. But again, not always. Adwin, with his long-standing and mystifying propensity for illness showed that we still had much to learn, though his case was, of course, unique. Not for the first time, I wondered if his health problems were psychosomatic, engendered by some defect in the workings of his brain, rather than his body.

I mulled at length too on the ostensible uniqueness of the human animal that Zelda and Kallan were so keen to defend and protect. I understood well that each human being is unique, with our individual background, upbringing, environment and development, but I failed to see how this would really differ even if a person was one of a clutch of people produced from the same fertilised egg. Surely all this would really mean in practice is that those genetically identical souls would only look very similar. Even if raised in the same Institute, with the same basic upbringing, surely each individual clone would have his or her unique development, following an exclusive and separate path through childhood and beyond, with different epigenetic pressures (the processes in our bodies that affect the way that genes are expressed, rather than the genes themselves), and with subtly different experiences and behaviours which would render each of them a person as unique as any other?

I tried to learn about the humans cloned before the Chaos, but there was almost no information about them, and what there was lacked sufficient detail to help support my belief in the individuality of each clone. I did, however, locate some fascinating ancient documentation on the nature of twins. Apart from my sisters, there were no twins in the world of my childhood. As part of the general antipathy towards foetuses produced from the same fertilised egg, it was only permitted to allow a single embryo to develop from each fertilisation, and if, as happened occasionally, the fertilised egg split naturally in two, only the one viewed as most viable was allowed to develop. But in the ancient, pre-Chaos world, twins were a normal occurrence, and scientists and sociologists were fascinated by them. Thus there was a huge amount of documented research into twins: genetic, behavioural, social.

The most extraordinary thing about twins, as far as I could discern, was that, although they were genetically identical, and nearly always physically indistinguishable at birth, their individual paths through life often led to them becoming less and less alike as they grew. And this was especially true in the rare cases where they were brought up apart. It seems that two identical humans can gradually become less so due to a range of pressures, environmental, social, cultural and even epigenetic where identical genes can nevertheless be expressed in different ways in different organisms. I was fascinated by the influence of epigenetics, how these factors seem capable of pushing a wedge between two people who are genetically identical, who look indistinguishable at the start of their lives, causing them to gradually diverge not only in behaviour, thoughts and attitudes, but even in their physical or facial appearance. I knew from my reading of this research that I must be correct in my understanding of human clones: each one would still be a unique human being who would follow a different and separate passage through life. The obsessive hostility to human cloning which seemed to reign in my world was not based on science, but founded on emotion rather than logic.

I shared my cogitations on these matters with Adwin, who could not find fault with my reasoning.

"Emaleen and Safya should be identical, yet they're really different," he agreed. "And they even look a bit unalike. Emaleen is a bit taller and thinner, and her eyes are slightly bluer". I could nor help but agree. Wryly I noted that despite Zelda and Kallan's hostility to cloned humans, they seemed unable to perceive a problem with the twins, the genetically identical children that they were bringing up in their own home. Zelda even seemed willing to find explanations to reassure herself that they were unique.

I was wary of sharing my ideas with my sisters. On the one occasion I tried Emaleen scoffed that I was "just wasting my time on such matters." And even Safya added that there "seems little point spending so much time worrying about things that can't be changed." And with Kallan or Zelda, I did not dare broach the subject, so emphatic had they been in the rightness of their views on the matter.

In any case, before I could explore the ideas any further, Zelda decided that we were ready to learn the details of her plan.

"I received a message from the Council this morning," she announced to us all one day after breakfast. "A good deal more polite than the last few," she added with a chuckle. "Obviously they are not really being polite, but they do not know what else to do to get me, to get us, to attend one of their meetings, so they are playing the game at least. I shall send them a message in a day or two to inform them that we will come and meet with them, and give them some dates we are free to do so. I shall leave them waiting a few days before I reply, just to annoy them," she added with a smile. "In the meantime, I shall fill all of you in on my plan."

And she did just that, speaking in quiet, conspiratorial tones as if we could be overheard in our own home, our estate so tightly sealed off from the outside world. We were all filled with excitement and apprehension for our meeting with the Council, our carrying out of Zelda's plan, and the lesson it would teach the Council. Zelda's antipathy towards the Council and her enthusiasm for her plan were contagious, and we all waited anxiously, with huge anticipation, for the actual day when I would port us all to the great Council Chamber to face those enemies of Zelda about whom we had heard so much, and for so long.

Chapter Twenty-Four

The day arrived on which we were due to attend the Council chamber, in truth not long after we had learned the details of Zelda's plan, yet seeming an age, so impatient were we for the events to unfold. Kallan instructed us to dress simply, yet elegantly, so we donned our smartest, brightest clothes, wanting to look dignified yet create an impression. When I was younger, I gave little thought to clothing. Everything I wore was provided for me, was just *there* when I needed it. Apart from Kallan when he left the compound in his finery, the rest of us dressed simply and plainly. Only after we had received visitors did I begin to wonder more about the clothes people wore, partly in response to the mixture of garments worn by our guests, to me an odd mixture. I learned that, although very simple clothes such as trousers, shirts, dresses, tunics, were acceptable dress in the outside world, many, if not most people, ransacked the distant past for sartorial inspiration. This led to a bewildering variety of styles abounding. During one of Marna's visits, Adwin and I had subjected her to a round of our usual questions about this very topic, our interest being what we would wear when we finally met people outside.

"You can wear what you like, my dears," she began, her chubby cheeks rounded with a smile. "And sometimes it's just absolutely bizarre what you see when you walk through a town or city. You see garments from all sorts of times in the distant past, but all together now at the same time. So you see ancient Roman togas, huge skirts almost two metres across, tall hats with trailing veils, silk kimonos. All sorts. It's absolutely bewildering to the senses of a poor old woman like me." Though we did not understand all of her words, Marna's indication was clear enough: our world's fashions were random, haphazard, highly eclectic, an indication of people with nothing better to fill their time with. And Marna finished her comments with a loud laugh causing her large belly to wobble. "And the really bizarre thing is that people pay no attention to who wore the clothes in the past - so you see women in the men's togas, men in huge wide skirts. Outrageous! Hilarious to anyone with a sense of history!"

We children were ready long before the time Zelda indicated we would leave. My sisters sat quietly, each with her long pale hair pulled back into a single thick plait, their similarity of look being further accentuated by their identical long-sleeved, knee-length pale blue dresses. Adwin and I shuffled restlessly around the living room waiting for Kallan and Zelda, unable to settle to doing anything else, incapable even of sitting down, pulling at the unusually tight and constricting jackets we had decided to wear which chafed against our necks, the kilt I had chosen to wear flapping around my thighs. Zelda arrived before Kallan, and I was astonished to see her looking so groomed. She had pulled her hair back even more tightly against her scalp such that not a single strand dared to stray beyond its confines. And amazingly, she had applied a little colour to her hair to hide some of the grey, creating a more uniform dark brown, and had even dyed her normally greyish eyebrows a deep brown, giving her an even more severe and forbidding appearance than usual. But the most remarkable thing of all was that she was wearing a suit, an outfit from the old world which we had seen in pictures: trousers, a jacket and a waistcoat over a crisp shirt and even a tie! Marna had told the truth. The trousers and jacket were made of dark gray silk, the trousers showing a sharp line down the front of each leg from where they had been pressed. The waistcoat, which we glimpsed through the front of the jacket as Zelda walked into the room, also of silk, was the colour of ripe plums, a shimmering burgundy, set off by the creamy cotton shirt and lighter purple tie beneath. We all gaped at Zelda, never having seen her in any such clothing before. She was brisk as she entered the room, but seeing our reaction to her, smiled slightly, almost bashfully, and shrugged.

"Well what do you think?" she asked. "Will I make enough of an impression?"

Before any of us could respond we heard Kallan approach the door, and we all looked up sharply. We expected him to outshine all of us, and we were not disappointed. He swept confidently into the room without a trace of shyness on his handsome tanned face. He had chosen an outfit of iridescent material which shifted colour from gleaming deep blue to emerald green with each tiny movement of his body, setting off the vivid azure of his eyes. Tiny glimmers of light rippled across the material, endlessly reflecting flashes of blue and green luminosity which danced over every surface of the room - the walls, the ceiling, the floor, and even off our own clothes. Kallan had parted his thick silver hair and had wound a thin silvery chain dotted with small sapphires around his head. His sleeves were long so he had not bothered to put on bracelets, but strung beneath the high collar of the magical raiment were silver ropes of sparkling cut sapphires. These adornments also caught the light, and to me Kallan seemed to be more than human, a glittering, shimmering being encased in a field of light so bright that it was impossible to say where he ended and the space beyond him began. Did such garments hail from the ancient world, or were these specific to our own times?

Kallan smiled complacently as he noted our dumbstruck expressions. We had seen him on occasion dressed up to leave the estate, but had never witnessed such splendour. I could not decide which of Kallan or Zelda I found more astonishing.

Kallan looked at us all critically, Zelda included, then nodded.

"You all look quite delightful," he said. We smiled, and Zelda once again seemed abashed. She quickly overcame her shyness, and briskly asked us,

"Well? Are you all ready?" We nodded our assent, still too overwhelmed by Kallan's appearance to speak. Zelda turned to me, fixed me with a penetrating stare, drawing together her strange dark brown bushy brows, and queried,

"Samek, my son, are *you* ready?"

I was deeply moved by her calling me 'my son', something I was not sure she had ever done before. It was an indication of her heightened state of emotion, and of how much reliance she was putting on me to successfully effect her stratagem. So moved was I that speech was impossible, so I simply looked her straight in the eye and nodded vigorously.

"Good," she said by way of response. "It is time."

I gulped with nervousness at the prospect of teleporting the five most important people in my life at the same time, yet steeled myself to make the attempt.

"Do we need to hold hands?" Safya asked me shyly.

"Yes," I replied. "I can't move other people without being in physical contact with them."

"And that's a pity," chimed Zelda, "It would look much more impressive if we just appeared in front of the Council standing apart, strong yet individual. Popping up in front of them grasping each other's hands might be perceived as weakness, as needing moral support."

Kallan opened his mouth to contradict Zelda, but before he could speak she continued.

"First impressions are crucial, Kallan, and having gone to such effort to look so resplendent as you do, we do not want anything to undermine that."

Kallan's mouth snapped shut, a small smile on his lips, mollified by Zelda's extravagant compliment.

"But all of you, remember to let go of each other the moment you appear before the Council," said my mother. "Perhaps that way we can safely teleport and still give the impression of being apart when the Council first sees us." We all nodded vaguely.

"Well?" Zelda directed at me suddenly, prompting me. "Now is the time!"

I swallowed loudly, but garnered my energies. We all moved close together, hands touching arms, a chain of linked bodies. Just before I began the teleporting process Kallan cried out.

"Wait! We need to arrange ourselves the way we want to appear."

"Yes, yes, of course," added Zelda agitatedly. "I should have thought of that." She looked at us all for a moment, and then gave us short, sharp directions as to how and where we should stand. She moved us around in order of size. Adwin and I stood at the front, side by side. Just behind us, and to our sides stood our sisters, and filling the gap in between and at the back were Kallan and Zelda. Once again, we made contact, hands touching arms, arms draped lightly across shoulders.

"Can you make us appear facing the Council?" Zelda said to me.

I considered this for a moment, then nodded.

"I should be able to sense which way we are facing just before we arrive, and move us around if I need to," I said quietly. Zelda nodded with satisfaction, and then nodded again to indicate that the time had come to make our entrance in the Council Chamber.

Once again, I assembled my thoughts, pulling my energies inwards. I closed my eyes and began the process of teleporting. As always, the actual event was brief and unremarkable. The digital memory had provided me with the exact three-dimensional coordinates of the Council Chamber earlier, so I knew where to take us. And from images I had seen of the Chamber in the digital memory I knew its basic layout. As we began to materialise before the assembled Council I perceived them all sitting impatiently in their chairs, behind a long table, and shifted our position very slightly so that we would make our final appearance looking straight at them, boldly and confidently.

As we appeared out of the blue, barely two metres in front of the Council members, they let out a collective gasp of astonishment, their surprise giving us a chance to break physical contact. The Council had expected us to travel via the teleportal, situated just beyond the doors to the Council Chamber, and to make our way into the Chamber as everyone else did, on foot. Our abrupt arrival was totally unexpected, and startling. I saw the look of triumphant smugness on Zelda's face from the corner of my eye as she contemplated the shocked expressions on the faces of the Council. She had achieved the stunning first impression she had hoped for.

For a long moment, nobody spoke. Zelda had instructed us not to speak first, but to let the Council make the first overtures. She explained that this would give us the advantage, putting pressure on them. And she was correct. I could sense the confusion and consternation in the members of the Council sitting stiffly before me. They did not seem to know how to begin.

During the heavy pause, I took the opportunity to survey my surroundings. I began by quickly running my eyes along the row of twelve well-dressed adults sitting in front of me. Nearly all of them had looks of concern, even anxiety etched onto their features. All except two. In the middle sat Rannald whom I recognised from pictures I had seen of him, his arrogant features unmistakable as he gazed at us. The only other person not looking worried was a very short, stocky woman sitting beside Rannald, glaring at me with open hostility. I turned my eyes away from her to survey the chamber.

The Council Chamber was a beautiful room. Zelda and Kallan had both fulminated about its opulence, believing such to be unnecessary, and merely a reflection of the self-importance of the people who inhabited it. Yet as I looked swiftly around, I was glad of it. It was not an enormous room, perhaps twenty metres at its greatest extension lengthwise, and ten or so metres wide. I did not need to look around to ascertain that it was an almost perfect semi-circle. We stood facing the single long translucent green table behind which were arranged the twelve surprisingly simple Council chairs. Behind us was the long, flat wall, the bisecting line of the semi-circle. This flat wall was made up of five wide doors with pillars in between. When the Council were in session, as now, the five doors were opened fully, and were cleverly engineered that when this was the case, they disappeared, telescope like, into the pillars. I could feel a gentle breeze against my back flowing through what was, in effect, an open wall.

From each end of the flat wall behind us began one end of the arc of the semi-circle, and it curved all the way round the rest of the room, encircling the open space in front of the Council table in which we stood, all the way round behind the table itself. This semi-circular wall was entirely of glass, real glass as I perceived on a quick scan. The walls of the chamber were about eight metres high, topped with a domed roof of opaque perspiglass, darkened slightly today due to the bright sunlight outside. But the curving wall was a marvel. The middle of it was a long rectangle stretching the whole way around it, and this was of clear glass, giving an extraordinary view of the city arrayed on the other side of it. The Council building was on a hill overlooking the city, the Chamber jutting out over the crest of the promontory, affording a spectacular view of the burgh as it cascaded away down the hill, across the plain below, the sea glittering in the distance. I did not have time to appreciate the view of the urban spread - the first I had ever seen, or the sea beyond, also my first glimpse of such a thing, as all my attention was focused on the crystal wall.

Apart from the clear glass rectangle, which seemed to be a viewing panel, the rest of the wall was entirely formed of small interlocking panels of glass in abstract curling, swirling patterns, vaguely reminiscent of leaves, branches and vines. The panels were coloured either sky blue or sea green, the thin lines joining the panels made out in purple. The colour scheme perfectly complemented Kallan's clothing, a fact that Rannald, the leader of the Council seemed to notice. He surreptitiously moved his hand across a flat panel on the surface of the table in front of him, and the colours of the glass shifted, now yellow and mauve, the lines between indigo so dark it was almost black. He moved his hand again, and the clear glass viewing panel darkened slightly, making the view of the city more opaque. I sensed in him an irritation that the view he had hoped would distract and even overwhelm us instead only gave us pleasure. And this could not be countenanced.

Zelda raised her dark bushy eyebrows at Rannald's petty gesture, a slight ironic smile playing on her lips. Before Rannald or any other member of the Council could speak I mindspoke to Zelda, including my siblings and Kallan in the message.

~*Shall we start?*~ I asked, referring to the plan Zelda had confided to us.

~*Yes,*~ replied Zelda, using the channels of direct mindspeak that I had opened and would keep open for us all to communicate through without anyone else knowing we were doing so. I sent the briefest of indications to my siblings, and we began to fuse our powers.

This time I did not close my eyes, and made every effort to appear as if I were not doing anything at all. My siblings followed my lead. Zelda glanced briefly round at us, and indicated her approval of our apparent nonchalance with the slightest nod of her head. The Council had absolutely no idea what we were about, even those who had some gift themselves. Our combined talents were so far in advance of anything the world had ever seen, that we were able to mask perfectly what we were doing. And the plan was so audacious that it would not have crossed the minds of any member of the Council what it was that we were putting into effect. So audacious yet so simple.

With my sisters' help, I took control of every single transmitter of visual narrowcasting in the world. Despite the fact that our world possessed the technical ability to narrowcast directly into the minds of citizens, most people still preferred to see news, reports, films, documentaries, public information and so on in large scale form, and in a shared forum. Thus, all such information was sent around the world via a small number of powerful transmitters, to be shown in three dimensional realistic holograph form both in large public spaces, such as town and city squares and parks, as well as directly into people's homes, or to their mobies. Zelda had told us exactly where the transmitters were situated, and it was surprisingly easy to locate them, and then to co-opt them to our purpose. Without the Council having the faintest idea, we took control of every transmitter and immediately began to narrowcast to every single home and public place, live, exactly what was happening at that very moment in the great Council Chamber. I made sure I included images of me and my siblings, to show the world the young and innocent faces of the children we were.

And in case anyone was busy or otherwise occupied and would miss what was being narrowcast, I took the much bolder step of informing every single person on the planet of what was happening, sending a message from the transmitters directly into the mind of each and every citizen via the small chip implanted in their brains.

I could almost sense a hush descend on the world outside the Council Chamber as people were made aware of our live narrowcast, stopping what they were doing as they realised what was happening. A nagging thought crossed my mind that perhaps Zelda had made a massive error of judgement in formulating and carrying out this plan. She was doing it, so she had said, to show the world what the Council was really like, how they really behaved. Yet I wondered if the result would simply be that the entire citizen body would turn against *us* and not the Council. After today, they would know who we were, what we were capable of, and what the Council thought of us. I just hoped that this knowledge would not rebound against us.

I sighed, knowing that I had no option now but to continue with the plan as we had discussed it. I just hoped that Zelda was right, that when people saw that we were 'just children', as she had called us, and that the Council believed itself to possess authority and power far beyond what the general population had ever granted it, that public opinion would swing decidedly against the Council, and in our favour. Though if Zelda were right, I wondered by what means we could make use of such public opinion.

Eventually, Rannald realised that Zelda had no intention of making any sort of verbal overture, and, losing patience, the Speaker himself began.

"Nice of you all to come," he said in a strong, deep voice dripping with snide sarcasm. I sensed Kallan wanting to laugh at his childish attitude, but controlling this desire.

"Our pleasure," replied Zelda, in a bright, upbeat voice which clearly irritated not only Rannald, but several other members of the Council. Despite the intense concentration I needed to maintain control of the transmitters to narrowcast live what was happening, I had enough energy to spare to perceive clearly the attitudes of the Council members. Beyond the three most hostile (including Rannald and the tiny woman sitting beside him), all visibly irritated by Zelda's manner, I felt some measure of antipathy from two of the others. Another two seemed less interested in us or the proceedings at all, their faces showing mild concern. The remaining five were showing various levels of support and sympathy for us, for us children that is, though not for Zelda. Even these five, though not as hostile to Zelda as some of the others, I suspected felt that her actions in creating us had been wrong, but they were at least fair enough not to blame us for the fact of our own creation. One of these I guessed to be Lenora, from Zelda's descriptions of her as a "giant, well suited to felling trees and wrestling bears with her own hands if she felt the desire."

Another pause ensued, as Rannald waited for Zelda to add to her two word greeting. But Zelda had no intention of doing so, forcing Rannald to begin again.

"I assume you know why we've summoned you, sorry, *asked* you to come here today?" said Rannald, clearly having intended to use the word 'summoned', despite correcting himself.

"To chitty-chat about old times, back at the Institute?" asked Zelda disingenuously. Kallan struggled to restrain a chuckle at this, his blue eyes twinkling, and had to work even harder when he saw the thunderous look on Rannald's surprisingly handsome yet supercilious face. Rannald breathed in and out deeply, barely able to control his rage, and before he could compose himself sufficiently to continue, the tiny stocky woman sitting to his left, her features almost matching Rannald's haughtiness, said abruptly in arch tones,

"To discuss your actions in breach of the Rulings, and what to do about it."

A silence ensued as Zelda considered how to answer the woman's comment. Before she could muster an appropriate response, Kallan spoke up in a loud voice.

"What do you mean Helna, 'what to do about it'?" he demanded, glaring at her. "What could there possibly be that you could do about it, assuming by 'it' you mean the existence of these four children?"

Helna did not reply, merely stared imperiously at Kallan, sitting higher in her seat as if to try and augment her tiny stature. I sensed annoyance towards her from the other hostile members of the Council, as if she had given away too much information, and too soon. Zelda suddenly stepped towards the seated Council, and, fixing first Rannald, then Helna with a penetrating stare, said in an ominous tone,

"I think you mean whether you should order these children to be destroyed, to be killed. Whether or not to abuse your authority to commit the murder, yes the *murder*, of four innocent children."

The hush which followed Zelda's statement was the most profound I had ever experienced. The entire room stilled, nobody moved a muscle, every breath was held. The word murder was so shocking as to be almost a taboo term. To utter it at all was unprecedented, and to accuse the Council, the highest body in the world, of contemplating the murder of anyone, let alone children, was a formidable insult, scandalously offensive. As far as I knew, there had been no murder in our world unless one went back to the very old records, certainly not for many hundreds of years. Such violent tendencies had simply been bred out in the process of creating multi-parent babies, and as such, crimes of violence had all but disappeared, and people were conditioned to obedience from a young age through social pressure and a process of shunning. We considered such atrocities to be symptomatic of the barbarity of the old world, something we, in our glorious, civilised times, no longer indulged in. Truly, the old world was savage, not only with its wars and genocides, its slaughters, killings and murders, then to add insult to injury, through most of its duration and in the majority of its regions its ruling bodies also imposed the sanction of judicial killing, of execution, on its citizens. We considered ourselves to have truly emerged from its darkness into our own self-created light.

"Well?" Zelda insisted darkly, persisting with her enquiry. "Have you or have you not considered murdering these four innocents?"

No member of the Council spoke. I used what spare energy I had to scan their thoughts, incautious as to whether they could sense me doing this, and what I found out was so shocking that I could not refrain from shouting out.

"They have! They have! They've thought about killing us, destroying us!" I cried in a plaintive voice. I quickly reined in my emotions, fearing that they would disrupt my control of the transmitters and affect the live narrowcast.

Rannald turned a look of such malevolence on me that I took an involuntary step backwards. I realised with a flash that he knew I had looked into their minds. Not only did it appall him that I could do this, but even more was he incensed that I had dared to do so without permission. Even among those people who had such powers, entering the private thoughts of others without permission was considered a dreadful breach of privacy, an offensive and harmful act. I quickly shared my concerns privately with my family, and felt a twinge of dismay from Zelda. But before we could react to Rannald's discovery, or he could speak out to reveal what I had done, there was a sudden disturbance behind us.

Someone was rushing towards the open doors at our backs, more than one person, and they were in a great hurry. Before any of us could turn to see what was happening, we heard many footsteps enter the chamber, stop dead, and a loud, nasal voice we all recognised shout in outrage.

"They're showing this, all of it, live, across the entire world!"

I remained quite still but knew the voice: Devid. When I had sent the message out to the citizenry at large, informing them of the live narrowcast, I had not thought to exclude him. It had simply not occurred to me. I did not know if he had already been somewhere else in the Council building or whether he had teleported here as soon as he could, but either way, he was now at the entrance to the Chamber, shouting out what was happening. I turned around to see that Devid was accompanied by around twenty other people, all sturdy young men dressed in curiously similar suits of a shiny black material, almost a uniform.

The collective outrage from the Council was so great that I nearly lost control of the transmitters, but with my sisters' help, I quickly grasped them again. Before anyone could do anything else, I made another deeply shocking discovery.

"They're carrying weapons!" I shouted, turning to face the new arrivals as I did. "All of them are carrying weapons!"

I knew that carrying weapons in any public place was strictly forbidden. The only permitted use of such instruments was against dangerous animals when out in the wilder parts of the world. Carrying weapons around the city or at a Council meeting was surely an unprecedented outrage?

"They're only stunners," whined Devid with a sneer on his face, though something in his eyes, behind the superficial expression of contempt, told me that he was seriously discomfitted to have had his weapons revealed, and not only to the people in the room, but to the world at large.

Chaos ensued as everyone began talking and shouting at the same time. The Council members were yelling, not just at us but also at Devid and his companions, Zelda and Kallan were shouting at the Council and at Devid, and Devid and his group were clamouring at us. The level of noise threatened to throw me off balance, so I had to cut myself off from all of it, taking my siblings with me. We stood silently, protected from the pandemonium all around us by a quiet, calm, circle of protection, enabling us to maintain our control. Outside our circle of control it was bedlam.

Devid made a move towards us, his footsteps drawing my attention to his oddly tiny feet. Behind him he was followed immediately by his coterie. Zelda sent us an urgent mind-message.

~*Can you stop them, stop them moving?*~ she asked. I nodded, immediately sending immobilising waves of energy in the direction of the hostile intruders, who all stopped in their tracks as if glued to the ground. Despite the seriousness of the situation, it was almost comical to see the expressions on their angry faces as they found themselves stuck, as they tried in vain to lift their feet off the ground, their heavy black boots fixed to the floor. I flashed a tiny smile at my siblings, and sent another controlling wave in the direction of our would-be assailants. This one rendered them incapable of any movement at all, and they stood immobile, arms plastered to the sides of their bodies, eyes wide open, mouths gaping in the positions they had been as the controlling wave hit them. Zelda, seeing what I had done, nodded in approval, knowing that I had rendered them incapable of drawing or using their weapons.

"How dare you!" boomed Rannald suddenly, his practised voice rising above the tumult, which was in any case diminished now that Devid and his gang were no longer able to speak.

"How dare you," he repeated, his loud and resonant voice cutting through the other voices, silencing them. "You come here at our request to answer charges of breaching the Rulings year after year, and then you dare, you actually dare to enter our private thoughts, to narrowcast our meeting to the world..."

But before he could continue Zelda bellowed in an even louder voice,

"We dare? We dare?" she shouted in such stentorian tones that she silenced even Rannald. She continued.

"You demand that we attend the Council, we come and find that you have been planning the murder of our children, then Devid, your nephew, the spy that you sent to our home, turns up with a large group of heavies, all armed ready for a fight, and you say that we dare?" She was convulsed with anger, her mottled face flushed bright red, her arms held up in front of her, fists clenched.

"You!" she shouted, thrusting her finger directly at Rannald. "You have no authority to demand anything of me or of my family," she went on in a voice shaking with rage. "And no right to criticise anything we choose to do to protect ourselves from your murderous plans. Why is your nephew here? Was that all part of the plan to exterminate my children, to get him to rush in pretending he did so off his own bat, but all along it was part of your strategy, and then for him and his cronies to attack us, *murder* us right in front of you, and claim it was in self-defence?"

I wondered if Zelda had gone too far. I sensed that the entire Council, even Rannald, had no idea Devid would turn up, and that arranging to kill us there and then, in the Council Chamber, was so outrageous that even the most hostile Council members would not have countenanced it. But given that a group of obviously aggressive young men had burst into the Council Chamber, armed and appearing ready for action suggested that Zelda may have been right all along: our visit to the Council would benefit us more than the Council. People would see what was happening with their own eyes and at the very least suspect the Council of conspiring with Devid. Devid's intrusion, unplanned as I believed it to be, would surely fuel antagonism towards the Council.

Nobody in the Council reacted to Zelda's accusations. Rannald must surely have known what the situation would look like to the world outside, and it did indeed seem as if he and the rest of the Council had planned to bring us before them, and then create a setting perhaps allowing them to rid themselves of all of us once and for all. All the Council members knew that there was nothing they could say at this juncture which would help them, and any attempt to explain would merely be read as justifying the unjustifiable. Wisely, none of them spoke, yet I saw an expression of despair rippling along the row of faces in front of me, a look of helplessness, a realisation of being in a position none of them had ever experienced before. The only face showing a different expression was Rannald, unruffled, lofty and contemptuous as ever.

Zelda must have known that this was not a time to speak. She knew we had the upper hand, and decided that it was wisest not to push the advantage we were enjoying, but to extricate ourselves from the situation. She indicated to me that I should take us home immediately, cutting the control of the transmitters as I did so. Just before I teleported us all away from the Council Chamber, Zelda made one last statement for the benefit of the citizens who I imagined had been rivetted to the entire procedure as events in the chamber unfolded.

"We are leaving now," she began, fully calm again as she enjoyed the success of our meeting with the Council. "As we are obviously not safe here. We will not be returning, as it is clear that the Council wishes us harm. We expect to be left in peace to get on with our lives quietly, a right every citizen should enjoy. Goodbye."

And at that, I cut the connection to the transmitters and took us all home, leaving the stunned Council staring at the empty space that we had just occupied. As I ported us back to the house, I allowed for Devid and his gang of rough-looking men to be freed from their strictures, though I made sure they would be stuck and immobile for a considerable time yet. I chuckled to myself as I imagined them standing like statues, their minds filled with fear that I might leave them as they were, a permanent reminder of our day in front of the Council.

Chapter Twenty-Five

The mood in our home was most peculiar after we re-emerged safely from our trip. Zelda was elated, ebullient, talking fifteen to the dozen about what had happened, barely pausing for breath, behaving in a way I had never seen before. Kallan was quiet and pensive, yet visibly sharing Zelda's sense of triumph. We children were utterly exhausted. Despite our practising of our gifts individually, and then in concert with each other, we had never had to use these for such major actions, and for such a prolonged period of time. In truth, the meeting with the Council had been the final stage of our joint practice, and it had taken its toll. We had successfully controlled the transmitters to narrowcast the events live to the world, and at the same time had resisted succumbing to the waves of antipathy flowing from the Council, and from Devid and his followers, and we had physically controlled the would-be assailants at the same time. None of us had ever attempted anything like this before, and thus had no experience of the sheer volume of energy output required, no precedent for how to cope with such a thing.

Kallan perceived that the four of us were so profoundly drained from our labours that we were not even able to move. We simply stood, mute, as Zelda's relentless babble washed over us. Kallan held up his hand to Zelda, and she immediately stilled. He then used the quiet moment to shepherd us all out of the living room where we had re-appeared, and push us gently in the direction of our bedrooms. Alone in my room, I tumbled onto the bed, fully clothed, closed my eyes, and fell instantly into a deep, almost unconscious sleep.

I awoke some time later, with no idea of how long I had slept. I still felt weary, and slightly achy, and knew that such huge effort as I had undergone in the Council Chamber would need some time to recover from. The emotional strain was perhaps even more the cause of my exhaustion than the physical toll my efforts had taken on my body. Or perhaps the two were so intertwined as to be indistinguishable. I assumed my siblings would also still feel wearied, though not as much as me, given that I had taken the brunt of the effort.

I yawned and stretched my aching muscles, then realising that I was hungry, decided I would have to summon the energy to make my way to the kitchen to find some food. It was broad daylight, and I realised with surprise that I must have slept for the best part of twenty-four hours. We had returned from the Council Chamber during the afternoon of the day before, and now it was around midday of the following day.

I moved slowly through the corridors to the kitchen where I looked around to see what I could eat. But before I could find anything, I sensed that something strange was happening elsewhere in the house. I was astonished to realise that we had visitors, *five* visitors, and that they were sitting with Zelda and Kallan in the living room. I was so taken aback by this that all thoughts of food vanished, and I moved rapidly through the house to the living room.

As I approached the door to the living room, I stopped, hesitant to enter. I decided instead to conceal my presence outside the room, and to listen in on what was being said. Zelda and Kallan were sitting on one of the small sofas, and arrayed opposite them on a larger sofa and two chairs were five members of the Council. I found this idea so strange that I doubted the evidence of my own perceptions, but on a more detailed scan, I knew that the visitors were indeed five of the Council members. I quickly perceived that they were the five more sympathetic members of the Council, sympathetic to us children that is, not to Zelda. The only one I really remembered from the meeting at the Council chamber was the tall, wide-shouldered and robust Lenora.

The conversation was being conducted in hushed tones, and I had to ramp up my eavesdropping in order to hear clearly what was being said. But even without such enhancement, I knew that the mood among the Council members was one of extreme agitation and distress. Zelda and Kallan were much calmer, radiating an odd mixture of jubilation and suspicion at the same time. I quickly ascertained that these five Council members had urgently requested that they be allowed to visit almost as soon as our meeting with the Council had ended, and that Zelda had made them wait a day before acceding to their request. I tried to discern what they were hoping to achieve just from reading their moods, but the message I received was so unclear as to be impossible to read, so I decided that I had to restrict myself to listening to the actual conversation. It must have been the disturbance caused by their arrival that had just woken me from my exhausted slumber.

"What option did we have?" I heard Kallan say in a defensive tone, clearly having just been asked why we had put on such a global display. "We know how much you've disapproved of Zelda and for so long, and then demanding our presence before the Council, finding out that you considered murdering our children, having a huge group of aggressive attackers arrive armed..."

"You know we didn't all countenance eliminating the children," interrupted one of the men in a soft voice, a gentle-looking elderly fellow with a haggard face. I wondered if he always looked this way, or only as a result of recent events in the Council Chamber.

"Murdering the children Vradley," corrected Zelda, visibly irritated that the mild-looking man had used the euphemistic word eliminating instead of murdering.

"Well, whatever word you choose to use Zelda," continued Vradley in a more aggrieved voice. "You know very well that the five of us here would never consider or agree to such a thing." Zelda grunted in a non-committal way, but did not argue the point.

"And you also know that no-one in the Council had any idea that Devid would do what he did," said another of the male Council members, a much younger man with a shock of red hair and ruddy cheeks.

"We know no such thing Breyan," Zelda retorted in a sharp tone. "And it seems likely to us that Rannald had planned Devid's actions. He is his uncle after all."

None of the Council members had any answer to this, and I surmised that, for all their protestations of ignorance of Devid's behaviour, they all thought it possible that Rannald had indeed planned the intrusion of Devid and his followers exactly as it had happened.

After a tense pause, the tall and powerful woman Lenora spoke for the first time since I had started my eavesdropping. Her voice deep and sonorous, so much so that I heard a light jangle as the reverberations in her chest caused the large and showy gold chain she wore to shift.

"None of us are here to argue on behalf of Rannald. Please believe us Zelda, Kallan. We are not here to justify what he or any other members of the Council have been planning or doing. We are here to see what can be done now, to try and repair some of the damage that has been caused by what happened yesterday."

"Damage?" said Zelda angrily. "Damage to whom Lenora? The damage is to you, the Council, to your reputation, now that the world at large knows what measures you are willing to take to put an end to me, my work, my children. You are only here to see if we will help you in overcoming the hostility coming at you from all directions. And you know what I say to that? I say no. I say you can all fuck off and shovel your own shit!"

Nobody replied to this unexpectedly crude outburst from Zelda. The silence that followed grew more and more tense and uncomfortable, until at last, Kallan felt he needed to soften the hostile atmosphere.

"Perhaps we should hear what they have to say Zelda, before we judge too harshly?" he said in a gentle voice. Zelda could never resist such persuasiveness from Kallan. She grunted and I heard her sit back in her chair.

"Well?" she then asked in a loud voice. "What have you got to say for yourselves?"

I felt the five Council members shift in their seats, and then indicate that Lenora should speak for them. She had the greatest authority there, as she had the longest tenure on the Council of any of them.

"Nobody will be demanding your attendance at the Council for the foreseeable future, Zelda," she began in her rich voice. "No-one on the Council would risk such a thing after yesterday's debacle. And your children are in no danger either. If anything were to happen to them now, the hostility towards the Council would be so great as to risk not only the roles of all of us members, but the actual existence of the Council itself. None of us will risk that, not even Rannald. In any case, there are five of us, another five who are hostile to you, and two who are indifferent. Nothing happens in the Council with those sorts of numbers. Whenever possible, we like to be in full agreement, or as close to it as we can manage. And in any case, all we want is for the whole episode to blow over, so we can carry on with our real work as we should. If the world has lost faith in us, we can't function properly, and that benefits no-one."

Zelda was about to interrupt, but Kallan shot her a disapproving look, and she subsided. Kallan then looked directly at Lenora and said,

"That makes me, us, feel somewhat reassured, Lenora, but I assume you will want something from us in return for us being left alone?"

"Huh!" interjected Zelda. "Now we come to the truth, the real reason you are all here. It is not to put our minds at rest, but as usual to make demands on us!"

"Zelda, please, calm yourself," said Kallan quietly. "Let's hear the rest before we make such judgements."

Zelda sat back again, arms crossed, a look of grumpy suspicion on her face. Kallan fixed Lenora with a shrewd look, and asked,

"Well Lenora? Do you want something from us?"

Lenora breathed in deeply, then exhaled loudly. She fiddled with the hefty gold chain around her neck which jingled loudly before she continued.

"Yes, we do."

"You see? You see?" shouted Zelda, arms flying into the air, brows dancing. "I knew it!"

Kallan ignored her, and indicated to Lenora that she should continue.

"To begin with we need you to promise that you will never again pull a stunt like yesterday, showing live to the entire world what was happening at a private Council audience."

"Not going to happen!" interrupted Zelda testily.

"Zelda!" barked Kallan. "Let her finish!" Zelda seemed surprised at Kallan's tone, but sank back on her chair, anger blazing from her eyes, but maintaining her silence.

"What else?" prompted Kallan.

"And you cannot let that child of yours, Samek I think he's called, abuse his powers to look into our minds without our permission. That was an outrageous breach of protocol and manners..."

"Without which we would not have known that some of you had considered murdering our children," interrupted Kallan angrily, incensed by this demand. Zelda nodded vigorously in agreement.

"That's as may be," continued Lenora, looking unruffled, though her disquiet was evident in the way she twisted the gold chain between her strong fingers. "But it doesn't excuse his behaviour. And...and", Lenora continued, suddenly hesitant. "And Zelda must promise to abandon this work of hers, must never again create children out of more than five progenitors. Actually, she must never again create any children, as this is only within the remit of the authorised Institutes. Individuals, as you know, are strictly forbidden from engaging in any such activity as it is the Council, on behalf of all citizens, who must be in full control of the reproduction and education of the next generation..."

"No! No! No! No! No!" bellowed Zelda, leaping off her chair and shaking her fists at the Council members. "For all your talk of individuals, I am one of the only real individuals, not one of your tamed citizens spending her time in frivolity and uniformity. And I have created a generation of unique individuals. So no to all of your demands. We will do anything and everything we need to do in order to protect ourselves, and if this means showing the world what the Council is up to then so be it. If it involves looking into your perfidious minds, then so be it. And if you think I would give up my work just because you want me to, you are living in a fantasy. And if that is all you have to say for yourselves, then there is nothing more for me to listen to."

And with that she moved rapidly towards the door, only just giving me enough time to race away, not wanting to be caught eavesdropping on the conversation. As I rushed back to my own room, I listened to the rest of the conversation between Kallan and the Council members from a safe distance. Kallan made it clear that Zelda would not relent on what she had just said, and that he agreed with her. Such demands were unjust and unworkable, and that given the historical antipathy from the Council towards our whole family, we had to reserve the right to protect ourselves in any way we saw fit. Lenora and the others entreated Kallan to speak to Zelda, to bring her round to their view, but Kallan simply kept reiterating that he agreed with Zelda. Eventually, the Council members accepted that they were getting nowhere, and took their leave, porting away from the house in a mood of despair and deep irritation, and of failure.

I could not but agree with Zelda and Kallan: the demands made on us were preposterous. And what was the Council offering in return? That they would not demand our presence again? Given the outcome from our recent meeting, this was the last thing the Council would want anyway. And to agree not to murder us? What sort of ludicrous pledge was that? But I could not help feel that the antagonism that had existed between us and the Council before yesterday would now continue in much more extreme form, and despite the fact that we would be left alone in the foreseeable future due to the Council's fear of us, what would be the long term effect of such profound antipathy?

The last thought I had before going into Adwin's room to wake him up was that the Council would surely work hard now to vilify us, to present us to the world as the offending party, to blacken our names and cause the citizens to be even more afraid of us than they already were. I shuddered at the thought of this, at what effect it could have in the long term, and decided then and there that I no longer yearned to join the world at large, to mix with ordinary people. I would not be able to trust them, and must therefore keep myself far away from them, safe in the bosom of my family.

Chapter Twenty-Six

After the visit to our home of the five Council members just before my tenth birthday, the years passed quietly. Guessing that there was likely to be a great deal of fear and mistrust towards me from the outside world, I decided that I could not risk visiting ordinary people in the towns and cities of my world. I had so little experience of dealing with other human beings that, despite my abilities, I knew I would find any overt hostility impossible to manage, creating a deeply confusing atmosphere if ever I were to find myself surrounded by strangers. I was glad I had the freedom, and safety of the estate. Perhaps I was wrong to see the fence as something keeping me in?

I spent my time at home, studying and learning, passing the time with Adwin and sometimes with my sisters or Kallan, and occasionally even with Zelda. Marna began to visit us again, which delighted me. Adwin too was overjoyed to see the return of Marna.

"I've missed her so much," he would say. "I have so much to tell her about what I've been learning, and the forest, and everything." I smiled at his childlike comments, simply glad to be able to enjoy Marna's benign company, her sense of humour, her tales of the outside world. She never again asked to bring anyone else with her: she had learned that lesson the hard way. So apart from Marna, I met nobody else outside of my family for quite a few years.

After the emotional meeting we had experienced with the Council, Adwin fell ill, probably as a result of the enormous effort he had made to support me in carrying out Zelda's plan. As always, his illness manifested itself in fevers, aching muscles, befuddlement and exhaustion, and he needed to spend several weeks in bed, gradually recovering his strength over a prolonged period of time. I tried again and again to scan his body to see if I could find the cause of his ailment, or at least to work out exactly how it was manifesting itself at a cellular physiological level. But all to no avail. Perhaps I simply lacked sufficient knowledge of the intricacies of the functioning of the human body? Or perhaps it was a demonstration of the limits of my abilities? Or was it, as I had thought before, that Adwin's problems had their source in his mind, and not his body? Was it his mental development that had been impaired as he floated in the gestation tank, and not his body's progress?

Emaleen and Safya, more secure than ever in the knowledge that other people were not to be trusted, continued in their regular trips into the natural world, travelling further and further afield, and remaining longer and longer away each time. Some days I would realise that I had not seen them for weeks, and when they returned, I was always keen to hear what they had been doing. Although Emaleen was still wary of sharing what they had been about, Safya regularly spoke to me of their adventures. I made an enthusiastic audience for the tales of her activities with her sister, climbing hills and mountains, wading through streams and rivers, fighting their way through forests and jungles. Adwin too enjoyed the tales of their exploits, sitting quietly, eyes shining, as he drank in all Safya had to tell him. My sister's descriptions of the wilds of the natural world set in motion a desire in me to explore the same, and I began to think about this more and more, wondering where I would most like to explore. Despite my profound desire never to be among strangers, the idea of widening my acquaintance of the natural world held great appeal.

With Safya, Adwin and I had achieved a fairly calm and affectionate relationship. Even with Emaleen the mood between us was placid, marred only by the usual flashes of irritation on her part. My brother and I would never be close to our sisters as we were to each other, or they were between themselves, but we got on reasonably well, wished each other well, and with Safya at least, happy to share our experiences and thoughts when we were together. For all the differences between us, even Emaleen was keenly aware of a profound connection that kept pulling the four of us back together. We were unique, the only young people in the world to have experienced the type of upbringing we had. All other people in our world had been raised in communities of children in the Institutes. We had not. Our ancestry too made us unlike anyone else: all other children were created from between three and five progenitors. We were formed from much larger numbers than this. This genetic manipulation to create our super-human powers gave us abilities and talents far beyond anything enjoyed in the world at large, beyond anything ever seen before, and this linked us in a deep way. In addition to all of this, we were pushed together by the force of public opinion towards us, the hostility and antipathy of many people, and the confusion and bewilderment of others. I occasionally wondered what would become of us, what we would be like as adults, would we have to stay on the estate because people considered us aloof or even freaks? But as I had no answers to such questions, I briskly pushed them from my mind.

Kallan was the only one of us to leave the compound and was thus, as I only learned later, the only one of us to have regular, and varied, social interaction with a wide group of friends.

Zelda, once she had calmed down after the emotional agitation of the visit to the Council, took up her work again, in direct contravention of the Council's wishes, as if nothing had happened. One difference in her was that she spent more time with me, teaching me as much as she could about the science lying behind my talents, about cloning, multi-parent embryos, teleportation and many other things. Her whole attitude towards me had been transformed by my success in the Council Chamber, and she now saw it as one of her primary missions to ensure I understood as well as possible everything there was to know not only about my own abilities, but also about her work. Given the centrality of my efforts in trumping the Council, perhaps she now looked on me as her successor, as the person most likely to take up the mantle of her work when she was no longer able to continue. I had very ambivalent feelings towards actually assisting her in her work, but no such ambivalence in enjoying the attention she was devoting to me, or joy in the expansion of my knowledge. I loved to learn, and could not soak up facts and ideas quickly enough, and relished the fact Zelda was behaving more like a mother than a jailer.

My life in those years after our visit to the Council Chamber passed quickly, busy as I was with studying and learning, playing around the estate with Adwin, occasionally flitting short distances beyond the fence. But these short trips did not satisfy me, and I began to wonder where I might like to travel to, somewhere more distant from the estate. I spent copious amounts of time studying the wild places on the planet, viewing endless films of these taken either from satellites, or even better from much closer by unmanned flying robot surveyors which swooped across the vast expanses of wilderness, storing the images they recorded for anyone to access.

I gazed in amazement at vast deserts, some with scattered plants and a few animals, to others seemingly devoid of life of any sort, endless expanses of golden dunes of sand shifting slowly in the wind. Or tropical jungles whose flora was so dense as to almost prevent any glimpse of the interior beneath the green canopy, yet clearly burgeoning with life of so many different types. Mountains were surveyed, some bare and snowy, others covered with pines and conifers, and the more verdant, river-fed valleys in between, hives of animal life. Desolate uplands, moorlands stretching away into the distance, devoid of trees or large plants, but enveloped in a uniform covering of short, green or purple foliage. But my favourites were the cold, northern forest valleys, mountains mauve in the distant mist, the forests themselves thick with conifers, spruces and pines, cut by rivers which froze solid in the winter, overflowed in cascades of frothy white water in the spring, dotted with ponds and lakes which also hardened into white flooring in the winter, blue-grey mirrors the rest of the year.

Adwin often joined me in my contemplation of the miracles of the natural world, and he sighed wistfully when I explained to him that "the animal and plant life was much more diverse before the Chaos."

"That's so sad," he replied, his innocent boy's face forlorn. "And so many people died too."

"But despite the lack of variety," I countered, to try and cheer him up. "Our world is filled with life again, all sorts of plants and animals, wild abundance everywhere. And isn't it better for nature that there are not nearly as many people? It was people who so nearly destroyed everything only eight hundred years ago."

Adwin seemed almost persuaded that the small number of humans alive was indeed a huge advantage for the flora and fauna of our time compared with the situation which prevailed in the lead up to the Chaos.

"I suppose," he mused in slightly uncertain tones, "that this leaves almost the entire planet to everything else since we only take up a tiny bit of the available land".

And it was a fact that the rest was truly wild, in a way that had not been seen since long, long before the Chaos, before the human population really began to expand. Such vast expanses of wilderness had not been seen since before the agricultural revolution, ten thousand years or so before the Chaos, when the human species began to reproduce at an unprecedented rate.

The climate of our world, then and now is warmer than it was in the period preceding the Chaos. This fact, and the relative paucity of human population means that nearly everyone lived, and still lives in two fairly narrow bands of latitude stretching around the planet, one to the north of the equator, the other to the south. These occupy a region stretching from the warmer temperate zones on one side, to the subtropical zones on the other. The tropics themselves are generally considered too hot and unpleasant to live in, and nobody seems willing to brave a permanent existence in the cooler temperate or cold zones of the world. Why bother, after all, living somewhere which is a struggle due to the climate, when there is so much space available in the comfortable and pleasant zones for the small number of our species.

Chapter Twenty-Seven

Zelda continued to monitor my studies, especially in the science underlying her own particular interests, as if she wanted me to one day take over from her. As I knew, her particular fascination was in the production of multi-parent embryos, and she went to some lengths to ensure I understood how the Institutes produced cohorts of siblings. I wanted to know more about the internal workings of the Institutes themselves, but she always fended off these discussions, telling me they were not interesting, and instead returned to the scientific basis of her main work.

I learned that immature human eggs, oocytes as Zelda called them, were always removed from the female foetuses as they approached full term, and stored for future use. And that a similar process was carried out on the male foetuses, with spermatogonia (the precursors of actual sperm) being removed from the immature testicles, also for future use.

Although Zelda did not patronise me, she nevertheless always explained the science in terms even a child could understand, and I understood it well enough to question its morality. When querying whether such actions were ethical, Zelda merely scoffed, and said that we were all required to make 'donations' for the common good. She went on to explain that when a new cohort was required, a small number of immature eggs were thawed and induced to mature, and these were then fertilised by sperm which had been produced from the spermatogonia. This selection of fertilised eggs was allowed to develop for about three days, until they had each reached the eight cell stage. These eight cell embryos were then split into individual cells, and cells were then recombined from different embryos, giving an identical number of eight cell embryos, but this time each one made up of cells from more than the original two 'parents'.

Cohorts differed in size, but were always in multiples of eight, and only ever twenty-four, thirty-two or forty individuals. And each cohort was created from sperm and eggs of three, four or five progenitors, depending on what was required. Many cohorts were all male or all female, produced only from sperm which had either XX or XY chromosomes and thus only leading to single sex offspring, and these, as Zelda explained, were simpler to produce, as the individual cells after being split from the first eight cell embryos would all contain either XX or XY chromosomes only. But it was easy enough now to ensure that only 'male' or 'female' cells were combined with each other after being split from the first embryo even where these cells were of both sexes. When I asked Zelda why mixed sex cohorts were produced, and not just the simpler single sex variety, she told me that it was now considered healthier, psychologically, for children of the same age to be of both sexes, and that it helped children become better adjusted to adult life.

Some niggling unease nibbled away at the back of my mind during my discussions of this process with Zelda, and eventually it came to me what the problem was. On one occasion, as Zelda was waxing lyrical about the beauty and almost simplicity of splitting cells from an embryo and reconstituting them in different combinations, I suddenly interrupted.

"But why do we still have men and women?" I asked.

Zelda stopped in mid-sentence, looking at me with great surprise.

"What on earth do you mean?" she queried, genuinely puzzled by my question.

I paused, collecting my thoughts so I could clarify my query. In truth, I was not entirely sure what I meant, but knew that it was important.

"I mean," I began slowly. "Why, if babies are produced this way, or people could easily be cloned, did people decide, after the Chaos, not to just get rid of one of the sexes. Wouldn't it be easier, simpler, just to have one? And wouldn't it remove some of the complication of social life?"

Zelda stood quite still, shocked into silence by my question. I could not tell whether she thought my query incredibly obtuse or highly perceptive. I waited quietly for her reply. Finally, she answered.

"We have discussed human cloning at length, and I have explained why we do not do that," she said tersely, preventing any further discussion of the issue by what seemed a change of topic, or a refusal to answer my question directly. I nodded, and decided not to share my lack of true comprehension at the decision made by our post-Chaos ancestors never to clone human beings. Zelda and I had argued that point often enough with no satisfactory outcome to our disputes.

"And I told you," she continued. "We need sperm and eggs to make embryos. That is the most basic bit of biology which surely you have known for years?" she added in a slightly sarcastic tone.

Again, I nodded, slightly stung by her tone. She looked at me again, still puzzled, so I felt a need to clarify my thoughts.

"Yes of course I know that, but it's not what I meant. It's not what I asked. Surely if we wanted we could still create male and female embryos, let them develop a bit, long enough to be able to harvest their oocytes and spermatogonia, so we could produce more embryos later on, but then only actually bring to full term one sex or the other. If it's more problematic socially to have two sexes, as you seem to be suggesting, why not just have one?"

Zelda looked bewildered by my comments and stared at me for a few moments before replying.

"But that would mean making a conscious decision to abort all the foetuses of one sex. Always." She said breathlessly.

"But you told me already that any foetus with any problem or imperfection is always aborted anyway, so what would be the difference," I countered. "And how is that so different from aborting all those of the 'wrong' sex?"

"But that is simply outrageous!" stated Zelda, adopting a high moral position which was totally unjustified, given what I knew of her experiments, and, gripped by a demon who demanded consistency, I could not help myself but add,

"But you have a whole huge room full of aborted foetuses, and you didn't think they were good enough to let *them* live!"

On seeing Zelda's appalled and angry reaction to my final comment, I instantly regretted my outburst. But as she stood in front of me, her fists clenched in anger, her face flushing red, I knew I was right to criticise her. She could not adopt such an ethical position on the one hand, while carrying out such unethical experiments on the other. I had shown up her hypocrisy, and perhaps this is what had angered her more than being reminded of what she had done. I did not believe she had any sense of guilt or wrongdoing whatsoever in relation to the rows of dead foetuses in her laboratory, so there must be another cause for her rage. She hated being caught out holding contradictory views by anyone, and perhaps especially by me, a pre-pubescent child of her own creation. She glared at me, the blotches of dry skin on her face livid, the heat flushing through her skin palpable from where

I stood. I sensed a most peculiar emotion run through her as she stared at me unable to speak: perhaps she had created a little monster, a being that she should be able to control but who was showing signs of being outside her charge.

After a tense, angry stand-off, during which we both glared at each other without speaking, she finally managed to find her voice.

"I think it is time you left," she said in a quiet but vaguely menacing voice. Needing no further encouragement, I turned and fled. But as I did so I knew I had won the encounter. I had shown up her contradictory attitudes, demonstrated to her that some of her apparent morality was built on sand, and she had no answer to my criticism. It was the first time I had ever bested Zelda, and it felt marvellous. I knew that I would probably not be invited back into her company for a long time after this, and I would miss the discussions we had had, the intimacy we were beginning to develop, but this was outweighed by the sense of victory, of triumph over my own creator. It seemed that one could win battles simply by asking for consistency in one's opponents.

In the end, even as Zelda had been bringing me further and further into her confidence, I had never really trusted that she did so through increased affection for me. Instead, I always felt as though even this change of behaviour on her part was merely part of a long-running experiment, and that I was simply an object, a tool which she would use in her experiments as she saw fit and as it suited her. It seemed to me that she did not look on me, or my siblings for that matter, as real, full human beings. Perhaps she did not see anyone like that, not Marna nor even Kallan. Perhaps human beings were simply artefacts, like any other, animate and inanimate, which Zelda used or discarded according to her needs.

My sense of triumph lasted throughout the rest of that day. Zelda's quiet rage pervaded the house, and this endured far longer than my sense of triumph. We did not see her at meals for days, as she locked herself away in her laboratory.

My life returned to normal, minus the meetings and discussions with Zelda. I continued to learn all I could about cloning, multi-parent embryos, teleportation and everything else that interested me. I became intrigued by meteorology, enthusiastically studying weather patterns now and all the way back to the pre-Chaos era, and was especially fascinated in learning how the Chaos had itself permanently altered weather patterns throughout the world. It was sobering to realise that human activities, carried out on such a huge scale by such vast numbers of people, could actually create a durable alteration to the weather systems of an entire planet, that although the planet was able to repair itself, it was never to be the same again. It carried the scars of human activity.

Chapter Twenty-Eight

Time passed much as before, with few changes to our daily routine. Four years passed since our visit to the Council chamber, and we now found ourselves in 2813. Adwin and I remained as close as ever, and he watched with great interest as I underwent the changes wrought by puberty. Our sisters had become women some years before, they being five years older than me. I had not been aware of the changes to my sisters' bodies. Perhaps it was because the gap in age was so large, or they were so often away from home, or that the differences were not so blunt with girls as with boys. Their voices did not change, and their growth was gradual. The main change my brother and I noticed was the growth of their chests (as Adwin called them), until one day we realised they were much the same shape as Zelda, though taller and slimmer, not as stocky.

But me, shortly after my thirteenth birthday I suddenly grew at an astonishing rate and in a period of only half a year or so I shot up by more than thirty centimetres, my voice becoming that of a man, almost overnight it seemed to me. The ten year old Adwin laughed as he watched me learning to control my newly elongated limbs, and for some months I was clumsy and gawkish, as if new to the processes of walking, running and managing my long, gauche legs and arms.

"You're so much taller than me!" Adwin said. "But you're so gangly, like a spider with four legs. It's funny when you walk with your arms dangling down and your feet almost missing their step. Walk in front of me," he ordered as we walked through the forest one day. "So I can have some fun watching you trip over or stub your toe. It's nice of you to give me so much laugh at!"

"Ha ha," I replied, forcing myself to sound as if I joined his merriment, deciding this was the best attitude to take. "But I suppose I must look funny to you, as if I've suddenly stopped being able to walk normally." I laughed, pretending to find my own incompetence entertaining. I knew if I let my brother think he had needled me with his comments, he would just carry on teasing me.

When we swam in the pond in our forest, he could not help but stare at the little thatch of black hair above my genitals. When I noticed him staring, he blushed and mumbled, "what is that? Down there?" I merely shrugged.

"It'll happen to you soon enough," I said, a thought which seemed to shock him.

"I don't know if that idea is appealing or appalling!" he retorted. "To have hair sprouting where it didn't before."

"No point worrying about it," I replied. "You won't have any control of it. And I rather like it," I added smugly. "It shows I'm becoming a man, and I'm not just little child like you." Adwin scowled slightly at this comment, clearly irritated, but instead of deigning to reply, lifted his head high, arched his dark eyebrows, and strode away, ignoring my giggles behind him.

Zelda took me back into her confidences again once she had overcome her anger at being caught out holding contradictory thoughts. In fact, over the years we regularly engaged in altercations over all sorts of issues, and it became a routine part of our relationship, arguing, not talking to each other, then picking up where we had left off as if nothing had happened. Kallan and Marna were both experts at managing Zelda's ill temper, and often acted as go-betweens when Zelda and I had quarrelled. Neither Zelda nor I ever asked them to, or ever mentioned their intervention, but without them the periods when Zelda and I did not communicate would certainly have been much longer.

One time, during a visit by Marna, she asked me to come for a walk with her in the garden, alone. I was surprised at her request, but readily agreed. We walked quietly for a short period, before Marna turned to me and spoke in a curiously earnest voice.

"I have something interesting to tell you," she said. "Something you need to know." I perked up, alerted by her tone that she had real news to impart.

"I met a very interesting man recently. He makes programmes about people's lives which he calls docudramas. He's really rather famous. Haari's his name. And when he realised that I was a friend of your family's, he was fascinated, telling me that he's been trying to contact you, Samek, for years, ever since you first went to the Council. He wants to meet you and make a programme about you."

I was speechless. What a bizarre idea.

"And," continued Marna, oblivious to my surprise. "He politely queried why Samek had never replied to any of his many, many messages."

"I never got any messages," I replied. "Not from him or from anyone else."

"That's what I told him must be the case. I said you were a well-raised boy who surely would not have simply ignored his messages. And I promised him I'd ask you when I next spoke to you."

"But why didn't I get his messages?" I wondered out loud. "If any came to the house, I'm sure they would have been passed on to me."

"Hmm," mused Marna. "I know that messages get through to Kallan and to Zelda, as I've contacted both of them many times. I wonder where he sent the messages?"

"What do you mean?"

"Well, I'm sure Kallan would have let you know if any had arrived for you. But Samek, my dear boy, even I assume that Zelda would have done no such thing. You know how she wants to keep you all locked away, protected' from the wickedness of the outside world. I can only imagine that if the messages went to Zelda, she would have made sure they never ended up with you, or that you even knew that you had received any."

I knew Marna must be right. I did not know this Haari, but why would he have lied to Marna? The only explanation was that Zelda had received, or intercepted, all of the communications from Haari, expunging them, ensuring I never had any inkling of their existence. I felt a surge of anger towards my mother, a hot flush spreading across my cheeks. Marna must have seen my reaction, and guessed that I was on the brink of storming off to rail at my mother.

"But Samek my dear, what benefit in confronting your mother on this? She is so stubborn, that it would only make her dig her heels in. And get angry." I was not persuaded, opening my mouth to argue with Marna.

"Samek, Samek! Listen to me and heed my advice," she said, holding a chubby hand up in front of my face. "If you must have a go at her, bide your time and pick your moment. But leave it alone for now. And in the meantime, why don't *you* contact Haari directly? I'll give you his location. And Zelda doesn't even need to know," she added with a chuckle and a conspiratorial wink. I felt my anger abate in the face of Marna's impish suggestion. And at the shocking idea that I could make direct contact with a stranger, an outsider, the first such person I would ever know in the world outside the compound. After this, Marna and I chatted for a while about other things, but my mind was focused on Haari. Should I contact him? When should I contact him? What would be the point?

After a few days of deliberating, my inquisitiveness got the better of me, and, on a day when Kallan was away from the estate, I stole into his room. I stood in front of his vidiscreen and spoke the location of Haari's apartment that Marna had given me. The screen glowed brightly, and without warning a face appeared.

A man's face came into view. His age was hard to determine, though with my extremely limited experience of other people, perhaps this failing was mine. But he was somewhere between late youth and early middle age. I thought he was probably around forty or so. His features showed a man who had lived life to the full, surprisingly deep wrinkles etched around his eyes and the corners of his mouth, and furrowing his brow. He was good-looking in a rather worn sort of way, with mid-brown, messy hair which was cut fairly short. But his eyes, which were a highly unusual colour of light golden-brown, almost amber, shone with a rare intensity, a penetrating look that caused me a sharp intake of breath as he stared straight into my eyes. He had a kind face, though wore what seemed to be a permanent look of irony, of world-weariness, underneath which I sensed shadows of sadness which he tried hard to hide.

I was surprised that I recognised him, though it took me a few moments to recollect from where. I had in fact seen him a number of times presenting programmes on the 3DV. He occupied his time producing and then showing highly personalised films of the lives of citizens, some famous, but many not. He had presented the lives of Council members, great artists, musicians and writers, but more often the lives of interesting but humble people. His work had made him one of the most celebrated people on the planet, and I knew that he was admired and respected by many, but disliked intensely by others for what they considered his over-intrusive and idiosyncratic presentations of the lives of others, lives which he had a tendency to dramatise for effect.

He smiled broadly at me, his face lighting up, the expression of irony effaced by the fullness of the smile.

"I finally get to meet you," he said. His voice was strong and resonant, not exactly loud, but with a carrying power that pierced the noise. It rumbled strongly in the lower register as it seemed to emerge from deep in his chest.

"After so many messages, ever since I first saw you five years ago with the Council. You've never replied to me."

He smiled again, though his deep voice carried a faint tone of criticism, of hurt feelings. I frowned slightly in confusion.

"Marna told me. But I've never received a message from you," I said. "Never."

He looked surprised, not knowing whether to believe me. I too did not know whether his claims were true.

"Why have you sent me so many messages?" I asked directly.

"Because I wanted to meet you, to persuade you to let me follow you, get to know you, make a presentation about you and your life to show the world," he answered frankly. "As you may be aware, that's what I do."

Even though Marna had spoken of this possibility, I was still taken aback. A presentation of me and my life? Present me to the world the way I had seen him do for other people? What a strange idea.

"Why would you want to do that?" I queried in puzzlement.

"Because you are the most interesting, the most fascinating person in our entire world. Believe you me, nobody else comes close. I would give anything to be able to get to know you and then to show the world who you really are."

"Why would they want to see that?" I countered, genuinely confused.

"Surely you're aware that the entire planet is obsessed with you? They have been for years, ever since they first saw you as a child making fools of the Council. And the gamers have produced a whole world of virtual reality adventures in which you are the star, the hero, or actually sometimes the anti-hero. But I have to tell you, not all the feelings towards you are positive," he said, merely confirming to me what I already knew.

"What do you mean, the hero or anti-hero?" I queried, feeling vaguely irritated by Haari's words.

"In the thousands of adventure games that so many citizens love to play, alone and together. You are sometimes the saviour of humanity, sometimes its nemesis." I frowned in confusion.

"Why should I be the anti-hero?" I asked. This time it was Haari's turn to frown.

"Many people are wary of you and your gifts, which you showed so clearly as a small child at the Council Chamber. And I think lots of them are worried about what you're really capable of, what you plan to do with your gifts. Whether they've got anything to fear from you."

"You're rather blunt," I replied, peeved by what he said.

"Perhaps", he replied. Then he peered at me keenly through his amber eyes and added, "But you must know I'm right."

I could not deny it. I knew full well that most humans were emotional creatures. And how would they not have been fearful of a small boy controlling the world?

"But why would working with you help?" I asked.

He paused, smiled, and said, "I could show the world who you really are, the real person, the ordinary human lying beneath all those phenomenal abilities and beneath the completely erroneous image they all have of you of some kind of devil or demi-god, or both at the same time."

He had a point, yet I was wary.

"What would it entail?" I asked. "What would it mean if I said yes?"

His golden eyes lit up with excitement, as my question suggested I might be considering his offer.

"I'd have to spend time with you," he said quickly. "Really, a lot of time. I'd have to visit you at home many times, seeing where you live and how you live."

I must have looked so shocked at this suggestion that he laughed. A strange laugh full of genuine humour, but underpinned with something else, a darker emotion, as if his humour were tinged with...what? Irony? Cynicism? The smile accompanying the laughter disappeared as quickly as it had appeared.

"And you'd have to come and visit me, come to where I live, meet my friends, and I'll take you out and about, around Beyra, to any other places you want to go, towns, cities, the seaside, concerts, parties, other events, anywhere and everywhere you want to go, just to see you and know you in as many different environments as possible."

I stood transfixed by his words. The shock of contemplating him visiting my home was great, but it was nothing compared to the prospect of visiting his home, meeting his friends, travelling, going to parties! Such things were totally outside my experience, outside what I thought I would ever experience. They were such ordinary things really, yet not ever intended for someone like me. They tripped off his tongue so easily, obviously everyday events for him. Did he have any idea how outlandish his suggestions sounded to me, outlandish yet irresistible? Did he understand me so well, know my restricted life to such a degree that he knew that I would find it almost impossible to refuse his offer?

"But how can I trust you?" I said quietly, trying to keep the obvious desire to do so from my voice.

"Why don't you look into my mind? I know you can do that as I've been reading as much genuine information about you as I could find, scant though such material is. And you know that I can't hide my intentions if you do that, that you'll be able to see everything."

"You'd let me do that?" I asked incredulously. I had been led to believe that such mental penetration was deemed one of the most undesirable things a person could undergo, that it was seen as a violation, a transgression of the most basic sense of personal integrity and freedom, and yet here was Haari cheerfully offering to let me do it.

"Of course, if that's the only way you'll trust me,", he said, smiling his ironic smile once again.

I nodded, and quickly entered his mind, before he could change it and tell me not to. I had never done this from such a distance, but found it easy, perhaps aided by being in contact with him, and by his willingness to succumb. I probed gently, as he stood calmly in front of me on the other side of the screen. I was surprised by what I felt. He seemed to like me in a way that was completely unexpected. I had hoped to find him reliable, trustworthy perhaps, but really only interested in me for the purposes of his activities in creating a presentation about my life. What astonished me was that he felt a genuine desire to show me to the world in the best possible light, to dispel the suspicions and fears of so many citizens towards me, and to do this out of his own feelings of warmth towards me.

As I probed his mind, surprise showing clearly on my face, I watched his features register my reaction with obvious pleasure. He knew that I was seeing what he really felt towards me, and his craggy, lined face crinkled in a huge grin which took in every part of his visage from his forehead to his chin, from ear to ear, this time chasing all hint of irony from his features. His humour was contagious, and as I withdrew with a snap from of his mind, I found myself also grinning like a fool, not even sure why I did so. Perhaps it was simply the novelty of meeting a stranger who demonstrated such simple, yet clear warmheartedness towards me, and so unexpectedly.

"Yes," I said simply.

"Yes what?" he asked.

"Yes, I'll agree to what you suggest," I confirmed. "Or at least, I'll agree to us getting to know each other, and then later I'll decide if I want you to show me to the world. But on that second point I make no promise."

His expression of delight was like a warm summer breeze, and I stood basking in it.

"And will you really take me to all those places, anywhere I want to go?" I asked breathlessly, still hardly able to believe it. I would never dare to visit such places alone, prevented from doing so by my fear of the outside world. But with a friend, one experienced in the ways of the world, I could take this much-desired step.

"Yes. I promise. But first I'll come and visit you at home," he replied.

I nodded, though I knew if I told Zelda I was to receive a visitor, a storm would erupt. But in the end, there was nothing Zelda could do to stop it happening. I would go and collect Haari myself, regardless of Zelda's feelings. Zelda would just have to be her rude, brusque self.

As I thought about Zelda, an unpleasant thought about her struck me. Before I acted on it however, I told Haari that I would contact him very soon, directly, by mindspeaking to him. I then smiled at him and cut the connection.

As I did so I returned to the thought I had just had about Zelda: that she had intercepted all my messages from Haari over the years. And not only intercepted them, but destroyed them and never told me I had received them. Zelda's desire to control my life was so complete, that I knew this must be what had happened. And her profound mistrust of all 'outsiders', as she called them, would have added more zeal to her isolation of me. But if Haari's messages had all been destroyed, how many others had I not received? How many other people had tried to contact me, only to be thwarted by the barrier Zelda had erected as she acted as my jailer? As I contemplated Zelda's actions, a rage entered me which I quickly suppressed.

I pushed my anger deep down inside, left it alone for the moment, but not forgotten. In contemplating what I thought was Zelda's betrayal of me, of my independence and basic rights, I smiled to myself as I contemplated, with great relish, telling Zelda that I was soon to have a visitor, and that there was absolutely nothing she could do about it.

Chapter Twenty-Nine

During the years following our fraught visit to the Council Chamber, we heard very little from that body. Zelda occasionally informed us that she had received some contact from one or more of the amenable members of the Council, usually Lenora or Vradley, but nothing ever seemed to come of this. The only thing of real interest that cropped up in conversations, mostly between Zelda, Kallan and Marna, was the fact that a new Council would shortly be chosen, the present one having almost reached its five year term. From discussions I had heard over mealtimes, it seemed that the lengthy process of selection was about to begin, and that by the end of the year, there would be a new Council. This did not, of course, mean that the new Council would be any more friendly towards Zelda or our family. And, according to Marna and Kallan, it looked likely that at least some of the hostile members would be chosen again, including Rannald as Speaker, for yet another term.

Zelda always dismissed the Council as irrelevant, believing them to have been sufficiently cowed by our visit. Kallan and Marna, however, did not share her dismissive attitude, and believed that our troubles with the Council were far from over. Marna particularly, found the Council's apparent silence towards us disconcerting, believing that the hostile members were biding their time, and almost certainly planning something in the meantime. She and Kallan could not accept that they had closed the door on us and would meekly allow us to live our lives in peace. Marna, more sociable and politically astute than my mother, often tried to warn Zelda about Rannald and his allies on the Council, and tried to get Zelda to consider what their next move would be, but Zelda relentlessly dismissed Marna's concerns, even when Marna was supported by Kallan. Zelda was utterly unmovable on this issue, which exasperated Marna who accused Zelda of burying her head in the sand.

"Just because you want something to be a certain way Zelda, doesn't mean it is!" Marna would state on many different occasions, rubbing her chubby hands together anxiously as she spoke, but to no avail.

As the day for choosing a new Council approached, Marna's warnings to Zelda became more urgent. When Zelda tetchily asked Marna why she was becoming more strident in her cautioning about the Council, Marna explained that it seemed obvious to her that the present Council would want to act before it was too late, before they were no longer in power. They did not have long to make their move, and Marna was convinced they would do so before they were replaced. Zelda, arrogant as ever, continued to scoff.

Marna tried another tactic in relation to the Council's plans, asking me to look directly into the minds of Rannald and his supporters to see what they were planning. As the Council scared me, I was initially wary of doing this, remembering the outrage this engendered the first time I had done it. But Marna was persuasive, and eventually I agreed. I did not trust the Council, and felt that breaching their privacy was the lesser evil even if they were aware of me doing so, if this would warn us of any danger they posed towards us. But to my utter astonishment, when I tried to locate the haughty Rannald and the other hostile Council members, in order to scan their thoughts, I could not actually find them. I searched and searched, but there seemed to be no trace of them, no hint of the Speaker or his four cronies.

I scanned over and over again, confused by my inability to locate the five inimical Council members. Suddenly, all of them appeared to me. I surmised that they must somehow have been able to block my location scanning, and I guessed that they had been shielded by something that allowed them to hide. I tried to ascertain what this was, but all I could sense, vaguely, was a small chamber fully enclosed by a metallic material I did not recognise and which my gifts could not penetrate. I was stunned, as I had believed myself capable of seeing through any barrier, but clearly this was not the case. I reminded myself to look into the material enclosing the chamber at a future date, and in the meantime I rapidly scanned in turn the minds of our five adversaries on the Council while I had the chance. I hoped they were unaware of my intrusion, having to be subtle to achieve this. In order to be successful, I had to substantially reduce the clarity of my own probing, such that I could not get a clear sense of what was happening inside their heads.

Despite this, I found images of our family in their recent memories, and was taken aback to discover that we still figured so strongly in their minds. Yet their thoughts were now unfocused, with little of substance for me to dig out. Their hostility towards us was so clear however, that to perceive this I would not have even needed to enter their minds. Yet the thoughts I encountered were inchoate, and I wondered if they were deliberately not allowing clear considerations of my family to form. But the feeling of menace was almost palpable.

After wondering for a few moments about what I had discovered, I realised that they must have deliberately obscured themselves behind a protective wall to discuss specific plans, and that having now left the enclosed chamber, they were disciplined enough to abandon the clear ideas they had been discussing, leaving only a shadow of general antipathy towards us behind, nothing specific I could grasp. They obviously feared my ability to read their minds, and had taken extreme measures to protect themselves. Or perhaps someone else had assisted them in this. I was unable to report anything of clarity to Marna, a fact which disappointed her greatly.

"Keep trying Samek, and see if you can work out how to penetrate the chamber they hide themselves away in," Marna encouraged.

I did as she bid, and tried again and again to read their thoughts, but they did not give away any information of substance which could help us. I decided instead to try and pierce the shield of metallic material around the chamber they used to discuss secret matters.

It proved harder than I expected, especially at such a great distance. The material used to create the chamber must have been specifically designed and created for the very purpose of blocking mind scanning. If Zelda had been more amenable to discussions about the Council, I could perhaps usefully have asked her for her thoughts on the matter, and for suggestions as to what exactly the material was. In the meantime, I was planning to move closer to the chamber to see if proximity would make it more permeable. Before I had a chance to suggest this course of action to Marna, disaster struck, a calamity on such a massive scale that all other thoughts and considerations were forced from my mind.

I was walking with Marna, Kallan and Adwin in the garden one morning during Marna's visit. The weather was fine and dry, a cool clear autumn day. We were chatting and laughing, simply enjoying the stroll and each other's company. I was struck, suddenly and without warning, by a wave of such intense horror from Emaleen that I was literally felled, collapsing to my knees on the garden path. I screamed as Emaleen's terror and pain invaded me, putting my hands over my ears as if this could block out her distress.

The others stopped dead, staring at me aghast, knowing instantly that something was dreadfully wrong. They all shouted at me at once, desperate to know what was causing me such anguish, but I was rendered mute by the ferocity of Emaleen's torment. Her thoughts were so powerful, and so unformed that for long moments I was unable to make any sense of what had happened. Abruptly I knew.

"Safya, Safya, Safya!!" I shrieked, making the others around me jump backwards with the volume and tone of my cries. I stared at them all, wide-eyed, incapable of saying anything but repeat the name of my sister.

“Safya, Safya, Safya!”

“What, Samek? What is it?” shrieked Adwin, his high treble voice close to cracking as he felt my profound distress. “What about Safya?” he yelled.

I could still not enunciate the messages that Emaleen was hurling out in all directions. I remained on my knees on the ground, shaking my head with disbelief, so shocked I could barely respond. Adwin began to shudder and shake, so caught up was he in my own emotional state. Zelda came racing across the lawn from the house, having been alerted to the fact that something momentous had happened by the almost uncontrolled waves of anguish which were pouring out of me. She stopped in front of me, panting for breath, shocked to see me in such a state. She fumbled for words, but found none, and simply stood stock still beside the others, waiting for me to gain sufficient composure to tell them what had happened. Kallan stared silently at my behaviour, though as yet he had no clear idea what was causing it.

After what must have seemed an interminable pause for the people standing like statues around me, I whispered through bared teeth.

“Safya is dead! She has been killed!”

Chapter Thirty

A horrified silence met my declaration. So aghast were my family and Marna, that Adwin's shaking abruptly stopped. All breath was held.

After a prolonged moment during which all motion around us seemed to cease, all sound muffled to the point of utter hush, the world frozen in stillness, I uttered the words again in barely more than a whisper.

"Safya is dead."

I knew I was right, yet had to repeat the phrase several more times, as if to convince myself of the veracity of what I was saying. Kallan collapsed onto the ground, tears flowing, loudly sobbing and shaking his head. Adwin stood completely still, staring at me in disbelief. Marna and Zelda simply looked bewildered, as yet to really hear what I had said.

Finally Zelda shook her head lightly, thereby dragging herself out of her shock. She fixed me with an intense gaze, bushy eyebrows drawn almost completely together, hand rapidly passing over her hair as if to calm herself with this familiar gesture. She cleared her throat once and whispered,

"What do you mean Samek? What do you mean?"

I stared back at her, blocking much of the energy of Emaleen's intense distress.

"Safya, she's dead," I managed to force out. "Emaleen is there. She's...she's been injured. She can't react, can't do anything but scream and scream for help."

"Where is she?" Marna asked, gathering sufficient control to be able to think practically.

"I'm not sure," I replied. "Somewhere in some mountains."

"Well find her!" Zelda snapped at me angrily. "Find her!"

I nodded, realising that I was not thinking sensibly. I quickly followed the channel linking me to Emaleen and managed to locate her though her thoughts were jumbled and twisted with pain and distress. I nodded again when I had done so and Zelda said,

"Take us there, now."

"No, no, no!" Kallan shouted, blue eyes flying open, silver brows raised high, as he gained sufficient control to realise what I was about to do. "I can't see it. I just can't see it."

"Very well Kallan," said Zelda. "You do not have to come. But some of us have to go now and see what happened, quickly, before anything changes, so we can find out what really happened."

"And to help Emaleen!" Adwin said loudly, glaring at Zelda as he shook himself out of his shocked torpor.

"Of course, of course," replied Zelda, without looking at my brother. "That's what I meant."

"Adwin, stay and look after Kallan," she continued, holding up her hand as Adwin began to object. "Samek, Marna and I will go now and see what happened." She then added, looking at Adwin. "And bring them home."

I glanced at Adwin and he indicated that this was alright with him. I felt that he did not in truth want to go and see the sight of his dead sister. He had felt that it was the right thing to do, but was actually glad to have the excuse of caring for Kallan so he did not have to witness such an awful spectacle. I had no desire to see such a thing either, but knew that my presence was essential, both to accurately port us to the exact location, and to have any chance of discovering what had really happened.

"Ready?" I asked Marna and Zelda. "Yes," they both replied instantly.

Without pause I grabbed their hands and set the porting process in motion, and an instant later we materialised on a flat, grassy meadow, high in the mountains my sisters had been climbing. I was vaguely aware of trees and bushes behind us, but was only interested in what we saw before us. The grassy plain ended some six or seven metres in front of us with a cliff, a sheer drop, plunging hundreds of metres straight down to a stony slope which extruded from the base of the cliff. The plain was empty. I rushed to the edge of the cliff, followed by Zelda and Marna. I looked over the abrupt drop and saw Emaleen lying, part way down the steep side of the cliff, on a small ledge.

She was quivering with anguish but no longer screaming. Her mental distress was undiminished, and I retained the block I had put in place, lest I be unable to function under the onslaught of such intense mental agony.

Marna began to lean over the edge, but I quickly stopped her by placing a hand on her chest.

"No," I growled in my newly adult voice. "We need to be careful. The ground here may not be stable."

Marna stepped back from the side of the cliff to stand beside my mother. I gently allowed a message to flow from my mind to Emaleen's, quietly informing her of our presence and attempting to reassure her. I had some success in this, and felt a slight abatement in the level of her distress. Simply knowing that we were there, that help had arrived, provided some small comfort. I knew she was injured, badly. At a glance I could see her leg was broken, and there was a bloody gash on her head, blond hair matted in the scarlet liquid still flowing copiously from the wound.

Emaleen was gazing downwards, leaning so precariously that I feared she might topple from the tiny ledge that had surely saved her life. I followed her line of vision, down the stony slope below where she lay. I gasped in horror at what I saw, and jerked backwards so as to block the sight from my eyes. About halfway down the cliff, dangling from a sharp rocky outcrop, was Safya. She was on her back, which, from the angle of her body, was clearly broken, her arms and legs flopping loosely over the edge of the outcrop, her long blond hair flapping pitifully in the breeze, her grey eyes wide, still showing the horror of her plunge over the cliff's edge. Blood flowed from the back of her body, trickling slowly down the bottom half of the cliff. It was clear she was dead.

"Safya is dead," I whispered, confirming what I had already told my family. "And Emaleen is badly injured."

Marna spoke from behind me and asked in a quiet, anxious voice,

"Can you do anything? Bring them up. Can you save Safya?"

I burst into tears at her question, shaking my head as I did so.

"No," I replied in a tear-thickened voice. "I can rescue Emmy, and try and get Safya's body. But I can't bring someone back from the dead."

"Why not? Why not?" shouted Zelda, grabbing me by the shoulders and shaking me as she did so. The force of her gesture almost toppled us both over the side of the cliff. "How do you know?" Continued Zelda angrily. "You have not even found the limits of what you can do!"

"I just can't," I replied tearfully, woebegone to have to make such a confession. "Nobody can. I wouldn't know where to start, and it's just too late."

Zelda stopped suddenly, her arms dropping from my shoulders, as if realising that I spoke the truth, that her aggressive manner was unwarranted.

"I am sorry," she said more quietly. "I am sorry. I did not mean, I just, I...," and she fell silent, unable to finish her sentence.

We stood in melancholy silence, heartbroken at what we witnessed. Emaleen gazed almost vacantly, unable to react to our presence, only capable of staring blankly over the edge of the ledge to where her sister lay unmoving. I could simply not accept that Safya was dead, that she would never again enjoy life, walk and talk, spend time with her family. It was too great a concept to cope with so suddenly with no warning.

I spoke softly to Emaleen, both out loud and into her mind at the same time, to ensure she heard me.

"I'm going to bring her back up, Emmy, so we can take her home. And you too."

Emaleen's quivering halted for a moment, and I knew she had heard me. I leaned gingerly over the cliff, looking keenly at its almost sheer face, until I noticed a tiny ledge close to the outcrop carrying Safya's body. I gathered my courage and ported myself to the tiny ledge. There I balanced as well as I could, feeling slightly dizzy as I tried in vain to ignore the long drop beneath me, then stretched over as far as I could, my finger tips finally making contact with my sister's shoulder, the only part of her body I could reach. I quickly carried us both back to the cliff top before I lost my precarious footing. I then carefully repeated the process with Emaleen. She seemed unaware of the extent of her injuries, oblivious to pain in the depth of her distress. I lay her beside Safya whose broken body lay sprawled on the grass, and Emaleen turned her bleeding head to stare at her sister, torn between the horror of contemplating Safya's damaged corpse and the relief that she had at least been rescued from her perilous position on the cliff side.

I knew I had more important work to do. I was aware that asking Emaleen what had happened would be useless. She was in such a profound state of shock that she would not be able to answer me, and even if she did, her words would be incoherent. I gently scanned her mind directly. After I had done so, I relayed what I seen to Marna and Zelda.

"They were both here, on this grassy meadow, enjoying the view, when they heard something, something loud, right behind them. They turned round and to their huge surprise, a flyer was landing just behind them, literally only metres from where they stood. Before they could react, four big brawny men jumped out of the craft and rushed towards them. Safya, standing upright near the edge of the cliff, was unable to stop the men rushing her and pushing her without warning straight over the top of the cliff. Emaleen reached out to grab her as she fell, overbalancing and following her over the cliff. One of the men, who seemed to be the leader, shouted again, and they all rushed back to the flyer waiting for them at the back of the meadow. They leapt in and the vehicle lifted into the air and sped off."

"Did she recognise any of them?" asked Marna.

"She's not clear on that," I replied. "But I might be able to sense if any of them are known to us."

I turned slowly, then walked around the meadow, scanning all around to see if I could pick up any indication of who the men were. I gasped loudly as recognition hit me.

"The leader of them, and one other," I said quickly. "They were some of the men who rushed in with Devid, armed, when we met the Council!"

Zelda instantly flushed purple with rage, her fists clenched, her whole body shaking with outrage.

"I knew it!!" she bellowed. "I just knew it!! It had to be them. The Council. The Council did this! The Council killed Emaleen!"

Marna and I could not argue with this. Marna had tried again and again to warn us that these people were dangerous. And the evidence of my own senses told me that this had to be the Council's doing, and even if this had not been the case, who else could possibly have arranged such an atrocity? Who else would have wanted to?

We stood in stunned and outraged silence, not knowing what to do next. Marna was wise enough not to tell Zelda that she had warned her, many times, and that Marna's warnings had been ignored, scoffed at by Zelda. I knew our friend was as devastated by Safya's death as we were, but assumed that she felt nothing would be gained from laying blame at my mother's feet for not taking her warnings seriously. In any case, what difference would it really have made? Nothing could have stopped my sisters leaving the compound for their regular outings into the mountains, and the Council would have found a way to perpetrate their hideous act somewhere or other.

"This is aimed at me!" growled Zelda suddenly, pushing back a lock of unruly hair from her angry face as she spoke.

I glared at her in astonishment, livid that she would immediately turn Safya's murder into an attack on her. She sensed my outrage, and added hastily.

"An attack on all of us, on our family."

I was not appeased.

Marna intruded into what seemed about to become an explosive argument between me and Zelda, at what was, in every respect, a most emotional time. She actually moved to place her substantial form between me and my mother.

"What do we do now?" she asked, prompting both me and Zelda to return to more practical matters.

I looked at Zelda, questioningly. I had no answer to Marna's query, and knew that Zelda would have to make the decision. After a few moments of reflection, Zelda quickly spoke.

"We demand, and I mean *demand* an immediate meeting with the entire Council, in their Chamber. We all go there and we confront them with this horror. Like last time, we show the whole world, show them what the Council has done, narrowcast globally every moment of that meeting." She looked at me and asked,

"You can do all of that, can you not? Shout to the Council now straight into their heads that we demand a meeting, then take us all there, and show the world like you did before?"

"Yes, of course I can," I replied. "Adwin and Kallan will want to come too," I added.

"Naturally," Zelda said. "And Emaleen. And Safya."

"Safya?" I queried sharply, not understanding what Zelda meant.

"We shall take her body with us and lay her at the feet of the Council. We need the world to see exactly what a murder looks like, to see exactly what that vile organisation is capable of. And beside her will lie the injured and battered form of her sister."

I was horrified at the idea of putting my sister's dead body on display to the world, yet at the same time saw the sense in doing so. If we were to point the finger of blame at the Council, to tell the world that they were guilty of one of the greatest outrages in post-Chaos history, nothing would bring home more vividly what they had done than the sight of the broken corpse of a young woman actually carried into the Council Chamber and placed in front of them. The blame would thereby be laid at their feet both literally and figuratively. And this would be enhanced by the still-living but badly wounded body of Emaleen.

Marna too understood Zelda's motives, and though she was shocked at Zelda's audacity, the Council's actions had been so egregious that no response by us would be too extreme.

I prepared to take us all home, but before I did so I shouted out to each Council member our demands: that they attend the Council Chamber later that day. I would not be disobeyed in this, and if they refused, or did not present themselves, I would transport them there myself, against their will. I ensured that my mindspeak was loud and aggressive, that it would so violently pierce their consciousness as to cause them real pain. I not only wanted them to suffer, I also needed to ensure there was no risk of them not hearing me. After I had ascertained from their shocked and outraged reactions to my mental intrusion that they had indeed heard me, I took us all home.

Chapter Thirty-One

We arrived home almost instantly to find Adwin and Kallan sitting in silence together in the living room. Adwin sat beside our uncle lightly holding one of his hands in his lap. Kallan seemed to be almost as incapable of reaction as Emaleen, and Zelda frowned with worry when she saw this. She moved rapidly to the sofa that Adwin and Kallan occupied, and sat immediately down beside our uncle, so she and Adwin now flanked him, providing him with protective columns: support on one side, affection on the other. Zelda took his other hand and squeezed it. He turned his head slightly, and seemed to notice her for the first time. He was no longer crying, but the marks of his tears scarred his face. He had not even attempted to wipe them off. Zelda started slightly to see the haunted, desolate look in his vivid turquoise eyes. She frowned, cleared her throat, then said in the most gentle and tender voice I had ever heard her use,

"My dearest. We need you. We must all go now to the Council, taking Safya with us. We have to show the world what they have done, what they are capable of."

She did not need to explain what I had related to her and Marna on the cliff top. Kallan seemed to know what she meant: that the Council were to blame. Zelda's compassion was so intense that it pierced Kallan's unresponsiveness. He sighed, a long, loud sigh, then nodded slightly. He seemed to understand what we needed to do, and that his presence was required. I always found it hard to appreciate that Kallan was Zelda's rock, given that Zelda seemed so emotionally self-sufficient, and so unneedy of others. From her earliest years, as long as she could remember, he had been by her side, supporting her, standing up for her, loving her. No-one else in her life came close. Marna she was clearly fond of, and their connection went back as far as Zelda's with Kallan, yet it was merely a fondness, a liking, and Zelda's feelings for Marna were not on the same scale as those she harboured for Kallan. All of her children she seemed to have some feelings for, though it was always difficult to be sure if these demonstrated real affection, or whether it was simply that she was used to us, familiar with us, given that we had shared a home with her for so long. In my more cynical moments, I told myself that her only feelings for us were scientific interest and an intense feeling of owning us. We were, after all, in the strongest sense of the word, her creations.

"When do we go?" Kallan asked quietly in a slightly hoarse voice, understanding that we were all to travel together to the Council Chamber.

"Soon, very soon my dear," Zelda replied softly.

Kallan nodded and sighed again, more gently this time.

"Shall I go and wash my face, clean myself up a bit?" he asked. Zelda hesitated for a moment, then replied,

"No. It is better that they see what we are suffering, see what they have done to us. The world needs to know what it means to...to...," and she could not finish her sentence.

"To have your sister murdered," Adwin added, unnaturally loudly as his anger added volume.

We all jumped slightly at his words, at their tone, and even more so at their meaning. The word 'murdered' was one so rarely used in our world that it felt almost archaic, as if only used to describe an action that happened in the distant past, that should no longer occur in our present day. Yet it had occurred, and had been perpetrated by the august body responsible for running our world. It was still almost impossible to comprehend.

Zelda then spoke quietly in her deep, gravelly voice. "Emaleen needs to come too. She is absolutely crucial." My sister had been bustled off the moment we arrived home to have her injuries tended to by one of our domestic automata which carried out medical procedures, Zelda not wanting to need the services of human doctors from the outside world. Although many such procedures were carried out by automata, a substantial number of people still preferred the human touch when it came to managing illness or injury.

Marna, still standing, turned to glare at Zelda. I wondered how my uncle would respond to Zelda's suggestion, and was surprised at his reaction.

"Yes. She *must*," he said, seeming to understand Zelda's intent. Marna turned a look of confusion on my uncle.

"She was there when it happened," he explained. "The only witness. And Safya was her sister, her twin. Her loss is the greatest of all. And the world must see her anguish. And her injuries."

After a few moments of silence, my brother spoke. "Will we take Safya too?"

Kallan was shocked by the question, but before he could answer, Zelda interrupted.

"Yes. Of course. We must. The world needs to see what the Council has done, witness the same horror we are all dealing with. Otherwise all we have is words."

After another pause, Marna nodded her agreement. We remained for long moments in absolute silence as I tried to understand what had just happened, how it would affect us. For all of us Safya's death was an atrocity, an act filled with distress, yet we would, eventually, get over the horror of it. But for Emaleen we all knew this was not the case. I feared she would never recover from this blow, this utter disaster. She and Safya were inseparable, and had been since birth. They only really needed each other, relied on each other, were everything to each other. One without the other was unthinkable, as if half of a single person had been brutally ripped from the other half. I turned to Zelda and asked in a quiet yet determined voice,

"How shall we do it?" I wanted revenge.

Zelda thought for a moment as she and I contemplated the others, each of them struggling to deal with his or her grief, and then she replied to me, softly enough so as not to interrupt the private silence reigning in the room.

"I shall carry Safya," she rumbled, and seeing my surprised look, she added, "You, young man, will have to help me support her, without it looking like that is what you are doing. I cannot carry her comfortably on my own but if we appear before the Council, Safya lying pathetically in my arms, that will create the most powerful impression."

I was astonished that she could think so clearly in the circumstances, that she was considering how best to present the hideous facts for greatest impact. I wondered if she was truly a heartless monster to be able to do so, but saw from her face that she was in fact deeply agitated and upset. Despite this, she seemed capable of responding with a brisk, rational plan. I had to concede I was glad of this, as none of the rest of us would have been able.

"We shall, as before, appear facing the Council," Zelda continued, this time in a louder voice as she needed to give us all clear instructions. "None of us will wash our faces or change our clothes. We must show the world what we are suffering. I will lay the body of poor Safya at the feet of Rannald, and I will tell the world what he has done. What *they* have done. They will not recover from this. After people see the atrocity they have carried out, their days will be over on the Council."

We listened in silence to Zelda's words, adding nothing as we had nothing to add. But after a long silence, we were all taken aback to hear Adwin's high boy's voice piercing the quiet.

"But that's not enough," he said quietly, yet with real asperity. "They need to be punished."

I was very surprised by what he said, but could not deny that merely being forced off the Council would not be sufficient punishment for having planned and carried out a murder. But what were we to do? In the distant past, a murderer would, at the least, have been subjected to a long period of imprisonment, perhaps even for the rest of his or her life. And in many times, and many places, a convicted murderer would have been executed by the state. But in our world we have no such state, no central authority that could contemplate such a thing. The only authority we have is the Council, and they were the perpetrators. We have no police, no judges, no courts of law or even system of law. We have no prisons, no executioners, no formal punishment of any sort that can be imposed on a citizen. The only way to control the occasional wayward citizen is a form of shunning. So how does one contemplate a punishment appropriate for murder without any infrastructure whatsoever to carry out such a penalty?

I looked around, and saw confusion and consternation on all the faces around me. None of us knew how to address the issue Adwin had raised. I felt that his words were accepted by everyone in the room, but that no obvious solution presented itself.

At length, we were all startled when Kallan suddenly spoke, loudly and with force.

"*We* will have to impose a suitable punishment."

We all stared at him in shock, and I was astonished to see his hard expression, harder than I had ever seen on his normally benign face. But I knew that if we did not impose a punishment, then the perpetrators of this horrific crime would escape without sanction, and this was not acceptable. Yet to take it upon ourselves to impose a punishment on citizens, and especially on members of the Council, this was almost unimaginable, and it would be impossible to judge the reaction to such a measure from the population at large. But then murder too had been unimaginable, and to let the killers walk free with impunity, this surely was the greater of two evils?

"I agree Kallan," Zelda said abruptly, looking round at all of us with an expression of challenge, to see if anyone would disagree. Nobody contested Kallan's view, not even Marna. Although she seemed rigid with discomfort at the idea, she had no alternative to offer and could see no other reasonable conclusion. She did, however, add a thought by way of tempering the severity of what we would do, this time addressing only Zelda and me, the others having withdrawn again into their own private grief.

"We must first ascertain exactly *which* Council members actually planned the whole thing," Marna said. "Can you do that, Samek?" she added, addressing me directly. I nodded, believing I could determine, with reasonable accuracy, the guilt or otherwise of each and every member of the twelve person Council.

Zelda grunted her disapproval of Marna's suggestion, not feeling inclined to generosity toward any member of the Council. But Marna persisted.

"I cannot imagine they were all involved," she said sharply, looking directly at Zelda. "Not all of them are your enemies, as you well know Zelda. But I concede that some of them hate you, hate all of you. I've been warning you about Rannald and his allies for years, so I have absolutely no doubt they're behind this, though of course they got other people to actually carry out the heinous deed. And though I shudder at the thought of taking on the responsibility for their punishment, I agree they need to be punished. What they have done is so...so...monstrous, that it cannot be allowed to just pass by. But it has to be just those who actually ordered it." She glared at Zelda and asked sharply,

"Zelda, do you agree?"

After a brief moment of reflection, Zelda replied.

"Yes, but only if we also punish those who knew about it but did not stop it."

Marna was irritated by Zelda's expanding of the list of Council members to face punishment, but knew she had no argument to counter what Zelda had said. Knowing such a thing was being planned and would be enacted without trying to stop it was not, after all, so very different from actually being involved in the plan itself.

"Very well," Marna said at length. "But not the innocent people."

Zelda nodded, and then looked at me for confirmation, which surprised me. I nodded too, not knowing what else to do. Zelda did not ask Kallan and Adwin to indicate their assent as she seemed to assume they would not gainsay her. And surely Emaleen, if asked, would not deny whatever punishment we chose to impose, nor upon whom we chose to impose it. Zelda seemed unwilling to finalise the actual punishment until we were in front of the Council members, judging the appropriateness of it at least in part by their reaction to the evidence of their guilt.

Time had moved on, and we knew we needed to take ourselves to the Council Chamber. I quickly scanned the Chamber from afar, and relayed the fact that the entire Council had indeed turned up. They had clearly believed my threat to teleport them against their will if they did not attend voluntarily, and they had seen demonstrable evidence of my powers, and that of my siblings, before. I knew that I could not teleport another person unless in direct physical contact with that person, but the Council had no inkling of this limit on my powers. The vague thought entered my mind that people just believing in one's gifts almost made them as effective as if they really existed.

I knew that the Council members felt that dragging them to the Council Chamber against their will would be humiliating for them, and they all chose to avoid such indignity. I caused Safya's body to lighten, such that Zelda could easily carry her. At Zelda's insistence, Emaleen had been brought to join us by the robot medic who had attended her. She was still in shock, sitting quietly in a wheelchair, head swathed in bandages, broken leg stretched out in front, wrapped in a hard protective covering. With grim faces, we arranged ourselves in the pattern in which we wished to appear in front of the Council. Even before we went, with Adwin's help, I took control of all the narrowcast stations, and prepared to inform the entire citizenry at the same time, so that we could show the world every moment of the bitter fruits of our second visit to the Council in their Chamber.

Chapter Thirty-Two

Mere moments later, we appeared in front of the Council. Zelda stood in the middle of our little group, seeming to struggle under the weight of my dead sister. As I was actually supporting most of her weight, this was an act. Even at such a time of intense, heightened emotion, Zelda was able to control her responses, to think logically, and to manipulate the situation to gain maximum advantage.

Emaleen sat close beside Zelda, one hand draped lightly across her dead sister's shoulder, emphasising both her connection to Safya and the enormity of her loss. I noticed a patch of blood which had seeped through the turban of white bandages on her injured head, and wondered if the medical automaton had done its job properly, or whether it had attended too hastily to my sister. I stood on the other side of Zelda, Adwin close beside me, supporting me in my control of the narrowcast stations and the live images I was sending out to the entire world. Emaleen I had not asked to assist us in this, as I was wary of trying to rely on her, given her extremely delicate emotional state. Flanking us were Kallan on my side, Marna close beside Emaleen, her bulk seeming to offer its own succour to my sister. Marna had joined us to give us support, but also because she had witnessed the immediate aftermath of the actual murder, seen the body of Safya hanging halfway down the cliff side, her sister dangling injured on a tiny ledge.

The Council members were in turmoil. Even those we counted as friendly, or at least not hostile, who did not yet know why I had summoned them, knew that something extraordinary and unprecedented must have happened. Lenora, sitting tall and straight, frowned, her hands jangling the heavy gold chain she always wore. Old Vradley's kindly features were twisted into a look of utter confusion. Breyan's ruddy face was even more flushed than usual, consternation wrinkling his brow between thick red eyebrows and stiff orange hair.

And from our enemies among their number the turmoil was no less profound - it was just of a different nature. Squat little Helna sat stock still, trying to mask her concern with a look of disdain. Only Rannald, the Speaker, almost succeeded in hiding his worry, his usual arrogance making his handsome features ugly.

Before Rannald or any other member of the Council could utter a word, Zelda stepped forward, staggering, as if weighed down both by the physical strain of supporting Safya's corpse and by the burden of emotional suffering she carried. My mother's clothes were askew, her gray hair escaping in many messy tendrils from its usual tight confines. As she moved slightly towards the twelve Council members who sat on their chairs behind the long glass table, they all, involuntarily, drew back as far as they were able. It was obvious from the way Safya lay in Zelda's arms, that she was dead. No living body could drape in such a manner. Everyone could see her back was broken, her head bobbing and lolling grotesquely as Zelda moved towards the Council members. She was covered in blood, so much of it that congealed lumps of red dripped from her to leave a slight, yet clear, trail of scarlet across the exquisite creamy marble floor of the Council Chamber.

Despite the effort I needed to narrowcast the entire scene to the world, I imagined that the entire population of the planet would be quite still, transfixed by what they were watching. Even from their more distant viewpoint, it was obvious that Zelda carried the corpse of a young woman, thick globules of blood dripping from her lifeless, damaged body.

Zelda stopped a few feet in front of the table, lowered Safya's body to the ground with what seemed a great effort. She then straightened suddenly, lifted her right arm and extended her first finger straight towards Rannald. She fixed him with a glare of absolute fury and spoke a single word in a voice which cracked like a whip.

"Murderer!!"

Pandemonium erupted. The entire Council leapt to their feet as one, all shouting and gesticulating at the same time. I was forced to intensify the protection around me, and I included all of us in it this time. That single word, aimed directly at the speaker of the Council, inside the Council's own Chamber, and backed up by the presence of a bleeding, mutilated corpse, was the most shocking experience most people had ever undergone. Murder was unknown in recent times, an ancient concept, something from the distant past, and to see Zelda standing beside a dead woman brought by her into the Council Chamber, and to accuse the Speaker of murdering her would be the most profoundly distressing thing most people had ever witnessed.

After a period of chaos, I sensed other people rushing to the Chamber from elsewhere in the building. I mindspoke this to Zelda who instructed me to stop them at the doors of the room. A large number of people, mostly sturdy young men, many of them in the shiny black outfits they had worn the first time we had come to the Council, tried to enter the Chamber. I held them immobile in the large, open doorways behind us. I recognised that the actual killers of Safya were amongst them, the ones I had seen when I had looked into Emaleen's memories on the cliff top. These four were armed with knives and weapons usually used against wild animals. They were not the only armed guards. I quickly mindspoke all of this to Zelda, letting her decide how to use the information.

As the more antagonistic members of the Council perceived that their rescuers were being held fast at the doors of the Chamber and would not be able to offer any assistance, Rannald clearly felt it necessary to impose some control on the turbulent situation. His booming and authoritative voice cut through the angry, distressed vocalisations of his colleagues.

"How dare you!" he bellowed, pulling himself up to his full imposing height and pointing directly at Zelda, fixing her with a look of malicious rage. "How dare you!" he repeated.

Zelda flushed purple, genuinely furious this time with no hint of theatrics. She rapidly mindspoke to me, telling me to silence the cacophony of voices. I did so without hesitation, much to the surprise and outrage of the Council members who found themselves unable to utter a single further sound. I saw the expression of shock on their faces, even on Rannald's smug features, their mouths gaping silently, then opening and closing like fish out of water as they tried in vain to produce sounds.

"How dare *we*?" growled Zelda in a quiet yet menace-laden voice which flashed across the now silent room like a bolt of electricity.

"How dare *we*?" she repeated. Then she looked straight into the eyes of each Council member one at a time, moving down the line of mute, floundering officials. When she had finished, she drew a deep breath.

"How dare *you*! How dare *you*!" she intoned ominously, her voice louder now, its pitch higher, sweeping her hand along the entire line of Council members. "How dare you murder my child." And as she voiced the awful word I felt a shudder pass through the entire Council.

"We are innocent, the aggrieved, the injured party. We have never done anything to threaten you, to attack you. Yet you have planned and carried out the most heinous, the most monstrous act the world has seen in centuries. Not only have you committed the first murder in hundreds of years, but the very first, the first and only murder carried out by the Council. By the body given the role of protecting and looking after the citizens. A more hideous act could not be imagined. And we cannot let you get away with it."

The entire Council visibly winced repeatedly at Zelda's words, her final comment causing a sharp jerking backwards among them. What could she mean when she said they would not get away with it? This was clearly a threat, but what could she possibly be threatening?

Once Rannald had overcome his shock at Zelda's speech, he tried to speak. Zelda silently indicated to me that I should allow him to do so. Rannald found his voice, and the slight delay in doing so allowed him to collect his wits. He looked scornfully at Zelda, then addressed her directly.

"Get away with it Zelda?" he boomed, enunciating each word slowly and carefully. "Get away with what? All you do is bring a dead young woman here, dump her at our feet and then accuse us, *us*, the Council, of murdering her. I've never heard anything so outrageous in my life. What possible proof could you have?"

Zelda's slight, derisory smile by way of response to Rannald's comments clearly disconcerted the other members of the Council. Rannald too was perplexed by Zelda's reaction, but too much in control to let it show. I noted that Helna and the other hostile members of the Council were particularly agitated by Zelda's response. The other members of the Council merely looked bewildered, still not truly understanding what was happening.

Zelda turned slowly to look at me.

"You can show us what happened, can you not young man? Show the whole world what happened on that cliff top?" she said in a quiet voice which cut through the silence in the room.

I nodded. I quickly mindspoke to my sister, warning her that I was about to enter her thoughts to recover the sequence of events leading to Safya's death. She balked at the prospect of having to experience the entire scene again, watch her beloved sister being hurled to her death, as if for a second time, suffer again her own frantic tumble and injury, but she indicated that I could do so as only thereby would we be able to fully inculpate the Council. Through her pain and distress, I sensed her making a huge effort to arrange the awful images as clearly as she could in her own head.

I closed my eyes and entered my sister's mind. As I did so Zelda briskly explained out loud what I was about to do, that I was going to narrowcast to the world exactly what had happened in that distant place which had ended with the first murder in centuries.

I quickly accessed Emaleen's visual memories of the awful events and relayed them to the entire planet. The landing of the flyer, the four black-clad muscular men leaping out of it and rushing towards the two young women, hurling them both off the cliff top. And as if this were not enough, I then went further and showed the image of Emaleen dangling precariously on a tiny ledge of salvation, leg broken, head bleeding profusely. And my final coup was relaying the image of Safya's broken body draped across the outcrop half way down the cliff, mouth and eyes gaping wide in horror, blood flowing from there to the bottom of the cliff.

I snapped the image off. There was nothing else they needed to see.

After a moment of utter silence, Rannald again gained his wits. He was a cold, calculating man, seemingly devoid of normal human emotions, but I almost had to admire his ability to cope in a situation of such crisis as this. It seemed as if nothing could fluster him, or at least not for long.

"That's all very tragic, child," he said in his usual loud voice, fixing me with a look which managed to be both nasty and patronising at the same time. "But what has any of it got to do with any of us?" he added in a disingenuous tone, gesturing towards the other Council members as he spoke.

I was nonplussed, not having an answer to this question. But if Rannald showed calmness in a difficult situation, he had met his match in Zelda.

"Those four men, the ones who killed my child," my redoubtable mother interrupted. "They are here, in this very room. And they are armed".

She turned around and pointed slowly at each of the four men, each outfitted in identical glossy black clothing, all of whom were clearly and instantly recognisable as the ones who had rushed towards my sisters, their leader being the very one who had hurled Safya to her death. And it seemed clear that they had rushed into the Chamber earlier in an attempt to protect the Council. They were Council guards, in a world where the idea of having to guard anybody was ridiculous. Why would the Council need guards, if nobody ever committed any crimes of violence?

"That still proves nothing against *us*," countered Rannald.

The other four hostile Council members nodded vigorous assent. I noted that the remaining members of the Council, now fully apprised of the facts of the death of Safya, and of the reason for our presence in the chamber, had edged very slightly away from our enemies on the Council. I suspected they did not do so consciously, but felt a desire to distance themselves physically from the five possible perpetrators of so heinous an act, thereby distancing themselves in terms of culpability.

Zelda looked again at me.

"Can you make them talk?" she asked, gesturing towards the four guards as she spoke. "Or just go into their heads and show us their meetings with whoever told them to act?" she added. I nodded.

"Yes, I can do both. But I don't think I can hear what was said. I can just find images. But one way or the other," I added with venom, "I can force them to reveal who ordered them to murder my sister."

A collective gasp sounded from the Council.

"You wouldn't dare!" shrieked Helna, speaking out for the first time, her ability to do so indicating that I had lost some grip on silencing the entire Council. "You wouldn't dare enter their minds without permission and force them to talk against their will. That is...that is...an outrage!"

"An outrage?" bellowed Kallan suddenly as he took a step forward to tower over the tiny squat form of Helna, and moved to such anger that he could not contain himself. "You talk to us of outrage? We who have just suffered the murder of our child!"

Helna opened her mouth to counter what Kallan had said, but was abruptly silenced by Kallan bellowing. "Be silent!" Helna's mouth snapped shut and she recoiled, so stunned was she by Kallan's tone.

Zelda turned to me, and said quietly, yet audibly,

"Keep them quiet," and by them she clearly meant the Council. "And make *them* talk," she added, nodding towards the four now horrified guards.

I silenced the Council members again, much to their obvious distress and offence. I walked slowly towards the four black-clothed guards, flanked as they were by their colleagues, all of them held in stillness by me. I quickly scanned their minds to see what I could ascertain.

"I only need to get this one to talk," I said. "He's the leader. He was given the instructions and the rest just followed his orders."

I felt his resistance as I began to compel him to speak out loud. He looked helplessly towards Rannald, and could not stop his eyes shifting across to Helna. I sensed them fighting uselessly against the energy which held them still and mute, silent rage boiling inside them. And something else too, even before the guard spoke: fear. A palpable, physical sense of fear flowing from them.

"He told me to do it," the guard began, looking directly at Rannald, and speaking in a curiously flat voice, as if he were reciting something as mundane as a list of household chores. "He called me in to a tiny little room, with only a door and no windows. A strange little room with shiny metallic walls, and the ceiling and floor of it were made of the same material. I wondered what it was all about. He was there with those two," he added, indicating Helna and the male Council member sitting next to her with the direction of his gaze.

"Not with Henrek and Katia too?" Zelda interrupted sharply, nodding in the direction of two of the other members.

"No, only those three," confirmed the guard. "They explained to me what they wanted me to do. I said I wouldn't do it, I couldn't kill anyone, but they insisted that the two people, two young women they wanted me to kill were enemies of the citizen body. They said it was my duty to eradicate such enemies, that I had no choice. So I instructed my subordinates, and, having been told where the women were, we went there in the flyer, but only managed to kill one of them. I knew we would have to get away as quickly as possible, as the Speaker had warned us that any delay would bring others - would bring you immediately," he said, looking at me. "We rushed away before we could finish the task properly."

A silence fell on the room. Nobody questioned my ability to uncover the truth and to reveal it to the world, but I sensed a powerful surge of doubt, especially from the masses watching rapt in the world outside. The evidence seemed complete: a dead body, the images from Emaleen's mind shared, the view of the corpse dangling half-way down the cliff, Emaleen still alive but badly injured on a ledge above her sister, the guard's simple factual story told in an almost expressionless voice. And in the background the well-known hostility towards us from certain members of the Council. Yet could I be entirely trusted to tell the truth? Could I not be manufacturing the words the guard spoke to suit my family's purposes? Could we not have bandaged Emaleen up as part of our theatrical presentation? Would this not be the perfect opportunity for us to deal with Council in a way we had wanted to for some time?

"But you are sure Henrek and Katia were not there, did not also give you instructions?" persisted Zelda eagerly. The guard shook his head and replied simply,

"They weren't there. But I don't know if they knew."

Zelda looked back at me and said quietly, "Find out."

I moved away from the guard and back towards the still unmoving Council members. I scanned the minds of Henrek and Katia, outraging all the other Council members by my intrusion. I knew even before I did so that they were fully conversant with the plan, even if they had not attended the actual meeting with the guard where he received his instructions. I knew by the air of deep anxiety and guilt surrounding them, patent on their faces even to a person with no gifts. After a quick scan to assure myself of my initial perception, I turned to Zelda.

"They knew. They knew all about it. They didn't want to actually get too much involved, but they did nothing to try and persuade the others not to do it, and did nothing to stop it. And they don't disapprove."

"Then they are as guilty as the other three!" yelled Emaleen totally unexpectedly, her voice cracking with emotion. We all turned to her in surprise, amazed that she would intrude into the proceedings in this way. But her anger was growing all the time, as was her obvious desire for the culprits to be punished, a desire for revenge.

"Yes I agree Emaleen," Zelda said quietly. "And they will face the same consequences as the three who actually planned it all." She then turned to me again and asked,

"What about the others?" I knew she was referring to the other members of the Council, those who were either indifferent to us, or even relatively friendly.

I walked slowly along the entire line of deeply anxious immobile officials, quickly scanning their thoughts. As always, I felt their outrage at what they perceived as a violation of their most intimate privacy. But I cared nothing for their feelings. I did not need long to find out what I needed to know. I turned back to Zelda.

"They didn't know anything, none of them. They only learned the truth today, here in the chamber, at the same time as the rest of the world."

"But how do they feel about it?" Zelda queried sharply.

I did not understand the point of her question. Either they knew or they did not know, that was surely the measure of their culpability. What did it matter what their attitude to the murder was after the event?

"Well?" persisted Zelda. "What do they think of what happened?"

I frowned slightly, turning back to the seven members who had been ignorant of the plan. Again, I quickly scanned their minds. I was actually surprised at the level of distress, horror even, that they all seemed to feel at what had occurred.

"They are as outraged and disgusted as anyone else," I relayed to Zelda and the rest of my family. "In fact, they seem barely able to comprehend what has happened, the enormity of it, and especially that it is other members of their own Council who planned and ordered the deed."

Zelda nodded slightly, a peculiar expression on her face. I could not tell if she was satisfied with my answers, or disappointed that the whole Council was not involved. I knew she felt hostility towards the Council as a body, despite the fact that only five of the members were overtly inimical towards us. Perhaps she had hoped to be able to punish all twelve of them, perhaps even destroy the Council in the process.

As if aware of Zelda's turn of thought, Marna spoke for the first time.

"Zelda. You promised that only those responsible would face punishment. You know what Samek says is true. So the ones who didn't know anything cannot be punished too."

Zelda glared at Marna, conflicting emotions showing clearly on her face. She knew that Marna was right, but seemed to regret the loss of opportunity to bring down the entire Council. After a short, tense pause, she nodded once, consenting to Marna's reminder.

Another pause ensued, longer this time. We were all aware of the need to consider what punishment was appropriate, and to put it into place, yet what could possibly be the correct penalty for such a heinous crime? And in a world with no crime, no criminal justice system of any kind, how to carry out the sanction? Perhaps we should have discussed this before we left our home, before we came before the Council, but we had not done so, at Zelda's specific behest.

Very rapidly I mindspoke to my whole family, including Marna in the discussion. I asked what we should do, and suggested we needed to decide quickly, as the world was watching. Zelda replied, using the silent channel I had opened between us all.

~*We cannot put them to death, much as I would like to,*~ she began, causing us to recoil in shock that she had even considered such drastic retribution. Before any of us could respond, Zelda quickly continued.

~*I said we cannot, so let us not waste time on that. I suggest though, that the five perpetrators are removed from society, completely removed. They need to be sent somewhere isolated, sent into the middle of nowhere, banished to the back of beyond, to the wilds. Let them stew in their own wickedness with no hope of salvation. Anyone disagree?*~

We all considered what Zelda had said. It was clear she had given the matter some thought before meeting the Council, though she was simulating that her ideas had come to her spontaneously. Her solution seemed appropriate, though perhaps a little harsh. The five Council members, left with nothing to do but fend for themselves, struggle to survive, remote, totally isolated from the world at large, this would serve as a real punishment. It would be like an extreme form of shunning, writ large. It could, in the end, drive them to insanity. Most people in our world were endlessly and relentlessly connected to others both physically and virtually, almost without cessation. My siblings and I were unique in living a life of segregation from the outside world, and even we had far more connection with it than Zelda was recommending for the guilty Council members. We could perhaps cope with such utter isolation, but I doubted Rannald and his co-conspirators could. But I truly did not care. They had murdered my sister, and for this atrocity the punishment did not, in the end, seem unduly harsh.

~We should kill them really,~ said my mother, interrupting my cogitations. *~Banishment is better than they deserve, but I suppose it's as much as we can get away with. Ostracise them completely in the extremes of our world to live alone, with no society, no technology. And if they die, then they die.~* She paused very briefly, then added,

~Are we all in agreement?~ and she looked pointedly at Emaleen when she mindspoke this question. My sister hesitated for a moment, and I sensed she was still wondering if we could get away with putting Rannald and his colleagues to death, but she knew that it was inconceivable to kill them all, and that Zelda's suggestion was probably the most we could impose on them without causing the rage of the entire citizen body to come crashing down on our heads. But Emaleen did not feel that the punishment was severe enough for Rannald, the ringleader of the plan to murder our sister. She mindspoke her concerns, but only to me, deliberately leaving the others out of the silent conversation.

~That's not enough for Rannald,~ she said, struggling to speak even in mindvoice. *~It's alright for the others, but not for him. He has to die.~*

I did not reply immediately to my sister's bald statement. I was conflicted. On the one hand I understood her desire for revenge, but on the other was fearful of taking such drastic measures. If we killed Rannald, surely this would create such hostility towards us among the people that it was not worth doing? I knew Zelda would have no such doubts, so chose to exclude her from the discussion between my sister and me. As I deliberated with myself, Emaleen pressed her point.

~What's wrong?~ she asked in a distressed and angry mindvoice, the pain of her injuries obvious to my senses. *~Why are you hesitating? Don't you think he deserves it?~*

I looked at her, pierced by the anguish clear on her fine features, distorted further by a look I had never seen on her face: a twisted look, a desire for revenge.

~Yes he does deserve it,~ I replied. *~I'm just worried what will happen if I do it, what will happen to us. People fear me enough as it is, and if I do this, what will they think then? What will they do then?~*

~Can't you do it without it being obvious you've done it?~ she asked me. *~Without anyone knowing?~*

~What do you mean?~ I queried, genuinely unclear.

~Make it look like an accident, maybe something natural,~ she persisted, still keeping the conversation only between the two of us. She looked at me with such eager desperation that I simply could not refuse. I replied, almost without hesitation.

~I suppose I could. I could stop his heart, or something like that. Nobody would know I'd done it, or be able to prove it. It could just look like a heart attack.~

Emaleen's look of gratitude mingled with relief as she slumped back in the chair outweighed any qualms I had about taking such a bold step.

~I won't do it now,~ I suggested. *~I'll wait till we're gone from here, or at least going. I'll make it look like a heart attack, brought on by the stress of what's happened today.~*

Emaleen nodded once to indicate her agreement.

~That's decided then,~ she said, by way of conclusion, but this time including the others in the comment, though of course none of them had any idea what had just been decided between my sister and me.

At this point, Zelda turned back to the as yet immobile Council members, preparing to deliver our verdict to them. But just before she did so, a thought seemed to cross her mind. She mindspoke to me.

~Can you block what I am about to say, somehow distort it so that the outside world can still see us, but cannot hear what I am going to say? But it needs to seem like an accident, some sort of interference which is not deliberate.~

I nodded, though did not know why Zelda made this request. She then added, *~You can let them speak again now. And do not let the sound through again till I tell you.~*

I created an electrical charge which would interfere with the sound being transmitted to the world, but still allowing the images to be narrowcast. I made it sound like natural distortion caused by weather conditions, or electrical interference. I indicated to Zelda I had done this, and she turned to the Council members. I still held them stationary, but freed their mouths to allow them to speak. Zelda briskly explained the punishment that would be imposed on Rannald and his co-conspirators, though of course she knew nothing of the private agreement between my sister and me in relation to the Speaker himself. As my mother spoke the Council stood mute, rendered voiceless now by their outrage at having such a sanction imposed on some of their members. No such penalty existed in our world as we had no formal system whereby to punish wrong-doers. The fact of imposing a penalty alone was sufficient to stun the Council, and the fact that it was being foisted on members of that august body added another layer of indignity and affront. If only they knew what I was planning for their leader, I thought to myself, then they would truly have cause for outrage.

Rannald and the other four convicted members were stunned to the point of utter silence by what Zelda said. The other seven, those who had escaped punishment, rallied more quickly. Breyan seemed to find his voice, and said in a hoarse, tense whisper, flushing even more brightly all the way up to his mop of red hair as he spoke.

"You can't do that Zelda. You have no right to impose such a penalty. Such things don't exist."

The other blameless members vigorously nodded in agreement, but Zelda was unmoved.

"*They* had no right to murder my child, to nearly succeed in killing the other one. Murder is not supposed to exist. They took that upon themselves, just as we take this punishment upon ourselves," she replied.

"Actually," she continued, after a brief moment's reflection, "*You* are going to take it upon *your*selves".

Breyan and his six guiltless colleagues looked bewildered at Zelda's final comment, genuinely not understanding what she meant. I caught her meaning immediately, and instantly understood why she did not want the citizens to hear what she was saying to the Council. She wanted the world to believe the punishment came from the Council, not from us.

"You, the other seven Council members, will be the ones to impose the penalty," Zelda explained simply. "You are correct when you suggest I do not have the right to do such a thing. You do have authority, however, and if you want the world to believe you seven are blameless of this atrocity, it might even benefit you to be seen to be the ones to punish the miscreants among your own number. If you expect the citizenry not to lose faith in your governance following a Council-approved murder of a child, you will understand why you need to impose this punishment."

Breyan opened his mouth to speak, but quickly snapped it shut again. His conflicting thoughts were transparent on his ruddy face. The other friendly Council members, as well as the two who had no strong feelings towards us all clearly shared the same struggle of emotions and deliberations as Breyan. They were incensed at being compelled to do something so utterly unprecedented as impose a penalty, especially on other members of the Council, yet what Zelda said about thereby exculpating themselves in the eyes of the citizens made sense. Though I had stated clearly to the world that these seven had no knowledge of the murder, doubts would surely linger that this was not true, that *all* members of the Council were involved, were implicated in this, the most atrocious event in many hundreds of years.

Breyan was clearly livid, his cheeks glowing like hot ripe tomatoes. He was livid that Rannald had planned and carried out such a hideous act. Livid that Zelda had backed him and his colleagues into an impossible corner. Before he could collect his thoughts sufficiently to answer my mother, the impressively-built Lenora suddenly spoke up, a strange, almost hesitant tone in her normally confident deep voice.

"If your boy here, Samek, can do so much, why can't he learn to travel back in time and undo what has happened, make sure this horrific crime never occurred?" she asked.

I was so surprised by her suggestion that I almost lost control of what I was doing. Adwin looked equally taken aback. But Emaleen's response was electric. She jumped in her chair. Such a possibility had not occurred to her any more than it had to the rest of us. She spoke to me in a rasping voice.

"Could you do that Samek? Could you learn to go back in time and...and...save my sister?" she asked hoarsely, the last three words in barely more than a whisper.

Her tone of voice was heart-rending, filled with dread that I might say no, yet at the same time alight with a faint hope that such a thing might be possible. I did not reply immediately, and Zelda pursued the issue.

"Well young man? Do you think you could?" she queried, genuinely intrigued at the idea.

"I...," I began tentatively. "I don't know. I really don't know. I've never thought about it."

I felt Emaleen's hope deflate like a burst balloon, and her palpable misery rocked me.

"But I could work on it, look into it, see if it might be possible, see what's been written on it before," I added quickly, more to assuage my sister's suffering than in the belief that I really could achieve such a thing. I nearly added that, even if I could learn to travel back through time, which obviously seemed impossible, this would not guarantee that by doing so I would be able to alter what had already happened.

Zelda returned us abruptly to the present, and ignoring Lenora's query, demanded of Breyan and his colleagues,

"Well? Do you accept what I say, that you seven have to impose the punishment on those five wicked colleagues of yours?"

Breyan glanced briefly at his six colleagues, and seeing that they all agreed, however unwillingly, nodded to Zelda. Zelda mindspoke to me, telling me to restore full sound to the narrowcast. She then turned to Breyan and indicated that he should pronounce the sentence on Rannald and his four culpable colleagues. Breyan looked at Lenora, raising his eyebrows to indicate that she should be the one to address the room. She frowned in irritation, but as she was the most senior member of the Council after Rannald and Helna, had little option but to comply.

Lenora spoke loudly and clearly in her resonant deep voice to the chamber, and unwittingly to the world beyond, simply but clearly elaborating the exact punishment to be imposed on Rannald and his four Council colluders. She went on to explain why such a punishment had to be imposed, despite there being no precedent for such a thing. The Council existed to protect the citizens, to assure the well-being and safely of the people, and when members of the Council, including the Speaker, organised and effected such a horrific act, they could not be allowed to escape without sanction. As she spoke, Rannald and his colleagues were initially too stunned to react, and when it seemed as if they would contest what was being said I took it upon myself to render them incapable of speech yet again. That they could even consider trying to argue against their punishment, despite their clear guilt, so incensed me that I felt they had no right to be heard. They had lost that right when they first put their unspeakable plan into action.

As Lenora spoke, I knew that the citizenry must be transfixed, silent and still, aware that they were witnessing history. In a world with no system of law, no courts, and no formal punishments, they were seeing the first imposition of such a punishment, a banishment, for the first time in thousands of years, the last time it happened being so long ago that it was more mythical than real. And as if this were not extraordinary enough, the people being outlawed were none other than the Speaker of the Council and four of the other Council members, the most important people in the world. What a historic event to witness.

After Lenora finished speaking, I prepared to take us home, wanting nothing more than to be away from the Council Chamber. I terminated the narrowcast, and just before I ported us all, Emaleen said suddenly in a surprisingly strong and piercing voice.

"What about them?" indicating the four thickset guards who had actually carried out the attack.

We all turned to face them, amazed that we had all but forgotten them in our desire to punish the guilty Council members. They stood immobile, looks of distress and fear on their faces. I glanced at Zelda, leaving it to her to decide. She smiled slightly, an unpleasant, lop-sided smile. I wondered if she was actually about to chuckle.

"They can join their friends out in the wilds," she said in a darkly amused tone.

"But they were only carrying out orders," Lenora snapped with a tinkle of her showy gold necklace, irritated by what Zelda had said.

"I do not care," Zelda continued. "No citizen should murder another citizen, even if under orders from the Council. Those guards knew full well that no-one, not even Rannald, had the right to order somebody's murder, so they should simply have refused to do it. They are just as guilty as far as I am concerned, and that is the end of it."

Lenora and Breyan both began to speak at once, to object to Zelda's comments, but they were silenced but Emaleen's surprising loud, harsh voice.

"They killed my sister! They need to be punished too!"

I stared at Emaleen as she cried out, and as I did so the thought occurred to me: we can kill these ones once they are out in the wilds, and the guilty Council members too, but gradually, one at a time, so nobody knows we have done it. I was shocked that such a thought had come so easily into my head, and chose not to share it with my sister at this point, lest she push me into carrying out this act immediately. But I could not help feeling that it was appropriate to take such action in the light of the heinous crime these people had committed.

Emaleen's tone of anguish mixed with fury rendered the remaining seven members of the Council mute. They knew that Zelda was correct: nobody had the right to order a citizen to kill another citizen. The guards should not have done what they did, and their guilt in the matter was beyond question. Breyan nodded once curtly at Zelda and again at Emaleen indicating that he would do as told, yet with deep anger showing on his ruddy face at what he was being compelled to do.

I hastily ported us away from the Council Chamber, releasing all the transfixed members and guards as I did so. As I made ready to port us, Emaleen threw me the briefest of glances, her brow furrowed beneath the bloody white bandage, silently reminding me of what I had promised to do.

So as we made our brief journey back to the safety of the compound, I put into place the secret, silent agreement made between my sister and me. I threw a short sharp wave at Rannald, directly into his heart. It felt as if I were thrusting my actual fist into his chest, grasping the beating organ and with the force of my grip squeezing the very life out of him. My last hazy image of the Council Chamber was of Rannald grasping his chest suddenly and crying out in pain, all the other Council members rushing to his side to help him. But I smiled slightly to myself in the knowledge that their assistance would be to no avail. He would be dead by the time his body hit the floor, before we had fully emerged in our own home. I felt a surge of sheer dark pleasure at what I had done, at this evidence of my talents, this tangible vision of what I could do when I set my mind to it. I mindspoke a simple message to Emaleen.

~It's done. He's gone.~ I sensed deep satisfaction from my sister, along with the same feeling of jubilation I myself was enjoying. But I knew the world would never be the same again. And neither would I.

Chapter Thirty-Three

The Council was in chaos, with only seven members left in position, and officially it was they who had imposed the sanction of exile to the wilds, though the initiation of it had come from Zelda. From the endless barrage of news and other programming transmitted to the world in the wake of our visit to the Council, it was clear that the world at large was in turmoil. I watched with fascination the emotional turbulence swirling through the population, almost unbearable in its intensity. Some of it was a sense of general outrage, that the Speaker and other Council members had planned, ordered and effected an actual murder, and that they had used other people to carry out the deed, and then on the other hand that the remaining members of the Council had ordered their banishment. Much of the anger was clearly aimed at Rannald and his murderous colleagues, some at the other Council members for having the sheer audacity to impose a harsh and ancient penalty without any real authority to do such a thing. Yet it was clear to me that we too were the targets of some of the anger and indignation. Many citizens were fearful of Zelda and her 'creations', afraid of what we were capable of, particularly alarmed at what I could apparently do. If I could control the entire narrowcast system on our planet, and could carry off what I had done in the Council Chamber, what else could I achieve? And more crucially, what else would I actually want to achieve?

But the anger aimed at me seemed incoherent in the sense that it had no clear goal or aim: it simply showed a deep anxiety among many people about my potential. The rage aimed at the guilty Council members and the four guards was focused and specific, and even though some citizens seemed to feel that *any* punishment was not acceptable, the entire population appeared to share the general outrage at what the perpetrators had done.

A few days later I entered the dining room, having collected Adwin from his room on the way. When we entered the dining room, the adults were all already there. Emaleen, however, had not appeared.

"She needs to be here too," Kallan began. "We all need to be together this evening."

Zelda nodded at this, and turned to me.

"Ask her to come, now. Tell her she must join us," she said.

I did as she bid, mindspeaking gently to my sister. She was trying to block my attempt, but with so little resistance that I was easily able to penetrate the feeble barrier she had erected. After her anger of a few days before, she seemed to be reverting to the almost catatonic state she had shown just after Safya's murder. I had no success in persuading her to join us. She simply did not respond to my request, and I sensed scant emotional energy even in her internal thought patterns. I was deeply concerned by this, and quickly relayed my concerns to the rest of my family.

"She *must* come, my boy," Zelda insisted, and Kallan backed her up with this.

"Yes, Zelda's right. We all need to be together," he added.

I looked at them helplessly, not knowing how to proceed. Kallan sighed loudly and impatiently.

"This isn't a time for niceties Samek. Just bring her here!" he snapped at me. I was shocked. Kallan was usually so courteous, so respectful of other people's wishes, that I could hardly believe he really wanted me to port Emaleen against her wishes.

"You mean just teleport her here, even though she doesn't want to come?" I asked hesitantly.

"Yes," confirmed Kallan. "And do it now," he added in even more impatient tone.

I glanced around the table, and saw that Zelda and Marna were clearly in agreement. Adwin looked as astonished as I was at Kallan's insistence. I swallowed noisily, and turned to my angry uncle.

"No," I said simply. "I won't do it." Kallan looked at me with hard eyes. "I can't do it," I added, wilting slightly under his unexpectedly grim stare. "I can't move another person without being in contact with them, and I refuse to go and drag my sister here. She's injured and suffering, in a terrible state in her head."

Kallan, Zelda and even the usually genial Marna glared at me, amazed at my resistance. But from that position I would not be budged. Eventually Kallan sighed loudly.

"Well I suppose we'll just have to go to her then," he snapped. "Unless you think even that's too much for her delicate sensibilities?" he asked me in uncharacteristically sarcastic tones. I shook my head, seeing no real reason why we should not go and visit my sister in the comfort of her own room.

We went to Emaleen's room, letting ourselves in. My sister mounted a pathetic attempt to try and stop us, but was simply too weak to succeed. We stood around her bed. She had removed the bandages from her head. I tried not to stare at her, so unused was I to her shorn hair, shaved so that her injury could be treated, golden stubble marred by a vivid red gash.

"My dearest Emaleen," Kallan said, in what he thought was a more gentle voice, but which was still tinged with annoyance. "We needed to see you. We have things to talk about." I realised from the tone of his voice that much of his irritation was caused not by my sister's resistance to joining us, but by his own attempt to suppress the emotional turmoil he himself was suffering from.

Emaleen stared at Kallan, as if not understanding his words, but eventually frowned. She looked at each of us in turn, and with sudden anguish in her grey eyes blurted out,

"Where is Safya? Where is my sister?" she whispered.

For an awful moment I wondered if, in her trauma, she had already forgotten what had happened, had expunged it from her mind, and that she was actually looking for her twin in their shared room. But I quickly sensed that all she meant was what had happened to her sister's body.

Kallan looked at her with enormous tenderness in his wide blue eyes, all trace of impatience vanished.

"She's resting in the small room behind the kitchen Emmy. She's at peace."

I realised that I had been so drained on returning home from our meeting with the Council, that I had not even noticed what had happened to Safya's body. I had brought her home along with the rest of us, but after that I only had the energy to find a little respite alone in my room.

The room behind the kitchen was cool, fresh air circulating through it from small vents in the walls. Usually we stored fruit, vegetables, cheeses and other fresh foods there - unnecessary when we could always order what we wanted whenever we wanted, yet deemed essential by Zelda who wished to be prepared for the unlikely eventuality that such a system ever broke down, or worse, was made unavailable to her and her family for whatever reason. This cool room was the only place to store a recently deceased corpse. I wondered briefly if whoever had placed her there had thought to remove the food first, but quickly pushed such thoughts aside. As the thought of food entered my mind, I realised I was hungry, and did not want to be reminded of death and cadavers as I contemplated eating.

I knew I needed to eat soon, to replenish some of my diminished stores of energy. As with my first visit to the Council Chamber four years before, the exertions of controlling the entire situation had utterly exhausted me, deprived me of all energy resources. And this time, even several days later, I still seemed unable to restore my sapped strength.

Zelda cleared her throat. She clearly had something she wished to discuss.

"We need to think about where to bury our child," she began, her voice low and gravelly, unusually laden with feeling.

Chapter Thirty-Four

The next day, I awoke late, desperately thirsty and ravenously hungry. I had eaten and drunk copiously the evening before, but since my exertions in rescuing Emaleen and Safya's corpse, followed by the extraordinary scenes at the Council, it seemed as if I could simply not eat enough. I hastily leapt out of bed and raced off in search of sustenance.

In the empty kitchen I downed several large glasses of water, then carried another into the dining room, along with a plate overflowing with as much food as I could pile onto it.

Zelda and Adwin were already in the dining room, both silently tucking in to large quantities of food, obviously also hungry. I nodded to them, sat down, and began to eat. Kallan soon joined us, having just taken food and drink to Emaleen in her room. I assumed my sister would not be joining us, given her emotional state at the end of the day before, and the extent of her injuries.

After a period during which all four of us replenished our energies, Kallan spoke quietly.

"We need to bury Safya today," he said. "Emaleen won't want us to, but we can't put it off."

I stopped eating, and stared at him. I had known that this moment would come, but the actual idea of committing Safya's body to the cold, dark earth was appalling. It felt so disrespectful, and so final, and yet we had no other option. I knew that some people chose to be cremated, but this did not seem to be an option as far as Kallan was concerned. Despite developments many centuries ago in cryogenic freezing of bodies in the hope that they may one day be brought back to life, this had long been strictly forbidden due to the deep fear of population growth, one of the prime movers of the Chaos.

"Where will we bury her?" Adwin asked in a high quavering voice, as upset by the prospect as I was.

Kallan looked him tenderly, and replied. "Somewhere beautiful. Quiet. Peaceful. Somewhere we know she would like." He then addressed all three of us.

"Do you have any suggestions?"

We all considered his question, and then began to discuss possibilities. In the end, we chose a spot not too far from the house, so she would not be too distant from us. Safya had not been keen on the forest, nor even particularly interested in the meadows around the house, but she had loved the well-kept gardens in the immediate vicinity of our home. And in particular, she had been wont to sit and read, or just chat with her sister, on the grass beneath a small cherry tree, which could be seen from the front of the house. It carpeted the ground around it with dense pink blossoms in the spring, and was weighed down with small scarlet fruits in the summer. We knew she would be at rest there, and that Emaleen would not object, at least not to the location.

The discussion of Safya's burial had pushed all further thoughts of food from my mind, and I saw that Adwin felt the same. In truth, I wanted to get on with the burial, get it over and done with as soon as I could. I was so disconsolate at the idea of abandoning my sister's body to the dank soil that I tried to wheedle my way out of being involved, but Kallan would not hear of it. He became cross, and we knew from his tone of voice that he would not countenance me not participating in the burial itself. When Adwin complained that he was beginning to feel unwell, the usually compassionate Kallan merely glared at him, silencing my brother.

The burial itself was a simple affair. Emaleen had simply stared at us in mute resistance when Kallan and I had gone to fetch her. Kallan wanted Emaleen to join us, wheeling her out on a sick bed whether she wanted to or not. In truth I sympathised with my sister. I did not want to attend the interment, but knew I had no excuse not to. Even Adwin's excuse of regular poor health had not been enough to move my uncle to pity. But Emaleen's poor physical and emotional state was such that she would only be able to participate if she was forced, and dragged there against her will. I told Kallan I had no intention of helping him, and eventually he relented, saying to Emaleen in a sharp tone,

"You'll regret it. You'll regret not having made your final farewells to your sister, but that's your choice."

I felt Kallan's words were unnecessarily mean, and transmitted my sympathy silently to my sister. Through Emaleen's fog of unresponsive misery, I sensed a murmur of gratitude coming from her. I knew that she would *never* make her final farewells to Safya, and that it would not make a jot of difference to her whether she attended the actual burial or not.

Kallan insisted that we prepare the hole ourselves, so we males struggled with spades and the damp earth to dig a large and deep enough resting place for our sister's body. As I completed it, I realised that he could simply have instructed one of the estate robots to do it. I glanced at Kallan, angry, believing that his insistence on me and Adwin helping him do it was some sort of punishment for us having tried to wriggle out of attending the burial.

We stood beside the hole, Zelda, Kallan, Adwin and I, as one of our domestic automata gently transported Safya's body from the house and lay it as delicately as it could at the bottom of the forbidding pit. We could not see her face as Kallan had wrapped her from head to foot in a long shroud of crimson silk. We had invited Marna to attend, but she had said that she was too exhausted from the events of recent days. I also assumed that she simply did not want to witness such a sad affair after so much recent emotional turmoil.

Adwin and I stood in mute horror as we looked down at the silk-wrapped body lying so still at the bottom of the dark, dreary pit. It would not be covered with soil and the grass replaced until we had all left: it would simply have been too much to bear to actually witness such finality. My brother and I had no idea what a funeral entailed, and waited for Kallan or Zelda to take control. Kallan spoke a few quiet words over the grave, saying how much we would miss Safya, what a gap it would leave in our lives. As he spoke Adwin wept unashamedly, unable to control the tears which flowed copiously down his face. I felt too tired to respond in like manner. Zelda stood in stony silence, a fierce, almost passionate anger radiating from her, but underpinned with a surprising depth of unhappiness. Kallan began speaking in a strong voice, but after a while his voice cracked, and eventually his grief was so great that he simply stopped speaking in mid-sentence, and broke down in sobs which convulsed his whole body over and over again.

We stood for a long time, how long I cannot remember as time took on a peculiar quality. I could not judge if we were there hours, or mere minutes. I felt dizzy with exhaustion and sadness, having to lean against Adwin to stop myself fainting, falling to the ground or even into the hole itself. Eventually Zelda turned abruptly and shuffled away, her rage leaving a trail of heat behind her. Kallan, whose sobbing gradually abated, ending in occasional shudders and whimpers, indicated that we should all leave Safya now, commit her to her final resting place. I was desperate to flee the awful scene, but at the same time almost incapable of doing so. I had to muster a huge amount of willpower to drag myself from the foot of the cherry tree, and back towards the house.

The three of us walked slowly towards the building, Kallan in the middle, holding each of our hands, his anger dissipated. As we traipsed back to the house, Kallan instructed the automaton to begin to replace the soil and the grass. As I heard the thump of each batch of moist earth landing on the silken wrappings behind me, I winced, and felt that we were abandoning Safya to the sombre, damp earth, betraying her as we committed her poor broken form into the eternal dark bosom of death.

I was so perturbed by what we had done that I could do nothing more that day than return to my bed, bury myself under the covers, and, finally, weep. After some hours, Adwin crept into my room and joined me. We attempted some consolation with our shared grief, our physical presence and contact, but with only minor success. For the hours we sobbed and grieved together beneath the bedcovers, we felt as if we would never again feel happy, never be able to live our lives once more in the blithe way we were used to. All the trauma of the ordeals we had endured in those few days came tumbling down around us, overwhelming us, rendering us utterly incapable of rational thought, children who had endured a murder, one of whom had in turn committed a murder. We lived in that moment, unable to see anything beyond it. Our first experience of the ugliest realities of existence was unbearable, and we thought we would never manage to free ourselves from the anguish we felt at that moment.

Chapter Thirty-Five

The following day the house was filled with a mood of despondency, sombre and mirthless. As was often the case when forced to endure a stressful situation, Adwin's health showed signs of weakness. He was listless and weary, and remained in his bed. He seemed to have a slight fever, and complained of feeling nauseous. It was more that the death of Safya, the anguish of the burial, had all taken such a toll on his emotions and energies that he was simply unable to function. It was a clear sign to me that his physical infirmities were likely to flow from problems in his mind. Kallan made sure he was comfortable, and regularly supplied with plenty to drink, though he was uninterested in food.

~I'm fine, I'm fine,~ he insisted in slightly tetchy tone when I mindspoke to ask him how he was. *~I just need to hide away after all I've been through in the last few days.~* I asked him if he wanted some company, and to my surprise he said no. *~I want to be on my own,~* he insisted, but relented a little as he registered my reaction. *~But maybe you can come later in the day, if I'm feeling better. I'll let you know.~*

I could discern nothing physically wrong with him. He seemed in fairly good health. I could only surmise that his spirit was damaged.

Zelda disappeared into her laboratory, and I was glad to be away from her. Her rage at what the Council had done had reappeared after her enjoyment of the theatrics at the Council Chamber waned, surrounding her like a hot cloud. Nobody could get through to her in such a mood, not even Kallan. He did not try to, and wisely left her alone. Kallan himself seemed unable to react properly to much around him. He politely but absent-mindedly engaged with me, almost as if he did not know me, and this was so strange that I preferred to be out of his presence too.

I tried to mindspeak with Emaleen, but she would not respond. All I could sense was a misery so profound that I worried for her sanity. But what could I do? She would not see me, or anyone else, nor permit anyone to help her. She had sealed herself tightly up into an emotionless box, closed the lid, and withdrawn from the world. When I tentatively asked Kallan what we could do to help Emaleen, he turned to me, looking at me as if I were a stranger asking a foolish and irritating question, and replied simply,

"Nothing. Nothing can be done. Only time will help. And she needs time for her body to heal as well as her mind."

I wanted to ask him more, ask him how he knew time would help, how long it would take, what would happen if time did not help, but he seemed so distant that I did not feel able to pursue the issue. I sighed, and quickly removed myself from his presence.

I was at a loss as to what to do with myself. I was so enervated by recent events that even if I had been able to concentrate sufficiently, I would not have had enough energy to practise any of my abilities. My concentration was in any event so poor that I was not able to settle to studying, or even to reading. I shuffled aimlessly around the house and the gardens, and even the thought of a trip to the woods raised no enthusiasm in me.

After some wasted and aimless hours, I wondered if perhaps I could distract myself with something on the 3DV, but even this offered no respite from my aimlessness. In fact, it made things worse as the offerings were still replete with fraught discussions of me and my family. I silenced the machine and racked my brains to think of something to do to occupy myself, to distract my attention from the events of recent days, but all to no avail.

As I sat on my bed, I was surprised to see Zelda appear in the open doorway of my room. Her anger seemed much abated, or at least had been replaced by something else: a steely determination. I waited in silence, assuming she would soon apprise me of the reason for her unexpected visit.

"Tell them I want to see them now young man. Make them come here," she said without preamble.

"Who?" I asked, having no idea to whom she referred.

She stared at me as if I were being deliberately obtuse and replied, "The fucking Council of course. Who else?"

I considered asking her why, but one glance at the hard expression on her face and I decided against this course of action. I sighed quietly and mindspoke directly to the seven remaining members of the Council. They were shocked by my intrusion into their thoughts, and filled with trepidation at the reason for it. But I simply told them that Zelda wanted to see them all, at our home, now. When they clamoured to know the reason for such an abrupt summons, I was able to tell them, honestly, that I had no idea. I asked them if the present moment was acceptable to them, and they all, grudgingly, said yes. I did not know if they agreed out of fear of what would happen if they refused, or out of curiosity, or assuming that I could teleport them to our home without their consent in any case.

As I was unable to teleport them without touching them, they used the teleportal in Zelda's laboratory, though I refrained from informing them of this limit to my powers. Sensing the slight surge of energy, I raced to the portal myself to see my mother standing as each Council member emerged from the machine, her face grim as she met them in silence.

I mumbled an apology to the line of anxious and irritated faces as I entered the room, only to receive an angry scowl from Zelda for doing so. She had no intention of excusing her behaviour, and did not thank me for doing so on her behalf. As far as she was concerned, we were in the right and we held the upper hand. I could not help agree with her in some ways. We had never harmed the Council, yet some members of that governing body had set about killing Zelda's children. But I did not think it politic to treat the remaining seven members in such a high-handed, discourteous way. It would surely be better if we could retain the goodwill we enjoyed from these people, such as it was, rather than antagonise them to the point that they too became hostile towards us. But Zelda did not care, and felt that we had so much control, wielded so much power, that we could, in effect, behave as we wished towards them, with impunity. From behind Zelda's back, I flashed the tiniest of embarrassed smiles at the three members I recognised - the imposing Lenora who ignored me, the elderly and gentle-looking Vradley who responded with a ghost of a nervous smile, and ruddy-cheeked Breyan, his red hair a messy mop atop his head, who nodded once in acknowledgement of my greeting.

Zelda offered no welcome to our guests, nor invited them to sit. I followed her lead in this, not wanting to make her more irascible than she already was. Perhaps it would be best if this meeting could be concluded as quickly as possible, and for this it was preferable that nobody settled in and became comfortable. Zelda and I stood in front of the assembled members as they waited anxiously to see what Zelda had to say to them.

"I have asked you all to come here to discuss something with you," Zelda began, punctuating her words with thrusts of her first finger at each Council member in turn. Her choice of the word 'asked' caused a few raised eyebrows, as she had done nothing less than command that they come to our house, without any hint of request. But they held their tongues.

I felt a trace of sympathy for the people arrayed before me. They were important people, certainly among the most important in the world, yet recent events had been difficult for them. And despite all citizens in our world being equal, everybody knew that some were more equal than others: members of the Council were the most distinguished, the most significant citizens of all. They were not used to being forced to do and say things at all, especially so much against their inclinations.

Zelda continued. "I want to talk about the forthcoming selection of the five new Council members that will need to be appointed. I do not know which of you, if any, will be reappointed, but I assume some of you will. That is what usually happens, at least. And since you have all responded so...so...efficiently to the murder of my daughter, I imagine many citizens will be happy to see most of you back on the Council."

Nobody said a word, though I noticed Vradley's kindly face wince at the word 'efficiently'. Zelda waited for a moment to see if her words would evoke any verbal reaction, but none was forthcoming.

"Well then, since none of you has anything to say, I shall speak and you will listen." Angry emotions flowed across the faces of the mute Council members in front of me at the way Zelda addressed them, Breyan flushing even redder than usual, but they were wise enough not to let these show as they masked their facial expressions. The only sign of tension was Lenora fiddling with the large gold chain around her neck, causing it to jingle lightly. My mother looked up at her, having to tilt her head back to do so, and snapped, "stop making that racket Lenora. It's irritating." Lenora's hand fell immediately to her side, her expression becoming even grimmer than it had been at being spoken to in such a peremptory manner.

"I want to make sure," my mother continued. "Absolutely sure, that the new Council will not be hostile to me, to us, to my family. I have no intention that we will suffer again what we have so recently suffered. Am I understood?"

Silence met her question, and she glared at each member in turn, awaiting an answer. After a very tense pause, Lenora cleared her throat and spoke, her usually deep voice rendered higher-pitched by the tension she felt.

"I'm sure we all understand your desire to have a Council that is more sympathetic to you Zelda, but I don't know what *we* can do about it. As you know, we have no control over who is elected to the Council." Zelda sneered at Lenora's reply.

"Don't be naive Lenora." Zelda scoffed, thrusting her finger almost up into Lenora's face as she spoke. "We all know that you have a great deal of influence over the election. Why would you not? Who would want to be on a

Council with a whole lot of idiots or people you cannot stand? So I insist that you do what you can, what I know you can, to influence the choice and to make sure not a single member of the Council hates us the way Rannald and his cronies did. I ask again, am I understood?"

"Yes," Breyan replied, as tetchily as he dared. "We understand you, but as Lenora said, we have no control over the way the appointment process works." Zelda laughed scornfully.

"If you wish to maintain that squalid deceit Breyan, then by all means do so," she sneered as she moved to stand right in front of him, this time actually poking him in the chest as she spoke, his red brows lifted high in silent outrage. "As long as you promise me that you will do all you can, openly or in the background, as you see fit. Are you willing make me that promise?"

The seven Council members stood utterly still, not really knowing how to respond to Zelda's question. Her tone of voice and body language clearly told them that they had no option but to accede to her 'request', and they could not fail to apprehend the veiled threat behind her words. Rannald's sudden death must surely be hanging unspoken yet heavy in all of their minds. And yet they could not be seen even to be attempting to influence the choice of new Council members, even to be heard discussing such a possibility, and especially so if any of them were then reappointed. Such behaviour would create a scandal, a crisis in the authority and prestige of the Council, a body desperately needing to bolster its image in the wake of recent events. Finally, Lenora decided that a promise could be made, but couched in tentative language. She coughed slightly before she spoke.

"I believe, Zelda," she began hesitantly, glancing at the others as she did, "That we can promise you to do everything within our power to ensure that the new members of the Council are not your enemies. Does that satisfy you?"

It was clear that Lenora was still holding fast to the claim that they had no power to affect the outcome of the appointment process, and that nothing would make her say otherwise. But my mother nodded and indicated that the promise was satisfactory, adding,

"But be warned: if any of you break your promise, there will be consequences." The members blanched at her words, hardly daring to consider what such consequences might entail.

"Oh, and by the way," Zelda continued, "If any unwelcome members of the Council are appointed, we will have to do something about that too."

Several members physically flinched at Zelda's final comment, at the sheer audacity of what it implied. But not a single one of them disbelieved her, not for a moment. They knew Zelda well enough to be convinced that she would act on any threat, and were well enough acquainted with my abilities to know that I was capable of carrying out any of Zelda's threats.

The mood of despondency in every Council member was profound, a pall of gloom pervading the entire room. I suspected that more than one of them would be very happy indeed not to be reappointed to the Council at this juncture, but they claimed that they had no influence over this. In truth, I was not sure if they were being disingenuous in making such a claim, and that they did, in fact, wield substantial leverage over the choice of new Council members. I dared not try to enter their minds in case they knew when I did so, as I did not want to make this deeply uncomfortable meeting any worse for them. But I suspected that they may well have influence over the choice of new members, as this could explain how members were so often reappointed, leading to mumblings among some citizens that the appointments sometimes seemed to be for life. I had no knowledge of the frankly uninteresting workings of the process to appoint new members, but assumed Zelda did. Zelda would always think the worst of the Council, and of all humanity for that matter, but on this issue perhaps she was right.

"Well," Zelda said abruptly. "That is that then. That is all I had to say, so you can all go home now and do what you have promised. But mark my words, I shall be following the appointment process very carefully, every step of the way, and if I feel that any of you are trying to go against what you have promised I will not hesitate to act. And the same goes for any new member I feel is against us. Now off you all go," she added, dismissively.

I wanted to offer my apologies again to the seven angry yet also dejected and humiliated adults standing before me, but did not dare with Zelda standing beside me. I did, however, politely ask if they were all ready to port away, and threw a vaguely apologetic thought towards them, silently, for the way Zelda had treated them as I gestured towards the portal. The moment they disappeared, Zelda turned to me.

"That was good," she said. "We've really got them by the balls now." I was surprised at her crude language, appalled at her treatment of the members of the Council. We needed allies in the Council, needed them to be on our side, and the way to achieve this was not to cow them into submission, threaten them, frighten them into carrying out our will. I knew Zelda was right in her insistence on a Council that was not made up on members inimical to us, but she was wrong, oh so wrong, in her methods of achieving this. I sighed, wondering if there was anything I could do to change her behaviour.

As I looked at her, I realised that she was triumphant, relishing the image of the defeated Council members as they stood in fear of her. Her attitude was grossly inappropriate given the atrocity committed against a member of her family so recently, and I knew I had to speak up, try to make her see that her methods were misguided.

"You should try to get them on side Mother," I began. "They're not our enemies, but treating them like that might make them so."

"For such an intelligent boy," she replied tartly, bushy eyebrows rising scornfully. "You can be a bit of a cretin on the sly. They will *never* be our friends. They are the Council and think they run everything, actually think they own everything. The only way to control them is through fear, with threats. Anything else simply will not work. It might in the short term, but believe me young man, in the long run their real natures will come to the fore and they will turn against us too."

I disagreed, and was convinced that we were at the perfect juncture to woo the Council, to win them to our side with respect, and by leaving them with what remained of their injured dignity intact. Zelda's treatment of them undermined what self-respect they still retained, and I felt this to be a disastrous course of action. In their situation I would dig my heels in. But nothing I could say would persuade Zelda - this I also knew. Her jubilant arrogance as she lorded it up over the Council, her obvious relish at humiliating them, these irritated me beyond measure. And as my anger grew, I suddenly remembered what Haari had told me about the messages he had sent me.

"And why did you conceal all those messages?" I demanded without preamble in a voice now shaking with fury.

"What messages?" she asked, caught unaware by the sudden change of subject. Her eyes glanced away from mine as she continued. "What on earth are you talking about now boy?"

"All those messages from Haari, and perhaps from other people, that were sent time and time again, year after year, yet not a single one of which ever reached me," I stated.

"I do not have the faintest idea what you are talking about," she mumbled, uneasy at the turn of the conversation.

"Yes you do!" I snapped, infuriated by her reply. "You must have intercepted them, all of them, and destroyed them," I said. "How dare you. How dare you treat me like this. I'm not your 'creation', as you call me. I'm not your property. I'm a person, a human being, and as entitled to receive messages, to have friends, to have visitors as any other person. You are a monster Zelda, the way you've treated me, treated Adwin and my sisters. You don't see us as human. You see us the way some of the outsiders see us, as creatures, creations, non-humans. And I've had enough of it. I'm not putting up with it any more. In future if you get any more messages you *will* pass them straight on to me. And also, though I can't force you to change the way you act towards Lenora, Breyan, Vradley and the others, you will not tell me how I should treat them. I will behave politely with them, treat them with respect and will apologise for your awful behaviour. And you will not stop me!"

Zelda was flabbergasted at my outburst, and had no response. She simply turned heel and shuffled briskly off towards her laboratory, leaving me shaking with a mixture of anger and agitation, underpinned by a surge of triumph. I had bested her, backed her into a corner from which she knew there was no escape.

But in truth it was a hollow triumph. My family was in turmoil. Safya was dead. Emaleen was badly injured and grieving alone in her room, withdrawn to a place nobody could reach her. Adwin had taken to his bed, made ill by the trauma of recent days. Kallan was in a state of such deep grief that he was acting like an automaton, behaving towards me as if he barely knew me. Zelda was more outraged and angry with me than I ever remembered.

And I was overwhelmed by my recent experiences. By the horror of Safya's death which I had been the one to discover, but I had also been forced to re-play Emaleen's experience in showing it to other people. By the suggestion that I could learn to travel in time, to go back and undo what had been done on that cliff top only a few days before. To return to the scene of the crime before it happened, and to prevent it taking place.

Was this really possible or just a wild idea? I had never given it any thought, but it now firmly planted itself in my mind like a tenacious weed, a seedling that would not go away until I had allowed it to grow to fruition. My instinct told me that it was not possible. Travel to the future was surely unfeasible - after all, how could one travel to a place and time that had not yet happened, had never happened? And travelling back in time, what of that? I was less sure of the answer to this, and knew that there were theories supporting the possibility, all based ultimately on the proposition that there was no real difference, or no differentiating, between time and space. Thus, given that physically travelling in space was easy for me to achieve now, why should travelling in time not be just as easy? But how would I ever practise it? If I sent inanimate or even animate objects back in time, if I could ever learn how to do this, how would I know that is where they had been? Even if I could bring them back again to the present, I had no way of ascertaining if I had indeed moved them in time, or merely in space. The only way to know would be to go myself, but the dangers in that were transparent. If it did not work, I would not know until it was too late, and I would either die in the attempt, or be stranded at some time in the past with no possibility of return to my own time.

And yet, and yet…the lure was immense. But even if I could learn how to safely move between different time periods, this did not mean I could alter the past and save my sister. In fact, if one were able to alter the past and therefore what followed it, the repercussions of this would be unknowable, far too dangerous to attempt, and would in fact make time travel so inherently perilous as to render it off limits. Even if one altered something that seemed harmful, perhaps even aspects of the Chaos, there was no guarantee that such alterations would not lead to even worse outcomes.

But how could a person alter the past? The past has already happened, and cannot happen differently. Surely this was the only possible solution to the conundrum of whether time travel could alter the past?

I assumed there must be copious literature on the possibility of time travel, scientific theories as well as philosophical musings. I would have to immerse myself in these to see what had already been written before I took another step towards any attempt to make it a reality.

I shook my head, clearing it of the reveries of journeying about through time, of the cogitations on the dilemmas thrown up by the ramifications of going back to the time of past events. I did not really believe that moving through time was possible in any event, and in truth, I had more than enough to concern myself with in the present. My family, my home, the Council, my future and my place within it. I decided, then and there, that I would overcome my fear of the world outside and begin to make steps towards it. When I felt calmer, and my grief and shock had abated a little, I would contact Haari. I would invite him to visit me, and I would visit him, finally see the city, meet his friends, begin to do all those things that other people took for granted. I would finally escape the confines of the velvet prison I called home.

Chapter Thirty-Six

A few days later, Haari leapt into my mind. I had told him I would contact him, but in truth I was wary of doing so, wary of making contact with anyone, especially with a stranger. But perhaps this would be the best thing to distract me from my feelings of purposelessness.

I located him easily. I mindspoke to him, asking him shyly if this was a good time to talk. He immediately replied that it was a perfect time, and I felt his chirpiness that I had contacted him as promised.

~I'm really pleased you've made contact Samek. Believe me, I wasn't sure if you would,~ he said in an upbeat tone.

~I said I would didn't I?~ I asked slightly petulantly, unfairly so as I had in fact almost forgotten the promise I had made.

~Ok, ok,~ he laughed, not at all bothered by my petulance. *~I'm just happy you've done so. How are you feeling?~* he asked. I was taken aback by the question, and even more so by the concern in his voice. I could not collect my thoughts to respond.

After a few moments of silence, Haari spoke.

~Are you still there?~ he said tentatively.

~I'm sorry,~ I said, embarrassed by my silence at the unaccustomed concern shown to me by a stranger. *~I'm just not used to being asked how I'm feeling.~*

~No need to be sorry,~ he replied in a gentle tone. *~I just wondered if the connection was cut, or if perhaps you'd changed your mind. I wouldn't have been surprised if you hadn't contacted me, or got cold feet. With your background, and all that you've just been through, that would have been quite a normal reaction in my opinion.~*

I sighed at his words, immediately grasping what he was saying. He was telling me that I was ordinary, normal, not some oddity or freak. Little did he know that I had killed the leader of our world, and that I had enjoyed doing so.

It was so strange. I had no friends. No friends in the usual sense of the word. Adwin and the rest of my family were not friends, they were family. They were the people who made up the whole of my world, who had been my world throughout my life. Of course Adwin was my best friend, the best friend a person could have, but he and I had no choice in the fact of each other's constant presence. I had never had the chance to meet outsiders who I could become the friend of. Marna I loved, but she was like a member of the family, and as Zelda and Kallan's friend, I had had no choice in the fact of her presence in my life either. But Haari, whom I barely knew, was independent of my family, and, feeling his warmth towards me, had chosen for him to be my friend. And in this choice lay the crucial difference with all the other people in my life.

I had no experience of friendship, but knew that the fact of being chosen, and choosing, these were of fundamental importance. We have no choice in the members of our family, or even in those who we meet through the other members of our family - all these people are simply unavoidable parts of our life. But there is no compulsion in friendship: a friend is chosen, and can be unchosen. That is what makes it so powerful, and so special. When a friend likes us, or loves us, we know that they are under no obligation to do so, not even to spend any time with us. Every time they contact us, wish to talk to us or be with us, they make a choice to do so. This idea was utterly novel to me, and so profound, that I was almost overwhelmed by it. Something that to others, brought up in the world of people, was so ordinary, so everyday, was to me marvellous to the point of being almost magical. I sighed with the sheer joy of it, and asked Haari when he would like to visit me.

He suggested that we should wait a while, until the storm of grief raging in our house abated. I was impatient for his visit, but had to agree with him. My home was so consumed with unhappiness, and in Zelda's case, fury, that this was not a good time for something so novel as a stranger's visit. We agreed to speak regularly, and I assured him that he could contact me whenever he wanted on the channel I had opened between us. He did not at first understand what I meant by this, so I told him that he would understand easily once contact was broken. To prove the point, I informed him that I was about to rupture the connection, and that he should then immediately re-engage with me. He was not convinced by my assurances, but after I had disconnected from him, and mere moments later his voice reappeared in my head, I had to smile at the surprise in his voice when he said *~It was so easy!~*

~Yes, I told you that didn't I?~ I replied in amused tones, though with the barest hint of irritation. *~You need to believe me when I tell you things. It won't do if you keep being so skeptical.~*

He laughed again, and promised that from now on he would believe me. We chatted for a little longer, eventually disconnecting, but with the promise that we would speak again very soon.

Some weeks passed, during which time I spoke often with Haari. At first he seemed tentative in making contact with me, perhaps out of respect for my grief, or perhaps still wondering if I was serious when I promised I wished to get to know him better, and that I might let him make a programme about me. But gradually he gained confidence, and began to regularly engage the channel, sometimes only to ask how I was or what I was doing, other times leading to much longer conversations.

During the early days, I enjoyed the contact with Haari with no disruption, but as Adwin's health slowly recovered, I shared with him my joy at having a new friend, relaying long snatches of the conversations between me and Haari, telling Adwin how extraordinary it was to have a friend, someone outside the family to whom I seemed to mean so much.

The response I received from Adwin to this news was unexpected. I had assumed he would be happy for me, share in my excitement and enthusiasm, but I could not have been more wrong. He was silent as I told him about the chats with Haari, and when his lack of response continued on the second and third occasion I spoke to him about Haari, I asked him "What's wrong?"

He frowned slightly and replied "There's nothing wrong. I'm very happy that you have a new friend, someone else in your life apart from me." It was transparent from his tone and his facial expression that he was anything but happy, and I was puzzled by this. I asked again what was the matter, but he merely repeated that he was fine, and then said "I'd like to be left alone now if it's not too much to ask."

I was astonished. Adwin had never requested that I leave him alone in this abrupt way. I could not understand what was wrong, though it was clear that my friendship with Haari was the cause of the problem. I did not want to exacerbate Adwin's sulking towards me by reading his thoughts, so all I had to go on were my perceptions of what he was feeling. It was clear to me that Adwin was unhappy at the fact I had a new friend, but the outward signs of his emotions did not provide me with any detail of the reasons why.

After this uncomfortable conversation with my little brother, I asked Haari what could be the problem. He seemed surprised I had no idea. *~I assume he's jealous Samek. Jealous of you,~* he added.

~What do you mean?~ I asked, none the wiser from Haari's reply. *~Why would he be jealous?~*

~You really haven't a clue, have you?~ Haari asked. I indicated that I did not. Haari's amazement was palpable.

~He's always had you by his side, and you him. From what you've told me before, you two seem to be incredibly close, and now you tell him that you have a new friend, someone else in your life that you like, that matters to you. He hasn't got anyone like that.~

~But he still has me,~ I insisted. *~That hasn't changed.~*

~He fears it has, or it that it might. And to some extent he's right. Before you had me as your friend, he always had you, at home, whenever he wanted or needed you. And you always needed him because you are closer to him than to anyone else in your life, and have so few people in your life.~

I was so perplexed by this idea that I told Haari I needed to think about it. I cut the connection so I could consider the matter quietly. I knew what jealousy was, of course, but had no experience of it. I realised that the relationship between Emaleen and Safya could have been seen as involving a large dose of jealousy, as each of them had cleaved to the other, but as they both felt exactly the same way, it had not been obvious. I wondered if jealousy only shows itself when one party to a relationship begins to distance him or herself from the other, only then allowing the other person's intense feelings to come to the surface. I wondered about Zelda's desire to keep her children closeted away from the world, isolated from the rest of humanity. Was this jealousy? I decided it was something different. It was more like a sense of ownership, of having a right to control what she had created.

I tried to broach it with Adwin, but he maintained his unconvincing attitude of "I'm fine and there's no problem", while persisting with his sulks towards me.

One day I made the mistake of suggesting to my brother that his "reaction wasn't normal." He stared at me as I dug myself even deeper. "It's not normal," I continued, "to react like this. It's not as if I've done anything to you. I've just found a friend, a new friend outside the family. And you...you are behaving like a child, sulking and pouting and not wanting to talk to me..."

"You're so mean!" he snapped at me. "Telling me I'm behaving like a child. I've told you I'm fine and there's no problem, so just leave me alone and go and chat to your wonderful new chum. Don't mind me. I'll be fine on my own."

"But Addy," I replied. "I know you're not fine. You're unhappy and I think it's really unfair on me. And to be honest, it's not a normal reaction to the fact that I just..."

"Not normal?" interrupted Adwin loudly. "Not normal? What a horrible thing to say again, that I'm not normal..."

"I didn't say you weren't normal," I complained. "I said your reaction wasn't normal. Don't twist my words."

"Oh, and now I'm twisting your words as well as not being normal am I? That's so unfair Samek. And you're one to talk about not being normal."

"What's that supposed to mean?" I asked.

"You're the one with all the gifts and powers, the golden boy that Zelda and everyone looks up to and admires so much. Not the...the failure, the one that went wrong, the one that didn't work out the way mother wanted." Adwin looked so upset by his own words, that I had no reply. I was amazed he thought of himself in this way, that he had the perception to know what Zelda really felt about him. And in truth, I could not deny his words. Our mother did think of him as a failure, as the one that had gone wrong. My heart went out to my brother, all recent irritation melting as I contemplated his unhappy face. I reached towards him to give him a hug, to assure him of my continued affection for him, but he threw up his arms, defensively, almost snarling at me.

"No!" he shouted. "Go away and leave me alone. I don't want any false attempts at consoling me."

"But Addy," I replied. "I want you to know that...it's not false. I still..."

"Just fuck off and leave me alone!" he snapped, then turned and ran off before I could say another word. I was nonplussed and had no idea how to react, what to do to bridge the gulf that had opened up between me and my brother. Before that day, I had no idea how he felt about himself, that he was bitter about his lack of gifts and my abundance of the same. That he thought he was seen as the failure in the family, me the success.

Haari offered much sensible advice when I discussed all of this with him, but was too distant from my family, and actually a major part of the problem. Emaleen was still locked away in her casket of grief, and in any case, I had never been able to discuss such things with her. On the few occasions I had tried, she had just scoffed with derision and mocked me. If Safya had been alive, she might have been willing to help, but this was no longer an option. And Zelda: I did not even consider asking her. She had barely emerged from her part of the house since the visit to our home of the Council members, and was never any use in discussing personal or emotional issues in any case. I decided I needed to talk to Kallan.

I had to bide my time until Kallan's behaviour towards me had returned to something closer to normal. He was still a little distant, but the bizarre way he had treated me as a stranger just after the burial gradually ebbed. One day, I came across him about to leave the house. I asked him where he was going and he replied that he just needed some air. I asked if I could accompany him, and though he seemed surprised by my request, he acceded to it readily enough.

We walked in silence in the garden, and soon came to the cherry tree under which we had laid Safya to rest. The grass had been returned to a state close to how it had looked before being disrupted, but it was possible to see the faint outline of a sad rectangle at the foot of the tree.

"It would be nice if we marked the grave," said Kallan, his mellow voice underpinned with sadness. "Perhaps a big stone on top of it, engraved with some appropriate words?"

I nodded my agreement, and said that I would find and arrange to transport a large stone from the forest, and that we could all decide what words would best describe Safya.

"Thank you Samek," Kallan said. "You're a good boy." And with this I felt his attitude towards me return almost to normal. Now was the time to broach my problem with him.

I said that I had something I wished to discuss with him, something I needed his advice on. He seemed pleased that I was seeking his counsel, and indicated that we should sit on a bench a little way across the grass, from where we looked directly at Safya's cherry tree.

There I poured out the whole story of Haari, how he had met Marna and how Haari and I had begun to communicate with each other. I explained to my uncle what Haari wanted, and he seemed about to interrupt, doubtless to warn me not to accede to such a request. I held up my hand.

"Please uncle, let me finish before I lose my train of thought," I requested. He closed his mouth, and I continued.

"Haari likes me," I continued. I was slightly irked to see a look of skepticism on my uncle's face at my comment. "He let me enter his mind," I continued. "And you know that I'd see if he was pretending." My uncle conceded this point with a little nod of his head.

"And I like him. It's so nice having a friend. My first friend. The *only* friend I've ever had." As I said this I saw Kallan's face flood with a look of sympathy towards me. He knew how alone we children were, how isolated had been our upbringing on the estate, and he himself had frequently berated Zelda about this, saying that we desperately needed to make friends, to meet people, to go out into the world. Despite this, I sensed his disquiet.

"And now I don't know what to do about Addy," I continued. "When I told him about Haari, I thought he'd be happy, but he reacted oddly. He went cool on me and now doesn't seem to want to spend time with me. And we had an argument, about Haari and about...other things too. Do you think he might be jealous?" I asked. I did not tell him that this was Haari's opinion, as I felt this would not impress my uncle. It was better that he think it came from me.

I stopped talking, and a long silence ensued, as Kallan considered what I had said. Eventually, he looked at me through gentle blue eyes, and spoke tenderly.

"Samek, my dear. You know I've been more than keen for you and your siblings to get out into the world and to meet people. To make friends. So in this I'm very happy. I'm not sure a man that age, and one who does what he does is entirely suitable, but I suspect, from your manner, that nothing I say will persuade you otherwise. And anyway, I know that despite your innocence in dealing with strangers, you are more than capable of knowing if someone is deceiving you, or is genuine, certainly when they let you into their mind, so let's just accept that this man...Haari, did you say his name was?...is your friend. And you're probably right about Adwin. He may be jealous. He is worried what your new friendship may mean. You might go away, or at the very least you won't be around so much, won't be available for Adwin when he needs you."

"But I'll still be his Samek. None of that changes," I protested, feeling a little guilty at not sharing with my uncle the other cause of the argument between my brother and me, though deciding that it was best to keep this between the two of us.

"None of what you feel changes, or who you are, but it's naive to think *nothing* changes. If, as you've told me, you plan to spend a lot of time with Haari away from here, then Adwin will be alone. And with Safya... gone, it'll be even quieter here, not that he spent much time with her before. But if you do as you plan, what time will be left for you to spend with Adwin? From the time of his earliest memories he's always had you here, with him, beside him. You two are bonded together. And he is not as robust as you, and you know I don't just mean physically. Frankly he's rather highly-strung, and he relies on you for most of his emotional support. He lacks your confidence."

"But what am I to do?" I asked. "Am I to give up my friend? Am I to give up ever having friends, ever leaving here? Am I to be locked up in this prison for the rest of my life?" And surely there was nothing I could do to soften Adwin's perception of himself as a mishap in comparison with my own success.

I felt unhappy as I considered my options. I could not see a good solution: either lose my friend and possibly all future friends, or cause my brother great distress. And even if I gave up my new friend, how would I persuade Adwin of his worth? Kallan felt my mood.

"Yes, my dear. You are, as they say, caught between a rock and a hard place." He looked straight at me, his azure eyes filled with compassion. "Whichever decision you make will cause distress."

"But I don't want to cause distress. What should I do?" I queried.

"I can't answer that for you Samek. It's a choice you have to make for yourself. But for what it's worth, I don't believe it's right for you to spend the rest of your life here on the estate. And frankly, it upsets me to hear that you feel as if you were in prison. You need to get out into the world, need to meet people and learn how to cope with them. And you need to make friends, to have more people in your life than just us. And Adwin needs this too. For all that he is feeling anxious at losing you, he cannot remain imprisoned here for ever, however comfortable this prison seems."

I felt Kallan was clearly indicating the decision I should make, despite his claims not to be able to make it for me. I knew he was right, and he had merely confirmed what I had felt. I could not remain in this comfortable jail for ever. I had to escape. And Haari was offering me the perfect chance to break free.

"I've made a decision," I announced. "I *will* continue my friendship with Haari, and when I've got to know him better I might let him make a presentation about me, despite what you think of that! As you say, I can't stay forever in this prison, no matter how safe it is. I feel bad that I might be hurting Adwin, but I'm not doing it to hurt him. And I'll still be here often, will always be his brother and, while he wants me, his closest companion."

Kallan nodded his approval at my decision, though he was clearly still unconvinced at the idea of a presentation about me being transmitted across the world.

"And perhaps," he added tentatively as a final thought before we made our way back to the house, "This will be the best thing to happen to Adwin, the thing that forces *him* to get out and about in the world and make his own friends."

Chapter Thirty-Seven

After many weeks, during which my friendship with Haari flourished and my relationship with Adwin floundered, I decided that the atmosphere in the house was sufficiently calm for Haari to make his first trip to the estate.

I told Kallan of my decision, and he seemed unperturbed. When I mentioned it to Adwin, he flushed with emotion, looked on the verge of tears, but merely said "Fine. Why should I care?"

"Addy," I replied. "I just want...I...I hope that you..."

"Oh don't bother," was my brother's curt reply. "Just enjoy your wonderful new friend. Samek the golden boy, with all the gifts and abilities and now a visitor all of his own too."

I left him alone after this, having no idea how to react. In fact, during the weeks since the burial, Adwin and I had not spent nearly as much time together as usual. When we were together, our previous perfect harmony was strained and uncomfortable, and I did not know how to change this, how to begin the process of returning us to how we had been before. I was not willing to give up Haari, and Adwin knew this. The problem for Adwin did not just concern Haari. In fact in some ways it was not really about Haari at all. It was clear that I was moving into a different phase in my life, one which might alter my relationship with Adwin forever as it was a phase from which there would be no return to the past. I planned to spend time away from the house, out in the world, and would never again revert to being the biddable, house-bound child I had been. Adwin knew he had no option but to accept what was happening, and knew that he needed to find his own solution to it, but he seemed unable to see a path through the maze. In the past we would have freely discussed all of this, and moved forward into the unknown future together, but the tension between us made this impossible. It crossed my mind that perhaps I should have invited Adwin to get to know Haari, to include him in our conversations, even to consider letting him accompany me when I finally left the compound to visit Haari. But I knew I did not want to share Haari, not even with my brother. Haari was *my* friend and I was jealous of him, cleaving him to me. And even if I had taken this course of action, how to solve the deeper problem of Adwin's negative view of himself, or his envy at my perceived status?

On talking further to Kallan, he counselled patience, saying that time would show Adwin how to manage the new situation. He felt that it was not always necessary to discuss everything in every detail, and that sometimes things found their own equilibrium if allowed the time and space to do so. I was not convinced by what he said, but as I could offer no other solution to the problem, I accepted his advice.

I felt I needed to tell Zelda that we would soon be receiving a visitor, yet harboured great ambivalence towards doing so. I knew that her reaction would be fierce and hostile, and this I did not relish. Yet I also knew she could not prevent Haari's visit, and in this I took great pleasure. Demonstrating to Zelda my new-found independence would be most enjoyable.

Zelda spent almost no time with us during this period, but I managed to corner her one day as she made her way from her room to the laboratory. I spoke without preamble.

"Zelda," I began in a firm voice, despite my trepidation at her response. "I've invited a friend here to visit us. He'll be coming either tomorrow or the day after. I'd like you to meet him."

Zelda stopped in mid-step, staring at me in utter astonishment. She looked comical, one foot raised off the floor, her amazement so intense that she forgot for a moment to lower it to the floor. I nearly laughed at the expression on her face, but wisely kept my features neutral. She would be angry enough without adding my laughter to her outrage.

"What??" she finally managed to squeak out, her usually abrasive voice shrill with shock.

"I'm having a visitor, a friend, who's coming to see me. Here," I repeated.

"I heard you," Zelda said in a tight voice, her tone dropping closer to its norm. "But that does not mean I understand what it signifies."

"Just what it says," I continued, showing her no sign of my fear. "A friend is coming to visit me."

"A friend?" she said, this time in a much louder voice, anger beginning to tinge its tone. "What friend? You do not have any friends!"

"Yes, actually, I do, and his name is Haari," I countered, irritability tinting my own voice.

"How? You never go anywhere, never meet anyone. How could you possibly have a friend?" Zelda asked, in a tone of genuine incredulity.

"I spoke to him on the vidiscreen a while back after...after I found out he'd been sending me messages for ages," I went on, gulping as I realised how close I had been to divulging that Marna had told me this. Zelda would have been livid with our old friend if she ever discovered the fact. "And we've been in contact ever since, often, and for long conversations."

Zelda just glared at me, trying to exert her usual control over me just by the intensity of her expression, by the fierceness of her dark eyes overshadowed by menacing mobile bushy brows, but this time I would not be cowed. I stared back at her, defiant and clearly unwilling to bow to her dominance. She frowned, and I suspected she was trying to work out how I had come upon the information.

"You will not invite this person here, to our home," Zelda commanded. "I forbid it."

I felt a surge of trepidation at her words, and nearly gave in to her. But I steeled myself, pushed back my shoulders, and replied in the most manly voice I could muster at the tender age of thirteen.

"You will not forbid it, cannot forbid it. I've invited him and he's coming, and there's nothing you can do to stop it."

I stared at her, adding an emotional thrust to the challenge of my words. She pulled herself up to her tallest, leaned towards me so our faces were mere inches apart, close enough for me to see the flakes and crusts of her throbbing eczema. And she then spoke in a tone of intense, yet quiet, growling rage.

"You dare disobey me? You dare try and influence me with your mind tricks? You are *my* creation, and you will do what you are told. You will not have any guests here, not now, not ever. Do you understand?"

I almost wilted under the weight of Zelda's ire, but from somewhere found the strength to resist it. I stood my ground and replied.

"Yes I understand you, but I will *not* obey you. Haari *will* visit me, and there is nothing you can do to stop him."

"Oh yes there is," Zelda replied in venomous tone. And after a moment's hesitation continued. "I can...I can...I can dismantle the portal so nobody can visit."

I laughed directly into her face. "You know you'd never do that. Kallan wouldn't allow it. And what would stop me ordering another one and keeping it in my room? Or I could just go and fetch him and bring him here myself."

A hint of doubt suddenly suffused Zelda's rage. She knew I spoke the truth.

"Then I will physically stop him when he gets here," she said, but with a trace of hesitation in her voice. "I will tell him to leave, and if he does not I shall...I shall fight him!"

I guffawed at this childish comment, knowing that Zelda was beaten. But I could not help adding,

"If you try anything like that, I will personally ensure that you are rendered immobile throughout his visit, and out of sight. I will not be embarrassed in front of my guest."

Zelda stepped sharply back as I said this, eyes flying open, bushy brows popping upwards, appalled that I would contemplate such drastic action, yet under no illusion that I was perfectly capable of such, and that I might even carry out my threat if I felt it necessary.

We stood in silence, eyes boring into each other. She sensed she was defeated, but did not want to show this by being the first to leave. I suddenly remembered something else, and my own anger rose inside me.

"And you still haven't answered my question about those messages," I added, in a voice beginning to shake with fury as I remembered.

"What messages?" she asked, suddenly breaking eye contact with me. "What on earth are you talking about?"

"You know perfectly well what I'm talking about," I replied.

"I have no idea what you mean," she mumbled, her tone showing unease at the turn of the conversation.

"Yes you do!" I snapped. "And I've had enough of it. And I'm not putting up with it any more. You can either meet Haari when he comes, and any other visitors I invite here, or you can absent yourself, or I will ensure you are absent. But you will not stop me!"

Zelda was flabbergasted at my outburst, and had no response. She simply turned heel and marched off towards her laboratory, leaving me shaking with a mixture of anger and agitation, underpinned by a surge of triumph. I had bested her again, backed her into a corner from which she knew there was no escape. I stood for a few minutes until my trembling abated, then quickly mindspoke to Haari, telling him he could come the next day during the morning. He was delighted at finally having a definite day for his visit, and I told him to let me know when he was ready so I could meet him by the portal before Zelda even knew he had arrived.

The next morning I awoke excited about Haari's visit. We had been in contact many times over the past weeks, had chatted at length about nothing and everything, had learned much about each other's lives, interests, passions. I almost felt butterflies in my stomach at the prospect of his visit, my first ever visitor. Haari was my first and only friend, so the event felt important, momentous even.

Kallan seemed pleased at the prospect of meeting Haari, and even Adwin had reluctantly agreed to do the same. He knew Haari would visit whether or not he wished it, that it was a situation over which he had no control, but I suspected that he was motivated by sheer inquisitiveness, and certainly not by a desire to please me. Our relationship had not recovered. We were cool and distant with each other.

Around mid-morning Haari let me know that he was ready whenever I was. I told him that I would meet him at the portal, and shortly afterwards welcomed him to our home, hurrying him out of Zelda's rooms and into the living room.

He sat down on the sofa and I poured him a drink of juice from the jug on the table. As I was doing so, Kallan came in and Haari sprang up to greet him politely. They rather formally shook hands, and Kallan also sat down. As we chatted about everyday matters, Adwin appeared in the doorway, hovering uncertainly as if wary of entering. I looked up, but before I could react, Haari jumped up again, walked briskly to the door and took both of Adwin's hands in his.

"You must be Samek's brother, Adwin. I've heard a lot about you from Samek and wanted so much to meet you."

Adwin blushed slightly at Haari's words kindly spoken words. I tried hard not to be irritated by Adwin's manner, feeling a surge of possessiveness towards Haari as Adwin smiled at him. I noticed, for the first time, that my little brother was winsome, cute in his boyishness. I sat down quickly beside Haari on the sofa, forcing Adwin to sit next to me where Haari could not see him without straining around me to do so.

We all chatted for a while, though Adwin and Haari could not easily talk directly to each other without effort, and mostly Haari spoke to Kallan sitting opposite. Adwin remained quiet through the conversation, only occasionally adding some childish comment or other which I did my best to ignore.

After a while, Kallan said that he had things to do, and left the room, telling Haari that it was a pleasure to welcome him to our home, and hoping he would join us for lunch. I hoped that Adwin would follow Kallan, leaving me and Haari alone, but he showed no signs of doing so. I considered forcing him to leave, but in the end, Haari made this decision for both of us, asking,

"Will you two show me around? I'd like to see the house and gardens, and the forest that Samek has spoken about so often." Adwin agreed immediately, and reluctantly I nodded my approval. I did not want Haari to think me mean-spirited and jealous, but I felt irritated with him that he had invited my brother along.

I spent the next few hours taking Haari all around the house and gardens, the meadows and the forest. Haari showed great interest in everything, asking questions about each and every room in the house, about the various plants outside, pausing to show respect to Safya's burial place where now stood a fine slab of golden-brown sandstone inscribed with the simple words suggested by Kallan at the top: "Safya. Sister. Friend. Beloved family member. She will be missed for ever". And below which, to Haari's obvious surprise, the harsher addition Zelda insisted we add: "Murdered by order of the Council".

Haari was fascinated when I showed him the fence marking the boundary of the estate, explaining how it worked, and how, all those years ago, my siblings and I had managed to cross it. And he clearly enjoyed the forest, seeming to show the same sense of wonder as I did, especially when we visited our favourite place, the woodland glade with its waterfall and pool. Looking back now as an old man, I smile as I consider how naive I was. I cannot imagine Haari was truly interested in much of what I showed him, especially the forest. He was an urbane city-dweller. I think now that he was humouring us though in a kindly way as an adult might do towards enthusiastic children. Adwin was still only ten years old, and though I liked to think of myself as a young man, I was not yet fourteen. Perhaps Haari just wanted us to like him. He had an amazing ability to make people like him, to make them think they were the most important people in the world while he was with them.

But at that time as we sat in silence on the dense grass of the glade, enjoying the sounds and smells of the forest, I simply enjoyed the unique experience of being there with a friend. Adwin too seemed happier than he had for some time, though he and I did not speak directly to each other much, tension between us hanging in the air. Haari seemed able to ignore this, talking easily to both of us. I should have enjoyed this time so much more than I did, showing my first friend around all of my favourite places, but my brother's presence marred my pleasure, grated on my nerves, making me almost seethe with silent anger whenever he and Haari laughed together, or seemed to share a common delight at something they contemplated.

We returned to the house for lunch, a simple meal for which we were joined by Kallan. Zelda made no appearance, and Haari did not ask about her. I suspected he had no desire to be confronted with Zelda, fully aware of Zelda's attitude to his visit, and of her reputation. Emaleen too made no appearance, remaining in her room from which she had rarely emerged since her sister's death. Haari also did not ask after her, knowing from what I had told him of her state of mind. I appreciated his delicacy in this, and throughout his visit felt nothing but warmth towards him. The only thorn was my brother's constant presence, his attempts, as I saw them that day, to sidle his way into Haari's affections. Kallan seemed to like Haari. I had not heard my uncle so jolly and happy since before Safya's death. Haari was a master at making people feel comfortable, and at finding what made them laugh. Kallan thoroughly enjoyed his risque sense of humour, and his gentle flirtation, to which, to my great confusion, my uncle readily responded.

During the lunch, as Kallan laughed at one of Haari's spicy comments, flushing with pleasure as he did so, I realised with a start that my uncle was attracted to him. I watched Kallan subtly, I knew I was right. The slight blush, the fluttering blue eyes, the almost forced laughter, all indicated that he found Haari appealing. I found the idea disconcerting, and felt a hint of irritation, almost jealousy. Haari was *my* friend, not Kallan's. It was irksome enough to be forced to share Haari's company with my brother without my uncle taking his ration of Haari's attention. I should have been delighted that Kallan liked him so much. It would make his visits that much easier for everyone, so much more pleasant. I also realised that this was part of Haari's charm, his desire to make people like him. And he seemed able to use different aspects of himself to appeal to different people. With Kallan he made use of his sexual energy, his appeal as a man. Adwin he made feel important, indispensable, and I remembered that he had listened attentively to everything Adwin had told him, as if Adwin's words were too valuable to miss a single one. I knew that I could bear my uncle's liking of Haari as it did not truly affect my own relationship with my new friend, but I could not support my brother's intrusion. It suddenly occurred to me "What does Haari do to get me to like him so much?" But I did not have a clear answer. Perhaps just the simple fact of being my first friend, perhaps that was enough.

I snapped my attention back to the present as Haari thanked us all for our warm welcome and hospitality. He said he should probably leave now, and not outstay his welcome. I was not sure exactly what he meant by this, but as I had no experience of a friend visiting another friend's house, I relied on his greater knowledge to decide when a visit was over.

Kallan left us, and Adwin too followed shortly afterwards, to my great relief. Haari told me what a great time he had had, how glad he was to have seen where I lived, to 'see me in my context' as he described it. We then discussed my visit to his home, something which filled me with excitement and a little trepidation. I said we could decide on the actual day later, not wanting to be pushed into taking such a huge step before I was ready. He accepted this, but urged me not to leave it too long.

"I so want to show you where I live, take you out round the city, introduce you to some of my friends. I promise you you'll love it, Samek, believe me."

I did not disbelieve him, but felt a flutter of anxiety at the prospect. Just visiting another person in their home would be a totally novel experience for me, let alone wandering around Beyra, and then actually meeting some of Haari's friends! He smiled slightly at my apparent apprehension at doing things that to most people were mundane and ordinary, but was sensitive enough not to push the issue. He would leave it to me to decide the day.

We stood, and just before I ported him home, he leaned towards me and hugged me, a strong, affectionate, brotherly embrace that took me totally by surprise. I gingerly wound my arms around his back in return, surprised at how warm and firm he felt, and how he had a different odour from any member of my family. An earthy, masculine smell, pleasant and comforting.

Chapter Thirty-Eight

One day, after a long mind-conversation with Haari, during which he teased me about my apparent reluctance to make the trip to his home, I decided, simply, that I could no longer put it off. I hastily mindspoke to him, telling him that I would come and see him now if that was convenient. He laughed at my sudden change of heart, saying that I ought to come straight away, before I changed my mind. I quickly ported myself to his abode.

I appeared a mere metre or so from him, finding him standing looking out of the window wall of his living room, gazing at the view across Beyra to the sea. He turned and beamed at me, his genuine smile lighting up his slightly worn features, moving quickly across the room as if to embrace me in a hug of welcome, but at the last moment changing his mind and holding out his hand instead. I shook his hand, surprised at the slightly formal welcome.

"It's great that you're here Samek," he said in his loud voice. "I've so looked forward to your visit."

I looked down as we released each other's hands, and he seemed to notice my glance.

"I thought I'd give you a manly handshake," he continued with a wry smile. "Instead of a hug. It just seemed right somehow. You're almost as tall as me. Quite the man!" I could not help smile slightly at his compliment, feeling pleasure at the comment despite knowing that it was exaggerated, an attempt to make me feel welcome. He had no idea that he need make no effort with this: he was my only friend, so how could I feel anything but warmth towards him.

He stood back as I gazed in fascination around the room. I had never been in another person's home.

"It's so small!" I blurted out. He laughed and replied,

"Yes, but why would I need bigger? As you know, I live alone."

I had no answer to that, but was still amazed at how tiny his dwelling place was. He offered to show me round, and smiled at my look of surprise: such a showing would surely not take more than a few moments. The whole flat occupied a single floor, oval in shape. About half of the oval was taken up by the living room I had first appeared in, the other half divided between a bedroom and a shower room. There were no other rooms.

"Where's the kitchen?" I asked, confused.

"The kitchen?" Haari replied, chortling as he did so. "Who has a kitchen?" I blushed slightly.

"We do," I said, slightly defensively. "Quite a big kitchen actually, and store rooms for food and such behind it."

"Yes," he said. "I remember now. But why do you have a kitchen? Surely nobody uses it?"

"Of course we use it. We make food in it." I replied simply.

He roared with laughter at my reply, filling the apartment with his deep tones. I felt slightly offended. I could not see what I had said to cause such hilarity. I stared at him without speaking until his amusement had abated.

"I'm sorry Samek, but you have to understand: nobody *makes* food. We all just order it."

"We order it too," I replied, still feeling offended. "But we make it too. Especially Kallan."

"But why?" he asked, genuinely confused.

"Because he likes to cook," I replied. "And," I continued with a slightly defiant tone to my voice, "So do I." He stared at me for a moment, then said,

"I'm sorry I offended you Samek. I really didn't mean to, believe me. It's just that nobody I know has a kitchen, and I don't think I know anyone who cooks."

"Nobody?" I asked incredulously.

"Well, there are some people who like to cook, as a hobby, and some even think it's some sort of art form. But it's rare, and certainly none of my friends do it. I've done presentations occasionally about people who cook, but it's always seemed such a hassle, so much effort for so little. You spend hours making something that's just going to be gobbled down in minutes. Why bother when you can order whatever you want whenever you want, and everything I've ever ordered has always been good."

I stood mute, feeling slightly foolish, the realisation of how removed I was from the world at large hitting me hard. Of course we often ordered food centrally, as we ordered everything else, but we also prepared food, cooked, and Kallan especially took great pleasure from this. To me it was a normal activity, but to Haari it seemed outlandish, something only very strange people did. I felt dismayed that in the first few minutes of my first visit to another citizen's home, I had already learned how unprepared I was to find a place in society.

"We also grow food," I continued, slightly defensively. Though this probably compounded my oddness, it was important to me that Haari know this fact. "We have fruit and nut trees, a vegetable garden, and even a kitchen garden with herbs."

Haari looked pensive as I said this, his amber eyes narrowing slightly as he filed away the information for future use. I shrugged. If he wanted to know me properly, he would have to know everything. What he said next surprised me though.

"I know people who grow things they can eat, out at their country places. They seem to enjoy it, the whole process of planting things, tending them, watching them grow. I sometimes get given vegetables, or fruit that they've grown. It's nice. You'll see," he continued, "that I have a balcony covered with plants, and there's a garden I had built on the roof but these are managed by automata. Like most people, I wouldn't do it myself."

"But it's wonderful to eat things you've grown yourself," I insisted. "They're not nutritionally any better than any others, but there's something really special about eating something you've grown with your own hands, with your own care."

He nodded in a slightly non-committal way, and then showed me round the rest of the apartment. It really was very small, but it was quite exquisite. It occupied the whole of the top floor of an oval-shaped building, eight storeys high. It was situated quite high up the steep slope at the very edge of Beyra, not far from the Council building. From the window, the Council edifice with its curved viewing window could clearly be seen, on the other side of the Neyr river.

Haari's building was very close to the river, just at the point where it tumbled down from the high plain above towards the delta below. It cascaded in white frothy torrents, just audible when standing on the balcony of the apartment. The entire oval of his home was surrounded by a wide terrace, with doors opening onto it from each of the rooms - small doors from the bedroom and the shower room, and a huge sliding double door from the living room. The walls were almost entirely made of perspiglass, as were all the walls of all eight storeys of the building. The whole edifice was a huge ellipsis, each floor smaller than the one below. And around each entire floor the inhabitants enjoyed the same continuous balcony as on Haari's floor. On a voice command or from a panel on the wall of the apartment, each balcony could be covered by an awning, in sections, so that inclement weather or very hot sun could be kept away from the terrace at will. Haari's balcony was filled with containers of plants, large and small, some green, others covered with flowers, bestowing on the entire balcony, and the apartment inside, a cool greenish light, as the sun filtered through the foliage of the copious plant life.

Most of the walls of the entire building were also made of huge panes of perspiglass, and this could be darkened or lightened at will, or made to change colour section by section. The architect had only given the option of colour change along the blue-green spectrum, so the only choices the inhabitants had were hues of nature or the sea: aquamarine, azure, sky blue, leaf green. This was to ensure that even when each inhabitant chose a different shade for their windows, they would all form part of the same spectrum and not create clashes the one with the other. This added to the effect created by the terraces on each floor overflowing with plants, many cascading down from the edge of the balcony towards the flat below. And the blue-green effect was further enhanced by the fact that the only visible parts of the edifice which were not perspiglass were thin columns supporting the floor above, columns made from a super-strong artificial material, but faced with lapis lazuli which had been manufactured and included seams of pyrites, sparkling gold in the midday sun. Haari assured me that the effect of the building was spectacular, perched as it was high on the hill behind Beyra, especially when it caught the bright light of the sun, causing the entire edifice to glow green and blue, interspersed with flashes of gold.

In the corner of the living room I was surprised to see a simple wooden staircase leading up to the ceiling. Haari saw me contemplate this in confusion, turned to me and said with a smile, "I had it put in a few years ago. Follow me and I'll show you why."

I did so as he ascended the stairs, though I could see nothing at the top of them but the flat ceiling. But as he approached the top of the staircase, a large panel in the ceiling slid silently open, sunlight flooding in. We emerged from the living room onto the flat roof of the building, on which, as Haari had indicated, was located another tiny garden, much like on the balcony. It was utterly delightful, though hot with the glaring summer sun. At a word, an opaque pale blue screen slid halfway across the entire space, offering pleasant shade from the beating sun. Haari led me to the southern edge of the roof garden and as I contemplated the view, I sighed with sheer pleasure. The whole of Beyra was laid out below. The gushing river to my right which then slowed as it entered the delta plain, the flat expanse of the city, every space between the houses and other buildings filled with trees, bushes, shrubs, parks and lakes. The scintillating sea beyond, flecked white at the wave tops, sparkling across its surface. I could make out in the distance what looked like a port or a marina filled with sailing boats.

"I thought such things were of the distant past!" I exclaimed, as I also noticed many of them racing to and fro across the surface of the sea.

"They are," replied Haari. "But they've made something of a comeback recently. And amazingly they're still powered by the wind. That's what people seem to want: to enjoy the feeling of being carried across the water by nothing more than the breeze and their skill."

I was transfixed. It had not occurred to me that such ancient artefacts would be resurrected and used, and for no purpose except pleasure. I shivered in anticipation at the myriad things I had to learn about daily life in the world outside my home.

As I stood and drank in the view, I quickly turned away as my eyes fell on the Council building. I did not want to think about unpleasant things on this marvellous day. We sat for a while on benches beneath a climbing honeysuckle, enjoying the heady scent of the blooms, and Haari explained more about how his building functioned, saying that most larger buildings in the world had similar workings. There were not many tall buildings in Beyra, or any other city. People generally preferred to live closer to the earth, and the majority of dwellings in Beyra were actually bungalows. There were, however, a handful of tall buildings on the slopes leading away from Beyra which encircled the northern side of the city, on top of which was located the Council building. Because of the fairly steep slope, buildings could be erected which would not overlook anyone, and not obscure the light, air and views of any other dwelling. There were restrictions, firmly enforced by common consent, on the height of such edifices, on their location, and even on their position in relation to adjacent tall buildings. In Beyra, for example, it was forbidden to erect any building more than ten storeys high, or which obscured, in any way, an uninterrupted view of the city and the sea. I saw sense in the rules about views, but not about the height of buildings.

"But in the past," I mused, "buildings became huge, more than a hundred storeys high in some cases. Why don't we do that any more?"

"I'm not really sure," replied Haari. "Perhaps they are just seen as a symbol of the bad old days, or maybe they're just viewed as ugly. In my humble opinion, it's nice that this city is so green, and if there were lots of tall buildings, that wouldn't be the case, even if they were all like this one, this hanging garden."

He also explained that the plants were all irrigated from above, either directly by the rain as the terraces were mostly left uncovered, or by water which was pumped up inside the columns to the roof, and then allowed to flow by gravity through an irrigation system connecting every floor and balcony. I asked him where his portal was, and he said that big buildings generally had communal portals, and that there were four in the entrance hall on the ground floor. I was surprised at this, assuming that every dwelling in the world had its own portal, but Haari assured me that this was not the case.

"In fact, many homes don't have a portal, and not just apartments in places like this. Lots of people just use the public portals I'll show you when we go out later. That is, assuming you want to go out later," he added hastily as he saw my look of alarm.

"Most people don't really teleport all that often, so it's a bit pointless and wasteful having portals in every home. It would be easier if we all had your abilities!" he added with a slight smile.

"But if you don't have a portal," I asked, perplexed. "How do you get up to your flat?"

Haari laughed at my obvious consternation at what I saw as an insurmountable problem. I, of course, would simply port myself in and out of an apartment on the eighth floor, but Haari, like other people, had no such ability.

"There are lifts from the ground floor," he replied. "And they even go all the way as far as my floor!" he added with a chuckle.

"Lifts?" I queried. "What do you mean? How do they work?"

"They look like a door in the wall. You step into one and it's activated either just by the motion of you stepping in, or you can control it verbally. You step onto a hovering platform, which then sort of floats you softly up to whichever floor you want."

I stared at him, amazed. What a lovely idea, to be floated up to your home.

"But how do you get back down again?" I asked.

"The same way," he replied. "The magnetic force is reversed so you float downwards instead of upwards."

I contemplated this simple yet elegant solution to moving people up and down inside tall buildings, and as I did so, Haari interrupted my thoughts.

"Would you like to go out?" Haari asked suddenly. I squirmed as I considered his question. Yes, I did want to go out, but I also feared doing so. He sensed my trepidation, and suggested that perhaps we just go for a short walk around the foot of his building, so I could see for myself how beautiful it looked from a short distance away. I saw no reason to refuse his suggestion, and nodded my assent.

"As long as I can try the lift!" I said.

He smiled and said that I would enjoy it. We climbed down to his apartment and as we did so I realised that I could not see where the lift could be. The entire floor was taken up by his flat. Before I could ask, he showed me what looked like a large rectangular box, taller than a man, as wide as it was high, discreetly located beneath the staircase. I had not noticed it before. As he approached it he said "Lift. Up,". I sensed rather than heard a sound, and moments later the front of the box slid open to reveal what looked like an empty hole, the base of which was filled by a metal platform. We stepped in, he said "Lift. Down," and without warning, we began to float slowly downwards. We passed a closed door on each floor, and Haari explained that these were the entrances to the other apartments. The top four floors had a single dwelling on each floor, the bottom four being divided into two apartments, one occupying each side of the building. There was another lift on the other side, servicing only the four residences on the first four storeys on that side.

I was astonished to learn that we could stop at any of the doors and let ourselves into the other flats. I found it almost impossible to believe that this could be true, that such a lack of privacy, of privateness, existed in the world. As I voiced my astonishment, Haari turned to me with a look of genuine surprise on his face.

"But of course we can let ourselves in anywhere, to any building, any house. Surely you know that?"

I shook my head, shocked into silence by Haari's revelation, and by his almost innocent assumption that this was completely normal. My own upbringing in a house run by a woman who was obsessed with privacy to the point of neurosis could hardly be different. And I felt deeply uncomfortable with the idea that anyone could enter anyone else's private dwelling whenever they wished. It seemed a violation to me, and certainly something

I could not imagine ever being comfortable with or getting used to. I voiced my concerns to Haari and he found my attitude as bizarre as I found his. To him, such lack of privacy was totally normal, how he had been brought up and how he had lived his life.

"Of course," he said, by way of trying to bridge the gap between us. "It would be considered impolite to enter someone's home when they are actually there. You'd always ask permission."

This did little to calm my agitation at the very idea: that if I ever lived out in the world, anyone could simply enter my home whenever they wished, even if I was there, and only courtesy might prevent them doing so if I were actually inside the dwelling! I secretly decided that I would not live like that, and I knew I could easily set up my own home to prevent such unpermitted intrusion. I suspected such actions would be considered unacceptable, offensive even, but thought this the lesser evil than the total lack of privacy the generally accepted option entailed.

We were deposited gently at the foot of the shaft, the door sliding silently open as we did so. We stepped out and made our way through the wide, spacious entrance hall. It was as lovely as everything else I had seen in this building. The floors, walls and ceiling were of a cool deep blue marble, shot with seams of metallic yellow. There were flowering plants in huge containers dotted here and there, filling the space with their perfume. The perspiglass walls were coloured a pale blue, filtering out the strongest rays of the summer sun, bathing the entire hall in soft azure light.

We left the building, walking a little way along a tree-lined paved area. We stopped and turned so that I could see the building from a distance. It was just as Haari had described, a tall almost circular edifice reaching into the sky, each storey narrower than the one below, trailing plants cascading from each floor's balcony, wall after wall of blue and green glass reflecting the glare of the sun, the whole supported by thin pillars of gold-seamed lapis lazuli. The sight took my breath away. I marvelled that so much effort had gone into creating a single edifice of such beauty and form, and wondered if this was normal, whether I would be gazing again and again at the architectural diversity I saw, delighting in each effort at differentiation.

I looked around me, and through gaps in the trees could just make out a few other tall buildings in the vicinity. To the south, away from these edifices, I glimpsed the sparkle of the sea across the top of the tumbling greenery of the city. I almost wept as I contemplated so much beauty, at the fact that people had made such effort to create a place to live that was so exquisite, so magical. And this was only one city. Surely others would be just as remarkable, perhaps even more so since Beyra was the world's biggest and most populous city. Smaller cities might be even more exquisite.

We wandered slowly, but not far from Haari's home. I knew he was allowing me to acclimatise gradually to the novelty of being outside my home, and especially as this was the first time I had been anywhere in the vicinity of human habitation simply in order to enjoy myself. The two previous occasions had been distressing and exhausting, leaving me overwhelmed. I began to get a glimmer of what life could be like in the big world.

After we had walked and talked for a while, Haari turned to me. He seemed to judge the time was right to nudge me gently in the direction of a more elaborate experience.

"Well, Samek. How about a trip to the centre of the city? To meet a couple of my closest friends?" he asked, peering at me with anticipation and also a slight tension, fearful that he had judged the moment badly and that I might refuse.

I looked back at him, touched that he seemed so concerned at what my response would be. I trusted him, and knew that he would keep his word, that at any point on any of our trips out and about he would not try to persuade me to stay any longer than I wanted to. I put my shoulders back, looked straight into his eyes and said,

"Yes, alright. Let's do it."

Chapter Thirty-Nine

Haari indicated that it would be most pleasant to walk from his building to the centre of Beyra. The weather was fine and at a moderate pace it would take well under an hour. And walking, rather than porting, would give me the chance to experience the city at a slow pace as I meandered through the leafy streets and lanes, the verdant squares and parks, seeing, smelling and experiencing the sights, odours and sounds of a city for the very first time in my life.

I felt uneasy at the prospect, yet did not really understand why. I was in the company of an experienced city-dweller in his home town, and I knew there was nothing to fear in Beyra. Yet the simple experience of walking through a city was so novel for me, that I felt tense and ill at ease. As I was beginning to understand, Haari was a most perceptive man, and again it crossed my mind that he might enjoy some of the abilities I possessed. He clearly sensed my anxiety, throwing an arm lightly across my shoulders for a brief moment, and saying gently,

"There's nothing to fear, believe me. Just enjoy the day."

I smiled wanly at him, trying to dispel my anxieties. His wide, reassuring smile did much to help assuage my fears.

"Do you want to walk beside the river, or through the city itself?" Haari asked me. I had seen the River Neyr from his flat, from where I could see the point, beside the Council building, that it reached the edge of the plain above Beyra and tumbled out over the lip of the hill. From there, it briefly crashed down in white water cascades and eddies, soon slowing to a more leisurely pace as it reached the gentle slope of the Beyran plain beside the sea. It meandered through the city, opening widely as it began its final approach to the ocean, and in its final elongated triangle lay a number of small islands, all clearly visible from Haari's flat. All but one of the islands were connected either to the river banks, or to each other, or both, by plant-filled footbridges.

Haari explained that the island furthest from the sea was isolated, to allow water birds to nest in peace.

"The Neyr looks lovely, but it didn't look like there were any buildings along its banks," I replied.

"No," said Haari. "The entire route alongside it has been left for strolling and enjoying the river, so no houses or other buildings have ever been built there. The buildings begin a little way back from the river."

"Then I think I'd prefer to walk through the city itself. I've seen rivers, or at least streams, but I've never seen a city," I declared. Haari nodded his agreement, a look of surprise on his face as I informed him just how strange, how reclusive, had been my upbringing. It must have been difficult for him to imagine never having seen a city at my age. Even though he, like all other children, had been brought up in an Institute far from urban areas, there were regular trips made to towns and cities from a very early age, all part of the normal socialising of young people towards the day they would take their adult place in society.

Our stroll took us ever downwards, across the gentle slope towards the sea. I realised that in such a city it would be hard ever to get lost. All that would be required would be to orientate oneself either downhill towards the sea or uphill away from it, and it would be easy to find a path to one's destination. The whole city was truly beautiful, and I gaped in wonder at everything I saw, astonished that people had gone to so much effort to create a metropolitan area with such concern for every detail of how it looked. When I shared my thoughts on this with Haari, he seemed confused at what I said.

"But why wouldn't people want to live somewhere beautiful?" he asked. "What would be the point of building an ugly city?" I did not really have an answer to his questions, but persisted with the point I was trying to make.

"In the old world, cities often had lovely parts, but were also a byword for dirt, squalor, overcrowding. How is it that all of this seems not to be the case any more?" I asked. Haari laughed, and answered in an ironic tone.

"By the gods, Samek, it really is time you got out and about in your own world, and away from so much reading about the old world. After the Chaos, with so few people, and so much meticulous planning of everything, there was no way cities would ever be allowed to just develop in the chaotic, higgledy-piggledy ways they had in the past. Before anything is ever built in our brave new world it is discussed and agreed, planned down to the last detail. That's how it's been done ever since the end of the Chaos. Beyra was designed to look the way it does, from before the very first brick was laid. Why would anyone have done it differently?"

Again, I had no answer to his comments, but was still amazed at the perfection of all I saw around me. As Haari had told me, most buildings were single-storey bungalows, each separated from its neighbour by gardens planted with a profusion of flowering plants, bushes and trees, many with ponds, streams, fountains. And as if this were not enough greenery, we barely walked more than a few minutes before we passed by or through a park with even wilder plant life, even taller trees, larger ponds and lakes, and some with streams and small rivers winding their way through them. Birds flitted everywhere in and out of the trees chirruping noisily, or swam in leisurely fashion on the many waterways. Flowers blossomed luxuriantly everywhere, in particular profusion on the many climbing plants that enveloped walls with their scented, many-coloured, meretricious glory. The smells of nature were everywhere: on the surface the heady, unsubtle aromas of the flowers, underlaid by the quieter, yet all-pervasive smells of the moist earth itself.

The buildings were all made of wood, and when I queried if this was normal, Haari told me that in this district this was the case, though in other districts many of them were made from artificial materials, or brick. Haari's own building was made from artificial, or partly artificial materials. Some of the houses we passed were dark, almost black, others of pale pine, and every shade of natural wood in between. I was surprised at how plain they mostly looked, their facades being largely undecorated. Haari explained that the people who liked this type of dwelling tended to opt for homes that were simple, at least in terms of how they looked. Obviously each one would enjoy every modern convenience in the way it actually functioned. Apparently, other districts of the city were filled with far more ornate buildings and that another day we would be able to explore these at our leisure. Today we were taking the most direct route to the centre which passed almost entirely through districts filled with simple wooden houses.

After forty minutes or so, during which I gazed around me and Haari explained as much as he could of the background, history and present of what I saw, we entered an area where the wooden buildings began to be replaced by those built of other materials; brick, stone, a range of man-made masonry. On querying this, Haari told me that we were nearing the centre of Beyra, and that some of the buildings we now walked among were not private dwellings, but had other purposes. I could not imagine what such other purposes might be, but Haari went on to explain.

"We have many, many organisations and societies Samek, for everything from the learning of ancient languages and crafts, to dancing, to sports and other physical activities, to the sciences, to natural pursuits, to rock collecting, to painting and so on and so on. Hundreds of them, thousands probably."

"I know that," I replied. "Though I didn't know people would meet in places like this. And I don't understand why people do it at all," I continued, in genuine confusion. "Why would people learn all these things, and especially things like ancient languages?"

"Boredom," was Haari's laconic reply. On seeing that I was no less confused, he continued with his explanation.

"The major problem for people in our world is boredom. Crushing, all-encompassing boredom, since nobody has to work. Nobody has to actually *do* anything."

"But lots of people work. Zelda, Marna, people who run the Institutes, *you*," I interrupted.

"True," replied Haari. "But that's part of my point. None of these people, including me, actually has to work. We have everything provided for us, from birth to death. But humans can't spend a lifetime doing nothing. No intelligent animal can. And we live a long time. Barring accident, most people live to well over a hundred, some as much as a hundred and twenty or so, and in a good state of health and fitness for nearly the whole of their lives. You have to do something with those hundred years or more. Obviously the early years are organised for you - the Institutes, the years you live with your uncle or aunt from the age of fourteen, finishing your education. But after that? Each person has to find his or her own way to fill the rest of their life, and at least with a pretence of purpose and meaning."

"You have a purpose. Making presentations about people you then share with the world."

"Yes," he replied hesitantly. "Though whether this is really meaningful or purposeful is moot. Perhaps I'm just filling time. But it's better than when I was a young adult." He grimaced as he recalled his earlier life, and I was piqued with curiosity.

"What did you do then?" I asked. "How did you find meaning?"

"I didn't find meaning, though it seemed like it at the time," he replied in a quiet, sombre tone. "I left my uncle's home as soon as I could, when I turned eighteen. By the way, we're going to meet my uncle shortly as he is keen to meet you, and I'm still very close to him. He's one of my best friends."

"Yet you left as soon as you could?" I prompted.

"Yes. I felt I needed to be free, to live without restriction. Without disapproval." I made no comment, merely stared at Haari, willing him to explain further. He sighed, and with a touch of reticence, continued.

"I was a wild young thing. Even in my last few years at the Institute I was always getting into trouble, and dragging others along with me. And poor Bartrem - that's my uncle, by the way - he didn't really know what he was getting when I turned up on his doorstep at what he thought was the tender age of fourteen. I was almost uncontrollable. I had no interest in continuing my education, or not my formal education at least. I was elated to be free of the extremely controlled and regimented life in the Institute, much as I'd enjoyed my time there. And I went wild." He glanced at me to see if his words were enough to satisfy me, but saw that this was not the case. He sighed again, and reluctantly continued, embarrassment, perhaps even shame tingeing his words.

"I was out all the time, drinking, taking every narcotic, opiate, pharmaceutical of any type - and believe you me Samek, we have hundreds of them! Coming home at all hours of the day and night, often not alone, sometimes bringing home groups of rowdy friends, sexual partners - and I do mean partners in the plural - causing havoc in Bartrem's nice, quiet, ordered life. I don't know how he stood for it."

"Didn't he tell you to stop?" I gasped.

"All the time," laughed Haari without humour. "But to little effect. Oh, sometimes even I felt sufficiently contrite about my behaviour to repent, and I'd tell myself that I would change, I wouldn't behave like that again. And for a week or so all would be well. But it never lasted and I rapidly returned to those crazy, damaging, self-destructive behaviour patterns, beginning the cycle all over again."

"Why didn't your uncle force you to leave?" I questioned.

"Force me to leave?" said Haari sharply, genuinely shocked by the suggestion. "Nobody throws out a nephew or niece under the age of eighteen. Where would they go? There's no place for such a person in our society." I was so perplexed by Haari's comments that I did not even know how to frame a response. He saw my deep frown, and felt further explanation was needed.

"Until a person turns eighteen, they are not a full member of society. I've never, in my whole life, heard of someone under eighteen living alone. I'm not even sure if they can claim a property at that age, not sure if the central allocation systems would recognise them even if they tried. I have heard of a few instances where someone moves to live with a different adult before they reach eighteen, but it's really rare. And frankly, no-one in their right mind would have taken me in! The only ones who might have done are those as bad as I was, or maybe the ones who've abandoned living normal lives."

"What do you mean?" I asked, surprised by Haari's final comment. "Who have abandoned living normal lives?" Haari glanced at me out of the corner of his golden eyes to see if my question was sincere. After fiddling with his hair for a moment he seemed to decide it was, so he explained.

"It's all about the boredom really. Most people still try to fill their long lives with other people, with activities, but there are quite a lot who just seem to give up all of this."

"But what do they do?" I intruded.

"Patience Samek," Haari replied with a wry smile. "I was about to tell you."

"They get into a world of virtual reality," he continued. I was none the wiser, so he continued. "Surely you've heard of the mobies that people use to watch narrowcasts and things like that?" he asked. I nodded, encouraging him to continue. "Well, lots and lots of people use them, though some get...addicted and just withdraw into a world of mobie reality, spending all their time linked up to a huge range of games, competitions, other activities, even other people doing the same thing, though of course always at a distance. I think I already told you that you are probably the most popular subject of many of the virtual reality adventures that people play."

I nodded, but then continued. "I don't understand," I said. "What do you mean about people spending all of their time doing this?" He sighed and paused as if searching for the best way to explain it to somebody as naive as I was at that age. I had only heard of the things he was talking about from his brief comments on a previous occasion. Presumably Zelda had removed all reference to such from the digital memory, the same way she had blocked our access to anything she wanted us to know nothing about.

"I don't really understand why they do it," Haari continued. "Though of course I tried it for a while when I was younger. But basically, instead of going out and about in the world, among people, occupying themselves with real humans, real activities, these 'mobie maniacs' spend nearly all their time sitting at home, actually alone, but constantly linked up to a huge network of others doing exactly the same. They claim their virtual world is more exciting, more fulfilling, more *real* than the real world. And they control what they do in it at all times. The really extreme ones never even connect with other people, but only with robots, artificial humans with artificial intelligence. And they say it's so much better than having to deal with the dull old real world, with the annoying and uncontrollable natures of real people. They believe they can do everything we can but much more efficiently, and that they're in control."

I was flabbergasted. Never having heard of such a thing, it seemed almost beyond belief to me. In truth, Haari's description of these people baffled me. I had spent my whole life isolated from the rest of humanity. I yearned to spend time in the world outside my prison home, to mix with real people, to learn to enjoy real activities. I simply could not comprehend why anyone would choose to remove themselves from all of this when they had the option of belonging to the world offered to them on a plate. I was silent for long moments as we continued to walk through the more densely packed buildings near the centre of the city. After a while I realised that I had no response to Haari's comments, so shocked was I by his revelations, so I decided instead to return to our earlier conversation.

"So your uncle, 'Bartrem' was he called? He was just stuck with you for four years?" I asked incredulously. Haari laughed, a harsh, bitter laugh.

"Yes," he replied. "The poor, long-suffering soul. And by the gods I'm so ashamed of how I was. As soon as I turned eighteen I left, partly, as I said, to be free of all restrictions, but to be frank, partly so he didn't have to suffer me any longer. Oddly, he tried really hard to persuade me not to leave, perhaps believing that he could help me, that I'd calm down and manage better under his stable influence, but I wouldn't hear of it. He was probably right, but there was nothing he could do to stop me. I got myself my own place - the very one I'm still in now - and took myself off there." There was a pause as he finished speaking, interrupted by my next question.

"And then what? What happened when you lived alone?" I asked.

"I carried on as I had been, but even worse as there were absolutely no restrictions on me whatsoever. I spent the next few years in a drug haze, pursuing crazy and dangerous activities, having huge amounts of sex with so many people of both sexes, in pairs, groups, indoors, outdoors. I won't appal you with the details, innocent as you are. But believe me when I tell you that it was all really about boredom."

"Boredom?" I echoed in shocked tones. "All of that because you were bored?"

"No," he replied, then paused in thought. "Not because I *was* bored. Because I was terrified of *becoming* bored, terrified that if I stopped long enough, sober, I would realise the crushing reality of a long and boring life." He laughed again, a harsh, barking laugh. "And then what would be my options? Kill myself or withdraw into the sad world of virtual reality!"

I stared at him, my eyes wide in astonishment. I had never known a moment of boredom in my life, and could not imagine ever knowing one. There was so much to learn, about the old world, the present world, about people and animals and nature, and inanimate things: how could anyone ever be bored? I felt a wave of pity for Haari at that moment, something I never imagined I would feel for him. He seemed so sophisticated and urbane, so in control of his life and his pleasures that I found it difficult to contemplate him as a young man, his feeling that his future opened up a vista of nothing more than profound emptiness and aimlessness, which he tried to fill with wild and manic behaviour. As if following my train of thought, he interrupted them.

"In the end I realised that what I was doing wasn't helping. Actually, it was just bringing home how empty my life was, and that trying to fill it with a lot of noise and people just wasn't working. So I stopped it all. Dropped all my old friends, who, it turned out, were not really friends at all, and took stock. I got back in contact with Bartrem who, bless him, seemed delighted to have me back in his life, and from there I began the slow process of building a life with meaning." He stopped walking suddenly, turned to me and looked at me through serious amber eyes, saying quietly,

"And what you see is all I managed!"

Despite my youth and lack of experience, at that moment I felt older and wiser than him. It was a most bizarre sensation and for a moment I could not respond. Did he really mean those last few words, that he had merely managed to become someone adequate, not special? I looked up to him as a model of a well-adjusted person, someone who would show me the world, explain it all to me, yet protect me from its worst aspects. A true friend. I was appalled to realise that he did not see himself like this, that in his own eyes he felt inadequate. As I looked at him, I allowed a flow of energy to drift out of me and into his mind, gently encouraging him to believe in himself, to see himself as the fine, true man that I saw. I admit that my actions carried a strong element of selfishness: I was so inexperienced in the ways of the world that I needed someone strong and self-assured to show the world to me. I could not bear the idea of a flawed Haari.

After a long pause, we began walking again. I felt that he was calmer now, more self-confident. A thought occurred to me.

"How did you pull yourself out of the life you were leading? How did you break the habit?" I asked him. He smiled slightly, in an almost sheepish way.

"I discovered something, an ancient philosophy of how to live your life, though I'm slightly embarrassed to admit it," he replied. I glanced at him as we walked, surprised by his words.

"But I'll leave that for another time, Samek, and tell you all about it then. It might help you too! Anyway," he continued, all trace of his dejection seemingly gone. "Most of these buildings are used by the groups, the recreational societies and such like, for their meetings. That's why they look different. They tend to only have a few large rooms, unlike the houses. And they are often nearer the centre of cities, though there's no real reason for this to be the case. People like to congregate near centres, as you'll see shortly." He glanced at me as we walked.

"I hope you will be alright with the crowds," he said with concern in his voice. "There are always lots of people milling around the centre, especially here in Beyra".

"Doing what?" I asked. He paused for a moment before replying.

"Nothing really. Or nothing much. Just filling time. Trying to pretend they're not bored to death." He smiled at this comment, though I sensed he meant what he said. I was perplexed. Did he really mean that many people wandered aimlessly, without purpose, around a city centre, simply in order to assuage their boredom? Simply in order to pretend they had something of purpose to do with their day? I feared that this was exactly what he meant. And as I considered these aimless wanderers, a flicker of comprehension at the 'mobie maniacs' and their attempt to find meaning by removing themselves from the world sparked in my mind. Haari interrupted my thoughts.

"Surely you're aware lots of them will be amazed to see you there, out and about in the world, and lots of them will try to talk to you, to meet you? We'll do our best to keep them away from you, but you need to be prepared."

"We?" I queried. "Who is we?"

"Bartrem," he answered. "As I told you. And also his niece, Lisvet. They are probably my two closest friends, the people I know really care for me."

"How old is Lisvet?" I asked. "The same as you?"

"No," Haari replied. "Nobody would have two nephews or nieces at the same time. It's unusual to be allocated two in your lifetime, but as it's random, it does happen. She's in her early twenties I suppose, though I'm not sure of her exact age. She chose to stay with Bartrem after she turned eighteen. And I'm glad. She's a good influence on him, and they are very close. And because of my relationship with Bartrem, she and I have become good friends too."

"What are they like?" I asked, as we moved into an area that clearly felt different, with buildings now much closer to each other, not separated by gardens and parks, and with ever increasing numbers of people on the streets, most of whom, on noticing me, whispered to each other, pointed, stared. I moved closer to Haari.

"You'll find out what they're like soon enough, Samek. I won't spoil the surprise," laughed Haari with touch of irony. "But I'll say one thing. Whatever I told you about Bartrem and his suffering of my awfulness, don't pity him too much. He's a difficult man, not popular with most people. Perhaps that's one reason he was able to cope with me. But don't be put off by his manner. Underneath the gruff and frankly rude exterior, he has a heart of gold. You just have to dig a bit to find it."

We turned a corner and I stopped in my tracks. Yet again, what I saw literally took my breath away.

Chapter Forty

I stood absolutely still, sensing Haari stop beside me. I stared at what I saw before me. But what made me stand and gape was not so much the buildings, though these were remarkable enough, but the sheer number of people, and the apparent disorder in their arrangement.

We stood on the edge of an ornamental lake, long and thin, much longer than wide, and I saw that a small stream entered one end of it, right beside where we stood, and sensed another similar stream exited it the other end. The entire length of the narrow lake was occupied on both sides by a flat terrace filled with trees and bushes, large pots with flowering plants, and here and there groups of tables and chairs. Many of the tables were filled with people eating and drinking, chatting, socialising. Behind the terrace rose a single-storey continuous building in which I could discern doorways narrow and wide, mostly jarred open, though I could not ascertain exactly what went on behind the doors. Above the terrace there seemed to be another long, flat patio, very similar to the one below, and also with an unbroken one-floor building behind. The edifice behind the second terrace was the highest point of the centre, and its roof seemed to be covered in grass and other plants. Climbing and trailing plants cascaded from the roof, and from the upper terrace to the lower. The buildings and floors on the lower terrace seemed to be made of stone slabs, in various geometric patterns of the gentlest tones of cream and pale pink, whereas the terrace above was in cream and the lightest green. The lake boasted many plants too, bullrushes, reeds, purple and yellow iris near its margins, the surface of its centre peppered with yellow and pink water lilies. Ducks and swans glided over its calm surface.

As with everything else I had seen, the effect was magical. It was hard to discern any edges, any corners, such was the profusion of plant life on the roof, the terraces, the lake. It was as if the very stones of the buildings were trying to free themselves from the lush green bounty of the earth, with limited success. And the verdancy worked ceaselessly to restrain the rock from escaping its bonds, except as far as was absolutely necessary to provide a comfortable setting in which humans could meet and socialise.

And so many humans! And in such disorder! I could discern no pattern in their movements. Apart from the pairs and groups sitting chatting animatedly around some of the tables, everyone else seemed to be milling haphazardly in each and every direction, no clear purpose or aim directing their trajectories across the terraces and along the sides of the lake. I had only encountered strangers a few times in my life. Twice at the Council Chamber and the few occasions when we had visitors at our home. The meetings with the Council had been fraught and antagonistic, but I was in control of them. This huge crowd in front of me now, stretching further than I could see in all directions, was aimless, as far as I could tell.

I had never been among so many people. As my eyes moved across the throng, I was astonished at the variety of clothing I saw. I knew that at that time people wore fashions from a vast span of ancient human history, plundering the digital memory for inspiration from the pre-Chaos era. On the two previous occasions I had been among strangers at the Council Chamber I had been too focused on controlling the situation, on narrowcasting the events to the world, to really notice the clothing. All I could remember clearly was that the guards had worn shiny black uniforms. The effect in front of me of the Beyran hordes was dazzling, and confusing. Colours and patterns danced before my eyes, the impression of sartorial and chromatic chaos being intensified by the fashion of the time for iridescent materials in shimmering multi-hues, sparkling and flashing as they moved and reflected the bright sunlight. Obviously such materials were rare in the distant past, and I realised as I gazed at the finery in front of me, that people's attempts at recreating realistic-looking old-world garments did not stretch to using authentic textiles. As I had been told by Marna, certain time periods seemed most in vogue and I noticed quite a few people draped in what, for all the world, looked like ancient Roman togas, but not the plain white with discrete strips of purple of the ancient world. Instead in a blazing array of colours, patterns, lustrous materials. And as I had been informed, the other period in vogue seemed to be Europe in the sixteenth century, and despite my trepidation at the crowds, I almost laughed as I watched people clumsily manipulating huge wide skirts which must clearly have been supported beneath the material by frames of some sort. One or two of these jutted a metre in each direction from the hips of the wearers, and I wondered how they managed such cumbersome garments. Then I saw that, as with the use of modern materials, the fashions made the most of current technology. As one of the wearers of a two-metre wide skirt approached a tight space between groups of chatting bystanders, to my astonishment the entire skirt suddenly contracted, drawing itself tightly to the hips of the person wearing it, popping out again to full magnificent width the moment the obstacle had been negotiated.

Why not? I thought, though I did wonder whether it was simply boredom combined with access to technology at no cost that led to such profusion of styles and materials. But why not dress oneself in the fashions of the ancient world, but without the weight, the bulk, the discomfort and inconvenience of such clothing, not to mention the narrower range of colours and fabrics? And as Marna had explained, the wearers paid no attention to the original gendering of the clothing. Women here were as likely to be togaed as the men, and the wearer of the amazing telescopic skirt was a tall, well-built man who seemed to be unaware that his dress would have been strictly female attire in its original time.

Haari sensed my discomfort at the throng, but not the reason for it. He knew I was unused to crowds, and to unknown people, and these aspects of what I gazed at were indeed disconcerting. But he had no idea I was more unsettled by the sheer fruitlessness of all the bustling activity I saw before me. I simply could not begin to comprehend why these people were doing what they were doing. I decided that the only way to cope would be to simply accept what was happening, and not try to understand it. I sighed deeply, and Haari took my elbow in his hand, guiding me gently forwards.

"Don't worry, Samek," he whispered. "Nothing will happen."

I sighed again and allowed him to steer me through the great milling crowd which, amazingly, parted to let us through, huge skirts telescoping in and out as we passed. I was intensely aware of the reactions all around me as people gradually began to realise who I was. It took some time for this knowledge to spread through the crowd, but I sensed it rippling across the sea of people like the wind through a field of wheat. My efforts in narrowcasting the recent Council encounter had ensured that my face was known, especially as I had deliberately included myself and my siblings in the images transmitted to the world in an attempt to evoke sympathy. Haari had told me that stories about my exploits were continually being narrowcast, endless conjecture about me and my family, much of it invented. In addition to this, I was the protagonist of a huge number of virtual reality games, playing sometimes a force for good, others a force for evil. And all of this made me easy to recognise. Some people merely stood aside, silently, to let us pass. Others gasped as they recognised me. Many whispered to their companions, or dug them in the ribs with sharp elbow jabs, pointing to me or indicating me with jerks of their heads. One or two could not contain loud exclamations of surprise as I passed. I threw up a barrier soften the uncomfortable effect of passing through crowds of people all of whose attention was focused directly on me, a few hostile, a few intrigued, but mostly simply astonished to see me in person, walking so close to them.

Haari could not help but sense my profound disquiet, glancing at me with a look of concern on his face.

~It's alright Haari. I'm alright. I've put up a barrier to block some of it,~ I mindspoke to him, as much to try and persuade myself as him that I was not on the verge of panic.

~Are you sure?~ He replied, using the open channel between us so that we could speak to each other in silence. *~We can leave if you want. Go home. Just say the word, or better still just port us away if it all gets too much.~*

I glanced at him, and smiled nervously, indicating that I understood I could just remove us without warning if I felt the need. We carried on walking through the silent crowds, and I was gratified to sense that after we had passed, people quickly gathered their wits and seemed to carry on with what they had been doing. The initial shock of seeing me rapidly replaced by the habits of everyday life, especially as I seemed to be doing nothing of interest. My clothing too was dull and dowdy, simple in the extreme. Apart from Kallan who took pleasure in extravagant clothing (though only when he left the compound), the rest of my family always dressed in simple, comfortable clothes, 'practical', as Zelda had described them. I had always assumed that Kallan's wardrobe was the oddity, a quirk of his, but a short walk in the middle of Beyra showed me clearly that we were the oddities. Our visitors had always presented themselves in simple clothes. Marna, I knew, deliberately dressed badly to deflect attention from herself, to create a public persona which appeared harmless, risible even. Yenifa was a scientist, and her flat, dull personality seemed always to be reflected in clothing of the same description. Devid, perhaps, had deliberately dressed in plain, though high-quality, clothes on his visit, but I could not know this.

After we had walked for a few minutes, during which I was so focused on the reactions of the people around me that I could not enjoy the surroundings as much as I would have liked, we came to an opening in one of the buildings behind the terrace surrounded by a perspiglass frame. We stopped and I turned to Haari, querying with my expression.

"We're meeting Bartrem and Lisvet on the floor above. It's quieter than here. This is the lift up a floor," he explained.

I nodded and we stepped through the doorway, Haari saying "up one floor" as we did so. The door glided shut, and from there we were lifted gently to the terrace a floor above. We stepped out a moment later, and I was glad to see that this first floor terrace was indeed much less busy than the one below. I breathed a small sigh of relief to be away from the heaving, milling throng, though there were still more people on this floor than I could feel comfortable with.

We walked a short way along the terrace, experiencing the same initial silent shock from the people we passed. We turned a curve in the terrace, and Haari said,

"There. At that table. There's Bartrem and Lisvet."

I followed Haari's line of sight and saw a few tables arranged in some sort of order along the outside of the terrace. Only one of the tables, right along the handrail marking the very edge of the terrace, was occupied. I saw a man and a woman at the table who I assumed must be Bartrem and Lisvet, deep in conversation. As we approached, Lisvet happened to glance in our direction. On seeing Haari, she beamed and waved at us, and said loudly to Bartrem,

"Look uncle. It's Haari."

She leapt up and rushed over to us, grabbing Haari in a warm embrace. Bartrem did not leave his seat. After a moment, Lisvet released Haari and turned to me, a wide smile on her face.

"And you must be Samek," she said in a bright, cheerful voice. "We've heard so much about you, and have been dying to meet you, haven't we uncle?" she said, addressing the last comment to Bartrem who sat in silence at the table. I smiled shyly at her, her friendly, open demeanour making me like her immediately. Before I could actually speak to her, she turned sharply to Bartrem.

"Uncle!" she barked, and then with an easy, natural laugh continued. "Say hello to Samek, even if you're too grumpy to greet your nephew!"

Bartrem merely stared at me without speaking. He had a slight scowl on his face, yet despite this, he seemed interested in me, and I sensed warmth behind his eyes. I could not understand the mismatch between his overt behaviour and his underlying emotion, though I remembered Haari's warning that he had a heart of gold, though it took some digging to find it. If I had not been gifted the way I was, I would have assumed he was not in the least happy to have been dragged here to meet me, a total stranger. Yet I knew that this was not the case. I decided to try and ignore his manner, and offered my hand as I stopped beside the table.

"I'm very pleased to meet you, Bartrem. Haari has told me about you, and I wanted so much to meet you myself."

I noticed both Haari and Lisvet smile at my words, knowing I had backed Bartrem into a corner by my courteous greeting. Even Bartrem, to his credit, looked mildly abashed, and mumbled, as he gave my hand a quick shake,

"Yes, yes. Very nice to meet you too I suppose."

Haari and Lisvet both burst out laughing at Bartrem's greeting, causing the scowl to return instantly to Bartrem's face. I could perceive that the warmth towards me had in fact grown stronger after my very civil greeting.

"Well," snapped Bartrem abruptly to all of us. "Sit down then!"

We did as we were told, and I glanced surreptitiously at Bartrem as I did so. I had already had a good look at Lisvet, seeing she was small, petite even, yet strong and fit looking, sporty. She had short dark hair cut in a simple style, wore no make up or jewellery of any kind, and was dressed in tight-fitting orange trousers and a matching top, the sort people used for outdoor activities. Her clothing was in marked contrast to most of the other people I had seen that day. Her large blue eyes were bright and alive, her face easily and rapidly forming into a smile as she looked at me, or Haari, or Bartrem. She had an open, honest face. A face that inspired liking and trust. Bartrem could hardly look more different.

He was much older than Lisvet, or even than Haari. I found people's ages hard to judge, but I thought he looked older than Zelda or Kallan, so I assumed he must be at least sixty, and probably more. He was scruffy, with ill-fitting garments, the colours of which did not seem to indicate any attempt at coordination. His hair, badly coloured a straw-blond hue, was unkempt, but thick and luxurious, sticking out in all directions from his large head. In some ways he reminded me of Zelda: the scowl and the poor dress sense in particular. Yet there was a profound difference. Zelda almost never showed warmth or affection, rarely towards me, and never towards strangers, yet this is precisely what I sensed from Bartrem. I was fascinated at the contrast between the way he seemed to feel and the way he seemed to want me to think he felt. I could not fathom why he presented this false facade. Was it fear of seeming weak? Fear of not receiving the same warmth in return? Or simply a deeply ingrained habit of behaviour which he was either unaware of, or simply unable to change? I could not believe he was ignorant of the effect of his facial expressions and body language, and my perception of this fact was rapidly bolstered by Haari as he laughingly spoke to Bartrem.

"Uncle. Stop frowning at our guest and be nice to him. We all know you wanted to meet him as much at Lizzie did."

I turned to Haari, a look of query on my face at his use of the name Lizzie which I did not recognise.

"We usually call our dear Lisvet 'Lizzie'. Lisvet is a bit of a mouthful," he explained. It seemed no more of a mouthful to me than Lisvet. Lisvet turned to me and said kindly,

"You can call me Lizzie or Lisvet. I've no preference. Whichever you like best."

"And if Bartrem is a bit of a mouthful, just call him Grumpy," laughed Haari.

"Or Grouchy!" guffawed Lizzie.

"Or Crabby!" howled Haari.

"Ha ha ha," interrupted Bartrem, with a ghost of a smile at the corners of his lips trying to intrude through the scowl. "You two are just hilarious, and I'm glad to provide you with so much entertainment. But that's enough now, you rude buggers."

Lizzie and Haari pretended to look contrite, but after a moment burst out laughing again. Bartrem made a rumbling noise of irritation in his throat, but his eyes showed an underlying amusement. I realised that such interchanges must be common between these three people, and were actually evidence of their affection for each other. I found it deeply odd that people who I assumed really liked each other should speak to each other in such a way. Their words suggested dislike, or hostility, yet their manner indicated affection. As they spoke, Haari and Lisvet laughed and smiled, and even Bartrem's frowns and occasional scowls seemed put on, artificial. I sighed as I was reminded just how much I had to learn about other people, and how they managed their social interactions.

"Shall we get something to drink? To eat?" asked Lizzie suddenly.

I was confused by her question. I had noticed other people with food and drinks at some of the tables on the terrace below, but I could not see where they had acquired them from. I had assumed they had brought them with them. Haari turned to me.

"Well Samek? A drink? Some food?" he asked.

"A drink," I replied, feeling thirsty from the long walk through the city. Haari waved his hand across a tiny red panel at the side of the table, and moments later I jumped as a strange, tinny voice spoke loudly beside us.

"Yes?" it asked. "What can I get you?"

I turned to see an automaton beside the table. I had not noticed its silent approach, though this was not surprising. It was very similar to some of the domestic helpers we had in our house on the estate, which moved around in total silence. I had not seen where this machine had come from, but I assumed it must have emerged from one of the doors at the back of the terrace, and that it had been summoned by Haari when he passed his hand across the red panel. The robot waited patiently for instructions until Haari told it what drinks we would like, then it turned and disappeared through an open door in the wall of the back of the terrace. As it did so, I remembered a conversation I had had with Zelda and Kallan about automata, when I queried why we did not make them to look like people. Zelda and Kallan had been almost scandalised by my question, telling me that it would be grotesque to produce working machines that mimicked the look of a human. When I persisted with my queries, they explained that a human is unique, and could not be reproduced in artificial form. It would create all sorts of problems with our sense of self, of identity, if we made fully realistic robots in our own image. I did not understand their comments at the time, and still could not really agree with them. How could it affect my sense of who I was, or of my worth as a person, if there were robots which looked like people? As there was a lull in the conversation at the table, I asked Haari, Bartrem and Lisvet why it was considered so awful to have human-like robots. I had always thought it would be nicer if our working automata looked more like people.

"As you may be aware," began Haari slightly pompously as I realised that he was used to being listened to. "The usual answer is that it somehow undermines the essential dignity of being human. Most people believe they are unique and can't be copied, so shouldn't be."

"What a load of absolute bollocks," stated Bartrem brusquely.

"I didn't say I believed it," replied Haari in a mildly defensive tone. "I said it's the usual answer and what most people believe."

"You know the real reason?" said Bartrem, turning to me. I shook my head.

"It's because if we made robots that looked and behaved like people, they'd be used for all the wrong things. Highly inappropriate things." I was none the wiser by his reply, and my frown made this clear.

"Sex," he stated simply.

"Uncle!", snapped Lizzie loudly. "He's just a boy."

"Grow up Lizzie," grumbled Bartrem. "He's not that young, and anyway, he's not 'just' anything. He is special and unique. I'm sure he can cope with some adult truths." I nodded at Bartrem, encouraging him to elucidate further. He did not disappoint.

"If," he began, looking straight at me. "If we had perfectly human looking robots, the main thing they'd be used for would be sex."

"And why would that be?" queried Haari. "Pray put us out of our ignorance uncle. It's not as if it's hard to find willing sexual partners, so why would we need machines that look like people?"

"Because, boy," continued Bartrem, patronising Haari by calling *him* a boy. "Unlike real people, a robot will do whatever you tell it to do. Anything at all, any time of the day or night, no matter how gross and disgusting the command, and..."

"That's enough uncle," said Lizzie abruptly. Bartrem stared at her, irritation showing on his face.

"It's enough when I've bloody well finished!" he snapped. "As I was saying before I was so rudely interrupted," he continued more quietly, addressing his comments to me. "Automata don't complain, or object, or disapprove. Real people are cussed, difficult, put obstacles in the way of satisfying desires. And they moan and gripe, they make you feel guilty, or they want something in return. Robots would be a better option for most people, and that's why we don't make them looking like people. And now I've finished," he said, staring at Lizzie. She glared back at him, and the slightly uncomfortable silence reigned at the table until the mechanised server returned and stopped beside us, its arms extended with four drinks balanced on the flattened extensions at the tips of the limbs. It deftly slid the drinks onto the table, turned, and walked silently away. Bartrem downed most of his beverage in one gulp, one which contained a good deal of alcohol from the smell of it. He sighed with pleasure, slammed the large blue glass loudly onto the table, and said,

"Well? Where had we got to with our conversation?"

"You were going out of your way to outrage our young guest," replied Haari. "And now you've shown him what an ornery old bugger you are, perhaps we can have a more civilised conversation?"

Bartrem looked back at him, and I sensed he wanted to smile, but covered it with an odd expression almost of disingenuousness, as if he did not understand Haari's criticism. Lisvet snorted slightly at the two men, shaking her head slightly as she did so, though I could not tell if she was irritated or amused by them. Then she turned to me.

"How do you find our city, Samek? This is your first time here, isn't it?" I took her cue to ignore Haari and Bartrem, and turned to her.

"Yes," I replied, returning her smile. "To the city itself. I've been to the Council building twice though."

"Yes, I know," she replied. "I saw both trips to the Council. Well, everyone did actually and saw you and your, um, your family there."

I was surprised at her use of the word family. I had understood that it was not in common usage, and certainly the members of the Council, even those not hostile to us, seemed to balk at referring to us as a family.

"You think we are a family?" I asked quietly. Lizzie looked a little surprised at my question. She paused briefly, a tiny gathering of the middle of her well-shaped dark eyebrows evidence that she was considering how to reply.

"Yes of course," she answered gently. "What else would I call you?" I shrugged, and replied,

"I didn't think people used the word. I thought it was just Zelda and Kallan who referred to us as a family. Do you know who they are?" I added, realising I had assumed she would know their names. Lizzie laughed lightly, blue eyes dancing as she did so.

"Yes of course I do. Everyone does. You're the most notorious people in the world." I frowned at her reply, not sure I liked to be reminded of the fact. But it was as much my fault as anyone else's that this was the case. I had, after all, forced the entire world to witness our trips to the Council. Before I could say anything else, Haari snapped out of his staring match with Bartrem, and spoke.

"A lot of people don't use the word family, but some of us do. For example, Bartrem, Lizzie and I are a family, and we call ourselves that sometimes. Even Bartrem, for all his grouchy exterior. Believe me, he'd be lost without us, wouldn't you, you grumpy old git?" he said, turning to Bartrem. Bartrem shrugged slightly, but then replied,

"Yes, I would. You two matter to me more than anyone else, anything else in the world. You are *my* family." He stopped abruptly and looked away, though I could not miss the look of affection for Lizzie and Haari flash across his face as he spoke. He seemed disconcerted, unused to voicing such feelings. Haari and Lisvet looked amazed, perhaps unfamiliar with hearing Bartrem express such emotions openly. After a few moments of embarrassed silence, Bartrem suddenly looked up from the table.

"Some of those arseholes at the Council, including the ones you and Zelda so neatly got rid of," he said, turning to me. "Especially what you did to Rannald," he added with a mischievous wink, causing me to blush and look away. If he was able to joke about Rannald's death, suggesting by his behaviour that I had had a part in it, then surely many others in the world believed the same. Of course I had caused Rannald's heart attack as punishment for being the ringleader in the murder of my sister, but I was appalled at the idea that such conjecture was common. "Even some of them have families," Bartrem continued, interrupting my thoughts. "And call them that."

"Who?" I asked in amazement.

"That Rannald for one," he replied. "He had a number of nieces and nephews. More than he should. I assume he arranged it, though it's supposed to be random."

"Yes, that's right," added Haari, turning to me. "And surely you know one of them? Devid. Isn't that his name?" I nodded, starting slightly at the name Devid. He, who had wormed his way into our home, and had then reported back all that he had seen to Rannald and the rest of the Council. I shuddered at the memory of this vile man who judged me and my siblings as living forms of grotesque experiments.

"Devid?" queried Bartrem. "I know that name. Have I met him?" he asked, addressing the question to his niece and nephew.

"I doubt it uncle," replied Lizzie. "You and he hardly mix in the same sort of circles."

"But I know his name," insisted Bartrem.

"As Rannald's nephew, surely most people do, don't they?" replied Haari.

"I suppose so," replied Bartrem. "As you say Lizzie, he and I are hardly likely to mix socially."

We sat quietly for a moment, sipping our drinks, enjoying the warmth of the sun and the smells of flowers, plants, the earth. I watched small birds flitting in and out of the foliage, butterflies flapping uncertainly across the spaces between plants. Bartrem broke the pleasant silence.

"It's interesting about families," Bartem stated, intruding into the silence. We all looked at him sharply, something in his tone attracting our attention.

"In the past of course everyone, or pretty much everyone, lived in a family," he continued. "The information we have is awash with this, and with endless stories of the feeling family members had for each other, powerful feelings, though not by any means always good feelings. Love, passion, commitment, loyalty. Betrayal, hatred, murder - the list of nouns goes on and on. Yet after the Chaos, as we began to re-make the world, the world of people, decisions were taken to try and undermine that basis, the fact that the family was the basis of society. It was felt that it was too divisive, that it cut societies up into too many tiny parts. As the survivors began to reproduce, this ability was fairly quickly taken away from individuals and put in the hands of the Council. Though of course it was always expressed as being in the hands of the people. It was in everyone's interest that individuals could no longer reproduce, and that all new life was created in laboratories. In fact, it didn't take long before even the *possibility* of individual reproduction was removed. From many hundreds of years ago, even if we wanted to, we couldn't make our own babies." He turned to me.

"You know all this I assume?" Bartem asked me.

"I know that female foetuses have their eggs removed before birth, and these are then used in the laboratories which make multi-parent zygotes, and the same happens to male foetuses, to their reproductive cells, their sperm cell precursors," I replied, causing slight amusement in Bartrem's face by my use of such technical terminology. "And because of this," I continued. "All humans in our present world are, in fact, infertile, having no reproductive cells by the time the baby is brought into the world. All reproduction is entirely in the hands of the Institutes and their laboratories, under the control of the Council." I stopped for a moment before remembering something else Bartrem had said.

"But I didn't know the real reason, that families, old-fashioned families, were felt to be too divisive, cutting society up into tiny parts. Is this really why we aren't allowed them any more?" I asked. Bartrem nodded, his straw-like hair catching the breeze as he did so.

"But," he then continued. "Despite natural families being a thing of the distant past, and impossible now, nature, evolution, still pushes us back in that direction." I looked at him, frowning, not really understanding what he was saying.

"Samek looks confused, uncle. Lizzie and I have heard it all before, many times," said Haari, resignation in his voice. Bartrem turned back to me, a look of eagerness on his face, ignoring Haari's tone. He seemed happy to have a new audience to whom to expound his views. He continued.

"Despite there not being families any more, not in the old, natural sense, we still feel the need for them. Even now we gravitate towards the small number of people with whom we feel we have a special bond, a deeper bond than with anyone else. We even still use words like uncle, aunt, niece, nephew, though we don't quite dare to make the leap into using such scandalous terms as mother, father, daughter, son. Or most of us don't," he added with a tiny wink at me. "Evolution made us into the social animals that we are, the family-based creatures that we still are, despite so many centuries of traditional families no longer existing."

"Uncle," interrupted Haari suddenly, his deep voice cutting through Bartem's higher tones. "You surely cannot expect to be taken seriously spouting such rubbish. Evolution and social animals and family-based creatures! Stuff and bloody nonsense!"

"All true, boy," countered Bartrem, genuine irritation in his voice.

"All rubbish," replied Haari. "Absolute rubbish. We've moved on from all of that, assuming it was ever true in the first place. We've moved beyond being creatures of evolution, out of control..."

"Oh?" interrupted Bartrem. "And in your great wisdom, what are we instead?"

"Social. Cultural. We're purely creatures of society and culture. We make ourselves. We aren't just animals subject to the whims of mother nature, of father evolution," replied Haari. "Lisvet," he continued. "Back me up here."

Lisvet threw up her hands. "No Haari I can't. I'm on uncle's side, as you should know by now if you ever bothered to listen to me."

Haari looked surprised at Lisvet's reply. "You surely don't believe we are still creatures of nature, of evolution?" he asked incredulously.

"Yes I do", replied Lisvet. "At least to a large extent."

Haari stared at her in silence, his amber eyes wide with disbelief. Before he could muster a reply, Bartrem took the opportunity to continue his explanations to me.

"As I was about to say before I was interrupted again, some researchers think that thousands of years ago, long before the Chaos, before humans began their experiment with agriculture, our hunter-gatherer ancestors didn't have small families the way they did later, even these researchers agree that we are drawn to small social units with whom we feel an intense bond of kinship. They think that children were probably brought up almost communally, at least once they were weaned, with groups of related adults, mostly women and old people, looking after them. I'm not sure I agree with such research, and there's no way they can prove this of course, but it could explain why our present system of Institutes seems to work, up to a point. If it's not so different from what our distant ancestors had, their ideas could explain why such a system still just about works now."

"You've just undermined your own position old man," said Haari. Bartrem turned to him.

"How so?" he replied.

"If we didn't live in families so long ago, then later we did, how are we limited by evolution? Either we are and it's unchanging and eternal, or not," stated Haari. Bartrem merely laughed.

"I never said evolution was unchanging and eternal. If you engaged your brain Haari you'd see that the word evolution implies change. Things evolve, people evolve. Nothing is unchanging and eternal. But what it does show is that as humans we have always been compelled to be part of small social units with whom we feel kinship. That *is* eternal and unchanging. And we are no less so now than we were before the Chaos, and thousands, probably hundreds of thousands of years before that."

Haari merely stared at Bartrem, unwilling, or unable, to pursue the argument further. I had sat in silence throughout the entire exchange, amazed at how quickly the mood of levity had shifted into one of disputes. I watched the debate as if looking at two competitors engaged in a sport, an antagonistic combat sport. Both parties seemed to need a pause. After a long, tense moment, Bartrem clearly decided to change the mood, perhaps having noticed my surprised expression.

"Anyway," he went on. "I doubt if an old world father could have felt any more for his natural children than I do for Lizzie and Haari," he said quietly, blushing as he expressed his strong feelings. Lizzie and Haari blushed too, unused to such declarations from Bartrem. After a brief pause, Bartrem cleared his throat and continued in an artificially gruff, loud voice.

"Anyway. Nature will out. Whatever social experiments humans try, and our present society is just one of many social experiments, the natural conservatism plus the atavism in our species so prevalent in so many aspects of evolution, these always force themselves through whatever surface we have imposed on a society, and our deep natures reassert themselves." He glanced at Haari as he made these statements, but Haari merely stared back at him, arms crossed, seemingly unwilling to engage in further debate. I suspected that my own obvious shock was the reason for Haari's present silence, and his expression clearly showed he thought little of Bartrem's most recent pronouncements.

"So I doubt," continued Bartrem, realising that Haari would remain silent. "Whether the way we make babies now will last for ever. Our present society is so odd, so weird. And even more peculiar is that we've ended up with a social set-up that nobody really seems to control."

"But doesn't the Council control it?" I interrupted, astonished by Bartrem's final comment.

"Not really, my boy," Bartrem replied. "Or they shouldn't. It seems like they do, but in truth they should really only be the administrators of what already exists when they come to power. Sometimes they take a more active role, depending on who the members are, and the Council over which Rannald presided was like that, but through most of their history they've been rather inactive, passive even. And things seem to have just developed themselves. So how one would go about changing anything is hard to see - how do you do that if you don't really know who is running things?"

"But there are groups who try to change things," interrupted Lizzie, once again joining the conversation now that the argument had passed. "Those societies and organisations calling for something much more like traditional families, with babies allocated to people as soon as they are born, brought up from the start in homes, not in the Institutes."

"Yes," added Haari, his irritation seemingly abated as interest in the new topic took hold of him. "And those really strange groups, the ones that live out in the wilds and claim they are returning to a natural life, the way our ancestors lived. Though of course they still want most of the comforts and luxuries of modern life, so it's all just a huge fantasy of theirs, just make-believe, that they're returning to an ancient and natural way of life."

"I agree with you on that," said Lizzie. "And nobody really wants natural birth any more. Women certainly don't. Yuk," she shivered. "What a horrible idea, it's so...so...farmyard!" Haari laughed loudly at her description, and even Bartrem allowed himself a little chuckle. Haari picked up the theme.

"Also, women were never truly able to be equal to men as long as they were burdened with pregnancy and childbirth, and the bulk of the work in rearing children for that matter. It always weighed them down, literally and figuratively. Taking this away from women truly liberated them. You'd have to be insane to want that to be forced back on you."

I had sat through the debates between Haari, Bartem and Lisvet in silence. I had never considered that evolutionary pressures could still be at work on modern humans. I had assumed that it had ceased to affect us, that with our technology we had risen above it, as Haari clearly believed. Yet what Bartrem said made so much sense, and explained why I felt such an intense bond especially with Adwin and Kallan, also with my sisters, and even with Zelda despite my not really liking her. And it showed why Devid was so bonded to Rannald, and why Bartrem felt so strongly towards Lizzie and Haari. Did Haari really believe that his feelings for Lisvet and Bartem were nothing more than cultural, imposed upon him by the society he lived in? Surely he could not really believe this? Surely he had to know that such feelings were much deeper than mere cultural constructions?

I was truly surprised by the revelations that there were groups in our society calling for change, calling for a return to a more natural family, in effect for the abolition of the Institutes and the entire process of rearing children. And even more astonishing was the discovery that there were others who lived out in the wilds, pretending to be returning to a life like the one enjoyed by our ancient ancestors. I pondered my own upbringing, which was surprisingly similar to that experienced in the old world, a home with a mother, a father, and children. I knew I would not swap it for the world, and the idea of being raised in an Institute to the age of fourteen filled me with sadness for those who had endured such a childhood. I felt sorry for all those thousands, millions, of children denied the security, the warmth, the stability, of the upbringing I had had, for all its problems. But could our society change? Did the fact that no-one seemed to actually be controlling it, that it trundled on under its own steam, oblivious to pressure for change, did this make it difficult, impossible even, for real change ever to occur? All of these new ideas tumbled around in my brain, making my head ache with the novelty, with the wealth of revelations I had witnessed on my first trip into the world of ordinary people. Would it always be so? Would I find every visit felt like sitting under a waterfall of new ideas?

Chapter Forty-One

As I sat reeling under the onslaught of so much new information, so many novel ideas, I perceived a slight commotion near our table. I turned to see a group of about seven or eight people in a wild array of colours and clothing approaching gingerly, seemingly egging each other on with nudges and giggles. They moved ever closer, and I heard comments such as "It's him, it's really him", and "Go on, talk to him. Ask him something."

I realised with alarm that the group was intent on talking to me, yet I was not ready for such social interaction. I tensed visibly as they neared where I sat, their whispered comments and laughter gaining volume as they did so. I saw Haari frown as he saw my reaction, but before he or I could say anything, Bartrem turned to the approaching gang and said in a loud, aggressive voice,

"Clear off! Just bugger off the lot of you!"

They stopped in their tracks, stunned by Bartrem's tone of voice and offensive words, the glittering surfaces of their clothing rippling in the sunlight and light breeze as they did so. They seemed unable to decide what to do, but after a moment of complete stillness, one of them, a woman in her middle years in a gaudy yellow and emerald toga leaned forward slightly, a cross look on her face.

"How dare you speak to us like that friend," she said in an quiet but angry voice, her one free arm waving about wildly as she spoke. "Do you think it acceptable to address strangers in such a way?" she continued. Bartrem was unmoved by her comments.

"You're not my friend," he replied in a growl. "None of you are, so just bugger right off back to where you crawled from and leave us in peace, especially you," he said, addressing the leader of the group directly. "You hideous old sow in that disgusting outfit."

I gasped at Bartrem's invective, my gasp echoed by the entire group of strangers. Such offensiveness seemed uncalled-for, and yet I suspected that Bartrem was speaking this way to protect me. He must have seen the obvious anxiety on my face as the unwanted assembly approached us, and responded in his own way to put a barrier between them and me. I was touched by his concern, but somewhat appalled at the way he spoke to complete strangers who, in truth, had not really done anything wrong. I glanced at the people standing in mute shock close to our table, assuming that they had never been spoken to in such a way before. Social interaction was clearly never carried out in such manner and they were so stunned that they did not know how to react. Bartrem turned away from them abruptly and addressed the three of us at the table, as if the silent, shocked group beside us no longer existed.

"Where were we, before we were so rudely interrupted?" he asked. The strangers tensed further, not sure if being rebuffed in this way was even more offensive than Bartrem's previous abusive language. Cutting people so abruptly out of a conversation in this way, turning one's back on them, perhaps this was even more discourteous than swearing at them. My lack of normal social interaction made it impossible for me to judge. After a few moments of intense silence, they began to shuffle away from the table, muttering quietly as they did so. They seemed deeply affronted and angry, and I found their antipathy unpleasant to experience.

I wondered if I should say something to Bartrem, or at least ask him if he really considered his behaviour appropriate, but I was shy to do so. In addition, I was moved by his leaping to protect me, a boy he barely knew, realising at that moment that he would be a fierce friend or a fierce enemy. I glanced at Haari and Lizzie, to see if I could take a cue from them. They did not look shocked, or even surprised at Bartrem's outburst, merely resigned and Lisvet perhaps mildly disapproving. I suspected that she and Haari had witnessed such behaviour many times before, and were not put out by it. So taking the cue from them, I tried to act as if nothing out of the ordinary had happened.

Our conversation resumed, and when I regained my composure sufficiently, I enquired further about the groups of people living out in the wilds. Bartrem turned to Lizzie on hearing my question, indicating that she should reply.

"There aren't that many of them," she began. "But they are all people who for various reasons don't feel they fit in. They claim they don't want all the rigidity, the control, of our modern lives, and say they are returning to a more natural state, as our distant ancestors lived. But as Haari said, it's all a bit of a fantasy as they have houses built for them before they go, and these houses enjoy most, if not all, of our modern comforts. They might look like ancient rural hovels, but they have heating, air conditioning, running hot and cold water and so on. But they haven't got much chance of creating a new society wherever it is they live. They can't reproduce, as Bartrem explained, so unless they keep recruiting new members, they'll just die out. And I can't imagine the women would dream of wanting to do anything as 'natural' as gestate an embryo and give birth. Such an idea would appall them as much as it appalls me. But they're still a great irritation to many people, including the Council, turning their back on the society they were brought up in, the perfect world many people think we've created for ourselves. If it's so perfect, why would anyone reject it? Why would anyone want to change it?"

"Some people just write them off as lunatics," added Haari. "But they don't seem mad, just odd or eccentric. And believe you me, many many citizens have a sneaking admiration for them, and ask themselves, in quiet private moments, whether they don't have a point." Haari turned to look at me directly, and continued.

"You remember our discussion about boredom?" he asked. I nodded. "Well, despite the modern comforts they have there it's still a harder life than the one we have here. They grow or collect, or catch all their own food, for example. Many people wonder if those wild-livers haven't found an ideal solution to the stultifying boredom. Perhaps they've found the answer to the sheer mind-numbing ease and comfort of our lives. They have some of the most basic comforts, but without the endless days which have to be filled. Without the aimless and pointless occupations most people fill their time with. And this is what alarms the Council and other citizens who are very happy with the status quo. Groups who not only call for change, but actually show this by their actions, these are potentially dangerous people. At least the ones who waste their lives immersed in virtual reality are no threat to the status quo." I could not help wonder if these people were misguided in their desire to effect change: perhaps the very act of removing yourself from normal society guaranteed that you also thereby removed yourself from any possibility of influencing it for the better. I knew for sure however, that such a life held no attraction for me, a person who had spent his whole life secluded from most of humanity, isolated on an estate in the countryside. Yet I was intrigued.

"Those other groups and societies," I suddenly asked. "The ones who are calling for babies to be allocated at birth to uncles or aunts. Are they big? Do they have any influence?" I asked.

"There are lots of them, and their numbers are surprisingly large," replied Bartrem. "The Council tries to ignore them, not to engage with them, though I think this is a mistake. They won't go away, and they keep increasing in number. The Council and others should engage with the debate, and explain why our present system is the best - that is, if they really believe it. Just ignoring it doesn't make it disappear."

"What do you think yourself Bartrem?" I asked shyly, nervous at asking him such a direct, and possibly intrusive question, and using his name for the first time. He did not seem to object to being questioned in this way, and paused for a moment in thought, scratching his head and causing his messy fake-blond hair to become even more tousled.

"An interesting question young man," he replied, in a quiet, almost kindly voice. "I love the relationship I have with these two here," he said, indicating Lizzie and Haari with a nod of his head. "And sometimes I wonder what it would have been like to have had them with me from the moment of their birth. Frankly, I'm not sure I'd have been a fit parent of such young human beings, but I understand why many people feel it would be a wonderful thing, a life-changing and positive experience, not only for the parent, but also for the child."

"It sounds like a nightmare to me," interrupted Haari. "Imagine being lumbered with a mewling and puking baby taking up all your time, demanding all your attention, ruining your life. I fervently hope I never even get allocated a niece or nephew at all. I can't imagine the disruption in my life of being responsible for a fourteen year old, let alone someone even younger."

"I'm with Haari on this," said Lisvet. "At least as far as having a baby is concerned. It sounds like hell. But I'd be very happy with a niece or nephew some day, but I hope not till I'm a lot older. I'm having far too much fun at the moment!" She and Haari smiled broadly at each other. Bartrem feigned a look of disapproval.

"But think for a moment," Bartrem continued in a slightly crabby tone. "How amazing it would be to be brought up from birth in a small home, by one or a few people, like parents in the old world. Like you have, Samek," he said, nodding in my direction, a hint of a smile lightening his features. "But it's hard to imagine it really," he sighed. "Having been brought up in the Institute till I was fourteen, like everyone else in the world with a few exceptions," he added, smiling again at me. "I can't envisage a different childhood. I truly can't picture what it would be like to raise a baby. But think what it might mean to the baby."

"I really enjoyed my childhood," intruded Haari with a touch of defiance. "Being surrounded day and night by a huge gang of other children, having all my friends with me all the time. We romped and played, got into all sorts of trouble, yet all within a safe, comfortable environment. And there were always lots of adults around, our carers, teachers and so on. And from the age of five, I had Bartrem in my life. He used to visit me often, and I visited him at his home. So I knew the affection, the love, of an individual adult." As he spoke, Lisvet nodded vaguely in agreement, though the look of uncertainty on her face suggested she was not as convinced as Haari and perhaps thought wistfully of how different her childhood could have been, if it had been spent entirely in the bosom of a small family. My thoughts were interrupted by Haari.

"I'm sorry if this sounds rude, Samek, but from what you tell me, your childhood hasn't been perfect."

"No," I replied hesitantly. "It wasn't. Isn't. But I think that's because of Zelda herself, her personality, and not because of the family set up. She's always been obsessed with privacy, with keeping us away from the world, and this is what has made my life so odd, so isolated. And the fact that, frankly, she's just not a very nice person. If she were more normal, kinder, then my life could have been wonderful. As it is, much of it has been good."

Haari sensed my defensiveness, and smiled at me. I knew he had not intended to be offensive, and was basing what he said on my own words. I smiled back.

"Anyway," interrupted Bartrem. "Whatever the rest of you think, I have some sympathy with those who would like a family life more like in the old world."

"Perhaps the answer," added Lizzie. "Is letting those who want it have it, and those that don't can keep the system we have, with the Institutes."

"Always the peacemaker," laughed Haari.

"Or compromiser," stated Bartrem, less politely.

Lizzie frowned at him, though her frown lacked any real conviction.

"Shall we have a wander?" suggested Haari brightly. "I'm sure the old man is getting stiff sitting here, and this conversation is far too serious."

Bartrem glowered at Haari for being called an old man for the second time. But we all stood up. As we moved off, the serving automaton appeared immediately, moved over towards us and cleared the table. I had not seen it watching or waiting, and was impressed by the neat system in place to ensure comfort and hygiene with no apparent effort.

We began to walk along the terrace, away from where Haari and I had entered it. I gazed in wonder at my surroundings. It was truly lovely, the soft green and cream of the stone pavement and buildings, the luxuriant greenery of plants on the terrace and cascading down from the roof above, the gentle sounds of birds, of water, of human conversation. But as we walked, I became more and more aware of the acute focus of the people we passed. Even when they feigned indifference towards me, I felt their interest. Much of it seemed to be simple fascination at my presence. Some of it came across as warm and kindly, smiles and nods made towards me. But there was a notable undercurrent on many people's faces of hostility and even fear. I found such feelings aimed at me distressing, knowing that I had never done anything to harm these people, had never even met them. Why did they feel such antipathy towards me, such suspicion and aversion?

Most of the people on the terrace were polite enough to leave us alone, contenting themselves with stares and whispered comments. But not all of them. As when we were at the table, small bands of individuals felt a desire to approach us, presumably with the aim of talking to me, meeting me.

At first my companions seemed oblivious to the rising fascination all around. Yet, as we continued our walk, taking the lift down to the lower floor, the weight of humanity milling all around me began to oppress, and the other three could not fail but to notice the increasing crush. The lower terrace was much busier, and the groups approaching us were larger and more frequent. Even the wild array of colours, fabrics, patterns in the often flamboyant clothing began to feel oppressive. And as news spread by gossip of my presence, the mood became more intense. As it did so, Bartrem began to respond with the same aggressive rudeness he had shown before. Interest slid towards outrage at his behaviour. People began to press towards us in ever larger numbers, leaving us little space to walk, or even move. We gathered close together for security, and Bartrem's loud, shouted swearing increased in intensity and aggression, becoming almost continuous. The atmosphere became more and more charged, more unpleasant, until I felt I could stand it no longer.

"I have to take myself away, now," I said to the other three, having to speak loudly simply to be heard above the hubbub of the thronging crowds pressing around us. "If I don't, I fear what I might do." Haari turned to me, anxiety clear in his face. He seemed to intuit what I meant: that I might lash out through my fear and really hurt somebody.

"Yes, a good idea. Do it now. Take us all away, back to my place."

The crush intensified, and before I could muster the energy needed to remove the four of us a particularly rowdy group in the crowd swelled forwards towards me. Without thinking, with no intention, I lashed out with my mind to protect myself, to protect all of us. The first few people in the swell reeled backwards as my mindlash struck them. They shrieked in pain, their hands moving up to protect their faces, confused by what they felt. They had seen nobody strike them, and there was no wound, no blood, yet the perception of agony around their heads, even inside their heads, was very real. They seemed mystified by what had just happened.

Without properly warning Bartrem and Lizzie to prepare to be ported, I grabbed Haari's arm, instructing him through mindspeak to take hold of Bartrem and Lisvet. I took us all away, back to Haari's apartment. As we vanished from sight, I sensed the shock and disquiet of the crowd: those at the front were outraged that something seemed to have struck some of them, and they were not used to people simply disappearing from view before their very eyes.

Chapter Forty-Two

A moment later, we materialised in Haari's small, neat living room. Haari had known what to expect, but for Bartrem and Lisvet this was their first experience of flitting. They stood quite still, blinking slightly in surprise at how quick and smooth the process had been.

"You hardly feel a thing!" exclaimed Lisvet, her eyes dancing with excitement.

"It was marvellous," added Bartrem, his eyes also shining with the sheer delight of his experience. "I would give anything to be able to do that," he continued, turning to me. "Do you think you could teach me?" Before I could reply, Haari spoke.

"Leave him alone uncle. He must be exhausted." Bartrem began to remonstrate with Haari at this comment, but Lisvet leaped to my defence.

"Haari's right, uncle. Leave the poor boy alone. He's just finished his first ever trip to the city, and being mobbed like that was thoroughly unpleasant even for us. Imagine what it was like for him." And I noted that she pointedly did not mention the fact that I had lashed out, mindstriking a few of the crowd. Perhaps she had not connected the crowd's shrieks and yelps of pain with me.

"And just imagine," continued Haari with an expression of mock disapproval as he looked at Bartrem. "As if the crowds weren't enough, he also had to endure you pontificating on and on!"

"You can bugger off too," replied the gruff Bartrem in a sharp tone. Haari merely laughed, as did Lisvet.

"You can ask me another time," I interrupted, looking at Bartrem. "Though I don't know if I can. Now, as Haari said, I'm exhausted and I really have to go home." In truth I was truly worn out by my experiences of the day.

Not only my first trip to Beyra, to any city, but the crowds wanting to meet me, the endless waves of emotion crashing against me from the seemingly limitless sea of humanity, and I had conflicting feelings about my lashing out at the crowd. I also, in all honesty, was weary from being with strangers, and I include Bartrem and Lisvet in this description, for all that they were polite and kind to me. Even Haari, whom I had known for a little while and with whom I had enjoyed distant conversations using mindspeak, I had spent very little time with and did not know well. For me, a youngster who had met so few strangers in his life, even spending time with friendly strangers as I did that day was wearying and stressful. And I had much to think about having listened keenly to the debates about the dissent in the outside world, a fact I found most disconcerting. I felt an intense desire to be away from Beyra, away from everything and everyone unfamiliar, to be home.

"You're safe here," said Haari, looking at me with an expression of concern. "You should feel this is your home in the city." I turned to him and smiled tentatively. It seemed important to him that I feel at home in his home, but I could not express the overpowering need I had for familiarity, though I smiled inwardly at the irony of my emotion. I had been desperately trying for years to escape the comfortable prison of my home, yet here I was, on my first proper trip away from that jail, desperate to rush back there as quickly as I could.

"I know that, Haari," I assured him. "But I have to go. I have to be at home, in the place I know. I can't explain it really, but I have to go." He nodded, though still looked disappointed.

"Thank you so much, Haari," I said. "For such a wonderful day. For inviting me to your home, showing me the city, and introducing me to your family. And despite the problems with the crowds in the centre, I've had one of most amazing days of my life, truly." He seemed to some extent appeased, nodding and smiling slightly. I then turned to Bartrem and Lisvet.

"And I really enjoyed meeting you both, Haari's family, and thank you for making me so welcome." Before I could continue, Lisvet turned and kissed me lightly on the cheek. I was surprised, not knowing if such action was normal on a first meeting. But her gesture seemed natural and spontaneous, appropriate to her open and friendly character.

"We loved meeting you too, Samek," she said. "And we hope to see you very soon. Perhaps you'd like to visit us at our house?"

"That's a nice idea," added Bartrem, slightly unexpectedly. And to my surprise, he moved close to me, smiled almost shyly, and patted me several times on the shoulder. Lisvet and Haari looked surprised at this gesture.

Clearly he rarely, if ever, showed any affection for someone he had only just met.

I stepped slightly away from the three of them, smiling, and said simply, "Goodbye and thank you again," and then ported myself home.

Moments later I re-emerged in the comforting familiarity of my own room. I quickly mindspoke to Kallan, letting him know I was home, but that I was so wearied by my day's activities that I needed to rest. A pang of sadness crossed my mind as I realised that in the past Adwin would have been the first person I contacted in such a situation. Kallan replied, telling me he was glad I was back, and wished me a pleasant repose. I took off my shoes, but otherwise fully clothed lay on my bed, my head filled with the myriad novel images, sounds and smells of my first day out in Beyra. Before I fell asleep, less pleasing thoughts slipped unwanted into my mind. I remembered, with sudden clarity, the moment I had used my mind to slap the front line of the crowd mobbing me. I had simply reacted without thought, without planning, and I had caused real pain. I shivered slightly as I realised that I had been lucky: if I had struck with more force I could have caused real damage, or even killed someone. I knew that I could kill a person if I struck with sufficient energy. After all, I had already put Rannald to death with the force of my mind. It was probably only my confusion and distress in Beyra which had saved the mob from genuine harm. It had been such an unwise thing for me to have done. Given my celebrity, I knew that everything I did would be minutely scrutinised, and shared rapidly across the planet. I fell asleep with these worrying reflections bustling around in my head.

Some hours later I awoke, feeling somewhat refreshed and rested. Before I rose from my bed, I looked slowly around my room, enjoying the friendliness of such well-known surroundings. I bitterly regretted my action in mindstriking citizens without warning, and as I gazed at all that was familiar, I wondered if I had been unwise in leaving the security of my home in the first place. I thought of the other rooms in the house, the gardens and meadows surrounding the building, and even the woods just beyond, wallowing in the sensation of ease and acquaintance, the sheer constancy and lack of novelty of it all. Might it not be better, I thought, to simply remain here for ever, never leaving the safety of the known? But as quickly as the thought entered my mind I tried to cast it out. I was determined not be afraid of the world outside. I must grasp it with both hands and make myself learn to know it, even to love it. But for another moment or two I would simply lie here, cocooned among the artefacts of my everyday life, swaddled in the plush velvet of my comfortable prison.

But in the end I forced myself off the bed, and went to find Kallan. I needed to be with my uncle. Another twinge of sadness rose in my mind as I realised that in the past I would always have rushed to find my brother when

I had things to share, but the tension that reigned between us was such that this was simply not an option. Kallan was in the garden tending to the herbs he grew behind the house. It was beginning to get dark, yet he seemed unaware of this as I came across him kneeling beside a bed, digging energetically to remove weeds from his precious herb garden. He looked up as I approached and smiled broadly, raising his elegant white eyebrows in query.

"Did you have a nice day, my dear?" he asked me in his mellifluous voice. "Shall we sit, and you can tell me all about it," he continued as he stood up. We sat on one of the nearby benches which flanked the path. As we sat, I noticed that Adwin was close by, kneeling on the lawn behind us, feeding birds out of his hands. I knew he used his gifts to calm the tiny avians, and felt another twist of unhappiness as I remembered that this had been a game we used to play together. As he saw me, he stilled, perhaps hoping that I had not seen him. He was close enough to hear what was said between me and my uncle.

I tried to ignore Adwin behind me, and focused instead on recounting to Kallan my experiences of the day, from my first moments in Haari's flat, to porting myself away from the same place later. He sat quietly, drinking in the descriptions and images as I filled his mind with sounds and odours to enhance his experience. I did not quite dare fill Adwin's mind at the same time, not being sure of the reception such an intrusion would receive. But I projected a large three-dimensional image into the air in front of us, clearly visible to my brother, showing Haari's tiny jewel of a flat, his exquisite building, the homes of Beyra and the city centre, even the meeting with Bartrem and Lisvet (minus the debates!). The huge, magnificently attired crowds milling around were clear to see, but I chose to omit the alarming final moments, the menacing throng, my ill-judged lashing out at the crowd. Such details would only serve to worry my uncle. Kallan sighed lightly, saying,

"Beyra is lovely, all of it. The centre, the lakes and rivers, the homes. And I'm glad you saw the area with those delightful wooden houses - that's especially pretty. And you'll get used to the people and the crowds. I remember the first time I was taken to a city when I was a boy. I must have been about six or seven, and though I can't for the life of me remember which city it was, it was a much smaller place than Beyra. But I clung onto my aunt as if my life depended on it. I was so frightened of all the people, everywhere. Compared to the relative tranquility of the Institute, the city seemed chaotic and disordered, fast, as if everyone felt compelled to run around all the time, talking, laughing and shouting. I was terrified and wouldn't let go of my aunt's hand. She laughed at my fears, but didn't let go of me. And the next time she suggested another trip I cried, not wanting to go at all, but she gently coaxed me into it, and it wasn't nearly as bad as the first time. And by the time a third trip was suggested, I was quite keen. After that I loved visiting the city, and we went to lots of them, eventually to Beyra." He turned to me and smiled.

"You'll get used to it quite quickly, I promise," he said. He then turned round and said loudly to Adwin who had remained motionless during my presentation to Kallan. "And what do you think of Beyra, Addy?" he asked. It might be nice if you thought about going there too. I know you're only ten years old, but if you went with your brother, he'd look after you."

Adwin seemed taken aback by Kallan's blunt speaking, but did not reply. He frowned heavily, his lidded eyes narrowed, shaking his dark curls. He stared at Kallan, then even more intensely at me, and without a word stood up and walked briskly away. Kallan was visibly annoyed by Adwin's response, and shouted after him,

"You come back here child. Don't you dare run off without answering me." But Adwin ignored him and continued his hasty departure.

"How rude!" snapped Kallan. "He's become impossible recently. I just don't know what to do with him."

I too had no idea what to do about my brother. I had naively thought that presenting Beyra to him might inspire him to accompany me on my next visit. But if anything, my images seem to have caused further tension. In my innocence I had not considered that seeing me out of our home, enjoying a free life, and especially spending what seemed such a delightful afternoon with Haari, all of this would simply exacerbate Adwin's jealousy of me, envy of what I now enjoyed in my life.

"Do you think I should go and try to talk to him?" I asked my uncle hesitantly, though with no desire to do so. After a moment's pause Kallan turned to me and replied,

"No. Leave him to stew. If you go and talk to him, or if I do, it'll just make him feel important. He's a silly little boy and I have no time for such nonsense."

"It's nearly dark," he said suddenly after another pause. "No point trying to wrestle with any more weeds today," he added with forced levity. He stood up, stretched, and then put an arm around my shoulders, gently guiding me back towards the house.

"Time to find something to eat I think," he said with false cheerfulness as we strolled back to the front door, a hint of a frown between his bright blue eyes the only sign that he was still irritated, and concerned, by Adwin's behaviour. Despite my own disquiet at my brother's mood, saliva filled my mouth at the mention of food. I realised I had not eaten since breakfast. The day had been so full of newness that food had been far from my mind. But not now. Now I was ravenous.

Chapter Forty-Three

A few days passed, during which I spent most of my time alone. The atmosphere between my brother and me was worse than ever after my trip to Beyra, and by mutual silent agreement, we barely communicated at all. If I entered a room he was in, he stood up pointedly, huffed loudly and left, without a word of greeting. At mealtimes, though we sat beside each other, he did not direct a single comment at me. If I tried to talk to him around the house or gardens, which I did a number of times, feigning nonchalance to try and mask my irritation, he simply looked at me, raised his eyebrows and then walked away. Only once did he deign to reply with a single word. I came across him sitting on a bench in the garden and tentatively asked him if he would like to join me on a walk in the forest. He glanced at me and simply said, "no," before standing up and leaving me gaping with surprise. I was astonished at his ability to maintain his attitude towards me, and sadly wondered if it would ever be the same again between us. I was lonely, missing Adwin's company, and as I thought about his persistent sulks, I worried for his mental stability, to have overreacted in such a way to a change in my life that in truth did not seem great enough to warrant such a response. And truly, I had no notion how to bridge the gulf that had opened up between us, no experience to draw upon to allow me to find a way to even begin to heal the rift.

One afternoon, as I returned from a trip to the woods, I was met by Kallan as I entered the house. I had gone alone, and though reminded at every moment of Adwin's missing presence, I enjoyed swimming in the woodland pond, gasping under the waterfall's cold frothy flow. The familiarity of the trip calmed me, transported me far from the clamour of Beyra, from the uncomfortable atmosphere in my house. Kallan frowned slightly at my damp hair and patches of moisture on my clothes where I had pulled them on after my dip in the pond, then smiled, saying,

"Marna is coming to see us this evening. And she'll be staying a few days."

He knew the news would delight me, as I adored Marna. His own pleasure at the prospect was transparent on his face and in his body language. I smiled broadly at my uncle and could not resist shouting "Hurray!", and raced off to change into clean, dry clothes. Kallan smiled at my enthusiastic reaction as I left him standing in the hallway.

Marna arrived shortly before supper, and as always, I rushed to hug her. She reciprocated with a huge, affectionate bear hug, pulling me into her ample bosom and even more ample belly. She told me how much I had grown. I chortled at her comment, it being what she always said, even if she had only recently seen me, and it could not possibly be the case. As usual, she bathed the room in a radiant smile even as I hugged her portly, matronly figure, noticing her usual unkempt and ill-fitting scruffy clothing, such a dramatic contrast with the extravagant garments I had recently seen in Beyra.

"Look at you, Samek," she said as she stood back to observe me. "All grown up. And what a marvellously pretty young man you are!" I was not sure I liked being described as pretty.

"Pretty? Don't you mean handsome?" I asked, with a hint of a pout. Marna merely laughed and ruffled my thick brown thatch of curly hair.

"Pretty, handsome. What difference does it make. Good looks are good looks, and always welcome." She laughed again. "But what would I know? I've always been a bit of an ugly toad!" Kallan entered the room at that moment, and also laughing, replied,

"Not ugly my dear, just homely." They smiled broadly at each other before embracing. At that moment Zelda arrived, and to our surprise, even she moved swiftly to Marna, clasping her in a brief, intense hug.

"Back again so soon, you old reprobate?" asked Zelda in a voice of forced gruffness, not fooling anyone that she was not pleased to see Marna.

"An absolute joy to be here, as always," replied Marna in an artificially sweet tone. She then immediately asked, "Shall we go and eat?" We all guffawed at her sudden change of subject, including Marna herself. I had never known anyone who enjoyed her food as Marna did. Even in periods of crisis or great distress, nothing put her off eating. As we laughed, she patted her large belly, the bottom of which actually protruded from beneath her ill-fitting and too-small shirt, shrugging expansively, as if to say what can you do?'

We made our way to the dining room as Marna asked me about my recent trip to Beyra. I filled Marna in with the details of my trip as we walked, and completed my story as we sat at the table, where food had already been laid out. This time I included details of people's interest in me, but still stopped short of describing the final moments of menace, my lashing out. When I finished, Marna said nothing for a moment, and then spoke.

"I'm glad it was mostly good Samek, though I'm sorry you found it so utterly exhausting. But people will get used to seeing you out and about if you're there often, I promise". We carried on eating, Marna with her usual gusto. She suddenly stopped and looked up.

"Where are the others?" she queried. "Emaleen and Adwin. Are they here?" A tense silence met Marna's innocent question. She looked perplexed. After a short pause, Kallan explained.

"Emaleen has rarely been out of her room since...since...the awful event. Adwin - well Adwin, I'm not sure about. He should be here," he added with a touch of irritation in his voice. "It's rude of him not to be here. I'll go and fetch him."

"Absolutely no need my dear," said Marna, picking up on the slightly tense atmosphere in the room, keen to try and smooth it over. "He'll show up when he's hungry I imagine."

"Hmmph," interjected Zelda. We waited for her to elaborate, but no further comment was forthcoming. I wanted to tell Marna why Adwin was not with us, that he and I were in a state of almost rancorous tension, that he worked hard not to be with me if he could possibly help it. I opened my mouth to speak, but Kallan, sensing what I was about to do glared pointedly at me and indicated, with the tiniest shake of his head, that I should hold my tongue.

"Adwin and Samek have had a row," Kallan interjected by way of explanation. "Nothing serious," he added. "Just a brother's tiff. I suspect Adwin is sulking somewhere." He spoke airily, as if of nothing important, but Marna was not fooled. She had known Kallan far too long to be so easily manipulated.

"A tiff?" she enquired. "About what?" Kallan did not reply, so Marna turned to me. "Well Samek? What on earth did you argue about?" I gulped nervously, darted a quick glance at Kallan's menacing face, then spoke quickly.

"Adwin doesn't like me having a friend. And he didn't like me going to Beyra with my new friend." Marna looked surprised at my comment, but before she could speak, Zelda intruded into the conversation.

"And I didn't like him going to Beyra either, especially not with that 'new friend'," said Zelda bluntly, staring at me ominously as she spoke. "It's not safe. Too many people hate me, and by extension, hate him," she added, still referring to me as 'him' even as she stared straight at me. "You heard what happened to him in Beyra, that lots of people recognised him, and that was only his first trip. I want him, all of them actually, to stay here where they're safe." I cringed at Zelda's words, knowing how much more resistant she would be to us leaving the estate if she knew the full extent of what had happened in Beyra.

"What on earth do you mean?" Marna asked her old friend, so surprised that she actually put her knife and fork down. "To stay here for how long?"

"Forever," replied Zelda simply. "Forever."

Marna slumped back in her chair, all thoughts of food pushed momentarily from her mind. She stared at Zelda, then looked at me, then at Kallan.

"What do you think, Kallan?" she asked in an unusually peevish tone. "Do you agree with Zelda?" Kallan glanced slightly nervously at Zelda before answering.

"No," he replied quietly. "I don't agree with her. And as you can imagine, there have been more than a few angry words between us about this. As you know better than anyone, she doesn't like people disagreeing with her." Zelda spluttered, and seemed about to remonstrate with Kallan, but he cut her off before she could speak by continuing, in a stronger voice.

"The boys, and Emaleen," he added, a look of concern crossing his face as he mentioned my sister's name, "need to get out into the world. They're growing up, even Adwin though he's only ten. They need people, more people in their lives. They need to know what the world is, and even with its risks, they need to be out there. Samek has made the first step."

"And Emaleen?" queried Marna gently. "How does she feel about this? She's a young woman, no longer a child. She needs to live an adult life."

Nobody replied to Marna's question. A slightly embarrassed mood pervaded the room. Marna glanced around, confused. After a pause, Kallan spoke up.

"I wanted to get Emaleen some help, psychiatric help, as she's been so withdrawn since...since...since it happened. But," he added with a dark look at Zelda. "Zelda refused point blank to allow any such person into the house."

"Charlatans the lot of them," mumbled Zelda. "No help to anyone. Best to let nature take its course."

Of course, she knew all about Emaleen, about my sister's withdrawal from the world after Safya's murder, but Marna had hoped that the process of healing her mind would by now have begun, with or without bringing somebody in. She looked questioningly at Kallan, deep concern on her face. My uncle merely shook his head slowly, sadness etched on his handsome features, resigned to Zelda's intractable nature.

"Maybe you can help her Marna," I interrupted suddenly.

"Help her how?" asked Marna, a confused look on her rotund face. "I thought she barely came out of her room."

"That's true," I pursued. "She doesn't seem to *want* to see anyone and only comes out occasionally, but anyone can go to her room, and she doesn't stop you going in. She just lies there, not responding, refusing to engage. But if you went to see her you might get through to her. I'm sure she trusts you. And you're good at that sort of thing." My tone was pleading, desperate even.

"I'm more than happy to try Samek," Marna replied gently. "But you shouldn't get your hopes up. Emaleen trusts all of you too, but that doesn't seem to have helped much so far." We were surprised at Marna's words, which could be interpreted as a criticism of our efforts with Emaleen. But I could not imagine that this was her intention. She was merely stating the truth, and warning us that her influence may be no greater than ours where Emaleen was concerned. I was downcast by Marna's reply, and she, big-hearted and compassionate as ever, felt a need to lessen my despondency.

"I'll go and see her Samek," she said softly. "And see what I can do. See if I can help. But you have to remember that I don't really know her that well." I nodded slightly.

We continued to eat in silence, something Marna never liked. After a short period, she looked up and spoke, clearly deciding it was time to change the subject.

"The new Council members have been appointed," she said through a mouthful of food. "And they all seem fair, decent, if a bit insipid. But that's probably for the best isn't it? It's what we wanted. We don't want a repeat of Rannald!" I was slightly surprised at Marna's final comment, raising the spectre of Safya's murder, when what she was trying to do was to lighten the mood. As if sensing her error, she continued briskly.

"And there is good news," she added.

"Oh?" queried Zelda, as she continued to pile food onto her fork, her attention only half on what Marna was saying.

"Yes," went on Marna. "There was apparently talk of putting Devid on the Council, by way of replacement for Rannald, but this was roundly rejected." Zelda stopped toying with her food, and turned to stare at Marna, a look of disbelief on her face, rapidly replaced by one of outrage as her bushy grey eyebrows began to wiggle.

"You call that good news?" she said ominously.

"Y..yes," stammered Marna, not sure why Zelda was so incensed. "He was rejected, not voted for. That's good news, isn't it?" she asked, turning to Kallan for support. Kallan had no reply. Zelda appeared speechless, such was her anger, her mouth gaping open and closed. She slammed her knife and fork loudly onto the table top as she finally found her voice.

"How is that good news?" she bellowed, grabbing and then hurling a glass to the floor where it smashed loudly into many pieces, causing us all to jump. "How could he even have been considered? He's Rannald's nephew for fuck's sake! He has to have known what Rannald was up to!"

"We don't know that," replied Marna, attempting to calm Zelda down. "He can't help being Rannald's nephew. After all, he had absolutely no choice in the matter." Zelda stared open-mouthed at Marna, her face purple, her rage almost palpable in its intensity. Marna needed no special abilities to feel the fury coming from Zelda, and she wilted under the onslaught, holding her hands up as if to ward it off. My mother was rendered mute by the sheer intensity of her own ire. She stood up suddenly, hurled her plate at the wall where it shattered, leaving a trail of brown sauce in its wake. She waved a fist in Marna's direction. I leaped to Marna's defence, fearful that Zelda might actually strike her.

"Don't you dare!" I snapped at Zelda. "It's not Marna's fault that they considered Devid. She's just telling us the news. Just leave her alone!" Zelda snapped her attention towards me, her fist still clenched. I cringed momentarily, before remembering that I was at no risk - I could deflect any blow from her with a mere flick of my mind. I was immune from attack. Zelda knew this, and merely shook her fist at me, her impotence only fuelling her rage.

"And you young man," she snarled at me, poking vigorously in my direction with the first finger of her other hand. "You...you need to get on with that time travel stuff we were talking about and stop wasting your time gadding out and about with your wonderful new friends. Get on with it and help your fucking sister!" And with this completely unexpected change of topic, she stormed from the room as fast as her shuffling gait could carry her, leaving a wake of almost visible anger behind her. Silence reigned in the room for a long while. Eventually Marna spoke.

"Perhaps it's best if I leave," she said quietly. "I've never known her so angry with me."

"No! Don't leave!" I pleaded. I turned to Kallan, imploring him silently to back me up. He turned to Marna, a gentle, concerned look on his tanned face.

"Marna, don't leave" he implored softly. "Zelda won't come out of her rooms now for days. And she's not angry at you. Or not only at you. She's angry at so many things. As you heard, she hates the idea of her children leaving the house, going out into the world. She hates what happened to Safya, and how Emaleen is. Devid was just the last straw."

"And she hates the fact that she can't do anything about me," I added with a pout. "She can't stand the fact that I'm out of her control now, that she's impotent where I'm concerned." Marna turned to me and nodded. Zelda always wanted to be in control, to be the puppet master of everything in her life. She had made me, created me, and yet here I was free of her constraints. And the irony was that she had created me with precisely the unprecedented abilities that ensured I could be controlled by nobody, not even by her.

"That's enough now," interrupted Kallan in a quiet, yet determined voice. "Let's change the subject. And Marna, you must stay with us for a few days as planned. Let Samek take you to the woods, spend time with him, with Adwin if he'll agree. And with me," he added with a smile. "And please, go and see Emaleen. See what you can do. It certainly won't do any harm. And who knows, perhaps you will get through to her in a way none of us have been able to." He spoke this last comment in a sad, almost resigned tone, his voice little more than a sigh. We finished our meal, talking sporadically about other matters, though with no enthusiasm and a forced manner. I was not unhappy for the meal to end, and to be able to excuse myself. I leaped up and headed off as fast as I could to my own room.

Marna did indeed stay with us for a number of days, and despite the strained dinner of her first evening and the undercurrents of tension and unhappiness in the house, the remaining days passed surprisingly pleasantly. I did as Kallan suggested, and took her to the forest. Marna managed to persuade Adwin to accompany us, and she tried gamely to keep the atmosphere light and frothy, though even she found this a strain, her efforts becoming more and more forced as the day wore on and she singularly failed to help mend the rift between me and my brother. I suspect she was as glad as I was when we returned to the house. Kallan too spent a good deal of time with Marna, even managing to persuade her to help him prune bushes and fight feisty weeds in the flower beds. I laughed to see Marna's ample form on her knees, hands forced into gloves that were too tight for her pudgy fists, wielding a gardening fork with such lack of dexterity that it was hard to see what possible help she gave to Kallan. But I loved her for her willingness to share all our domestic activities and chores, her happiness in simply being part of the group.

As Kallan had predicted, Zelda did not emerge during Marna's visit, confining herself to her laboratory. In truth, I always preferred it when Zelda was absent, as the mood in the house was at such times calmer and more pleasant, lacking the air of tension that usually reigned when Zelda was out and about.

True to her promise, Marna visited Emaleen in her room. She told us, after her first visit, that she had simply sat on the end of her bed and spoken quietly to her, surprised to see that she had kept her blond hair shorn short, the red wound clearly visible. She had spoken about everyday matters both inside and outside the estate, and had even talked of Safya, telling Emaleen that Safya would not have wanted her sister to suffer in this way, that Safya would want her to carry on with her life, live it to the full, and not allow her grief at her sister's death to ruin another life. When I questioned Marna, she could not say if Emaleen had even heard her words, let alone be moved by them to change her ways. But she went into her room several times each day, softly chatting about this and that, each time reminding her towards the end of the visit about Safya, what Safya would want from her.

Adwin was unable to hold himself aloof from Marna, joining Kallan and me at mealtimes. My brother even managed to spend some time alone with Marna, something I suspect she went along with to try and ease tensions in the house. But after the forest walk, my brother would not join in with other activities if I were present. I felt pity for Marna as she made a great effort to keep everyone happy, her time and attention being dragged in different directions.

On Marna's last night, as she, Adwin, Kallan and I sat in the living room after dinner, talking about nothing in particular, a slight tension in the air caused by the fact that Adwin and I were in the same room together, I heard a strange sound approaching the door. I glanced up, and to my astonishment, I saw Emaleen standing shyly at the threshold, undecided as to whether to enter, swaying slightly on the crutches she was using to help her walk, a tremulous look of apprehension on her face. I had not seen her outside her room since the day of Safya's death, yet here she was, wrapped in one of her sister's green silk dressing gowns, feet bare, hovering outside the living room, looking strangely beautiful with her shaved head making her big slate-blue eyes appear enormous. Even her large ears did not detract from her stubble-headed loveliness. The others caught my mood, and followed my line of gaze. There was a mutual gasp of surprise as they saw Emaleen. We all held our breath, fearful that even the slightest sound or gesture would cause Emaleen to flee like a skittish doe.

Indecision racked us all, but after a few moments of absolute stillness Marna simply smiled gently at Emaleen. This mild, everyday gesture was all my sister needed. She manoeuvred herself clumsily into the room, unused to the crutches, and with tiny, hobbling steps, crossed to the sofa Marna was sitting on. Marna began to get up to help my sister, but Emaleen scowled lightly at her, seeming not to want any assistance. Marna sat back down as Emaleen turned, then dropped with a thump onto the sofa, laying her head delicately on Marna's shoulder. Marna reached her arm around my sister's shoulder, and with the lightness of a feather, pulled her closer. She stayed like that as we tentatively resumed our chatter, quietly at first, but gradually with more vigour as we realised that Emaleen was not about to flee, or try to as surely such would be impossible with a broken leg. The mood in the room was extraordinary. On the surface it was ordinary, apparently easy-going, no more than a group of friends prattling on about nothing of importance, all differences between Adwin and me forgotten in the moment. But underneath swirled a profound, unspoken joy that Emaleen had made the first step out of her grief and back towards a normal life. Kallan, sitting on the other side of Marna on the sofa, looked quietly ecstatic, surreptitiously taking Marna's hand in his. Marna responded by gripping it tightly.

We chatted long into the evening, staying up later than we normally would, none of us wanting to break the spell that had been woven by Marna. But eventually, as we noticed Emaleen's head lolling gently against Marna's shoulder from where it had not moved, Kallan decided that this was enough for one evening.

"Time for bed I think," he said, addressing in particular Adwin and me. "And Emaleen, my dear heart," he continued. "I think it's time you rested too." My sister opened her big sleepy eyes on being addressed by name. As she focused, she looked at Kallan, and to Kallan's enormous delight, actually smiled at him. A small, hesitant smile, but a smile nonetheless. Kallan visibly struggled to contain his tears, as it occurred to him that this was the first time Emaleen had smiled since the day of Safya's death.

Emaleen nodded slightly at Kallan, and then stood up, this time allowing Marna to help her. They were both stiff from sitting so long in one position without moving. As they stood, my sister leaning heavily on Marna for support, she leaned forward suddenly, kissing Marna on the cheek. As she did so she uttered two simple words. "Thank you." Marna merely nodded and smiled, also struggling to hold back her tears. As Marna helped my sister get her balance between the crutches, Emaleen then kissed Kallan too, to Kallan's enormous delight, and as she did so, Adwin and I stood up. We wished Marna and Kallan a good night, and then we left the room, followed by our sister as she swung forward between the wooden braces.

Adwin and I walked slowly in silence back towards our rooms, letting Emaleen catch up with us. As we arrived at Emaleen's room, she turned to us before she went through the door. She said nothing, merely flashed us a tiny smile, the look on her face saying it will all be alright now.' I sighed with relief and, leaving her to enter her room, again seeming not to want any assistance, my brother and I made our way back to our own rooms, not uttering a single word to each other as we did so, merely revelling for the moment in the profound change to our home in the last few hours, in the time since Marna had come to see us and had worked her benign magic. But as I left my brother to enter my own room, I knew that the short truce between us was temporary, engendered by our shared happiness at Emaleen's change of mood. The tension would not be long in making its return.

Adwin maintained his attitude of silent rancour towards me. Kallan tried a number of times to talk to my brother, to persuade him to put away his childish sulks, to accompany me on my next trip away from home, but with no success. After a number of such attempts, Adwin took to his bed, complaining of illness. It was hard to question this, as he was prone to such, but I knew that this time Adwin was not suffering from fevers or stomach problems, though he did a surprisingly good impression of the lassitude he generally complained of. I wanted to tell him I knew when he really was sick, and to tell Kallan that on this occasion he was merely feigning malady, but decided that this would only serve to intensify the already fraught mood that governed our relations.

I complained to Haari about Adwin's pretence on a number of occasions, and he suggested,

"Perhaps I can visit? Maybe I can bring your brother round to being less...less...difficult with you, maybe even cajole him into making a trip away?" I was reluctant to accede to Haari's suggestion, wondering if this might not make things worse, but as he pointed out, "Things are in such a parlous state anyway, what harm could it do?" I eventually allowed myself to be persuaded and brought Haari to see us.

I had not known that Kallan had invited Marna to visit on the same day. As Haari and I sat talking quietly in my room shortly after his arrival, musing on what to do about Adwin, I sensed Marna's use of the portal, and her presence in the house. I wondered whether they would like each other. I thought it unlikely anyone could dislike Marna, though with my limited experience of people I might be wrong in this. Perhaps her jovial bonhomie would grate on some people, be seen as superficial, forced even? And Haari, charming, smooth, urbane, I recognised how this could be perceived as slick, perhaps even artificial. I took Haari to meet Marna, and they seemed to take an instant liking to each other.

Kallan was not in the house when Marna arrived, so she, Haari and I withdrew to my room and talked. Marna first enquired about Emaleen, and I was able to report that she was beginning to take steps into the world again, slowly, tentatively, but with real progress. Marna nodded in satisfaction, saying that she would go and see her as soon as we had finished our conversation. I then shared with Marna my fears about Adwin's behaviour, hoping Marna would be my ally in this. She was adamant that all three of Zelda's remaining children must escape the confines of the estate, and from Zelda's control. Close as she was to her old friend, Marna did not feel Zelda's on-going influence over us was beneficial.

My portly friend listened quietly as I spoke of my recent problems with Adwin, and his current faked illnesses. Haari said nothing, perhaps feeling that it was not his place to intrude. I sensed Marna's liking of Haari grow even as I spoke, and as Haari held his tongue. It seemed odd, that one person could feel more for another person even where neither of them spoke. Marna seemed to enjoy no special gifts, yet I was beginning to learn that many humans enjoy a subtle, almost sixth sense, of the mood and attitude of another person even where that person remains quiet. I felt that Marna appreciated Haari's respectful silence, reading in Haari's face and his body language that he was our friend and ally in trying to solve the problem of Adwin.

When I finished speaking, Marna merely said "Hmmm," then sat quietly, thinking. After a few moments she looked at Haari.

"And are you here to try and help with Adwin?" she asked. Haari nodded. "And are you hopeful?" She continued, still addressing her comments to Haari.

"No, not at all," replied Haari. "Quite the reverse in fact. I thought I might be able to help, but now I'm here, I'm not at all sure." He glanced at me, raising his eyebrows, his amber eyes wide with query. I felt he was asking silently whether I could divulge our earlier conversations to Marna. I nodded slightly, indicating that he could.

"Adwin is worried," Haari continued. "He doesn't like that fact that Samek is beginning to move away from this place, fearing that he'll lose him." He paused for a moment. "And he resents the fact that Samek has a new friend, a good friend I hope. He's frightened that Samek will abandon him."

"I see," mused Marna, and then continued. "But that's absolutely ridiculous. Samek and Addy are closer than anyone I've ever met. Even though they are three years apart in age, they're inseparable."

"But that's exactly the problem," replied Haari, voicing my own thoughts. "Samek is separating himself from his home, and from his brother, at least in some ways. And Adwin knows it, knows it's inevitable and that there's nothing he can do about it. I think it's causing him so much concern that he doesn't know how to deal with it."

"Kallan wants him to make a trip with Samek, doesn't he?" asked Marna.

"Yes," I replied. "But he refuses. Or actually won't even consider it. And if I try to talk to him about it, or anything, he just refuses to answer me."

"But he has to make the leap. He absolutely must get away," insisted Marna with an expansive gesture of both her short sausage-like arms. Her insistence was surprising, and something in her tone alerted me to an underlying issue which I perhaps did not know about.

"I know he has to get away, Marna," I said tentatively, not quite knowing how to put my thoughts into words. "But why...why now?" I stared hard at my family's oldest friend, and was shocked to see a look of deep consternation on her face, a serious, concerned expression I had never witnessed before. Haari sat in silence, aware from the looks on both our faces that something important was happening, but ignorant of its cause. Marna glanced at me, a look on her face that I could only describe as guilt. She quickly looked away, uncomfortable with the intensity of my gaze.

"What is it?" I finally asked, unable to bear the suspense. Marna looked at me briefly, sharply, before allowing her gaze to drop again. "Tell me!" I insisted. She sighed.

"All Adwin's illnesses," she began. "You know he suffers from strange illnesses." I nodded, perplexed by what seemed a change of subject. "You've never found out what the problem is have you?" she asked, glancing at me. I shook my head, still none the wiser on the reason for her comments.

"Well they all stem from his provenance, from where he comes from. Or more accurately, from how he was made by Zelda." She glanced up at me, noting the look of confusion on my face. Zelda had commented on occasion that Adwin had been an experiment which had not worked the way it should. She had even described him as 'an experiment that went wrong'. I had not paid much attention to her words, had not given them much credence. I assumed she simply meant that some part of her plan with Adwin had not come to fruition. He seemed, apart from his tendency to sickness, his recent overreaction to the change in my life, to be little different from me or my sisters. He did not enjoy the same level of gifts as I did, but neither did either of my sisters. I assumed Zelda had used more progenitors with Adwin than she had with me in the hope of producing a person even more gifted than me, but for some reason this had not happened. This is how I interpreted her words 'a failed experiment'. I gave them no more weight.

"The illnesses stem from what Zelda was trying to do with Adwin," continued Marna, as if reading my thoughts. I sat back in surprise, but quickly realised that this made sense. I found it hard to understand Adwin's tendency to sickness in a world where sickness barely existed. And despite my best efforts at looking inside my brother's body, I had never been able to find the cause. More and more I had begun to wonder if his various maladies did not have their origin in his mind.

"I won't bamboozle you with the technical details," continued Marna. "But suffice it to say that there were problems during your brother's gestation. Things didn't work out the way Zelda had intended. I think she was trying to be too ambitious, and I told her so at the time."

"But," I added, then paused. "But if there were problems then why...why..." and I choked on my words, barely able to force out what I needed to ask. Marna peered at me with concern. I managed to squeeze out the ugly thought that had entered my mind. "Why," I whispered, "Did Zelda allow my brother to be born?"

Marna sat back abruptly, shocked by my question. Haari's rugged features showed confusion until he suddenly remembered what I had told him previously about the room full of aborted foetuses floating in tanks of yellow liquid. His eyes and mouth popped open in unison as he realised what I meant. Marna stared at me for a moment before replying.

"With your brother it wasn't the same as it was with all the others," she replied in a voice trying to sound calm, but tinged with distress. "With them, the problems were obvious. They were visible. With Adwin that wasn't the case." I furrowed my brow in confusion, so Marna continued with her explanation. "Adwin looked absolutely normal, seemed absolutely normal, as he still does. It was only later that the problems started to emerge, the illnesses, the weakness, the lack of anticipated gifts. And it's still not clear that all of this may stem from problems in his mind, not actually in his body."

"Is that all?" interrupted Haari suddenly, joining the discussion for the first time in a while. Marna turned slowly to face him, looking directly into his worn but handsome face.

"It's enough for Zelda," she replied with a little shrug. "She doesn't tolerate imperfection, especially not in herself, in her own work that is."

"When did Zelda first realise that Adwin wasn't...perfect?" I asked, my voice still little more than a hoarse whisper.

"When he was a few years old. When it seemed clear that his illnesses were not a short-lived anomaly, but something more serious, more permanent. And by then of course it was too late to..." and Marna stopped abruptly mid-sentence, her face registering surprise, and guilt, and anger with herself at having said so much.

"To what?" I asked. She looked down at the floor, twisting her chubby hands together, unwilling or unable to look at me. She stared fixedly at the floor, silent.

"To what??" I repeated more sharply. This time I would not accept silence as a response. I threw out a wave of coercive energy, something I would not normally have contemplated with Marna. But my urgent need for a reply outweighed my sensibility towards her feelings. She continued to stare at the floor, but had no option but to reply in a tiny voice.

"To terminate him. To terminate Adwin."

A deep silence met her words. Haari was as shocked as I was, perhaps more so. I had seen the aborted foetuses, some of them almost full-term babies. Haari had not. I knew Zelda well. Haari did not. To Haari the very idea of 'terminating' a small child, killing it simply because it offended Zelda's sense of her own worth, her own infallibility, was so shocking that for a few moments he held his breath. Finally he gasped loudly as his body forced him to breathe. He stared at Marna as if he had imagined her words, but he knew he had not. He then turned to me, and I saw the startled look in his wide-open eyes. I stared back at him, then something dragged my attention back to Marna.

She sat utterly immobile apart from the tiniest twitching of the tips of her stubby fingers, her gaze still fixed on the same spot on the floor in front of her. I knew in that moment that there was more, something she had not yet divulged.

"What is it Marna? What else is there?" I asked, so worried that I forgot to compel her to answer. She did not answer. She remained as she was, with the tiniest slow shake of her head from side to side as I heard the barest mumbling of the words "no, no, no," from her lips. I lost patience and entered her mind, an outrageous breach of privacy especially towards someone I felt such affection for.

"Oh no!" I whispered hoarsely as I read her primary thought. Then more loudly, "oh no! No! No!"

Haari snapped his head round to look at me, concern wrinkling his face.

"What is it Samek? What's wrong?"

For long moments I simply could not reply, so great was my distress. My mouth was dry and I had to swallow several times before I could find any voice. I turned to Haari and answered him.

"She thinks Zelda might yet get rid of Adwin. Terminate him," I moaned. Haari snapped his gaze back to Marna.

"Is this true?" he asked incredulously. "Is this really true?" Marna finally roused herself, looking up suddenly, her eyes filled with unhappiness.

"I don't know. I just don't know. But it's possible."

"Why?" persisted Haari. "It just doesn't make sense. Adwin is like a son to Zelda, one of her own. How could she do this, or even think it?" Marna continued to stare at Haari.

"Because every time she looks at him, she sees her own failure, her own incompetence mocking her. And she can't stand it."

"But to terminate, to *kill* a child because of that. It's...it's...monstrous!" replied Haari.

After a brief pause during which time I tried to assimilate what Marna had suggested, a thought suddenly occurred to me.

"Does Kallan know?" I asked Marna sharply. "Does Kallan know what Zelda might do?"

Marna shook her head slowly, gathering her thoughts before answering. "No," she replied quietly. "Or at least, I don't think so. I can't imagine how he would react if he did. Obviously he knows about the problems with your brother," she continued, looking up and straight into my eyes. "And Zelda must have complained about him being a failed experiment, probably on many occasions, but I don't imagine Kallan has ever really thought through what Zelda might mean by that."

"We have to tell Kallan," I announced. "If he knows what Zelda might do, he can stop her," I added, a hint of desperation in my voice. Marna and Haari both stared at me, wondering if what I suggested was a good idea or not.

From the perplexed expression on Haari's face, I saw that he could not decide, but Marna's face quickly cleared as she replied,

"I don't think that's sensible Samek."

"Why not?" I snapped. "How can it not help? Kallan is the only person who's able to reason with Zelda, to get her to do things. She doesn't listen to anyone else, not even to you," I added, scowling at Marna. She sighed loudly.

"That's as may be my dear," she replied, trying hard to maintain a calm tone. "But imagine what Kallan will feel if you tell him such a thing. And what I said about Zelda, I'm not really sure whether she would actually consider such a thing. It's just a thought really and..."

"You said," I snapped, jumping to my feet. "That Zelda might still choose to terminate my brother. That's what you said. That's what she said, isn't it?" I said, looking at Haari for confirmation. Haari looked uncomfortable to be getting dragged into the dispute, but backed me up, tentatively at least.

"That's what it sounded like you said Marna," he confirmed in a surprisingly hesitant voice.

"I was only voicing a thought," she replied defensively, but I was not to be put off.

"But you've still thought it, so it must at least be a possibility!" I replied. I stood quite still in front of Marna, unsure what else to say. She was clearly regretting ever having said anything, her face dejected as she once again stared down at the floor, shaking her head slightly from side to side, jowls wobbling as she did so. For all the distance that existed between my brother and me, I wanted to protect him from our mother, but Marna was surely right to be concerned at Kallan's reaction to being confronted with the possibility of Zelda terminating Adwin. Would it really do any good to inform my uncle, or would this simply cause him great distress without achieving anything concrete? Would Zelda really pay heed to Kallan's views on the issue? But I felt an urgent desire to do something. But what could I do? How could I possibly protect my brother from my mother, if she set her mind to something?

Chapter Forty-Four

Several years rolled by. Some time after my fifteenth birthday, more than two years since the murder of my sister, Haari was making one of his regular visits to my home and I sensed he wanted to say something but was wary of doing so. After a chat about nothing in particular, I could not withhold my curiosity.

"Haari. Tell me what you want to say," I encouraged.

"What do you mean?" he asked, surprised at my directness, and even perhaps at my perceptiveness. But he should have known by this point that it was impossible to hide things from me. Even without entering someone's mind, I could get a sense of what a person was feeling by their unconscious emotional signals. Over the past few years, I had worked on this skill, so it was becoming ever keener. I looked at him, saying nothing, but raising one eyebrow as if to say 'I know you want to say something!' He smiled slightly, knowing he was cornered.

"Alright," he continued. "I have a suggestion for you, but I'm nervous you'll say no." I was intrigued, and sat in silence waiting for him to say more. After a pause, he plunged in.

"I think you'd be really interested in a trip to one of the Institutes," he said. "The one I was brought up in. I'm still friendly with the woman who runs it. She's run it for years and years. What do you say?"

I was surprised at his suggestion, not having guessed what he would say. I knew all about the Institutes from my conversations with him, yet I had never been to one. I had ambivalent feelings towards them, these places where babies were produced in batches, called cohorts, in foetal tanks, and then raised in these cohorts to the age of fourteen. There they lived, played, were schooled, learned what it was to be human. This experience seemed alien to me, far removed from my own passage through childhood. Yet at the same time, I was intrigued by such places. They had, after all, produced the older members of my family, as well as Haari, Bartrem, Lisvet.

Despite my interest, my initial feeling was to say no, as such a trip would involve meeting a large number of people all at the same time. I was about to refuse, but, glancing at Haari's face, I hesitated. He looked anxious, perhaps that I would refuse, yet also showing such a keenness that I should acquiesce, that I did not reply immediately. I considered briefly, wanting to find a way to agree. Would it really be so bad? True, there would be many people at the Institute, but most of them would be children, many of these very young. And I was interested in such a visit, intrigued to see the foetal laboratories, and the places the children lived and played, spent the entirety of their lives before puberty and just beyond. Haari waited in silence, tension clear in the stillness of his body, the slightly anxious look on his face.

"Alright," I said eventually, with a trace of hesitation. "But you'll be with me?" I added.

"Of course, of course," reassured Haari, relief flooding his face and voice at my agreement. "And perhaps we can ask Adwin if he wants to come too." I frowned at his last comment. Through the course of the two years since my friendship with Haari began, the mood between me and my brother had calmed somewhat, was no longer fraught with tension as it had been. But it was not close, and I had never managed to return us to the relationship of brotherly love we had enjoyed previously. We had gradually negotiated an unspoken truce where we could spend time together, sometimes even just the two of us, but we spoke mostly about light and superficial topics. We studied together, played together, even renewed our trips to the woods, but no longer did we discuss matters of any significance, not even our favourite musings on what it must have been like to have lived before the Chaos. I tried, time after time, to raise more personal and intimate topics, but was rebuffed on each occasion. Eventually I knew that in order to have any relationship with Adwin I would simply have to avoid such topics, as each time I raised one, the tension quickly reasserted itself between us. And in particular Adwin did not want to hear about my trips outside the estate, my friendship with Haari, my meeting of people in the world. And Adwin spent more time alone than he would have done before, though quite what he spent his time on I did not dare enquire.

With my sister, things were much better. She gradually emerged from the depths of grief, once again taking her place in the family, and even started going out of the estate on trips into the countryside and elsewhere, sometimes even visiting Marna in her home. Emaleen and I, never really close as children, were less distant than before. Perhaps it was simply that as I grew up, the age difference between us seemed less important, or was it that with the loss of her sister, her other family members took on greater importance?

But when Haari suggested we invite Adwin along to the Institute, frankly, I did not want him to come. Perhaps Haari was trying to be helpful, but I did not want to share him with my brother, especially as Adwin seemed so resistant to hearing my tales of trips outside the estate with Haari. And I certainly did not want my first trip to one of the Institutes ruined by Adwin's mood, by the tense atmosphere which would surely reign between us if we were together outside the estate. I felt mean as I considered Haari's suggestion, and chose to keep the real reasons for not asking Adwin to myself: and for the first time since I had known Haari, I told him a lie.

"Adwin isn't very well," I mumbled, adding a thrust of coercive mental energy to make Haari believe me. He was a cynical man, prone to disbelieve people's words. And given that I had been brought up in such a tiny community of other people, lies did not come easily to me. But even with the mindthrust, Haari looked a little surprised at my statement.

"That's why you've not seen him today. He's in bed," I added hastily. This was a blatant lie. He was actually out in the garden with Kallan, but Haari could not know this. In case Adwin returned soon, and I would be discovered in my falsehood, I lifted my gaze from the floor where I had focused it as I had voiced my deceptions.

"Shall we go soon?" I asked. "Now?"

Haari laughed in surprise at my sudden eagerness, but did not question it. He probably assumed I was merely impatient to see the Institute. At least in this, there was partial truth. He nodded, saying,

"Yes ok. Minnie is expecting us any time. That's the woman who runs the place, who brought me up in fact. I asked her a while back if I could bring you some day, and she said just to turn up any time." He sighed in a theatrical way and continued. "Back to the hive which spawned me!" he said with a smile. I looked confused so he explained that the children in the Institutes often referred to their place of origin as a hive, producing large batches of similar creatures to carry out the communal will, much like in a bee hive.

Haari provided me with the location of the Institute, and I was astonished to discover how far it was from any towns or cities. He assured me that this was quite normal, and that it was considered most appropriate for a child's early years to be spent deep in the countryside, away from the world of adults. I knew that adults, of course, ran the Institutes, but that in each such organisation there would only be found the minimum number of grown-ups required for adequate supervision, education and upbringing.

Children's lives were mostly spent in each other's company, and this was one of the reasons why each child was allocated an uncle or aunt, from the time the child was five years old. The uncle or aunt regularly visited the Institute, took the child for visits to his or her home, to cities and other places, gradually increasing the exposure to the outside, grown-up world as the child grew older. And shortly after the child's fourteenth birthday, he or she would go and live with the uncle or aunt at least to the age of eighteen.

Haari lay his hand on my shoulder and I ported us to the coordinates he had given me, appearing moments later on a well-tended lawn in front of a large building. I stood for a moment to get my bearings, then slowly looked around.

The building before me, two storeys high, was solid and well-built, made of stone in various colours, its surface patterned to look like winding, creeping foliage, the stone made up of pieces of various shades of cream, light and dark greens, with an occasional burst of colour to represent blooms of reds and blues. Huge perspiglass windows ran the whole way along the front of the building, on both floors, tinted in various colours, though some clear. Many of the windows were open. Right in the centre of the building was a large door made of deep brown wood, jarred wide open to let the warm summer air flow through the house.

"That's the main building," explained Haari as I gazed at it. "It's got most of the classrooms, the educators' offices, the administration. You can't see it from here, but at the back is the large communal eating room and the kitchens, and behind them is another garden like the one we're in. The adults all live in a big building at the edge of that garden."

I turned around and saw a large, flat lawn, beautifully tended, with a number of buildings all around its edge. These were mostly one floor only, and Haari explained that these were where the children actually lived, where they slept, played in bad weather and spent much of their time. Each was made of wood, painted a different colour. The effect was strange, the grass encircled by long, flat buildings, red, blue, green and purple. Behind the bungalows large trees reared up and I assumed these marked the start of woodland.

"Yes," confirmed Haari when I asked. "But it's not like the forest surrounding your home. This is more like managed woodland, if it's woodland at all. It's really just a nice shady place for the children to walk, run, and play. And a little way into it, there's a stream and a small lake where we used to swim and go out in little boats. There's a rope across the lake, suspended between two big trees, and you can go from one side to the other on a wheel system attached to the rope, or just drop half way across into the water."

As Haari spoke, I remembered how he had told me how happy he had been here, how much he had enjoyed his childhood at the Institute, that he was glad he had had *his* childhood and not mine.

I heard a sound of voices, excited voices, mostly high-pitched, and suddenly children appeared, rushing out of the colourful bungalows around the lawn, laughing and shouting as they did so. I moved closer to Haari at the onslaught of so much noise and movement. He laughed lightly.

"Don't worry. They're just coming out to play before lessons start."

"Are they always so noisy?" I asked, still standing very close to Haari. He laughed again, more vigorously.

"Yes they are. As we were. As I told you, being brought up with so many children there's always noise and bustle, laughing and shouting. I loved it!" I stared at the groups of children as they raced across the lawn, or stood around in groups, thinking that there must also always be arguing and fighting, bickering and scuffling, struggles for ascendancy within each cohort, but I kept my thoughts to myself. Haari was so obviously happy, immersed in his nostalgia, that I did not want to intrude into his mood.

I tried to keep track of the various groups of children, remembering what Haari had told me about this Institute (and all the others, as they functioned on very similar lines). The laboratory attached to the Institute produced a batch of children, a cohort, once every three years for a particular Institute. Due to the method of disassembling and reassembling fertilised eggs to produce each cohort, cohorts were always numbered in eights, usually thirty-two or forty children. Fifteen embryos were produced from between three and five progenitors. When these had reached the eight cell stage, four or five of them were chosen, the most viable, and according to whether the cohort was to be all male, all female, or more usually, a mixture of male and female. As the number in a cohort was most commonly thirty-two, and a mixture of male and female, four embryos were generally chosen, two with double X chromosomes (the female) and two with XY (the male). These eight cell embryos were divided into their individual cells, each one of these then being used as the basis of a new embryo. This meant that every cohort was in effect made up of four or five groups of identical octuplets. When I asked Haari more about this, he shrugged, saying that in the cohort nobody really cared who was identical and who wasn't. The entire cohort was closely related anyway, as they were all produced from a maximum of five progenitors. I remembered wondering out loud what it would be like to meet all seven of Haari's octuplet 'twins', but he seemed to think that me wanting to was so odd that I quickly dropped it.

Since a cohort was produced only once in three years for a specific Institute, and children under five were raised in a different part of the Institute, where I was standing now there were only three cohorts. And from what I could see, there seemed to be one group a little younger than me, perhaps thirteen years old, so there must be another around ten years old, and the youngest would be about seven. This is indeed what the three chaotic groups on the grass appeared to be. With the milling and racing around, I could not do an accurate count, but reckoned it must number around a hundred children. No wonder there was such a cacophony and apparent mayhem. But as I looked more closely, I saw that for all the noise, each cohort, and smaller groups within the cohorts were in fact well organised. The children in the two younger cohorts were playing games the rules of which they clearly understood, though I had no way of knowing what such rules, or games, were. The members of these two cohorts interacted a good deal with each other, apparently not perceiving much difference between their two ages. The older children, some of whom were pubescent, or on the verge of puberty, held themselves aloof from the younger ones: I suspected they considered themselves to be closer to adulthood, and therefore did not want to engage in the undignified raucous play. But I saw that they had splintered into clearly demarcated smaller groupings, ranging from two to around five or six youngsters.

I was fascinated to watch normal children interact with each other, so limited was my experience. But my contemplation of them was interrupted when a girl, almost a young woman really, from the oldest cohort, spotted us. She was wearing emerald green shorts and a baggy short-sleeved bright red shirt. I noticed that all the children were dressed in a fairly similar way, not quite a uniform as there was a profusion of different strong simple colours, but all in simple practical clothing. Her dark blond hair was pulled back from her open and friendly face into a plait behind her head, though messy tendrils escaped at the front. She smiled and waved at Haari, and then crossed the lawn to greet us.

"Hello Haari," she said confidently. "It's good to see you back at the hive," she added, standing on tiptoes to kiss him lightly on one cheek. "And who is your friend?" she asked, turning to me.

"This is Samek," he replied, and facing me, he said, "This is Elza, Samek. She's the niece of one of my brothers from my cohort. Sometimes he's brought me along when he's visited her, and I've taken her out when he's not been able to."

"Nice to meet you Samek," Elza said in a confident, friendly voice, looking at me with great interest as she did. "I recognise your name. Is it a common name?" she asked. Before I could reply, Haari explained.

"There are a few others around with the same name, Elza," he said. "But surely you've heard of *this* Samek? He's the most famous person in the world and anything but common!" I reddened slightly at Haari's words, not happy to be described in this way, especially as Haari's voice carried a tinge of showing off, of showing *me* off.

"We get little direct news of the outside world here, but even I've heard of you Samek," stated Elza. "Aren't you the one who's been brought up outside an Institute, and if I remember rightly, you're made of lots and lots of progenitors?" Before I could reply, Haari interjected.

"Yes, nineteen of them. He's unique!" I frowned at Haari's description, but he seemed oblivious to my discomfort. "And his abilities are absolutely extraordinary, not like anything you've ever seen, or anyone's ever seen, for that matter."

"Well," replied Elza. "I'd love to know more, but we have to go in to class now." She smiled at me and Haari, and as she began to move towards the large building, she turned and asked me, "Would you like to join us?"

"Yes I would," I replied eagerly. "I've never been in a class before." Elza looked surprised by my comment and queried,

"But from what I've heard about you, you're well-educated, isn't that so?"

"Yes, but I've been educated, am still being educated actually, at home, by the adults I live with, often alone, or in the company of the other children in our house." I avoided the words mother, uncle, siblings, having no idea what reaction such words would be met with. Even what I said caused a sharp reaction of surprise on Elza's open and friendly face. I hastily continued. "What we've learned has been deep and wide, but basically unstructured."

"Why unstructured?" queried Elza. "Don't the adults you live with have a plan of what you need to know?"

"Not really," I replied, feeling curiously defensive even though Elza's query carried no hint of censure, merely curiosity for something unknown to her. "As long as we cover the basic subjects, we're free to follow any path to knowing anything we want in any way we want. So I've no idea what it's like to be in a structured class with lots of other people."

Elza smiled again and replied, "how extraordinary! Well come along then and see how our classes work. You're more than welcome."

"I'll come too," announced Haari suddenly. "It'll be weird being back in class again after so many years! I'm not sure it'll be entirely pleasant. I never was the best student." And he laughed wryly as he and I followed Elza through the open door, up the stairs to the first floor and into a classroom off the corridor which ran the full length of the building.

There were about two dozen small tables in the room, each facing the same way, and with a chair beside each one. The outline of a 3DV was visible hovering above each table, and as the youngsters took their places, they moved a hand in front of each one, causing the edges of the machines to become more defined, glowing slightly, awaiting further instructions. I was surprised to see only about half the cohort in the room, but Haari explained that classes often had half, or even less than half, of a cohort. A little above twenty was a maximum number considered appropriate, even in subjects like the one these young people were about to engage in: the history of the early post-Chaos era. Haari and I found places at the back of the class, sitting at two of the vacant tables.

As the young people settled, a very tall man with thin lanky legs, and long skinny arms dangling from narrow shoulders entered the room. He was around thirty years old, as far as I could tell, though I still found it hard to judge. I thought this seemed young to be an Institute educator. The class quietened down as they saw him move around the tables to the front of the room. He turned, and caught sight of Haari and me. He raised his eyebrows, but before he could speak, Elza spoke up.

"They're with me, Margan. Haari is my uncle's brother, and the other one is a good friend of his. His name is..." but before she could speak my name, the teacher, Margan, interrupted.

"I know perfectly well who he is. He's Samek." His tone was unpleasant and I sensed his dislike of me. I flinched slightly at his patent animosity. Margan said nothing more. He just glared at me, hostility transparent on his face. Surprised at the strange reaction to me by their educator, the entire cohort turned to look at me. I felt uncomfortable being the object of such attention, and heard whispering as the youngsters stared. Some of them knew who I was, and before long these had informed the others. I felt uncomfortable with their scrutiny, but took heart that none of the young people seemed to be showing dislike or antipathy on their faces. They simply looked interested, nothing more.

"Front!" said Margan loudly, causing all twenty pairs of eyes to snap back towards him. I breathed a sigh of relief. Despite their lack of animosity, I still found the intense stares of so many strangers disconcerting. I settled back in my chair as Haari glanced briefly at me with a tiny smile, by way of reassurance.

The class proceeded quietly as Margan spoke, and images appeared and moved through the 3DVs. Sounds and even smells produced by the machines added to the students' experience of the new world of those intrepid pioneers in the years after the Chaos, as they emerged from their shelters into the shattered remains of what had once been a beautiful planet. I watched over the shoulder of Elza, who sat in front of me, as images were shown of the first contact between the tiny dispersed groups of survivors, as they shared their fears, discussed the very real dangers they faced, the existential threats they had to deal with on a daily basis. But gradually they came together and after much disagreement, found a path towards salvation and survival. Many sacrifices had to be made, and many changes to the ways things had been done before the Chaos, some out of sheer necessity, others in an attempt to avoid setting out on the same trajectory which had led to the Chaos in the first place. I watched fascinated as images of greenery slowly spread once again across the world, assisted by a programme of reintroduction of the plant species that had been destroyed in the Chaos, yet whose seeds or DNA had been salvaged before the final throes of disaster. And then the same process with the re-created fauna was put into place, gradually repopulating the world with animals, though with far less diversity than before the Chaos, as most species had not had the benefit of having their DNA sampled and saved.

The founding narrative of our society was endlessly retold it seemed, and I was enjoying the class, apart from the continuous antipathy Margan seemed to show towards me. I had no idea why he felt this way, but it did not require any special gifts to know his feelings, so often did he flash me looks of malice. The rest of the class tried to ignore his mood, but it pervaded the room, and I sensed that it distracted many of the students from fully benefitting from their education. I considered entering Margan's mind, to ascertain the real reason for his dislike of me, but decided against it. I did not know if he enjoyed any special gifts himself, and knew that he would be outraged at such an invasion of his privacy. I decided to avoid the possibility and not give him any more reason to dislike me. I wondered why he did not simply demand that I leave the room: this was his classroom after all. Perhaps he feared what would happen if I refused. And how would he make me do so? The whole world knew of my gifts, so surely he was aware that I could not be compelled to do anything I did not want to do. And if he told me to leave, and I refused, his authority with the students would be undermined, his credibility brought into question.

The lesson reached the point where the new citizens raised the possibility of multi-parent children, and to my surprise, Margan instructed his students to turn their 3DVs off at this point, so they could engage in a verbal discussion of the issue. Something in Margan's tone alerted me to danger, and I sat up straight in my chair, fully attentive to what he was saying.

Sensing my sudden change in mood, Haari tensed, wondering what had happened.

Margan began innocently enough, merely explaining the decision to take reproduction away from individuals and to put it in the hands of the Council, or as he explained it "in the hands of all the people, and not just as a result of a sporadic and haphazard encounter between two sets of genitals". He then asked a series of questions about the actual techniques used to produce the embryos, and appeared satisfied with the students' replies. I was amazed at the level of knowledge these thirteen-year-olds had in this area. As I was considering this fact, I heard a communal gasp from the youngsters sitting in front of me. I had been so busy thinking that I had missed something Margan had just said, but it had clearly caused a stir. I noticed Haari staring at me, trying to gauge my reaction, and I was cross with myself for drifting off into my own world at what must have been a crucial juncture. But I had no need to berate myself for missing Margan's comment, as he had every intention of continuing in the same vein.

He was telling the class about the abortive early experiments in producing foetuses from more than five progenitors, explaining why such experiments were such a disaster, forcing the Council to ban them from that time forth. But instead of focusing on the scientific reasons for the problems, he instead spoke mostly of the morality of producing such foetuses. I sat in stony silence as he pontificated about the distortion of nature, the unnaturalness of foetuses "and even children" created from "too many progenitors". I could not understand the points he was making - surely taking reproduction away from people in the first place, producing foetuses in tanks, and using the gametes of up to five people were all unnatural acts, distortions of nature, albeit ones that our whole society accepted and agreed on? How could using the sex cells of more than five people be any more unnatural? Surely this was merely a question of detail, and not of principle? Yet Margan clearly felt there was a deep divide between what happened in the Institutes, and what Zelda had done. And despite the fact that Margan did not mention Zelda or me by name, there could be no doubt to anyone in that room that the object of his invective was me, sitting quietly, at the back of his classroom.

I became more and more angry, until I sat fuming, but with no idea what to do, whether to storm out of the room, stand up and argue with him, or even silence him. I was so incensed that the idea of hurting him came into my mind, punishing him for his words, and the thought felt pleasurable. As if following my thoughts, Haari looked across at me anxiously, fiddling with his earlobe, as I opened and closed my fists. His glance distracted me momentarily from my anger, and for a fleeting moment I wondered whether hurting Margan would only serve to underpin the educator's words, perhaps suggesting to some of those present that he was right. But my brief moment of relative calm was abruptly shattered by Margan's next words.

"And we all know that a child produced from too many ancestors is utterly abnormal, monstrous."

I could not contain myself. At the word 'monstrous' I leaped up from my chair, shaking with rage as I did so. My action caused the heads of all the youngsters to swivel instantly in my direction, apprehension mixed with excitement showing on their faces as they contemplated my livid features.

"How dare you!" I bellowed. "How dare you! You stand there as an educator, trusted by your students, and fill their heads with such...such wickedness. You have no idea what you are talking about, yet you go on and on, knowing how offensive your comments are to me, a guest in your class." I strode towards him, the young people in front of me leaning aside as I forced my way through them. I stood right in front of Margan, pulling myself up to my full height, still almost a full head shorter than him. Yet I saw fear in his eyes, real fear. He knew very well what I was capable of. He must have seen my performances at the two Council events, at the first of which I was still a small boy. And the virtual reality games about me had created all manner of stories about my gifts, leaving people in some confusion about the full extent of what I could do if I chose to. I knew that rumours abounded that I had caused Rannald's fatal heart attack. Margan trembled visibly as I glared at him, and I knew he was regretting his barely veiled attack on me. We locked eyes, mine blazing with anger, his wide, unblinking, filled with foreboding.

I had to force myself not to lash out at him. All eyes were fixed on me, watching what I would do. If I punished Margan in any way for his comments, my guilt in this would be clear for all to see. I breathed in and out loudly in an effort to become calm. Haari had moved up beside me, and laid a hand on my forearm, which now was stretched in front of me, my fists clenched with agitation and rage. His presence was enough to remind me of what I could do if I chose, yet what I must not do. But I had to speak.

"You are a nasty, wicked man," I said. "You tell your students that people like me are monsters, when I'm sitting in the very same room. You think you can get away with it. How do you dare? How do you dare? I...I..." I had no idea what else to say. As I spoke, my anger flared once more. I felt Haari's grasp strengthen on my arm and shook it off. I knew I should leave the room, but before I could force myself to take a step, without planning it, I thrust a mindslap in Margan's direction, causing him to reel backwards so hard that his head crashed into the wall behind him with a loud thud and a shout of pain. He slumped to the ground leaving a scarlet snake of blood from the back of his head all the way down the wall. He lay unconscious on the floor and through my rage I wondered if I had not gone too far. But I could not have left him unpunished. I turned and fled the room as fast as I could before I lost control and unleashed something even more damaging on him, on this person who felt so secure in his bigoted beliefs that he felt no compunction in insulting me to my face. Well I had wounded him in return, I thought with a surge of satisfaction, as I raced away.

Chapter Forty-Five

I rushed headlong down the stairs, and did not stop until I stood in the middle of the lawn. I halted my hasty steps, standing still, taking deep breaths as I tried to calm my beating heart and outraged feelings. I struggled to control my desire to hurt Margan further.

Moments later Haari rushed up to my side, accompanied by a flushed and animated Elza. I was shaking with anger, and with the effort to control my hunger to inflict more pain and harm on that dreadful man. I lifted my head, looking Haari in the eyes. He saw my conflict, fearing what I might do.

"No!" he said in a firm but quiet voice. "Don't. Don't do it. Don't do anything."

I stared at him, war waging within me. On the one hand a yearning to use my powers to crush that insect. On the other hand, reason trying to force its way into my emotions, calming me, telling me that Haari was right. After a few tense moments, reason gained the upper hand. I breathed out loudly, not having even been aware of holding my breath. I was grateful for Haari's soothing presence, steering me away from an ill-judged action, the repercussions of which I could not predict. Gradually my breathing returned to normal, my fists opened, my body ceased its trembling.

"Come and sit down," suggested Haari. "Over here. There are benches around the lawn." I allowed him to shepherd me across the grass to a brightly painted bench situated in front of the red bungalow. Elza followed us slightly nervously, not knowing if her presence would be welcome at such a fraught moment, but as Haari and I sat down, she plucked up the courage to ask in a small voice,

"Shall I go and tell Minnie you're here?" Haari nodded, and flashed Elza a tiny smile. She trotted off briskly towards the big building, her tightly braided hair bouncing on her back as she moved. Before I could say anything, Haari leaned towards me and spoke quietly.

"What he said was disgraceful, and so offensive. And that blatant change of topic from history to genetics just to be able to make his views about you obvious." I opened my mouth to speak, but Haari interrupted. "But surely you know you can't lash out every time someone says something you don't like?" I scowled, but remained silent, my expression clearly saying 'Why not?' Haari was not put off by my sulks, merely continuing quietly.

"In my humble opinion and for what it's worth, I think that Margan is a nasty piece of work, and personally, I'd happily give him a good smack. But we don't do that. And especially *you* can't do that. You have to control yourself."

"Why?" I interjected angrily. "Because I'm a monster and monsters need to behave?" I knew it was a childish reaction, but I had to say it. Haari sighed, shaking his head slightly.

"No," he replied, ignoring my puerile tone. "Because of what you're capable of. As you told me yourself, you can kill someone with just the tiniest flicker of thought. As you're well aware, people are nervous of you because of this, and with good reason, so you need to show the world that you won't misuse your abilities." I continued to sulk, though with less conviction. I knew Haari was right. I should never reveal my powers to the world in this destructive, damaging way. To do so only gave credence to those who claimed I was a monster, adding fuel to their conviction that a person who did not conform to their eugenic principles was an abomination, for whom such behaviour was normal.

Haari continued to sit quietly beside me, his calm manner acting as an easy balm to my agitated emotions.

"You know what you need?" he asked abruptly. I turned to him, curiosity in my face. I tried to maintain my scowl, but for some reason I was never able to do so for long with Haari, and now his tone of voice captured my attention, sweeping my sulks away.

"You need to find some system, some technique to use when people like Margan insult you," he said. I looked at him queryingly. He continued. "Do you remember when I told you ages ago that I'd got over my wild period during my youth by using one of the ancient world's philosophies?" I nodded, remembering his words well. "Well, perhaps you could try the same?" he suggested tentatively. I looked at him, my brows knitted.

"This isn't really the time or place for a full discussion," he went on. "But a few comments now might help, and we can chat further later." I looked at him keenly. He smiled slightly at my change of mood, and spoke.

"I read lots of old philosophies during my youth, and quite a few made sense, but the one I liked best, that I found the most accessible and manageable was Stoicism. I think it might have had its origin in the even more ancient Buddhism, but I'm not really sure. I just read that somewhere." He paused to look at me. I had heard the words Stoicism and Buddhism, but knew little of what they meant. I waited quietly for him to continue, which he did after a moment's pause as he scratched his head, collecting his thoughts.

"In a nutshell, you have to realise that some things are out of your control, so there's no point letting them worry you. Believe me, even you can't control everything - you can't stop people thinking things you don't like or saying things that irritate you or make you angry. So there's no point even giving these things much thought, if any at all. If you can't change something, drop it, let it go. There's no point doing something pointlessly. So when an idiot like Margan goes out of his way to offend you, laugh at him, or ignore him, but don't let him make you so angry that you lash out at him. As the stoics might have phrased it - don't allow him to disturb your tranquility."

"But I *can* change things," I replied, a hint of a pout re-establishing itself on my bottom lip. "I have control. I can punish him, hurt him, stop him saying things like that again if I really want." Haari ignored the pout, but replied to my comment.

"True, but as I said, you can't stop what's in his head or whether he says it in the first place. And even you can't control the minds and thoughts of the entire world."

"And even if you could," he continued. "You mustn't. If you controlled everyone's thoughts, what sort of person would that make you? Worse than those who insult you. You'd be the supreme being in a world full of non-people, non-humans, beings who had had their freedom, their will, taken away from them. What sort of world would that be - one you'd like to live in? And what sort of life would it be for you?" He stopped, and I stared at him. I knew he was an intelligent man, but I had rarely heard him addressing such profound questions, questions touching on the nature of what it meant to be human, of the point of being alive.

"And there is no point living a life it it's not a good life, a well-lived life. You need to find a place for yourself in this world, Samek, but not mis-live the one life you have." He tailed off, and fell into silent thought. I gazed at him in total surprise. The expression in his deep golden eyes was so sincere, and his eagerness to share his thoughts with me to help me live the best life I could was so transparent, that I was moved.

"We can discuss another time," he said, as if wishing to change the subject after so much seriousness. "I see Elza coming back with Minnie."

I followed his line of sight, and saw the brightly-clad Elza walking towards us accompanied by another, very different woman. One very young, barely out of childhood, the other old, the oldest person I had ever seen. As they approached I watched them carefully, especially Minnie. She was substantially older than Zelda and Kallan, even than Bartrem. I remembered Haari saying that she was the director of this Institute throughout his childhood. Given his current age of around forty, or perhaps a little more, I tried to work out how old she might be. I imagined that no-one would be allowed to achieve the position of director of an Institute without substantial experience of children beforehand. And I surmised that very young adults would not be allowed to occupy positions even of junior educators or carers of children, this being one of the most important jobs in the world. Margan was probably about as young as anyone working in the Institutes would be, and he looked to be at least thirty, possibly more. If Minnie had been director over forty years ago, and had built up substantial adult experience for years before that in more junior positions, I estimated she must be at least seventy-five, and probably a good deal more. Before I could ask Haari, Elza and her companion reached our bench. Haari leaped up, and I followed his example.

"Haari, my dear boy," said Minnie in a surprisingly strong voice. "One of my favourite students!" Haari laughed as he gently embraced the elderly woman in front of him.

"Hardly," he replied. "As you well know, I was nothing but trouble when I was here at the hive."

"True," said Minnie with a hint of a smile on her face, still healthy-looking despite her age. "But we all loved you anyway. No matter what shenanigans you got up to, you always had a charm about you that was hard to resist." Haari blushed at her words, looking down at the ground, shuffling his feet in a surprisingly childlike manner. Minnie then turned to me.

"And welcome to you Samek," she said, holding out both her hands. As I grasped them she continued. "Haari has told me a lot about you, and I've been very keen to meet you." I was pleased at her words of welcome, and at her discretion in not saying that she knew all about me from my unwanted fame in the world. She was delicate enough of my feelings to suggest her only knowledge of me came from Haari, though I knew this could not be the case.

"Thank you, er...," I replied, unsure how to address this person so much older than me.

"You can just call me Minnie," she said with a little smile. "All my friends do, and as a good friend of my dear Haari, I hope we too can become friends."

"Thank you, Minnie," I said, and did not know what else to add. She sensed my slight hesitation, and continued.

"Elza has been telling me about Margan, his unacceptably rude comments about you just now. I am so sorry that you had to experience this, and I promise you I'll have words with him. It won't happen again. Elza also told me that he slipped and fell, and hurt his head. I hope it's not too serious." I glanced at Elza and wondered if she had lied to the director of the Institute. But I realized that she could not have known what I had done, and must really believe that Margan had simply stepped backwards away from my anger, and that his 'fall' was an accident.

But Minnie's words also brought back my anger, and I could not refrain from speaking out.

"I want him dismissed," I said simply. Minnie looked confused.

"Dismissed?" she asked briskly. "What do you mean?"

"Dismissed," I snapped. "Removed from his position here." Minnie was shocked at my words, at their meaning and their intensity. Elza too was visibly taken aback. I felt Haari tense beside me, perhaps in disapproval of what I had said. I ignored him.

"He's not a fit person to be educating children," I added, sounding confident despite my total lack of experience of normal education. "So he must go. Be removed from office." Minnie stared at me, unsure how to respond to my demand. I was fifteen years old, still a boy in Minnie's eyes, barely older than the children in the oldest cohort under her direction, and she was not used to being spoken to in this way by one so young.

"I understand your feelings, Samek," she began, in a tone intended to sound sympathetic, but actually coming across as patronising. Understand my feelings she might, but dismiss them she certainly did. "But this is something you know nothing about," she continued, in a sharper tone. "And with respect, it has nothing to do with you."

"With respect," I replied archly. "It has *everything* to do with me. He is not fit to teach, so shouldn't be teaching. And I'm sure there is no shortage of other people. Far better people."

"Are you sure, child," replied Minnie, using a tone of voice I assumed she used to silence dissent from among the children in her care, "That you're motives aren't more about revenge for your own hurt feelings rather than any concern for the children Margan teaches?" I paused before replying, considering whether her words carried truth. I decided that she was half-correct. I did indeed wish to punish Margan further for the outrages committed against me, but I also, sincerely, did not consider he was fit to mould young minds, to be responsible for what the next generation would think, and in particular, what they would think of me. Before I could formulate a reply, Haari intruded into the conversation. I cringed as I heard him draw breath to speak, wondering what he would say.

"Samek," he said in an unusually quiet voice. "I agree that Margan isn't necessarily the best person to be teaching suggestible youngsters. But surely you know his views aren't that uncommon? If we sacked everyone who thought like him we might struggle to get enough people to train our youngsters in the hives."

I glared at him, angered by what I felt was a betrayal. And I did not appreciate being reminded of just how many citizens found my existence troublesome, offensive even. I did not know how to respond.

Minnie looked gratefully at Haari, a faint smug smile on her face. Behind Minnie, Elza was scowling slightly. I sensed that she disliked Margan, and would be happy to see him dismissed. I wondered if some of the other young people felt the same way.

"We'll that's that then," said Minnie dismissively, assuming the matter to be closed. I struggled to contain my anger but one glance at Haari showed me that he too seemed ready to move on to another topic. I drew a deep breath in preparation, but for what? To physically remove Margan from the Institute? To what end? He would surely simply come straight back when I was no longer there. And if what Haari said was true, any replacement for him might be no better. I scowled, squirming with frustration as I realised I had no suitable options in this situation, no outcome I could engender which would please me.

Haari looked at me keenly, anger clear on my face and in my posture. He shook his head very slightly, almost imperceptibly as he mindspoke.

~No Samek. Don't do it. Don't do anything. It will only cause problems for you.~

I continued to squirm for a few more tense moments before the realisation hit me that I was, in effect, powerless in this situation. Powerless to achieve a result that would satisfy me without creating a backlash against me among the citizens. I closed my eyes and forced my anger to subside.

Minnie, assuming the conversation to be at an end, nodded at Haari, then turned a supercilious smile on me.

"Let's hope your next visit, child," she began. "If there is one that is," she added. "Will be less...fraught." She turned to move away, turning her head to add a final comment. "And that you will be less...demanding about things which have nothing to do with you."

Before I could muster a reply she pushed brusquely through a group of youngsters hovering, fascinated, nearby, who had followed me out of Margan's class. Despite her apparent air of haughty victory, the set of her shoulders suggested she was irritated, annoyed by a child making demands on her in her own Institute.

As soon as Minnie had disappeared through the doors of the building, the whole group of Elza's colleagues rushed towards us, crowding around us, asking questions, chatting to me and to each other, a mobile rainbow of bright cheerful-coloured clothing. In my usual plain and sensible garments, I felt like a dowdy sparrow in a flock of birds of paradise. They had heard the interchange between me and Minnie, and though they had great respect for their director, it seemed that none of them much liked Margan. I saw in their faces that they were disappointed that he was not going to be dismissed, and perhaps even admired me for standing up to Minnie as far as I did. As I also sensed no hostility to what had occurred in the classroom, I could only surmise that these youngsters had all interpreted the event according to the evidence of their own eyes. I had merely stood angrily in front of their educator, he had stepped backwards and had fallen, hitting his head. Despite all of them knowing who I was, it did not seem to occur to any of them what I had actually done. Perhaps they knew little of my full abilities? Or was it the innocence of childhood transferred to the behaviour of another child?

My initial reaction to being surrounded by strangers was one of panic, reminding me as it did of my distressing first trip to the centre of Beyra. But I quickly overcame my disquiet as I realised, to my utter astonishment, that these strangers were on my side, were friendly, sympathising with me for not getting my way with Minnie, simply happy that I had come to their home today. As I looked round at the smiling, encouraging faces, I smiled back, tentatively at first, but then more broadly. I saw Haari hovering in the background, wondering how I would react to being in a crowd, sensing perhaps that I was still irritated with his lack of support for me with regard to Margan.

"Come on," said Elza loudly enough to be overheard by everyone. "Let's show Samek around. Show him where we live. Would you like that?" she asked, looking at me.

"Yes I would. Very much," I replied, putting the frustration of Margan behind me. She smiled and grabbed my hand, dragging me off as the others all followed. I glanced round nervously to see if Haari was following. He merely stood beside the bench, tension in his manner.

"Can Haari come too?" I asked, smiling at him slightly to show that I harboured no grudge. Elza and the others turned to look at him, Elza cocking her head to one side.

"Yes why not," laughed Elza after a fractional pause, though I suspected more for effect than through genuine deliberation at my question. "Bring the old man along too!" We all chuckled, Haari as much as anyone else as he moved to catch up with us. We moved off as a group, chatting and laughing, and I realised that this was the first time in my life that I was involved in something in which I was merely a part, no more or less important than any other part, and the feeling was good.

Chapter Forty-Six

We began in the living quarters of the children, those brightly painted wooden bungalows which encircled the wide expanse of lawn. Each cohort slept in a long dormitory lined with beds along each wall. And there were bathrooms, and a range of other rooms I assumed were used for a variety of indoor leisure pursuits. I was surprised at the simplicity of the bungalows' interiors. The furniture was functional and practical, of good quality, yet lacking any hint of luxury. Each child had a locker and a small wardrobe for personal items, but these could not hold many objects. I realised that these children were raised surrounded only by the most basic comforts, without extravagance. Despite being brought into a world in which any object could simply be ordered via a central distributor, children in the Institutes did not appear to enjoy access to this service. When I raised this with Elza, she found my questions strange, almost laughable.

"But we have everything we want," she said with a smile and an expansive gesture of her arms around the inside of the bungalow. "What more do we need?" I had no answer to this, but I found the contrast between the sparse personal artefacts in the Institute and the luxury of the few places I had been in the outside world amazing. At what point did a young person, recently liberated from the Institute, develop a taste for comfort and luxury, opulence even? Were there people who eschewed this throughout their lives? Perhaps those strange people I had heard about who lived off the land out in the wilds were reacting in a way that was consistent with their childhood? As I considered this point, I remembered that Haari's home was fairly simple, at least where furniture and other household objects were concerned.

"Come on," said Elza, interrupting my thoughts. "Let's go and see the rest of the hive."

We returned to the main building, and I was shown the other teaching rooms, the administration section, the large communal eating room and the kitchens where the food was received. On our way through the kitchens, Elza and her colleagues liberated a whole tray of small cakes sitting beside a large portal, much to the irritation of a large red-faced man I took to be in charge of provisioning the Institute. He shouted at us, but the youngsters merely laughed as he shooed us out of the door. I had to react quickly to catch a cake Elza threw at me as we exited the kitchen. Haari followed behind us, looking vaguely embarrassed by our behaviour, mumbling apologies to the angry man, though Haari surely must have got up to much worse in his time at the Institute.

We walked back across the grass and through the trees to the small lake where I saw canoes and rowing boats tied up to the shore. I glanced up to see the rope Haari had reminisced about, stretched across the open water from one tall tree to another. A brook entered the lake at one end, exiting the other. There were no children here at this time, all the others still being in class. The twenty or so accompanying me now were in high mood, having escaped Margan's class in pursuit of Elza and Haari. I was astonished at the continuous talking and laughter, banter and general bonhomie. What must it be like to be endlessly surrounded by so much joviality, so much companionship, so much noise? I could not help but contrast this with my own childhood, locked away as I was in my quiet prison. A comfortable prison, all in all, but a prison nevertheless. I was conscious, however, that for all the conviviality of the Institute, these youngsters were also prisoners. I knew they were not permitted to leave these environs before the age of fourteen unless accompanied by an adult. Was this simply another type of jail? Were children always incarcerated in this way? And if so, which prison was preferable - my peaceful, luxurious isolated one, or this loud, jolly, sociable yet spartan one?

From the lake, we walked further through the light woodland, towards what Elza called the Laboratory. This was the group of buildings where the actual creation of the foetuses took place, where they were incubated, then brought out into the light, and where the babies remained until they joined the older children shortly after their fifth birthday. I felt deeply ambivalent about visiting the Laboratory. Part of me was fascinated by the idea, to see where life began for everyone in this home so unlike my own. Yet I also felt on edge that I might find some aspects of the Laboratory distressing, that I would be reminded of Zelda's experiments with multi-parent embryos which she had forced me to witness in her laboratory on the estate.

As I glimpsed the laboratory buildings through the trees I fell silent. I remembered the long rows of foetal tanks in the locked room at my home, the line of grotesque, preserved remains of Zelda's abortive experiments suspended in their pale yellow liquid. With a shudder I recalled foetuses, some near birth age, with hideous deformities, with two heads, with spines that extruded through their skin, with hair covering their tiny dead bodies. Elza seemed to notice my sudden change of mood, and Haari's reaction to it, but she could have no idea of the cause. She turned to me and smiled slightly, cocking her head, a trace of query on her face. I forced myself to return her smile, but did not want to share the reasons for my anxiety.

As we reached the edge of the trees, we had to pass through a gate, barred across its top. The gate sat in the middle of a sturdy wooden fence which stretched in both directions, curving slightly away from the woodland as it did. As we passed through the gate, Haari explained that the smallest children, those under five, were not allowed access to the woods, the brook or the lake, as these were too dangerous for them. And the gate was locked in such a way that a tiny child would be unable to open it. I wondered whether children of six or seven were perhaps also too young to be allowed unfettered access to the lake, but when I asked this question, my query was met with laughter and blank incomprehension. None of the youngsters, nor Haari, could see any problem with allowing any of the older children the free run of the rest of the Institute.

We walked across another grassy area towards a large, unattractive, square building in front of us. Some attempt had been made to relieve the sheer outside walls by painting them in bright patterns, yet this did not hide the fact that this building was ugly. It looked to be made of concrete, or something similar, and was a simple elongated rectangle in shape, perhaps a storey or two high, though this was hard to judge as it did not have a single window. The building was long, stolid, almost menacing. We moved around one side of it, and I saw that behind it there was a brighter aspect. Close to the concrete block were a few painted wooden buildings, almost identical to the living quarters of the older children I had recently visited. And stretching away beyond these colourful bungalows was an attractive grassy lawn, surrounded by flower beds and bushes.

Elza explained to me that the low level bungalows were where the tiny children slept and lived, and the other buildings were their play areas, eating areas and so on. When I glanced at the huge concrete edifice beside us, she explained that this was the Laboratory itself. She asked if I would like to visit it, actually go inside. I was surprised that we needed no permission to do so, but Elza explained that the oldest children in the Institute were encouraged to take an interest in the process of creating babies, and were always welcome to enter the Laboratory in order to further such interest. I swallowed hard, once, then nodded, indicating that a visit would be most informative, though in what way, I dreaded to contemplate.

As we passed through the only door into the building that I could see, a double, opaque perspiglass entrance that slid apart automatically at our approach, I suppressed a slight shudder as I contemplated what I might be forced to confront inside. I was surprised that the entrance hall was bright and spacious, not dark and gloomy as I had anticipated. As we entered, we encountered a youngish man wearing the sort of white gown that Zelda wore when in her laboratory. The man smiled on seeing us, and spoke.

"Hello Elza, and the rest of you. That's a lot of you for a visit. What is it you want to see?"

"Hi Arnil," replied Elza breezily. "This is Haari who was brought up here. Though years and years ago, obviously," she added with a wink in my direction. "And this," she said, pointing at me, a hint of bragging colouring her voice, "Is Samek. He's visiting for the first time with Haari. He wanted to see the Laboratory." Arnil glanced first at Haari, showing little interest, but then turned to me, staring at me keenly for a moment. He seemed to know who I was.

"A good idea. Shall I show you round, or do you want to do it?" he asked, his tone suggesting he preferred the former.

"It's better if you do it," replied Elza. "Samek might have questions I don't know how to answer." Arnil nodded, turned, and led us out of the entrance hall.

We walked down a long corridor lined with small rooms. A few of them were brightly lit and in these could be seen scientists sitting at equipment-covered tables, or bustling about at activities I could not discern. Arnil explained as we passed these busy rooms that we could not enter them in such a large group nor without undergoing a sterilisation process. These were the small laboratories in which the actual genetic work was taking place - the fertilisation of the ova after choosing the appropriate sperm, the breaking up of the eight-cell embryos into eight separate new embryos, the earliest stages of the process of producing the new lives that would soon take their place in the life of the world. I stopped and pressed my face up against the perspiglass of one small room, amazed at the apparent simplicity and ordinariness of what appeared to be happening. New life was being made here, in almost miraculous fashion, yet all I could see were a few men and women in white overcoats sitting quietly at tables, manipulating small objects in front of them. Arnil gently coaxed me to follow him by explaining other aspects of the Laboratory's work.

"And shortly," he said, "We'll be in the main hall, where we have all the tanks, where we are gestating the next generation of children." I was slightly confused by his comment, and by the fact that there was such busyness in the small genetic laboratories.

"I thought you only created one generation every three years for each Institute," I began.

"Yes that's right," he replied, nodding.

"But if you have one-year-olds and four-year-olds in this Institute," I continued, judging that this must be the case from what I had seen so far, "Then why are the tanks gestating babies now? Don't you have to wait another few years?" He smiled in a faintly patronising manner at what he clearly thought were foolish questions.

"Not every Institute has a Laboratory," he explained slowly, as if speaking to a small child, or an idiot. "That would be terribly wasteful. All that effort and equipment for only thirty-two or forty babies every three years! What would we do with it in between, and with all the scientists? We provide babies for a number of Institutes, so we are busy all the time, and when one generation is brought out of their tanks, we are preparing to fill them again with the next batch."

What he said made sense, though I was surprised to hear it. It made the whole process seem even more like industrial production than I had initially supposed: automated production of factory babies. Where was the uniqueness of each human life, when it began in such mechanical, dispassionate fashion? But was my origin any more special? In one way I was unique in the world with my nineteen progenitors, but did this mean I was more of an individual than any of the youngsters crowding around me, all of whom had been manufactured in this high-tech, mechanised and impersonal way? I knew I could not claim such uniqueness, and that I was in no way any more human than any of them. What does it matter a person's provenance? Surely all that matters in the end is what sort of human being each person becomes?

We entered what I surmised was the main hall, passing through another automated perspiglass door. I stopped in my tracks just inside the entrance to the room, causing a bottleneck as the other youngsters tried to crowd in behind me. I was rooted to the spot as I found myself in a room eerily similar to the ghastly one at my home: a long hallway, little more than a wide corridor really, lightly lit foetal tanks positioned in regular rows all along its walls. I breathed deeply, trying to calm the agitation I felt as I was transported back to the dreadful day in Zelda's laboratory, the day she had physically forced me to witness the semi-human debris from her years of failed experiments. The horrors of her failures arrayed in neat rows, little twisted and deformed corpses floating lifelessly forever in their fluid-filled tanks, as she held me fast, forcing my eyes to witness abomination after abomination.

My moment of distress was obvious, even to the youngsters who had only just met me. But they were confused by what they saw as a bizarre reaction to simply entering a room they had all been in many times before.

Haari, however, knew the cause of my distress, as I had spoken to him of Zelda's aborted foetuses before. He spoke silently to persuade me to move further into the room, using the telepathic channel I kept open between us.

~It's not the same Samek, I promise you. This room is full of life, not death.~

I heard his words and took comfort from them. He was right. This was totally unlike Zelda's array of grotesqueries: this was a room filled with new beginnings. I pushed back my shoulders and indicated to Arnil that he could lead on and I would follow. As we passed the tanks, he explained the processes of taking the tiny embryos from where they had been created, and when they were sufficiently well-developed, they were transferred into the foetal tanks in these rooms. Here, they were attached to the artificial uterine walls via coloured pipes passing through the circle of jelly on the wall of the tank. Nutrients were provided through the coloured pipes, just as they had been in Zelda's laboratory. As this Institute was creating babies for a number of other similar locations, there were embryos at different stages of development. The smallest of them were little bigger than my thumb, tiny curled things with only the barest indications of the limbs and other body parts budding out of their almost fish-like little bodies. The largest were near full-term, babies ready to emerge into the light, each part of them fully developed. And these were tranquil, calmly dozing in their manufactured, translucent wombs, blissfully unaware that they were shortly to be dragged from their man-made sanctuaries, so typical of this stage of humanity.

The room truly was unlike Zelda's hall of horrors. Here was nothing but calmness, life and expectation of life, peaceful origins of tiny beings that would grow to become full and functioning members of their society. I was calm in this place, content to gaze at the wonders in front of me, to contemplate the happy futures stretching out before these tiny creatures. All thoughts of Zelda and her experiments faded to nothing. I turned to Haari and smiled, noting the relief on his face as I did so.

Eventually we left the Laboratory, emerging back into the strong sun of the late afternoon. Elza could see I had enjoyed my visit to the source of life immensely, but she must have had no understanding of why I seemed to be filled with such profound relief. For her, such a trip was commonplace: pleasant, but not particularly special. For me it had been a transformative experience, profoundly affecting my view of the miracle of life, and of the workings of my own society.

The rest of the afternoon, before Haari and I left the Institute, was spent playing with the smallest children. For the first time in my life I met a large number of babies, held them, crooned to them, grew alarmed when they cried. In my isolated life on the estate, the only baby I had ever met was

Adwin, and at the time I was little more than a baby myself. In addition to this, my brother had been a very quiet, intense baby. These warm, cuddly, noisy creatures were a mystery to me. I found it hard to imagine they would grow up, walk, run, speak, emerge from their incompetent and dependent state into fully-functioning human beings, autonomous and independent. Haari and Elza, as well as the other youngsters who remained with us, found my behaviour with the babies enormously amusing. My clear surprise, shock even, at the simplest antics of the tiny creatures, so ordinary to those accustomed to babies, created huge entertainment for my companions, and I did not mind in the least that I provided them such hilarity. It was benign, well-intentioned, and I even began to play up to it. The sense of belonging, of being teased in this gentle, almost affectionate way, was so unique to me, that I wished it to go on and on, and I made sure it lasted as long as I could manage.

And we played with the four year olds as well. As with the babies, I had almost no experience with tiny humans of this age, yet at least they seemed less unfamiliar to me. They were mobile, running around, speaking perfectly in their high-pitched tight little voices, and as such were small versions of older children, of adults even. They pestered us to pick them up, bounce them, swing them round, and seemed to relish surprisingly rough treatment, causing them to shriek with laughter, begging us again and again, without a break, to carry on with this physical play. Haari particularly was badgered constantly, as he was by far the biggest and strongest of all of us. He showed extraordinary patience with the tiny pests, and seemed to thoroughly enjoy the endless childish games. He laughed and joked, and I realised I had never seen him so relaxed, so abandoned in the pursuit of simple, child-like pleasure. I wondered if little children perhaps brought out this sort of mood, this state of being, in all adults, or was it only special grown-ups who responded to the tiny people in this way?

But all good things must come to an end, and as the light began to fade slightly into early evening, the carers of the four year olds, who had been content to step back and allow others to take some of the burden of their care away from them for a few hours, stepped in. Against the howls of outrage from their wards, they stopped the games and politely requested that we leave, to allow them to prepare their tiny charges for supper and bed. We thanked them for giving us so much latitude with the children, and they laughed, thanking *us* for giving *them* such a peaceful afternoon. They warmly insisted to Haari and me that we should return whenever we wished, and we promised them, and the children, that we would return.

We walked a little way from where we had played with the small children, accompanied by Elza and the handful of her cohort who had remained with us all afternoon. I did not want to port us away in view of the four year olds, as I did not know how they would react to our sudden disappearance from before their very eyes. But as we approached the gate into the other part of Institute, we said our goodbyes to Elza and the others, as they bade their own friendly, easy-going farewells to us. As I ported us away, I basked in the feelings of good-will and camaraderie that I had experienced this day, and realised that it felt so intense, so enjoyable, that it pushed the hostility of Margan, the dismissive attitude of Minnie, far into the background, rendering them almost without power. Was this what Haari had meant when he had spoken of not letting people upset my tranquility?

Chapter Forty-Seven

After my first trip to the Institute, I returned there regularly, despite Minnie's frosty reception towards me each time. Generally she avoided encountering me on my trips, which suited me very well. I suspected she would like to have banned me visiting, but that she feared my reaction were she to do such a thing. Haari insisted, however, that this was not the reason she did not forbid me visiting. He explained that nobody was ever banned from an Institute, and that Minnie would not have felt she had the right to do so. He added that citizens were expected to take an interest in how their society replenished itself, since most people would never have an individual child to care for. In my early trips I was always with Haari, though as I became more confident of spending time with groups of people, I occasionally went alone. Haari even managed to persuade me to invite Adwin to join us on one occasion, though seeing my obvious discomfort at having to share Haari with my brother and the tense atmosphere that pervaded the entire trip, he never suggested inviting my brother again.

"You need to patch things up with Adwin. Believe me Samek, you really must," Haari would exhort time and time again. But I did not know how. The rift between us seemed permanent and I had no means to bridge it. Though we had gradually arrived at a place where we could mostly engage with each other in a fairly calm way, ostensibly without tension, I knew it was not the same as before, and I feared that it would never be the same again. As I spent more and more time away from home, my brother became ever more isolated. He withdrew into himself, spending much of his time alone, and on the rare occasion I, or anyone else for that matter, tried to discover what it was he did with his time, he became secretive, shifty, and prone to giving vague answers to direct questions. I remember one particular day when we were studying together, working on a mathematical puzzle Kallan had set us, as he was wont to do in his attempts to force us back together.

I must have been around seventeen at the time or perhaps a little older, my brother three years my junior. I tried, obliquely, to discover what he occupied so much time with when not with me, but he skilfully batted away each indirect enquiry. Eventually I became exasperated.

"But what do you do all day when I'm not here? Just what do you do?" I asked.

Adwin turned to me, his dark-ringed eyes even more hooded than usual, his expression guarded and slightly irritated at the same time. I noticed that he had grown his hair out such that his near-black curly fringe fell across his brow, covering his eyebrows. For a long moment he simply stared at me through dark eyes, then spoke, quietly.

"That's none of your business," he replied, his new baritone voice surprising me with its masculine tones. Nothing more. Not another word of explanation passed his lips. He looked away as I continued to stare at him. I was nonplussed. Should I persist with my questions? But what would be the point. He showed no intention to elaborate further. Should I try to enter his mind to discover how he occupied his time? I briefly considered this though I was not sure of success with my brother who possessed some powers of his own. He must have known I was considering such an action, which was hardly surprising as he was well aware of my abilities. He lifted his eyes and glared at me from under heavy lids.

"Don't you dare," he growled. I tried to look innocent, as if misunderstanding his meaning. "Don't you dare," he repeated. I opened my eyes wider, in a futile attempt to enhance my feigned innocence.

"If you try to go into my head," he continued in an almost menacing deep tone at odds with his soft, still childlike face. "I will never speak to you again. Never." And I knew he meant it. I looked away, finding it impossible to hold my gaze in the face of this Adwin that I did not know. I knew he was hiding something, deliberately keeping a secret from me, but I was at a loss how to winkle it out of him without committing the outrage of entering his mind against his express wishes. My brother had grown a trim, dark goatee beard and short moustache, wispy at his young age, but much fuller than anything I could have managed at his age, or even at the age of seventeen. How odd I had not noticed this before. Where did he get the idea from? I wondered if he had taken inspiration from the paintings of the ancient playwright Shakespeare we had looked at together. Was that his role model? Was he acquiring fashionable affectations he had seen in images of people outside the compound?

As we resumed our joint efforts at the puzzle in front of us, I was invaded with a profound sadness as I remembered how close we had been as small children, and with a sense of helplessness at how to remedy the present coolness between us, how to take us back to that time of happiness and camaraderie.

After a few moments working on the puzzle, Adwin rendered me speechless with an additional comment.

"If you must know," he began in a quiet voice. "I often go out too. Out into the world." For long moments I simply could not respond, so astonished was I at my brother's words.

"But...but where...where do you go?" I finally managed to stutter. A tiny, barely perceptible, enigmatic smile played at the corners of Adwin's lips. He was enjoying my amazement. Without even glancing up at me, dark eyes fixed on the puzzle in front of him, he replied.

"And that is also none of your business." I was simply too taken aback to pursue the matter, certain as well that he would not divulge any further information. How unlike me he was. I was happy to share my experiences.

I enjoyed my trips from home, especially to the Institute. I got to know many of the children there by name, developing real friendships with some of the older ones, then telling my family about my encounters. Only a year after my first trip, Elza's cohort left the Institute and went to live with their uncles and aunts in cities and towns around the world. A few of them, Elza included, I kept in regular contact with, visiting them and even bringing some of them to the estate. Elza was a regular visitor, fascinated by the life I had led as a child. Elza was eight years younger than Emaleen, but she helped Emaleen come out of the grief she had suffered from since the death of Safya. Elza was an inexperienced young woman, keen to spend time with another woman, only eight years her senior, whom she felt to be worldly. In truth, Emaleen was hardly any more worldly than Elza given her isolated upbringing on the compound, but to Elza she must have seemed mature, sophisticated, full of arcane knowledge of what it meant to come into womanhood. And Emaleen responded eagerly to the attention, almost always joining Elza and me on Elza's visits. Kallan was delighted with Elza, not only for herself, but also for the effect she had on Emaleen. Curiously, my sister chose to keep her hair shorn, barely a centimetre long, despite the fact that her head injury was long-healed. And I noticed that she walked with a slight limp, something rarely seen in our world, presumably due to the hasty patch-up of her broken limb after her tumble from the cliff, so keen had Zelda been to drag Emaleen along with the rest of us to accuse the Council of murder.

Emaleen enjoyed telling us about her trips from home, into the wilds she had enjoyed so much with her sister, or to visit new friends. She and I grew closer as we exchanged stories of our lives outside the compound. A topic we often discussed was teleportation, and we even broached the subject of time travel, wondering if it would be possible for me to acquire this skill. Was it really so different from teleportation? Could similar techniques be used to take the far more impressive step of not only travelling in space, but also in time? Left unspoken, but hovering in the air between us was the spectre of Safya's murder: if I were able to travel back in time, could I prevent my sister's death? We reached no conclusions in our chats and avoided raising the tantalising possibility of saving Safya, but we continued to eagerly explore different aspects and problems of travelling in time.

My enjoyable experiences at the Institute assisted me in gaining the confidence to try again to get out and about among ordinary people, and, accompanied by Haari, I braved the Beyran hordes, gradually becoming inured to being among milling, noisy, gaudy crowds. As people saw me often in Beyra and other cities, they gradually became accustomed to me, so the problem of them crowding me diminished. On some trips I would pass an entire day without seeming to create much of a stir, and Haari even joked that people were beginning to get bored of me.

Haari introduced me to the social world, to concerts, to theatrical productions, to organised sporting events, to a wide range of virtual reality events, to parties, galas, dances, and other festive occasions. At some of the events we attending Haari was a keen participant in the various dances that people seemed to enjoy so much. I was not a good dancer, despite Kallan's attempts to teach me and my siblings the basics which, according to our uncle, "you'll need when you join the world." On complimenting Haari for his skills, he shrugged slightly, disingenuously, replying, "oh it's nothing. Nothing important." I suppressed a smile at his not-quite-true answer: he was clearly very proud of his dancing abilities.

I was astonished at how many people Haari knew, and I struggled to keep up with the endless introductions to new individuals. I was also amazed at how much time people spent pursuing leisure activities, and even more in doing nothing more than socialising. When I queried this, he reminded me of what we had discussed long before: in a world in which nobody has to work, and most people live a long, healthy life, there is a huge amount of time to fill. I could not understand why more people were not filling it with things I perceived as useful, but he laughed ironically, saying,

"Since everybody dies in the end, ultimately, there's no such thing as useful."

Clearly the musicians at the concerts we attended had spent a great deal of time learning their craft, as had the actors and other performers, including those in virtual reality performances, and also the sportsmen and women we saw. And I knew many people were erudite in a wide range of academic disciplines, modern and ancient. Others were expert scientists. Some spent a great deal of time studying dead languages from the old world, meeting regularly in social groups where they conversed only in these ancient tongues. Many others immersed themselves in producing works of art and craft of myriad diverse types, some very old-fashioned, others highly technological. Yet despite all of this, Haari insisted that the majority of people did not engage in such activities, did not do anything I would consider useful or purposeful. And I also remembered what he had told me about the huge numbers who just withdrew into a world of virtual reality, sometimes even with a representation of me as the protagonist in their unreal adventures. I simply could not fathom the mind-set of any of these people, brought up in a world where most human knowledge from the old and the new world was available at the touch of a button or a simple voice command, a world in which there were no obligations of work eating into one's free time, why would most people then spend the bulk of their existence merely filling all that marvellous time with chit-chat, with gossip, with bland, pointless entertainments? Why would anyone spend a long life pointlessly, merely treading water until death? Haari again reminded me,

"Since we all die, aren't all pastimes just a way of filling time?" I could not understand how Haari reconciled his deep cynicism with his view that it was vital not to mis-live.

I spent a good deal of time with those closest to Haari, especially Bartrem and Lisvet. I could never quite work out what Bartrem spent his time doing, though I surmised that he was an intellectual dilettante, reading and learning widely across a huge range of topics, a generalist with no special interest in any one subject. Lisvet, for all that I liked her very much and spent many happy hours with her, seemed to like nothing better than socialising, spending almost endless hours doing little more than attending events and chatting to friends. As time passed, she and Elza became good friends, even though Elza was not Haari's niece. I enjoyed spending time with these two delightful young women, but always felt, after a few hours, that we really should be doing something more useful, or at least talking about more profound issues. They would laugh brightly at me if I mentioned such feelings, rendering me silent. I had to limit the time I spent with them, as it always felt as if I was wasting my life if I spent too much time in doing nothing. Bartrem informed me that the ancients had a concept of, and even and expression for such endless, aimless activity: the sweetness of doing nothing. Such an idea was alien to me, though I did think that in the old world, when so much time was occupied in the soul-destroying activity of earning a living, perhaps the quiet time, the leisure time, perhaps this really would have felt sweet. To have spare time to simply do nothing in an enforcedly busy life, must surely have been wonderful. But to graft such an idea onto *our* lives, lives in which nobody was ever obliged to do anything, this seemed to give permission to spend a wasted lifetime, to achieve nothing, to have no purpose in ever having been born.

During the years I spent learning how trivial was most of my world, I began to look more seriously into the possibility of time travel, my interest piqued in part by my regular discussions on the topic with Emaleen. Zelda began to badger me about this, telling me that I needed to learn to travel in time, so as to try and undo the tragedy that had befallen my sister Safya. She had no qualms about stating such an aim bluntly.

I read copiously around the topic and discovered, to my surprise, that before the Chaos there had been a good deal of work published on the theme of time travel, fiction in which characters managed to move to different times, sometimes deliberately, on other occasions by accident or even against their will. I buried myself in these works, enjoying the tales they spun, never entirely convinced that such was actually possible. Yet some of them were well-crafted, well-founded in physics, at least of the theoretical type.

After the Chaos a long period passed during which there seemed to be no interest in time travel, nothing on the topic being published either in fiction or fact. The survivors simply had more pressing matters to attend to than muse on the possibility of moving through time. When it did tentatively reappear, it was not met with much enthusiasm, and over time, this degenerated into a good deal of hostility. There was some discussion of whether travelling backwards could avert, or at least ameliorate, the Chaos. This discussion, minimal in quantity, was nevertheless fierce and inconclusive. In the end, opinion seemed to take the firm view that time travel was either impossible and therefore not worth wasting any time on, or simply too dangerous to try as its results could never be known, never be predicted. Eventually, the Council forbade any experiments in travelling in time, such that the interest in it waned to the point of disappearing, at least in terms of any record being left of an interest.

Individuals such as Marna and Zelda found the idea interesting, though given their general willingness to entertain taboo subjects, this did not necessarily reflect a general desire to discuss such a topic. I often discussed the issue with Zelda, sometimes joined by Marna, and occasionally even with Haari on his visits to my home (though Zelda never warmed to him). We discussed the dilemmas involved in travelling back in time, most particularly the fraught issue of whether one could alter the future by what one did while visiting the past. Marna was especially interested in whether a person could alter their own future, or even cause themself not to exist, insisting that such a possibility led to a paradox which she called the ancestor paradox. She asked me and Zelda one evening to answer a question.

"If you went back in time and killed your own ancestors before you had been created," she began. "Does that mean that at that very moment you would simply disappear because you could never have come into existence in the first place without that ancestor?" Zelda and I considered this for a moment, though Marna spoke again before we could answer.

"And surely if it meant you couldn't exist, then it wouldn't have been possible to travel back in time in the first place as you would never have existed! And if that were the case, then you couldn't have killed your ancestor as, by doing so, you made it impossible for you to exist. Now that's what I call a paradox!"

Marna and Zelda seemed to enjoy such hypothetical discussions about the effects of a person travelling back in time. I found them interesting up to a point, but ultimately believed them to be tangential to the possibility of time travel. My own view was quite clear. What had happened had already happened, and as such could not be altered. It not only had already happened, but it had always happened the way it had happened, it *must* always have happened that way because it took place in the past, which was by definition unalterable, immutable. In other words, the past has *always already* happened the way it happened, and nothing could ever alter this fact. Zelda and Marna, especially Marna, seemed to find my views on the matter irksome, simplistic, and ultimately uninteresting. I pointed out to them, however,

"But isn't it better this way? If you could alter or affect the past by travelling back to it, surely this means you shouldn't go there? You'd have no idea what effect your being there could have, so the only safe way to deal with this issue would be not to go there at all."

Marna pooh-poohed my comments, but had no real answer to them. I knew I was right, that I *must* be right, and this gave me the confidence to consider trying to travel to a time that was in the past, secure that nothing I did there could alter or affect the present, because whatever I did there had already happened, had occurred the first time in the way it had, the only way it could ever happen.

Initially, such discussions were merely academic as I was convinced that time travel was an impossibility. Zelda kept pressuring me to study it, insisting that I do so rather than dismissing the possibility out of hand. To curtail Zelda's pestering, I agreed to continue my research into the issue. I dug out even more information than I had uncovered so far, and was surprised at the volume of work that existed. To my even greater surprise, I also discovered substantial academic discussion of the issue from before the Chaos. It seems that scientists from the twentieth century and beyond began to seriously entertain, and explore, the theoretical possibility of time travel, supported by theories in emerging branches of physics. These scientists were perhaps encouraged, or pressured, by certain writers of fiction who had been writing time travel stories for some time. At first, scientists more or less disbelieved the possibility of travelling through time, and many tried to disprove its feasibility by using science. But to their surprise, the more they researched it, the more they began to come round to the idea that it may, in fact, be realisable.

I knew that if I were ever to learn to travel in time, I did not want to have to rely on machines to do so. My studies took me down other routes, and curiously, into the ancient philosophies that Haari had mentioned to me. I learned of the stoic practitioners of the ancient Greek and Roman worlds, some of whom were able to endure extraordinary hardship with fortitude. And from this, as Haari had suggested, I worked back towards the even more ancient Buddhism, whose links with Stoicism seemed clear to me. It was particularly the ability of the buddhist practitioners to induce in themselves a state of meditation so profound that it was almost a trance, verging on a self-induced coma state. Surely such a removal of the mind from the distractions of the outside world would be needed if I were ever to be able to engage with time travel? I began to experiment with trying to induce the trance-like state of the buddhists, the better to concentrate all my mental energies on the problems of moving through time. It was frustratingly difficult as I found my concentration simply inadequate, and often, just at the point of passing from full consciousness to an almost sleep-like internal state of dreamy contemplation, I would be rudely brought back to everyday reality. But I persisted and slowly, very slowly, I improved my skills in this unexpectedly difficult endeavour.

Several years passed as I kept myself busy studying time travel, honing my ability to induce a trance-like state of deep meditation. I also gradually enlarged my social circle and familiarity with my world, and with learning as much as I could about the world I lived in. My home life continued as before, though with some profound differences. I now regularly invited guests to my home - Haari, Bartrem, Lisvet, Elza and others. And despite Zelda's irritation at this, she grew gradually accustomed to it without ever really accepting it, knowing there was nothing she could do to stop it, and as Kallan often reminded her, it was better to still have me living safely at home than alienating me to such a degree that I moved out.

My relationship with Adwin rumbled on as before, a cool, distant feeling pervading all our interactions. I had watched from afar as my brother underwent puberty, painfully aware that I should have been helping him cope with the changes to his body, his voice, his emotions, but he never came to me for assistance and I did not feel able to offer it.

One day. On returning home from a trip to Beyra where I had met Elza and Lisvet, and I bumped into my uncle as I emerged from my flit.

"Nice to have you home, Samek. It's very quiet here."

When I queried what he meant, he informed me that Zelda was visiting Marna and that Emaleen had taken herself off to the hills as she so often did. I did not pay much attention as Kallan spoke, eager as I was to go to my room to rest after a busy day. I turned towards my room, but what my uncle said next stopped me, my attention fully engaged.

"And Adwin's gone out somewhere too. He said he was going to meet a friend." I turned with a snap and stared at Kallan as if he had said something bizarre. He looked back at me, raising his elegant silver eyebrows, a quizzical little smile on his face as he contemplated my shocked expression.

"Gone out to meet a friend?" I managed to squeeze out in a tight voice. "What friend?"

"How would *I* know," replied Kallan with a shrug and a tiny purse of his lips. "Nobody ever tells *me* anything." And with that he turned and walked off, leaving me standing still, rooted to the spot with surprise. As I got over my surprise, I realised that it was good for Adwin to have a friend on the outside. It would allow me to feel less guilty leaving him alone at home so much of the time. And perhaps he would be less morose, less melancholy, less unpleasant to be around. Yet I realised too, with a start, that I was jealous of Adwin. I felt almost irritated that he had found somebody else to replace me. I did not feel comfortable leaving him at home, yet at the same time was irked that he was not pining alone for me. I pushed such thoughts quickly from my mind, not happy with what they meant about my attitudes.

Emaleen also began, slowly, to spend time away from home with other people, mostly with Elza after Elza's pestering on this point finally succeeded. Elza introduced her to her own friends, those from the Institute and others such as Lisvet. Marna too managed to persuade Emaleen to visit her on a number of occasions.

As I moved into my late teens, it seemed as though my life would be calmer, more pleasant, ordinary even. But I had been lulled into a false sense of security which was soon to be rudely shattered by an event in the outside world which would once again raise the spectre of who I was, and what many people felt about me and my family.

Chapter Forty-Eight

One spring day in 2818, some time before I turned nineteen, I sat drinking tea in the centre of Beyra with Marna, Kallan and Haari on a day out, we noticed the usual hubbub of voices around us grow more animated. I remember the very moment as I had just been distracted by the incongruous thought that I should have made use of the laser shaver that morning as I passed a hand over my rough and stubbly chin. I had come surprisingly late to shaving, and regularly forgot, often having to be reminded by Kallan who considered stubble on the chin to be most unattractive. I glanced over the balustrade of the balcony where we were sitting to see what had caused the minor commotion. I saw people had stopped to watch the huge 3DV broadcast beside the lake below us, clearly captivated by what they saw. I squinted slightly to better see what they were all watching so avidly.

"They're about to announce the new Council," interjected Haari, who kept up with current affairs more keenly than the rest of us. I tensed slightly at his words, as I always did at mention of our world's administrative body. I calmed myself by recalling that my family had had no problems with the Council for years, not since we had forced the removal of Rannald and his allies. Yet there always remained the nagging fear that such a state of peace between the Council and my family would not endure, and Zelda fed my lingering doubts on this matter, retaining her deeply-engrained hatred of that entire lofty assembly. Her view was that the recent lack of hostility from them was merely a hiatus, and did not represent a permanent thawing of relations between us.

But years had passed during which we had been allowed to live in peace, having little to do with the Council, and they having nothing to do with us. I realised that it was just over five years since my sister's murder, and was shocked at how quickly the time had passed. After Safya's murder a new Council had been appointed to fill the five gaps left by those members who had been banished to different corners of the wild parts of the world. Today the new Council would be announced, and this was always an event of major importance to the world, despite the fact that, as a rule, Councils merely administer our society, and are not supposed to govern it in the way the ancient world's ruling bodies did. Rannald's Council had been more intrusive than most, more active, and this was another reason why Zelda had hated it so much. She felt that the Council should do no more than passively administer our society, leaving citizens to do what they pleased, especially her.

All four of us stood up and arrayed ourselves along the balustrade facing the giant hologram, falling silent to better hear what was being said. Some of the names being announced we already knew, as it was common for existing Council members to be chosen again. Lenora was confirmed as retaining her position as Council Speaker. Ruddy-cheeked Breyan with the shock of red hair was also reappointed, along with Binyamin and Tanya whom I knew slightly from past encounters. The elderly Vradley was not, though I did not know if he had wanted to be or not. The names of most of the remaining twelve members were spoken aloud, none of which we knew. But the final name was only too well-known to us, and caused all four of us a collective gasp of surprise as it resounded around the centre of the city: Devid.

I stood stunned, unable to respond, barely able to breathe. I felt my companions flinch too, almost as appalled as I was. Devid! That odious creature who had wormed his way into our home. Zelda was convinced that Devid had been part of the plan to murder my sister, and she tried to force the old Council to banish him to the wilds along with the other perpetrators, but there was no clear proof against him, and in the end we had no option but to leave him at large. I never thought that he would manage to get himself appointed to the Council, though I assumed that his connection to Rannald had helped him in this. I shuddered as I remembered that this meant that many people still considered the exile of the Council members and the actual killers of my sister to be wrong, immoral, a punishment no-one had the right to impose. And I could only imagine what they thought of Rannald's untimely heart attack at the end of that fraught Council meeting in which we accused them of murder, and yet at which I had actually murdered the Speaker.

Eventually, I managed to shake myself out of my shock, and looked at my companions. They were well aware of the antipathy I felt for Devid, which was shared with my mother. And I had told them on more than one occasion that we knew he saw us as freaks, as monsters. Haari was upset by the choice of Devid, mostly on my behalf. Marna and Kallan both looked outraged and distressed.

"We must get home," Kallan said in a tight, tense voice. "We must get back and tell Zelda." I nodded and after ensuring we were all touching, immediately ported us all back to the estate.

Zelda was not in the main house, and we assumed she must be in her laboratory. When this was the case, usually no-one would disturb her. But today's news was so momentous that we were compelled to forgo our usual reluctance to disturb her. I mindspoke to her directly, something I almost never did. She was initially irritated by my intrusion into her private thoughts, but the urgency of my voice asking her to come and talk to us quickly persuaded her to rush to meet us.

A few moments after I had mindspoken to her, my mother bustled into the living room where we were all waiting. I had urged my brother and sister to join us too, and Emaleen had arrived moments before. Even Adwin, who I knew from his reply was not at home, was persuaded to return immediately by the urgency of my message.

"Well?" asked Zelda in a voice tinged with anxiety at the worried faces that greeted her. "What is it? It must be important." Adwin and Emaleen were also eager to hear the news, but those of us who had been in Beyra moments before were suddenly reluctant to divulge what we had heard, none of us wishing to be the one to apprise Zelda of something we knew would cause her to explode with outrage. We all glanced nervously at each other, but eventually Kallan sighed impatiently and took the plunge.

"Zelda, my dear," he began hesitantly, forcing himself to speak in a calming tone. "We've just heard...we heard in Beyra...we need to tell you something..." he stammered.

"Just tell me!" barked Zelda, reaching up to smooth a wayward lock of hair that had made a bid for freedom in her haste to meet us. Kallan looked to me and Marna for support, or in the hope one of us would pick up where he had left off, but we both avoided his gaze, not wanting to be the one to give Zelda the awful news. He swallowed loudly and continued.

"The new Council has just been announced," he said in a slightly tremulous voice. Zelda stiffened at his comment, her facial features freezing, her breath held, the hand smoothing her hair stopping in mid-gesture. "And I hate to have to tell you this, but Devid has been appointed."

Zelda did not move a muscle. She was so still that she seemed made of stone. For a long moment she simply stared at Kallan, not breathing, not blinking. We all held our breath. The room was utterly silent, not a whisper of sound escaped our lips, not a hint of movement in our bodies. Finally Zelda breathed out loudly, a rough, rasping sound grating in her throat.

"Devid!" she said in a strangely quiet, almost strangled voice, slowly lowering her hand. "Devid. Devid. Devid," she repeated, as if trying to get her mind to accept what she had just heard. She stood quite still, her face flushed with anger, the dry patches of eczema white against the livid blood-infused skin of her cheeks and forehead. She shook her head slowly from side to side, her disobedient locks of hair seizing the opportunity to escape from their rigid confines. She said nothing, merely emitting a low growling sound from her throat. After a few moments during which none of us knew what to do, she looked at me sharply, her eyes narrowed.

"You have to kill him boy," she stated baldly. I gasped, and the others in the room stared at Zelda as if she had gone mad.

"What...what do you mean?" I stuttered. Had my mother concluded that I was responsible for the death of Devid's uncle?

"What I said," Zelda replied in an ominous tone. "You have to kill him." I said nothing, merely stared at Zelda, my mouth gaping open, my eyes wide.

"I...I can't," I finally managed to squeeze out in a strangled voice.

"Yes you can," Zelda replied enunciating each word carefully with a jab of her finger. "You have told me before that you can easily kill a person with the tiniest flick of your mind." I nodded vaguely.

"I can, but I mean I can't," I replied.

"Speak sense!" Zelda snapped at me. "Either you can or you cannot."

"I mean I can *physically*, but I won't. I can't, I mean I won't just kill someone in cold blood," I replied. Zelda glared at me. I did not dare even glance at Emaleen lest my look give away the fact that she and I shared a secret: that Rannald's death had not been accidental. But for all that I hated Devid, he had not killed anyone, had not taken the life of someone close to me. Killing him in this way would be a much bigger step than what I had done to his uncle, the man who had arranged the murder of my sister.

Zelda's expression then changed abruptly, a sly, pensive expression replacing her anger.

"Not even Devid?" she asked, moving closer towards me. "Devid, who despises you, despises Adwin and Emaleen. Devid, who was certainly part of the plan to murder Safya." I backed away from her as she spoke, as if I could escape the truth of what she said by distancing myself from her. But she could see from my face that she was gaining the advantage, and continued to approach me, finally coming face to face with me as I was backed up against the wall with nowhere else to go, her dense mobile eyebrows menacing me as she spoke.

"Kill him Samek, kill this creature who thinks you are a monster, an abomination," she goaded, a twisted, nasty hint of a smile on her face, each word punctuated by a sharp jab of her finger into my chest. "Kill him the way you killed Rannald." I gasped at her final comment, colouring with shame that Zelda had shown to Haari that I was not the person he thought I was. It was surely only a guess on my mother's part, a stab in the dark, but her aim was deadly accurate.

"No! No! No!" I shouted, lifting my arms in front of my face. "I can't. I won't. And nothing you can say will make me." I threw up a barrier to shield myself from some of Zelda's intense anger and pressure, and she felt it immediately, knowing herself beaten, at least for the moment.

"You'll regret it my boy," she snarled, adding a few final, painful jabs into the already tender spot in the middle of my chest. "Mark my words. All of you," she said as she spun around to confront the appalled faces in the room. "You'll all regret not acting now. And you, Samek, you especially will rue the day you refused to do what you needed to do."

And at that, she barged her way through the bodies between her and the door, and marched out of the room as fast as her shuffling walk would carry her. A stunned silence reigned, finally broken by Haari moving across to me and laying a hand on my shaking shoulder.

"You made the right choice," he said quietly. "Believe me, you can't kill someone in cold blood just because you hate him. We can't behave like that." I looked up at him, his strange golden eyes showing deep concern. "But what did she mean about Rannald?" he continued, genuinely confused. I blushed furiously, but ignored his question.

I turned to look at each of the other people in the room, feeling their mood as I did so. For Haari the issue was simpler than for my family, simpler even than for Marna who had for so long been deeply involved in our lives. I sensed from the hard look on Emaleen's face that she would have no compunction in killing Devid: he was so intimately connected with Rannald. Kallan and Marna would probably agree with me, but I wondered if they saw sense in what Zelda had said. Would I, would we, come to regret not acting decisively at this juncture? As with Haari, they looked confused by Zelda's final comment.

I looked at Adwin and was surprised to see a most bizarre look on his face. He seemed confused, perhaps at the reference to killing Rannald, but there was something else in his expression, something dark and veiled, almost angry, which caught my attention. I could not fathom the meaning of such a strange and cryptic look, but as my brother noticed my frown, he immediately masked the odd expression on his face, replacing it with a studied blandness as he stared back at me through impassive inky eyes. I wondered briefly at the meaning of his earlier, unguarded mien. Was he more squeamish than I thought, or was there something else behind those dark eyes? Incongruously, I noticed that his trim little goatee beard and moustache were now thick and dense, surprisingly so for a lad of only fifteen years.

My attention was drawn away from Adwin, however, by the mood in the room, by the anxiety and distress on the faces of Kallan and Marna, even of Haari, by the ugly eagerness clear in Emaleen's features. I shuddered a few times, and quietly left the room. I had a strong need to be alone, to consider the morality of taking it upon myself to kill Devid, a human being whose very existence seemed only to create dissent, to cause unhappiness and misery. Would it really be wrong to extinguish Devid's life, if such an act would make many other people's lives so much better?

Chapter Forty-Nine

After Devid's appointment to the Council, the next few months were almost anti-climactic. Nothing happened. We received no word from the Council, and life continued much as before. It was a strange and curiously tense time as we all seemed to be waiting for some action from the Council, some further, unwelcome, intrusion into our lives.

After wrestling with my conscience, I finally decided it would be wrong to kill Devid, a decision I was to bitterly regret. Zelda was so angry with my refusal to kill Devid on command that she did not speak to me for weeks, but as the time passed with no change to the way the Council appeared to be functioning, the frost between us thawed. In fact, our rapprochement was such that I began in earnest to consider the practicalities of time travel, as much to please her as myself.

Whilst I did not have Zelda's grasp of physics, I realised that I would need to ascertain much more clearly what seemed to actually be happening when I teleported, the better to transfer such knowledge into my experiments with time travel. To this end, I spent a great deal of time making short trips, during which I would open my mind to the actual process. And after each trip I would sit quietly contemplating exactly what had just happened and how it had felt. It was a fascinating operation, trying to bring to my consciousness a procedure I usually underwent without active thought, without really engaging in. As I progressed, I realised that to travel in time would need a different quality, and would, as I had begun to guess, require a total withdrawal from the ordinary world around me, a full immersion in an isolated, individual mental world of dream-like trance.

As my understanding of the process of teleporting continued and I tried to relate this to my thoughts about time travel, I shared my thoughts regularly with other people, especially Haari and Zelda. Haari was fascinated but worried, especially as I could give no assurances that my trip back in time would succeed. Teleportation only varied part of the here and now. Travelling in time would surely mean varying both dimensions.

Zelda seemed to lack the concern Haari felt, and showed interest only in my conjectures and practices. She regularly asked how I was progressing, showing an unprecedented fascination with me, with my activities. Her enquiring was so regular that it felt almost like badgering, an obsessive concern with my progress. Ostensibly, her interest arose out of a desire for me to return to the moments before Safya's murder, so as to be able to avert the dreadful crime (something I did not believe possible). But I sensed that this was a front, and behind this overt reason for learning to port through time lurked other motives. I considered looking into Zelda's mind to see if I could winkle out her real fascination with time travel, but decided against this. I knew such an intrusion would outrage my mother, and I would presumably find out what I wanted to know in good time.

In the meantime, I enjoyed the closer relationship I had with her. She was a very difficult woman, frequently grumpy, ill-tempered, morose, and she rarely smiled, seeming to lack a sense of irony or of humour except for the occasional outburst in relation to some dark matter that tickled her. Yet she was hugely knowledgeable, intense in her discussions, and time spent with her was valuable to me. I explained to her what I had learned about teleporting, then took her with me to show her. She understood the science lying beneath teleportation far better than I did, but lacked the perceptual apparatus to see and feel it as it happened. Apart from the very first day I had learned to teleport people, she had only ever teleported by means of a machine, never paying any attention to the actual process. After our joint flits, I was rewarded with a rare smile from her, a real smile of simple pleasure, and of gratitude for what I was showing her.

"It is as if I am actually inside an experiment my boy," she said animatedly. "Not just watching from outside, or seeing what happens at the end, but actually immersed in the process itself. What a strange idea, and so amazing!" I basked in what I felt was praise, something she so rarely gave.

"And you think you might be able to jump through time like this, using what you have learned about teleporting?" she asked me one day in a slightly tense voice, showing how eager she was for me to do this.

"I might," I replied hesitantly. "Though I can't guarantee it," I added hastily, as I saw her eyes glint with excitement at the prospect, her expression almost greedy. I reminded myself that her true motives were yet to be revealed, telling myself not to be deceived into feeling happy with her praise. She was up to something, and only time would show me exactly what. Whatever her real motives in showing such an interest in my progress, it was amazing to me that she even listened attentively to my discussions of buddhist trance-meditation as a necessary precursor to time travel, a fact which surprised me given her usual hostility to such abstruse topics.

"But surely science is the only way forward, young man?" she would ask, frowning as I tried to explain the sensation of inducing a trance.

"Yes," I agreed. "But it's a question of how to access the science," I tried to explain, though not very clearly. "I need to cut out all distraction, all input from the world outside. I'm sure this will be essential for me to succeed." She had no real reply to this, so merely nodded. I could control the here, but also needed to control the now.

One strange side-effect of spending time with Zelda in this way, flitting with her all over the world, was that she spent time away from home. This was something she rarely did, such was her profound distrust of humanity. Yet to fully demonstrate what I had uncovered, she was willing to allow herself to be taken to many different places. One day we found ourselves high on the plateau overlooking Beyra, close to the entrance to the Council building.

We were so immersed in our animated discussion of teleporting and time travel as we strolled along the edge of the plateau, that we did not notice ourselves approaching the Council building itself. Just outside the main entrance, our discussions were rudely interrupted by a whiny voice we instantly recognised.

"Zelda and Samek," it sneered, the very tone of it making my skin crawl. We stopped in our tracks, little more than an arm's length from Devid, who was leaving the Council building. I looked up into the scornful face of that awful man, wondering as I did who Devid reminded me of. Before I could remember, Zelda scowled, a low growl emitting from her throat. Devid was accompanied by Lenora, the statuesque and imposing Council Speaker, and three tall and burly young men who looked to me to be guards. I could just make out another person behind the three sturdy men, obscured by the sheer size of the guards. I was so astonished to see the guards that I paid scant attention to the person hidden at the back of the group. I remembered that during Rannald's tenure of the Council Speakership, he had employed a group of armed guards, and that they had been dressed in the same glossy black uniforms that I now saw on the three men before me. And it was a small group of such men who had actually carried out Safya's murder.

"Guards Devid?" Zelda growled. "You think people hate you so much you need guards?"

"What guards Zelda?" replied Devid disingenuously in his grating nasal voice, a light sneer on his face. "These are just Council advisers," he said, indicating the three young men behind him with a sweep of his arm, adding a little sniff as he did so. Lenora looked embarrassed, but said nothing. I knew the 'guards' were not actually armed, and wondered if Devid was right, but something in his tone, and in the body language of the three men told me this was not the case, as well as their near-identical clothing and heavy boots.

"Lenora," said Zelda, turning to the Speaker. "What in the name of hell are you doing with this viper?" Lenora flushed red, and did not immediately reply. I noticed that she now wore several showy chains of gold instead of her usual one, surely to indicate her elevated status as re-elected Speaker. And to this she had added a number of large glinting rings of such size that only someone as big and strong as she could carry so easily. As it became clear that Zelda had no more to say, the Speaker finally spoke, her usually deep tones higher due to her defensive manner.

"If by that you mean Devid, then why shouldn't I be with him? He's a Council member now, as I'm sure you know. We have a lot to discuss. We have huge responsibilities running this world of ours and..."

"Oh spare me the holier-than-thou platitudes Lenora," snapped Zelda. "I have no doubt you have plenty to be getting on with. But why with him? And why is he on the Council? Actually," continued Zelda before Lenora could even reply. "More to the point, *how* is he on the Council? He is very young for the role, and is it not an amazing coincidence that he is Rannald's nephew? And you, Lenora," she added with a jab of her finger upwards towards Lenora's gold-laden chest. "Did you have anything to do with his appointment?"

Lenora flinched slightly at the barrage of questions from Zelda, and I watched in fascination at the expressions flowing across her face at each query. Especially interesting was her deep blush at Zelda's final question. I sensed strongly that she did indeed have some involvement in Devid's appointment to the Council. But she rallied quickly.

"What nonsense!" she retorted, her deep voice still higher than usual, betraying her forced confidence. She lifted a heavily-ringed hand as if to fiddle with the chains around her neck, but perhaps sensing that this would indicate tension, she quickly dropped it again. "You know that appointments to the Council cannot be influenced by anyone, least of all by any existing Council member."

Zelda snorted in derision at her claim, laughing out loud to show she did not believe a word of it. Lenora reddened more deeply, this time more in anger than embarrassment.

"You should show more respect for members of the Council Zelda," interrupted Devid. "Especially for the Speaker." Zelda turned to him, a look of such contempt on her face that, against my will, I was impressed by Devid's ability to show no sign of being cowed.

"Respect?" snarled Zelda, turning back to Lenora. "None of you deserve respect. The whole lot of you are contemptible. Even you Lenora and your cronies like Breyan and Binyamin, the best of you, even you are a huge waste of space, a bunch of total arseholes. The only really worthwhile one among you is no longer on the Council - old Vradley. And you Devid," she added, her eyes darting back towards him. "What can I say? A nastier piece of work would be hard to find. The quicker you shuffle off this planet the better. We can only hope you quickly meet some fatal accident..."

"You threaten me?" snapped Devid angrily, the nasal tones accentuated by his sudden ire, and actually stamping one of his little feet. "You dare to threaten me you dangerous madwoman? What will you do?"

"Stop it both of you," said Lenora loudly, her usual deep tones reasserting themselves as she issued the command. "This is unbecoming behaviour, especially from you Devid as a member of the Council." Devid stilled at the reprimand, colouring slightly with the affront from Lenora. Whether Lenora felt any real respect towards Devid or not, I suspected that *he* did not hold *her* in high regard. His manner towards everyone suggested there was only one person in the world he admired: Devid. I imagined he would prove a thorn in the side of the entire Council.

A very tense silence ensued. I wanted not to be there, to be away from the hatred which swirled around the space between Zelda and Devid. But I was transfixed, pinned to the spot by the animosity also flowing towards me from Devid. Apparently time had not tempered his venom towards me. As I stared at him, an unwelcome thought thrust itself suddenly into my mind: perhaps I should kill him after all. I could arrange for him to have an accident. Perhaps Zelda's comment had been a hint to me to arrange such a thing. I shook my head, trying to dispel the notion, but it persisted, almost talking to me, telling me: why not? What would the world lose if I were to remove this despicable person from it?

Lenora decided that the painful, hate-filled silence had dragged on long enough.

"Actually Zelda, I'm glad we ran into you," she began in an obviously affected normal tone of voice. Zelda dragged her eyes away from Devid, looking sharply at Lenora. "There's something we wanted to discuss with you," Lenora continued. Zelda said nothing, but merely stared at the Speaker, thick eyebrows raised in surprise. I saw that Lenora was anxious, and sensed that she was wary of what she was about to say. She kept her arms pinned firmly to her sides, lest her anxiety be betrayed by agitated fingers. Her eyes darted to Devid, and she gave him an almost imperceptible nod of her head, giving him permission to speak.

"We, the Council that is, have heard," began Devid in a pompous tone, looking directly at me, "That you are contemplating time travel, working on techniques to achieve it." I jumped slightly at his words. How on earth did he know this? Who had told him? Zelda frowned deeply as she contemplated the same questions. I felt betrayed but had no idea how the Council had learned of my experiments. On Zelda's insistence I had only revealed my work to a few people outside my family, only to Haari and Marna. I had never even mentioned it to Elza and the other youngsters from her Institute, nor to Bartrem and Lisvet, and I am sure that Haari would not have told them as I had made it clear to him how important it was to keep the plans a secret. The very idea of time travel was such an unprecedented process, that I knew if my attempts to master it became known then people would talk about this, discuss it with friends. I had already learned that such idle gossip could spread with the speed of an epidemic. I continued to stare at Devid, wondering not only where he had gained his knowledge, but also where his comments would lead.

"And we're not happy with it," he continued with a little sniff after his words, answering my silent question. I did not reply, and merely raised an eyebrow in query. He continued.

"We want you to stop. Actually, we forbid it. We forbid any further experimentation in time travel."

Zelda snorted scornfully, and replied in a loud voice. "Forbid? Who the fuck do you think you are to forbid anything? You are not our rulers Devid. You are just the Council. Your job is to run this world, *administer* it, according to the will of the people." And with each repetition of the words 'you' and 'your' she jabbed aggressively at Lenora and then Devid with her finger. Lenora opened her mouth to speak, but was cut off by Zelda. "You forget yourselves," she continued, her relentless jabbing gaining vigour with each 'you' and 'your'. "You think you govern us, but you do not. That is not your job and never has been. So do not spout any more rubbish about forbidding us. We shall do as we please."

A silence ensued. Devid's face showed anger and even more: intense hatred. Lenora seemed not to know what else to say. Zelda sneered at the two of them. I sensed that the three 'advisers' standing behind Lenora and Zelda were readying themselves to step forward. As they did so, I heard a little shuffling of the feet of the person hidden behind the guards, as this person attempted to keep his or her face obscured from us. I was about to ask who this was obscuring him- or herself behind the guards, but Zelda had noticed the slight movement of the guards and spoke to them directly.

"And you three can stop right there. If you try to make any sort of move towards us, he will stop you," she said, pointing in my direction. I nodded in agreement, indicating I would do just that. The three stopped dead.

"Zelda, be reasonable," interrupted Lenora in an attempt to diminish the tension between us all. "Time travel is just too dangerous. We don't know what sort of chaos it would cause if Samek succeeded. If he went back and changed the past, what effects might that cause into the future, to now?" Zelda turned to her, and I was very surprised to hear her next words, echoing clearly my own views on whether going back in time could affect the past.

"Don't be so foolish Lenora," she said patronisingly. "The past is the past. It has already happened the way it happened. It cannot be changed. So nothing a person did then could affect the present because it has already occurred." Lenora looked unconvinced, but had no real reply. Devid, however, did.

"That's missing the point Zelda," he said with another irritating sniff, his whiny tone grating more and more on my nerves. "This is not some sort of philosophical discussion of whether the past can be altered, it's a question of the here and now and what is and isn't allowed. We are the Council, and we forbid you or any member of your family from attempting to travel in time. We forbid you from even investigating it. And we are supported by a huge number of ordinary people." I jumped at his final statement. Was he right? Did many people find the idea of time travel worrying, frightening even? I imagined that this might well be the case, and that in this Devid might be speaking the truth. But how did they know of our intentions in the first place? Zelda was unmoved by Devid's comments, maintaining her sneer.

"And I repeat," replied Zelda, glaring at Devid, bushy eyebrows dancing menacingly above dark eyes. "You cannot forbid us anything, so you might as well give up trying. Look what happened to Rannald and his cronies when they crossed us. And most of them got off lightly." Devid was so incensed by Zelda's comments, her threats in all truth, that he could not formulate a reply. Lenora too was appalled at what Zelda had said, but before she could muster a response, Zelda turned to me. I was still in shock at Zelda's words, almost admitting that Rannald's death had not been an accident. Before I could react, Zelda spoke.

"I am feeling queasy in this company. Take me home," she ordered.

I was about to do as bidden when a thought which had been nagging at the back of my mind suddenly made its presence felt with great clarity: just who was the mysterious and shadowy person so assiduously veiling him- or herself behind the heavy curtain of the guards? I knew, with an intense certainty, that I needed to find out, that this was somehow important, vital even. I tried to ascertain who the person was, using my gifts, and was astonished to discover that his or her identity was being deliberately masked.

"Who are you?" I asked sharply. "You, hiding at the back. Show yourself," I demanded. But nothing happened. The guards remained stolidly in place, concealing the mystery person completely. I sighed impatiently. I had had my fill of irritation for one day, so instead of asking again or trying to breach the barrier protecting the person, instead I emitted a thrust of energy, physically forcing Lenora, Devid and especially the three bulky guards apart, leaving a clear pathway between them to the person so carefully ensconced in their shadow. As I did so, the screen protecting the person melted away. And what I saw literally took my breath away.

Adwin!

Zelda gasped loudly, then began to splutter and stutter, so aghast that she could not formulate a single coherent word. I was no less stunned, but stood in absolute silence, still as a statue, my breath suspended. Adwin, my brother, remained as still as me, staring defiantly straight into my eyes, though I saw a veiled hint of shame on his face struggling to show itself despite his best efforts to suppress it. Zelda continued to burble and mumble inarticulately, her hands opening and closing rapidly as my brother and I remained immobile, glaring at each other. Time seemed to stop. Everything around me faded from my immediate perception as all I could focus on was my brother's face. It was as if we stood alone in the world, encased at each end of an invisible, yet impenetrable, tunnel. Nothing else existed for me but my brother's face. For long moments we stood in utter stillness, the only thought in my head being "Why?"

Abruptly the silence crumbled, the world outside the tunnel intruded into my consciousness. Zelda having found her voice, but still only able to utter the single word "you, you, you," over and over again, as she jabbed her finger towards Adwin. The guards made a move to hide Adwin again, but I stopped them at their first step, holding them still. I glanced at Lenora to see a look of concern on her face, perhaps concern at what I would do. I dared a look towards Devid, but wished I had not. He sneered, with a look of what? Triumph? On his face. I had to use all my will-power not to lash out at him, to mindstrike him, even to kill him. I forced my gaze back to my brother. I suddenly saw that the familiar goatee and moustache adorning Devid's sneering face was exactly the same as the one around my brother's mouth. Adwin had copied Devid, imitating the way he looked, and had been sporting the beard for some time. Why had I not made this connection long before? Suddenly I realised that Devid was the friend my brother had been leaving the estate to visit. But how had they met? Surely Devid had engineered the meeting, and must have worked hard to persuade Adwin to spend time with him. And with another flash of insight I knew how the Council had discovered my working towards time travel - my brother had told Devid. And once Devid knew, it was inevitable that the rest of the Council would find out, and from there, large swathes of the citizen body. And surely Adwin had told Devid that Zelda wanted me to kill him.

My heart crumpled. I felt I had been struck in the chest as I had struck Rannald. My brother, my own dear, sweet little brother, had turned against me. But why? Why had he done this? My thoughts were interrupted by Zelda mindspeaking to me urgently, finally able to enunciate more than a single word.

~Kill him. Kill him now,~ she ordered.

"Who?" I gasped, spinning round to face my mother. "Adwin??" forgetting to use mindspeak, such was my shock at Zelda's instruction.

~No,~ she snapped. *~Devid. Kill Devid.~* But then, almost as an afterthought, she added, *~Adwin too. He betrayed us.~*

I was so stunned by what Zelda had said that I froze, unable to move a muscle, to react in any way at all. Kill Devid? And kill Adwin?? I tried to force my mind to work, to take in all that I had just learned, to process the fact of Adwin's actions, of Zelda's insistence that I should put Devid to death, and worst of all, that I should end the life of my brother.

I turned back to face my brother, seeing clearly the shame that had now forced its way into his features. He was desperately trying to maintain his look of defiance, but his mortification that he had been discovered gained the upper hand. I stared at him, misery clear on my face. He could not hold my gaze, dropping his eyes to the ground, his thick dark fringe falling across his forehead masking his eyes. I knew, for all that he had broken faith with me, this was not a reason to kill my brother. My mother's reaction was extreme. It was most likely her simply making use of the situation to rid herself of what she saw as a failure on her part in producing an imperfect being. But Adwin was my baby brother, the companion of my childhood. I shook my head sadly, sighing loudly as I did so. I sensed Zelda about to exhort me to act against him, but I silenced her before she could speak.

~No!~ I mindshouted. *~I will not kill my brother. I can't do it, and I won't do it. I'm not sure I can just kill Devid either in cold blood,~* I added, turning to face Zelda. Once again her outrage rendered her a spluttering and incoherent babbler, but this time her ire was aimed at me. I was about to remonstrate with her, explain further why I could not act when Devid suddenly forced himself into the emotions swirling between me, Zelda and Adwin. He would have been wiser to have kept his mouth shut.

"Well?" he cajoled in a voice that seemed to come straight through his nostrils. "Come on then Samek. Show us what you can do. Show us what you're made of." He smiled openly as he spoke, a nasty sneer which caused a flush of anger to invade me. My irate expression seemed to amuse him, to encourage him in his goading.

"Scared are we? Can't bring yourself to do what you need to do?" he urged. "You're pathetic, boy, just pathetic. If my brother had betrayed me *I'd* know what to do. *I* wouldn't hesitate. If I were in your shoes I'd..." but before he could say another annoying word, my anger flared suddenly, tipping me beyond reason. I turned to him and, without warning, without plan, hurled a bolt of energy at his head, intending not merely to hurt him, but to kill him, with no thought to the consequences.

The energy bolt bounced off him, shattering into hundreds of harmless invisible shards. I was stunned. How had he done that? How had he even known what I had tried to do?

He merely laughed out loud, the first time I had ever heard him do so, a braying, horsey, jarring sound. When he stopped, he turned a contemptuous, almost pitying look on me, and simply said,

"So now you know."

I was so shocked I could not react. From the corners of my eyes I saw confusion on the others' faces. None of them had any idea what had just happened. They could neither see nor sense the energy bolt I had hurled at Devid, and equally had no way to perceive the way he had so skilfully deflected it. As he had said, now I knew: I knew that he must be highly gifted to have been able to detect the energy, and even more so to have so deftly flicked it aside. Suddenly unsure of my own abilities, I knew the only sensible course of action at this juncture was to leave.

~We need to go now mother. Now.~ Before she could respond I grabbed her hand and began to port us home, flicking a final, sad, look towards Adwin as I did so. But he remained as he had been for some time, eyes cast down to the floor, unable to look me in the face.

Chapter Fifty

"Well what just happened boy?" demanded my mother as we emerged in the hallway of our home. "Tell me!" she barked, her gruff voice darker than usual.

I stood in silence for a few moments, collecting my thoughts. Zelda continued to glare at me, bushy eyebrows squeezed together.

"Devid is gifted, really gifted," I finally managed to squeeze out. Zelda looked confused.

"What on earth are you talking about?" she snapped.

"I lost my temper when he was goading me," I continued. "And just lashed out without thinking. I sent a wave of intense energy at him, at his head, which probably would have killed him." I paused for breath. "But he knew it was coming and just knocked it aside." I stopped and Zelda continued staring at me, this time her expression one of deep shock at what I had said.

"But how...how...I don't understand...how...?" she began, stammering as she tried to put her thoughts into words.

"I don't know mother. I really don't know how. But I know for a fact that he sensed what I did and was easily able to stop it. Easily." Zelda frowned as she considered my words, her scientific mind taking over and pushing her shock and outrage into the background.

"Do you think he knew before you did it?" she asked abruptly. I did not at first appreciate the importance of the question, but quickly realised what she meant: if he had sensed my intentions *before* I put them into effect, this meant he was able to enter my mind, or at least to know what I was thinking. This was a deeply worrying possibility, even worse than my initial fears.

"I...I have no idea mother," I replied slightly sheepishly. Zelda frowned again.

"But could you not tell if he went into your mind? Would you not have known? And why did you not watch out for this happening?" she queried brusquely. I squirmed slightly.

"It never crossed my mind," I replied defensively. "Why should it? I thought I was the only person in the world with my gifts, as you've been telling me all my life, so it never occurred to me that anyone else could be trying to read my thoughts."

"Hmm," was Zelda's only reply to this. She continued to glare at me, and I felt compelled to keep talking.

"But I imagine he can't go into my mind. I think I would probably have known, probably have felt something, unless he's so powerful that he can do it without anyone knowing. But I doubt he could do it without me knowing even if he could do it with other people." I knew I was babbling in an attempt to exculpate myself from Zelda's accusations, but found it almost impossible to stop myself due to a combination of discomfort at her hard stare and my own fears over Devid's abilities. If he were able to enter my mind without me knowing, the implications were awful. Had he been reading my thoughts all the time he had been with us on the estate?

"I don't even know if he can do it at all. I'm just guessing. But even if he can I can't imagine..."

"Could he hear us when we mindspoke?" Zelda interrupted sharply. I stopped talking abruptly. It was an excellent question. A deeply worrying question. I shuddered at the very possibility. It would mean Devid had eavesdropped on many private, secret conversations between me and members of my family, without even going to the effort of entering our minds to do so. I tried to recall his reaction when we had used mindspeak, and answered, in a quiet voice.

"I don't think so."

Zelda sighed loudly, her frown intensifying so much that her unruly eyebrows actually met between her eyes. "You do not think so?" she growled. "Why not?"

"Because he never showed any sign of reacting when anyone mindspoke in front of him, and I'm sure I, we would have noticed something if he'd heard us."

"Unless he's a master dissimulator," snapped Zelda. I shrugged very slightly. Perhaps Zelda was right, but I felt, strongly, that even with his best efforts to feign not hearing us mindspeak, Devid would not have been totally successful. After all, he had failed to dissimulate his contempt for me from the time of our very first meeting.

"I'm sure I would have noticed if he could hear us," I asserted confidently, as much in an attempt to convince myself as Zelda.

"I hope you're right young man," said Zelda, then paused. "Can you enter his mind now to find out?" she asked suddenly.

"No," I replied bluntly. "I wouldn't dare. He would know in an instant." My mother scowled at this less than satisfactory answer.

"Well see if you can learn to do it without him knowing," she said as she turned and began to walk away, considering the conversation at an end. Before I could do the same, she turned suddenly to look at me again, an expression of befuddlement and anger on her face.

"But how in hell did he get those abilities?" she asked, as much to herself as to me. "Where did they come from?" I stood in silence, having no answer to her questions. I was perplexed. I had assumed that nobody had gifts anything like mine. My sisters enjoyed some abilities, as did Adwin, though to a much lesser extent than me, and we had been engineered to be gifted. And I understood that many people had very low level talents of a similar type. But I was the only person in the world, the only person ever in history, who enjoyed such developed and wide-ranging abilities. And yet here was Devid clearly demonstrating that I was not alone in my talents. So where had he got them from? Before I could think further on this, Zelda gasped loudly as a thought occurred to her. Her shock at what went through her mind was so great that she stumbled slightly, and had to put out a hand to brace herself against the wall to prevent herself falling. She looked at me with a look I had never seen on her face, one of such horrified distress, that my blood chilled. She opened and closed her mouth over and over again, trying to force her lips and tongue to pronounce words, but such was her emotional state that the only sound I heard was a strangled, gargling as she grappled with her undisciplined speech organs. I stared at her in silence until she brought her voice under control.

"There is only one way Devid could have those gifts," she whispered hoarsely. "He must have been created, engineered like you." I looked at her in confusion, not understanding her meaning. Her wide open, anguished eyes continued to stare directly into mine as she continued.

"From lots and lots of progenitors, like you. And they must have been chosen for their gifts, as were yours. So somebody else has been breaching all the rules on reproduction just as I have. Somebody else knows how to do it, and has been doing it for a long time. Longer than me as Devid is older than Emaleen." I gasped at the implications of her words. My siblings and I were not the only babies made from large numbers of progenitors. There were others like us in the world. Devid at least, and who knows how many more.

"But who could have done it?" I asked in hushed tones. "Who else knows how to do it?"

Zelda stared at me. "Marna, but she would never have had the courage to do it. And she would have told me if she had anyway," replied Zelda, fully regaining her composure. "I am not sure who else. I shall have to give it some thought. But," she continued, her expression shifting suddenly into one of almost sly anger. "This changes the game!" And before I could ask her what she meant by this, she turned on her heel and stumbled away, leaving me standing gaping like a fool. I was exhausted. The day had presented far too many surprises and shocks for me to cope with, so I took myself off to my room and threw myself onto my bed, pulling the covers over my head in a futile attempt to shut out the world: a world which had suddenly become a great deal more complicated, and dangerous.

My encounter with Devid and Adwin shook me. Finding my brother with Devid and realising that Adwin had turned his back on me so completely was distressing. I could not even bring myself to think about it, burying it deep within my mind for contemplation at a later date. And as always after time spent in Devid's company, I felt sullied by the experience. His contempt for me was so transparent, so powerful, that it washed over me like a stream of filth, of effluent, and after bathing in such feculent waters I felt an intense need to be cleansed, both literally and figuratively. And as I fell into a fitful sleep, all I could see were identical dark trim goatee beards and short moustaches arrayed around treacherous red lips.

I spent the next day in the forest, alone, trying to enjoy the simple pleasure of revisiting familiar haunts. Unusually, my trip did little to calm me. Everything I saw reminded me of Adwin, of our regular outings together, especially as children, when we had been close, when the world had seemed simple. And Devid featured prominently in my thoughts as I wandered without aim through my woodland retreat. His determination to forbid me from continuing with my work towards time travel did nothing but steel my resolve to perfect my experiments. He clearly believed I would be cowed into submission by the Council's edict on the matter, but his pronouncement had exactly the opposite effect.

Later that day Zelda and I ate a quiet dinner together, talking very little, each lost in private thoughts. Towards the end of the meal I announced to my mother my new resolve to intensify my efforts to travel in time. She stopped eating, put down her cutlery, and looked at me directly. I was amazed at the emotion in her eyes as she stared at me. The warmth in her eyes showed approval of my words, and more: they glowed with real affection. I blushed and wanted to look away, but was unable to break the connection between us, so rarely had I experienced any affection from Zelda, from the woman I called mother.

We stared at each other in absolute silence for long moments, my knife and fork frozen in mid-gesture between plate and mouth, until the moment was interrupted as a large piece of gravy-laden potato fell from my fork, splashing loudly onto the table as it did so, spattering me lightly with warm brown sauce. And as if the potato had given Zelda her cue, disrupting the almost magical mood with its moist splat onto the table-top, Zelda spoke, and what she said destroyed any vestige of the warm atmosphere that prevailed between us.

"And when you go back in time young man, I want you to get DNA samples from a long list of people, special people whose genetic material was not saved," she said in a brisk, business-like voice. I stared at her mutely, incomprehension showing on my face.

"So I can use it in my next batch of embryos," she continued, on seeing my confused expression. "Even better if you can get it from people before the Chaos. Great people. People with special skills and abilities." I continued to stare at her, my features registering utter befuddlement. She assumed I simply did not understand what she was saying, so continued to elaborate.

"I need more samples, more people's DNA, so I can push onwards, carry on where I left off after making you and your siblings."

She stopped, as if she had explained enough. My look of confusion slowly shifted into one of disbelief, and then anger. She raised her grizzled, tufted brows as she watched the expression on my face change. She clearly had absolutely no idea why I seemed irate, why her comments had annoyed me so much. For a long time we remained quite still, me glaring at her, she gazing back at me in confusion. Finally I spoke.

"Now you reveal your hand," I said in a quiet, tight voice. Her eyebrows rose even higher as her incomprehension grew. "Now you show your real motive in pushing me to try and time travel," I continued, my voice beginning to tremble with emotion and quiet rage. "You're not interested in me going back to the time of Safya's murder, to try and stop it happening. You're only interested in me getting you some precious DNA samples from people from the distant past." She began to splutter slightly, and I sensed she was about to begin trying to persuade me that I was wrong. But I would hear none of it. I knew her too well.

"I should have known all along," I continued quickly, my voice shaking now. "I should have known that you wouldn't have any concern for my sister. That you were only interested in what *you* could gain for yourself by me going back in time. What *you* could make use of. You don't care about anyone else. You're so predictable. And I'm an idiot for not seeing it earlier."

"Samek, my dear boy," Zelda began tentatively, lifting a hand to smooth her hair, but I did not want to hear her excuses, her feeble attempts to exculpate herself.

"Shut up Zelda!" I snapped. "I don't want to hear it. You are the most selfish, the most self-obsessed person and...and...and I've fucking had enough of you."

And at that, I stood up and marched out of the room before she could react. I rushed down the corridors of the quiet house, wishing that there were someone else at home I could talk to, Emaleen or Kallan, or even Adwin I thought with a pang of sadness.

I stormed into my room, slammed the door shut behind me, and threw myself onto my bed. I sensed Zelda hesitantly approaching the door of my room, and quickly sealed the door tightly shut, erecting a barrier around me so I could not hear what she had begun to say from outside the room. I knew she would be desperate for me to continue with my efforts to travel in time, but I simply did not want to hear what she had to say. I turned onto my back and lay quietly, calming my breathing and my anger.

As I did so, I was astonished to realise I still had an intense desire to continue with my work on travelling in time. Such a desire had nothing to do with Zelda, it simply happened to coincide with what she wanted. And I had to admit to myself that trying to save my sister was also not the only impetus to my desires. I had spent so much time and effort in my endeavours that I did not want to throw it all away, and I needed to prove to myself that I could succeed. A tiny part of me, a childish petulant part of me, briefly considered abandoning my work simply to spite Zelda, but I hastily quashed such foolishness, knowing that I would be the one to lose the most by such an action. I knew, with absolute clarity, that I harboured a deep yearning to overcome the obstacles I faced in learning how to travel safely back in time, and to be able to return myself to my present world. Exploring the world of my time had ceased to interest me.

And so I persisted with my endeavours, my studies, my engaging with deep trance-like meditation, and my contemplation of the practicalities of time travel within the trance, coming up against obstacle after obstacle, or at least that is what I kept telling myself. The truth was, as I had finally admitted to myself, that despite my desire to visit the past, I was fearful, terrified even, of making such a huge leap into the unknown, unable to know with certainty whether I would succeed in doing so, and even if I did, whether I would ever be able to get back home again. And my fear of failure to return was even greater than my fear of failure to travel in the first place. The safest thing to do was to explore my own consciousness of time. Every part of consciousness existed either in the tiny here and now or in the massive horizon of memory on the one side, expectation on the other.

Chapter Fifty-One

After the awful meeting with Devid and Adwin, I engaged ever more with exploring my consciousness through entering the trance-like state I had learned to go into. I hoped that by doing this I would learn eventually how to travel in time. In theory this should work, though one of the insurmountable problems was that I would not know whether my endeavours were successful until I actually made a leap into the dark. And the possibility of failure was an eternal spectre, floating ghost-like in the background of all my work. A total failure, such that I simply did not move at all, would be disappointing, but at least I would be unharmed. But there were so many other frightening possibilities. I might manage to travel through time but be unable to stop my flight, hurtling endlessly backwards until I died of natural causes, most likely of something as mundane as thirst. That is, assuming that bodily functions continued as normal when the body was racing through time. Perhaps all functions would simply fall into a state of suspension during the trip? I did not see why this would be the case, but in truth, I had no idea. Or perhaps I would succeed not only in making the trip, but also in braking my trajectory, coming to rest at some distant time in the past, only to discover that the process had somehow damaged my physical self, or perhaps I would immediately be subjected to an ordeal so violent that I would be killed, maybe by humans (or other animals) so terrified by my sudden appearance that they reacted without thought. Or I would simply be unable to return. Perhaps time travel was a one-way journey, that for some reason I did not understand, it was only possible to travel backwards and not forwards, leaving me to eke out the rest of my life as a stranger in a strange land, an eternal foreigner in a place so alien that I would never fully understand it or fit in.

"And what happens if I die in the past?" I asked Haari when we were discussing my imminent visit to the past. He shrugged with apparent nonchalance, though I saw real concern in his eyes at my question.

"If I die," I continued. "Or am killed in the past, does that mean I'm dead here and now? Or would I only be dead there, and still alive here? Could I still come back home and be alive here? But if I was dead, how would I bring myself back?" Haari had no more answers for such questions than I did, but to him they were merely hypothetical. For me, they were real, very real. And nothing I had read provided answers to such simple, yet profound questions. Nothing I had read even offered a definitive view as to whether I would be able to return home at all. I spoke to Marna and Zelda too about these conundrums, but they were as unable to provide clarity as anyone else. Kallan I never spoke to about my concerns. On the rare occasions he actually partook in a conversation about time travel, he became so antagonistic that I chose to exclude him from all further discussions. He simply could not understand why, given the raft of unanswerable problems, I would still be seriously contemplating embarking on such action, even if such were to help save Safya. "I've lost one of you," he would moan. "I can't lose a second child."

Yet, despite my fears, as I became more immersed in my studies and my plans, my excitement at the possibility of travelling back in time grew and grew. Nothing seemed able to deflect me from my aims, notwithstanding all the unknowables standing in my way.

At length, there was little more to say, and little reason to agonise further. I decided that early the very next morning I would make the leap and transport myself back in time. Haari, who had been visiting me at the estate, returned to his own home, and I went to find Zelda. I told her of my decision, and she was elated, though clever enough not to show it too obviously, lest it irritate me so much that I change my mind. But in truth, I was by now so enthralled by the idea of going back in time, that nothing Zelda, or anyone else, could say or do would deflect me from my plan. I made my farewells to my mother, as I had already done to Haari. I sensed Zelda wanted to remind me to try and collect genetic samples from extraordinary people I encountered, but wisely kept her counsel, remembering my angry reaction the last time she had made such a suggestion. I could not face talking to Kallan, knowing how distressed and irate he was as the prospect of me travelling back in time. I knew such a meeting would achieve nothing but upset him further, and cause me unhappiness, and possibly disequilibrium. I did not want to cause Kallan anxiety, but I would not be diverted from my chosen path.

As I said goodbye to Emaleen I asked her to talk to Kallan after I had gone, and to explain why I felt unable to make my farewells to him personally, noting as I spoke to her that she still maintained the shaved head that had been forced on her after her sister's death. It was as if she was a living memorial to Safya. Emaleen's attitude to my decision was peculiar. On the surface she seemed cool, almost indifferent, but I sensed that this was a front. Beneath the feigned nonchalance, she seemed agitated. I did not think it likely she felt the same anxiety as my uncle, and could only surmise that perhaps she was envious of me, envious that I was able to embark on such an astonishing adventure. Or was her attitude a suppressed hope that I would succeed and be able to prevent the murder of her sister? I chose to accept her superficial show of minimal emotion, rather than delve deeper into the motives for her mood. I had neither the time, nor the inclination to do so at that point.

One thing Emaleen said to me, almost in passing however, raised another fascinating aspect of time travel I had not really considered.

"Why do you want me to talk to uncle after you've gone?" she asked, rubbing a hand over her blond stubble, a habit she had acquired, seeming to enjoy the sensation of shorn hair on her palm. "Can't you make sure you come back just moments after you left, so he won't even know you ever went?" I stared at her, impressed by the astuteness of her off-hand queries. On brief reflection, I realised that she was probably right. On the assumption I could return at all, and control that return, I could choose the time of my reappearance, such that my absence could be kept to the bare minimum, moments even if I so chose. I smiled at my sister.

"What a strange idea," I said. "I could come and go without anyone knowing, even if I spent ages back in the past. I could always return to the exact time and place I'd left." She looked back at me, maintaining her almost indifferent exterior, but the tiniest of wobbles in her voice as she spoke again revealed to me her underlying perturbation at my imminent travels.

"If you stay away ages, will you have aged when you come back, or do you think that when you return you'll be the same age as when you left?" she queried. I looked at her keenly, a slight frown drawing my dark eyebrows together.

"I don't know," I replied. "I really have no idea. But surely if I've aged, then I've aged, and that cannot be turned back? If it did, it would be so bizarre. I could live a whole life in another time, then come back to my own era and carry on where I left off. And I could keep doing it, having endless different lives in different periods." My sister's veneer cracked and she smiled tightly.

"That would just be so weird," she countered. "And so unfair!" I nodded, believing the matter to have been settled. But as with every other aspect of time travel, I could not state anything with certainty. The entire concept was theoretical, and would remain so until I took the leap and subjected myself to its reality. I was not even sure I could go back in time at all, nor that I would survive if I did succeed in travelling through time.

As I was about to take my leave from Emaleen, a distressing thought entered my mind.

"If anything goes wrong," I began quietly, looking directly into her big pale slate-blue eyes. "Then I won't return." She looked pensive, her eyes opening wider. "And if that happens," I continued. "Then you will have to talk to Kallan. And to the others. Will you do that for me?" I added. She hesitated for a moment, then nodded once, turned, and left me the room, her slight swaying gait a reminder of her erstwhile injuries.

But what to do about my brother? I desperately wanted to talk to him, to make my farewells. If disaster should occur, I would never see him again, never talk to him again. This thought brought a lump to my throat and made it hard for me to breathe. As was often the case in those days, he was not at home, though I knew I could contact him directly to tell him what I was about to do. But I would not do so: he might tell the Council. I was still so hurt at his betrayal of me that I could not bring myself to speak to him, knowing I would not be able to contain my anger if we spoke. It pained me dreadfully to take my leave of the time I lived in, with all the risks this entailed, without a final talk with my little brother, but such was the intensity of my damaged feelings that I would not do so. After all, he was the one who had gone behind my back, spent time with Devid. Devid! Of all people! And to reveal to that serpent my time travel plans...I was not sure I would ever forgive my brother for his duplicity. If he was now excluded from my final preparations and farewells, then so be it. He had only himself to blame. And if he were apprised of my plan, surely he would rush straight to his new friend Devid to blab everything.

The night before my grand adventure I had to force myself to sleep, such was my excitement at what I would do at first light. As I lay in bed, trying to calm my breathing and the clamour in my head, my heart beat faster as I contemplated that shortly I would travel in time, that I might make the very first such trip ever made by a human being in the history of the world. What an unsettling idea!

Just before dawn I awoke, and such was my anticipation that I could not remain in bed even at that early hour. I had decided not to take anything with me, nor have contemporary clothes made for me. Fashions changed so fast in the ancient world, and I was not sure the exact year I would arrive in any case. I would acquire suitable garments on my arrival. And it seemed safer to introduce as little matter into the past as I could. I had no idea of the effect that bringing things into another time might have, so chose to keep them to a minimum. I considered making the leap naked, but felt that this would surely attract too much unwanted attention on arrival.

I planned to leave before any of my family was awake, though I sensed Emaleen had already woken. She was in her room, and showed no indication that she would come and see me off. I was slightly disappointed at this, but perhaps it was better to have no distractions as I made my first jump in time. As my sister showed no desire to see me, I chose not to contact her.

Glancing around my room I tried, with little success, not to wonder if I would ever see it again, then took a few deep breaths. I summoned my courage, focused my mind, and began the process of entering the trance-like state which would enable me to travel back in time, linking me directly with some time in the past, a past that no longer existed and yet which I would, in mere moments, inhabit. Or so I hoped. Using the techniques I had worked on for so long, I removed my mind from the world, plunging into the dream-state I had practised so many times. As I felt the pull towards this condition, other thoughts and sensations diminished until I entered a state of sensory dissociation, my surroundings breaking down from objects into bare sensations, the sensations fading into greyness. This was the final stage as I steeled myself for the enormous, world-changing leap back in time.

At first, I could see nothing. Literally nothing. Just the slightest sensation of movement, a floating feeling with no resistance of the ground against my feet. All around me was greyness. Or rather, nothingness. Not even a true greyness. Greyness suggested substance, *something* that was grey. But what I perceived was a complete absence of matter, of anything at all but a foggy, emptiness all around me. Panic gripped me, and I had to exert all my mental energy to quell my terror. I practised mind-exercises I had learned for this very eventuality, gradually gaining control over my alarm. After a little while, I was calm enough to survey my diminished yet expanded consciousness in an effort to try and perceive anything at all in the void which enveloped me, though there seemed to be nothing there. It was as if I had tuned out all objects, all thoughts, all memory, apart from the tiny focus of my attention.

I had no idea how fast I was travelling. And though there was no wind, no physical sensation in any direction, my mind sensed something: a small streak of light in the distance. It appeared for all the world like a tube of light in a fog of greyness, sparkling with a tiny white light tinged with flashes of icy blue. I focused all of my attention on it and it grew brighter. I sensed that I was moving towards it, then alongside it, though it is hard for me to say exactly how I knew this. But it grew bigger or came closer, occupying more and more of the field of greyness. It was my only measure of my speed and location. And then, without warning, it was behind me. I had rushed past it, leaving its tail in my wake. At that instant I knew that the twinkling track of luminescence was a person, a *gifted* person, somewhere out there in the world I was hurtling past. I gasped in shock as the realisation hit me. And then I laughed. A curious, dull tinny sound, without an echo in the emptiness I sailed through. I laughed at my own success. I was travelling in time, and had found another person like me, someone with special abilities marking them out as different.

But as I was congratulating myself, I was filled with immediate dismay. The sparkling streak was so far behind me now I could barely see it. The first person in the past with extraordinary abilities I had ever encountered had only been shown to me for brief moments. I knew nothing about them, their age, their sex, where they lived, when they lived. And how would I actually meet one of them? What did I have to do to stop my breakneck regression through space and time? I calmed myself again and began to experiment with altering the speed of my trajectory. After a few abortive attempts, the first of which caused me another burst of panic when I failed to slow my hurtling voyage, I managed to alter my speed slightly. Or at least, that is what it felt I was doing, as I was able to change the sensation of pulling on my body, and then increase it again. But nothing I did seemed to give me the ability to do more than marginally slow my speed. I was not able to stop. With dismay I realised that I had no control over where I would end up. My desire to travel a little way back in time to help undo the horror of Safya's murder was thwarted.

After a short time I began to peer around me once more, searching keenly for another twinkling human emanation in the form of a stream of brightness. And I did not have to wait long. I realised that if I concentrated, I could just make out a few other such luminous tubes dotted around me in the misty gloom, apparently in random order. As I worked my way through a number of the starry streaks of twinkling light, I wondered how far back I had travelled. I assumed, or perhaps merely hoped, that I was moving in a direct chronological line backwards from my own time, initially through the post-Chaos era. As I continued, the number of shining beams diminished rapidly. I did not understand why this was so until I remembered that the population in the immediate post-Chaos era had been tiny, so the number of gifted individuals would also be minuscule. I surmised that I must be approaching the time of the Chaos itself.

Suddenly, I saw no more of the shooting stars. Then a curious thing happened. My trajectory became less smooth, and I was buffetted slightly as if travelling through cross-winds, or across a choppy ocean. The effect only lasted a few moments, to be replaced once again by the perfectly serene grey nothingness of before. Had I just passed through the Chaos? As I made myself calm once more, I saw a few bright twinkling beams of light out of the corners of my eyes. I focused on them, and suddenly found myself hurtling towards one of them.

As the bright tunnel rushed towards me I knew I was exhausted, weak from the exertions of travelling in time, dizzy from the experience. I had no way of resisting the pull towards the light. It grew bigger and bigger, evermore bright and luminescent, filling my perceptions until I was enveloped in a world of dazzling brightness. With no warning I collided with an object I could not discern. Incandescent brilliance erupted all around me, so intense that I was blinded. I lost consciousness.

Chapter Fifty-Two

I came slowly back to consciousness. I was lying in a messy heap upon hard ground. I remained absolutely still, eyes closed, until the dizziness and nausea I was suffering passed. As I waited for my mind to clear, the enormity of what I had just done struck me: I had travelled in time! For the first time in history a human being had successfully moved himself from one time period to another, and I was that human being. I calmed my pounding heart, and then opened my eyes by the tiniest crack. It was the early-afternoon, judging from the light and the angle of the sun still high in the sky. The day was warm, though with an edge to it, as if chilliness were not far away.

I moved my head to look around. I was lying slightly to the side of a small green space. Slowly I stood up, dizziness threatening to render me once more unconscious as I unfurled my body from the ground. After a few moments standing quite still I risked lifting my right foot, and giggled slightly as I contemplated myself standing almost still on the edge of the small green square, one foot lifted slightly off the ground, almost too timid to put it down again lest I break the spell and find myself unable to do so. But when I lowered it gingerly to the ground in front of my left foot, it came to a rest just as it would have done in my home world. I laughed out loud, causing a few passers-by to glance at me sideways. A few of them showed signs of vague interest in me, glancing up and down briefly at my obviously unusual clothing, and perhaps slight concern at a stranger laughing to himself who had only just dragged himself from a lying position on the grass. But not one of them slowed their pace, or looked back again, and I realised I had learned the first lesson of wherever and whenever it was I had landed: strangers show little interest in each other's behaviour. One woman, walking briskly across the square I was in, changed her trajectory slightly as if to walk a little further from me than she would otherwise have done. She frowned slightly as she contemplated my simple emerald-green tunic and baggy leggings, cinched by a silver belt at my waist, but she merely shook her head slightly as she continued with her brisk steps. I looked around me, taking in the activities I saw. The square was a thoroughfare, and a number of people seemed to be passing across it, all in very much of a hurry as far as I could see. On the pavements surrounding the square on all sides I noticed other people, also rushing past. Noisy wheeled vehicles raced around the square on all four sides, disappearing from sight past the square or into side streets. Another lesson, it seemed: people here are always in a hurry, so unlike the meandering and aimless crowds in Beyra. Time seemed to be more valuable to these people, unlike those in my time with their long and idle lives. Why hurry anywhere if you nothing in particular to do?

But there were others taking a more leisurely approach to life, or at least to this moment. A few wooden benches dotted here and there in the square were occupied, one or two with couples chatting quietly, but mostly with individuals sitting, as far as I could tell, as distantly the one from the other as they possibly could within the confines of the arm rests on each end of the bench. They were squeezed up against the edges of the benches, despite there being space to spare in between, and they studiously ignored each other with a skill that seemed well-practised, competent, each occupied with their own activities. This was in marked contrast to my trips to Beyra and other cities of my time. In the twenty-ninth century nobody seemed to want to be alone, at least not when out in public where everyone wandered about in leisurely fashion in noisy, chatty groups. Many of the people in this square seemed to be eating, and I surmised that this must be a mealtime. One or two had their heads buried in books, but most appeared mesmerised by small electronic devices they held in one hand, which I quickly ascertained were portable communication devices, though even on a cursory survey of them with my mind, I knew they had many more functions than mere telephony. But how clunky they looked! And as I scanned their workings, I laughed at how primitive these devices were. My chuckles once more evoked a flutter of mildly disapproving glances.

A few people sat on the grass, and as with the benches, there were a few groups but mostly lone individuals. And the single people were dotted in what appeared random locations, but on closer inspection I saw that they were in fact rather precisely situated to be as far from others as possible, a ring of grass around each one, each person almost exactly the same distance from the person to their right and their left. I was reminded of bushes growing in deserts, which look almost regimented in their spacing from their neighbours. I wondered if these people managed such precise distancing from each other consciously, or whether it was simply years of practice. Were they aware of it at all? And I could not help wonder if people in my time ever sought solitude in this way. I had never seen it, though I had a small sampling to draw from. Perhaps a desire to be alone was considered socially inappropriate in my time, though I knew that some people chose to live alone. Haari for one. But even he spent little time at home, always out and about with his friends and family.

Most amazingly of all was the fact that nobody really seemed to notice that a person had just appeared out of nowhere, popped up in a spot where moments before there had not been anyone. Did people here really have so little interest in what was happening around them that nobody noticed my arrival? Or could they possibly have already mastered teleportation? I doubted this was the case as this must surely be a time before the Chaos, and teleportation was not invented until many centuries after the Chaos. As I looked at these people, on the benches and the grass, scampering across the paved areas, I could only assume that humans here were so immersed in their own little worlds, their clumsy communication devices, that a stranger could literally materialise before their very eyes without them seeing it. I sighed. These were primitive people indeed.

I quickly scanned the minds of the people around me and discovered that I was in London, which, if memory served me correctly, was the capital of the island nation of Britain situated off the north-west coast of Europe. It was the year 2012: I had travelled eight hundred years! I learned this fact from one of the people squashed onto the end of a bench who was specifically thinking about this date. The man seemed to be trying to find out whether there were still any 'tickets left for the olympics' on his device which involved him contemplating specific dates in August of 2012, though I guessed he was having little success due to the tetchiness in his mind.

Within mere moments of arriving in 2012, I committed my first act of theft: I had noticed that the man seeking tickets for the olympics was accompanied by a number of large bags on the ground beside him, each carrying several items of clothing. I emitted a slight thrust of energy, causing him to lose awareness of what was happening around him, and quickly removed a shirt, jumper, trousers and shoes from his bags. I had no moral qualms about taking the clothing, but did not want to attract unwanted attention. In fact, the man had been so immersed in his electronic device, that perhaps I had had no need to use my gifts, but I certainly did not want to be caught stealing clothing within my first few moments in London!

As I walked to the edge of the square, I ducked into some bushes where I quickly changed my clothing, leaving my own garments in a pile on the ground. I should have liberated a bag from the man too, I thought, but decided that I could simply abandon my own clothes. My new garments were too big for me, but not by too much, simply hanging loosely off my limbs. As it was not cold, I tied the jumper around my waist. By luck, the shoes fitted fairly well, enough to allow me to walk without too much discomfort, though I wished I had worn socks as I travelled as there were none in my bag of thieved booty.

I emerged from the bushes and walked out of the square I had landed in. I located a name plaque on one of the walls just outside the space.

'Bloomsbury Square', it informed me. I stood on the pavement with the aim of crossing the road encircling the green. I was very wary of the vehicles rushing up and down both sides of this road, being almost totally unaccustomed to such things. We had vehicles in my own time, but these were almost silent, and clean, producing no filthy emissions. In addition, they were never used within towns and cities. Most people used portals to travel and walked around the urban areas, vehicles being reserved mainly for trips to the wilder parts of our world where no portals existed. And of course, our vehicles were engineered such that it was impossible for them to crash or even collide with anything else.

I had to wait at the side of the road, and then dart between the dirty, noisy, smelly cars and vans that seemed in such a hurry to be somewhere else. I managed, finally, to reach the pavement on the other side of the street, though not without several vehicles making loud beeping noises at me, presumably to warn me to get out of their way. I stood to catch my breath, feeling foolish that I had barely been able to cross a road, despite having travelled eight hundred years to get to the road in the first place!

I was aware of feeling weary, sluggish from the exertions of time travel as I walked. I turned into a small street leading away from the square, for no reason but that I felt a need to move, to stretch my legs after the sensations of time travel. As I walked, I constantly had to jump to get out of the way of other pedestrians, all in such a hurry and apparently so oblivious to others that they may as well have been hurrying alone through the quiet countryside. I could not understand how they themselves did not endlessly bump and crash into each other, but mostly they did not. Again, I could only surmise that their years of practice at negotiating the relentlessly busy pavements of this bustling city had rendered them expert in this. The only ones who seemed to collide with others were those walking and manipulating their small portable telephones at the same time. Why did they persist in using these hand-held machines if they were unable to do so and walk at the same time? This struck me as singularly foolish behaviour, especially as they crossed roads as they walked, seemingly oblivious to the racing, noisy vehicles.

As I walked I saw a glass-fronted building whose window was filled with a display of the portable telephones, and saw that they were called mobile phones or just mobiles. How clunky and cumbersome they were, occupying not only the hands but also, so it seemed, the focus and concentration of their users as they stared intently at the tiny screens. Some of the people were talking into these mobile phones, presumably to another person doing the same in another place, and these people were as adept as managing the thronging pavements as others. Or almost as adept. The fact of having a conversation at a distance seemed to distract them to some degree from their immediate surroundings, and they occasionally had to swerve swiftly to avoid a collision. This sort of behaviour I had seen in Beyra as people used the implants in their heads to communicate with friends at a distance, but with implants (as with actually speaking on a telephone), the speaker still had full use of his or her eyes to watch where they were going. But the other people here in London, the ones who were tapping away busily on the surface of the telephones, these people seemed completely unaware of their environment, and were often involved in minor accidents with other pedestrians, usually those who themselves were as occupied with their own mobiles. When such a collision occurred, a few of them tutted in irritation, or mumbled a brief yet insincere apology, but to my amazement, most of them hardly seemed aware of the jolt, and simply continued on their way as if nothing had happened. The only time I saw one of them react strongly was when the force of the bump caused the telephone to tumble from a woman's hands to the ground, shattering it into its constituent parts. This led to a loud verbal altercation which I heard continue as I moved past the two people involved.

On another occasion I witnessed a more serious accident. On the pavement somebody had left open what looked like a trapdoor leading underground. The door itself was quite large, easy to see, if a person were looking, that is. But a rather portly woman in red shoes with very high heels was teetering along the pavement some way in front of me, immersed in whatever it was she was doing with her portable telephone. I assumed she would see the open door on the pavement so did not think to shout a warning to her. But she did not see the door, crashed straight into it and fell headfirst into the gaping hole, the last thing to disappear being the shiny red heels of her unsuitable footwear. The image was so unexpected, and comical, that I guffawed, then quickly clapped my hand over my mouth to stifle the sound. Laughing at another's misfortune, while still a regular occurrence among my own people, was surely looked upon with the same disapprobation in 2012 as it was in my own time? For a moment I wondered if I should stop to help, but as I approached the open hole, I was amazed to see the large woman emerge from the hole, clambering up with the help of a ladder leading down into the hole, but struggling to do so as she could only use one hand to haul herself up with: the other hand still clutched the telephone! And from the look of concentration on her face, I guessed that she had not even paused in whatever it was she had been doing with the device before her headlong plunge through the open trapdoor.

I crossed a junction shortly after the amusing episode with the fat woman. The junction was wide and chaotic. After a few more minutes of fighting through the thronging sea of humanity, something grabbed my attention with a snap. My senses were invaded by the presence of a gifted person close by, a woman. My eyes darted all around until they alighted upon a shuffling figure some thirty or so metres away from me moving surprisingly rapidly away down the pavement. Her back disappeared from view among the crowds, reappearing briefly and disappearing again as she walked. The sensation of gifts and abilities took my breath away both because of their intensity but also the sheer unexpectedness of them.

I hastened to follow the woman using a mixture of simple vision and my own gifts. When she disappeared from view I worried that I would not be able to follow her due to the immense throng of humanity moving in disordered disarray in all directions on the pavement. I hurried my step, following the woman for some time along streets and down alleys, over junctions and crossroads.

Suddenly, my quarry stopped. I sped up to try and reach her, but as I arrived at the spot from which she had just left, my focus was drawn sharply to the display she had been gazing at in the huge window of what I assumed was a shop. A bookshop. Something in the window drew my attention as if almost shouting at me to be looked at. A display of books by a writer called Ruth Firestone, and at the front of the display her "Newest and Best", the "Seventh instalment of the compelling World's End saga".

I was mystified that this book, and what I assumed were the first six instalments of the saga arrayed around it, should so demand my scrutiny. I felt as though I had no option but to investigate further. I was so distracted by the books' silent appeal that I lost track of the woman I had been following as she wove her disappearing way through the crowds. I could think of no way to locate the woman again, so decided instead to investigate what it was that had drawn me to the books in the window. I entered the bookshop.

I gazed up at a notice board indicating the layout of the shop. It was a big building and I did not understand most of the descriptions of different types of book. As I stood sighing with frustration, a young woman approached me, asking me if I needed any help. I turned to see a cheery face smiling at me. She wore a label of some sort with her name, Hannah, and what I guessed was the name of the shop. I nodded and opened my mouth to speak. At first, nothing came out, causing the woman's cheerful smile to fade slightly. I had not uttered a single word since my arrival, and was suddenly frozen in my first attempt to do this.

My own language, the *only* living language in my own world and time, was a direct descendant of this same English spoken shortly before the Chaos, with a minor sub-stratum of influence from a few other languages. Many of the survivors of the Chaos were themselves native English speakers, given the realities of the world order before the Chaos. And even more importantly, most of the others spoke English as a second language. In this world I found myself in 2012, just before the Chaos, English was the dominant world language, with no competitors. It did not enjoy the largest number of native speakers (although it was second or third in this list as far as I remembered). But what it enjoyed was the status of the unrivalled world language, the lingua franca that everybody else scrabbled desperately to learn. So when the tiny groups of survivors emerged from hiding after the Chaos, English was the only realistically usable language in those terrible early years. All other languages spoken in small numbers by some of the survivors quickly died as it was essential that all remaining members of the human race be able to communicate easily and freely with each other. Within a generation or two after the Chaos, English was the only language spoken natively by all remaining people. And this has continued to be the case right up to the time I write these memoirs as an old man. Though many people still enjoy studying other ancient languages even today, as I commit my memories to paper nine hundred years after the Chaos, these tongues are all dead, every single one of them. And I knew from my studies using the digital memory just how much my own English resembled that spoken at the time I had travelled to. I spoke with a slightly different accent, and occasionally used odd words or expressions, but this would be nothing out of the ordinary in a city with so many people from so many parts of the world.

After a few moments of hesitation as the woman's smile faded more and more, I finally found my voice.

"Yes," I forced out hoarsely. "I am looking for the books you have over there, in the window. By Ruth Firestone." The woman nodded, relieved that I had finally broken my silence and that my request would be so easy to answer. If she had noticed an odd accent or manner of speaking on my part, she made no issue of it.

"Of course," she replied politely. "Up the stairs over there to the second floor then at the top turn right and follow the corridor until you reach the section called Science Fiction. You'll find the books you're looking for under F."

I nodded my thanks and followed the young woman's instructions.

I stopped directly in front of a tall wooden bookcase, laden from top to bottom with books, each one's coloured spine facing outwards, the name of the book and I assumed the author emblazoned on it. I perused the bookcase and discovered that almost the entire contents of the middle shelf were books by Ruth Firestone. I read the name out loud to practise speaking, attracting a tiny glance from a young man in spectacles at the next bookshelf. What a pretty name, I thought. Firestone. I took one of the books out of the bookshelf and held it in my hands. I was then suddenly struck with a realisation: the woman I had been following *was* Ruth Firestone. I was not sure how I knew this, but felt sure that this was indeed the case, that the author herself had stopped on the pavement to gaze at the display of her own books, the central place being taken by the seventh instalment of her saga. Was she merely checking the way this bookshop displayed her work, or was it simple pride to see her name so prominently on show? I picked up one of the books, entitled "What World Lies Beyond?", and opened the first page. The publisher's name was given as Guillemot, along with the address of Guillemot, in London. This book, according to the information inside the cover, was the first in a series of science fiction novels in which the author recounted the tales of the horrors of the world during, and then after, an almost total disaster of such epic proportions as to destroy everything and everyone. I shuddered slightly as I read the description, and then skimmed through the first few chapters of the book.

I became more and more astonished, and disturbed, as I did so. And as I selected the second, the third, the fourth of the series and right through to the seventh, the most recent, I was utterly dumbstruck. What I read seemed almost to be a description of the Chaos, or at least many aspects of it, and then of the world of the survivors. Some parts of the Chaos were omitted, and its fictional progression was not identical to fact, nor was the post-Chaos world described exactly how it had actually happened, yet the parallels were so close that I knew that the apparently ordinary shuffling woman that I had followed as she moved through the world, must surely have foreseen much of what really was to occur, and then decided to write about it. Her abilities much be extraordinary, to allow her access to such foresight. Could she have any inkling that she wielded such a gift? I suspected not, yet something had driven her to write about what she saw, record what she perceived, even perhaps hoping that what her books described might serve as a warning. An unheeded warning, as history would show.

I memorised the address of Guillemot, determined to locate its offices where I might discover the whereabouts of Ruth Firestone. As I walked down the stairs of the bookshop another thought jumped into my head. Surely the white and blue starry streak of light I had crashed into on my arrival was Ruth. Surely, somehow, I had been dragged to her location though not by any deliberate design. Her gifts were so great that, even without her knowledge, her cry for help had acted as a magnet, pulling me into its sphere of influence, forcing me to stop, and to find her.

Chapter Fifty-Three

On my way towards the door of the bookshop, I noticed a large table covered in books about London. One of the most prominent was a street map. I opened it, wondering how to locate the address of Guillemot. I flicked through its pages as if hoping that the location of Ruth's publisher would simply pop out of the mass of coloured maps. My frustration grew and I dropped the book back onto the table. As it fell it opened to reveal what looked like a list of street names at the end of the book. I quickly found the street I sought then the page it was listed on. After a few moments of scanning the correct page my eyes fell on the name of Guillemot's street. On the previous page I found the location of the bookshop I was in and was able to trace a line with my finger from Guillemot to where I stood. I glanced around me, deftly slid the book under my shirt and hastened out of the shop before I was apprehended in my second theft.

Once a safe distance from the bookshop I removed the book from its hiding place, opened it to the correct page and briskly followed the line I had traced to Guillemot, so intent on my goal that I barely noticed the hustle and bustle going on all around me.

Despite the assistance offered by the map, I found its symbols and squiggles difficult to decipher. A number of times I lost my way, or had to retrace my steps. I even sat down on a welcome bench for a while on one occasion, so frustrated was I by my apparent inability to do something as simple as read a map.

Eventually I arrived in front of the publisher's offices, breathing a sigh of relief as I did so. What should surely have been a fairly short brisk walk had taken me nearly two hours! I stopped in front of the building and looked up. It had a glass and metal door set in a facade of yellow bricks. The entire length of the street was occupied by what appeared to be a single, long, building. It was four storeys high, or perhaps five - I could not quite see the top from where I stood. Each storey had a perfectly straight line of windows, each window identical to the next. The roof was not visible, obscured as it was by a small wall built in front of it. This wall had no obvious purpose, and seemed to exist simply to hide the roof behind. Each sequence of four windows on the ground floor was interrupted by a door. Most of these were of brightly painted wood, but a few, like Guillemot's, were made of gleaming metal and glass. Every door was accessed by a short flight of steps, each one sided with a curved railing of metal painted a glossy black. I glanced down to my right, and noticed another, longer flight of stairs leading to a lower floor, almost below ground, the top frame of whose windows was at foot level. I dredged up from my memory some of the history of cities like London. I recalled that in these old houses, the servants had lived below stairs, down in the semi-dark bowels of the building, with the owner's family occupying the bright, airy floors above. I assumed that such a social set-up no longer existed in 2012, and wondered who now occupied the lowest floors.

I was far from being an expert in English architectural history, but called dimly to mind something I had come across in my studies about many of these buildings filling the centre of London. They dated from approximately two hundred years before the time I now found myself in, and I remembered that the unembellished facades and semi-obscured roofs were hallmarks of that time. They seemed beautifully preserved for such old buildings, and I surmised that they must have been in constant use, subjected to continual upkeep to have remained so perfect. The sheerness of the facade was such that the entire terrace looked like one long building, and only the existence of the regularly spaced doors indicated that there were many separate dwellings in this one unbroken edifice.

I gingerly mounted the steps to the entrance, and had to struggle somewhat to open the heavy glass door by pushing hard against its brassy handle. It felt unusually heavy. Perhaps I was still weak from my journey through time and space. I entered and stopped in the hallway. Inside it was beautiful. A sturdy staircase in the shape of an L led from the left-hand side of the hall to the first floor. The floor itself showed an intricate pattern of tiles in black, white and dark green. There were large pots of tall ferns in several of the corners. The light was subdued, mostly entering through the door, or the round window above the door which was made of coloured glass. I noted with surprise how much this entrance hall reminded me of buildings in my own time. I stood marvelling at this fact and so enjoying the experience of this shady, cool hallway, that I had not noticed a small table on my right, behind which sat a very small, thin woman dressed in a garment of almost exactly the same moss-green as the tiles of the floor. Given that the paint on the walls was another shade of green, slightly paler than that on the floor, this tiny person blended with her surroundings, a little chameleon sitting still on a leaf. Thus I jumped slightly when a voice seemed to emerge, bodiless, from the very fabric of the building.

"Can I help you?" the voice asked, more loudly than one would expect from such a small frame. I span round and stared, not knowing how to respond. The woman peered at me over the flat top of her dark-rimmed spectacles.

"Can I help you?" she repeated, more sharply. I did not imagine that she led a busy life here in this quiet hallway, yet her tone carried more than a trace of impatience, as if I had somehow disturbed her in the middle of some activity of great importance. While I thought about what to say, I smiled. I cursed myself for not having properly planned my visit to Guillemot Publishers. I conjectured that a smile should at least give me a moment to think. The woman did not return my smile. She pursed her lips and raised her eyebrows, emitting the tiniest hint of a sigh from her nostrils. I finally managed to babble a reply.

"I...I...you...you have an author," I began, still hesitant to speak and made nervous by the woman's manner.

The little woman behind the desk sighed overtly at my foolishly obvious comment.

"We *are* a publishing house," she replied acidly, and said no more. Clearly my comment deserved no more response than this.

"Ruth. Ruth Firestone," I continued.

"Yes," snapped the bird-like woman. "What about her?"

"She's one of your writers, isn't she?" I asked.

"Yes. But I repeat: what about her?"

"Do you know where I could find her?" I asked.

"What do you mean, 'find her'? Is she lost?"

"No. I mean, where does she live?" I blurted out. The little woman gave me a look of such arch disdain that I almost bolted for the door. After a long, tense pause, she finally deigned to reply.

"We cannot possibly give out such information," she stated in an official tone, finality seeping out of her as she did so. She seemed to believe our interaction was at an end and looked down at some papers on the table in front of her. I, however, did not, and remained where I was, rooted to the ground, staring at her, though at a loss as to how to progress. The woman sighed again as she realised I was not going to leave, the index finger of her right hand drumming impatiently on the desk in front of her. She looked up sharply, again glaring at me across the top of her spectacles.

"And who are you?" she finally asked in a tight voice.

"I'm her nephew," I replied, without hesitation, though surprising myself at how easily this lie came to my mouth, without pre-meditation. The woman's manner shifted infinitesimally, the tiniest diminution of hostility flowing from her.

"And your name is?" she asked, her tone not quite as acidic as before. Almost, but not quite.

"Same..." I began, tailing off before finishing my name, as I wondered if the name Samek existed in this time. If it did not, I might attract unwanted attention by using it.

"Sammy what?" the woman interrupted impatiently, accompanying her question with yet another sigh of frustration and a tiny drum roll of fingernails on the table top. I hesitated for a brief moment, caught out by this unexpected question, but relieved that Sammy at least seemed to be proper name for the period, even though that is not quite what I had said.

"Sammy Firestone," I said on the spur of the moment, giving the only second name I could think of, and using the form of name the little woman had used.

I wondered if I had chosen well. Did nephews in this time have the same second names as their aunts? I found the family relations in the old world hard to keep a track of, though I knew that the second names were family names, thus shared by a group of related people. I quickly thought about how I could carry the same family name as Ruth. I remembered that a woman usually took her husband's family name on marriage, so if Ruth were married, and used her husband's family name, then I would have to be the son of one of her husband's brothers to have the name Firestone, or the son of a sister of her husband, but not if that sister were also married and had taken *her* husband's family name. And if Ruth were not married, or wrote under her own family name, then I would have to be the child of Ruth's brother, or unmarried sister, or sister who still used her own family name. I tried, rapidly, to sort all of this out in my mind. Apparently, my relationship to the author was sufficient for this tiny, yet fierce, custodian of the entrance to Guillemot, to allow me access to the hallowed inner chambers. She picked up the top part of a device on her desk, also green, and pressed some buttons on the part which rested on the table.

"Mr Schapps?" she asked after a moment. "I have a Sammy Firestone in reception. Ruth's nephew. He's asking about her, where he can find her. Shall I send him up?" She replaced the top of the device, which I realised must be a communication device, though not one that could be carried, and turned to me.

"Mr Schapps will see you," she said with raised eyebrows. I looked blankly at her. She frowned in renewed irritation.

"Mr Schapps is the director of Guillemot," she explained. "He knows Miss Firestone well. Go up the stairs over there and follow the corridor round to the front of the first floor. You'll see his name on the door. But make sure you knock before you go in," she instructed, as if I were a child. Her tone indicated that she was glad to be passing the burden of dealing with me on to somebody else. I smiled tentatively at her, as eager to be away from her as she seemed to be to wash her hands of me, and moved towards the staircase. As I mounted the first step, she said in a loud voice.

"You've very lucky. He doesn't see most people. Not without an appointment." I smiled again and mumbled my thanks, quickly mounting the stairs. I followed her instructions and soon found myself standing in front of a large wooden door with a brass plaque, the name "Simon Schapps" engraved on it in solid letters. I knocked.

"Come in, come in," called out a friendly, yet weary voice. I was relieved to hear the tone, having had enough of the hostility of the ground floor guardian. I pushed the door open and walked in. The room I entered was large and wide, with two windows facing me. In front of the windows was a huge desk of very dark wood, covered by what looked like dark green leather. Whoever was responsible for the decoration of Guillemot had a strong preference for green, it seemed, as had the designer of Beyra I noted with a small pang of homesickness. The desk was loaded with piles of paper balanced precariously on stacks of books. The walls of the room were filled with bookcases groaning under the weight of more books. And there was barely any space on the carpet (also green!), this too being covered with heaps of books stacked haphazardly across the whole room.

"Mr Schapps?" I enquired politely.

"Simon, please, call me Simon," said the genial-faced man sitting behind the desk, facing the door. I estimated his age at about fifty, though this was little more than a guess. He was short, bald on top with only a line of greyish hair encircling the lower half of his head. He had large, kindly brown eyes, and as I entered he took his glasses off, placing them on the table in front of him as he looked directly at me. "Come in and sit down," he continued, beckoning me to a leather chair placed in front of the desk. I smiled inwardly as I noticed the chair was brown. Clearly the decorator had overlooked this object when greening the rest of the building. The chair had its own complement of books, and Simon blushed slightly as I stood beside it, not quite knowing what to do.

"Just put them on the floor," he said with an embarrassed laugh. As I did so, and sat down, he carried on talking.

"Penelope said you are Ruth Firestone's nephew?" he asked in a kind voice. I smiled at him as I sat down, noting that he seemed harried, stress sitting only just behind the genial exterior, a slight flush on his cheeks.

"Yes," I replied, not knowing what else to add. I was saved the effort by Mr Schapps' next question.

"You must be her brother's boy, Samuel," he said. I was confused. I felt relieved by the question, as it implied that Ruth must only have one brother. This made my purported relationship to Ruth easy to hold in my head, but why had Mr Schapps called me Samuel? Before I could reply, perhaps committing some sort of gaffe thereby, I was saved again by Mr Schapps.

"I remember she told me that her brother's called Samuel, so I imagine you were named after him?" he asked. I just nodded, assuming that Sammy was a short form of the name Samuel, just as it was for Samek in my time. History told me that parents sometimes gave a son the same name as the father. How confusing that would be in the home. How would you know which Samuel was being referred to? Perhaps the son would be given a nick-name, or use a short form such as Sammy. I was hugely relieved that my off-the-cuff lies had so easily settled into the truth.

"You're looking to find your aunt?" Mr Schapps asked. I realised he was someone who did not leave many silences, and would fill any gap in a conversation. It would be safest to let him do most of the talking. I nodded, and mumbled "Yes."

"You don't know her address?" he queried, frowning slightly. But before I could think up a plausible reason why I did not know my own aunt's address, I was rescued once again by the garrulous Mr Schapps.

"Well I'm not really surprised. I know she has almost nothing to do with her family. She's told me a few times how she doesn't get on with any of them." I restricted my reply to a nod, and an appropriately despondent expression.

"I'm glad you're trying to find her," Mr Schapps went on. "Family's important and it's not right for you not to know her, even if she and her brother, your father, haven't spoken for years. When did you last see her?" he asked me suddenly.

"I can't remember," I mumbled. "Years ago."

"Sad. Very sad. She's a wonderful woman," he added, though as he said this an odd expression crossed his lined face. A wistful, unhappy look. "She was only here this morning visiting me, discussing plans for her next novel," he added. I almost winced with frustration that I had missed her.

Mr Schapps then paused and I sensed he was considering whether to share with me what had crossed his mind. He seemed to decide that he would, or perhaps he was just someone who found it difficult to keep his thoughts unspoken.

"She's had a lot of problems," he said quietly. "Problems of a...psychological nature," he continued in an almost conspiratorial tone, leaning across the desk towards me as he spoke. I followed his lead, leaning towards him, looking directly into his surprisingly pretty brown eyes, noticing how dense his lashes were, his eyes framed by thick but well-shaped dark brows.

"Yes," I said softly. "So I understand from my father." Mr Schapps sat back, a look of slight surprise on his face. For once, he remained quiet.

"I'd love to see her again," I said, feeling I needed to take the initiative. "I think perhaps I could help her, or at least get to know her. After all," I added, "she *is* my aunt. And as you said, family is important." Mr Schapps remained silent, and I sensed conflict in his mind. But eventually he seemed to resolve his dilemma.

"I'd love to help you young man," he said in a vaguely dejected tone. "I really would. But I can't give out my authors' addresses without their permission."

"But she's my aunt," I pleaded in a slightly whiny tone, frustrated.

"Yes, yes I know, but without Ruth's express permission I can't give out her address, not even to family members. It's a matter of privacy, and professionalism. I'm sure you understand." I sat for a moment, wondering what to do next, and as I considered, I noticed, as if for the first time, what I assumed was a computer of some sort on the side of Mr Schapps' desk, partially obscured by the mounds of papers and tomes. I realised that Ruth's address would be stored somewhere in Guillemot's records. Obviously a publisher needed to know where its authors lived.

I had never tried to access information from an ancient computer. In fact, I had never seen a real one before, and wondered if I would be able to access its memory. I needed to create a little time for myself however, so I used the techniques I had developed as a child in controlling the minds of animals and put Mr Schapps into a state close to hypnosis, freezing his mind in mid-thought. I had used a similar technique in the Council Chamber when I had forced the murderer of Safya to speak, and a weaker version on the man whose clothing I had stolen so recently in Bloomsbury Square. I had only just recovered sufficient energy to be able to carry out this simplest of tasks. Mr Schapps froze, mouth open, about to speak. I felt truly sorry for him, for having to resort to such measures, and hastily got on with the task of accessing Ruth's address, the quicker to return Mr Schapps to normal.

Its technologies being of such antiquated type, I had no idea how to begin to understand the ancient computer. And to be honest, I had never shown a great deal of interest in the workings of machines except at the most basic level. I was flummoxed. I sat for a few moments, wondering what to do next, when I realised that Mr Schapps might know Ruth's address. It was certainly worth a try. I used my slowly returning reserves of energy to enter his mind, though I did so with a twinge of reluctance at invading this kindly man's privacy in this way. I could not at first find Ruth's address, though with a little delving, intruding more deeply than I felt comfortable with, I unearthed it. It seemed that Mr Schapps had a keen memory for such things, something I was grateful for. I committed the address to memory, withdrew from Mr Schapps' mind, and at the same moment, removed the control holding the unfortunate Mr Schapps in his unanimated state. As he sprang back to life, he picked up exactly where he had left off.

"As I was saying," he said kindly, shaking his head slightly as if to rouse himself. He paused for a moment, frowning slightly. "Actually, I feel rather odd. Have we met before today?" he asked me suddenly. I shook my head.

"No," I replied. "Why do you ask?"

"I've just had the most powerful sensation that we've met before. A real sense of déjà-vu. Are you sure we've not met before?" he repeated. Once again, I shook my head, wondering if my entering his mind had caused him to believe we had met previously. But before I could think further on the matter, Mr Schapps shrugged slightly and continued to speak.

"I do hope you can find your aunt. Can't you ask your father, or your grandparents. I think Ruth's father might still be alive, isn't he?" he asked. I nodded vaguely, not wanting to commit myself to an unequivocal reply. I smiled at Mr Schapps, not wanting to impinge upon his time, or his kindness, any further. In any case, I had what I had come for. I stood up, smiling.

"I understand Mr Schapps...Simon," I said. "Obviously you can't invade my aunt's privacy. I'll ask my father. And thank you so much for your time today, it's been a pleasure meeting you." He also stood up, clearly embarrassed not to have been able to help me more, and seemingly even more so at my polite comments.

"I'm so sorry not to have been able to help more, young man, but I'm glad you understand," he said, proffering his hand across the desk. I leaned across and shook it warmly, smiling all the time.

"Thank you," I said again as I walked away from the desk, closing the door of Mr Schapps' office as I left the room, seeing him standing behind his messy desk, a look of regret on his face. I tripped down the stairs and across the tiled hallway. As I pulled the glass door to the street open, I could not help turning to the acerbic Penelope (whose name I had learned from Mr Schapps), throwing a parting shot in her direction.

"Penelope," I said brightly. "Thank you so much for your help. You're a ray of sunshine." And as I left the building I laughed out loud at Penelope's confused scowl at my blatantly insincere words.

Chapter Fifty-Four

I ported myself back to Bloomsbury Square. It was beginning to feel like home, as if this were the doorway to London, the only place I could have entered the city from. That I had entered through here the very first time I travelled in time lent it a strange status in my mind. I felt comfortable in this square, as if more securely connected to the future from this spot than from anywhere else I had been this day. Perhaps the fact of being so distant from my own time and place made me grasp at anything which felt even the slightest bit more familiar than the otherwise chaotic newness of everything else. Bloomsbury Square became my point of orientation.

I found a vacant space on a bench, though this time was forced to share it with another person. I glanced briefly at the man at the other end of the bench, as far from me as he could manage. He was dressed smartly in matching jacket and trousers, a blue shirt and rather garishly multi-coloured thin item of clothing tied tightly around his neck. He paid me no attention whatsoever as I sat down, so immersed was he in tapping away at the tiny rectangular toy in his hand. His furious tapping on the screen accompanied by regular beeping intrigued me, but I did not know if this was a game or some kind of vexed communication with another person. But I did not feel I had the luxury to enquire further. I had to find the woman I had followed earlier, and to do this I would have to travel to her home. I had no idea where it was, despite having memorised her address. I needed a map of the area. I assumed I could find other maps in the bookshop where I had stolen the map of London. I wondered if this time I should resist stealing again. My two previous thefts could have drawn unwanted attention to myself. I wanted to avoid this, as well as the risk of being caught. After all, this society's economy did not permit people to get something for nothing. In my own time theft was almost non-existent, and this is still the case as I write as an old man. It is not that people are necessarily more honest in my time (although in truth they probably are as we have been selectively bred for centuries to be that way). But when one can simply requisition anything, what cause is there to steal? The whole idea is simply redundant. Theft is surely predicated on some people having what others want, and those without believing that the easiest way to acquire the object is to take it, without permission, from those others? In my time such a thing would be laughable, and even if someone took an object belonging to another, the other person would simply order a replacement, confused as to why the thief had not done that in the first place. I had to force myself to remember that in this year of 2012, theft was considered to be a serious moral issue for most people.

I decided it was safer to buy the new map. But money! There was a slippery concept which I had studied at length. I was sure that most people in the world I was visiting understood it almost instinctively, so pervasive was its influence, so ubiquitous its presence, yet to a person brought up in a society without money, it was a remarkably difficult idea to get to grips with. I understood the idea of exchange of goods or services, bartering to find an acceptable interchange of value of something offered by one person to another. Even in my own world, we sometimes engaged in something similar, one person offering to make an artefact for another in return for some other object or service. Such actions happened naturally and easily, and this I understood. But money was different. In itself, it had no value. I knew that in the twenty-first century coins did not have any intrinsic value, but not long before this time, coins did have intrinsic value, being made of precious, desirable metals. Though even this was only because people attached value to those metals. Without such attachment of value, even the use of gold or silver coinage representing goods or services was arbitrary. And later, the gold and silver were replaced by much cheaper metals, and eventually just paper! The value inherent in the means of exchange bore no relation to the content of what was being exchanged. I found it hard to grasp that people would happily accept a pile of fundamentally worthless pieces of paper and in return give up goods of real value, or devote substantial amounts of their precious time in providing a service in return for bits of paper. And by 2012 most transactions were carried out electronically, so the people never even saw physical evidence of the money side of the bargain.

I remembered discussing the concept of money at length with Bartrem who had a particular interest in the workings of such systems in the old world. He had described it in a way which helped me understand it more than anyone else. He had called it a surrogate.

"Money represents the goods or services exchanged," he explained. "It functions as a surrogate for the actual goods or services. And as long as everyone understands the value of the surrogate, and accepts it, and it is backed up by some real authority, then it's an effective system. It is much quicker and easier than barter and exchange, and can be done at a distance."

Be that as it may, I needed money, and quite a bit of it, though I knew I would struggle to understand why goods and services were valued in specific ways in this world of 2012. I knew that there were methods available of transferring money without using money - as if money itself were not tricky enough - but decided that I would stick to using cash. But where to find it? And I would have to steal it. I knew that I would need to find a machine to control so as not to draw attention to myself.

I glanced around from my vantage point on the bench, and saw that there was in fact a bank just outside the square. Bartrem had explained to me at length about banks in the old world. I strolled over to it, and watched from a distance as a number of people approached a brightly coloured panel built into the wall outside the building. Each person seemed to be able to extract paper money from the panel by interacting with it, using a small plastic card. I took a brief scan of the internal workings of the machine to see how it worked. Luckily it was simple enough even for me to understand. I waited until the machine was free, and quickly positioned myself in front of it, obscuring the front panel with my body lest it be noticed that I was not interacting with it in the same way as the other people by use of a card. I instructed the machine to pay me the maximum it could in the unit of currency here, and moments later, a large pile of paper notes extruded from the wide slot on the machine's front. I had little idea of its value, but this seemed to be a substantial enough sum to see me through the next few days at least. I quickly gathered up my booty and moved away.

I came to a junction, a crossroad from which flowed four busy streets. As always, pedestrians abounded in all directions, traffic raced noisily to and fro between the crowds of walkers. I stood for few moments, gazing along the four axes. As I did so, I was struck by something I had not noticed earlier in the day. As I had made my way to Guillemot Publishers, I had been so focused on the task, and on not being mown down by the people marching along the pavements usually distracted by their portable electronic toys, that I had paid little attention to much else. Now, I took the time to survey my surroundings, especially the people rushing in all directions along the many pavements I could see. I was astonished to see such variety in humanity. So many different skin tones and colours, so much variation in hair type, eye colour, height and width of body. I knew that London at this time housed many people from other parts of the world, so I would not expect to see uniform skin colour, but the sheer number of those who clearly hailed from distant lands was amazing. And even those who looked to be European of origin were as often as not from outside this small island. I scanned their minds hastily as each one passed me, causing a slight frown on each face as I did so, and was presented with language after language. And I found it hard not to stare at those who looked the most different from the people in my own world.

After the Chaos, the tiny numbers of survivors who emerged from their refuges were predominantly light-skinned. Overwhelmingly so. This was a reflection of the economic and political reality of the world just before the

Chaos: the populations of the richest countries, those most likely to have prepared safe havens in the case of disaster, were predominantly fair-skinned. And even within these countries, the citizens most likely to have access to the refuges were light-skinned. It was no surprise therefore that most of the survivors had pale skin. And even though, during the centuries after the Chaos, the breeding programmes utilised genetic material from people who had not survived, again, due to the political and economic reality prevailing in the lead-up to the Chaos, most of these people were also white. The few who had hailed originally from other parts of the world, and whose skin tone had been darker, had been rapidly subsumed into the general post-Chaos population. In fact things went further than this: in the post-Chaos years a form of eugenics was practised to produce a single race of people, a deliberate project to ensure that in the future the endless problems of race that had dogged humanity before the Chaos would never again rear their ugly, disruptive and divisive selves.

I was reminded, as I surveyed the variety of humanity surging around me, of the fact that in my time, not only was there far less variation in the surviving flora and fauna compared to the pre-Chaos era, but also in the different types of human being. My own species reflected all the other species which had managed to emerge in the post-Chaos world: we were still there, but our range of types was substantially reduced.

I was fascinated by the different skin colours, hair types, eye colours, facial features and even body types I saw pass on all sides of me. I forced myself not to stare, for, although these people rushing along the pavements appeared oblivious to their surroundings, I quickly discovered that they were more aware than I had first thought. They seemed to discern with remarkable acuity if someone was staring at them, even if only for a few moments longer than acceptable. Thus I received many surprised looks, and even angry glares, before I disciplined myself not to stare. How extraordinary, I thought, to be able to act as if nothing around you impinges upon your consciousness while at the same time being acutely aware of the other people in your environment. How much practice was needed to master such apparently conflicting skills, to engage them simultaneously?

And not only were the differences of origin of the people fascinating to me, but also the divergent body types. In my world, after centuries of selective breeding of human beings, there was far less diversity in body type than I saw all around me. Here, people were tall, short, thin, muscular, and most astonishing of all, quite a few carried substantial amounts of excess body fat, a thing rarely seen in my world except on a few individuals who had chosen to be this way, almost as an affectation, like Marna who felt that her avoirdupois diverted attention from her dubious activities and friendships, leading people into believing she was harmless. Again, I had to force myself not to stare like a rude child at all the mixed and motley humanity all around.

I chided myself at my distraction, remembering that I needed to find Ruth Firestone.

I walked briskly through the streets looking for a shop which sold maps, eventually finding one, outside of which was a stand containing a range of maps, mostly of London, but a few of other parts of the country. Knowing now that such a map would contain an index, I skimmed through the index at the back of a map of England until I found the location of Ruth's home, then turned quickly to the page indicated. I saw that it was situated on the east coast, slightly to the north-east of London, in an area that looked almost devoid of habitation. I checked several times, but each time with the same result. I supposed that Ruth had chosen an isolated spot as she seemed not to be a person who dealt easily with other human beings, not even her own family. Without further delay, I ported myself to the co-ordinates of Ruth's beach home.

I emerged a little way back from the beach, turned to face the sea, and walked the short distance to Ruth's home. Here, so close to the water's edge, the land was wild, with no sign of agriculture. The road ended abruptly, and I stepped off it onto sandy shingle, dotted here and there with tough-looking plants tenaciously flourishing in the endless wind and salty spray from the sea. I did not recognise any of the plants, wondering if any of the species I saw had been saved before the Chaos and brought to life again after the disaster. The air was marvellous after the pollution of London: clean, fresh, invigorating. Despite my trepidation at the forthcoming encounter, I felt happy, walking with a bounce in my step.

As I approached the lone wooden building, my perky footsteps slowed, my feet dragging ever more reluctantly along the sandy ground as I contemplated how to introduce myself to Ruth. I had given little thought to the reality of meeting her, not knowing how much to give away at the start of who I was, where I had come from. Clearly I could not barge in telling her I had travelled from the future and had come to her home to meet her, perhaps even help her. She would likely consider me insane or dangerous, or both, and avoid all contact with me. And who could blame her? Perhaps I could claim to be a fan of hers, though I had no way of knowing how she would react to this either.

I gingerly approached the house, more like a cabin really, made of dark wooden planks. It was a one-storey home, though there was a small extension upwards over part of the cabin, perhaps a single room upstairs, mostly glass, which I imagined afforded a wonderful view across the sea. I sidled around the building, locating the main door which faced the water. In front of it was nothing but an expanse of pale yellow sand and then the ocean. What an extraordinary place to live, I thought. The front of the house seemed to have most of the windows, there being only two very small ones at the back. This meant that from within the building, all one would see would be the beach and the ocean, nothing else, no sign of humanity whatsoever. A perfect solution if one sought to avoid the rest of the human race.

I stood in front of the door, a sturdy and solid wooden object with no glass. Before I lost my nerve, I lifted my right hand and knocked loudly several times. The noise resonated inside the house and I wished I knew of a less intrusive manner of signalling my presence, but I could not see any other way of doing so short of simply porting myself inside - something that would hardly endear me to Ruth.

From a cursory scan inside the building, I knew that Ruth was at home. And the energy she emitted told me that she was the woman I had followed earlier in the day through the streets of London. She must have returned straight home just after I lost her. She stood immobile, presumably ceasing all activity in the hope that whoever was knocking at her door would simply go away, believing nobody to be at home. But I was not going anywhere. I waited a few moments, then knocked again. Once more, absolute silence within. After a few moments I heard movement inside the cabin. I put my ear to the door and heard light footsteps approaching the door. But the occupant could not see who was on the other side of the door without looking out of one of the windows on either side. As this would also allow the person outside to see the person inside, she refrained from such an action.

The footsteps stopped immediately behind the door. I leaned as close to the door as I could and spoke loudly enough to be heard, yet not so forcefully as to evoke anxiety.

"Ruth?" I asked, adding a thrust of calming energy to accompany my voice. I hoped my calming energy helped a little to assuage the worst of her fears, but I did not want to make it too strong. I wanted her to remain alert, and herself, so that when I finally got to meet her I would not do so under false pretences. It was important to me that she know me for who I really was, right from the start.

"Ruth?" I queried again. "I know you are there, and I really want to talk to you." Utter silence greeted my words.

"My name is Sammy," I continued. "I've come to talk to you, to help you." No sound broke the silence. I knew I would have to say more, but was unsure how to proceed without frightening Ruth even more. After a pause, the length of which threatened to add to the air of anxiety, I plunged ahead.

"I know about you Ruth, about the things you've seen, the things you've foreseen that you've written about in your novels." I paused, not certain what else to add. I was taken aback when I heard a delicate rattling sound of metal, and the door opened a fraction, a chain securing it tightly so it could not open by more than a small gap. And a voice spoke through the crack.

"Many people have read my books," said the voice, a tight, tense voice tinged with fear and anger. "Many people think they know about me from my books. So what do you want? What do you want of me?"

"I want to meet you, to talk to you," I answered as I pressed my face as close to the crack as I could. It was fairly dark in the hallway of the house, and I could not see Ruth's face clearly. Mostly, I perceived a pale face with large dark-ringed deep brown eyes, wrinkled at the corners, full red lips, and a mass of messy dark brown curls surrounding what I could see of Ruth's face. As I had pursued her previously I had only ever caught glimpses of her back.

"Many people want to meet me, but I don't meet fans. I can't."

"I'm not a fan," I replied, though instantly regretted the comment as I saw a jolt of fear on the sliver of face the other side of the door. If I was not a fan, then what was I? What on earth was I doing here?

"I mean, I'm more than a fan," I hastily added, aware how weak my comment sounded. Before I could say more, I was interrupted.

"What do you really want?" Ruth asked, and by her tone I sensed tears were not far from her eyes. "And how do you know where I live? Where did you get my address?" She was terribly upset, her voice quavering with a mixture of anger, outrage, and real distress. I sighed, knowing I was not managing the encounter very well at all. I had no option but to offer more information, more of the truth of who I was and my reasons for being here.

"I'm like you," I said after a short pause as I tried to find the right words. I wondered why Ruth was unable to sense who I was, but had to assume that her gifts were of a different nature from mine, or so inchoate and uncontrolled that she did not always understand what she sensed. "I see things that other people don't see. I sense things other people don't sense." This was as close to the truth as I could manage without divulging the full facts of who I was.

I saw Ruth jerk backwards, away from the crack in the door. My words had clearly struck a chord.

"How do you know I see things and sense things that other people don't?" Ruth asked in such a quiet voice that I strained to hear it.

"I can pick thinks up," I replied. "And your gifts are clear from your books."

"My gifts!" she snapped in a voice laden with bitter irony. "Is that what you call them?"

"Yes," I affirmed. "They are gifts, real gifts."

"Curses more like," she replied before I could continue. "I am plagued with seeing things and hearing things. I hear voices. I am accursed."

"You hear voices?" I queried, astonished at this revelation I had not considered.

"Yes," she snapped. "I hear voices, all the time, all around me, whenever I'm among other people. Why do you think I can't stand being with them? It's why I have to be alone."

I felt a surge of sympathy for this remarkable woman who had gone through her life hearing voices, seeing and sensing things nobody else did, without any understanding of the origins of her abilities. What a difficult and distressing life she must have led. My heart went out to her.

"Will you let me in Ruth?" I asked, perhaps slightly abruptly. "It's hard to talk properly like this." I saw a look of near panic on Ruth's face at the prospect of opening the door, allowing a total stranger to enter her home, even one who seemed to understand her in a way nobody else ever had. Yet she did not immediately slam the door shut or back away. I peered even more avidly through the gap in the door, and saw the ambivalence on Ruth's features as she warred with herself: to open the door or not to open the door. In the end, her lifelong wariness and caution seemed to win out.

"No," she replied. "I can't. Nobody has ever been here before and nobody has ever been inside my house when I've been here. Even workmen have to arrange to come and let themselves in when I'm away. I can't let you in." My disappointment was profound, and even more so when Ruth then slammed the door shut, removing from me even the tiny sliver of her face I had been able to talk to.

"Please Ruth," I wheedled. "If you won't let me in, please let's just keep talking. I have so much to tell you...I can..." But she suddenly shouted, interrupting me.

"Go away. Just go away and leave me alone. I don't want to see you. I don't want to see anyone!" I knew from her voice that she was determined. I stood for a few moments, filled with indecision. Should I simply port myself inside her home, force her to listen to what I had to say? It was in her interest that she hear my words, yet such an action might, probably would, destroy any hope of ever gaining Ruth's trust. I sighed. I knew I had no option but to leave. I was not, however, beaten. I would try again. And again. And eventually she would relent and agree to meet me. Surely she *must* relent.

I wandered a long way up the beach, enjoying the solitude and the simple pleasure of the bracing breeze, the sparkling sea, the crowing calls of birds as they circled above my head. I looked keenly at the circling birds, wondering if they were the same species as in my own time. In the twenty-ninth century we had a few species of seagull, but here I counted at least five different types, and other birds I simply did not recognise, some flying, some wading in the shallows, others hopping animatedly over the beach. I had to dampen down my sorrow as I thought about the Chaos, how it would wipe out nearly all life on earth.

It had been a long day already. It was not yet dark, though the tones in the light presaged dusk. As the day began to wane in earnest, a glorious sunset erupted, the heavens filled with hues of deep yellow, red, pink and purple. I sat in front of a small dune, leaning my back against the sandy support, gazing out at the ocean. I wished that the coast faced west, the better to immerse myself in the colour show of sunset, yet it was spectacular enough as the dusk pigments gradually faded into deeper purples, reds and oranges, the sky finally coming to rest with a canvas of uniform deep blue, dotted copiously with stars. As I gazed at the twinkling lights in the sky, I was stunned to realise that I knew all of the constellations. I saw Orion, the Big Dipper, the Seven Sisters. The reality of what I had achieved this day struck me with a hammer blow: I had travelled in time. I had successfully travelled across eight centuries. The first person ever to do so. And this truth was evidenced by the proof of my own eyes - that I was looking at exactly the same starry groupings as I had done in my own time, the immutable and unassailable confirmation that this was indeed my own world. This society would soon be destroyed, but the universe would not care.

After my somewhat abstract and philosophical contemplations, more mundane and prosaic bodily needs began to impinge insistently upon my awareness. I was hungry and I was thirsty. I smiled at this, at the fact that despite my mind's engagement in such lofty considerations of my extraordinary and unprecedented triumph, my body imposed its own basic needs emphatically into my thoughts. I ported myself quickly back to London where I found a small shop open. Here I bought a large bottle of water, several sandwiches, and some chocolate. I ported directly back to the beach, 'my beach' as I was already beginning to think of it, where I enjoyed an impromptu picnic.

I lay down in the sand, wriggling my body to create a small indentation in which to insert myself, making a small pillow of grasses for my head. I lay directly in front of the dune, on my side, from where I could look out over the empty sea, hear the waves at they lapped gently over the beach. I threw a shield around myself, keeping myself warm and dry and which I hoped would also protect me from any chance of discovery. I was worn out by my day's adventures, and though my heart pounded a little from the unaccustomed meal, I quickly fell asleep.

I awoke sharply in the pale light of early morning. I was unsure of the exact time, but given the month, and the nature of the light, I knew it was not long after dawn. I looked around, noting that the beach was as deserted as it had been the day before. It promised to be another beautiful day, though at this hour it was chilly, a fact I discovered abruptly as I removed the protective shield, even through the jumper I wore.

I stood up and stretched my limbs. I then removed all of my clothing and walked into the sea. The temperature of the water quite took my breath away. I waded in until the water reached above my waist, and here I stood, gasping for breath as the shock of the chill sea pervaded my body. I took calming breaths, choosing not to protect myself from the cold. How invigorating it was! I dived forward, immersing myself fully under the water, swimming out a short way before hastily returning to the shore. As I splashed out onto the beach, I caused my metabolic rate to spike, my increased body temperature quickly drying me. This I had learned to do years before after taking dips in the forest pond on the estate, where even in mid-summer the water was chilly from the stream which cascaded into it from the rocks above.

I finished my food and water, and then decided to try and see Ruth once again. As the day before, she simply refused to see me, this time not even opening her door by the small crack of the previous occasion. I left her home and sat on the beach nearby.

After a short while, I began to feel vaguely irritated by Ruth's manner. I had sympathy for her, for the difficult life she had endured, yet I was here to help her, to offer her guidance and information that nobody else could possibly offer. Her blank resistance to my efforts irked me slightly, so I made a decision to coerce her into allowing me into her life. I stood up and walked the short distance back to her front door, feeling less resolute in my decision with each step. It was important to me that Ruth trust me. Yet it was vital for her that I meet her. I was conflicted. As I approached her door, I made a choice: I would coerce her. But I would do this as gently as I could, and not compel her to open her home to a stranger.

I knocked at her door for the third time. As before, I knew she was in the house despite her ceasing all movement.

"Ruth," I said loudly, confidently, bossily. "I am not going to go away until you agree to meet me. I'll just keep coming back again and again. So you might as well agree to see me." I was met by absolute silence on the other side of the solid door. I sensed the slightest hesitation from Ruth, so stood quite still, waiting for her to respond. After a long pause, during which neither of us spoke, or moved, Ruth finally roused herself to action. She moved to the other side of the door, and I sensed her mere centimetres away from me as she spoke.

"You can't come in. I already told you that," she said in a quiet yet determined voice. But...but I can meet you somewhere else," she offered. As she made this suggestion, I sensed her own anxiety and vague confusion as to why she had said this. But she continued. "We can meet and talk in person, but not here. Somewhere public."

"Very well," I conceded. "Where? And when?" A silence met my questions, though I imagined that she was simply considering the options.

"Not too far from here, in a village about an hour's walk, there's an inn. Do you know it?"

"No," I replied. "I've only come to this area for the first time in my life yesterday, and I don't know where the village is." I added, smiling slightly as I considered the truth: I had never come to this *time* before! Ruth then surprised me by opening the door, though the small chain still held it open by only a crack. She peered out at me through the tiny gap.

"You can't miss the village," she explained. "It's on the only road away from here. Didn't you come that way?" She queried suddenly, but then continued before I could come up with a plausible answer. "The inn is called the Traveller. It's the only one in the village, right in the middle. I'll be there tomorrow at three in the afternoon. It will be quiet then."

"Could we not meet sooner?" I asked, disappointed at having to wait until the next day. "Later today perhaps?"

"No, I'm sorry. In the evenings the pub is quite busy, and at lunchtime tomorrow it will be too. I can't be there when it's full. There's too much noise in my head." Her tone was regretful, yet adamant. I had no option but to agree to her terms.

"Very well," I replied. "I'll see you in the Traveller tomorrow at three. Will you recognise me? You can't see me too well through that tiny crack."

"Yes I'll recognise you," she said with what seemed to be a trace of humour in her voice, much to my surprise. "There are so few strangers in these parts that I imagine you'll stick out like a sore thumb." What an odd expression she had just used. What did a stick have to do with a sore thumb? But before I could think further on this, Ruth spoke again.

"And now, please, go away and leave me alone. I'm not used to having people here, and I'm finding it difficult." And at that she closed the door loudly.

I nodded to myself, and left Ruth in peace. As I walked slowly away from her home along the beach, I wondered what on earth I would do with myself between now and the following afternoon. I wondered about the possibility of returning to the twenty-ninth century, but as I had no clear idea of how I had arrived in 2012 I had no way of knowing if I could return home. And even if I were able to do so, there was no guarantee I could return to exactly the right time and place in the twenty-first century to fulfil my promise to meet Ruth the following day.

Chapter Fifty-Five

I considered my options. Should I return to London, or perhaps make my way to the Traveller Inn? I could simply return to London and procure food as I had done the night before, but decided instead to visit the inn I would meet Ruth in the next day. I might as well find my way there beforehand, and allow myself to be comfortable with the environment.

Ruth had told me that the Traveller was about a hour's walk along the road leading away from her house. I ported myself in small flits along the road, unsure how to locate the inn by a more direct route. After a number of such jumps, I saw a cluster of buildings a short way in the distance. This must be the village Ruth had mentioned. I strolled the final stage to the inn so as not to appear out of the blue in the middle of the village, terrifying any locals.

The village was tiny, really nothing more than a cluster of houses around a small green space with a pond in the middle. Around the pond grew a few small trees of types I did not recognise. One of them had a striking silver-coloured bark, something I had never witnessed in my own time. And growing all around one side of the pond were tall plants, clearly water-lovers as the bottom parts of their stems disappeared below the edge of the water. One stand of plants particularly caught my eye, covered as it was with large yellow flowers almost in the shape of bows. These I had seen in my own time in the lake in the middle in Beyra, and also on one of my trips to an area north of where I lived with Haari and Lisvet. That area enjoyed beautiful natural contours of hills and valleys, and we had stopped beside a lake in one of the most sheltered vales. I remember having seen exactly the same plant growing along the bank there too, which Lisvet informed me were yellow irises. The memory caused me a pang of longing to be with Lisvet.

On one side of the green space was the only large building in the village, outside of which swung a wooden sign with the words 'The Traveller Inn' in large faded red letters. I entered the building through a door overlooking the green. The building seemed very old, with sagging wooden beams, small windows, and some sort of creeping plant growing over most of its whitewashed facade. There was a surprisingly large number of people inside, and a good deal of noisy chatter. I paused for a moment to get my bearings, and saw a long counter running almost the whole length of the large room I found myself in and which itself made up most of the inn. On this were what looked like large shiny copper taps, behind it rows of brightly lit bottles. A single woman stood behind the counter, chatting quietly to an obviously drunken man perched precariously on a stool in front of the counter. I approached the bar from where I could order drinks. The smell of stale food and alcohol hung in the air.

I approached the bar, and as I did so the woman looked up at me, stopped talking to the drunken man, and moved slightly away from him. As she looked at me directly, I could still hear the man muttering away, apparently oblivious to the fact that his conversation partner was no longer listening.

"Yes dear, what can I get you?" the woman asked me in a brisk, penetrating voice, the kind of voice that has spent years making itself heard. I looked at her, a tall, sturdy woman, flushed in the cheeks with the heat of the room, or perhaps from a lifetime of overindulgence in alcohol, a mass of messy artificially blond hair escaping in all directions from her head, but with a jolly expression on her features. I realised that I did not know what drinks were available.

"I'd like a drink," I said, and paused. She eyed me keenly.

"Yes I assume you do," she said. "This is a pub after all," she added, with a twinkle in her eye. I surmised that an inn was also called a pub. I also realised that what I said was not sufficient.

"Cider," I added, as I glanced at the list of drinks and prices. "Do you have cider?"

"Yes we do!" she laughed. "Draft or bottle?" she continued. I was flummoxed by her question, but she took my confusion for lack of knowledge of precisely which brands of cider she offered, rather than lack of understanding of the question itself. She listed rapidly, in a practised manner, a number of words I did not recognise as she vaguely indicated a glass-fronted cabinet behind her with her arm, though without turning round, then pointed to one of the large gleaming taps on the bar, giving me another name. Without any real preference, I ordered a cider from the tap without hesitation, so as not to appear as ignorant as I was.

"Large or small?" she asked. I did not want to appear stupid, so quickly replied.

"Small. Just a small one."

"A half then," she added, though I did not understand her meaning, unaware as to what the whole was of which I was being offered a half. Before I could show my ignorance by asking her what she meant, she peered at me keenly. "You're a bit young," she said. "Are you over eighteen?" she added, but before I could reply, she continued briskly. "I should really ask you for ID, but round here no-one bothers too much." I was taken aback by her comment. It had never occurred to me that I would need identification to buy a drink.

The woman turned around, picked up a glass from the shelf behind her and began to fill it from the tap on the bar.

She smiled at me as she filled my glass, and noticed my gaze as it wandered around the room, over the walls and ceiling.

"Wondering about all the beams?" she asked. I nodded. "They're all from an old ship. A really old ship. The ship itself was built around five hundred years ago, and when it had run its course, they took the beams and they ended up being used to build this place. And that was over four hundred years ago."

I stared at her in astonishment. This inn was over four hundred years old? That was half the time I had travelled to be here. Such an amazingly long period for something so ordinary as an inn in a village in the middle of the countryside.

"And it's only ever been an inn," the jolly woman added almost proudly as she put the full glass down on the bar, spilling a little of the amber liquid as she did so. Again, I stared in astonished silence. How much had this building seen, how many people had passed through its doors, how many events and happenings had it witnessed in the lives of all those people? And if a village like this could harbour such an ancient edifice, surely there were hundreds, thousands like it all over the country, all over the world? My mind could barely encompass such an idea, and the dark shadow of the destruction so shortly to be unleashed upon this world filled my mental horizon.

A growling sound in my belly brought me back to more ordinary thoughts with a bump.

"You want something to eat love?" the friendly woman behind the bar asked, surprising me by calling me 'love'. It seemed a curiously intimate word to use to a complete stranger. She had now called me 'dear' and 'love'. I wondered if I should copy her linguistic usage, but judged it risky to do so - I really had no idea of the appropriate time and place for such terms, so it seemed wiser to refrain. I smiled at her, however, and asked her if they served food. She said they did, and nodded towards a large sheet of plastic-coated paper on the bar, on which I saw descriptions and pictures of a wide range of meals. The sheet seemed to be covered in small dirty lumps of such meals left there by previous guests, so I did not actually pick it up, perusing it from a distance as it lay on the bar, questioning as I did the wisdom of eating somewhere so unsanitary. I did not dither, and ordered fish and chips with something called mushy peas. This meal was listed as the 'house speciality', so I decided to give it a try. I paid for the drink and the food, surprising the woman slightly with the large wad of notes I drew from my pocket to do so, and then took my drink to the only spare table in the room, a tiny round one wedged into the space in front of one of the windows. I squeezed myself in, sitting on a small wooden chair. Both table and chair wobbled, and I spilled some of my drink as I placed it on the table, such was its rocking motion. After about ten minutes the woman came bustling over to my table with a huge plate on which I saw a large piece of what I assumed was fish, coated in a yellowish crispy covering, a large pile of rectangular golden vegetables, and a blob of lurid green vegetable matter dotted with the occasional recognisable pea.

"Any sauces, love?" she asked. I declined, not knowing what sauces would be offered to accompany such food. I began to eat, my stomach grumbling loudly as it perceived the odour of the fish and chips. The food was heavy, filling, and greasy, yet appetising in its way. I quickly put away the entire plateful, washing it down with regular swigs of the slightly tart cider. Shortly after I had finished, the woman from the bar swayed over to where I sat to collect my empty plate and glass.

"All done?" she asked. I nodded. "Did you enjoy it?" she questioned.

"Yes, it was delicious," I answered, exaggerating slightly, though she seemed pleased.

"My husband's the chef," she explained, smiling. "Anything else?" she then asked. I said I did not require any more food or drink, but a thought did occur to me.

"Do you rent rooms here, to sleep in?" I asked, remembering from old Victorian literature that inns commonly did so.

"No," she said, in a tone of regret. "We used to, but had so little trade we gave up. The nearest place to here is in Southminster. You'll have to try there." And as she moved away from my table, she turned and said, "You need a cab?" I hesitated, not sure what to say by way of reply as I did not recognise the word. I shook my head, not knowing how else to respond.

"You have your own transport then?" the woman continued. I nodded.

"Yes. I have a vehicle," I replied, causing her to raise her eyebrows slightly, presumably at something odd in my choice of words. I did not want any questions asked as to where I would spend the night. With a vehicle, she would assume I would make my own way somewhere else to find lodgings. She nodded, and then spoke again.

"You're not from round here, are you dear?" I shook my head, and when I replied, I maintained the deception I had begun at Guillemot.

"No. I'm from London," I said. "I'm here visiting my aunt who lives near the sea. But she doesn't have room at her place for me to stay," I added hastily, before the woman could ask me why I was not going to spend the night at her house. She nodded and made her way back to the bar, passing into a room behind the bar to deposit the plate as she did. I quickly made my escape, before I was subjected to further questioning.

Nobody was about in the village, so I simply ported myself back to the dune from where I had contemplated the stars the night before.

After this, I spent the rest of the day wandering aimlessly up and down the coast, revelling in the freedom of this place so devoid of humanity. I took a detour at one point, slightly inland, finding a most odd landscape of dunes, sparse tough vegetation, and a patchwork of small ponds and pools of brackish water. As I meandered through this strange land, I disturbed the resident birds, of many different species, all of which quickly moved out of my way with a variety of outraged squawks and caws, twitters and tweets as I disrupted their usually untroubled existence.

I dozed in the late afternoon beside 'my dune', waking hungry as the sun was setting. I sat for a few moments as I woke up, again revelling in the glory of the sunset over the ocean. I flitted quickly back to the shop in London to procure more eatables. On a whim, I flitted to the bookshop I had visited on my first day in London where I bought (not stole!) all seven of Ruth's novels. Returning to the beach I ate hungrily as I perused the entire saga as it unfolded in Ruth's stories. I fell asleep book in hand, tired from the exertions of the past few days.

The next day I awoke early again to the cawing of seabirds and the gentle lapping of waves against the strand. I doffed my clothing and raced into the chilly sea, gasping with the shock. I swam a long way out, nearly panicked as I looked back at the distant beach, then smiled as I remembered I need have no worry. I felt tired, so just ported myself back to the beach. I dried myself metabolically, dressed again and sat down to eat the remainder of the food I had procured the day before.

The rest of the morning and early afternoon I spent exploring my surroundings a little more. I meandered without aim up and down the beach, through the salt marshes behind the dunes, simply delighting in the solitude, the freedom, the sense of achievement of having travelled across eight centuries without mishap, and now being close to fulfilling my main purpose in having come here: meeting and helping the amazingly gifted Ruth Firestone. After a light lunch once again bought after a speedy flit to the shop in London, I dozed beside my dune in the warm sun.

I awoke from my slumbers, and was surprised to find myself anxious about my forthcoming encounter. Why was I nervous? Surely I could not be fearful of the actual meeting? I could only surmise that I was so eager for the encounter to be a success, that this was making me trepidatious. And surely this Ruth woman was unpredictable. From the position of the sun, I estimated that it was close to 3 o'clock. I checked on the wrist watch I had stolen along with the clothing in London, and saw it was indeed only minutes to the appointed hour. I ported myself there without delay.

As the evening before, I entered the old inn by its main door. I was relieved to see that the woman I had encountered the day before was not at the bar. She had been most pleasant, but I did not relish the prospect of being grilled about my sleeping arrangements.

I stopped just inside the door, and looked around. As Ruth had said, the pub was very quiet at this time of the day, there only being one table occupied, and the same inebriated man occupying the same stool beside the bar as the evening before. Ruth did not appear to be there, and I wondered if she would renege on her promise to be here. I quickly quashed such an ungenerous thought. It was not quite three o'clock. I bought myself another small cider from the server. This woman was younger than the one from the night before, and seemingly less prone to being interested in her customers. She also seemed to have no intention of asking me for identification, for which I was relieved. I took my cider and made my way to a table in the far corner of the pub, isolated from any other by an expanse of open floor. I thought Ruth would probably appreciate a location as far from other people as possible.

A small clock above the unlit fireplace on the other side of the room chimed three. Moments later, the door creaked gingerly open, and through it slowly emerged Ruth, poking her head around first to survey the interior, before allowing the rest of her body to follow. She stood quite still just inside the room, pushing the door closed behind her. For a few moments she did nothing, allowing me to scrutinise her carefully before she saw me.

I had, of course, seen her before, but only a small part of her face through a narrow gap in her door, or her back disappearing into a crowd. Her general air of anxiety, of fretful fearfulness was as apparent as before, and she seemed to need to work up the courage simply to look around the room. I could now see that she was taller than I was, and slim to the point of being almost gaunt. She was dressed in plain clothing, a dark blue dress with long sleeves, the skirt of which reached down to just below her knees, the whole cinched with a plastic belt. The dress had a simple flower pattern in pale blue dotted over the material. Her legs were bare below this and I was surprised to see her shins sporting dark hair. I had noticed already that women in this time relentlessly depilated themselves, especially their legs. Ruth's feet were shod in blue sports shoes of some kind, old and battered, comfortable-looking. A large and clearly weighty handbag, also dark blue, hung off her right shoulder, pulling her down slightly such that she leaned towards the right. As she stood, her hands moved towards each other, her fingers intertwining as she wrung them together, clear evidence of discomfort. For all the ordinariness of Ruth's appearance, she was nevertheless crowned with a wonderful head of hair, a cascade of tumbling dark-brown curls which reached half way down her back. Her hair was not well-styled, being allowed to find its own route across her head and shoulders. But it was thick and glossy, so dense that she was able to use it to partially cover her face, something I was sure was not an accident.

After a few moments, Ruth slowly began to turn and look around the room. The last place her eyes fell was where I sat. Her dark brown deep-set eyes caught mine for the briefest of moments before she dropped her gaze, but in that moment there was a bright spark of recognition between us, not only of each other's existence, but perhaps of the connection between us, our shared difference. It was clear that she did not like to look at someone directly, and as she shuffled across to my table, she kept her eyes firmly fixed on the floor in front of her. She stopped right beside my table. As she stood beside me, I tried to gauge her age. Her posture was upright, almost too much so as she held herself stiffly, tensely. Her hair had no grey in it, though her skin showed signs of wrinkles, especially in what I could see of her forehead. But this might be the result of constant frowning rather than age. I thought she was perhaps in the environs of forty years old, but accepted that such a number may well turn out to be misjudged. For several moments neither of us spoke. Finally I decided I would need to take the initiative.

"Ruth?" I asked quietly, in the gentlest voice I could muster. Her eyes darted once from the floor to look at me, and then straight back down again.

"Yes," she whispered. "You're Sammy?"

"Yes," I replied. And then, after another pause. "Please Ruth, sit down." She slid into the chair opposite me, not looking at me as she did so. I noticed that her bottom lip was bleeding slightly, and saw the reason as she took her seat. Every few moments she seemed to chew quickly at her bottom lip with her top teeth, a nervous habit which she seemed unable to control. Her fingers continued to intertwine rapidly, only punctuated by one of her hands being lifted to scratch her head, or push the dark rectangular frames she wore back onto her face. I had seen glasses on the face of Penelope, the Guardian of Guillemot, and knew what they were in any case, as I remembered how much hilarity it had caused me and my siblings when we had learned that the ancients wore heavy artificial glass lenses to correct problems with vision. Ruth wore heavy, dark-framed glasses, but as I glanced at them I realised that they had no glass in them. They were merely frames. What a strange thing to do, I mused, to wear glasses that could not improve one's sight, being devoid of lenses! I could only imagine that their function for Ruth was not visual, but as a shield, a mask behind which to hide.

"Would you like a drink?" I asked, as much to break the silence as for any other reason. She shot the briefest of glances in my direction, though not quite meeting my eyes as she did so, and nodded.

"Port," she replied tersely. I stood up, but before I went to the bar to buy her a glass of the drink she had requested, one I had never heard of, I turned to her.

"Please," I begged. "Please don't run away." I sensed in her a strong urge to flee. She had kept her promise to be here to meet me, but the reality of it was so stressful for her that I feared she would simply bolt. She gave me the tiniest of nods as I went to the bar. As I stood waiting for her drink to be poured, I watched her carefully, ready to move quickly in the event that she made a dash for the door. She did not run away. She barely seemed to move at all, apart from the nervous intertwining of her fingers interrupted by the rapid movement of her hands from time to time to her head or the frame of her glasses. Her full hair prevented me from seeing her face clearly from where I stood, but I sensed the lip biting had increased in intensity.

When I returned to the table, I sat down, gently placing the glass of deep red, aromatic liquid in front of Ruth. Her right hand darted out, lifted the glass to her mouth, and she drank the entire contents of the glass in one gulp. I was taken aback by this, but without asking, quickly returned to the bar to have her glass refilled. This procedure continued for another two glasses, until finally, with her fourth glass, she seemed content to merely take a small sip before placing the glass back on the table in front of her. I endured all of this patiently, keen to allow Ruth to dictate the rhythm of this meeting which I knew she had not wanted. And yet despite her unwillingness, I sensed in her an intense curiosity mingling with the disquiet at being with me. She knew that I was not a fan, that I truly seemed to be something else. She did not as yet know what I was to her, but the fact she had agreed to our meeting, and had kept her promise to be at the pub suggested that she believed I would be important in ways she could not begin to imagine.

I decided I needed to take control of the situation, and began to speak.

"You like the port," I stated, in an attempt to lighten the atmosphere. Ruth's eyes darted up from where they were fixed on her glass, almost, but not quite, meeting mine. She clearly did not know if my comment was a criticism of her rapid imbibing. I quickly continued, adding as much sincerity to my words as I could.

"I must try it next time. It smells delicious." She seemed calmed.

"You've never had it?" she asked in a quiet voice.

"No," I replied. "Never." She raised her eyebrows slightly at this, surprised. She fell silent again, offering no further comment.

"Thank you so much for coming," I said, not wanting the minimal rapport I had created to be jeopardised by a lengthy silence. "I wasn't sure if you would," I added, not entirely truthfully as I had forced her to do so against her inclination.

"I said I would!" she retorted sharply. "So why wouldn't I? Did you think I was lying yesterday?" She was clearly irked by my comment, so I hastily reassured her.

"No, no. I didn't think you were lying, not at all," I said. "But I know how hard this must be for you, and how strange it must have been, me just turning up yesterday, saying the things I did, so I'm just really happy that you're here." She said nothing, but her hands stilled and she ceased biting her bottom lip, and I sensed a slight calming of her agitation.

"Is it too noisy for you here?" I asked. "We could go somewhere quieter if you like." Her eyes darted up to my face, and down again.

"No," she replied. "It's alright here." I was not sure if the possibility of being somewhere less public with me, a stranger, was not even more alarming than being in this public place. She suddenly looked up, very nearly into my eyes, her upper teeth once again closing in on her bruised lip.

"Why can't I hear voices from you?" she asked suddenly. "I hear them from everyone else. So why can't I hear them from you?" Her tone indicated suspicion, genuine suspicion at why I was silent in her head, unlike all the other people she came near. I decided to leap in, not keep her in the dark any longer. I took a deep breath.

"Ruth," I said quietly. "I have a story to tell you. About me. Please, please listen to me. Hear me out. What I have to tell you will sound unbelievable, crazy even, but I promise you it's all true. I promise I'm not crazy." She stilled, intrigued and alarmed in equal measure by my words, but intensely aware of the urgent sincerity in my voice. I stopped talking for a moment, collecting my thoughts, watching her keenly as I did so.

"I'm listening," she said simply after a short pause, and I began. I spoke at length, telling her all about myself, my childhood eight hundred years in the future, the fact that I had been created from nineteen progenitors, that I enjoyed extraordinary and unprecedented gifts of many and varied kinds, how I had learned first to teleport and then finally to travel in time. She listened in silence, immersed in the words of my tale. The only reaction was a tiny gasp and a darting look actually into my eyes when I said I had learned how to travel through time as well as space. I assumed she would have already arrived at this conclusion after I spoke of my childhood in the future, but perhaps it needed my bald and unequivocal words to bring home exactly what this meant. I continued with my story, telling her how I had read her novels, and had instantly recognised her as a kindred spirit, a person with remarkable abilities, innate and natural abilities.

I stopped speaking. Ruth glanced up at me once, then stared at the table, utterly still. "It sounds…it sounds…fantastical," she mumbled. I could not help but agree. I sensed conflict in her: a natural skepticism about my story mingled with a desperate desire to believe me. I sighed, wondering what I could do to persuade her. I glanced round and noticed the drunk man sitting on the stool beside the bar. He was muttering something, though whether this was to the woman behind the bar or into his own drink, I could not tell. Neither seemed to be paying him much heed in any case. Ruth followed my line of sight and I had an idea. Using my hypnotising technique, I compelled the unfortunate man to stand up and stumble over towards our table. When he was standing beside us, I made him repeat the parts of my story telling of myself, in my exact words. He spoke quietly, only loud enough for me and Ruth to hear him. As he spoke Ruth stared at him, thick dark eyebrows rising higher and higher on her brow as she recognised that he used my own words. The man's final words were new, but also mine: "And does that persuade you that what I say is true?" I had him ask as I looked at Ruth quizzically. She responded with a little shrug of the shoulders, not quite convinced that this was not merely some trick I had learned to perform, but calmer, more willing to suspend her disbelief, at least for the moment.

"And I'm really hoping," I said as the drunkard wobbled back to his stool, a look of vague confusion on his face as to why he was not there already. "I'm really hoping that I can help you." At my final comment she looked up again, once more briefly into my actual eyes.

"Help me?" she asked in the softest of voices, barely audible yet suffused with intensity. "Help me how?" she whispered. I felt in her tone a heartrending mixture of mistrust mingled with yearning. I could only imagine that many people had offered to help her, tried to help her, but all to no avail, and perhaps she believed that many of them were dissimulating their true intentions. Yet I hoped she knew I was not like them, and that I was, in fact, telling the truth. Perhaps someone with such abilities as mine, someone who had mastered the art of travelling in time in order to cross the centuries to help her, perhaps this person might be the only one truly able to offer her assistance. My words had ignited a small flame of hope in her breast which began to burn brightly, despite her lifelong distrust of other people, her endless difficulties in managing her everyday life.

"I...I...I'm not sure exactly how I can help you," I said, floundering slightly, and reeled under the impact of her disappointment, the flame spluttering, almost going out. "But I was drawn here to you after travelling across eight centuries," I added more brightly. Her disappointment receded slightly at my words, at the confident tone of them, the flame of hope flickering back to a state of brighter luminosity.

"I can help you with the voices to start with," I said suddenly, buoyantly. She looked up sharply, eagerness etched on her face.

"How?" she breathed.

"I can teach you how to block them, to put up a barrier to that sort of thing. I have to do it sometimes when I'm with people who are really agitated or upset, though mostly to block feelings and emotions rather than words. If I don't," I explained. "I can be completely overwhelmed by them, and they can make me unable to function."

"I get that too!" Ruth added, her eyes showing an animation I had not seen before. "It's like standing under a waterfall of other people's feelings. It's awful. Dreadful. I can't bear it. Can you really help me block it out?" she asked, desperate hope flowing out of her, hot and fiery.

"Yes I can. I promise. I can teach you how to do it permanently if you like, or just on each occasion you want to do it. I do it as and when I need to. I wouldn't want to block it permanently," I added. "That would be a shame, to cut myself off from other people like that, emotionally." She sat quietly, and I wondered if she agreed with my comment.

"I'd like to block the voices completely," she said, after a moment's thought. "They just invade my brain unasked whenever I'm around other people, chatter chatter chatter all the time, and mostly almost unintelligible. Can you block them, forever?"

"Yes," I said. "If that's what you want. She nodded again, and then abruptly stood up.

"Can we start soon?" she asked. "Tomorrow?" I was about to say that we could start straightaway, but Ruth spoke first.

"I need to be on my own now Sammy. I...I...would like to thank you though for today, for all you've told me and for what you will teach me. And I hope we can also think about the visions I get, the terrible images which you read about in my novels and my readers think are from my imagination, though I think they might be real. They feel real to me." At this, she actually stared at me, her fists clenched in tension, as if challenging me to deny what she said. But I felt unable to respond. I considered that she had been subjected to quite enough new information today without talking about the Chaos, and what happened thereafter. That would be a difficult conversation for another day. I was disappointed that she felt the need to rush away, hoping that her belief in my tale would allow her to relax a little in my company. But perhaps I should not expect too much too soon. After all, only a few days before Ruth had not even met me, and she surely had a great deal to think about, a huge amount of novelty to process. I considered asking if I could stay with her, in her cabin by the sea, but one look at her anxious face, at her expression showing eagerness to be alone, and I quickly shelved this idea. I was happy enough sleeping on the beach, under the stars. But I would pin her down to an agreed time to begin our work together.

"Yes," I began. "I am sure I can help you with all of that too," I continued, remaining somewhat vague in what I said. "But we should start tomorrow, as you suggested. And in the morning," I added, not wanting to give Ruth enough time to regret her decision to allow me into her life. She paused briefly, then nodded.

"Yes, tomorrow morning," she agreed. She then seemed to reach an important decision. "Come to my house around ten. If the weather's good we can go out walking. If it's wet, you...you can come inside." And she emitted a slight shuddering sigh as she said these final words. I felt a tiny surge of triumph as I realised the huge progress I had made since the day before. If the weather was poor, Ruth would allow me into her home while she was there, the first person ever to be granted such an honour. She turned on her heel and as she walked towards the door she said simply, "Till tomorrow."

I sat for a while in the window seat of the Traveller after Ruth had left, running through my mind all I had learned, all we had discussed. I indulged myself in another cider, this time a large one. As I asked the indifferent barwoman for this, she looked at me slightly quizzically.

"You mean a pint?" she asked in a tone less than polite.

"Yes," I replied with a touch of hesitation, then remembered that in this place and time the standard measurement of liquid was a pint. I realised with a smile that my 'half' of the night before had therefore been a half pint. As the youngish woman poured my pint from the tap on the bar, she glanced suspiciously at me. Did she think I was mocking her with my smile? Was I simple-minded? She was distinctly discourteous in telling me the price, grabbing my proffered money, and banging the change loudly down on the bar. I suppressed a further smile at her brusque manner, taking my drink back to the window table.

After I had drunk the full pint, I felt surprisingly giddy, and knew that cider must be stronger in alcohol than it tasted. Though it had an undercurrent of tartness, it was really quite sweet, its fruity origins clear in its rich, warm flavours. I considered having another pint, but decided against it. Better to keep my wits about me. Instead, I left the Traveller, bought some more food and drink in a tiny shop opposite the pub, and ported myself back to my beach. I stowed the food safely among some tall tufts of sea grass, though I doubted anyone would find them, this part of the coast appearing devoid of human life. But noticing the raucous birds wheeling above me, or hopping around on the beach, all clearly aware of my presence, I decided my food needed more protection, so I erected a shield around it, obscuring it from the view of my hungry, greedy feathered companions.

I spent the rest of the day wandering along the beach, meandering cautiously through the salt marshes behind the coast, once again astonished at the diversity of life even in this small area. I had known, before my trip back in time, that the pre-Chaos world had teemed with hundreds of thousands, millions of different species of plants and animals, but knowing of something is not at all the same as witnessing it. Here, on this relatively bleak and windswept part of the east English coast I saw more species of plant and animal than I could count, and most of them were unfamiliar to me. Some resembled those I had seen in my own time, but most were new to me. Various types of tough-looking grass (and similar plants I could not name) clung tenaciously to life in the sandy soil, their roots surely forced to manage not only the granular nature of the soil, but also the high levels of salt in the ground. And there were plants with fluffy pompoms looking like little pieces of cotton wool, others with small blue and purple flowers braving the sea-spray. And there were even small trees, *very* small trees, stunted and leaning uniformly backwards away from the incessant wind off the sea. And all around were birds, flitting and fluttering from plant to plant, wading in the small ponds behind the dunes, ducking under the water from time to time to emerge beaks full of trailing dark green plant matter, or an occasional tiny silvery fish glinting in the sun. Further back from the water I heard the plop of amphibians as they hopped for cover in the ponds. I gazed into the water and saw what looked like small frogs or toads swim down to safety away from the surface as they perceived the threat of my face looming over the water. I did not recognise their species, and assumed they had not survived the Chaos. And I heard insects, many insects, chirruping and buzzing, some of which I could see, like the bees busily rushing from flower to flower, most I could only hear. I sighed out loud at the sheer vitality of the sights all around me. I wondered how many species were supported just by this small patch of sparse and not very fertile land, and then compared how far I would have to travel in my own time to encounter such diversity of life, so many different species. My own time seemed filled with life, a planet almost totally dominated by wildness, flora and fauna. But the number of species was tiny compared even to this one small section of relatively sparse English coastland.

I wandered back to the sea, and even braved another dip in its chilly waters. As the sun set, I dozed a little, to be woken by an awareness of larger animal life in the vicinity. I cracked my eyes open a little to see a big red fox only feet away from me. Its amber eyes were fixed on me as it peered down its long nose. It did not seem fearful, merely slightly tense, its muscles ready for flight should the need arise. I did not need to force the little beast to stay. It seemed intrigued by me, so I spoke to it gently.

"Hello there," I intoned quietly. "You're a handsome creature. And you I do recognise - we have some of your type at home." It stiffened slightly at my words, but remained immobile. I suspected it smelled my food, which I had not bothered to shield again after eating some of it earlier. I did not see the need as I was sitting right beside it. I slowly moved my hand to the little pile of edibles, picking up a cooked chicken thigh. I held this out to the lovely russet creature in front of me.

"Are you hungry?" I asked. "Do you like chicken?"

The way the fox gazed avidly at the proffered titbit, its shiny black nose twitching as it sniffed the welcome odour, told me that it did indeed like chicken. I tossed the cooked piece towards the animal, missing the beast by a hair's breadth. It did not flinch, but immediately darted forward, grasped the thigh firmly between small sharp teeth, and raced off along the beach. It clearly did not trust that I would not attempt to retrieve my piece of food, so took immediate action to ensure I would not be able to do so.

What did a wild creature like this make of my act? Did he realise I was making him a gift of the food, a deliberate act of kindness? Or did he think I had slipped, casting the chicken by accident towards him? Or maybe he thought I was simply stupid, too dim to know what I was doing? When I had entered the minds of animals in the forest on the estate, it was usually difficult to ascertain exactly what a beast was thinking. The mood of an animal was easy enough to perceive, usually with some clarity, be it fear or apprehension, joy or pleasure, but more specific attitudes or actual thoughts were almost impossible to pin down with any precision. I decided not to bother with the fox, allowing it to simply make its escape along the beach, presumably pleased with itself at its acquisition, whatever the cause of its good luck.

As the sun set and I sat alone on the windy, deserted beach, I felt a pang of yearning for my home. I was, after all, so very distant from it, so alone in this isolated place, that it was no surprise to suffer such waves of homesickness.

I thought of Ruth, her unhappiness, her agitation, her fear of meeting me, and then remembered the surge of tremulous hope she had emitted on learning that I might be able to help her, and these pushed any doubts I harboured of the rightness of time travel out of my mind. Ruth needed my help. She deserved my help. I was the only person able to offer such help. And with that, I lay down in my homemade sandy bed, preparing for sleep.

But sleep would not come. Despite my genuine tiredness at the exceptional events of the past two days, my mind would not rest, thoughts and ideas, feelings and perceptions buzzing around inside it in an inchoate, undisciplined way. After a period of trying, unsuccessfully, to impose order on my mind, I conceded defeat, sighed, and sat up.

The night was exquisite. There was a large, though not quite full moon illuminating a clear, deep blue velvet sky, its glossy darkness only interrupted by a magnificent display of celestial bodies twinkling and winking at me from their far-distant vantage points. A light breeze blew across the beach from the sea, flowing softly around me. The only noise was the gentle lapping of small waves against the shore. If I cleared my mind, I was able, for a moment, to forget where I was: eight centuries from home with no guarantee I could ever return.

I looked out across the water, and, without warning, I was overcome with an intense sense of loss, sudden and heavy. I was once more back in the twenty-first century, and knew that all this quiet beauty would soon be destroyed, obliterated in the all-encompassing disaster of the Chaos. The beach, the dunes, the wild marshy land behind with its abundant flora and fauna, the village with its ancient cheery tavern, and the great teeming metropolis of London along with all its millions of inhabitants. Deep sadness and an almost wild anger arose in me at the sheer scale of the tragedy about to unfold, and at the inevitability of it, the inescapability of it as it moved towards the inexorable disaster.

These anguished feelings of tragedy and loss, piled upon my delicate mental state being so far from home and so alone, overwhelmed me. I leaned back against the dune and closed my eyes, trying in vain to control my shallow, rasping breath and pounding heart. What would become of me if I were to find myself stuck here, unable to return home?

After what seemed an age I managed to bring my heaving chest and erratic heart beat under control. But I was exhausted, wrung out physically and emotionally by the crushing knowledge of the catastrophe soon to be played out, by the awareness of the devastation soon to be visited upon this messy, noisy, smelly, untidy world which was nevertheless marvellous and glorious, animated, alive in a way my own time could never be. I lay down in my sandy bed, wrapped myself in a protective barrier, and fell quickly into a troubled and restless sleep.

Chapter Fifty-Six

I awoke early after a most unhappy night during which I suffered dream after dream filled with unpleasant and frightening images, pictures I had seen in the digital memory of the effects of the Chaos, of the utter devastation wrought by the actions of the people in the world I was visiting. I did not feel rested, but was nevertheless glad to be awake, to no longer be subjected to the parade of dreadful impressions which had filled my mind in sleep.

I stretched, undressed, and took my usual bracing morning dip in the sea. I lay on my back in the water for a short while gazing up at the pale blueish-yellow dawn sky, my mind much calmer now than during the night. Nothing ever seemed as grim in the morning, and I was glad to be able to put the hours of darkness behind me. I dried myself, dressed again and broke my fast. After eating, I knew it was still too early to make my way to Ruth's home, so I continued my explorations of my surroundings.

I walked further up the coast until I reached a spot where the wildness seemed to merge gradually with farmed land. I stood on the cusp between the untouched coast and the obvious human interference, just able to make out the line of the land to the north turning sharply to the left. I brought to mind the outline of this coast on the map I had looked at, remembering that this part of the country jutted out into the sea, being surrounded on three sides by water.

As the hour was early, I decided to move a little way inland to visit a small rectangular building I could just discern from where I stood near the sea. Something about it attracted me.

I splashed through a marshy area of dunes and brackish pools, almost slipping into the watery ponds more than once. I came to a large sign which informed me that it was forbidden to walk on the area I had just traversed, a 'preservation area' which was so delicate that any human interference would be damaging. I shrugged, knowing it was too late for me to unwind my steps.

I turned and looked at the small brick building a little way behind the sign, and walked up to it. It was simple: a small rectangle with a slate roof high above. I did a circuit of the building finding a wooden door on the side facing away from the sea. I struggled a little to turn the handle, the door creaking loudly open as I let myself in. I closed the door behind me and gazed at the space inside. It was a large single room reaching to high wooden beams below the slate roof. There were a few benches and a table with a small vase of flowers on it at the end furthest from the door, a cross on the wall behind. It was a church, or chapel of some sort, empty, quiet, peaceful. Its walls showed patterns in the brick suggesting that it had once been much bigger and later reduced in size, the original openings to its extensions having been bricked in. I was astonished to feel that the building seemed to throb with a sense of age, great age.

On a small shelf beside the door I found some information and was truly amazed to discover that this chapel, named 'Saint Peter's ad vincula', was nearly fourteen hundred years old! It had been built as a chapel in the seventh century, and was now once again a place of worship. It was built along the line of an ancient Roman fort wall, using some of the bricks and stones of the same. It had indeed been larger, and had also included residential buildings for monks. I shuddered at the sheer age of the simple, unassuming edifice I stood in, wondering fleetingly if, after surviving for fourteen hundred years, it would withstand the rigours of the Chaos soon to come. Perhaps here, isolated near the coast, standing in an area seemingly devoid of human habitation, it would remain standing for another fourteen hundred years? When I returned to my own time, if I were able to do so, I would have to visit the area to see if this remarkable little building still stood. If it did, it would surely have been reclaimed by nature, given that nobody in my own time lived so far north, at least not on a permanent basis.

I sat for a while on one of the benches, enjoying the quiet solitude of this special place, before I realised that the time of my appointment with Ruth was nearing. I reluctantly left the chapel, stuffing a wad of those meaningless bank notes into a locked metal box for 'offerings' as I did so, and made my way back to Ruth's cabin, this time avoiding desecrating the sanctity of the delicate protected area I had crossed earlier in the day.

I approached the house confidently, feeling very differently from the way I had felt the first time I had been there only two days before. This time I came under invitation. I rapped loudly on the door, and moments later it opened inwards, revealing Ruth. I smiled broadly at her, and was rewarded with a hint of a smile in return. Her eyes darted up from the floor, almost meeting mine, before dropping again. She was tense, toying with a strand of hair with one hand, her lip bruised and sore where she had clearly been nibbling at it.

"Hello," I said brightly. "I'm here!"

"So I see," she answered in a quiet voice. Despite my invitation, I sensed anxiety in her. I knew that she wanted to meet me, to talk to me, to avail herself of my assistance, but this did not completely assuage all her feelings of nervousness in spending time with an almost unknown person. But she had promised, so, visibly steeling herself, she continued.

"Let's go out. We can talk as we walk," she said.

The day was perfect, warm and sunny, the usual sea breeze ensuring it would not become too hot, small fluffy clouds passing rapidly high above our heads. I nodded, and she stepped hesitantly out of the door, pulling it softly behind her. She was dressed almost the same way as she had been the day before, but this time in an identical dress of dull dark green dotted with paler green flowers, though with the same battered shoes on feet which stuck out below hairy shins, the same well-worn handbag slung across her shoulder, so heavy it dragged her right shoulder downwards. She glanced up at the sky, then darted back into the house to rescue a large floppy pink hat, and a pair of sunglasses. I was glad to see she was not wearing the glassless spectacles, though wondering if this was actually due to her slight diminution of fear of me, or merely because she was planning to don dark glasses against the sun instead.

We walked for hours along the beach, first to the south which was new to me, and then back northwards as far as the end of the wild part of the coast. At the start of our meanderings we talked little, a tension reigning between us. I was unsure how to break the mood, and Ruth seemed out of her depth spending time in this way with a stranger. Little by little, however, the atmosphere between us shifted, assisted in great part by our regular simple comments about what we saw as we strolled.

"It's very isolated here," I noted. Ruth's eyes did not look at me as she replied.

"Yes. That's why I live here," she confirmed. "So I don't come across other people by accident. Just those who turn up uninvited," she added, though I could not tell from her guarded tone whether she said this with irritation or ironic amusement. "And I love the wildness of the beach," she added.

"It's beautiful, and not just the beach, but all the salt marshes behind," I commented. Her eyes, shaded by the dark glasses but still just visible, slid almost imperceptibly towards me for the briefest of moments, before looking away again.

"You've visited them?" she asked in surprise.

"Yes. Several times. The first day I came here, and again yesterday after our meeting. I wasn't sure what to do with myself. I didn't dare try to return to my own time in case I couldn't get back here again, assuming I could even get home at all. So I took long walks up the coast, along the beach, behind the dunes..."

"You mean here? Near my home?" she asked sharply, a strange tone in her voice - irritation? Anxiety?

"Yes," I replied cautiously. "Is that not alright with you?" She did not reply and I found it hard to discern what she was thinking. We continued to walk in silence, a tension palpable between us. It had not occurred to me that she would be upset by the fact that I had spent most of the last few days near her home. To me it seemed an obvious place to while away the time before our next meeting, but something about my choice clearly displeased her.

I considered tackling her on her reaction to my revelation, but wondered if this might not exacerbate an already tense situation. I chose instead to pretend to ignore it, and to act with forced jollity.

"The birds make me laugh," I commented pointing at some of the more raucous of them as they wheeled noisily in the sky over our heads. Ruth did not reply, nor glance at the birds. I tried again.

"Do you know what they're called?" I asked. "What species?" This time Ruth did respond.

"Terns, I think," she said, tersely, but at least she had spoken. I then spoke again.

"And last night I saw a fox," I added. Ruth stopped and turned to me, a surprised, and clearly annoyed look on her face.

"You were here last night too, on this beach?" she asked in a vexed tone.

"Yes," I confirmed hesitantly. "I slept here. Both nights." She looked shocked at my revelation.

"Outside?" she asked incredulously. "On the beach?" I nodded. She simply stared at me with such surprise that her luxuriant dark eyebrows were clearly visible above the top of her sunglasses.

"Where?" she finally managed to ask. I forced a small smile.

"Back there, in front of one of the dunes," I explained. She remained quite still, and after a moment, continued her enquiries.

"In the open?" she asked, her voice having lost its irritated tone, only incredulity left behind. I nodded. Ruth removed her glasses to peer at me more closely, the first time she had stared at me since we met. I saw only surprise in her deep brown eyes, and decided to explain further.

"I made a little bed in the sand, and a pillow out of grasses," I began. "And then I threw up a barrier which I think would protect me from any intrusions - weather, animals, humans, anything really."

She was clearly astonished at my disclosure, staring at me for long moments before she seemed to realise what she was doing, dropped her gaze, once again donning her dark glasses.

"I'd never have the courage to do that," she mumbled. "To sleep out in the open."

"But I felt safe inside my barrier. Nothing could harm me," I explained, though I was not at all sure of the effectiveness of the barrier. After all, I had never had to actually rely on it.

"I still couldn't do it," she replied, shaking her head slightly. "I wish I could," she continued. "I mean, I wish I had more courage, enough to do something like that. I envy you." Then she sighed lightly, and added, "I yearn for such freedom."

After this brief conversation the ice seemed to crack, despite the frosty reception with which my revelation of having spent so much time near Ruth's home had been met. We began to talk more easily. At our previous meeting I had told her my story, or at least the most pertinent parts of it, and today I was eager to hear the details of her own background and upbringing, the path of her life. She seemed wary of talking about herself, preferring to deflect my questions again and again back to my life. We sat down on the sand, gazing out over the sea.

"But you said yesterday something about your mother," Ruth prodded. "Tell me more about her, about your family." I did not want to waste our meeting on things I already knew, but had little choice but to indulge Ruth in her curiosity.

"My mother isn't really my mother," I began. Ruth frowned slightly. "I mean, she is one of my...my parents, but as I said yesterday, I was engineered from the DNA of nineteen different people." Ruth nodded as I said this, indicating that she remembered what I had told her the day before, but the expression on her face suggested she was skeptical.

"I really was made from nineteen people," I insisted, a hint of defiance in my tone. "In my time nobody is born any more. Everyone is created from a number of parents that we call progenitors. Don't you already have multi-parent babies in this time?" I queried.

"Yes," Ruth replied slowly. "Made from the genetic material of three parents I think."

"Well then," I continued. "It's the same thing, just more parents. And my mother, Zelda, is one of my parents, but she's actually the scientist who made me, who developed the techniques of using so many parents, and she raised me too in her house, my home, along with my uncle Kallan. Though he isn't really my uncle, we just call him that." I stopped, wondering if my explanation was helping or hindering. Before I could continue, Ruth interrupted.

"You said you had siblings too?" she asked, perhaps searching my story for familiar ideas she could latch onto. She then looked surprised at the dark expression which crossed my face on hearing her words. She removed her glasses again.

"Yes, a brother and two sisters, twin sisters. But I'm not getting on with my brother at the moment. In fact, our relationship has been cool and distant for years."

"I haven't spoken to my brother or sister for years either," replied Ruth. "Or my father for that matter. My mother is no longer with us." Before I could offer sympathy at Ruth's final comment, she suddenly changed the subject. "What about your sisters? Do you get on with them?" she asked. I winced visibly at the innocent question, a pang of sorrow slicing through me as I thought of Safya. Ruth could see my reaction, and her own face mirrored mine, sadness showing clearly on her dark features in sympathy with me, though as yet without knowing why. Or perhaps she was simply thinking of the loss of her own mother.

"One of my sisters, Safya," I began, then stopped as a wave of sadness passed through me. Ruth perceived this and leaned towards me, an evident compassion clear on her features.

"Safya was murdered," I stated. Ruth jerked backwards at my words with a gasp, her deep-set eyes flying wide open, her tattered crimson lips opening in a wide circle.

"Murdered?" she whispered. "Murdered?" I simply nodded, mute. "How?" she prompted in a tiny voice. I did not feel at all inclined to relive my sister's killing, but felt I had no option. I had dangled the awful idea right in front of

Ruth, so I could hardly now refuse to elaborate. I explained as briefly as I could what had occurred, about the Council and its attitude towards my family, about the murder itself, the injury of my other sister, and the aftermath. I withheld the fact that I had killed the Council Speaker in cold blood, not feeling that this would endear me to Ruth. She listened in absolute silence, her eyes staring resolutely at the ground, her only movements a clasping of her hands together and a gentle nibbling on her bottom lip. When I had finished my tale, she sighed deeply.

"That is awful Sammy. So awful. I don't know what to say. I don't get on with my brother and sister, but I just can't imagine what it would be like if one of them were murdered. It's atrocious." She then glanced at me, and added, "And what happened to the people who did it?"

"We don't have murder in my time, I explained. "So we have no system to deal with it. Why would we? But we knew they needed to be punished."

"Of course they needed to be punished!" Ruth exclaimed. "So what happened?"

"We had to invent a punishment, my family that is," I went on. "But we got the rest of the Council to actually impose it so it would have some authority behind it. They've all been banished, sent to live in the endless wilds, far from other people, the Council members who planned the crime, and the thugs who actually carried it out. And the ringleader...died shortly afterwards anyway," I added, withholding information on my part in his death.

After this, it seemed there was little else to say on the matter, and Ruth seemed wary of asking any more questions about my life, my home, my time. For the moment at least. I used the opportunity to get her to divulge details of her own history.

"I'm not going to tell you when I was born," she began with the tiniest hint of a smile. "And don't ask," she added. "After all, it's rude to ask a lady her age." I took her word for this despite not really understanding her meaning. She hailed from north London, where she had been born into a Jewish family.

"Do you know what a Jew is?" she asked me suddenly, after telling me this fact. I paused for a moment before answering, to give me time to recollect what I knew about this group of people.

"Sort of," I admitted, though hesitantly, aware that my knowledge of this people was patchy, to say the least. My reply seemed to satisfy her, however, and we resumed our stroll along the beach.

But as we continued to walk, I was able, gradually, to elicit further details from her about her life. What interested me most were her descriptions of the effects of her abilities. She informed me, with obvious distress and a bout of lip chewing as she did so, of the voices in her head.

"They started when I was really young, so early that to be honest I have no memory of a time before they existed. When in the company of other people, I was subjected to twitterings and witterings all around me, often incomprehensible and senseless, though peppered regularly with words, phrases and even whole sentences of clarity. As a small child, I didn't question the voices. I had always heard them and therefore had nothing to compare my experience with. But as I grew through childhood, and especially once I was at school, I rapidly learned that the endless utterances in my mind weren't normal, were, in fact, unique to me. For years I simply didn't dare divulge to anyone what I suffered, fearing the reaction this would cause. But all along I sensed that those closest to me, especially my mother, knew that something was wrong, very wrong. Eventually I mustered the courage to tell my mother everything, and my mother admitted that she had had suspicions that my mental state was unusual, to say the least. I was then subjected to a long series of doctors and psychiatrists, to scans of my brain, electrodes monitoring my mental activity. But all to no avail. The scans and electrodes showed slight elevations in certain brain activities, but nothing sufficient to explain the sheer magnitude of what I was describing. The medical professionals were flummoxed, but eventually pronounced that I suffered from an unusual form of schizophrenia. They prescribed powerful anti-psychotic drugs which I diligently took for some years.

"But the drugs had little effect, at least on the voices. What they did, however, was to dull much of the rest of my mental ability, rendering me almost impervious to emotion, making me care almost nothing about anything or anyone. As I entered adolescence, I made a bold decision: I would stop taking the drugs. Disaster! I was plunged almost immediately into a nightmare of feelings and emotions and endless chattering voices, though this gradually calmed enough for me to be able to function. But I never functioned normally. The voices were so endlessly distracting that normal human relations were not possible, and I also suffered chronic anxiety, fear of the world around me and especially of people. I was taken from my school and sent to a school for people with serious psychological problems, an institution in which the children lived as well as studied. That place was more hindrance than help.

"Imagine," Ruth said to me in an incredulous tone. "Being surrounded by nothing but lunatics, psychotics, schizophrenics. If you weren't mad before you went there, you would be by the time you came out!" Ruth's tone was tinged with a trace of irony as she said this, and I was pleased to note this unusual hint of humour from her. I did not make any comment at her observations. I had no context for the institution described, and chose to listen rather than offer what could be construed as insincere commiserations.

"At my 'special school'," continued Ruth, emphasising the term with a mirthless chuckle, "I withdrew from contact with everybody, not just at the school, but also my family who I blamed for abandoning me to that ghastly place. As I approached my late teens, reaching the age where I would need to leave the school, my family faced a crisis. Where should I live? What would I do with my life? But my mother came to the rescue, and I went to live with her. My mother tried to persuade me to start taking the medications again, but I refused point blank. As I grew into full adulthood, living quietly in my mother's house in north London, the voices diminished in intensity and regularity, but only because I kept myself away from other people as much as I could. My mother, bless her, tried to ensure we received no visitors, something that must have been really difficult for her as she was a very sociable, friendly person.

"But soon I began to notice other activities in my mind. I began to have dreams, incredibly vivid dreams of destruction and devastation, of the world ending, being subjected to famines and droughts, plagues and epidemics, wars and nuclear attacks. I despaired about what was happening in my overactive brain, at one point even toying with the possibility that I was experiencing the sort of revelations of an Old Testament Biblical prophet! But since I didn't actually believe in God, I quickly quashed these thoughts. But this left me floundering for answers to the source and significance of my visions.

"Try as I might, I could find no answers to the origins or meanings of the images showing themselves to my mind. I regularly discussed these with my mother, and between us we tried to contain and control the visions, but with no success. I despaired. My mother despaired. The voices I heard whenever I was around other people made it difficult, painful and distressing to go out and about in the world, and even in the refuge of my home I was constantly bombarded with harsh, extreme and violent images. I contemplated suicide on many occasions, but each time I let slip such thoughts to my long-suffering mother, that warm and loving woman was so distraught at the prospect that I could never actually go through with it. But it was actually my mother, that sensible, practical and down-to-earth woman who managed, in her way, to save my sanity.

"One morning as I shared my horrific visions of catastrophe from the night before, my mother offered a suggestion, a simple, almost off-hand idea which proved to be my salvation, or as near to it as I could hope for."

"Why don't you write down everything you see," my mother suggested. "Maybe turn it all into a book, or books. From the stuff I see on the television, people seem to love all that sort of violence, disasters, post-apocalyptic science fiction." I remember staring at her, astonished at the suggestion, but quickly deciding that my mother's idea was sound. I certainly had nothing to lose by recording my visions, and even if such an action didn't help my mental state, I might be able to make a living from it.

"And the rest," Ruth declared, "is history. I started to transcribe all the images and pictures each morning, typing them up while they were still vivid and precise. And before long I had so much material that I needed to start sorting it, arranging it into a coherent story. And to my amazement, as I began to do this, it seemed almost to sort itself. A clear pattern emerged of the process of destruction. And as I started to write it in the form of a novel, I soon realised I had enough to write lots of novels, a whole series of them. And when I'd done the first one my mother managed to get a friend who was a literary agent to give it to Simon Schapps at Guillemot, and he loved it. It was published, sold really well, and I've done six more since then. I've made a lot of money from them which has given me an independence I never imagined I'd have. I was able to help my mother financially which made me really happy, and I lived with her till she died, nearly five years ago. Since then I've lived most of the time here in the beach cabin as far from other people as possible while still being able to get into London when I need to."

Ruth stopped talking after this for a long time, and we sat quietly on the beach, each engaged with our own thoughts. After a while, I remembered something I had noticed in Ruth's final novel as I had skimmed through it.

"The stuff in your last book," I began. "All the things about the people who survived the Chaos and..."

"The chaos?" queried Ruth. "What is that, and why do you call it that? I've never called anything the chaos in my books. I didn't give the disaster a single name." I bit my tongue, angry with myself at having let the word chaos slip out. I did not want Ruth to know that the visions of disaster and destruction she had seen were not fantastical images, the result of serious psychological problems. Given her delicate mental state, I feared what the effect would be on her were she ever to learn that her novels were not fiction, but mostly fact, an already determined future. I tried to cover my error.

"I...I don't really know," I stammered. "It does all sound rather chaotic," I added lamely. Ruth looked at me oddly, but did not pursue the issue.

"Anyway," she continued. "You were asking how I came across the ideas for what happened after the disasters, the chaos as you call it.

"Actually," she added after a moment's reflection. "The Chaos is a good name for it. I wish I'd thought of it, but no matter. But to answer your question, I began to get visions of the aftermath of all the disasters, this Chaos, but really weirdly, not until I got to the end of my sixth book, the one where the world is more or less completely destroyed. So I just did what I'd always done and wrote them down as the next instalment of the series."

I was shocked by Ruth's revelation. Not only had she seen much of the truth of the progress of the Chaos, she had also been able to foresee, with reasonable accuracy, the immediate post-Chaos world, that devastated planet into which the tiny numbers of survivors so cautiously emerged, as they contemplated the destruction with heavy hearts and wondered how to begin to rebuild. Her abilities were so powerful that I was stunned, completely taken aback by the level and intensity of her gifts. No wonder she had struggled to cope with such astonishing abilities without any understanding of their source. I had first believed she only had the ability to hear other people's thoughts, the voices in her head, but her revelations this day made me realise that she was, somehow, able to foresee many aspects of the future, to take her mind beyond her own time, and to sense the horrors that were about to unfold. I was amazed at how different her gifts were from my own, my total inability to see what was to come. As I considered this I pondered: does this mean the future is already written, even if we cannot see it? That not only the past is unalterable, but also the future?

As I considered all that Ruth had told me, and struggled with myself as to how much of the future to reveal to her, she abruptly changed the subject.

"You promised me you'd help me with the voices," she said. "Can we do that now?" I looked at her, her face showing an eagerness, a cautious optimism tinged with the possibility of disappointment that I may not be able to make good on my promise.

"Yes," I replied, glad of the detour away from further discussion of the Chaos. "Do you want me to help you with the visions too?" I added. She was visibly surprised at my question, ambivalence clear on her face.

"I...I...I really don't know," she stammered. "They can be awful, but I've sort of got used to them. And writing them down has really helped me not get so upset by them. And without them, I'd have nothing to write about." She stopped talking, chewing her bottom lip vigorously as she thought about my offer, both hands lifted to her head as if massaging her temples. She seemed unable to make a decision.

"Well," I offered, helping her with her dilemma. "Let's just deal with the voices for now, and you can think about the visions later. There's no hurry. I'll be here for a while." And I smiled at her by way of reassurance. She glanced up at me, a faint smile of gratitude on her face. She stopped chewing her lip, and I saw a tiny drop of blood glistening scarlet on the rough and damaged skin of her bottom lip.

"Shall we begin?" I asked. Ruth nodded, her eyes glistening with nervous anticipation as she stared down at the sand in front of us.

Chapter Fifty-Seven

In truth, I was not sure how to begin with Ruth, to help her control the voices in her head. Where we sat on the empty beach, there were no such voices, no risk of them with no other people within many kilometres. From the very start, I had blocked my own internal thoughts reaching Ruth's mind, a fact she had picked up on at our earlier meeting. Perhaps I needed to remove the barrier between our minds, allowing her to hear my thoughts in order to teach her how to control this? Or would it be better to simply enter her mind and teach her that way, directing her attention to the internal workings of her brain by way of demonstration, getting her then to emulate my actions?

"I think," I began tentatively, "That we have a few options." She looked at me quizzically.

"Don't you know how to do this?" she asked, a hint of disappointment creeping into her voice that perhaps I was not who I said I was, or at least would not be able to offer her the help she so desperately craved.

"Not specifically," I admitted. "I've never done it before, but I believe I can help you, especially someone with your amazing abilities." Ruth seemed a little reassured, but I saw residual doubt in her face. I paused for a moment. Then suddenly the best way to convince her of my potential leapt to mind.

~I'm going to start by teaching you how to speak to me without talking,~ I mindspoke to her. She jumped as my voice resonated in her head, so taken aback that she turned and stared at me, directly into my eyes.

"You...you...just spoke straight into my head!" she stated, utterly confounded. I smiled at her astonishment, at the expression of almost comical shock on her face.

~Yes,~ I continued, maintaining the mindspeak. *~Why don't you try it? Why don't you try to talk to me the same way, from your mind directly into*

mine?~ I encouraged. She continued to stare at me, by far the longest direct look I had received from her.

"How?" she managed to squeeze out. "How do I do that? It didn't sound like all the other voices," she went on. "I've never heard voices from you anyway, but this sounded more...more...directed somehow, more deliberate." I paused for a moment at her comments. With a person who did not suffer the ailment of endless voices in her head, learning to mindspeak was so easy as to seem almost automatic. Haari had immediately begun to do so as soon as I opened a channel between us. But with Ruth, I needed a slightly more guided method of showing her, so she could always differentiate it from the normal babble her mind was subjected to.

~Can you feel where my voice is in your head? Can you sense its location?~ I asked her. She knitted her eyebrows in concentration, half closing her dark eyes as she struggled to locate the exact place in which my words resonated. After long moments during which I said nothing, unwilling to interrupt her concentration, her eyes flew open, and I saw an unusually bright smile light up her face.

~Yes!~ She exclaimed in silent words. And as she realised that she had, without even trying, managed to mindspeak directly to me, she was so overcome with emotion that she burst into tears. I was nonplussed, as I had not expected this reaction. But her tears were short-lived, merely a response to the shock of what she had done, the enormity of what she had achieved. Quickly she recovered her usual controlled poise. She glanced at me as she wiped the moisture from her cheeks, a tiny smile at the corner of her lips.

~I...I...this...I can't believe it!~ She managed to mindspeak. I smiled at her transparent joy as emotions flowed out of her, a surge of excitement, of anticipation, of hope. I knew that she now believed me, believed who I was, had faith that I could help her.

We remained many hours on the beach. From the outside we would have looked most peculiar. A silent couple sitting quite still, hour after hour, the only evidence of communication being our animated facial expressions, our frowns and smiles, our quizzical looks, our taciturnity punctuated by occasional chuckles and louder laughter. In all honesty, if there had been other people on the beach they would most probably have avoided us, looking as we did like crazy people sitting in silence, grimacing and contorting our features, laughing loudly and apparently randomly at absolutely nothing. But the beach was empty, devoid of human life. We regularly caught the birds on the beach by surprise, startling them with our unexpected outbursts, their raucous irritated reactions to us as they took flight causing us further merriment.

~If anyone saw us,~ mindspoke Ruth. *~They'd think we were deaf and using sign language, but wouldn't see the signs we were making!~* And she laughed, apparently finding this idea amusing. I looked surprised at her comment, and she asked,

~Don't you have deaf people? Sign language?~ I shook my head.

~We don't have anything like that any more. All of those...those...handicaps,~ I mindspoke, not knowing what other word to use. *~All of them have been bred out. We barely even have any illness any more, usually just the occasional very minor problem.~* Ruth glanced up at me, amazement on her face, astonished at my words.

~That's incredible,~ she said. *~What a fabulous thought: a world without illness or disease!~*

The day passed as I worked hard to teach Ruth how to manage certain aspects of the workings of her mind. She was an avid pupil, eager to control the wayward brain which had caused so much distress in her life. After her initial success with mindspeaking, I taught her how to do the same unprompted. Her first words to me simply flowed along the channel I had opened up between us. It was quite another thing for *her* to create the connection herself. I withdrew from her mind, asking her to connect with me directly, mind to mind. She struggled at first with this and began to become agitated, distressed at her failures.

"It's no use!" she snapped. "It's just no bloody use. Nothing's happening. I can't do it." And I feared she was on the verge of abandoning the attempt, so I was compelled to enter her mind again and gently draw her towards success. After many attempts, she suddenly seemed to find the answer to the problem, fabricating a clear line of connection between us. I was rewarded by a huge smile and a look of satisfaction on her face as she shouted "Eureka!" I had no idea what the word meant, but its intention was clear from her triumphant expression.

From this, we moved on to the voices. I had to almost artificially drive my own thoughts into Ruth's head in a way which I thought mimicked the voices she was normally subjected to. I was forced to work hard to jumble up my words, make my thoughts confused, incomplete, as close to those she usually experienced as possible, something that I found difficult as I had been directing my thoughts clearly to others for years. As with her creation of a connection to my mind, there were many abortive attempts, Ruth becoming irritated with herself and with me, discouragement seeping into her feelings as she struggled again and again to block my words as they careered around in her mind.

~Perhaps we should take a break?~ I suggested in the middle of the afternoon as her mood became more fractious. *~Perhaps we should have something to eat?~* I added, feeling hunger pangs invade my stomach.

~No!~ She replied loudly into my head, with little control of the silent volume. I flinched slightly as her refusal struck me.

~Ok, ok,~ I said, holding up my hands. *~But please don't yell like that. It hurts!~* She looked sheepish and promised to control the intensity of her outbursts. But she refused take a break, so intent was she to master the blocking of the voices, and we continued for some time after this without pause. Just as with her earlier success, this one too came suddenly, abruptly, almost without warning. I was maintaining a steady stream of garbled mutterings in my head, forcing these into her mind where they bounced around incoherently. Suddenly she looked up sharply, dark eyebrows drawn tightly together. She was so surprised at what she was experiencing that she forgot to mindspeak.

"Have you stopped?" She asked. "Have you stopped making the noises, the words?" I shook my head, maintaining the stream of babble even as I did so.

"No," I replied, also reverting to normal speech. "Why?" She was unable to answer immediately, finally finding her voice.

"I can't hear you," she whispered, her voice trembling. "I can't hear you anymore."

We stared at each other for a long moment as her eyes shone with elation. I felt a surge of happiness at the transparent joy on Ruth's face.

~Eureka!~ I said, using the word I had learned from her. *~You've done it! ~* I added, in silent tones of awe.

~No,~ she replied quietly. *~You've done it. You've silenced the voices in my head. For the first time in my life.~*

We sat in silence, quietly delighting in our triumph. After a few moments, I turned to Ruth.

~You need to practise it with other people, as soon as possible. Now, in fact.~ Ruth frowned slightly and I was not sure if she had understood what I meant. Or perhaps she understood it very well, and was fearful of what it signified: that we needed to travel to a place with other people. I sensed great hesitation in her, though it seemed to be mostly premised on the fear that she had not, in fact, truly managed to control the voices. Perhaps it was a

one-off, or only my artificially created voice that she could block. Perhaps when faced with the reality of many chaotic voices coming from all around she would find she had not mastered the skill at all. But this time I was adamant. It was essential that she try her new-found ability immediately, to reassure herself that it was real, before she lost the nerve to make the attempt.

I would brook no opposition from Ruth, and my tetchiness with her was not helped by the fact that I was tired and hungry and thirsty. I pushed her hard, subjecting her to the mental equivalent of a stamp of the foot, causing her to wince. But she knew I would not be thwarted. I even went so far as to threaten her.

~I'll just teleport us both somewhere if you don't agree. Somewhere absolutely full of people,~ I said peevishly. She was well able to sense that I was not making idle threats, so she wisely capitulated. After a brief and slightly irascible discussion we agreed to go straight away to the Traveller Inn. It was a good compromise as it was familiar to Ruth and there would be people there, though not so many as to cause her undue anxiety. Before she could change her mind I grabbed her arm and took us there.

As we appeared in a quiet alley beside the inn, Ruth gasped, leaning against me for support. I had forgotten that she had never teleported before, the experience being entirely novel for her. I felt a twinge of guilt that I had overlooked this in my haste to bring her here. But as I glanced at her, my sense of culpability evaporated. She looked astonished, yet full of excited happiness, like a child seeing the sea for the first time. Though she seemed a little off-balance physically, her eyes shone.

"That was amazing!" she said loudly, her emotion again causing her to forget to mindspeak. "I can't believe what we just did, what just happened. One moment we were there on the beach, and then whoosh, the next moment we were here. Is this how you usually get around?" she asked.

"Yes," I replied. "It's the only way to travel," I added with a grin.

"I could get used to this!" she stated animatedly.

We made our way quickly into the pub. As the day before, there were a few people in the large main room, several tables occupied. We approached the bar where, to my dismay, the large jolly woman with the tousled thatch of dyed blond hair from first night was back on duty. She looked at us attentively as we leaned against the bar.

"Hello again dear," she said brightly to me. Turning to Ruth, she spoke again. "And I've seen you in here a few times too haven't I? You're the writer who lives down by the sea." Ruth nodded. The woman behind the bar seemed about to ask further questions, but before she could do so I mindspoke to Ruth quickly.

~I don't want her to ask lots of difficult questions so I'm going to lie to her. Please go along with my lies.~ Ruth seemed slightly surprised at my words, but indicated assent with the tiniest nod of her head.

"I found my aunt's house," I said, nodding in Ruth's direction. "And I'm staying there now, with her." The woman at the bar drew her eyebrows together, and replied.

"I thought you said there was no room at her house, didn't you love?" I realised my mistake as she spoke. I had indeed told her this.

"I let him sleep on the sofa," Ruth intruded, surprising me as she not only backed up my lie about who she was, but elaborated the untruth.

"That's nice," replied the woman, seeming to lose interest in the matter. "And what can I get you?" She then asked, looking at both of us. I ordered a whole pint of the draft cider, and once again opted for the filling fish and chips I had enjoyed a few nights before, though this time asking for ordinary peas in place of the bizarre green pap of mushy peas I had the last time. Ruth joined me in a pint of cider, and ordered something called 'shepherd's pie'. We took our drinks and made our way to the same corner table we had first sat at, to await our food.

I felt Ruth's agitated emotional state as I followed her to the table, both of us walking carefully so as not to spill cider from the overfilled glasses. As we sat down opposite each other, I was concerned at Ruth's mental state, but when I looked at her, all my worries evaporated. She was shining with joy, happiness so clear on her face that she almost emitted beams of light, at least to my perception. I sat in silence, waiting for her to speak. She could not formulate words for long minutes, such was the depth of her emotional reaction to the situation. When she was finally able to find her voice, she leaned towards me, her luxuriant dark locks falling forward to frame her face. She looked me right in the eyes, and whispered.

"Silence. Just silence. The voices are gone!"

Chapter Fifty-Eight

After an hour or so in the Traveller, during which Ruth remained free of the voices in her head, she insisted we visit somewhere busier, more animated, for her to test her new-found freedom. I was slightly hesitant to accede to her demand, but she insisted, and in the end I realised that she was right: she needed to reassure herself that what she had achieved was complete, and permanent.

We decided to visit the nearest town to Ruth's seaside home, a small place called Southminster, so, hand in hand, I teleported us to a quiet spot in the town, amused at Ruth's almost childish enjoyment again of this method of travel.

~*Do you think you can teach me to teleport?*~ she asked as we began to walk around Southminster.

~*I don't know,*~ I replied, genuinely unsure if she had the right sort of ability to do this. I saw dismay on her face at my words, so added brightly, ~*But I'm more than happy to try, maybe a bit later on?*~ She did not seem entirely satisfied with this, but did not push the matter further. I was still keen to address Ruth's visions of the Chaos and the post-Chaos world, not believing that they helped her live in a tranquil state, though I understood her hesitation when I had offered to help her control the visions. She certainly did not want to lose access to her visions completely. But my aim would be to allow her to experience them only when it suited her, to control them, to prevent them coming unbidden as and when *they* saw fit. This seemed to me a much more important and urgent task than teaching my new friend to teleport.

We spent several hours wandering around the small town, in and out of shops. I had very limited experience of shops, only the bookshop, the place I procured victuals and the shop I had bought the map from, so was keen to see more. Throughout the time we meandered Ruth was able to maintain her peaceful mind, free from the voices that had plagued her life. I took the opportunity to experience a small slice of everyday life, fascinated at the places we visited. Ruth found my endless fascination amusing, and a little perplexing.

~*Don't you have shops in your world. I mean, in your time?*~ She mindqueried as we wandered from one outlet to another.

~*No,*~ I replied. ~*We don't have anything like shops. Some of our artists, jewellery-makers and other people working with crafts have small showrooms where they display the things they've made, but none of them are for sale. In fact, we have no concept of buying or selling in my time time, no exchange system of this type.*~

~*But if people make and display these things, what do they get for them?*~ Ruth queried reasonably. I paused for a moment before answering.

~*People do make works of art, jewellery, stained glass, lots of things, thousands of other artefacts others might want. But they don't sell them. Anyone can get them just by asking.*~

~*So nobody pays for them?*~ Asked Ruth in disbelief. ~*Why does anyone bother to make them then?*~ Again, I had to pause before answering, to collect my thoughts.

~*I think they are just happy to provide pleasure to others, to make things other people want. And it would be inconceivable to think of demanding anything in return. Some of the most successful artists do occasionally barter their work in return for other highly prized pieces, but this is just so that both parties can jump the queue of other people waiting for the objects. It's not a true barter or exchange system.*~ Ruth seemed nonplussed by my descriptions, rendered silent by them, perhaps trying to imagine a world with no buying and selling, no exchange mechanism for products, no money or any other type of currency. As if giving up the attempt, she shook her head over and over again, her thick dark curls flying in the breeze, a look of confusion on her face.

We visited shops selling food and drinks and other everyday items, others selling what appeared to be medicines, a huge range of what looked (and smelled) like soap, shampoo, perfume and the like; shoes, clothing. Other shops seemed to sell items I could not fathom the purpose of, knick-knacks and 'gewgaws' (as Ruth called them) which appeared neither useful, nor attractive to my eye. And in every shop we visited there were many, many articles I simply did not understand, did not recognise. I began by asking Ruth about them. She politely explained each one to me, but clearly found the process dull, so I quickly abandoned it.

Ruth managed to successfully maintain her block on the importunate voices throughout our entire trip, and this gave her an enormous sense of joy, and of triumph. She kept commenting on how extraordinary it was to be out and about with ordinary people and not to be suffering the usual vocal assault on her brain that had always accompanied her in such situations. She also repeated her thanks to me over and over again, until I told her, with a laugh, that she needed to stop.

When Ruth was satisfied she was fully in control of her new ability, we decided to leave the town and return to her home.

~Can we teleport there?~ She asked, eagerness clear on her face. *~Or what did you call it? Flit?~* She added.

~Of course,~ I replied with a grin. *~But do you mean actually back to your house, inside your house?~* I asked, wanting to be absolutely certain this is what she intended. She hesitated for a moment, as if wondering herself if this was what she had meant. Suddenly she seemed to make up her mind.

~Yes,~ she said. *~Why not.~*

I glanced around to find a quiet spot from which to port us, walked over to a row of bushes on the other side of the road we were on, and led her hastily behind them. Before she could have a change of heart and withdraw her invitation, I grabbed her arm and ported us directly into the hallway of her home. As before, she beamed with pleasure at the sensation of travelling in this way.

From the hallway, Ruth led me into a small living room on the left-hand side of the house which enjoyed a wonderful view of the sea, almost its entire front length being occupied with a large window. It was dotted here and there with old-looking furniture, a sofa and two armchairs, all well-worn, covered in shabby dark red material, many lumpy cushions of various different colours and textures, none of them matching, thrown haphazardly across the seating. At the back of the room, with only a tiny window in the wall behind, was a large wooden table and four chairs. These too were clearly old and well-used, the table top scratched and stained in many places, the chairs looking as if they did not sit evenly on the wooden floor. In addition, none of the chairs matched, each one being quite different from its neighbours. The dark wooden planks of the floor, which extended the whole width of what was, in effect a single large room, were covered, in the living room, with several large, rather grubby, mats. These must once have been beautiful and probably expensive, as I could just make out complicated patterns in wools of various colours, but they were so worn, and dirty, that they now merely added to the general air of shabbiness and lack of care of the rest of the room. The table at the back of the room sat on bare boards.

Ruth seemed oblivious to the condition of her living and dining areas, indicating with a vague wave of her hand that I should sit down. I picked the middle of the sofa as this seemed to be the least grimy part of the seating. As I walked across the mat on which the sofa sat, the soles of my shoes crunched on the copious pieces of I-know-not-what littering the surface. I forced myself not to show my distaste as I lowered myself onto the stained fabric of the sofa, putting a smile on my face as I did so in an effort to hide my feelings.

"I'll go and make a cup of tea," she announced, reverting to normal speech now we were in the safety and privacy of her home. She turned just before she left the room.

"Do you drink tea?" she asked. I nodded.

"I mean," she continued. "Do you drink tea from where you come from, in your time?" she asked.

"Yes," I replied. "It's still very popular." She seemed to find my answer vaguely amusing, though I did not really know why. As she left the room a tiny smile curled the corners of her lips. I followed her in my head so I could get my bearings in the house without seeming to be too nosy. She crossed the hall and entered a small kitchen at the back of the building. I saw that the other room at the front of the house, across the hall from the living room, was a small room with nothing in it but bookcases groaning under the weight of tomes, and behind this room was a small bathroom. This was the entire ground floor, but at the very back of the hallway was a circular metal staircase which led to the single room on the first floor I had noticed from outside, almost entirely surrounded by glass. As I visited this upstairs room with my mind, I saw that it was another bedroom, and at the back of it was another smaller bathroom with only a toilet, a basin and a shower, none of them terribly clean as far as I could see. This room seemed to be where Ruth slept, as it looked occupied, the bed unmade but covered in a pile of messy bedding.

After a little while Ruth returned to the living room with a tray on which were two surprisingly delicate blue and pale pink porcelain cups sitting on tiny saucers, a little jug of milk in a matching pattern, and what I surmised was a teapot covered in a strange dome of padded material. Ruth noticed my quizzical glance at the covering on the teapot.

"It's a tea cosy," she explained. "It keeps the tea warm." I had never seen anything like it, and laughed out loud at the idea of putting what was, in effect, a warm coat, on a tea pot. Ruth looked offended by my mirth, as if I thought the use of the cosy ridiculous.

"Actually," I said, once I had stopped laughing, and in an attempt to assure Ruth that I was not laughing at her. "It's a a sensible idea in a cold climate. I'm sure the tea gets cold quickly if you don't keep it 'cosy' like this." She did not look entirely convinced by my attempt at conciliation, but held her tongue.

We sat drinking tea and chatting for hours, Ruth pressing me for more details of the world I came from. In addition to further information about my own odd background, I also elucidated as much as I could about my world in general. I talked more of the Council, of its history and its current role, and gave further details of my own family's problems with it, including my brother's current friendship with the vile Devid.

"Why do you think your brother, Al...Ad...what was his name again?" Ruth asked.

"Adwin," I replied.

"Why do you think Adwin has become so chummy with this Devid, if he's as horrible as you say? What could be the possible reason?"

"I'm not sure," I replied hesitantly. "As I said before, Adwin and I have not really been close for years and haven't shared private thoughts with each other for a long time. And since I discovered him out with Devid we haven't spoken at all. In fact, he's not been at home much since then. I assume Devid made an effort to befriend him. Adwin was initially reluctant to leave the house, so I think Devid must have made all the effort and must have worked hard to meet Adwin and then manipulate him into thinking he was my brother's friend. After my brother and I fell out, poor Adwin must have been really lonely. I knew he was, but I didn't know what to do about it. I had my friends outside the house, but he didn't seem to want to make any effort to make any friends. And I didn't see why I should take him along with me when he was always so miserable in my company, so difficult to be with. I did a few times but it was always unpleasant."

"So you just left him alone at home? Who did he spend his time with? What about your sister? Or your uncle or mother?" Ruth asked, a hint of disapproval in her voice.

"My sister, Emaleen, is eight years older than Adwin and never spent time with him. Even when she began to get over her sister's murder, she and Adwin never really spent time together. They get on alright, but just aren't close. My uncle is lovely, kind and thoughtful, but like me he's been finding Adwin difficult for ages now, and Kallan's often away from home himself, especially now we're all older. And my mother! She's probably the last person Adwin would choose to spend time with, even less than with me. She wants him dead."

"What??" gasped Ruth in outrage at my final, almost throw-away comment. "What in God's name do you mean 'she wants him dead'??"

"Well," I began, wishing I had never made the comment. "She thinks he's a failed experiment, not like me and my sisters. His gifts are not well-developed, and he's often ill, weak, in a world in which such things barely exist any more. If she'd known he had so many problems when he was still a foetus, she would have terminated it, him." I stopped speaking before I could let slip the fact that Zelda had once even instructed me to put an end to my brother's life. That would surely be a step too far for Ruth.

"My God," said Ruth after a pause. "And I thought my family was dysfunctional!" I was not exactly sure what the word signified in this context, but guessed at her meaning. I blushed and squirmed at Ruth's disapproval. And I hardly dared imagine what she would feel if she knew that I had killed the old Council Speaker, that Zelda had told me to kill Devid, and even to murder my own brother!

I quickly changed the subject, talking about Beyra and our other towns and cities, the buildings, the beautiful environments we had created to live in. I spoke of the fact that citizens are provided with everything they want and require, from cradle to grave, and have no need ever to work. I explained, as far as I was able, how the central distribution centres worked, though I was somewhat vague on the specifics. In truth I was not sure how they functioned, and had never visited one, never really giving them much thought. I was however able to elaborate in more detail on the functioning of the Institutes, how our society created its babies and chose to raise its children to the age of fourteen, and what happened to them after leaving the Institute.

Eventually I stopped talking. Ruth sat in silence, her mind filled with the words and images I had given her. She was astounded that I was able to transmit, directly into her mind, actual pictures of the places I described, showing her my home, the forest on the estate, Beyra, the children playing at the Institute. She had never experienced anything like this before, she told me. Even her visions were much less clear than this, less well-formed or focused. And in truth, what I showed her were bright and happy pictures, completely unlike the dark and fearful visions she herself received. I specifically avoided showing any images relating to the attack on Emaleen and Safya, as I felt this would distress her for no purpose. And distress me too.

Later in the evening, Ruth prepared a simple meal of what she called macaroni cheese. "Or mac 'n' cheese if you're trendy!" she added with a chuckle, to my total confusion. We enjoyed the simple yet rich tasty food together, sitting on the wobbly chairs at the stained and scratched table, washing it down with a surprisingly pleasant bottle of white wine. Darkness began to fall, late, as was usual at this time of the year so far from the equator, unlike in Beyra or on the Estate. I felt the time to retire was nearly upon me.

"I'll take my leave Ruth," I said, making to stand up from the table where we had lingered long after our meal. She glanced at me sharply, and I sensed a surge of emotion from her even in the gloomy room where we had forgotten to put the lights on. I stayed where I was, immobile in my chair, sensing that Ruth was wrestling with something in her mind, with ambivalent feelings over something into which I did not want to intrude. She wrung her hands together in between raising one of them to twist strands of her thick hair. After a few moments, she sighed slightly, almost inaudibly, such that I felt the sigh rather than heard it.

"I'd like to let you stay here, but I'm not ready for that," she said in a tiny voice barely above a whisper, her eyes fixed on the floor in front of her. The curious expression on her face told me that she was surprised by her own words, as if they had made a decision for her that her mind had not yet quite reached.

"That's fine," I replied gently. "I can easily sleep on the beach. I don't want to cause you any distress."

She paused. "Yes," she replied. "Yes, that would be best," she continued. I was pleased that Ruth seemed to have considered inviting me to stay, even if she could not bring herself to do so, knowing what a huge step it was for her even to contemplate such an offer. As she had informed me earlier in the day, nobody had ever even entered her home when she was there, let alone stayed overnight.

I said I was tired and would take my leave. I followed Ruth into the hall, and wished her a good night as I opened the front door. She hesitated briefly before saying 'good night' to me, and then turned abruptly on her heel, making her way to her room upstairs.

I was truly weary after the exertions of the day, my energy resources being depleted by so much effort over such a long period, so I made my way briskly along the beach to the same dune I had slept in front of the night before. My 'bed' was still intact, even the pillow. Such was the isolation and emptiness of this region that nobody else had set foot on the beach that day. I lay on the sandy bed, wriggling a little to get comfortable, arms folded behind my head, staring at the near-black starry sky and listening to the gentle lapping of the waves on the shore. The moon was strong, and it cast an icy blue aura into the darkness all around it. I yawned, threw up the barrier I hoped would suffice to protect me, and fell quickly asleep, listening to the soft sounds of the sea licking the sand.

Chapter Fifty-Nine

The next morning I awoke early to the creamy yellow luminescence of a mid-summer morning high in the northern hemisphere. I stretched, noting to my great surprise that the protective barrier I thought I had erected seemed no longer to be in place, then stood up. I would have to look into the reasons for the disappearance of the protection I had set up. But for the moment I removed my clothes and skipped into the sea, gasping with the shock of the cold water. It seemed too early to disturb Ruth, so I returned to the beach, dried myself by raising my body temperature, and once again donned my clothing. I lay back on the sand, hands clasped behind my head, recumbent and comfortable on the soft surface as I watched the sky turn from pale gold to light blue, the only sounds the gentle, regular swishing of the waves against the shore interrupted by the raucous cawing of the sea birds as they made preparation for the day ahead.

I dozed a little, on and off, until I sensed movement in Ruth's home. I looked with my mind into the house, seeing that Ruth was awake and making her way down the spiral stairs towards the hallway, and thence to the kitchen. I took my cue, stood up, and made my way to her front door. I knocked gently and was quickly met by the sight of Ruth as she opened the door, dishevelled, her mass of dark wavy hair like the wild nest of some huge bird, sleepiness evident in her deep-set inky eyes, an ill-fitting and none too clean gown of a fluffy, dark blue material wrapped loosely around her.

"Good morning," I said cheerily as I stepped briskly across the threshold before she could stop me. She jumped on hearing my bright tone, her eyes sliding briefly upwards to my face. Had she forgotten I was staying so near her house? That we had arranged for me to come to her early in the morning? She quickly rallied, however and even managed to flash a small smile in my direction.

"Coffee?" she mumbled as I followed her into the kitchen at the back of the house. I indicated that I would prefer tea, and she set about preparing both drinks. We stood in silence as she did so, and I realised that she was not given to communicating in the mornings, hardly a surprise in light of the quiet, isolated life she had led in recent years.

"I'll go and wait at the table," I said quietly, not wanting to discomfit her with my presence. She nodded vaguely, as if she was not really listening, and I took my leave of the room. A few minutes later she appeared in the door to the living room, carrying two large cups. She sat opposite me, placing one in front of herself, the other in front of me. We drank the warm drinks in silence.

As the caffeine began to make its presence felt, Ruth became more animated, as if she were finally joining me in this day. I felt it might now be acceptable to talk.

"What shall we do today?" I enquired gingerly. She glanced at me from under her dark eyebrows, squinting slightly to see through the curtain of cascading unkempt hair. She offered no suggestion, remaining silent.

"Shall we take a trip to London?" I asked suddenly. She stared at me for a moment, then looked away. "I know I've already been there," I continued. "But I didn't see a lot last time as I was fixated on other things. And there's so much to see that I'm curious about. What do you think?"

For a long time Ruth remained silent, and I refrained from speaking, allowing her to think. She seemed nervous of the idea of visiting her capital city, yet at the same time almost eager to do so. Finally she spoke.

"Yes, alright. I've always found London alarming, with all those people, the voices, all the noise inside my head and on the street, so much dirt and pollution, hustle and bustle. But I suppose I need to see if I can manage there now, manage to control the voices, that is." She glanced at me with a tiny smile. "If I can go there and block the cacophony in my head, then I can do it anywhere!" I smiled back, pleased that Ruth had agreed to travel to the big city with me.

We ate a simple breakfast of toast liberally coated with butter and honey, then made ready to depart. I informed Ruth that I principally wanted to visit some of the buildings housing the great cultural artefacts, namely museums and art galleries. So many of the collections in these places had been destroyed in the Chaos, that in my time only a tiny proportion of them survived for us to enjoy. Even the digital memory only stored images of a small fraction of what had existed. I knew that great cities in rich nations of this time housed almost unimaginable quantities of such articles, many of them on display, giving the citizens the extraordinary opportunity to see them with their own eyes. In the front of the map of London I had stolen was a list of 'main attractions', the names of many of which I had memorised. As I listed the places I wished to visit, Ruth held up her hand as she laughed.

"We can't possibly visit all of those, or not in one day," she said with a chuckle. "Not even in one week." On seeing my look of disappointment, she quickly suggested, "why don't we prioritise, and then do a few today and maybe a few more tomorrow, and then see what else you'd like to do." I had little option but to agree with this plan, acceding to Ruth's superior knowledge. In truth, I had no idea of the size of these places, nor the extent of their collections. We finally settled on visiting the National Gallery and National Portrait Gallery that morning, followed by the British Museum in the afternoon, then the following day we would tackle the 'museums in South Ken' (as Ruth called them), or at least the Natural History and Science Museums, and what she referred to as the V and A. I thought that this seemed a disappointingly short list, but Ruth assured me that this was already more than enough to peruse in two days. Again, I had to bow to her greater acquaintance of the city.

I was eager to start, so gently encouraged Ruth to prepare herself for the trip, trying not to irritate her with my impatience as I did so. She did not in fact take long to ready herself, and soon appeared in the doorway of the living room in yet another dress of similar shape and pattern as on previous occasions - this time dark purple with mauve flowers. She noticed my look of surprise as she stood at the entrance to the room.

"What?" she asked, with a trace of annoyance in her voice. "What's wrong?"

"Nothing," I quickly countered, colouring slightly at having been caught gazing at Ruth in the first place.

"So why the strange look then?" she persisted, irritation stronger in her tone.

"I just...I'm just surprised...you seem to have lots of similar dresses, but in different colours," I managed to blurt out lamely. Ruth's dark eyebrows shot up. This was clearly not the response she had expected.

"Why not?" she countered sharply. "Why shouldn't I?" I had no answer so merely shrugged my shoulders.

"I learned years ago that it's just a waste of time to spend ages thinking about what to wear," she explained defensively. "So I have lots of clothes that are basically the same, just different colours. When I find something I like, I buy a whole range of the same ones. It saves so much time on shopping, which I hate anyway, and even more on never having to worry about what to wear."

"That's an interesting idea," I countered smoothly, keen to soften Ruth's obvious irritation at me. She looked unconvinced, but seemed to decide to let the matter drop. I noticed that Ruth had her customary large and heavy bag already weighing down her right shoulder. I had planned to take a bag, and considered asking her if we really needed two, but decided against such a query given that I had never seen her out of her house without this weighty receptacle.

"Can I help you with your bag?" I asked her, in a further attempt to smooth her still-ruffled feathers. She glanced up at me, a startled look on her face at such a simple question. She drew the bag more closely to her side, clutching it tightly, but said nothing.

"Ruth?" I persisted. "Can I help you carry it? It looks heavy. Maybe we can carry it in turns?" I offered. She stared at me for a moment, then shook her head, dropping her gaze to the floor. I was at a loss to understand her strange reaction.

"Why not?" I could not help myself asking. "What's in it?" She shot a look at me of real anger, but a moment later this was replaced by one which seemed to show embarrassment. She blushed slightly, shrugging her shoulders, but did at least deign to answer me this time.

"Things," she said baldly. "Just things." I was about to ask her 'what things?', but one look at her expression and tense body language silenced my question. I shrugged.

"Alright," I said. "If you won't let me help you that's alright." But as I moved past her into the hallway I could not help making a quick scan of the mysterious contents of her huge bag. Some of the items I did not recognise, but those I did seemed surprisingly mundane: a bottle of water, a hairbrush (which I thought very odd as she did not seem to tend regularly to her hair), a large selection of medicines for all sorts of minor ailments, an odd plastic receptacle with a long slit on the top filled to bursting with coins, another money-holder stuffed with paper money - far more money than I imagined we would need, a plastic wallet bursting with small cards the uses of which I could not fathom, a fat paperback book, several pairs of spectacles (though only one with glass in them), a toothbrush the top of which was carefully wrapped in a tiny plastic bag secured by an elastic band...at this point I gave up my scan, not having located anything of much interest. As I walked past Ruth I noticed that she had donned her glassless spectacles again, but chose not to question her on this. I assumed a trip to London was still sufficiently stressful to warrant such masking of her eyes from the public.

When I ascertained that Ruth was ready, and had told me the address of the National Gallery, I asked her for a map of London so I could get my bearings. I had left mine on the beach. I ported us to its location on the side of Trafalgar Square, the huge open space in front of the two galleries comprising our morning's project. As we moved through space, I tried to locate a quiet part of the gallery to appear in. Ruth had told me earlier that the area would be teeming with people, even at this early hour. I did not want to create problems by appearing out of thin air, even though I had seen a few days before how adept Londoners seemed to be at ignoring all that went on around them. As we materialised, hand in hand, in one of the only quiet spots I could discern inside the building as we ported, I was surprised to see we were inside what looked like a tiny cubicle. Ruth giggled as we emerged.

"We're in a toilet. Inside a toilet cubicle!" she laughed. I glanced down and saw she was right. I felt a frisson of annoyance at myself, aware of the indignity of arriving at our destination through a lavatory. Ruth seemed to simply find the idea funny, and continued to giggle.

"But how are we going to get through the rest of the toilet without being seen?" I complained. "And aren't the toilets gendered in this time, so one of us will be forced to hurry through a toilet of the wrong gender, and we might get caught?" Ruth did not seem to share my concerns, still amused at where we had entered the gallery.

"Teleporting seems so glamorous, so exotic," she said. "And yet we end up squashed into a toilet cubicle!" she added, with another giggle. She then glanced at me, noting my expression of slight irritation.

"Oh come on," she cajoled. "I can hear there's no-one else in the loo. Let's go." She grabbed my hand, gingerly pushed open the door of the cubicle, and dragged me into the main room of the toilet. We quickly crossed in front of the row of basins backed by mirrors, and had nearly made our escape into the main building when, to my dismay, the main door to the toilet swung open, and in shuffled a rather elderly woman, smartly dressed, who politely held the door open to let us leave, only noticing me as we sidled past her.

"Excuse me!" she snapped, in a surprisingly strong voice. "This is the ladies' toilet. What on earth is *he* doing in here?" I had been caught, and I froze, but Ruth strode through the door dragging me in her wake. As she did so, she turned her head to the elderly woman.

"He's a lady, madam, despite appearances to the contrary," she replied with a loud guffaw. Before the outraged woman could muster a retort, Ruth pulled me out into the gallery and away from the toilet door. I glanced round and shrugged a slight apology, but the poor woman's face was immobile, a mixture of would-be outrage and confusion etched upon it. When we had moved far enough from the toilet that Ruth judged us to be safe, she stopped. She was still laughing at the whole episode, though not joined by me.

We were in a quiet part of the gallery, but as a small group of people passed by us, Ruth's amused expression suddenly vanished, to be replaced by one of distress. She stared at me, eyes wide and anxious.

"The voices!" she exclaimed. "I can hear them." She seemed about to panic.

~*Block them!*~ I instructed sharply, mindspeaking loudly to cut through the babble in Ruth's mind. ~*The way I taught you.*~ I nodded vigorously, encouraging Ruth. She stared back at me, took a deep breath and put into motion the process I had taught her for blocking the eternal gibberings all around her. After only a few moments her eyes flew open, her expression suddenly bright and happy.

"It worked!" she exclaimed, forgetting to mindspeak, and speaking so loudly that a young man passing by us actually jumped. A huge smile lit up Ruth's face. I could not help but join her in her delight. We moved away from where we were standing, through the corridors of the gallery. I knew from the grin plastered on Ruth's face that she heard no voices. As we walked, a thought occurred to me.

"Why did you say I was a lady?" I asked, thoroughly confused by Ruth's words, and choosing to speak normally as I felt there was nothing we needed to obscure. "Was it just to shut the poor woman up?" Ruth glanced at me, humour returning to her dark eyes, not well-masked by the glassless glasses. She had to remove the spectacles and wipe away the tears of humour that still rested on her cheeks from her earlier laughter.

"Partly," she replied when she had recovered sufficiently to be able to talk. "But actually some men do say they're ladies. And some women say they're gentlemen, for that matter," she attempted to explain, leaving me no clearer. She saw my continuing confusion.

"Some people claim they were born into the wrong body," she continued. I frowned even more deeply as her comment made no sense to me.

"But you're born into the body you're born into," I said in an attempt to explain my confusion, to myself as much as to my companion. "It just *is*, isn't it?"

Ruth shrugged slightly. "I think so, yes," she replied. "But many people don't agree with me. And there's a growing noise around the issue."

"Noise?" I queried, not understanding her meaning.

"Discussion. Reports in the papers, on television and so on," she explained. "Lots of people seem to think it makes perfect sense to say that you're born into the wrong body. That you can have a man's body, but feel like a woman. Or vice versa." I stared at Ruth, astonished.

"Are you making this up?" I asked, suspicious that I was being toyed with in my naivety. "Are you teasing me?" Ruth shook her head vigorously.

"No, no. Not at all. I promise you that what I say is true. And some of these people even go as far as to have surgery. *Lots* of surgery. To change their bodies, alter what their bodies look like." I continued to stare in astonishment, so Ruth continued. "They have their genitals removed and new ones constructed, of the opposite sex. And if they were men, they have breast implants, operations to reduce their square masculine jaw lines, and to remove their adam's apples, and sometimes even implants to make their hips more rounded and feminine. And they have to take copious drugs for the rest of their lives to suppress their natural male hormones."

"How long has this sort of thing been happening?" I asked incredulously. "I've never heard of it, never came across it in my reading of the time before…of this time." Ruth was surprised at my comments, though I was relieved that she had not seemed to notice my slip of tongue in almost giving away the fact of the Chaos.

"Really?" she asked. "I would have thought it became more and more common, judging by the way things are going at the moment. I'd be surprised if it's just a short-lived phenomenon, a fashion as some people think." I did not answer her. I realised that I had nearly given Ruth enough information for her to ask questions about *why* I had never heard of these operations: that the Chaos was so imminent, that any cultural changes occurring now would, by definition, be short-lived. All of them. I quickly intruded before this highly intelligent woman could make the connection.

"I suppose there was a lot for me to read. I was bound to miss some things." I felt my explanation was weak, but Ruth did not seem to notice.

"Of course," she added by way of further comment about the operations. "They don't really change sex, gender. Most of them don't really look that convincing, especially the men. They still have big men's veiny hands and huge feet, and deep voices. And they don't have wombs or ovaries. They can't conceive. And if you tested their DNA, they'd have XY chromosomes, men's chromosomes. Not women's XX." I accepted all that Ruth said, and we moved off into the gallery proper in silence. I was astonished at what I had heard. With all our advanced genetics, I had never encountered the idea of a man believing he had been born into the wrong body, and that he was really a woman, or a woman feeling the reverse. It was such a bizarre concept that I did not know what to think of it, how to feel about it. As we entered the main hallway of the gallery, my final thought on the matter before I was distracted by practicalities was 'If you can think you are born into the wrong body, then are there people who think they're born into the body of the wrong species? Could a person believe that they were a wolf, say, or a chimpanzee, born into a human body, by mistake?'

Ruth insisted that we would not have remotely sufficient time to adequately view every painting on display in the huge gallery, and when I did a hasty mind-tour of the building before we began, I realised she was not exaggerating. It was enormous, with room after room filled on every wall with paintings large and small. I could of course, undertake a quick mind-tour of the entire building, but did not feel this would offer me a full enough experience. I wanted, *needed*, to see and experience the paintings for themselves, in the flesh as it were. I had only the vaguest idea of the history of painting in this world, and no sense whatever of what might be most rewarding to see. I turned to Ruth, a rather helpless look on my face.

"Do you have any suggestions?" I asked rather pathetically. "I have no idea where to start."

"What sort of art do you like? Is there any period you really want to see?" she asked, reasonably. I shrugged and pulled a face indicating my almost total ignorance on the matter.

"I suggest we just do a handful of galleries properly then," she replied briskly, "Rather than too many too quickly." I nodded my agreement, this suggestion concurring closely with what I had already felt. "And if you have no idea what you like or want to see, shall I just choose what I like?" Ruth continued.

"That's as good an idea as any other," I agreed. "At least that way one of us will definitely be happy!" I added, using a phrase I had heard Bartrem using on a number of occasions. Ruth looked surprised at my comment, wondering if there was a hint of criticism in it. I had not intended it to be received in this way, so I quickly qualified what I had said. "I'm sure I'll love what you recommend," I added. "Especially if you can explain to me what you like about it as we go."

We picked up a leaflet from a desk at the main entrance and Ruth quickly perused it.

"I specially like the oldest stuff," she said. "The Medieval and Renaissance. And we can add a few others too, perhaps from much later just by way of contrast. The Impressionists are always nice to look at and then maybe one much more modern, more abstract. How does that sound?"

"Fine," I said, trying to dredge from my mind what I remembered of the terms she had thrown so casually at me. She turned and moved off with me trailing in her wake.

Ruth led me for hours round hall after hall filled with all manner of wonders, and many pictures I found less wonderful, though probably more to do with the fact that I had no context for any of them than the inherent quality of the art itself. We shuffled slowly, stopping at most, though not every, painting. As I gazed at faces and landscapes, fantastical images and animals all gazing back at me, Ruth did a remarkably effective job of explaining the composition to me, placing it in its historical context, and then giving me her personal opinion of each one. She was, I realised, highly educated and very erudite. She seemed to have a wide knowledge of each painter, of the development of each one's work and style, of his place in the history of art and history in general, and even of the techniques used to produce the works in front of us. I was astonished to discover that all the painters were men.

When I expressed my surprise at her extensive knowledge, Ruth explained. "My father is an art historian," she said. "He still teaches at a university here in London, and has written lots of books on the subject. I spent a huge amount of time as a child being dragged around art galleries, before my parents got divorced, and he always tested me on what I'd learned at the end."

After a number of hours, we decided to leave the gallery and make our way around the corner to the National Portrait Gallery. I was intrigued at the very idea of an entire gallery devoted entirely to portraits. Ruth explained that it was not nearly as big as the National Gallery, and then turned to me.

"What did you like best here?" she asked suddenly. "Here at the National Gallery?" I considered her question for a moment.

"The oldest stuff of all," I said. "The Medieval galleries. I loved the colours they used, the vivid yet simple blues and reds, greens and yellows. And lots of gold! And the curious lack of perspective in many of the paintings. They looked almost flat and yet still managed to portray animation and life, a sense of movement."

"You didn't object to the fact so many of them were religious, Christian?" Ruth asked.

"No," I replied. "It doesn't mean anything to me, after all, religion. We don't have religion any more in my time. But doesn't the Christian stuff worry you?" I asked. Ruth looked confused by the question.

"No," she replied, a hint of irritation in her voice. "Why should it?"

"You told me you're not a Christian," I replied. "You're a Jew." She looked even more surprised at my comment, but declined to reply, merely frowning at me with the tiniest hint of a scowl, accompanied by a nibble of her bottom lip, the first time I had seen this nervous habit showing itself that day. Clearly I had offended her in some way, though I had absolutely no idea how or why. But sensing her annoyance, I let the matter drop, changing the subject.

"And after the really old paintings," I continued quickly. "I think I liked the really modern ones. The pictures are strange, hard to understand, but appealing, compelling. Are they supposed to mean something or are they just decorative?" I asked. My question seemed to amuse Ruth, and her irritation dissipated.

"I'm sure they're *supposed* to mean something," she replied. "The artists think so in any event, though the rest of us often struggle to see exactly what. To be honest, I think most people just look on them as decorative or pretty."

We continued to chat as we now perused the pictures in the Portrait Gallery, face after face staring at me from their flat prisons. I found this gallery less appealing, much of it seeming the same, repetitive, though some parts stood out. I did enjoy the small gallery titled 'Tudor' however, but had to ask Ruth to remind me what this meant. The faces here were strong, some of them unpleasant, especially the amazingly wide and overdressed man called Henry VIII. But the clothing he wore, and that worn by others in the gallery, especially Elizabeth I (Henry's daughter and England's greatest monarch, as Ruth informed me in a tone of pride I did not understand) was astonishing. Hugely ornate, liberally covered in jewels and pearls, the skirts billowing out far beyond the outline of the body, a ruff, a huge stiff lace collar.

"I wonder how anyone could walk, or move at all in such clothing," Ruth observed. She was astonished when I told her that dresses such as those worn by Elizabeth I were fashionable in my own time on women and men, though I hastily added that the materials used were different - light, comfortable, easy to manipulate. Ruth laughed as I described how the wide skirts could be pulled in with a pop to negotiate tight spaces, only to snap back out again at the will of the wearer.

"But," I noted. "No-one in my time wears the ruffs, or so much jewellery on the clothes themselves and around their necks, their wrists, all those rings, the lace, the extra bits."

"It's all about show," Ruth commented as we stared at the portrait of this redoubtable looking woman with her intelligent beady dark eyes and thin lips. "Wealth, power, control. It must have weighed a ton, though whether she was comfortable or not didn't come into it."

Ruth sensed that I was flagging after an hour or so in this gallery, and suggested that we leave and find somewhere to eat. I happily agreed. We ate nearby, and I experienced my first pizza. A strange meal, I thought, predominantly a huge stretched piece of hot bread, though pleasant enough. Big and filling, perhaps excessively so for the time of day, and not helped by the large beer I accompanied it with, but I felt it necessary to experience life as the locals did during my time in London. Ruth ate a small bowl of pasta, but did manage to consume two very large glasses of wine, something which surprised me.

Over lunch, I asked her about the voices. When I asked her, she stopped eating, her fork coming to a standstill halfway to her mouth.

"Oh my God!" she exclaimed, loudly enough for the couple at the next table to glance at us. "I'd completely forgotten about them." I looked at her in astonishment. Her blocking of them was already so efficient, and permanent, that she seemed to have forgotten to have considered them.

"That is wonderful," I said. "I'm so pleased." She looked at me quickly, then looked away.

"Yes it is," she agreed. But despite the liberation from a lifetime of clamouring in her head, she seemed suddenly on edge as I reminded her about the voices in her head. She stopped eating, fiddled with her hair, and chewed at her bottom lip. I recalled that she had never once that morning talked to another person properly or even looked anyone in the eye, even though with me she seemed relaxed, able to find enjoyment and even humour in the events of the day. But her thick-rimmed glasses remained firmly on her face throughout the morning, even now in the restaurant not being removed. I had taught Ruth to quieten the babble in her head, but I wondered if I would ever be able to help her with the disquiet and unease from which she suffered, the profound scars of a lifetime of distress. I had extraordinary abilities, it was true, but these had limits, clear limits. I had shown Ruth how to block the babble of voices, preventing them from reaching her mind, I could help her control the visions if she wanted me to do this, but I could not cure the pathological state of her mind, only assist her to manage some of its worst symptoms. I felt a deep disappointment in myself as I considered my limitations, a fact that must have been so clear on my face that Ruth saw it.

"What's wrong?" she asked. "Are you alright? Are you unwell?" I shook my head, not trusting myself to speak, or even mindspeak. I did not want Ruth to perceive the extent of my dismay, and especially not the reasons for it. I finished eating as Ruth drained her second glass of wine. Finally I trusted myself to talk again.

~*I'm fine,*~ I mindspoke, knowing I was better able to dissimulate my emotional state through mindspeech than normal speech. Ruth looked at me quizzically, and I sensed that she was not convinced.

~*Shall we go?*~ I suggested abruptly, wanting to distract her from asking any more questions, from delving any further into the reasons for my shift of mood.

~*Very well,*~ Ruth replied hesitantly, not pursuing the matter, at least for the moment. We paid and left the restaurant. I felt very full and a tiny bit dizzy, and as I glanced at Ruth I saw she was slightly flushed and walking a little unsteadily. We decided to make our way to the British Museum on foot, at least partly to work off the lunch.

It was not far, though as always in the centre of London, it took longer than it should due to the endless throng of people everywhere, rushing along the pavements, hurling themselves across roads between the traffic, bumping into us while they went as they tapped away at their clunky hand-held devices. As we approached the museum, I stopped to stare. It was a huge building from side to side, but surprisingly squat from top to bottom. It was surrounded by huge columns of the sort I thought only existed much earlier, in the old Greek and Roman worlds. We approached the entrance, climbed the steps and went in.

Ruth took me first to the central space where I admired a beautiful sheer round white internal structure inside a wide plaza, the whole covered in a dome of glass criss-crossed with thin metal meshing.

"Oh!" I exclaimed in surprise. "It looks like something we'd have at home." The building was old, yet the much newer glass and metal dome looked almost familiar to me, causing me a pang of homesickness. We walked all the way around the central space, discussing what we should see. Ruth explained that this museum was, like the National Gallery, far too big to visit in its entirety. Again, on asking me what I wished to see most, I was nonplussed, unable to offer any suggestions. In the end we decided to wander and simply stop wherever the inclination took us.

We spent the whole afternoon perusing room after room stuffed with artefacts from many different countries and across a huge range of epochs. Most of it was very old, even to the people of the twenty-first century, and ranged from tiny delicate works in gold and silver to vast monumental pieces carved from enormous slabs of stone. I could hardly process all I saw, let alone comprehend it, though Ruth helped as much as she could by trying to put everything on display into some sort of historical context, at least in terms of the broad brush of history. I was bowled over at the sheer age of much of what I saw, some of if dating thousands and thousands of years before Ruth's time. The small church I had found near where Ruth lived seemed ancient, but these objects were much, much older. The ancient Egyptian and Mesopotamian rooms were probably the most dramatic, though I was upset by the dark leathery skin of the mummies, refusing at first to believe they had ever been real people. They were creepy, eerie objects, and somehow deeply sad too. I hurried past them as quickly as I could. They reminded me of the dead babies in Zelda's laboratory.

Room after room, object after object, we gazed and gazed until I became so bemused by the variety that I could barely distinguish one thing from another, one era from another. A few things stood out. The exquisite boxes of gold and other precious metals, studded with gleaming jewels in which, so I read on the information panels, had been stored pieces of bone from real people, saints, revered holy people of the Christian religion. The coffers themselves were quite splendid, but I could not begin to understand the significance of storing bits of desiccated bone of long-dead people, revered or not. The rooms with coins, though difficult for me to understand well or even tell one apart from another, seemed to engage Ruth's attention. Only when she informed me that the oldest coins in the collection were two thousand seven hundred years old was I impressed: I gently patted my pocket, hearing the light jangle of the coins nestled there. Such a huge span of time, yet I realised that the ancient examples in the cabinets in front of me looked almost exactly like the ones I had been using that day. I even took one out, holding it up in front of its venerable ancestor, struggling to comprehend the continuity of history, of culture, that lay between these two similar objects. I quickly quashed the thought that the Chaos had not only destroyed the objects themselves, but all that weight of continuity at the same time. Things ceased to exist, but also the entirety of human cultures which had taken millennia or longer to grow and develop, all wiped out in a matter of a few generations.

Ruth and I both sniggered like children at the cabinet filled with objects in the shape of erect penises - lamps from the ancient Roman period formed to look exactly like large phalluses. They were beautifully made, but again I was at a loss to understand the significance of such bizarre objects described as 'Good luck charms to ward off evil'. How did a society ever develop the idea that a lamp made of multiple erect penises could act as a protector against evil? I simply could not begin to understand. At this display I learned once more how childish a sense of humour Ruth could display. I had witnessed this inside the toilet we had ported to, and again now as she giggled at the penis lamps. This time, however, I joined in with the merriment. But more surprising was what Ruth said to a boy of about seven or eight years old with a thick mop of almost white-blond hair and innocent blue eyes who had managed to find the display while his parents gazed into another, less scandalous, glass cabinet nearby. The boy stared at the lamps, not entirely sure what they were decorated with. He was probably too young to have even seen a picture of an erect penis, let alone the actual thing, but still seemed to have some idea that these might be male appendages. As he peered closer, Ruth turned to him, initiating conversation for first time that day to a stranger.

"Willy lamps," she said to him with a giggle. He turned to her, a look of astonishment on his face. "Prick lights," she continued. "Cute cock candles," and her alliteration sent her into gales of not entirely pleasant laughter, especially as she saw the look of shocked confusion on the poor child's face. He turned and ran off to re-join his parents. Ruth continued to laugh loudly, attracting the attention of the people around us, most of whom probably assumed she was merely laughing at the 'cock candles'. I noticed the little boy speaking animatedly to his parents, pointing at Ruth as he did so. After a few moments, the mother caught her son's hand, and, despite the father shaking his head as if to prevent the mother's next action, she dragged her son over to us followed by an obviously reluctant father, stopping close to the still chortling Ruth. As she saw them, her laughter abruptly stopped, one of her thick dark eyebrows rising in query.

"You...you...shouldn't say things like that," began the boy's mother, as the father tried to disappear into the background. "You upset him with your obscenities." Ruth just glared at the woman in response, and I was amazed at what seemed to be a new-found confidence. Ruth stared and stared, and the woman grew visibly more and more uncomfortable, but before she could find anything else to say, Ruth turned to the child.

"He's a liar. He lied. I never said anything." She turned back to the mother. "And you should be careful who you accuse, especially when you choose to believe that little fibber you're raising." She turned and moved off briskly, indicating that I should follow her with a flick of her head. As she did so, she winked at me, a tiny hint of a smile tugging at her lips. I was astonished. What a strange transformation from the normally timid woman I had begun to know. Was it the lack of voices in her head, the knowledge that she was now in control? Or was it simply the two large glasses of wine recently imbibed? I hoped I had not created a monster.

Eventually we tired of the endless stream of magnificent objects presented to our senses. We heard an announcement stating that the museum would shortly be closing, so we made our way to the exit in order to leave before the crowds of visitors came tumbling out. We moved a little way from the museum, and I suddenly realised that we were right beside Bloomsbury Square, my portal to London. I suggested we enter the square to rest awhile, and Ruth readily agreed, though she insisted on stopping at a small shop just outside the square to buy several small bottles of white wine.

We sat on one of the benches in the middle of the square, and I was hugely relieved to take the weight off my feet, and off my overburdened mind. I could not adequately handle the enormous wealth of objects that had passed before my eyes that day, and knew I would need to revisit it all in my head before I even began to grasp the significance of most of what I had seen. We sat in silence, enjoying the relative tranquility of the square. Ruth offered me one of the small bottles of wine, and I accepted, as much to stop her drinking both of them as because I felt a desire to drink. We screwed the tops off the tiny bottles, Ruth carelessly tossing hers onto the grass behind us, and sipped in silence. As we sat, I felt a sudden, unexpected surge of despair trying to enter my thoughts. All those fabulous paintings and ancient artefacts, all gone, all destroyed so soon after this time, obliterated in the Chaos! I was not in the right frame of mind, or the right place, to manage such desperate emotions, so I rapidly quashed them. But I knew that this suppression could only be maintained for so long, and that emotions of such intensity would intrude again and again until they were acknowledged. But for the moment I succeeded, though Ruth's curious sideways glance at me suggested that she had sensed my brief dark emotional surge before I managed to force a lid onto it.

After a short rest, we agreed that we had both had enough of London for the day. I was so exhausted by my experiences that I could not even be bothered to find a safe and secluded place from which to teleport. In fact, I only just had enough energy left to port us at all, so, leaning in to Ruth to ensure contact, I simply took us away from the square, leaving the few astonished people who saw us disappear to find an explanation for our sudden vanishing.

At Ruth's house, Ruth went to her room to rest, leaving me alone downstairs. She had not told me to leave, so I decided to stay. I lay down on the grimy sofa and fell asleep, only waking many hours later, noting the diminishing light of dusk. I lay quite still, though eventually roused myself as I heard Ruth moving around in the house. We ate very simply that night, finishing the macaroni cheese Ruth had made the night before, though I noticed that Ruth, once again, partook of a large amount of wine. At one point she seemed to become aware of my focus of attention on her glass.

"I must seem like a lush," she said, with a hint of a smile, though not with any amusement to back it up. "I probably do drink too much," she admitted. "But it's always been the only thing that has helped with the voices. It doesn't exactly silence them, but it dulls their effect. And it seems to dull the general anxiety I suffer from too, though only in the short term." She glanced at me, nibbling her bottom lip as she did so, apparently nervous at my reaction to her comments. I felt compassion for this woman sitting opposite me, once again reminded acutely of what she had suffered in her difficult, distress-ridden life. I forlornly wished that her future could be less anguished. Before I was able to formulate a verbal response to her comment, she laughed unexpectedly, though there was no humour in her outburst.

"I suppose I should cut down now that the voices are no longer there," she said. "But I probably won't. There's too much else still going on in my head. And anyway, I like it." I had nothing to say, no words of comfort, so I simply tried to look sympathetic, hoping this would help. After a pause, Ruth sighed, finished her glass of wine and stood up.

"I'm exhausted," she announced. "And we should get an early night. We're going to have just as busy a day tomorrow." I nodded at her words, filled with a mixture of excitement and dismay at our plans for the next day. Did I really want to force myself to witness another parade of glorious, extinct artefacts, knowing that they would not last long beyond this time? And yet I knew that I must, that I had to be witness to as much as I could, to record it in my mind, precisely *because* it was about to be wiped out.

"Can I stay?" I asked as Ruth left the living room. She turned and looked at me, her face befuddled with the effects of alcohol. "Here," I clarified. "Can I stay here, on the sofa." Ruth glanced at the sofa as if confused, then turned back to me.

"No," she said simply as she turned on her heel and left the room.

I stumbled out of the front door, offended by Ruth's refusal. After spending the entire day together, getting to know each other as we had, was I still not to be trusted enough to be allowed to sleep in Ruth's house, taking my rest on her grubby sofa? I strode angrily down the beach, as much as it is possible to stride over sand, found my 'bed', lay down, and was asleep in mere minutes despite my irritation with Ruth, too tired even to enjoy the sounds of the nocturnal ocean.

The next day Ruth and I repeated the process of the day before. A quick light breakfast, a hasty flit to London, this time to one of the huge museums in the area called South Kensington. On this occasion I managed to port us to a quiet corner of the museum but not inside a toilet. We emerged in a dark corridor, behind a tall glass box reaching to the floors above, affixed with a sign which read 'Lift out of order'.

This was the Natural History Museum, a most glorious massive building of blue-grey and pale yellow bricks, fabulous staircases everywhere, ridiculously high ceilings, light cascading in from so many windows. Yet I found the displays mostly distasteful, even sad. After many rooms of cabinet after cabinet stuffed with the preserved corpses of all manner of animals, I told Ruth I wanted to leave. What was the fascination this culture had with preserving dead things: humans in the British Museum and animals in this museum?

Ruth was surprised at my doleful expression, not able to understand my wretchedness as seeing such a parade of dead birds, mammals, reptiles and insects almost all of which had not survived the Chaos, had not made it into my own world. A few had been resurrected from their genetic material, but the vast majority were, to my people, gone, lost forever. And beyond this fact, I simply found it distressing to be surrounded by so much death. It felt as if the deaths of so many creatures during the Chaos were being foretold by the exhibits in this museum.

Ruth managed to persuade me to visit the whale room before we left, promising me it was worth seeing. In truth it was as depressing as the rest of the museum: a display of bones and bodies of magnificent, defunct marine mammals. I was, however, astounded to see the sheer size of the skeleton of the blue whale suspended from the ceiling. The largest creature that had ever existed, though not one that succeeded in surviving the Chaos nor one that my people had managed to bring back to life thereafter. A thought occurred to me that perhaps I should be collecting genetic material while I was here, not from the type of individual humans that Zelda wished me to, but from long deceased animals and plants that no longer existed in my world, to permit our scientists to once more bring them back to life. But I knew I could not do this. I had to be strict with myself, and not tamper with anything that had already happened. Such action would not, could not, lead to a happy outcome. What had happened had already happened. Had *always* already happened, and nothing I did could change this fact.

Ruth took me next to the Science Museum, and I found the exhibits interesting in an almost amusing way. I was no scientist in my own world, but seeing these ancient objects claiming to be, in their time, the cutting edge of scientific knowledge, was almost risible. They seemed so huge, cumbersome, clumsy and clunky. Ruth was singularly unamused by my derisive laughter at many of the exhibits, and the tutting and scowling of other visitors indicated their equal displeasure at my merriment. Ruth quickly hurried me through a hallway to another part of the museum, one dedicated to geology. This was much more to my liking, especially the galleries filled with examples of rocks and minerals, something that had always engaged my attention in my own time.

After a morning spent in these museums, we had a quick lunch nearby, though I noticed that Ruth declined to order alcohol, perhaps self-conscious of doing so after our brief discussion the evening before. Or perhaps more simply that she was suffering the effects of too much the day before? After this we made our way to another remarkable building almost next door to the museums we had perused that morning.

"This is the V and A," explained Ruth. "The Victoria and Albert." At my blank expression she explained who these people were, and that this museum, along with all of the others we had just seen, had been funded out of the profits from a great exhibition of objects, many of them scientific, from all over the world, held about a hundred and sixty years before, all housed in an enormous glass building named the Crystal Palace in a large park close to the museums. The Albert who had given his name to the museum, Prince Albert, had been the initiator and organiser of said Great Exhibition. As she spoke, I remembered some of what she told me from my studies.

This was an extraordinary museum, though I could not quite discern its theme, if it had one. It seemed to house paintings and sculptures, artefacts from countries all over the world, jewellery, silverware, stained glass, a whole gallery of glass objects and much much more. Objects and articles of all types from all time periods, and from many different nations. There was even clothing from a range of times and places. But this curious variety made this, in many ways, the most fascinating museum for me, offering me the widest view of this world, the most expansive glimpse into a long-dead life. We spent hours in this place of wonders, Ruth having to literally drag me away from one exhibit to the next, from room to room to room. She pressured me to keep up a brisk pace, the better to see as much as possible. And what did I like best? It would be hard to say, but the room of glass must surely rank as one of the most amazing, and one of the quietest. There was only one other person with us as we covered the two floors of glass objects, some of them from thousands of years before, others contemporary. I was stunned to see how little they had changed over the ages, and how well preserved were these most delicate and fragile of objects. Surely none of this would survive the disaster to come? And yet, these eminently breakable objects had already survived for centuries. As with the coins in the British Museum, I felt a surge of profound sadness as I contemplated the cultures that the glass objects represented, how each artefact had a train behind it stretching back centuries, millennia, and stretching forward in front of the object, each artefact a mere dot along a seemingly endless cultural path. And all of this endless, seamless cultural continuity would soon be eradicated in such a short space of time.

As the museum closed, and we were more or less shepherded out of the door, I was loathe to leave behind this house of marvels. And as I emerged into the still bright light of a late summer afternoon, the emotions I had forced down the day before would no longer be quelled, gushing and gurgling to the surface.

I sat down on the steps in front of the huge entrance door with a bump, surprising Ruth as I did so. All around me other late leavers parted to surge around me, some of them brushing me with their knees. I stared up at Ruth who had stopped, turning to look at me with a quizzical, worried expression. I knew from her face that I must be displaying severe distress. She did not seem to know what to do, remaining transfixed, immobile in front of me.

I was overcome with anguish, with a desolate sense of loss as the images of the two days in the museums and galleries flooded through my mind. The thought that all of this glory, these miracles of creativity and progress, of history and culture, could all, *would all*, so soon be eradicated, annihilated in the all-encompassing disaster of the Chaos. I thought too of the ancient church I had visited, of the glorious diversity of the natural world in this time compared with my own time. And not just the objects themselves, but even more so the societies and cultures that lay behind each object, cultures which had taken so many generations to grow, had endured for thousands of years, the sheer exuberant variety in human societies that existed in 2012, all of which would be wiped out. And my own time suddenly seemed flat and empty, superficial and dull. In only eight hundred years, what could we possibly have created to compare even in the tiniest degree, with this vibrant world of 2012? All we had to build on was what was preserved as DNA or in the digital memory. Everything else was lost to us for ever. This was all just too much for me. I lifted my hands to my head, cradling my aching mind between them. I emitted a loud high-pitched moan of such intensity that Ruth stepped backwards. She then sat on the pavement in front of me, staring at me in shock, her hands over her ears as if she could block the anguish entering directly into her mind. But to no avail: the ferociousness of my sorrowful lament rendered her incapable of blocking my distress from entering her head.

Passers-by stared at me, and a few of them even moved slightly towards me as if to assist, but the look of fierce, angry misery I turned on them caused them to veer away, unwilling or unable to approach. Ruth sat in open-mouthed affliction, feeling my pain as I felt it, unable to escape its clutches, her eyes squeezed shut in a futile attempt to block the outpouring of anguish.

After long minutes of moaning, the intensity of my distress began to wane. As I regained control of my emotions, my outpourings of grief abruptly ceased. Ruth slowly, tentatively, took her hands away from her ears, opening her eyes with the tiniest gap possible. She stared at me, her mouth still wide with shock, completely in the dark as to the cause of my profound distress. She finally closed her mouth as she perceived that my groaning lament was finished.

~Sammy,~ she mindspoke, in the gentlest tone she could muster. *~Sammy. What's wrong?~*

Though I had ceased my moaning, my emotional state was still severely affected by my misery, and before I could control my thoughts or my words, I blurted out,

~It's all going to be destroyed. It's all going to end. So soon. And I can't bear it, I just can't bear it. So much loss, so much destruction...I...I... ~ And as I looked at Ruth I was suddenly aware of having said too much. Her expression once again registered deep shock, her mouth and eyes flying open.

"What's going to be destroyed?" she asked in a tone of distress, so disturbed by my words that she reverted to normal speech. "What loss?" she added urgently. I stared at her, and then hastily dropped my gaze, fearful she may read my eyes and understand what I meant.

I had promised myself I would not tell Ruth about the Chaos, not give her any indication of the horrors into which her world was about to descend, had, in fact, already begun to descend. And yet, in my anguish in the face of two days of miracles and marvels and death, I had so lost control of myself that I could not stop these words about the Chaos tumbling from my lips. I was livid with myself and did not know how to proceed. Should I now come clean, tell Ruth everything, divulge each dreadful detail of the catastrophe to come? Or should I lie and make up some story to explain my bizarre outburst? But how could I possibly do this without appearing as insane to Ruth as she had appeared to others? What possible explanation could there be for my dramatic and distressing behaviour?

I stared at the ground for a long time, unable to move, incapable of deciding what to do. Eventually I realised I could not sit on that step for ever, Ruth waiting quietly on the pavement in front of me.

"Something terrible will happen to the world," I stated abruptly, without preamble. "To *this* world," I added. Ruth jumped at my words, distress flooding her emotions. Her teeth clamped down on her lip so hard that they drew blood, her hands flew up to bury her fingers in her luxuriant locks.

"What will happen?" she whispered. "And when?" I looked up at her, melting inside as I witnessed her distress, her confusion, her sheer unhappiness.

"I'll tell you everything," I said, deciding at that instant the she deserved to be told the truth, the whole hideous truth. She was not a child, did not need protecting. Or even if she did, I could not patronise her by acting as if I knew what was best for her. She would need to hear everything, each detail of the Chaos soon to come, but not here, and not now. Knowing the end was soon coming might make her change her priorities.

"We should go home now Ruth," I said dejectedly. "I'll tell you everything, I promise, but quietly, in the comfort of your home. Later." I sensed she was about to argue with me, to try and persuade or push me into divulging the entire story here and now on the steps of the museum, but one look at my determined face and she thought better of it. She nodded slightly.

"Let's go home then," she said in a quiet voice. "I need to be at home," she added.

Not caring who saw us or what they thought of our sudden disappearance, I placed my hand on Ruth's shoulder and took us instantly away from that place and back to the safety of Ruth's cabin on the beach. Safe for the moment, I thought, as we rushed through space. But not for long.

Chapter Sixty

That evening at Ruth's beach home, we passed a very quiet time. I was so irate at my own outburst, my inability to hide my anguish over what loomed on Ruth's horizon, that I had no desire to say more. Ruth was apparently so shocked by my behaviour outside the museum, and even more so by my revelations as to the cause of my distress, that she too showed little will for conversation. Only once or twice she tried, weakly, to get me to elaborate further, to provide more details of what I had revealed, but I would not be drawn, remaining taciturn to the point of being nearly mute. After a few abortive attempts, she abandoned the effort.

In truth, I knew I would have to tell her more, tell her everything I knew about the impending Chaos. She deserved this. And yet I was still so upset by what I had witnessed in the past two days, so distraught as I contemplated the scale of destruction soon to be unleashed upon the world, that emotionally I was in no fit state to tell the story of the Chaos. Ruth would be horrified enough when faced with the reality of her near future, without the additional burden of my afflicted mental state as I recounted the nightmarish reality.

I was relieved when Ruth announced, shortly after we had eaten, that she was going to her room. We had sat in near silence at the table, both toying with our food, neither of us showing much interest in what lay on the plates before us. Ruth seemed more intent on imbibing a substantial amount of wine than eating, putting away glass after glass in rapid succession until she had drunk well over an entire bottle on her own. I did not join her.

When she went to her room, I sat alone for a while at the table, then finally heaved myself off the chair, cleared away the plates into the kitchen, and returned to sit on the battered, dirty old sofa as the twilight outside gradually faded into obscurity. When the room was in total darkness, I finally roused myself enough to switch on a single small lamp, not wanting to suffer the intensity of any more brightness than this. I remained for a long time, immobile on the sofa, lost in my unhappy thoughts. Eventually exhaustion conquered me, and I toppled sideways on the sofa into a deep sleep, the first night I had spent in Ruth's home, though without her permission or knowledge.

The next morning I was glad to heave myself off the sofa, so much had I tossed and turned during the night, drifting in and out of unsatisfying sleep caused by the discomfort of the ancient lumpy sofa too short to sleep on, as well as the fact that my mind wrestled with the problem of what to do about Ruth. I knew for a fact that the world she lived in was entering its period of irreversible decline, hurtling headlong towards inevitable ruin. I knew she was only in her early forties, certainly young enough to witness the entire process, even the final awful destruction which would almost bring an end to the human race, an end to the Earth as Gaia - a living, breathing entity.

The house was silent. I tried to prepare tea in Ruth's kitchen in an almost mechanical way, defeated by the clumsy device used to heat water, and deciding in the end to simply cause the water to boil myself. I had no desire to eat.

As I sat at the dining table absent-mindedly sipping tea, I heard the front door of the house open. Ruth was coming in. She must have been up early to be returning at this young hour. She entered the living room, and seeing me sitting at the table at the back of the room, came over to me, taking the seat opposite. I put down the cup I was clutching and we looked at each other. I was surprised at her frank, hard stare, knowing that such behaviour was not normal for her. She seemed unsurprised to find me in her home, and I assumed she must have noticed my presence on the sofa as she went out. She indicated no approval or disapproval of my unpermitted night spent in her home. Outwardly, she appeared calm, calmer than was her norm, but I saw in the dark recesses of her near-black eyes the raging emotions that surged through her. I waited in silence, allowing her the space to collect her thoughts. She struggled to do this, to gather herself sufficiently to speak coherently. After a long wait, she finally spoke. What she said was surprisingly mundane, perhaps her way to overcome her hesitancy at speaking at all.

"I couldn't sleep," she began. "I didn't sleep well. I've been thinking about yesterday." She paused for moment, frowning slightly. "You were so upset," she continued, her voice betraying her intense emotion with its slight wobble. She breathed deeply a few times, and continued. "You have to tell me what is coming," she stated simply. She then dropped her eyes to the table, as if the effort to maintain her stare had tired her. Her hands intertwined, wriggling together with tension. She began to chew at her bottom lip. Now I sighed, so loudly that she glanced up at me.

"In truth," I began. "I'm not sure where to begin. I suppose I should ask you if you're really ready to hear everything. Are you sure this is what you want?" She nodded, but said nothing. "Very well," I continued. "But where to start?" I added, more to myself than to her.

"You have to bear in mind Ruth," I said, "That I'm not a historian. Obviously I know quite a lot about the Chaos that is to come. We all do in my world as it's such a vital part of our education. It's drummed into us from a young age, as much a warning about what can happen as anything else. But my understanding of it is probably not very well-organised, even in my own head. It's probably muddled."

"That doesn't matter," she interrupted in a quiet voice. "I just need to know. To see how close my visions are to what will actually happen. What the future holds." I nodded and continued.

"Well," I began. "The root cause of all the problems was population. It just kept growing and growing, faster and faster, each generation more than double the one before, and nobody seemed to think it was important. Nobody in a position of authority ever seemed to want to address the issue, to try and deal with it. There were, if I remember rightly, some organisations that tried to get governments and international bodies to take it seriously, but to no avail. All the governments and international organisations ever did was ask how many people the planet could support, discuss how technology and science could keep increasing food yields and so on rather than asking whether governments should try and control, or reduce their populations. I suppose the issue was just too fraught with emotional and cultural issues like the personal right to have as many children as you want, or so many religions forbidding contraception and so on. So the governments and other bodies didn't dare address the escalating numbers of people, or just didn't think it was worth it as they knew they'd never get anywhere. We're in 2012 now?" I said suddenly. Ruth looked up.

"Yes," she confirmed. I paused a moment, trying to remember any details about this particular year apart from what I had learned by entering the mind of one of the men in Bloomsbury Square the day I had arrived: that it was the year of the Olympic games in London. I had a vague idea that another man had made a mystical prediction that the world would end in 2012.

"So the population of the world is about seven billion or so at the moment, if I remember correctly?" I asked. Ruth nodded. "And already about a third of these people are underfed, huge numbers of them are out of work with no prospect of work, lots of people don't have proper homes to live in. And this will get rapidly worse. In the poorer countries the population is growing far too fast for them to cope. If I remember rightly, some of the poorest countries' populations will double in about the next twenty years or so, and these countries will then have the added problem of a hugely disproportionate young population, lots of whom have nothing to do, not enough to eat, but all needing food, and water, and space to live in. And the growth is geometric, which people seem to struggle to understand. If a country has a hundred million people now and doubles each generation of about twenty years, then in twenty years there'll be two hundred million, but twenty years after that there'll be four hundred million, and another generation later eight hundred million and so on. That's how the history of human population growth has generally progressed, but the problem is that now there is better health care, people live longer, food production has been increased - all good things in themselves - but disastrous unless governments and individuals realise that they need to limit population growth at the same time. Unchecked growth of any organism's population will rapidly lead to an almost total collapse in the numbers of that organism as it outgrows the space it has to live on, or the water or food available. It will implode."

I continued for quite a while on the theme of population. I discussed the rise of emigration from the more populous, poorer countries, to the richer countries, something that Ruth agreed was already well underway in 2012. The richer countries had initially welcomed quite high immigration, knowing that they had the reverse problem of the poor countries: a birth rate that was too low to sustain itself. But as the trickle of people became a flood, and then started to swell into a veritable tsunami, the borders began to be closed. The rich societies simply could not cope with such a level of immigration. Their infrastructures began to creak under the strain and eventually, unable to plan or adapt or expand fast enough, began to crack and crumble. The very lifestyles enjoyed in the richer countries, which the immigrants were supposed to help maintain, began to fail precisely because of the sheer number of new people. And there was, of course, a profound social effect too. No society can survive if it finds itself overwhelmed by huge numbers of other people who do not share its cultural values, even at such a basic level as its language, let alone more profound aspects such as religion, moral and ethical values and so on. Internal social problems began to erupt all over the richer world as antagonisms between different cultural groups grew more regular, more desperate, more violent. With the speed and level of immigration being so high, the immigrant populations did not assimilate, or even integrate, preferring to live and socialise within their own ethnic and cultural groupings. The richer countries began to turn into, in effect, a patchwork of ghettos with little contact or communication between the ghettos. The immigrant populations, usually the poorest even in these richer countries, wanted to take more and more economic benefit from the host culture without contributing to the cultural life of the countries they were living in, their ghettoised lives separating them as if behind huge walls. The native populations started to feel that their cultures were at serious risk of destruction, and that their governments would not do anything to help maintain them, always on the side of the immigrant communities (or so the native people believed), and the natives began to fight back.

Eventually, as civil unrest and internal strife grew unmanageable, governments had no option but to close the borders, and then themselves struggled to maintain internal control over fractious and fractured populations. The balkanisation of the people in these countries into separated ghettos rapidly exacerbated the social problems, and violence began to be a common aspect of daily life. Governments were forced into ever more brutal measures to try and prevent violence between the divided groups within their populations. As this was happening all over the world, international trade and transport of goods quickly dwindled, and then disappeared, and as imports of food and other essentials became more and more scarce, those liberal western governments eventually abandoned all pretence of liberalism, governing with an iron fist. But in the end, even this was not enough, and internal strife led to revolts and revolutions all over the western world, governments being brought down, reassembled with different parties involved, brought down again, and again, until no central order remained at all, each country nothing more than a patchwork of small internally organised areas, usually run by brutal overlords, and with endless hostility and violence between the tiny neo-feudal 'states'. Obviously by this point there was no remnant of the grand international bodies any more which had existed for many years and which had tried, in mostly futile attempts, to avert wars and other disasters.

And a similar pattern occurred in the poorer countries, though at a much faster pace and with more brutality due to the inherent weaknesses in those countries' governments in the first place, and the vast and unmanageable populations.

The burgeoning numbers of human beings used arable land to build dwellings, thereby further reducing the production of food. The young people had no work, and were eventually even prevented from emigrating, so had nothing to do but agitate and cause trouble. The arable land that remained was overworked, degraded year after year by overproduction, and as the world's problems increased, the import of fertilizer, pesticides, medicines for animals ceased, causing yields to crash and domestic animal numbers to diminish rapidly, adding famine to already undernourished populations. Insect numbers plummetted, a devastating problem given that so much human food is pollinated by insects.

And water was perhaps an even bigger problem. I remembered reading that even by the start of the twenty-first century, there were serious problems with overuse of water for agriculture and industry, especially in some of the countries with the biggest populations, namely India and China.

China's sources of fresh water were polluted, and became more and more so. India, though abundantly supplied with fresh water, extracted so much more of it than it received, that even quite early on warnings were being sounded of groundwater being reduced to levels that could not be replaced. Those two massive countries did in fact go to war against each other, a war fought for land, for water. China persuaded most of the smaller countries of south-east Asia to join it in attacking India, a necessary coalition as it would otherwise have been impossible for China to attack India directly with the Himalayas in between. The Chinese had had to sweep through south-east Asia as it prepared to attack India, dragging the armies of those countries along with it as it did so.

Some of the richer countries tried to increase their production of desalinated sea water. A good idea in theory, as only a few percent of water available on the Earth is fresh, the vast bulk of it being either tied up in polar ice, or saline. But this was expensive and not particularly efficient, and could only work for small countries. And I remembered reading about the problems around the Mediterranean. There were quite a few desalination plants here, but the production of such water naturally produced a great deal of salt by way of waste product. And what did these countries do with all this salt? They threw it straight back into the sea! So over a relatively short period of time this small, sealed ocean became so salty that most of its animals and plants could no longer survive, and even the desalination plants eventually stopped functioning due to the excessive salinity of the water.

Over time, though not very much time, I told Ruth, the entire human biosphere first creaked and fell apart, rapidly joined by what remained of the wilder parts of the world, the natural biosphere. Without sufficient water in the ground, the rivers and lakes either having been too much extracted from or heavily polluted, all life began to struggle for its very survival. This destruction, and the lack of pollinators, led to famines, small and localised at first, but spreading rapidly as the environment was degraded further and further, as pollution poisoned the air, the soil, the sea. Famines led to wars as governments, such as they were by this time, attempted to alleviate the immediate effects of the lack of food by taking it from their neighbours, or stealing the land or water from those closest to them. Famines also led to illness, and epidemics grew into pandemics which spread in waves around the globe, one replacing another, sometimes more than one disease at the same time. Some of the old horrors, scourges of humanity, once more reared their heads, typhoid and typhus, cholera, dysentery, tuberculosis. And huge numbers of people were wiped out by sweeping tides of influenza of all different types, avian flu, swine flu, bovine flu.

And of course the wars grew in regularity, in scope, in intensity. Some were fought at a distance, as weaponry by this date allowed conflicts to be waged without the combatants being anywhere near each other. Long range missiles and bombs, remotely piloted aircraft and other mechanised fighting machinery, all allowed countries to arrange the eradication of others from afar. But some wars were still fought by more conventional means, especially those between the poorer countries who, in general, had not been able to afford the most up-to-date assault weaponry. And sometimes even the richer countries, who did own such weapons, chose not to use them as they needed the physical damage to be kept to a minimum. There is little point in waging war for land to grow crops on, or for clean sources of water if your methods of warfare render the soil and water useless.

As countries became more and more desperate, and especially in the wake of the collapse of international trade and communication, internal structures failed further and further. Nation states no longer existed in any recognisable form, having instead fractured into thousands, hundreds of thousands of tiny mini-states, almost feudal in their structure. Some of these though, mostly through accidents of geography, retained control over the most potent weapons of all. The world was filled with nuclear warheads, dotted here and there across the richer countries and even some of the less rich ones which had stockpiled such weapons. Wherever these happened to be situated, those miniature feudal states took control of them. Tiny countries ruled by brutal and often crazed overlords which possessed enormous arsenals of destruction. And other tiny states possessed different horrors: biological weapons.

As the world order collapsed, as famines and droughts, wars and natural pandemics took their terrible toll on the human population and on the rest of the natural world, disorder spread, panic and despair grew, and eventually some of the tiny states made the final, fateful decisions to unleash the devastating ultimate weapons. We do not know which little feudal enclaves began the process, but the world suddenly found itself succumbing to the horrors of some of the worst diseases known to humanity. Biological warfare unleashed ebola, the plague (bubonic, and especially pneumonic plague with its massive rate of mortality) were inflicted on an already suffering and struggling population, wiping out millions, billions, in a very short space of time.

And then, almost inevitably, the final calamity came when one of the tiny states decided it would wage nuclear war against one of its neighbours. The neighbour, of course, retaliated with the same. And from this first salvo there was no return. All over the world the nuclear states reacted, panicked, button after button pressed, warhead after warhead thrust into the sky to descend shortly afterwards with its blast of massive destruction. So sudden was this descent into hell, and so overwhelming in sheer volume of warheads propelled into the sky all around the globe, that the combined effect set off earthquakes and volcanoes, in addition to their own tempest of destruction. And the earthquakes themselves caused massive tsunamis. In addition to the havoc caused by the tsunamis, especially in coastal areas, the world was filled with ash and smoke from hundreds of volcanoes, with the black carbon from the thousands of nuclear explosions. The sky fell dark for years, little sunlight reaching the planet's surface. Few plants grew and temperatures remained well below normal. Ozone levels were destroyed by the intensity of the storm of rockets, increasing damaging ultraviolet rays all across the globe, despite the lack of essential sunlight. A tiny number of people, almost all in a few of the richer countries, managed to get to pre-prepared shelters before the final holocaust, and remained in hiding for years buried deep underground or inside mountains. For the rest of the unfortunates left on the surface, those people who had not been carried off by the famines, wars and epidemics, there was no hope of survival. They had somehow managed to endure the catalogue of woes that had assailed them, mostly by fleeing to some of the more isolated parts of the natural world which still remained, yet now they rapidly succumbed to the radiation, the lack of light, the lack of food. They all died, every single one of them. And only years later did the few thousand survivors dare to emerge from their shelters into the tattered and battered remains of their once beautiful planet, to begin the arduous process of recovery, their very survival hanging in the balance, and remaining precarious for many years.

I finally stopped speaking. Ruth sat in silence, utterly still, her eyes having remained fixed on the same spot on the table throughout my dreadful monologue. She seemed in a state of shock at my elaboration, as if transfixed by the images I had created in her mind. I remained quiet, allowing Ruth to manage her emotions, her reaction to what I had told her. After a long silence, she suddenly looked up at me, holding my gaze with an intense expression on her face.

"Are you here to help?" she asked in a tight voice. I did not know what she meant, my eyebrows drawing together in confusion.

"Are you here to help?" she repeated. "To do something about it. To try and stop all of that happening. To stop the Chaos?" Her tone was sharp, though not with me. It was heavily tinged with despair, eager to receive my assenting reply. I sighed deeply.

"No," I replied simply. "That's not why I'm here." She glared at me, consternation mixed with anger on her face.

"Why not?" she wailed. "Why not? If you know all of this will happen, and how it will happen, why won't you do anything about it? Why did you bother to come back here if not to try and prevent all that...that horror."

"It's not that I won't do anything, Ruth," I replied in a quiet voice. "It's that I can't. I can't do anything to stop what will happen..."

"Why not? Why not? I just don't understand!" she interrupted brusquely.

"Because it's already happened," I stated. "Everything I described has already happened so it can't be undone, it can't be made to un-happen. It can't be changed." Ruth continued to glare at me, frowning heavily, despair and anger flooding her face. She clearly did not understand what I meant, so I was obliged to explain further.

"What I described," I began, "Is in the future for you, from where we are today. But for me that's not the case. For me, it all happened long ago. So it has all already happened. The next eight hundred years have already happened. And in fact, everything has always happened the way it happened. It's always already happened exactly as it did." Ruth said nothing immediately, but I saw her frown deepen, this time with the concentration of trying to understand what I meant.

"So you're saying," she finally said, speaking slowly and carefully, "That anything that has happened in the past can never be changed, can never happen any differently from the way it panned out the first time?" she asked.

"Yes," I confirmed. "That's exactly what I mean."

"But how do you know that?" she asked sharply. "How can you be so sure that's the case. You told me you are the only person in your world able to time travel, and that this is your first trip. So you are the first human ever to travel in time. So how can you be so certain of the...the immutability of the past?"

"It's the only logical conclusion I can reach," I replied. "The only logical conclusion anyone could reach if they think about it. It's already happened, it's past, it's in the past, so by definition it simply cannot be done in any other way."

"But you can't know that for certain," Ruth persisted. "You changed me, and perhaps my interaction with the world. Couldn't you at least try to do something else, something bigger, grander, for everyone and everything else?"

"I am absolutely certain I am right," I insisted, not letting Ruth hear the uncertainty that had entered my mind as I considered what she had said about changing her and her interaction with the world. Had I done more than I should? Had I altered the future in some unpredictable, unimaginable way? And worst of all, had I, by my meddling, perhaps even done harm? Even if I had not caused the Chaos, could I have created ripples in the fabric of space and time that exacerbated it, would exacerbate it? I simply could not, *would not* seriously entertain such an idea, and quickly quashed it. "And actually," I continued as I tried to persuade Ruth and myself. "I can't change history." Ruth looked at me quizzically, so I elaborated on what I was I had said.

"If I thought I might be able to change the future, alter it in any way, it would be incredibly unwise and dangerous to do so. Even if it were possible, it would surely be completely unpredictable what effect any alteration would have, both in the short and the long term. It could end up causing even worse problems than those which actually happened."

"Worse?!" exclaimed Ruth loudly. "What could be worse than what you described?! And you have altered it. You've altered me!"

"There could be no survivors at all," I said quietly. "And the world so completely annihilated that nothing survived, not a single animal or a single plant. The Earth as a blackened, burnt, empty shell. That would be worse, surely?" Ruth had no answer to this, as it had clearly not occurred to her.

"So," she said at length in a melancholy voice. "There's nothing to be done then? Nothing at all?" I shook my head, so saddened by the truth of what she said and by her dejected tone of voice and miserable expression that I could not speak. We sat in utter silence for a long time, neither of us capable of uttering a word. But eventually Ruth broke the silence, her words backed by a small but intense surge of hope, a tiny flame casting a weak, fluttering light in the dark despair filling her troubled mind.

"Can you take me with you when you leave, back to your time?" she whispered, tension in her tone, fear of my reply. I was taken aback by her words, words I had hoped not to hear from her lips. The prospect of having to refuse Ruth, to see the look in her dark soulful eyes as I did so, this was something I could hardly bear. But I had no option. She had asked me a simple, direct question, and I would have to respond.

"No," I answered in a soft, sad voice. "I can't."

"Why not?" she pleaded.

"It won't work. It can't work," I insisted.

"You mean you won't take me, not that you can't", replied Ruth with surprising acerbity, though more engendered by her profound disappointment at my reply than real anger at me.

"No," I said softly. "I really do mean I can't, that it won't work." The truth was I had no idea if I could manage to travel back home. I suspected that my trajectory the first time was random, my arriving in this time and place an accident. And even if I thought I might be able to physically take Ruth with me and actually manage to find my way home, I was sure that Ruth's mental state was simply not stable enough to cope with such an upheaval, with such an outright change in her life. I would not take responsibility for what might happen. And indeed, I did not want to accept the blame if the physical jump were unsuccessful, if something should happen to Ruth in the actual process of travelling in time itself.

"How do you know you can't take me?" Ruth asked sharply, interrupting my thoughts. "How do you know if you've not tried?"

"I know that it is impossible to travel forward in time from one's own place in time," I stated. This was close to being a blatant lie, or at least the certainty with which I said it was a clear deception. I *believed* this to be the case, but did not know it as a fact. But I felt sure that I would not be able to travel forward from *my* own time into *my* own future, and no more would Ruth be able to travel forward from the moment in which she now lived into *her* future.

"It's a rule of time travel," I said briskly, with forced conviction in an attempt to persuade Ruth to believe me. "It is only possible to travel *backwards*, into a time that has already happened, to inhabit a space in time which has already existed, really existed. It is simply not feasible to take yourself forward into a time that has yet to exist. For you, that would mean creating a version of yourself which has not yet existed, and cannot therefore exist in that time." I felt guilty feeding Ruth this theory as if it were proven truth, but I needed her to believe me, and to abandon any hope of being rescued in this way, of being plucked from the present to be whisked away to a future salvation. I assuaged my guilt, partially, by telling myself that my theory must *surely* be correct, that it was the only logical conclusion that one could reach. Yet a nagging doubt entered my mind: I could *try* to save Ruth. I could tell her that this was merely a theory, and relay my doubts about my own ability to return home, doubts about her ability to function in my world, and then leave the decision to her, let her risk a failure in the time travel itself causing her to die, or to cease to exist, or risk a mental breakdown as she unsuccessfully tried to adapt to life in my time. But I knew I would not take this option. I would not make myself responsible for Ruth's physical or mental well-being in this way. I lacked the courage to take this upon myself. And even were I to take such responsibility upon myself, I had no idea if I could actually get home anyway. I had stumbled into 2012, into Ruth, having no clear idea of exactly how I had got here. I hoped I would be able to return home using the same method, but was not at all sure I would succeed.

Ruth was once again staring fixedly down at the table, her eyes seemingly rivetted to a spot just in front of where her hands lay, trembling slightly, flat on the tabletop, her white skin contrasting starkly with the dark wood. I wanted to say more, to try and reassure her, to reach out to her with my mind, and with my hands, but did not know what I could do or say to comfort her. I had just told her, in essence, that I would abandon her to all the horrors and hideousness of the future I had related to her in such ghastly detail, leave her here to cope with it as best she could. And my offers of help to her, already controlling the voices in her head, perhaps assisting her with her visions of the future, these seemed feeble, pitiful in light of what I had refused to do for her.

Ruth stood up so suddenly that her chair toppled over, crashing loudly to the floor behind her. I jumped at the noise which shattered the painful silence reigning between us. Without a word, or even a glance in my direction, she left the room, and the house, the front door slamming loudly as she exited towards the beach. I wondered if I should follow her, to try and offer her some succour, but sensed strongly that she had no further desire for my company at that moment. She was a loner, and I assumed she would better manage the torrent of thoughts, ideas and feelings sweeping through her alone, as usual, and certainly not accompanied by the person who had caused most of her anguish.

I sat very still at the table for a long time, but finally stood up and made my way to the front door, and from there to the beach. Tonight I did not feel I would be welcome to stay the night in Ruth's home. I threw myself down in front of the dune where I had slept undisturbed for several nights, exhausted by what I had just gone through with Ruth, and also from the previous night's fitful and restless sleep. I dozed off. The bright and cheerful summer sun continued to blaze in a clear blue sky, unaware of how ill-fitting was its appearance, how inappropriate that it continued to create such joyful luminance despite the mood of the occupants of the little beach house, and the dark clouds of the turbulent tempest soon to be visited upon this bright and beautiful Earth.

Chapter Sixty-One

After an unsatisfying doze of a few hours, I came to consciousness slowly, cracking my eyes open gradually against the golden light pouring through the gaps between my eyelids. My sleep had been filled with ghastly images created by my own stories to Ruth of the progression of the Chaos, sights of famine and plague, pandemics of biological warfare and nuclear disaster, death after death, body after body, devastation and desolation. As I stood up I shook my head vigorously in an attempt to dispel the frightful impressions assaulting my mind.

I realised I was hungry, and remembered the little stash of food I had stored near the dune. I gave so little thought to what I ate that it was not a pleasant repast, but I had no interest in the flavours of what I ate, so immersed was I still in the images in my mind, and in Ruth's despair.

I was filled with guilt at what I had told Ruth. Not so much the detail of the Chaos, which she herself had insisted upon hearing, and for which I bore no responsibility, but rather my blank refusal to even attempt to take her back to my time, to try and rescue her from the forthcoming nightmare.

I wondered where Ruth was, as I knew, after scanning the building, that she was not at home. As far as I could tell, she was nowhere near her home. I sat quietly, wondering what to do. I decided to look for her first in Southminster, so flitted there, stopping briefly on my way at the Traveller Inn to confirm she had not gone there instead. I wandered around the streets of Southminster, in and out of the shops we had visited together, but there was no sign or trace of Ruth. I returned to the beach near Ruth's home, not knowing what else to do. I wondered if I could locate her using the same trance state I had used to travel in time. As it had been so effective in allowing me to traverse eight centuries and find an individual person, could it not function within a specific time to achieve the same result?

I struggled to enter the trance state. I was agitated, my mind buzzing with all that I had so recently experienced. I began to wonder if I would ever succeed, and as I wondered this, the unpleasant thought struck me that if I were not able to clear my mind I would never be able to return home when the time came. This thought did not help, but eventually I managed to slow my heart rate and breathing, empty my mind of external influence, and finally achieve the detachment needed to enter the trance. But nothing happened. I realised I had no way of controlling the effect. I had travelled back in time only a few days before, but now seemed to achieve nothing. I did not move, and could find no way to induce movement. Had it all been random the first time, an accident? Had my 'ability' to travel back in time been totally outside of my control or volition? Would I be able to return home at all if I could not find a way to utilise the trance state? Such thoughts destroyed the tranquil state I had achieved, and I found myself back in the world of reality with a bump. I pushed any other thoughts out of my mind on the possible repercussions of my failure to locate Ruth, or even move, in the trance state. This was a problem for another day.

I spent the rest of the day wandering aimlessly in the vicinity of Ruth's beach home. Up and down the strand I meandered, and through the salt marshes lying behind. What had so fascinated and delighted me on my first exposure to it now distressed me, as all I could bring to mind was how close it was to utter destruction. Sometimes I sat to rest or merely to watch the waves breaking against the shore, or admire the raucous activities of the sea birds as they fought for dominance. The weather was delightful, the day being warm and sunny with barely a cloud in the sky, the heat kept at a pleasant level by the gentle but persistent breeze caressing the land from the direction of the sea. This too only served to exacerbate my misery as I thought how transient it all was, how temporary.

As evening approached, and the light began its slow decline towards dusk, I made my way back to the house. Ruth was still not home, so I ported myself inside. There I prepared myself a simple meal, washed down with several bottles of a beer called India Pale Ale which I found most pleasant, a rich amber drink with many layers of flavour. As darkness began to slide its way into the house, I sat on the old sofa and turned the television on. I realised that I had not yet engaged in this activity, one I knew was a primary pastime of people in this period. I had no idea how to actually set the apparatus in motion so in the end had to enter the machine with my mind and somehow, though I was not entirely sure how, I managed to get it to light up, images and sounds suddenly appearing on the screen. I found that I could move from one programme to another, and as I was restless, I was unable to settle on one easily. I was bombarded with images and relentless loud music and other noise from the films, news reports, what looked like documentaries and many other programmes the basis or function of which I could not fathom. A large number of these involved ordinary people carrying out a range of activities, some mundane, some bizarre. One such programme had groups of people sitting watching television programmes and commenting on them. How peculiar, I thought, to sit watching an animated box on which images of other people doing the same passes before one's eyes. The comments from the people were sometimes amusing, though I struggled to understand the context of many of them, and the whole experience felt oddly self-referential. Another programme involved some sort of dance competition, though with competitors who did not appear to be able to dance, and yet another with singers many of whom appeared unable to actually sing. And one programme, which I was only able to look at briefly, involved subjecting people to frankly disgusting activities while being abandoned in a jungle, but none of this against their will as far as I could tell. I could not understand the purpose of any of these programmes, so did not dwell long on them. In the end I settled on watching some delightful programmes about the natural world, a parade of glory mostly long-extinct (in relation to my time, that is), land animals, marine life, plants. These offerings were enchanting, informative, captivating, yet at the same time deeply distressing as very little of what I witnessed with my eyes had survived the Chaos.

After many hours of surveying the offerings on the small black box, I grew tired of it so caused it to shut down. I was slightly concerned at Ruth's absence, and wondered why she had not returned. Was she really so angry with me that she could not face me? Or did she simply need time alone to cope with her raging emotions following my revelations of the Chaos, and my refusal to provide her with salvation? Eventually I lay down on the lumpy sofa, wriggled in an attempt to make myself comfortable despite having to keep my legs bent due to the shortness of the furniture, and eventually went to sleep, assuming that Ruth would not return that night.

I had a slightly more restful night despite the shortcomings of the sofa, and woke early, partially refreshed. I noted that Ruth was not in the house, had not returned during the night. This concerned me slightly, and I thought that I should travel to London myself to look for her. Although I had not found her in Southminster, perhaps I could succeed in this in London?

I ate quickly, and flitted to a quiet spot in the midst of a thicket of bushes in Bloomsbury Square, my portal to London. I noticed vaguely that the clothing I had discarded on the day of my arrival was still sitting in a little forlorn pile on the ground beneath the shrubbery. The hour was early, and there were few people in the square at that hour. The weather also agitated against trips to a leafy square, this being the first day since I had arrived in London to show rain and dark clouds, leaden skies and chilly winds. The leaves of the bushes into which I emerged were dripping wet, and by the time I managed to push my way out of the thicket into the open space, my clothes and hair were thoroughly drenched, the chill wind taking me by surprise. The rain itself was not heavy, more a light constant drizzle filling the air than true rain, but enough to cause discomfort. I raised my body temperature, allowing my body heat to force the water on my clothes to evaporate.

As I walked, I tried to find a trace of Ruth, but my ability to do this was still very poor. As I had expected, I enjoyed no success.

I was not sure what to do next, until it suddenly occurred to me to visit Mr Schapps at Guillemot Publishers to see if he knew anything of Ruth's whereabouts. He had refused to tell me her home address, but might be persuaded that to divulge her present location did not qualify as such an invasion of privacy.

I walked briskly to Guillemot's office, only a short walk from the square, though as I approached I slowed slightly. I remembered the tiny yet formidable Penelope, the guardian of Guillemot's gate, and was not eager to face her again. As I approached the entrance to the publisher, I had a stroke of luck. Walking towards me I spied Mr Schapps, making his way to work. I quickened my pace so I would arrive at the door to Guillemot before he entered. He could protect me from the diminutive doughty doorwoman I did not wish to face alone.

"Mr Schapps!" I said brightly as I approached him. He looked at me, for a brief moment not seeming to recognise me. He had been lost in his thoughts, and my intrusion caused him a flicker of disorientation. But his face quickly lit up as he remembered who I was.

"Sammy!" he said, in a friendly voice. "Nice to see you again. Did you find your aunt?" he asked.

"Yes," I replied. "I asked my father and he told me where she was living. I've been staying with her for a little while, since I was here last actually." The lies tripped easily off my tongue, though not all of what I said was untrue.

"Good," replied Mr Schapps. "I'm glad. And please do call me Simon," he reminded me. "Mr Schapps makes me feel so old!" he added, with a wry little smile. He turned to enter the glass door of his business, then stopped, looked at me, and asked,

"Is there something I can do for you Sammy?"

I nodded. "Yes, Mr Sch...Simon," I replied. "There is."

"Well come inside and we'll have a chat. It's not the weather to hang around on pavements."

I followed him through the door, as he swept me past the table by the door at which the fearsome Penelope already sat ready for her day's work, her preparations including the expression of pursed-lipped disdain she seemed to perpetually wear.

"Good morning Penelope," called Simon in a bright tone.

"Good morning Mr Schapps," she replied formally. "I see you have a visitor," she added, disapproval oozing out of her, though I was not sure if this was aimed at me personally or simply that her role of guardian of the gate had been supplanted by Simon as he himself granted me access to the inner sanctum of Guillemot.

"Yes," replied Simon, apparently ignoring her reproachful tone, inured to it after so many years of suffering it. "Can you bring us both some coffee," he added. "Or would you prefer tea?" he said, addressing me. I indicated I would indeed prefer tea, so he instructed Penelope to bring a pot of tea upstairs as soon as she could. Lips drawn together even more tightly, eyebrows arched, Penelope stood up, and as we made our way upstairs she disappeared through a door at the back of the hall, presumably leading to a kitchen. I followed Simon up the stairs to his office.

"Well young Mr Firestone," said Simon with a little smile as he took off his raincoat, shook it, and hung it over the back of his chair. "What can I do for you?" He sat down heavily and gazed over the apparently permanent pile of books and papers burdening his desk. I sat on the large leather chair opposite, which was so low I could barely see him. He pushed two piles of books slightly apart, the better to see me, almost causing an accident as the taller of the two wobbled precariously before it decided not to tumble to the floor. When the tomes ceased trembling, I spoke.

"I found my aunt, as I said, and I've been staying with her by the sea. But the day before yesterday she went off in the morning without saying anything, and she hasn't come home. We had a disagreement and I'm a bit worried about her."

"I can see that you would be," said Simon. "But I'm not sure how I can help," he added.

"I was wondering if she's been here in the last day or two," I replied. "Or if not, if you know where she might be." Simon looked at me kindly out of his surprisingly pretty eyes.

"I can tell you she's not been here, young man, not since just before the time *you* first came here. I haven't seen her or spoken to her since then in fact." He was about to add something else when the door creaked open.

Penelope entered without knocking, carrying a tray with a pot, two cups and a small jug. I was amazed at how quickly she had managed to prepare the tea.

"Will you do the honours Penelope?" asked Simon, smiling at the dour face of the guardian of Guillemot. She seemed to exude even more disdain at this perfectly reasonable request, but nevertheless placed the tray on a small table at the side of the room and prepared to pour.

"Milk?" she asked me curtly, in a tone of voice that I thought would surely curdle the same. I tried not to laugh at her manner, it seeming so exaggerated, as I did not imagine she was a woman who took kindly to being ridiculed. I nodded slightly and she poured two cups of tea. Silence reigned in the room as she handed Simon and me our drinks. I noted that she had chosen a cup for me with chips around its rim, whereas Simon's was in perfect condition. I shook my head slightly at this calculated insult. Simon did not seem to notice, but thanked Penelope and said that he did not need her any more for the moment. She reluctantly slid from the room, closing the door loudly behind her, but not before she had cast a final disdainful look in my direction.

"Where were we?" asked Simon after she had left. "Oh yes, I just told you that I've not had any communication with Miss Firestone since the day you came here, or maybe the day before? I can't remember exactly. And I'm afraid I don't know where she is now." I was disappointed at Simon's words, but persisted.

"But would you know where she might be? Where she might go when she comes to London? Could you try to contact her?" I asked. Simon paused for a moment before answering, a pensive look on his face.

"I'm afraid I don't know where she might be. I know she has a brother - your father - but I assume you've already tried there?" I nodded, though of course this was not true. From what Ruth had told me, and Simon himself on my previous visit, it seemed highly unlikely she would have gone to her brother Samuel's home, as they were estranged. "But I have no idea where he lives anyway," continued Simon. "The only address I have for Ruth is the one you're staying at. I've never been there as I don't think she welcomes visitors. She's so private generally, and we usually do business on the phone or via email, or her very rare visits here. I can try calling on her home phone, but you say she's not there."

A thought entered my mind. "Does she have a mobile telephone?" I asked, a flicker of hope in my voice.

"No," replied Simon simply. "She told me a while back that she'd hate to think people could contact her whenever they wanted, wherever she was. And she worries that she could be tracked via a mobile."

I was visibly discouraged by Simon's words, and being the kindly, helpful man he was, he seemed to feel guilty at his lack of ability to offer assistance.

"I'll try her on her home phone," he stated, then picked up the top part of the telephone on his desk, pressed some buttons on the static section then waited, hand pressing the moveable part to his ear. After a little while he joined the two parts together again, shrugging lightly at me and shaking his head.

"There's no answer," he said. On seeing my troubled face, he continued. "I'm really sorry," he said. "If I could help you more I would. I know I wouldn't give you her home address last time, but I think you understood why not? But if I'd seen her or had any idea where she was now, or if she had a mobile phone, I promise I would help." He stopped talking, struggling to find a way to assist me. His face suddenly brightened.

"Perhaps you could go to the police?" he suggested. "Report her as a missing person?" I started at what he said, having no desire to make myself known to any of the authorities in that time. He took my look of concern as a dismissal of the idea.

"Yes, yes, you're right," he said in a slightly discouraged tone. "They wouldn't do anything. She's a grown woman who lives on her own and likes to be alone. It's hardly a police matter if she goes off somewhere for a couple of days." He stopped talking, and appeared to have run out of ideas. We sipped our tea in silence. I noticed him glancing around at the stacks of books, the papers scattered over his desk and the floor, and realised I had taken up enough of this benign man's time. I put my almost empty cup down on the desk, having to balance it delicately on one of the only tiny free spaces near the edge, and stood up. I extended my hand, as I had learned to do. He stood up and shook it.

"Thank you so much for your time Simon," I said warmly, genuinely grateful for his kindness towards me. "I'm sure it'll be fine. As you said, she's a grown woman and quite used to being alone."

"Yes, yes," Simon assured me. "I'm sure she'll turn up soon. She might even be there when you get back later today," he added hopefully. I nodded and smiled.

"I'll show myself out, and thank you again," I said as I made my way to the door. The last I of saw of him was as I turned slightly on leaving his office as he sat down loudly, sighing as he forlornly contemplated the mound of work haphazardly strewn across his desk and every available space in his room. I tripped down the stairs and hastened across the open space of the tiled entrance hall. As I passed the desk at the front, Penelope spoke without even looking up from what she was reading.

"Finished so soon?" she asked acidly.

"And good morning to you too," I replied ironically, ignoring her question, but unable to restrain myself from throwing a thrust of energy in her direction, one which crashed into her mind causing her to jerk backwards in her chair and cry out in pain, a puerile act of petty revenge on my part and a waste of my gifts. But as I passed through the door to the outside world, I smirked with pleasure at having inflicted a cheap parting shot at this oh so unpleasant woman to whom I had done no wrong.

But my pleasure was short-lived. I stood outside the entrance to Guillemot, unable to decide what to do, how to proceed. I strolled without purpose back to my usual and now familiar square and sat on one of the benches, all of which were empty this early and on such a day. The rain had ceased, at least for the moment, but the bench itself was wet, a fact I only ascertained as I sat down on it with a squelching sound.

I truly had no idea how to proceed with my search for Ruth, and made to return to the beach house. I worked hard to try and persuade myself that all would be well. Ruth would return, she would accept what was to come, and be glad of my presence in her life, of the help I had been able to give her, the help I could still offer. I ported myself away from London, back to the coast, filled with a forced happiness and confidence, premature as it was soon to be shattered.

Chapter Sixty-Two

When I arrived back inside the beach house, I immediately sensed that Ruth was already home. I did not know when she had arrived, and chided myself for not having checked earlier. When Simon had telephoned her at home she may not yet have arrived back, or had simply ignored the ringing of the bell. I felt I had wasted time in London looking for her, when all along she may not even have been in the city.

I noted that Ruth was upstairs in her glass-bound bedroom, deep asleep. She seemed exhausted, and I wondered where she had been since I had last seen her, what she had been doing. I removed my shoes and crept around the house in silence. I ate a cold meal of chicken and boiled potatoes I had found in Ruth's refrigerator, not wanting to disturb my host with the sounds of kitchen appliances humming in the preparation of hot food, even assuming I could actually understand such primitive devices as to make them work. I tiptoed into the living room, and ate sitting on the old sofa. I was impatient to see Ruth again, to try and patch up the connection we had, so fragile, and damaged by my revelations of the Chaos, my refusal to save her by whisking her away to my time. I was not sure I could make amends. How could we return to our earlier warmth when I had nothing else to offer except despair?

I sat for hours on the sofa, thinking, just thinking, reviewing the images and feelings of my trip in time, of London, of Ruth, of the beach house on the beautiful empty coast with its abundance of exuberant flora and fauna, of Mr Schapps, even of the awful Penelope. I tried to imagine how all of this would appear to people of my own time but realised with a start that I could not put myself in their place, not imagine how they would feel about what I had actually experienced. I felt so far removed from my own world, not only in simple years but also in emotion, such that empathising with my own people eluded me. I realised with a start that my own time seemed almost unreal, distant in every way, as if I were imagining it, inventing it.

My reveries were interrupted by a slight noise above my head. I sensed that Ruth was waking up. I waited impatiently for her to make her way downstairs, which she seemed to take an age to achieve. Her movements were plodding and sluggish, as her mind took its time to return to full consciousness. As she dragged herself around her bedroom, I decided to prepare for her descent by making coffee, for her and for me.

When Ruth finally emerged into the living room, her dark hair wild around her head, her clothing (a plain red dress this time, patterned with pink flowers) crumpled and dishevelled from having been slept in, I was able to offer her a steaming cup of the aromatic brew from the large pot of coffee. I poured her a large cup, adding a generous splash of milk as I knew she liked, and placed the drink on the small table in front of the sofa. Ruth sat down heavily beside me, still groggy from sleep, and began to quietly sip from her cup, cradling it in both hands. She had not looked at me at all or acknowledged my presence in any way as she had entered the room and settled on the sofa, and I worried about her mental state.

She showed little except lassitude and fatigue, and I realised with a shock that she seemed to be blocking any further outpouring of emotion. When had she learned to do this? I had not specifically taught her to block the outflowing of her mental state in this way. I was truly amazed that from the few techniques I had imparted to her to control the voices in her head, she had been able, alone, to reverse the process, not only erecting a barrier to impressions entering her mind, but also screening what she exuded. I was deeply impressed by her native abilities, but at the same time disappointed that she had chosen to lock me out in this way. Had she decided that I was not, after all, someone to trust, not a person to rely on? I was itching to know what was going on in her mind that she was so eager to hide from me, and was about to enter her head to find out for myself when Ruth spoke. And what she said shocked me even more.

"Don't do that Sammy," she said. "Don't read my mind." She did not look up from her mug as she said this, and her voice was quiet but determined.

"What do you mean?" I managed to stammer out, disingenuously. I knew exactly what she meant. She glanced at me from behind a curtain of unkempt hair, a small, strange smile on her face, enigmatic, a touch sad.

"You know perfectly well what I mean," she replied. "Don't go into my mind. Please. Respect me enough to leave me my private thoughts." I blushed at her words, squirming with embarrassment at having been caught out in this way. And I was flabbergasted to know that Ruth was able to sense what I was about to do, to detect this as I attempted to enter *her* mind. But why should I be so surprised? I had pulled towards her precisely because of her remarkable innate gifts, gifts I had helped her to understand and control. Clearly she had spent much of the last day honing her ability to make use of the power of her brain.

"I won't," I finally answered, when I had recovered sufficiently from the shock. "I promise I won't enter your mind," I confirmed. And I meant it.

"Never?" Ruth insisted. "You promise you won't ever do it?"

"I promise Ruth, I promise. Not now and not ever." She nodded, satisfied that I would hold to my words. And I knew I would. My heart went out to this remarkable woman whose life I had forced my way into, dangling ideas and possibilities in front of her, only to snatch away salvation when she asked for it. I owed her at least this much. We remained in silence on the sofa, finishing our coffee. After a long period, I turned to Ruth.

"Where have you been?" I asked. "I was worried about you." She did not turn to look at me, but the small curious smile returned to her face, mysterious and tinged with melancholy. She did not reply, and I knew she had no intention of replying. I sighed. She was a grown woman, much older than me, and well able to look after herself. What business was it of mine to know her whereabouts? And was it not a little patronising to show such concern for her as if she were not able to fend for herself?

After this an uncomfortable silence ensued. I was at a loss what to say, how to break into her secretive mood. She stared down into her empty cup, not looking at me, not moving. The stillness dragged on and my disquiet grew.

"Anyway," Ruth said suddenly, in an unexpectedly bright voice. "Enough of all that. Enough gloom and doom and sad faces." She turned to look at me directly. "Let's have a little party!" she announced loudly, smiling openly as she did so. I was astonished at the abrupt change of subject, and of mood, the mercurial shift from quiet dolefulness to animation and enthusiasm. I stared back at her with a look of sheer astonishment on my face that must have been so comical that she laughed out loud. She grabbed my hand and leapt up off the sofa, pulling me with her.

"Wine!" she shouted. "We need wine!" And, letting go of my hand she raced off to the kitchen, to return shortly with two bottles of white wine and two enormous glasses.

"You pour," she instructed in a jolly voice. "I'll choose some music. What's a party without music?" I stood stock still, unable to react to the change in Ruth's demeanour. And I had never seen her like this, or even imagined she could behave in this way. She seemed like a different person.

"Come on!" she encouraged with a chortle. "Chop chop. Look lively. I'm gasping for a drink!" I roused myself and moved towards the table where she had placed the wine. I knew I had no option but to go along with her bright mood, despite the day's early hour. I opened one of the bottles by unscrewing its metal top, and poured some fruity white wine into each glass. As I did so, Ruth glanced round from where she stood, squinting at the glasses in my hands.

"That's pathetic," she laughed. "Twice that much. Go on. Be generous. We've got plenty more." I did as she asked, filling the glasses to the top, and noting that this emptied almost two thirds of the bottle. Ruth turned away, satisfied, and began to peruse some wooden shelves built into the wall along the side of the room. There were many books around the walls, but these shelves were not laden with books, instead containing large thin cardboard envelopes, each one filled with a stiff object I did not recognise. Ruth hummed a little as she ran her finger swiftly along the row of envelopes, then grasped one, pulling it quickly out.

"Here we are," she said as she looked at the large square envelope in her hands. "The Seekers. That'll do for a start." I had no idea what she was saying. The object in her hands was a mystery to me, her words even more so. From inside the cardboard envelope, which I now saw was emblazoned with a photograph of a group of about five people, and the words 'The Seekers' in large letters, as well as some other words, Ruth gently slid out another envelope, this time of white paper with a small black circle in its centre. From this, she once again extracted another object, this time a perfect rigid circle of a black shiny material, ridged all over its surface, and interrupted by a much smaller circle in the centre of matt paper with words on it, and a tiny hole in the very middle. I looked at the object perplexedly, wondering at the complexity of the procedure as Ruth flashed me a little smile. She then moved to a squat wooden cabinet near the shelf on which sat a device whose purpose I could not guess. She lifted the clear plastic lid of the device and carefully laid the plastic disk flat onto the surface below. She then pressed a button on the front and I saw a small arm move from the side of the machine across to the disk, dropping down to make contact with it near its edge.

Without any warning, loud music erupted into the room. I jumped slightly, and Ruth laughed at my reaction. The music was being produced from the disk, somehow passing through the arm, and emerging from two wooden boxes placed beside the device on the cabinet top.

"It's a record player," Ruth explained on seeing my still-confused face. "And these are records," she continued, indicating the shelves with the cardboard envelopes with a sweep of her arm.

"Well, don't just stand there like a lemon. Give me my wine," she instructed. I moved quickly to hand her one of the glasses, wondering why she had described me as a lemon. She took a huge swig, fully a third of the glass, then indicated with a jerk of her head towards my as yet untouched glass that I should do the same. I sipped, though more cautiously than she had. She tut-tutted.

"That won't do. I'm not getting drunk on my own, and I *am* getting drunk. So you have to as well. So go on, neck some of it. Be a man!" she said, her final comment seeming to cause her great amusement, though I could not understand either the intent of the phrase or her hilarity. What possible link was there with downing a large amount of wine in a short period and being a man? And what did this mean for Ruth, who seemed adept at quaffing large quantities of wine, though clearly not being a man? I did as I was ordered, taking several large gulps of the yellow liquid. It was pleasant enough. It had always caused me wry amusement that as the Chaos progressed and scientists and politicians ratcheted up the desperate race to save as many species of animal and plant as possible, they had made very sure to rescue a wide range of grape types, clearly feeling that good wine would somehow be essential to the well-being of the survivors of the Chaos.

As we stood drinking our wine, I attended to the music filling the room. In terms of melody, and harmony, it was surprisingly similar to some of the songs regularly heard and performed in my world. I remembered that Kallan once told me that our people were strangely conservative when it came to music, preferring a narrow range of styles, and that in the time before the Chaos there had been more variety. Though even in this variety, the music enjoyed by the vast majority of people before the Chaos was often of similar type, the more esoteric and arcane styles being limited to small social, economic or cultural groups. After the Chaos, in many ways an intense conservatism reigned in general as people struggled to survive, their focus on ensuring the continuation of the human race. Luxuries such as experimental music, art, even new thoughts and ideas could simply not be countenanced, at least not until humanity's future was on a more stable footing. But after many generations of living within a narrow, conventional and orthodox ideology, emerging from it was difficult, slow and stuttering.

As I listened, I engaged with the words of the gentle, vaguely melancholy song emerging into the room.

Walk with me through the long and lonely night.
Walk with me and my world is filled with light.
Here I stand feeling lost and so alone
Take my hand, don't desert me now,
please don't hurt me now.
If you walk with me though I know the road is long
I'll get by, with your love to keep me strong.
More by far than a guiding star above
I long for you.
Walk with me. Oh my love.

Somewhere the sunbirds fly
In a clear blue sky.
Only you and I there together.
Love me. Now and forever.

A song of struggle, hardship and pain, yet also of profound love, of loyalty, of the longevity of human affection. I found myself deeply moved by this simple song, its sweet, rocking melody, its gentle harmonies, its words of hope in a difficult world, hope underscored with fear, the voice of the woman singing it managing to convey both melancholy and optimism at the same time. Despite the familiar-sounding melody and simple harmonies, I knew that there was no such music in my own time, nothing with so many layers of meaning, so much ambivalence of message. My own time, for all its luxury, its comforts, its security, suddenly seemed to lose its lustre, to appear shallow and flat, lacking the depth, the complexity, the sheer abundance that this year of 2012 showed even in the simplest thing. I looked at Ruth, and saw her swaying gently from side to side, eyes closed, silently mouthing the words. I was assailed with an almost overwhelming sense of sadness as I watched her, lost in her enjoyment of the music, the lyrics. I had to force myself not to break down, as I had on the steps of the museum, but this time for much more immediate, narrow reasons. For the simple compassion I felt for Ruth as she managed, for a brief moment, to put her troubles away, to focus entirely on the pleasure of the tiny moment of music snatched from the awful reality of her internal world. I never imagined I could have been so successful in helping her.

As the song finished, Ruth opened her eyes. She was surprised at my forlorn expression, fixing me with a quizzical gaze, a curious half-smile lifting one corner of her mouth.

"That won't do at all Sammy. We'll have no sadness today. This is a happy day, a jolly day, a day to celebrate and rejoice," she cajoled.

"Celebrate what?" I queried, my voice wavering slightly. She shrugged slightly, her smile widening.

"Whatever you want," she replied. "Being alive. You being here. Us being here together. Me knowing who I am for the first time in my life." And then she paused briefly, before adding in a quiet voice. "Me being at peace with myself." And as she said this, she leaned across to me, lightly touching the side of my face with the back of her hand, stroking my cheek for a fleeting moment before withdrawing her fingers. Her gesture was so unexpected, so filled with emotion, that tears came into my eyes. Ruth was distressed by the reaction she had caused.

"I'm sorry," she whispered. "I didn't mean to upset you. I am just so relieved to know that I was never insane. "

"Then you need to make sure you keep screening your feelings," I managed to say in a thick voice. "I got such jolt of emotion through your fingers just then. And," I added. "You need to change the music. That song is so sad."

"You don't like it?" she asked.

"Yes," I replied. "Very much. But it's not right if you want today to be a happy day, a jolly day, a party day. Don't you have anything lighter?" She smiled at me, and went to change the record. After rifling through her collection of records, she suddenly said "Ah ha!" and pulled one off the shelf. She took the one playing off the record player, threw it carelessly aside, and replaced it with the new one. When its notes loudly began, I knew it was far more appropriate.

"Seventies disco," Ruth announced. I was none the wiser from her description. "Dance music from the nineteen seventies," she explained. "It was a great time for dance music, loud, simple tunes to jump around to on a dance floor, to sing along to."

"But you can't have been there?" I asked her.

"No of course not," Ruth laughed. "I was only a small child at the time. But I discovered it much later and have loved it ever since."

Ruth took my now empty glass and went to refill it, as well as hers. To do so, she had to open the second bottle. I knew I was becoming tipsy, but decided to go along with whatever Ruth wanted. This was her day. She handed me back my glass and we both took large swigs. She then took my glass from me, placing them both on the small table in front of the sofa.

"Come on then," she encouraged as she sashayed over towards me. "Let's have a dance." I laughed at her exaggerated swaying movements and animated face, as she extended a hand towards me. I took her hand and we began to move together, rocking backwards and forwards, jumping up and down, stepping from foot to foot. I was not an accomplished dancer. Kallan had tried to teach me and my siblings some basic dances, though with little success. We could all manage up to a point, though without real skill, unlike many people in my world for whom dancing was a serious pastime. Haari had taken me on a number of occasions to social events involving dancing, some more formal than others, and his skill had shown me just how inept I was. He insisted it did not matter, but nevertheless had seemed rather pleased with his own abilities.

I saw that Ruth was no better than I was, perhaps even less fluid, more stiff and ungainly. She seemed barely able even to follow the insistent pounding beat. But today it did not matter. We were simply enjoying each other's company, the wine, the music. If we clomped about in gawky lumbering fashion, inelegant in the extreme, well what matter? Nobody was watching, nobody else was there. We only had ourselves to please, and this we did mightily.

All of the rest of the afternoon and into the evening we danced and chatted, drank, and drank more. As darkness fell we decided to take a small break to fill our empty bellies. We sat at the table to eat, Ruth having simply thrown frozen pizzas into the oven. I grinned as I recalled that this was my second pizza since arriving in 2012 just a few days before. As I stuffed it into my mouth, the wine having given me a raging hunger, I thought it a marvellous meal for interrupting a drinking session: dense, doughy, fatty, and flavoursome. After eating, we sat for a short while resting before taking up our previous activities of drinking and dancing. As we became more inebriated, Ruth bellowed louder and louder to the music, shouting out the lyrics to every song. She had obviously listened to them many times as she knew them word perfect. I, on the other hand, was not familiar with a single one of them, though this did not stop me from joining in, making up lyrics or mouthing the words I thought seemed correct at the top of my voice. Sometimes my attempts were so ridiculous that they rendered Ruth unable to sing herself, so loudly was she laughing at my drunken efforts.

The evening moved into night, and yet still we continued to drink, to sing and to dance, sometimes moving together to dance hand in hand or with arms wrapped around each other's shoulders, backs or waists, other times parting and jigging alone on our own private spot, facing each other. Occasionally Ruth would excel herself by executing a swift twirl, which, when I tried to follow suit, just caused me to fall heavily to the ground, to our huge mutual hilarity. We listened to all sorts of music, but, upon my insistence, universally light, upbeat, jolly. As the night wore on and my state of drunkenness grew, I could no longer tell any of the music apart, and as the fog of intoxication seeped ever more thickly into my brain, all I ended up being aware of was a relentless thumping rhythm overlaid with an inchoate blaring orchestration.

After many many hours, and countless glasses of wine, I suddenly stopped. I had reached my limit, unable to move further, unable to drink more. I managed to mumble to Ruth that I could carry on no more and that I needed to fall over and sleep, preferably on the sofa rather than the floor. I am sure that my words were almost incomprehensible gibberish, little more than a "nya nya nya", yet she seemed to understand them, or at least their intent. She nodded and suddenly moved right up against me, our faces pressed together only inches apart. I was startled by this, though unable to react physically, not daring to move lest I take a heavy tumble. Ruth stared at me out of bleary, barely focused dark eyes, eyes filled with intense emotion, affection and perhaps even love for me, a longing for something from me or with me I could not clearly identify, and a transparent happiness mingled with profound sadness. I was overwhelmed, moved almost to tears by the intensity of Ruth's feelings. In her drunken state, her guard had dropped a little, her screen tattered and filled with holes. I held to my promise not to enter her mind to gain more clarity as to her inner feelings, and not even sure, drunk as I was, if I would be capable of doing so even had I wanted to. Ruth leaned into me even closer and kissed me on the forehead, as gently as the caress of a feather, filling me with such feeling that drunken tears began to flow freely down my face.

"No Sammy," she managed to enunciate. "Don't cry. It's good. It's all good." And at that, she took a step backwards away from me, peered at me for another moment, her eyes still blazing with feeling, though with emotions I could not clearly ascertain, then turned on her heel and stumbled out of the room. I remained where I was as I heard her lumbering across the hall to the staircase to her room. She managed somehow to mount the stairs, though I suspect, from the noise she made, having to do so on all fours to prevent herself falling. Moments later I heard her land with a loud thump on her bed, fully clothed. Then silence. She had passed out. I took this as my cue, making my own unstable way the few steps to the battered old sofa. I barely managed to reach it, so drunk was I, almost falling flat on my face as I lurched along. I knew if I fell, I would stay there, sleep where I had fallen, unable to rouse myself sufficiently to haul myself off the cold floor and make the short journey to the sofa. But I managed to reach it somehow, falling the last few feet directly onto the sofa. I wriggled to try and get comfortable, though in truth I could feel little, so numbed was I by the effects of the alcohol. I managed to plump up a couple of thin, saggy cushions into something resembling a pillow, and there, just like Ruth, I lost consciousness, my final thoughts being happy ones of the jolly, wild, wine-soaked evening I had spent with Ruth. I passed out with a smile on my face.

Chapter Sixty-Three

I slept soundly all night, or rather, I remained unconscious, only emerging from my drunken slumbers late the following morning. As I slowly came to consciousness on the sofa, lying quite still with eyes firmly shut, I could hardly believe how unwell I felt. I truly felt ill, and realised that this was what it was to suffer from an appalling hangover. At the age of nineteen I had obviously been indulging in alcohol for some time, but never had I drunk anything like as much as I had with Ruth the night before. Mercifully, the curtains were closed, though I knew I had not been remotely coherent enough to have remembered to draw them before crashing onto the sofa. Ruth must have done this at some time during the evening, though I had no recollection of the event.

I realised with a start that something was wrong in the house, very wrong. There reigned a stillness, a deep silence which filled me with foreboding, though I could not put my finger on the reason why. I sensed nothing coming from Ruth's bedroom upstairs, absolutely nothing. I shivered with dread at the lack of sensation, knowing that Ruth could not possibly have roused herself to leave the house already, she having been in such a state of advanced inebriation the night before. I stood quite still for a few moments, paralysed with indecision, before summoning the courage to leave the kitchen and make my way to the staircase at the back of the house. I stopped at the foot of the stairs, realising that I had never been physically into Ruth's bedroom, never climbed the spiral stairs to the glass room perched atop the building, only ever having made a cursory visit with my mind. This time I felt, I *knew*, that I needed to be there in body.

With much trepidation, I placed a foot on the first step, then slowly, with great reluctance, I mounted the stairs, one heavy tread after another. As I approached the top, my head emerged straight into the single room where the staircase entered it, and I then dragged the rest of my body up after my head. I gingerly put my foot on the floor of the bedroom, joined by my other foot. And there I stood, immobile, staring straight at a large double bed pressed up against the far wall. And to my horror, there lay Ruth, on her back, arms folded across her stomach, utterly still. I stared in disbelief at what I saw, unwilling to accept what my senses were screaming at me. That she was not breathing. That her body emanated no warmth. That she was dead.

With painful aversion, I forced myself across the room, feet dragging along the floor as if to prevent me reaching my goal. I stood beside the bed and gazed bleakly at the figure stretched out before me, Ruth's body still shrouded in the dishevelled clothing from the night before, hair a wild bird's nest forming a dark halo around her head. In desperation I scanned the lifeless body to see if I could sense any signs of vitality, but to no avail. I knew I would not succeed, but tried over and over again, until I could do no more. I stood absolutely still, the question coming to my mind: "Why?"

I remained beside the bed, legs quivering. My eyes were drawn to the small cabinet beside the bed, close to where Ruth's lifeless head lay so peacefully on its blue cotton-wrapped pillow. On the cabinet lay a small cream coloured envelope, the single word 'Sammy' written on it in large bold hand-written letters. I was aghast. A letter to me from Ruth, from beyond the threshold of life. I stood transfixed, staring mutely at the envelope, knowing I must open it and read what was written, yet terrified of doing so.

My curiosity finally overcame my fear and I reached down, gently picking up the creamy envelope between first finger and thumb. I held it in front of my face, turning it around in the light flooding through the glass wall, trying to discern its message from without, but not having the courage to open it. I could not see what was written, though knew that there was a hand-written letter to me within. With sudden decision I slipped my hand under the seal and tentatively extracted the paper inside, its colour matching the buttery envelope. I hesitantly cracked open the stiff paper, holding it in front of my face. It was covered in small, neat lettering, and I realised with a jolt that Ruth must have written it *before* our drunken party the night before. In her state of inebriated befuddlement at the end of the night there was no possibility that she could have even contemplated writing such a careful, neat missive, let alone actually execute it with such precision. I could only surmise that she had prepared the letter before I had returned to the house. While I was in London seeking Ruth, was she here planning her own suicide, committing her thoughts to writing for me to read after the dreadful event? And all through the evening before, as we drank and danced, talked, laughed and joked, she had known what she was planning, how she would escape from the horrors I had described to her. I found it almost impossible to believe that this decision had been made before we began our jollities, yet I had not sensed such a conclusion, had not perceived the slightest whiff of it.

I knew now why Ruth had insisted on me not entering her mind and why she had erected a barrier against me sensing her emotional state. She had feared that I would apprehend her underlying emotional state, discover her plan, and of course try to stop her from carrying it out. I had naively obeyed her wish for privacy blissfully unaware of its true purpose, and now I castigated myself for my innocence. If I had ignored her desires, forced myself into her mind, she might yet be alive. As I considered my error in respecting her wishes I was assailed by a wave of emotion, my breathing became shallow and difficult, and I had to force myself to return to a state of calm lest I lose my ability to respond rationally to the disaster I saw before me. As my heart rate slowed, I allowed my eyes to drop to the page before me, and, taking a deep breath, I began to read.

Dear Sammy,

When you find this letter, I will be dead. As you may have guessed, I took an overdose of a number of different drugs, all prescribed by my doctor, but not designed to be taken together, and in such quantity. And certainly not on top of so much wine. I have taken so many that there will be no chance that I will wake up, no opportunity to regret my action and to try and reverse it. As I'm sure you have also realised, I am writing this letter sober while you are out of the house, though I plan to get drunk tonight and hope I will be able to persuade you to join me in one final night of fun, a happy, joyous final farewell to this world, this world I have struggled my whole life through to understand and to come to terms with, though mostly with little success.

I am sure you will be cursing yourself, convinced that you could have done something to stop me, or perhaps that you could have offered me more help than you already have, perhaps even tried to take me away from all of this, save me by taking me back to your time. But I know you would have done this if you could, and I beg you not to blame yourself for anything.

I want you to know that the days I have spent with you have been some of the happiest of my life, and I thank you for them from the bottom of my heart. I beg you, do not be sad. I leave this life willingly, with a light heart, happy at last to understand who I am. You gave me this understanding. You taught me that there is nothing wrong with me, that there never has been anything wrong with me, that the voices in my head, the visions, all the other problems I have suffered throughout my life were entirely a result of me being special, gifted. And for this I can never thank you enough. But I cannot bear the thought of what is to come, the Chaos you described to me in such vivid terms, most of which I already know from my visions. I simply cannot endure all of that, and so must take my own life before it is too late, take my destiny into my own hands and not let fate work its dark magic on me.

I have a favour to ask of you - will you telephone my brother and tell him what has happened before you go? You can just tell him you're a friend. But I suggest you are not here when he arrives, or perhaps even the police if he chooses to call them. I think your presence will be impossible to explain. You'll find his number in the address book next to this letter. His name is Samuel Firestone. Funny that you both have the same name.

I have no more to say Sammy, except please do not mourn me. Just remember me, and know that your presence in my life was the greatest gift I ever received.

Yours in great affection,

Ruth

I dropped the letter, then collapsed onto the floor where I knelt, staring almost blankly at Ruth's cold corpse. I could not even cry. I felt a curious cold shock, a grief not permitting the release of tears. I remained on my knees, trembling with emotion, sweat breaking out on my brow, my heart pounding in my ears. When my mind eventually managed to control my body's reaction, I was overwhelmed with a sense of guilt so powerful that I struggled to breathe. Could I have helped Ruth more? Was telling her the truth the wrong thing to do?

I knelt on the floor so long that my body began to ache with the effort of holding such a position, my knees throbbing against the cool floor. I dragged myself to a standing position, then sat gingerly on the edge of the bed, carefully avoiding contact with Ruth's now cold cadaver. I opened the purple address book on the cabinet beside the bed. I found Samuel Firestone listed under S, after incorrectly looking under F to begin with. I looked at the old-fashioned telephone sitting next to the address book. Remembering Penelope's and Simon's actions on my visits to Guillemot, I lifted the top part of the machine and put it against my head. I heard a buzzing sound coming from the device. I looked at the other part of the telephone and saw a small panel with numbers. I pressed the numbers listed in the little book. I heard an electronic tone pulsing regularly, then a little click. I was wondering if this was the time when I should speak, when a voice preempted me.

"You've reached Samuel Firestone's phone. I'm not able to take your call at the moment, but please leave a message at the beep and I'll get back to you as soon as I can." Then a short electronic signal and silence. I needed to fill the silence with what I had to say, so I spoke quickly and quietly into the part of the device in front of my mouth, again emulating what I had seen Guillemot's guardian do. I explained as briefly as I could what had happened, adding, as instructed by Ruth, that I was a friend who had discovered her body. I gave my name simply as Sammy. I then reconnected the two parts of the telephone by placing the hand-held part into the cradle below.

I sat for a while, knowing that I would soon need to leave, before Samuel heard the message and put in place the necessary action to retrieve his sister's sad remains. I knew that my presence in Ruth's home would cause great confusion. The real Samuel Firestone would have no idea who I was, and I assumed that on discovering a suicide in this way, he would need to involve the authorities. They would try to locate me, to work out who I was and what I meant to Ruth. They might contact Ruth's publisher, Simon Schapps, and he would throw further confusion into the story by telling them that he had met me, twice, and that I had told him I was Ruth's nephew, Samuel's son. The fearsome Penelope would back up Simon's assertion. Samuel would of course deny this, saying he did not know me. I felt sad that Simon would know I had lied to him, and irked that Penelope would feel vindicated in her instant and intense dislike of me. "I knew there was something odd about him," I could hear her say. "I knew he couldn't be trusted." But there was nothing I could do about this now. I had done what I had needed to do, and in the end, Simon had shown great loyalty to Ruth by refusing to disclose to me her address in the first place.

In the end I supposed the verdict would be suicide, as there was nothing to suggest anything more sinister. I considered leaving the letter Ruth had written to me as proof of the fact that she had taken her own life, but there was too much in it that would merely add fuel to the fire of puzzlement over who I was, and the references to the Chaos might even suggest to readers of the note that her already fragile mental state was even worse than they believed. I did not want people to think badly of Ruth. I pushed the letter into my pocket, sighing as I realised that few people would miss Ruth. She was not close to her family, Simon Schapps was not really her friend, she seemed to enjoy no other close relationships. Only her readers would miss her, and they would soon forget her, moving on to new books, new stories, new authors.

As I prepared to take myself home, so immersed in my grief at Ruth's death and, perhaps even more so, in my guilt at refusing to save her from the Chaos to come, I barely registered the fact that I might not actually succeed in travelling forward through the eight centuries to my own time. If I had agreed to take Ruth with me, or at least to try, would she still have taken her own life? I imagined that she would not, at least if such an action had succeeded. I moaned out loud with the weight of my remorse. Who was I to play god, to lie to Ruth, to tell her that it was simply not possible to rescue her by transporting her to my own time? I thought of her apparent happiness the night before while she knew all along that this was her 'happy, joyous, final farewell to this world'. I began to tremble again, emitting a tiny whimper as I glanced at the stiff, white corpse lying so peacefully on the bed.

"This won't do," I sharply reprimanded myself out loud. "I need to focus if I'm to get myself home."

I turned away from the bed, gazing out of the huge window wall at the sea beyond, drinking in my final image of the deserted beach, or at least I fervently hoped it would be my final image. The weather seemed to share my mood, and for the first time I saw the sea choppy with blustery wind, the sky gray and overcast, a light drizzle running in rivulets down the window. I breathed deeply a few times, calming my emotions, slowing my heart beat. I closed my eyes to try and begin the process of entering the trance state needed to take me home.

With a soul weighed down with a heavy burden of guilt and failure I prepared to port myself away from the tragedy of Ruth's death, unsure if I would see my home once more, and even if I did, wondering if I would ever have the heart or the courage to travel in time again.

www.ingramcontent.com/pod-product-compliance
Lightning Source LLC
Chambersburg PA
CBHW071957110726
47910CB00005B/1560